# MABEL;

## OR, THE

# CHILD OF THE BATTLE FIELD.

## A ROMANCE.

---

Amid the din of war's alarms
A beauteous infant lay:
The shield of Heaven around it hung:
It 'scaped the fearful fray.

---

## LONDON :

E. LLOYD, SALISBURY-SQUARE, FLEET-STREET.

—

MDCCCLI.

# MABEL;

## OR, THE

# CHILD OF THE BATTLE-FIELD.

## CHAPTER I.

THE BATTLE FIELD.—THE HORRORS OF WAR.—THE CHILD OF THE DEAD.—THE MAD HORSE.

It was half-past nine o'clock on the evening of June the 18th, 1815. The battle of Waterloo had been fought and won. The power of Napolon lay scattered in the blood of those who, for his giant ambition, had bled in vain. Many miles of country were covered with a flying host, hotly pursued by those who had earned the laurels of that dreadful day.

The slant rays of the scarcely yet expiring daylight fell across the field of carnage, where lay thousands of human forms dabbled in gore—

"The weary to sleep, and the wounded to die."

The sharp rattle of musketry might still occasionally be heard, and now and then the sullen boom of some cannon fired from a height at the gasping, retreating foe. No time had there yet been to tend the wounded ; no time to look for friends ; no time scarcely to think upon the various events of that dreadful, but awfully necessary day's work—a day's work which England can never forget, and which France, by its writhing malice, still shows is fresh in its recollection, as if it were but yesterday she suffered a defeat unparalleled in the history of warfare.

There was one spot in particular where the slain and the wounded lay most thickly. The bodies of men and horses were intermingled in horrible confusion. It was a hollow of not many yards in extent, and it would seem as if many had crawled there to die : while others, writhing from their wounds, had rolled into it, and there breathed their last sigh.

A gigantic French cuirassier lay dead with his head nearly off, for our troops could only assail them conveniently about the neck. By his side was a light cavalry man, an Englishman, who was frightfully mangled, having been borne off his horse by a cannon ball, which had hit him in the chest, and disfigured him fearfully.

Many others lay in different attitudes ; in most cases the ghastly, horrible countenances turned upwards, and presenting the most horrible distortion of visage it is possible for the imagination to conceive, even in its moments of most active picturing of the horrible.

At the feet of a dead horse lay the body of a young man, who, by his splendid uniform, was an officer evidently of rank. His costume denoted him as belonging to the French army. A large scarlet cloak half hid him, and upon the verge of the cloak lay huddled up the form of a young female, who was either dead, or had fainted after seeking the battle field, and finding some loved object perhaps among the slain. Near to this group was an English officer, whose horse had been shot under him, and who had been cut down by a French cuirassier, before he could disengage himself from the wounded animal. He was a young man, although the quantity of blood which had flowed over his face, and become clotted in his hair, would have effectually prevented any one from recognizing him. The hurt he had received rendered him insensible. It had occurred during the final charge in which the French had suffered so signal a defeat.

Just as the sun absolutely dipped below the line of the western horizon, a cool air swept across the battle field, and perhaps he was so near recovering from his insensibility that that was sufficient at once to recover him from unconsciousness, for he certainly did open his eyes, though he remained for some moments in that drowsy state which immediately succeeds insensibility, when all objects have that hazy aspect to the mind, which makes us doubt if we are not still in the land of dreams.

Intense pain, however, soon convinced him that it was no delusion, but that he really had been wounded, although to what extent he knew not, and was recovering from a swoon on the field of battle.

A temporary accession of delusion came over the young officer as he made an effort to clear the blood from before his eyes, and to look around him on the dead and the dying. He called aloud on several names of well-loved persons, who were not there, but whom he had left in England when he sought the fortune of war in the duke's army.

"Where are you?" he cried. "Dear ones, where are you now ? why do you not come to me? Alice—Alice ! Oh, God ! could you look upon me now !"

A deep, sepulchral groan sounded near to him, and at once recalled him to a sense of where he was, and what he was.

"I am not alone here," he said, faintly. "Why should I fill the air with my complaints ? I am one of thousands—of thousands. The night is coming on, or my eyes are dimmed with blood and tears. Tears ! No—no. I am a soldier."

Again the groan came upon his ears, and then from immediately behind him, a quarter from whence he was sure the groan did not come, some one said, in a rich brogue—

"Aisy—aisy ! whist ! botheration ! The curse of Cromwell light on the divil who carved out to me this purty slice on the head ! It's myself that wonders now where one of my ears has gone to."

"An English voice," said the young officer.

"Who spakes? Did anybody say nothing ? —bekase, if he did, let him say it agin, anyhow ; or, if he didn't, why, thin, he needn't, and hold his peace, by the blazes."

This was certainly not the most intelligible speech in the world, and yet it was welcome to the ears of the young English officer, who, making a great exertion to speak loud enough to be well heard, said—

"My good fellow, is your name——"

Again the deep groan which had before come upon his ears sounded nearly close to him, and he finished his sentence by adding—

"What's that ?"

"Bedad, no, sir ; that's not my name."

"You heard a groan ?"

"Faith, thin, I've seen so many groans, and heard so many mighty queer things in the way of wounds to day, that I've got careless in my way, anyhow."

"You are English ?"

"English ! Irish, if you plase."

"I—I meant that you belong to the English force."

"True for you, sir, and never a word of a lie."

"And your name is——"

"Rafferty Brolickbones, at your honour's service."

"I—knew it."

"Did your honour? May I be so bould, sir, as to ask what regiment your honour sports your elegant figure in as an officer?"

"How know you that I am an officer?"

"Faith, thin, it's dark it is, surely; but there's a fire beyant yonder, and the smallest gleam of it comes and goes, like a jack-a-lantern, on your honour's shoulders."

"Oh, God, I am sadly hurt."

"Amin, sir."

"I fear I shall—bleed—bleed to death."

"Amin, sir."

"I am faint—dreadfully faint, with loss of blood—and—and a death sickness is coming o'er me."

"A——min, sir."

"Curse you!" said the young man.

"Go it agin, sir. Get in a passion. It's as good as a glass of brandy, when that same isn't to be had. Bedad, sir, you were givin' a catalogue of your grievances—now, I've lost one of my ears, there's a hole in my shoulder, and one of my legs is broke, in a manner o' spaking."

"How do you mean?"

"Oh, clane and easy, sir, that's all. The blood of the O'Connors of Meath, and the Sulivans of County Cavan, sir, is running about, sir, all round me, like peas in a shovel."

Again the deep groan came upon the young officer's ears, and raising himself as well as he could, although with great pain, upon one arm, he said—

"Speak—speak! Who groans so sadly? Speak, I implore you!"

"Mon Dieu!" said a voice. "Ma chere Louise—ma petite——"

Then there was a deep sob and a groan, as if it were the last that could come from a broken heart.

"Gracious Heaven!" said the young officer, and he let himself fall back again among his own blood.

"Sir—sir," said Rafferty.

"I hear," said the other, faintly.

"Some Frenchman that, I'm thinking, sir. Polly vous Frenchy. How are you, old fellow? Whist, sir, there's somebody coming."

Creeping along the battle-field, in a strange, crouched-up attitude, so as to be almost on a level with the heap of carnage that lay about, came a human form. It took a strange, wayward course, now turning a few feet to one side and then to the other. Sometimes stooping down so low as to be nearly lost to view, and at others rising higher, showing a large dusky bulk in the dim light that still lingered on that dreadful field of blood.

The young officer felt a strange sensation of alarm, and he made a sudden and ill-advised movement, by which his wound bled inwardly, and a gush of the ensanguined fluid came in his mouth, nearly choking him, and projecting a sudden faintness which reduced him almost to death; and yet, it was strange, of all his faculties he preserved his sight the last; and, as he lay totally and entirely bereft of all power of movement, he saw the strange, hideous-looking form coming by a devious track closer and still closer to him. Then he heard the voice of the Irishman.

"Whist, sir, whist! It's a female woman, sir. Eh! did you spake, sir? Eh—eh? Oh, bedad, he's gone to glory! Pace be to him, amin! and great glory above and all around, amin! Sir—sir! Oh, he's gone off. Quiet as a lamb. Pace be to all here, glory and amin!"

On, on, came the figure, slowly, but surely; and now, as it neared him, the young officer became aware that it was, as far as dress went, a female form, and that what had given it the huge, odd-looking, misshapen appearance it had worn at a distance, arose from the fact that she carried with her a large sack that, no doubt, was well filled with the spoils of the dead.

"By the holy!" he heard Rafferty say, "I know what she is now; she's got past the scouts, and is robbing a churchyard she is, or what's as good as one. Oh, the saints now! Here's justice. The poor devil of a man in the moon was put there only for picking up sticks on a fast day to broil himself a pork chop; and here's somebody coming—oh, the devil! Oh, oh, murder! By God, sir, it's a good thing for you you are dead already, sir. Do you see that? Now, by the holy power, sir, it ought to reconcile you to your own mighty melancholy decase, sir."

The young officer did see *that*. His whole soul was concentrated in his eyes.— He saw the robber of the dead pause before what seemed to be a heap of slain, and commence the task of rifling pockets, and cutting off costly ornaments from the uniforms. He saw her suddenly pause and start back a step. Then he saw the glittering blade of a long knife which she held in her hand. It was raised, and poised for a moment in the air; then, with a dart forward like a tigress, she buried it in some one's heart, for there arose simultaneously with the blow, one short, sharp shriek, and then all was still.

He could not speak—he could not move. He felt that next it might be his turn to be murdered in his helplessness. A cold perspiration broke out upon him—he felt a sort of consciousness now that his last hour was come. He could not have closed his eyes one half instant for the world's dominion, and life to enjoy it.

Desperate were the efforts to shake off the strange waking trance that had come over him, but they were all in vain. There he lay, with the power of fancying all the horrors of such an impending doom as that which seemed now certain to him, and yet without the power to move a limb, or to breathe one word of deprecation.

And Rafferty, too, thought he was dead, and so made no effort for him; and yet what could he do, sorely wounded and with a broken limb? He thought he heard a rustling behind him, as if the wounded Irishman were trying to creep away, and then again every sense that was left him became concentrated in watching the movements of the woman.

Now she was near enough that he could hear she was muttering to herself in a compound language of Dutch, French, and German, and he became convinced she was one of those harpies who infest an army, and, like vultures, hover on the outskirts of a battle to feed upon the slain.

That the incursions of these people were as much guarded against as possible, he well knew; but no human vigilance could certainly keep them out of the field of slaughter; and it was horrible, indeed, to think of escaping absolute death in the conflict, to meet it by the hands of a murderess, without even the small consolation of a struggle.

Now she paused at a body which lay not many paces from him, and he saw her lift up one of the hands of the dead man, upon which he supposed there was a ring, for he could perceive that she was shaving away with her knife at one of the fingers, as if it had been a piece of wood that it was necessary for some purpose to sharpen to a point.

All the while, too, she kept muttering to herself upon some indifferent topic, and when she had got the ring off, he saw her give it a hasty wipe, to get rid of the blood and pieces of mangled flesh that hung to it, and then drop it into the capacious sack, which was the receptacle of all her plunder.

Nearer—nearer still came the woman—she was close to him, and as she flung the sack beside him, he heard the jingle of its multifarious contents. She began humming the fragments of some song, while she lifted up first one of his hands, then the other, to see if there were rings. He wore none, and, with an oath at her disappointment, she tore open his vest, which was soaked with blood, and laid hold of a gold chain he wore. There was a difficulty in getting it, so she took a grasp of a handful of his hair, and jerked up his head, while she took it off him.

Something, then, seemed suddenly to strike her that he yet lived, and she placed her great brawny hand upon his heart. She felt its faint pulsation, and a chuckle came from her lips. The knife was immediately produced, and, stooping over him, she raised it the whole length of her arm above her head to give force to the blow.

Oh, what a moment of agony was that! Intense dread burst the fetters that bound his tongue, and, in a voice that might have been heard over half the extent of that battle field, he shouted—

"Help!"

"Coming, sir," cried the welcome voice of Rafferty, and in an instant such a tremendous report took place close to his ear, that he was nearly stunned with the concussion.

Rafferty had got hold of a musket by some means, and having levelled it over the dead horse, he fired it right into the face of the woman.

"Take that, my jewel," he cried. "Our side for ever and a day. Hurrrah!—hurrah! What a darlint you are, to be shure, anyhow. Fair and easy goes a mighty long way, sir. And so you ain't dead yet? It's a shocking thing, it is, sir, to have to blow the blessed head off one of the fair sex, sir."

———

## CHAPTER II.

THE WOUNDED FRENCHMAN.—THE OFFERING.—THE SACRED TRUST.—MORE DANGERS.

So stunning and so sudden, so close to his very face, and so utterly unexpected, was the report of the musket which had been fired by Rafferty Brolickbones, that the young officer for the moment scarcely knew whether it had saved him from the dreadful hands of the plunderer of the dead or not, or, indeed, whether or not he was the sufferer from the discharge of the deadly weapon.

The voice of the Irishman, however, recovered him to consciousness, and he bent his eyes in the direction where the woman had stood, who, in another moment, but for so timely an interruption, would have put an end to all his pains and all his expectations with that knife which, doubtless, had already found the heart's core of many a brave fellow.

The bullet from the musket had hit her in the mouth, and being, by contact with the teeth, deprived of some portion of its force, it had, instead of perforating the skull in its passage out, fairly lifted off one of the bones, and nearly literally, as Rafferty had expressed it, blown her head off.

Her death must have been instantaneous; and there she lay, presenting, from the freshness of the wound, and the nature of it, one of the most hideous spectacles even in that field of horrors.

The spot of ground on which this tragedy occurred was a slightly raised one, so that, as the body of the plunderer lay, her face and head seemed, to the eyes of the young wounded officer, to be on a level with a long strip of the western sky, which was still illumined by the last faint rays of the setting, or rather sunken sun.

It was this circumstance which enabled him to see an effect which made him shudder. A heavy, thick sort of steam rose from the mass of broken bones and blood which had been a human head. It was like the vapour that arises from a valley at sunset, and it hung over the ghastly spectacle like a mist of blood.

"And this is war!" thought the young

man. "Gracious God! this is what men call glory!"

"How is your mother's son now, sir?" said Rafferty.

"How is who?"

"Yourself, sir, of course, I mane. A swate piece of goods that, sir. Bad luck to her, and a warm place down stairs along wid the jontleman as estames the likes of her, sir!"

"You have saved my life, Rafferty."

"I hope so, sir; but, you know, as your honour is bad hurt, there ain't so much merit in the thing. It wasn't just the likes of a Brolickbones, sir, to see you murdered in that kind of way; and bedad, sir, the mighty elegant twist I gave my leg in getting a holt of that musket is one of them things to remember, sir, without a memyrandum, sir, any way."

"Ah, I should think so."

"Right for you, sir. It was an English musket, sir, and the poor devil who had a holt of it had been dead so long that he hadn't got into a habit of letting go of it."

"It was held by a corpse?"

"That same, sir, was the case. A fine young man, no doubt, sir, if one could have come to a judgment, only, as his two legs was gone, it wasn't aisy. Now, sir, if that had been a French gun, sir, bad cess to it! but it would have missed fire; and then, as sure as my name's Rafferty Brolickbones, that 'tarnel woman would have had two more murders on her soul, for she'd have just settled you and me, nate and aisy, before you could have said, 'Mike, how's your mother?'"

"My good fellow, I owe you a debt of gratitude."

"Thank you, sir."

"It is I have to thank you, Rafferty; and believe me, that if I survive the horrors of this day, I will not be unmindful that I owe to you my life."

"Faith! sir, that's not much. Pay me off when you see some poor fellow in a bad plight; and when you're walking about like a gintleman in the pride of your heart, and all's nate and aisy wid you, if you see some poor fellow hard up, and an Irish tongue in his cheek, give him a trifle, and tell him it's for the honour of ould Ireland and Rafferty Brolickbones."

"I will—I will."

"That's enough, sir. It's well paid I am. Did you see the cretur, sir, when she was hit?"

"No, no; I was faint."

"By the holy, sir, the bullet smashed her teeth like a box of dominoes gone mad, sir. Then, sir, she gave a kick that would have sent anybody to smash, sir, and sich a splutter as never was known the like. My belief, sir, is, as it's no woman at all."

"Indeed!"

"No, sir. That's a fact. It's one of the rascally suttlers, who has disguised himself like a young lady, sir, no doubt."

"I am glad of that."

"And so am I, sir, for the honour and glory of the sex, sir. Good luck to them, young and—well, we won't say anything about them as is ould, bekase they ought to have had all their luck, sir, long ago. Did you hear that, sir?"

"I did hear a strange noise."

The young officer listened, and so strange and terrific a half shriek, half howl, met his ear, that he involuntarily trembled, and exclaimed—

"Good God! can that sound be human?"

Again it came, louder than at first. Such a sound he had never in his life heard, or, indeed, anything approaching to it. There was something about it perfectly undefinable. It was like no other tone. It was too loud to have come from mortal lips—of that he felt assured: and where, then, could it have arisen?

At such a moment, if ever fears of the supernatural might be considered excusable in an educated mind, surely they were when they found a temporary home in the brain of that young officer. In a loud tone of voice he spoke to the Irishman, saying—

"Rafferty, do you hear it?"

"Surely, sir, wid my one ear I hear it."

"And can you guess what it is?"

"I think I can, sir. I was wounded at Salamanca, and lay all night half in a ditch and half out of it, sir. Well, sir, towards the light of the morning, I heard that same sort of sound, and I thought it was ould Nick, sir, himself, a playing a kayed bugle, sir."

"And what was it?"

"Aisy, sir. Well, there was a poor divil who had been kilt intirely close by me; so I says, 'What's that?' says I; and what do you think he says, yer honour?"

"I cannot tell."

"'It's a mad horse,' says he."

"A mad horse!"

"Yes, sir; and here he comes, kicking friend and foe, galloping along like thunder and turf. Oh, bedad, and if he comes this way, we're in for it, any way."

Again the dreadful sound, which to hear for the first time and not to comprehend was enough, and more than enough, to fill any mind with horror, came across the battle field, and then the heavy tramp of hoofs upon the soil: and, plunging, tearing, snorting, and dashing up the soil with its feet, came on the mad horse!

The creature was dying; but what mischief might it not do before that last pang came which was to close its earthly career—what wounded wretches might it not scatter more pain and a worse death among, as—under the influence of delirium—it rushed madly across that field of carnage, sadness, and woe!

"It's coming, sir," said Rafferty—"it's coming!"

"Gracious Heaven!" moaned the young officer, "is it not enough to endure all the danger of the fight, but there must be these superadded horrors to make war more terrible—to meet death with greater agony?"

"Faith, sir, then what you say is true; and I suppose the sum and substance of that same goes a long way to mean that you'd rather not be kicked, sir, by the horse, any way?"

"Rather not, indeed, Rafferty. Which way is he going?"

"Bedad then, sir, it ain't mighty plain I can see at all at all; but he's took a bit of a turn, sir."

"Thank Heaven!"

"Now don't hilloa, sir, till you are out of the bush. He's coming back again. It's a small thing that'll frighten many a Christian, sir, let alone a horse—I shall jist try the same on. Whist, he's a coming."

The mad charger now wheeled round suddenly, and reeling from approaching weakness, occasioned by loss of blood, it seemed for a moment about to fall, but still was there strength enough left for another charge, and on it come.

It was a noble animal, coal black, and of immense size and strength. Some of the soldiery trappings still remained—one stirrup only dangled at its side, and from the character of the saddle and its accompaniments, it seemed to have belonged to some of our own heavy cavalry. In less time than it has taken us to say so, it is on the spot where lie those in whose fortunes we are interested. It came from a direction which would bring it across the body of the wounded French officer and that delicate-looking female form which lay crouched up so close to him, as if he, even wounded, were a greater protection than all else from the horrors of that field of blood.

The steed stumbles before it reaches them, but with its whole weight it rolls over that sad group, and then makes frantic efforts to regain its feet. One of its hoofs came in contact with the already fearfully mangled head of the suttler and plunderer of the dead, he who had met with so well deserved a fate at the hands of Rafferty. It was horrible to hear the hideous crash which was produced by the concussion which hurled the body some yards off, where it lay, strangely doubled up, as if it were in an attitude prepared for a spring.

The young ensign shut his eyes, for in another moment he knew the horse would be upon or over him—he felt as if a sudden rushing wind was sweeping past his face. The mad horse had cleared his prostrate form at a bound, and the danger was over.

"Sir," said Rafferty; "sir!"

"Well, Rafferty."

"A mighty fine jump that, sir. The hind hoof of the creature, sir, was not a mile, if an inch was that same, from the top of your head."

The young man shuddered at the danger he had passed.

"Rafferty, he said, "can you hear no-thing? Surely there are parties sent across the field to succour the wounded. We shall not be left here to die, Rafferty, shall we?"

"No, sir. But only think what a lot of boys there are on the field, sir, and many of them worse off than we are."

"Not much worse, Rafferty—not much worse."

The same dreadful groan, which at such long intervals seemed to be forced by acute pain from the French officer, now came upon the ears again of the ensign and Rafferty.

"Do you hear that, Rafferty?"

"I do, sir."

"Poor fellow!"

"Yes, sir. He's a Frenchman; but then, you know, sir, we shouldn't be hard on him for that—he couldn't help it. It's his misfortune, sir, not his fault, poor devil! He couldn't make himself be born in that neat Irish town, Ballyobothershin, you know, sir."

The wounded French officer seemed to have heard what Rafferty had said, or, at all events, he heard the voice, if he understood not the purport of all the words. That he could speak English, however, he now proved, by saying a few words in that language.

"Who speaks?" he said; "who speaks?"

"It's me, Frenchy," said Rafferty. "Parley vous, Frenchy, how do you find yourself, old fellow?"

"Are you badly hurt?" said the young ensign.

There was something in the young man's voice which seemed to inspire the French officer with a feeling of confidence, as he said, faintly—

"I am dying—I am dying! But why should those I love die here—those who had all to lose and nothing to gain by this dreadful day of slaughter? We—we might be satisfied with what we call glory, but the happiness of those she loved, was ever her dearest delight—her last—last care in this world. I am dying—I am dying."

"I fear," said the ensign, "that we cannot aid you. I am hurt seriously, I think, myself."

"And a nice kettle of fish I've made of it, Frenchy," said Rafferty. "Parley vous Frenchy. Keep up your spirits."

"Who is that?"

"An honest friend of mine," said the ensign.

"Thank your honour. I'm as honest as most folks, I shouldn't wonder."

"You are both badly wounded," said the French officer. "When they pick you up, say you know Roucelli, of the garde cheval. In the French lines the name is not unknown and not unrespected."

"The French lines!" said Rafferty. "I wonder where there's any French lines now."

"The emperor has won the day."

"Has he, though? Parley vous, Frenchy. The emperor has burnt his whiskers, Frenchy, and been beat into smithereens."

"Into what?"

"I presume," said the ensign, "that you were wounded before the fate of the day was virtually decided. The English are the victors."

"Is—is that true?"

"It is so, on my honour."

"God—God! then all is lost! Oh, my Marie—my beautiful—oh, God—oh, God—all is lost!"

"Sir, you much lament the loss of this battle."

"It is to me the loss of home, friends, kindred, honour, all I hold dear. Where—where are you? It is very dark—very dark, and yet a confused mass of yellow light is dancing before my eyes. I am dying—where can I find you? Oh, the agony to move—the dreadful agony to move!—Horror—horror—horror! She is dead!"

"I am here, close at hand to you," said the ensign. "I cannot move though. Of whom do you speak?"

"The horse has killed her! The horse—the horse! Oh, to come by such a death as this! But we shall meet again—we shall meet again. Soon—soon—yes, soon. Now—now—hush—hush, little one, hush! Are you dead, too—are you dead, too?"

"It strikes me, sir," said Rafferty, "that that poor Frenchy, sir, ain't in his right mind and senses. Any one would think he was nursing a baby, sir."

Even as the sergeant spoke, the low, half-smothered cry of an infant came upon their ears, and he exclaimed:—

"Oh, murder! Talk of the devil, sir, and—"

"Hush—hush!" said the ensign. "Can it be possible that there is a child here? Is it some delusion, or was that the voice of an infant I heard even now?"

Suddenly he felt something touch him, and, as well as he could, he raised himself a little, when he found that the wounded French officer had dragged his mangled form close to him, and was looking in his face with such an expression of intense suffering and anxiety, that, the first impression of the ensign was, let him live as long as he might, he should never forget that sad and agonised countenance.

The effort which the wounded man had made to get so far, although the distance, as a distance, was nothing, must, in his condition, have been terrific. But what will not the body accomplish when the mind strongly incites it to some extraordinary action? Under any other circumstances, it would have been thought absolutely impossible for a man so badly wounded to move at all; and so it would have been, but now his soul was animated by a purpose which overcame, in its vast importance, all other considerations, and conquered bodily weakness and bodily pain.

He had drawn himself along by one arm, and, held tightly to his breast with the other, was as astounding and unlikely an object to see on that field of carnage, as could well be imagined. It was a young child, dabbled in blood—soaked in the ensanguined stream which had flown from the wounds of the officer who held it.

While the young ensign, faint and exhausted as he was, managed to see so much, with pain and difficulty the French officer spoke; but although we may give his words, we cannot paint to the reader the wild energy with which he spoke, nor the deep, pathetic tones in which he implored the ensign to grant him the boon he sought.

"You are my foe," he said. "My hand may have stricken you, or you may have done as much for me; but I am dying, and the fight is over. I can see by this faint light that you are young. Perhaps you have some happy home, where there are smiling faces to greet you—where there are fond hearts that love you. Look at this babe. Did you ever love a child? Did you ever take to your heart one of those dear, small treasures, and find joy in its innocent caress? Oh, if you have known affections—if around your heart are woven those invisible ties which bind all who are brave and generous to some loved objects, you will not refuse my prayer! I am dying. My last words are for your ear—my last thoughts may be elsewhere; but, Englishman—conqueror—on this field of blood I ask you to protect this child. It is not one which will disgrace you. It comes of fair lineage—it—it—it—oh, this faintness—this dreadful faintness——"

"Your child is it?" said the ensign—"your child?"

"I—I—am very faint. Save the little one—save it—save it!"

"On my honour, such kindness as I can bestow upon it, I will. You see I am wounded myself; but the succour that comes to me shall come also to this infant."

"You will—will befriend——"

"It shall never want a friend in me. God forbid that at such a time I should refuse so sacred a trust."

"I—I—have not words in which to bless you. Bless you; take—take the dearest, but——"

He, with a great effort, laid the infant down close to the young Englishman, who placed his arms around it, saying—

"I swear to you, on the honour of a soldier, that I will have this little one taken care of!"

It was a trivial circumstance, and perhaps accidental, but the young babe (for such it was) as if with a consciousness of the words that were uttered, placed one of its tiny hands into the young officer's, while with large, lustrous eyes, it seemed to look beseechingly in his face.

The man was much affected, as he said—

"Tell me, sir, the name of the child?"

"Mabel."

"And are you its father?"

"I—I—help—help! I die! Water!—

Oh, for one draught of water! Marie—Marie—Marie—my Marie!"

With a strange gurgling sob he fell backwards. Blood gushed from his mouth—there was for a moment a curious movement of the limbs, and then all was still. He was a corpse!

## CHAPTER III.

### THE RESCUE.—THE CHILD OF MYSTERY.—THE BATTLE FIEND.

EVEN as the French officer drew his latest breath, there came a strange, lurid light across the battle field. It fell upon the faces of the dead, giving them a supernatural appearance—a singular aspect of renewed vitality; and as shadows were produced by the movement of the light, one could almost have expected to see those stiffened corses lying in their gore rise up again to make that field of blood ten times more hideous than it was.

The light fell upon the sparkling uniform, too, of the French officer, and it fell upon the face of the living child, which the young ensign, who now felt a drowsiness creeping over him he dreaded to encourage, held to his breast.

The features of the child were beautifully regular, and whether it was a natural expression, or some consciousness of the terrors of that dreadful day and night had reached its mind, there was certainly upon its cherub countenance a look of gentle sadness, which sat upon so young and so beautiful a face most oddly, although most sweetly. The age of the child might be about one year, as near as, by so casual a glance as he could take of it, the ensign could judge. It did not cry, it did not sleep, but it nestled close to him, and looked earnestly in his face. Occasionally, too, it moved one of its little hands, and dipped the tip of one of the tiniest fingers in the world in the pool of blood which was close to it, and then it would look at the crimson stain, as if, young as it was, it could moralise upon that theme.

Already the ensign loved the child. We always love what we protect. There seems to be an innate feeling in the human mind to that effect; it is a kind and immediate recompense for a kind and good deed. He had promised to save the child—to protect it, and he loved it that it had no hope but in his protection, and closer still he pressed it to his breast, as he thought what might be its unhappy fate, if he had not had the heart to save it.

"Yes," he said, "I will keep my word. Fain would I have known more of it—I should have liked to hear its history; but still, known or unknown, I will protect it. My home shall be this infant's home; my friends shall be its friends; and, thank God, I know there are English hearts at home, which, for my sake, will do for this little stranger all that love can do or kindness dictate."

The light which had gleamed for one instant had faded away again, and the young ensign fell into a train of sad musing. He had uttered a word which in imagination carried him far away from that battle-field to happier, better scenes. That word was "home."

Home, with all its dear associations—when was he to look upon it again, if ever? Oh, why had he roamed from it? What demon had seduced him to think war glorious? What mad demon of ambition had forced him from all that was dear and full of excellence, to place him a mangled, bleeding wretch upon that dreadful plain?"

In fancy, he could hear the voices of those he loved—he could see the faces he knew so well hovering about him as he lay; and then he thought of what would be the pang—the gush of grief when they heard that he had fallen. What a poor recompense it would be to them to be told that he had fallen gloriously! How dull and harsh it would sound in their ears, and how sad a substitute it would be to them for the presence of a loved one whom they never more might see!

He was interrupted in this train of reflections by the sergeant, who suddenly said, with a groan—

"No luck, sir—no luck."

"What do you mean, Rafferty?"

"Oh, then, sir, parties are in the field, picking up the wounded; and they've got lights, sir: didn't you see?"

"I did: I saw a light just now."

"Well, sir, they were coming on this way as clean as a whistle, sir, when they met some other poor devil, and carried him off; so here we have to wait, perhaps a mighty long time, sir."

"We must take our turns, Rafferty."

"Bedad, sir, I suppose we must. So you've got the Frenchy's child, sir? Do you know, it strikes me you ain't a married man, sir."

"I am not."

"I thought as you wasn't, sir; but, however, if your honour goes on in this way, it will be a mighty great convenience to you when you do happen to marry, you know, sir."

"A convenience! How?"

"Why, sir, you'll have a nice little family ready made."

"Rafferty, you would not have had me refuse to take charge of the poor helpless child?"

"Refuse, sir! I have you refuse! Do you think I have no bowels, sir? Bedad, sir, I ain't Pagan, anyhow. Refuse, did you say, sir? I'd take the poor little small creature myself if you didn't like the job. Faith, then, in ould Ireland, it's iligantly off is the Brolickbones. It's an estate we have, sir—an iligant cabin built of potatoes, and the mud growing round it like the sweetest flowers in the universe, sir. Then, there's

Mistress Judith Brolickbones, a born lady, sir, and one of the great O'Shaugnesseys, sir, and then there's—Oh, murder! who's this now, I'd like to know?"

A tall, stalwart-looking man strode up to the spot. In his hand he held a strangely shaped sword; it was short, and wide towards the point. He was dressed in a costume more of a civilian than a military character, and as he came up, he said—

"I heard English voices. Where are you?"

"Here, my broth of a boy," cried Rafferty.

"Here, here," said the young ensign; "for God's sake, get us some assistance to take us off the field."

"I will see if I can mention you to any of the parties who are out. Have you seen any French about here? Alive, I mean?"

"Not that I am aware of."

"Confound them—I have not come across twenty alive. Those, however, I have finished."

"Finished!" cried the ensign.

"Do you mane finished," said Rafferty, "to be took as a polite name for murdering, sir?"

"My name is Sternholde. You may have heard of me."

As he said these words he walked away.

"Do you know the jontilman, sir?" said Rafferty.

"I do; I have heard of him. He is an *attache* in some capacity to the staff of Blucher, and came with despatches to the duke this morning. He is notorious for his antipathy to the French. Some of our men call him the battle fiend, for he never will knowingly leave a Frenchman alive. Even if he seriously wounds one, he will follow him up with relentless severity. He is a powerful man, and reputed one of the best swordsmen in Europe."

"Faith, sir, a lively sort of character; and your friend, who has made you sich a mighty handsome present, sir, of the child, would have stood no great chance, if he had not taken himself off to glory as soon as he did."

"I fear the Prussian, Sternholde, would have killed him, and we were too powerless to hinder it, Rafferty; but see, the light gleams across the field."

"And great glory to them, sir; they are coming this way, too."

A corporal's party now steadily approached the spot, and with a gush of joy that brought tears to his eyes, he heard the cry of, "Wounded — wounded? Any wounded?" uttered in an English voice.

"Yes, here," he said, faintly. "Here."

"And when you have nothing else to do, boys," said Rafferty, "you can come and see how the spalpeens have made game of me, and pick up all the pieces of me somehow."

The corporal who had command of the party, which was an offshoot from a much larger one, commanded by an officer, selected the ensign, and then, as he stooped to assist n placing him in a blanket which was stretched out by the men for his reception, he started with surprise to see the child clinging to the breast of the officer with the greater tenacity that strangers were present.

"A child!" he exclaimed.

"Yes, my friend," said the ensign. "It has been brought to me by some one who is now dead, and I have promised to take care of it. Can you assist me in so doing, and I will take care you are no loser by it?"

"My wife, sir, will see to it, poor little thing. We—we had one of our own, sir, once."

"You have lost it?"

The man turned aside, and a visible emotion shook his whole frame, as in a half-choked voice he said—

"It was blown to pieces by the explosion of an ammunition waggon."

The ensign shuddered, and, still holding the child, he was placed in a blanket, and slowly carried off the field; nor was Rafferty left behind, for he was taken likewise by four men of the same party, whom he wonderfully amused all the way by detailing, in his own peculiar manner, the various incidents that had occurred during the time that he and the young ensign had been lying wounded on the field, so that the men thought it no labour to carry him to one of the hastily arranged military hospitals which were formed for the wounded in every house between the plains of Waterloo and the city of Brussels which could be made available for that purpose.

The young ensign, before he reached a house, had some more conversation with the corporal concerning the child, and after receiving a solemn promise that he and his wife would take care of it, and let him know from time to time how it was getting on, he felt so overcome by the loss of blood, which had ensued from his wound, and the agony which the being carried from the field gave him, that he fainted, and remained for many hours in a state of perfect unconsciousness.

During that time he was taken to one of the hospitals, his wounds dressed, and himself placed in as comfortable circumstances as the resources of the army on the night of that day of most desperate carnage could afford.

---

## CHAPTER IV.

THE SEARCH FOR THE LOVED ONE.—THE MOTHER'S DESPAIR.—THE MEETING WITH THE BATTLE FIEND.

WE have before mentioned that, lying close to where the wounded French officer had originally fallen, was what appeared to be the lifeless form of a young and beautiful female. From the manner in which her arms were clasped round him, and from the interest he took in the child, it may be well gathered that it was in search of him she had come to that dreadful scene, and then died, believing him to be no more, or, at all events-as indeed he was, in too hopeless a condition for recovery to be possible.

That he had considered her to be dead, there can be no doubt; for he had made no allusion to her in the brief conversation he had had with the young English ensign. All anxiety on her account was over, and he had thrown all his energy of supplication into his prayer for protection to the child alone.

But it would appear that this opinion of her death was premature. All who have paid much attention to the various united occurrences connected with the battle of Waterloo, are aware that towards the grey light of morning—the morning after the battle had been lost and won—there fell for about ten minutes a smart shower of rain upon the dead and the few wounded who had been unwittingly overlooked in the exertions that had been made to recover all that were possibly imagined not to have breathed their last, from the field.

And when it is recollected that the French, being so completely routed as they were, abandoned their wounded to the humanity of the victors, and that our hospitals were crammed with wounded Frenchmen, the task of clearing such a battle plain of its occupants will be readily enough admitted to have been no easy one.

This smart shower of rain recovered several who had fainted, and were, to all appearance, dead, in consequence of it plashing upon their faces, and producing a slight shock to the nearly completely exhausted system.

Among those who thus awoke from a blessed unconsciousness of much misery, was this young and beautiful girl; for such she seemed who had lain so long in a trance on that fatal spot.

The rain fell heavily upon those fair features, which, no doubt, had been idolised by many a heart. It mingled with the blood which had already soaked her long raven tresses, and it made the slight clothing she wore cling more closely to her exquisite form. With a deep sigh, she awoke and looked upwards at the dull, grey sky, not yet sufficiently lighted by the rising sun to look otherwise than night-like, and not very dark. For some moments she lay profoundly still. Memory had not yet resumed its functions, but soon, alas! too soon must she awaken to a consciousness of where she was, and with that a remembrance of what had brought her there, and what harrowing sight had met her gaze when first she had reached the spot so fatal to her happiness.

A short, sharp cry of anguish announced that the time had come. Memory had re-assumed her sceptre, and that young girl knew now all that had for a few moments been so confused and dream-like.

"Rouselli!" she cried, "Rouselli! My child—my—my child, where are you? I had it here—I had it on my heart. My child—

Mabel—Mabel! Oh, God! where is my beautiful child!"

With frantic gestures she rose to her feet, and looked wildly around her. The dead only met her gaze, and again, in accents of the wildest despair, she cried—

"My infant! where is my child? Mabel—Mabel—Mabel! Rouselli, speak! If it be but a word, oh, speak to me. God! this is too terrible. All still—still as the grave. Ay, the grave; but who could kill the sweet little one, from whose eyes one glance would surely disarm the murderer's hand? No—no; it is not dead. Yet where—where can it be? Mabel! my child—my only joy—my darling child!"

Her eye suddenly fell upon the dead body of the French officer. The uniform must have been familiar to her, for, without a moment's hesitation, she now flew towards him.

"'Tis he—'tis he!" she exclaimed. "Found—found! Oh, 'tis I have strayed, not he. He has my child—my darling Mabel! He, he! Rouselli! dead—dead! and I living! where is the child? Not here—not—here! and he alone who could tell me of its fate—dead—dead! Oh, Heaven—Heaven—Heaven! Now, kind Heaven, send your lightnings on me, for I am a wretch weary of existence. Rouselli, I say, Rouselli, I demand of you my child."

She knelt down by the side of the ghastly corpse, and overcoming, from the stronger impulse of maternal affection, her dread of touching so fearful an object, she searched the folds of the cloak, which still partly hung around the body, with the hope of finding somewhere there the only object of her solicitude; but soon she became convinced search was fruitless, and what pen can describe the dreadful accession of despair which then came over her mind, and nearly at the moment drove her to madness?

For a moment she clasped her hands, and cast an appealing look to Heaven, as if she were about to utter some prayer, but the intention deserted her. Her mental agony was too much even for prayer to soothe, and with wild screams that brought more tears into the heart of many a poor fellow, who lay at his last gasp on the damp earth, she fled over the field of battle.

She had no hope of finding the object of her love. Her flight from spot to spot, and the frantic manner in which she called upon her child, were rather mechanical movements than dictated by reason.

In this state she neared the town of Hugue-mont, which had been the scene during the preceding day of so much hard fighting, and where so many corpses lay strewn about in the wildest disorder.

"Mabel!" she still shouted, "Mabel—my child! Give me back my child!—Heaven, give me back my child! Why, oh, why delight me with such a gift, but again to tear it from my doating heart? Mabel—Mabel! My child—my child!"

Suddenly, then, from among the ruins of the town house, there darted out the figure of a man, and heedless of where he trod, whether it was on the dead or the dying, he rushed towards the female form who there stood in such an attitude of woe.

With a fiendish laugh he seized her wrist, and throwing off the undress military cap he wore, he cried, in scarcely less wild accents than she herself had been speaking in—

"Do you know me?"

She turned her eyes upon his face for an instant, and then, at the same moment that she made a vain effort to escape from the clutch he had fastened upon her, she shouted the name of—

"Sternholde!"

"Yes," he cried, ferociously, "I am Sternholde, whom men call the 'Battle Fiend.' Where is he? I would not name him. Where is he?"

"Dead—dead. Beyond the reach of your vengeance. Give me back my child!"

"Dead? Rouselli dead! D——n!"

"Give me back my child."

"Death and fury! What mean you? Where is the child, ask I? Where is it—at Brussels—in France? Where, tell me where?"

"You cannot deceive me, villain. You, and you only, would snatch if from my arms. Restore it to me, Sternholde. The child, at least, never harmed you. Restore it to me. My Mable—my child!"

"By Heaven and hell, woman, I have not seen the infant! The knowledge of its existence added fuel to the flame of hatred which burnt in my breast already sufficiently fierce. Tell me where it is, and life shall not long linger in its frame!"

"You know too well. Why will you thus torture me by a pretended ignorance of that on which you are too well informed? Oh, Sternholde! surely you have some touch of human pity left for me? What have I done—what have I done?"

"Favoured and advanced the doings of others. In that way you have injured me. And now, by this pretended ignorance respecting the child, you would baulk me of my vengeance."

"Sternholde, you mock me. Oh, give me back my babe. Surely—surely, you would not keep so young a child from its mother? Remember, I am now its only friend."

"Its only friend, are you?"

"I am; for, on my soul, I do assure you he is dead."

"Curses on the hand that laid him low! A thousand curses on the arm that struck him down!"

"And yet you wished to kill him. The last time we met, Sternholde—it was in Paris—you told me that you had but one great pursuit in life, and that was the destruction of Rouselli."

"I did."

"And yet now you curse the hand that has accomplished your wish."

"I might wish him dead without wishing another to step between me and the long-cherished purpose of my soul."

"Horrible—horrible!"

"I wished him dead, but it was that I might kill him."

"Man—man, would you carry your resentment even beyond the grave? Oh, think of what you say. You, even you, Sternholde, cannot really mean so much wickedness."

"Not mean it! Ha, ha! You do not know me yet, Marie. You do not know me yet, I see."

"I know you too well for peace—too well for consolation. God knows you have been my bane."

"Indeed!"

"And you know it, you must know it. You know how relentlessly you have persecuted me and mine, Sternholde. The very fact that you heap anathemas on the head of him who has, in the chances of the battle, taken the life of Rouselli, shows how dreadful and how implacable are your resentments."

"Yes, implacable."

"I know you are."

"I tell you, Marie, I would give my own life to arouse Rouselli once again from the sleep of death that I might meet him face to face, and leap to my revenge. What is it to me that he is dead if another hand slew him? A thousand, ay, nearly a hundred thousand, better men than he, have this day shared his fate. The very air is heavy with the scent of blood."

"It is—it is!"

"And to me 'tis welcome. I have been a scourge even to the very country which gave Rouselli birth. I have, for my deep hatred to him, pursued his nation. If my soul can at all be sunk amid the curses of eternal perdition, it will descend to the mansion of the unblessed with the weight of the blood of four hundred and thirty Frenchmen."

"Gracious Heavens!"

"You are surprised; but I have been an exterminator. Rouselli was a Frenchman, and for his sake I have waged war against a whole nation."

"What wild insatiate rage!"

"Call it what you will—I did it. I had always a hope of meeting him—wherever France was engaged in warfare, there was I in the opposing ranks. Wherever a solitary traveller of that nation could be traced, I was on his footsteps like a bloodhound."

"Peace—peace!"

"Nay, you shall hear. I always had my knife ready; I would spring upon them unaware, and, like some avenging spirit, I would take the life of him who had no fault but that he spoke the native language of Rouselli."

"This is madness."

"It may be so; but yet was there a wonderful method in it. I have a charmed life!"

" A charmed life ?"

" Yes; and so men have called me the battle-fiend, and those who have been contending with France have never rejoiced to see me. Bullets will not touch me—swords turn aside when aimed at me. I am desperate from a conviction that I am fulfilling my destiny."

" Sternholde—Sternholde! Let me lead you back to that one subject which fills all my heart."

" What is that ?"

" My child—my child !"

" Oh, indeed ! '

" None but you would tear it from me. Sternholde, you have hidden it somewhere !"

" Ha—ha—ha !"

" You—even you could not have the heart to kill a child."

" I have the heart for anything !"

" And yet I have heard you talk of love and joy, and all the dear delights which true affection can bestow. I have heard you speak of hearts knit together in holiest ties; and I have seen the tear of sympathy bedew your cheek, Sternholde. I have marked your voice falter as you have told of some true lover's fate, who, loving with an adoration more than human, had fallen from the height of purest joy through falsehood—treachery——"

" As I feel—as I feel! By Heavens, how well you fan the flame of my revenge !"

" No, Sternholde, no! You are wrong! Recall, if it be but for a moment, those happier days, when you, a happy student, careless of all but of the beaming light that fell from the eyes of beauty unadorned, you spoke of the dear future as of some sunny dream, some dear resemblance to the golden haze of a rare old picture, fresh from the god-like hands of some master of his art !"

" Revenge—revenge !"

" Discard the word, Sternholde. You know not what you say. Young enough are you yet to repent you of that which you have done. Oh ! fill not up the cup of Heaven's wrath to the overflowing. Sue for mercy where mercy is as the very atmosphere which angel's breathe. Sternholde, oh, Sternholde, take better thoughts, and yet live to be a likeness of what once you were."

" God !" he exclaimed, " has it come to this !"

" You relent, Sternholde, you relent. Some vision of your better nature crosses you."

" Ha—ha—ha !"

" It does—it must. I feel assured it does. Your fancy, even now, carries you back to the door of the old house at Gottengen."

" Forbear—forbear !"

" Nay, I will not forbear to be to you as the better angel who shall drag you back to virtue and to peace !"

" It is too late, Marie, it is too late."

" Never—never !"

" And yet I am a man of blood."

" And yet can you repent."

" No—no—no !"

" I say yes. There is boundless mercy in Heaven—who shall limit it—who shall say it is too late for any human soul to cry aloud —' Great God I have erred ; forgive me !"

" I shudder, but I persevere. My guilt, if guilt it be at all—and are we not the mere puppets of circumstances ?—we cannot create any more than we can control—is as an ocean, submerging all thoughts of mercy in its fathomless depths."

" Let it be an ocean, and yet one drop of heavenly mercy shall change its nature, and tincture it with hope."

" No—no—no ! A hundred times no !"

" I say a thousand—ay, a million times, yes !"

" Oh, Marie, could I—but that is madness —madness. Death—death—death to all."

" My child, Sternholde, my child."

" Fool ! think you that if I had met that infant, it would have lived ? And think you I could refrain from exulting in its death ? You strove to move me, but my heart is adamant. But yet, Marie, if you would do me some grace—if you lay up one obligation to you now——"

" Yes—yes. I will—I will."

" You swear ?"

" So help me Heaven."

" Ha—ha ! Well sworn. Take me to the spot where lies Rouselli's body. I would feast my eyes upon the corpse—I would look upon his face again, even though it be in death."

" No—no."

" You have sworn."

" Not while such unholy passions are tugging at your heart. Besides, I have promised more than I have power to perform, for in my frantic eagerness to search for my lost little one, I have wandered from the spot, and now I know no more than you do where to search for his remains."

" I know it."

" You know what ?"

" I guessed it from the first. You would cheat me of my vengeance—but you cannot !"

" I cannot comprehend you."

" Rouselli lives—he lives ! The story of his death is a fabrication to cheat me of my revenge. To turn me aside from the path I have chosen, and which, sooner or later, must have enabled me to reach his heart and gratify my long nursed feelings of vengeance. I'll not believe it—Rousilli is not dead !"

" These eyes beheld him."

" And yet I'll not believe it. But let me test the truth. If Rouselli, who removed you from my heart, be dead, that tie is broken."

" It is broken."

" Well—if you have lost your child amid this scene of carnage, that tie is broken."

"No—no—no. Death has not claimed two victims."

"Doubtless he has. Will you fly with me, and let the past be as a dream, to which we will not again refer? Marie, will you fly with me?"

"With you, Sternholde—with you?"

"Ay, wherefore not?"

"Rather say wherefore. I will not think of such an act."

"Then I am convinced Rouselli lives. He who betrayed you—who betrayed another so dear to me——"

"Ah—you weep!"

"Weep—weep!—I weep! The fount of tears is dry. For years I have not shed one drop."

"They would be blessed tears if you could shed them over again!"

"I never shall. I alluded to my sister Bertha—the beautiful and the good. You hear I can name her without shrinking—without tears. Bertha, I loved her. Well you know how much I loved her. She was *his* victim. Can you wonder that I look for great revenge now? I have registered a vow in Heaven to exterminate him and all that belong to him. The branch of the family to which he belongs shall fall to rise no more. His means shall become the means of those to whom the law will give them. His name shall not live in the memory of the next generation of men."

"He is dead. What more would you? It may be madness to seek for revenge at all, but yet there is a something of human nature in it which discriminates between the innocent and the guilty: but it is the act of a fiend to punish, or seek to injure those who have done no wrong, but merely have the misfortune to be connected with the guilty."

"Seeking for no applause from men," said Sternholde, "I care not what terms they apply to my conduct."

"Nay—nay, you cannot be so indifferent."

"I am! And you but waste time in wasteless argumentation. Marie, I have made a resolution—we will not part now. You shall come with me. We will fly to Germany."

"Never! You will not, or you cannot, tell me of my child, and I must still prosecute my frantic search. Sternholde, farewell for ever! It is my prayer to Heaven that we may never meet again."

"Indeed!"

"Yes. Farewell—farewell."

"Not so, Marie. We part not thus. Your prayer might find compliance, while one of mine might meet rejection. Marie, I have a secret to communicate to you, and there is no more fitting time than this."

"A secret, Sternholde!"

"Yes, one which you cannot guess, and not to put you in suspense, Marie, I love you still!"

The young mother stepped back a pace or two, as she repeated the words—

"Love me still!"

"Yes, with all my ancient fervour. Therefore is it that I ask you to come with me. A dim shadow of my early dream of joy may then be fulfilled, Marie. You have no ties now. Away with all vain regrets. I love you still—I feel I love you still."

"And think you I could, for a moment, dream of yoking my fate to such a one as you? You who breathe an atmosphere of murders! You, who have not even the poor credit of being ashamed of your foul deeds! You, the assassin of harmless men because you were foiled in your revenge upon one who had really injured you! You, a man in whom cruelty became a principle because your revenge meant to be cruel! No! sooner would I pass away from this great world, and all its troubles, along with the heaps of slain that lie here around, than I would, for an instant, dream of uniting my fate to such as thou art!"

"Be wary—I am a desperate man."

"You ever were."

"I am more desperate than you have known me."

"That you cannot be, or, if you are, another feeling which you have been accused of has gone on increasing hand in hand along with your desperation."

"What is that?"

"Cowardice."

"Cowardice!"

"Yes, of which you give a noble example, by threatening a woman, and wishing to feast your eyes upon the sight of him dead, whom, notwithstanding all your boasts, I do believe you avoided while in life."

"Now, by Heaven——"

"What, by Heaven! what?"

"You will drive me to do some desperate deed to your own great prejudice. I am not used to taunts."

"You need not much driving, I calculate, by your own account, to do any desperate deed, provided you can do it safely. I have tried, and failed to awaken some better feelings within you, and now I know you as you really are. Farewell, for ever."

"I can act as well as threaten."

"Against me, doubtless. You are a man, and have a sword; I am a woman, and un-armed."

"Taunt me not. For your own safety's sake, taunt me not."

At this moment the low winding note of a bugle came upon their ears, and Sternholde started, as he strained his eyes in the direction from whence the sounds came. A body of Prussian troops, which had been pursuing the French for some distance, was returning, and taking the nearest route to Brussels, across the ensanguined plain of Waterloo.

Now, too, were to be seen in the dim, waning light, the dusky forms of the soldiers as they came on at an easy pace, not absolutely formed in rank, but so much together, that at a word of command they could take close order, and assume a stricter appearance of discipline. The first rank that was ad-

vancing consisted of a body of light infantry,
of some thousand or so strong. Each man
was carrying his musket as it best suited
him, and the ranks had the straggling appearance they present when troops are on the
march, and permitted to relax in the order of
their steps.

Now and then the bugle sounded to bring
up the stragglers, and, after this tolerably
strong body of infantry, appeared a dense
mass of cavalry, covered with dust and foam,
and bearing many external evidences of how
hotly they had pursued the retreating foe for
some distance, as well as what casual en-
counters they had had with some of the
hindmost of the flying host.

These troops had pursued the French some
leagues from Waterloo, and were only recalled when all effectual opposition was at
an end, and the remnant of Napoleon's army
was scattering itself over too wide a tract of
country to render pursuit at all available or
desirable. The rout had been most complete, and with the exception of very few,
who took the nearest roads to Paris, scarcely
a regiment was in order of discipline, or
knew whither it was going or where were its
officers. It was *sauve qui peut*, according to
the French, which freely translated into
English, means, " The devil take the hindmost."

Infuriated at the opposition of Marie to
his wishes, Sternholde drew a pistol from
his pocket, exclaiming—

" Before yon advancing column nears us,
choose between death and voluntary flight
with me."

" Voluntary !"

" Psha ! I have no time to cavil about
words. Make your choice—I swear that
you shall die by my hand, or follow me at
once into the ruins of this house."

" I will not purchase life," said Marie, " by
dishonour ; but while I have it, I will do my
best to retain it. Help, help, help !"

As she spoke, she rushed off in the direction of the advancing troops, and so sudden
and entirely unexpected was so expeditious
a movement on her part by Sternholde, that
he let her get a considerable distance before
he levelled the pistol after her retreating
form. Then he found, to his mortification,
when he pulled the trigger, that the recent
rain had damped the powder, and no discharge
followed.

Casting the weapon at his feet with an oath,
he produced another, but by this time some
of the foremost ones of the advancing soldiers
had seen Marie, and were running forward to
meet her, for her cries for help had reached
the ears of hundreds of them. One fleet
runner just met her, and caught her in his
arms, as Sternholde fired the second pistol,
which was fully discharged.

" Hit, by God !" he cried, as he saw the
soldier and Marie fall to the ground together.
" Hit, and her weight has knocked that med-
dling fool over."

A rattling discharge of musketry was im-

mediately sent after him, but he plunged into
the ruins of the still burning farm-house, and
was on the instant lost to view, apparently
quite unhurt from any of the random shots
which had been discharged after him.

———

## CHAPTER V.

### THE OLD FARM-HOUSE AT MONCKTON FRIARS. —FIFTEEN YEARS' LAPSE.—THE PROGRESS OF EVENTS.—THE FIRE.

FIFTEEN years had passed away since that
memorable battle of Waterloo had been
fought and won. Fifteen long weary years
to hundred of thousands, whose best and
fondest, dearest and noblest of hopes were,
during such a period, quenched for ever.
Fifteen years of sparkling joy to a much less
number, and to many who, with a sigh of
astonishment, would have heard that so long
a sunny lapse of time had passed away.

And what an age in the life of any human
being is fifteen years—a fourth of most
ordinarily long existences ; and were those
fifteen years to be thought over in the progress of their events at what period of
existence they may, their vast effect upon
the prospects and the position of all persons
must be soon apparent.

What man during such a period has not
something to lament ? We do not allude to
the small ordinary lamentations of life, for
those crosses will occur as naturally as we
draw breath, but larger and more serious
evils. Fifteen years may have given the
destroyer power, and the grave may have
closed over some fair, much-loved form we
would fain have had yet awhile to linger with
us on our earthly pilgrimage.

Fifteen years converts the child almost to
the man—the little prattling infant to the
young girl in all the pride and glory of her
beauty. They convert the young and the
enthusiastic into the staid, the serious, and
the calculating. They convert the strong,
hearty man into an old one, who sees the
ties that bound him to life contemporarily
all one by one severed, and begins to think
that he himself is lingering too long in a
world which is peopled by new faces and
with the thoughts, feelings, opinions, sympathies, and pleasures, of which he has no kind
of companionship.

Yes ; fifteen years have passed away since
Waterloo was fought and won. The dead
have become rotten who fell on that memorable day, and their glory is mingled in our
records somehow with the accounts we
have heard of how well everything grew
upon the plains of Waterloo after the battle,
for some years, in consequence of the earth
being so well manured with blood.

The political events which followed that
awful conflict had not then fully developed
themselves, but they were doing so rapidly.
Peace had been restored to Europe, but the
angry passions which many years had

fostered and generated, now only slept for a time, or felt themselves chained down by the force of circumstances.

But what changes, amid all those which have been produced by time and circumstances during those fifteen years, have occurred to those persons in whose fates we have become interested, from watching for a brief space of time what occurred to them on that field of carnage, when the name of Waterloo was fresh in the minds of men, and the account of the most sanguinary conflict of modern times appeared to Europe more like a dream than a reality, bringing in its train such important results?

What has become of the young ensign who lay there, so badly wounded, and thinking of the happy home he had left, to engage in such a scene, and make one of the miscalculating people who prefer doing the fighting abroad, to paying for it at home? Where is he, and how has he prospered or retrograded in his circumstances since that awful day?

And the young child whom, with a generosity of spirit we are proud to say is an acknowledged characteristic of our countrymen, he made so ready a promise to protect —where is she—Mabel as she was named? Fifteen years must have made great alterations in her, if still she be numbered among the living.

And the battle fiend—Sternholde, the wild, revengeful man, who had conducted an interview on the field of blood with the bereaved young mother, that said so little for his head or for his heart—does he still continue his mad career, or has the grim hand of death been laid upon him, and stopped him in the midst of his atrocities?

Was that man a great moral hypocrite, or was he labouring under a great moral delusion in destroying the members of a nation, only one out of which had injured him? Perhaps his feelings were a compound of the two states. He may have wandered from honour, because to do so was a more convenient mode of living before he entered the army than any which honest labour could present to him, and then he might have tried to stultify his own brain sufficiently to enable him to consider it a sentiment, and that the revenge he sought justified the diabolical proceedings.

And Rafferty Brolickbones, who feared to be picked up in so many pieces from the field of Waterloo, that some of them would be lost—where is he? Has fifteen years quenched the sparkling merry humour of his heart? Have they dimmed his perception of the ludicrous? Have they attacked in any way his love for whisky?

Let us cast about us for some chance of discovering the whereabouts of some of those whom we have mentioned, and whose fortunes we still propose for a time to follow. We will not travel for the present out of England, but we seek them not amid the hum of crowded cities, or busier haunts of man. With a foreknowledge of where to look, we cast our eyes upon one of the most romantic and delightul spots in Cumberland. It is summer time, and all is fresh and beautiful, and full of radiance, joy, and beauty.

But we will be more methodical, and fain would we, ere the storm of fate, which is hovering in the distance, expends its fury upon an innocent and a beautiful head, linger by that sweet spot, and in imagination conduct our readers to the every haunt of sylvan beauty which is to be found about its intricate and time-worn recesses.

In one of the most favoured spots that the country could present for many miles around, was an ancient, large, rambling, roomy, handsome farm-house. The house and farm attached went by the name of Monckton Friars, and since the memory of man, in the way of tradition, from father to son, it had never known any other appellation.

Monckton Frairs is one of those buildings —we say is, because it still exists—which, unhappily for the picturesque and the beautiful, are fast passing away from the land. Aged, without showing any evident signs of decay—venerable from the lapse of years that have rolled over it, and which appear only to have consolidated those structures they have not destroyed. For the greater part it was built of the old red brick of which such beautiful specimens can be seen at Hampton-court, and in some of the old houses in Kent which have escaped the hands of the despoiler.

The architecture of Monckton Friars would have puzzled a conjuror to define; but wherever there was much ornament, it was evidently belonging to the age of the Henrys, and of Elizabeth, when a more florid taste showed itself, and many of the nobility and wealthy yeomen had added to their buildings some new wing according to the fashion of the times.

The general character of Monckton Friars was, therefore, that of an Elizabethan building, although it presented an odd jumble, when closely looked at, of all ages, and all sorts of tastes. But time had, somehow, made the incongruous look beautiful, and had so rivetted, as it were, the whole mass, by the luxurious tints it gave to it, that no one could fail to look with pleasure on the house.

The creeping plants grew up prodigiously on some of the walls: deep latticed windows permitted the casual passenger to see into old oaken rooms, the ceilings of which had cost, or would now, at all events, cost, as much as would run up a modern house, in the lath and plaster style of 1850. The doorway was a perfect study of itself— massive and beautiful. You had to descend a step on going into the house, which certainly is a circumstance which gives a hall a cavernous appearance; but the beauty of the front, which was amazingly massive, was indisputable.

It was covered with rich carving, and supported upon columns, which, on their shafts, showed how little labour was grudged in the days when they were so elaborately fashioned. And all around this ancient edifice was a farm, and grounds of the richest produce, and tended with the greatest care. About two hundred acres lay in such a manner round the house, that, from some one or another of its windows, almost every meadow, every copse, and every little streamlet, could be fairly seen. In the front, and contiguous, precisely, to the grounds of Monckton Friars, was a lake of such clear, transparent water, that to look into it showed the Heaven above as clearly as it could be seen in reality, and gave to the mind that dreamy feeling of awe which results from the looking into some profound depth almost greater than human calculation can define.

The same family which now occupied Monckton Friars had done so as long as anything whatever was known of the house. They had been the original proprietors of the place, and from father to son had it descended as regularly as age after age, in the natural order of things, permitted it to do.

But very many important changes had taken place among the inhabitants of the old place, if the place itself had succeeded, through lapse of so many ages, in preserving its ancient character. The name of the family was Morton, and originally they had been but rude men, who had acquired for some good service rendered to some reigning monarch, the grant of the land comprising the Monckton Friars estate.

Some of them had been men-at-arms, and one had been an esquire; but the family had never been one of any great consideration, so that when England had become more powerful, and, consequently, more prosperous and settled in its affairs than it had been in early times, the Mortons of Monckton Friars became yeomen, and rather rough uncultivated tillers of the soil.

From age to age, however, the importance of the property increased, and additions had been made to the old house. Then the march of education, of course, found its way to the farm-house held by the Mortons, and we find among the inscriptions in the old church-yard in the vicinity, one which says—

"Here lyeth ye mortale remnante
of
Hugh Morton, of Monckton Friars,
a right cunninge clerke. Pray ye good
Christian for his soul.
1617."

Most probably the "cunninge clerke" was some member of the family who had a taste for literature, and was looked upon as a wonderful genius because he knew B from a bull's foot. Alas! those days have past away, when a man who could read was considered something wonderful, and be courted and admired, while one who could write was considered little less than a conjuror.

Now, in this confounded age, when everybody can do everything, no one has a chance. There is nothing to acquire but thousands will acquire along with you, and reputations are not to be had on such terms. But to return to Monckton Friars.

As the property increased in value, the Mortons became more important people, and shook off, along with many other trammels, the rough exterior that had for a number of years characterised them. They became quite civilised, and, at our own time, a more polite, highly educated, and more generally esteemed family did not exist.

\*     \*     \*     \*     \*

It is the same month, June, in which the battle was fought which laid upon the field of Waterloo Henry Morton, the young ensign who had been so badly wounded, and who was a much-loved member of the family we have been describing to the reader. Indeed, it was the anniversary of that day which is never recollected by an Englishman without pride, be he the greatest philosopher and condemner of war that ever stepped. The weather was delightfully serene. Without being by any means sultry, there was that pleasant high summer temperature, modified by a cool, brilliant kind of air, that made mere existence a pleasure, and produced a pleasant effect upon the spirits. Scarcely ever had there been such a year for vegetation as the one we are alluding to. Nature seemed to have done her best with all her multifarious productions.

There had been a plentiful supply of moisture from the skies—the heavens had been bountiful in its supplies, and the sun had shed an early and genial warmth with it, and the fields bore an ample evidence of the riches of the coming harvest. So it was, earth and Heaven teemed with goodness and joy—the gay-plumaged bird, and the beautiful songsters, flitted hither and thither in the joy that animated nature.

The sweet sounds that greeted the ear of the wayfarer were strong and numerous, not a hedgerow, nor a tree, nor a copse, but what had its own appropriated warblers, and even the heavens were inhabited by the lark. The fields were scarce less worthy the study of man; the grass was tinted strongly with the yellow flowers that cover the beautiful meadows of our beautiful land; the hedges were ornamented by the blossoms of the white thorn, though in many places this was on the decay—the time for flowering was fast going past.

The corn-fields presented a beautiful appearance; the tall and gracefully waving corn gave a pleasing and refreshing sensation to the sight, dazzled by the brightness of the sun. And, then, the beautiful contrast between the green and varied beauty of the meadows and corn-fields, and the clear and crystal waters of the streams, and the blue of the distant hills.

It is refreshing to gaze upon running water when in the heat of a noontide sun, so beautiful and covered with the white floating flowers of the woods, and the yellow water lily; the tall hedges and rushes all conduce to the beauty of river scenery, the most picturesque and the most beautiful in the world.

The sunset was beautiful, and the heat was excessive, and would have been suffocating, but for the cool breeze that sprang up as the sun declined, that breathed a refreshing breath over the parched surface of the earth. The sky was serene and bright, save here and there, where a fleecy cloud sailed slowly and imperceptibly across the heavens; these were gradually illuminated by the sun's departing rays.

The gorgeous tints that now bedecked the heavens, and gilded the declining day, were more beautiful than, perhaps, had ever been seen or noticed by any human being. The tall trees threw long shadows, and hill and dale were alike diversified by deep shadows and broad sunny spots.

The evening was drawing to a close, too, and the heat of the day was sensibly decreasing, still it was not doing so so

THE ENCOUNTER BETWEEN THE MENDICANT AND THE MASTIFF-DOG.

rapidly as to produce any unpleasant sensations. By the banks of the lake, which held its quiet place so near to Monckton Friars, had been planted a thick belt of wood, and although, from common prudence, to give space for the trees to spread and acquire their full growth, many had suffered from the axe of the woodman, yet it had ever been an object with the possessor of Monckton Friars to keep this belt of wood in a good state of preservation.

It was not only a pleasant object of itself, but it shielded the farm from any cold winds which in the dreary winter time might sweep across the lake. Through, too, the very centre of this thick plantation was a winding path that was well preserved, and had in course of years acquired amazing hardness and solidity. It was but narrow, and wound along like a long snake among the trees, now avoiding some stately chestnut, and now brushing closely past the trunk of some tall poplar, which seemed intent upon its head reaching Heaven.

In the heat of summer, at times when not a leaf stirred on a tree, and as the weary insects, who seem but to have their existence round the refulgence of its rays, sunk exhausted among the petals of some gorgeous flower—when all nature seems conquered by the temperature—when people move along languidly, and scarcely have energy to tell each other how hot it is—when the husbandman falls asleep from his labour, and the yellow corn may be almost seen to ripen beneath the scorching rays that fall so vividly upon it, then that walk in the wilderness, as it was called, was deliciously rural and pleasant.

And there were several things to make it so. In the first place it ran from east to west; therefore, the sun's rays scarcely ever could penetrate into the pathway; and, in the second, the lake was so close at hand that it always imparted some degree of coolness to the air, and if it did not that, when the sun's rays almost warmed its surface, it looked cool and refreshing, as it was seen glancing among the trees by any one strolling along that mimic forest-path.

One end of the plantation terminated in a meadow, which formed part of the Monckton Friars estate; the other end in some fields belonging to a neighbouring property, from which it was only divided by a hawthorn edge, for the Mortons were not troublesome, suspicious people, and sought not to build themselves up so completely as many do.

We have been thus particular in describing the wilderness, by which name it will be known during our narrative, because it is to that place we rush at first, and at once, to conduct our readers. The slant rays of the setting sun, then, were just streaming over the lands of the farm, and the glaring light of day had given place to the mellower, more welcome radiance that filled the evening air, when a solitary figure might have been seen wending its way along the winding pathway in the wilderness.

The form was that of a young girl, although from her stature, which was tall, no one would have thought her really so young as she was, until they had looked in her beaming and beautiful, yet childlike, gentle face, and then there could be no doubt but she was still only on the verge of existence. She was attired, not showily, or in costly garments, but her appearance had about it that ineffable grace which betrays at once the tenderly nurtured girl, who has been carefully watched and tended by the sleepless eyes of fond affection.

A straw hat was carelessly thrown back from her head, so that the whole contour of her face was visible.

Oh! how shall we hope to describe the world of sweetness and beauty that found a home on that countenance! Truly was she one of Nature's best and dearest works. It was a face to dream of for ever after once seeing—one of those sweet, chancelike countenances which are so full of idolatry that we can hardly believe that they really belong to earth.

Her eyes were of the darkest hazel; so full, too, of intelligence and power, that the bad shrunk from their gaze, while the good doated on their intellectual beauty; her cheeks presented the clear, transparent colour which health and pure air only can give; while her mouth, so beautifully curved, and so full of expression as it was, would have been a long study for the longest summer's day that ever dawned.

Her hair was not black; but it was so nearly so, that, while it had all the beauty that black could have as a contrast, it had likewise the silky fineness which seldom belongs to that colour. It hung evidently in masses of wavy tresses of Nature's own fashioning, about her neck and face, and then far down on to her shoulders, where, with a gentle springy motion, as she walked, it danced upon her snowy breast, as if proud of the resting-place it had obtained.

"And with all her beauty, all her intelligence, and all the tender care which had been bestowed upon her, there could have been observed by an attentive observer an air of sadness upon her face.

At times, too, this air of sadness would deepen into positive melancholy, and then a sigh would come from her heart, as if, despite all incitements to serenity and joy, there was still a something hidden there which marred the beauty of all things, and tempered the happiness of her young heart to a sedater feeling.

What could it be that interposed its cruel blight upon the joy of one so fair, and surely so good? Too young was she for those ill-impressed affections that bring more tears than smiles; too young to have yet discovered that the flowers of life only bloom in such rich beauty on the world's threshold, and that, after that, they are few and far between. And yet she was unhappy.

But now she raises her eyes to Heaven, and clasps her hands; she speaks, and her words fall like the lowest notes of some distant music on the ear.

"He will tell me all to-day," she said; "he has promised he will tell me all to-day; I am the child of mystery. I have no kindred—none to love me with that love which should spring from a mother's heart. I am very desolate—very desolate."

A tear stole down her cheek, and fell upon one of her small, exquisitely shaped hands. Oh! what beauty—what intelligence there may be in a hand!

She started as the pearly drop made its presence known by thus gently flowing from her eyes.

"For shame!" she said; "is this true? Is this grateful? Who has been so tenderly—so kindly, fondly nurtured as I have been—upon whom has so much care been lavished: upon whom have the eyes of true affection beamed more devotedly? And yet I weep and say that I am desolate. No—no—no! I may be sad at times, but I am not desolate, while warm, kind hearts exist beneath that roof which will ever, to me, be a hallowed spot, rendered sacred as the home of the dearest affections."

She was at a small opening among the trees, which commanded a view of the house, and now she paused to look at it; but she saw it through a hazy mist, for, all unconsciously, her eyes had filled with tears, and, as she brushed them from the long lashes that fringed those orbs of light and beauty, she said,—

"Now, I deserve some reprehension from those who have loved me so well for this. I do deserve their censure. It is a poor, a very poor return for all the kindness they have lavished on me to be weeping here as if that kindness had been harshness, and all that tender devoted care I have received but so much refined cruelty."

Alas! the struggle that was going on in her mind was not one of any touch of ingratitude. No human heart that ever beat could be more grateful than she was to the family of the Mortons; but, as she said, she was a being of mystery, and knew not even who she was.

That much of her history she knew—that she was the adopted child of the Morton family—that for some reason or another they had all lavished much kindness upon her—that they seemed never weary of their goodness to her. They had made her one of themselves; nay, she went by the name of Morton—Mabel Morton; but yet she knew she belonged not to them, and that some mystery, which had never yet, to her, been explained, enshrouded her, and her birth and friends.

No wonder, then, that she, with so sensitive a heart, should feel some touch of occasional depression. It was not that she appreciated not all that had been done

for her—it was not that deep, heartfelt gratitude did not form the very essence of her being; but it was the agony of suspense, and of doubt, that brought upon her face that melancholy aspect, and now had forced tears from her eyes.

"He will tell me all, now, to-day," she said again; "he has promised to tell me all; and yet, how little is that all, he says. And, when I wept upon his breast, and begged to know the story of my life, he said he knew so little that he had not told me, lest I should be unhappy by losing my spirits in wild conjecture."

A ray of sunlight, which had suddenly dipped from behind a projection of the house, fell upon her face, and she turned aside to avoid it.

On the moment she became aware of the presence of a stranger in the wilderness, who was leaning against the trunk of a tree at some distance, and who seemed to be most intently observing her.

The sunlight is impartial. It falls alike upon age and youth, beauty and its opposite; and as the man there stood he was completely enveloped in the golden rays of the setting luminary, which found its way through the opening in the wilderness that had been artificially made on purpose for the view of the house from that spot.

---

## CHAPTER VI.

THE STRANGER IN THE WILDERNESS.—THE THREAT, AND THE TERROR OF MABEL.—THE FLIGHT TO THE HOUSE.

So unusual a sight was a stranger in the wilderness of Monckton Friars that, for a moment, Mabel could hardly believe the evidence of her own eyes to the fact that there was with her on that spot, which she thought secure from all intrusion, one whom she knew not.

He did not speak. He looked tired, travel-worn, and exhausted. The apparel he wore had evidently seen much service; it was patched and re-patched clumsily in all directions; shoes he had none; and one of his feet was bleeding as if from some recent injury he had received from a flint casually trodden upon. Round his head he wore a coloured handkerchief, and above that again was a slouching hat of the most ragged and wretched description.

Take him altogether, a more unprepossessing man could scarcely have been found, or more likely to create alarm in the breast of one so far from immediate succour as was Mabel Morton.

And yet, without affecting all the qualities of a heroine, Mabel was not a coward, and the momentary feeling of terror almost subsided into one of compassion as she marked the wretched aspect of the man.

The sun was, too, strongly upon his countenance, and she perhaps was too little of a reasoner upon physiognomy for her to take up any prejudice against the man on account of the awfully sinister expression that sat upon it. Heaven knows, poor girl, she had afterwards ample opportunity of knowing every line of that dreadful face.

Poverty in rags is never very graceful, despite all that poets have said of it. There is not much inducement to a man in the lowest depths of pecuniary wretchedness to strive to arrange his rags neatly; and no wonder that, along with her feelings of compassion, Mabel should associate one of loathing for the object before her, who was one of the worst looking mendicants she had ever in her short life beheld.

When he saw that he was observed by her, he advanced a pace or two, and then he was out of the sphere of the sun's influence, and she was better able to see the face which before had been so obscure.

His eyes were small and ferret-looking. The forehead had that shelving shape which betokens in its possessor cunning without wisdom; and about the mouth there was some unfortunate curve which could not well be defined, but which gave an uncommonly villanous expression to the whole face.

The first impulse of Mabel was to fly from the spot when he now began to move towards her; but she checked herself in that, and paused, as his attitude was respectful, and he took off the slouched hat he wore. Then, in whining accents, which must have been the result of long practice in mendicity, he said,—

"Sweet young lady, take some pity on a poor man—an old soldier, one who has fought the battles of his country, and kept the domestic hearths free from the invader. Have compassion, dear young lady, on an old soldier."

Mabel was almost too terrified to speak, for he kept coming still nearer to her each moment. However, she mustered courage to address him in answer to his mock submissive appeal.

"If you go round," she said, "to the front of the farm, you will be relieved. No one is turned away from that door unrelieved, who is considered worthy."

"The front of the house, miss?"

"Yes. Go there."

"Lord bless me! if you knew how far I have travelled, and how long ago it is since I've tasted food, you would not ask me to go so far."

"It is a mile to the nearest place," said Mabel, "at which you could purchase food, were I to give you money. It is not a fourth part of that distance to the front entrance of the farm."

The fellow looked puzzled for a moment, and all he could say was—

"Oh, indeed!"

"Besides," added Mabel, "you are trespassing here, you must be aware; and, however charitable Mr. Morton may be, I know he does not approve of intrusions on to those parts of his grounds which are set apart for the exclusive use of the family."

"Morton—Morton!"

"Yes, Mr. Morton."

"Then, what place is this, miss?"

"Monckton Friars, it is named. I will go by a shorter route to the house, and see that you are relieved."

"Well, but—but I can go by the shorter cut, too."

"You would lose your claims to charity were you to do so. It is not permitted; and I should incur blame. I tell you again, no one is sent from here unrelieved; but it has become necessary on that very account to guard against intrusions on all sides."

The man advanced another step, and in a voice which betrayed some agitation, he said—

"Girl—I—I beg your pardon, miss—was Mr. Morton ever in the army?"

"He was," said Mabel, surprised at first at the question, although a moment's consideration told her she need not be, as that was a fact known to the whole country side. "He was, but is not now."

"He—he was, but is not now," repeated the man, as if the words possessed to him more than common interest.

Mabel was going away, but he called out to her,—

"Stay—stay. I—I want to know more—I must know more."

"You must!"

"Yes—I—no—that is, I humbly request to know more."

"I cannot remain to answer the questions of a stranger," said Mabel.

"By Heaven!—no. Pardon me, miss. Your father, Mr. Morton——"

"He is not my father."

"Not your father! Not—not—not your father! What then—what then, I say? You are too young to be his wife. What —what——"

"This is impertinence," said Mabel; and, feeling a degree of alarm which she would not show, she hastened to leave the wilderness. Fain would she have ran from the place, but a sense of pride and natural courage which she possessed, forbade her to do so, and she only walked at a rapid pace. Some distance lower down in the wilderness was a swinging gate, which led to a pathway direct to the farm-house, and it was that which she now wished to gain. Before, however, she had proceeded far, she heard the hasty patter of the man's bare feet upon the pathway behind her, and she felt assured that she was being actually pursued. A pang of fear came across her mind, and she quickened her speed. She knew that she was being overtaken, and that there was no time for her to open the gate and pass through it, so she at once turned upon her pursuer when she reached it, and with her hand laid upon it, and a face as pale as marble, she said—

"What means this conduct? Is this the way you advance your claims to the charity of those whom I can influence?"

"D—n their charity!" cried the fellow; "why did you run away from me in that way for?"

"How dared you pursue me?"

"Because it was my pleasure. I can see that you are obstinate enough to refuse me an answer to what I want to know, by fair means, but perhaps you will be wise enough to give it to me, if I threaten what you cannot but feel, from my superior strength, I can perform."

"Threaten!"

"Yes, threaten. I want a few plain answers to a few plain questions; and you had better give them to me at once."

"Beware, sir; I am not so far from home but what I think I could summon assistance. I pity your wretched condition, and am disposed to forgive even this outrage, if you at once desist from following me."

"Can you, indeed! By G—d, you carry it with a high hand; and the more I look at you, the more I feel inclined to insist upon an answer to my questions, the first one of which shapes itself into the words of who are you?"

"Who—who am I?"

"Yes, who are you? What's your name? Who are your friends, girl? Are you any relationship to Morton or none?"

Mabel looked fixedly at the man, and the idea crossed her mind that surely he must know something of her history, or he would not be so curious in asking questions concerning her. Forgetting for the moment, then, all prudential considerations, as her mind reverted to that which was to her the most interesting question in the world,

she cried, with sudden energy and animation,—

"Tell me why you ask. Tell me who you are. What, what do you know—what prompts you to ask of me such questions? Oh, if you know aught of—of the past——"

She checked herself, and with a flush of colour upon her face, she felt that she ought not to have said so much to a perfect stranger, and she added,—

"No matter, no matter; I—I do not want to know. Farewell! farewell! Go and get entrance at the front of the house; I have no more words for you. Go—go—go, I say."

"Not yet, girl. Your manner convinces me I am not wrong; that I have not been walking over England years for nothing. You are not a daughter, indeed; you are no relation of Morton's. Was he at the Battle of Waterloo?"

"He was."

"I knew it. The very man. D——n! what a treat. You are a beautiful girl, and you are like one whom I knew long ago. I thought so, when first you turned your head, and I saw your face; but, somehow, then the likeness vanished; but now it has come back again, and I know that I am not at all mistaken."

"Like one whom you know? Like who? like who?"

"Humph! You are ready enough to ask me questions, but far from willing to answer me any."

"No, no, I ask nothing—nothing. I demean myself by conversing with one, who, by some accident, has, of course, just become acquainted with enough of my history to enable him to prey upon my imagination. Follow me not, sir, or you will do so at your peril."

"I will not follow you."

"Farewell! farewell

"Nor shall you go. Attempt but to pass through that gate, and I will detain you here by force."

"You detain me here by force?"

"Such were my words, and you shall find that what I say I'll do, I will do; so take the matter easy. Make a virtue of necessity. Answer me what I would ask of you, and then you may go where you please, and as soon as you please."

Mabel made a hasty calculation in her own mind of the distance to the house, and she asked herself if her voice could really reach so far. It was a time of the evening when none of the farm labourers were about the meadows, as all were engaged in attending to the live stock of the place, so she had but little hope of success. Her heart beat with fearful violence; she wished, yet dreaded to hear what the mysterious man had to say to her.

"You are considering?" he said.

"No, no, no," she cried, "I am not. I have nothing to say to you."

"Very good; I have something, however, to say to you. What is your name?"

"My name is well known; it is no secret My name is Mabel."

"I guessed as much," cried the fellow, in a tone of exultation. "You have no friends; you are kept by Captain Morton—for he is a captain in rank—in charity. You know nothing of your own history."

"Gracious Heaven, who can you be who have acquired so much knowledge of what I am?"

"Ah, who can I be?"

"Tell me, I implore you."

"Oh, you are beginning to implore, are you? Ha! ha! what an odd thing, to hear a fine young lady, such as you are, so proud and haughty, imploring of a poor beggar, without a shoe to his foot."

"You shall be rewarded; you shall not long remain in such a situation, if you can tell me who I am. If you know the secret of my birth——"

"I do know it."

"Oh, tell me—tell me, I beseech you; keep me not in ignorance; tell me, I implore you, tell me."

"Hush! there are two words go to that bargain, Mabel; you must answer me some questions first."

"What? what?"

"You shall hear; and now remember, if you cavil over your answers, or refuse me the information I seek, I leave you, and you will never know who you are, for the secret is buried here, and nowhere else."

He struck his breast as he spoke, and eyed her fixedly. She trembled, and held on by the gate for support, as she replied—

"What questions I can and ought to answer to you, I will answer, with the hope that you will be explicit upon that subject which is so dear to my heart, and which has given rise in my mind to so much endless, painful, and all-engrossing conjecture."

"I will satisfy you."

"On your oath, swear to me that you will."

"I swear that I will. Answer the questions which I ask of you freely, and I will then answer you as freely all that you can ask of me."

"I will, I will. Yes, yes."

"By the bye, first and foremost, have you any money?"

"A small sum; you are quite welcome to it."

She produced her purse, and he at once snatched it from her trembling hands, and placed it out of sight in his bosom, as he cried, with a brutal laugh that made the very heart of poor Mabel turn cold—

"This will do for the present. Ha—ha—ha! This will keep the enemy at bay for the present. By G—d! it strikes me very forcibly that, in a short time now, I shall cut a very different appearance to my present one. D—n these rags, they become me about as well as a scarecrow."

## CHAPTER VII.

THE NEW ANXIETIES OF MABEL—THE DOG AND THE GUN.—THE DISCOMFITED RUFFIAN.—MABEL'S SWOON AT THE FARM-HOUSE.

ALREADY did Mabel begin to repent of the bargain she had made, when she saw what a state of brutal exultation it produced in the mind of the fellow who had so far induced her to hold a conversation with him on a subject upon which she had never opened her lips to any one save him who was her benefactor, and all to her that a parent could be.

Even now, could she have succeeded in doing so with any degree of safety, she would have flown from the spot, but she dreaded to make the least movement to undo the swinging gate, lest, in pursuance of his threat, he should rush forward and lay violent hands upon her; and what could she, young and delicately formed as she was, expect to be able to do against the reckless ruffian who stood before her?

When he had indulged himself as much as he wished in his contemplations of a change in his prospects, he bent his keen eyes upon Mabel's face, and in a voice of triumphant malice he cried—

"Come, then, is Morton rich?"

"I—I believe he is rich."

"Good. Is he married?"

"Yes," said Mabel, pleased to find the questions such as she could answer without any breach of confidence.

"Has he ever told you how he came by the care of you?"

"Never."

"Indeed; that's very strange. You don't know, then, any other name than that of Mabel?"

"They call me Mabel Morton; I know

no other name, although I know that to that one I am not entitled."

"How old are you?"

"I do not know, but it is generally believed that I am about sixteen."

"Right; the general presumption is correct, I happen to know. Ha, ha! What's at the end of that gold chain round your neck, eh?"

"A cross."

"A cross! let me see it."

"No, no; I have given you what money I had; that I do not value, but I will not part with this."

"Not part with it?"

"No, not except with my life. It is precious to me, for it was round my neck when I was an infant, and I have often been told by those who have been so kind to me, never to part with it."

"Indeed; you won't show it to me?"

"I will not."

"It is made of brilliants, set in a white-coloured gold."

Mabel started.

"You seem surprised, but, you see, I know a thing or two. It is of value—I mean, it is of intrinsic value. If you preserve it with any notion that it will assist you in discovering your parents or family, you are wrong; it will do no such thing—I know better."

"I will not part with it."

"Pho! pho! give it to me."

"Never! never to a living soul!"

"I can tell you more in one minute than ever you could discover by any one's recognition of that cross in a hundred years."

"I will not give it to you."

"Remember, I have as yet told you nothing."

"Then tell me nothing; I have promised not to part with this, and I will not."

"Now confound your obstinacy, girl, what a fool you must be; you know you will just give me the trouble of forcing it from your neck."

"You dare not do so," cried Mabel; "I tell you again and again, you shall not have it."

"And I tell you that I will."

"Help! help!"

"Ay, you may call, your voice won't carry to that house I see yonder; and if it did, I'm off before the fleetest runner in it could get here. Give me the cross, I say."

"No, no, spare me that; you shall have more money to-morrow; I will bring you its full value in gold, if you will name the sum."

"You will?"

"I will; but this I cannot, dare not, part with, but with my life. You would not murder me for what to you can possess no value but its worth in money?"

"Murder be hanged! I want only to look at it, if you will keep your word about bringing me the money to-morrow. The cross is worth fifty pounds."

"Fifty pounds?"

"Yes, if it's worth a penny piece."

"I have not such a sum. Good God! where am I to get fifty pounds? It is not possible, it is not possible."

"Then must I have the bauble."

At this moment, from some part of the plantation, there came the sudden and sharp report of a gun, and the stranger gave so alarmed a start, that Mabel seized the opportunity, and, opening the swinging gate, she darted through it. Recovering, then, from his momentary surprise almost immediately, he, with a furious bound, and an oath of the most diabolical character, darted after her; but scarcely had he got half-a-dozen yards from the swinging gate, when a large hound sprang into the middle of the pathway between him and Mabel. At so great a speed, however, was he coming on after the flying girl, that he could not stop himself till he was right upon the dog, who, although of a peaceable demeanour, did not seem to think such a step was proper, so he took a tolerable mouthful out of the fellow's leg, and then looked at him, as much as to say, "Well, my friend, what do you want?"

Rage, although excessive, by no means deprived the beggar of sufficient reason to make him thoroughly understand the propriety of falling back out of range of the dog's teeth, and he accordingly placed himself on the other side of the gate, with a quickness that would have done credit to a harlequin at any theatre in Christendom.

Well did Mabel know that she was safe the moment she saw the noble hound; for she and he were old acquaintances. Indeed, he not unfrequently accompanied her in her walks about the estate, and often when she had left the farm-house without him, he had sought her out, and walked along with her, as a body-guard of no unimportant character.

She immediately turned with a flushed face and confronted the fellow, who now found himself in a dangerous position, and as she rested her hand upon the head of the hound she said—

"If I were as full of the passion of resentment as you are of wickedness, I could, by a word, set the creature on you, and perhaps your life would fall a sacrifice to your wish to do a deed of violence to one as unable effectually to resist you as you would be to resist this honest creature."

The dog gave a very ominous growl, as if he understood what was said, and wished to signify his assent to it. Then he looked up in Mabel's face, to endeavour (for dogs are most acute physiognomists) to discover if it would be quite pleasant to her for him to fly at the fellow, who stood on the other side of the gate, or not.

"Keep him off—keep the dog off!" cried the discomfited ruffian. "Don't let the d—d brute fly at me. Keep him off!"

"You do not deserve that I should keep him off!"

"Look at him, will you? he's coming!"

"If you attempt to fly, he will pursue you."

"I know it—keep him away! Such a brute as that would kill a man; keep him quiet, now, do!"

"Your abject terror now, as well as your former brutality, proves your desperate cowardice. He shall keep guard over you, until some one comes to take you into custody for your attempted robbery."

"Take me into custody?"

"Yes. You are a thief. You would have robbed me, and because you thought yourself the stronger, you would not have cared what degree of violence was necessary to deprive me of the trinket which I told you I set the most intrinsic value upon."

"Ah, but, Miss Mabel, remember that I have something to tell you about your real name and your family, you know."

He spoke in a whining, cringing tone, which, if possible, was more disgusting than had been his former brutal style of discourse. He showed that he was a ruffian who could stoop to anything, and, when the stronger, was unmeasured in the amount of his wickedness, while, when the weaker, his abject timidity knew no bounds.

"I will hear nothing—I will hear nothing," said Mabel, "from such a man as you are'"

"Then beware!"

"I heed not your threats. Leo, boy, look at him!"

The dog advanced close to the swinging gate, and then sat down and stared the man in the face, while he now and then gave a low growl, and licked his immense tongue round his jaws, as if to warn him that if he attempted to move away,

another good grip would be the consequence.

"Mabel!" at this moment cried a voice, and a young lad, whose age might be about the same as hers, or possibly a year older, made his appearance, carrying in his hand a light fowling-piece. "Mabel, you here?"

"Yes, Charles, yes—yes. I have been frightened by that man."

"Indeed. Let him take care of himself."

"Leo has him safe, Charles, Leo has him safe. But I think I will let him go now."

"Go! No such thing. Hilloa, you fellow! Oh, look, Mabel!"

The man had produced a long, glittering knife, and, with a fiendish expression, he suddenly cried—

"Now send your dog on, and I'll soon let out his heart's blood."

"Drop that knife," said the lad, who had been named Charles by Mabel, as he presented his gun. "Drop that knife, or, as you are a living man, I'll send a charge of number four in your face."

"Let him go—oh, let him go!" said Mabel, who felt much terrified at the turn affairs had taken. "Leo—Leo! Here, boy!"

The dog came to her immediately, and she cried out—

"Go—go! you are free to go."

"If it's your wish, Mabel, to let him go," said Charles, "he may, but my brother Henry, I know, if he were here, would not."

"Hark you, Mabel," said the fellow, as he turned away, "the wisest thing you ever said in your life, you said just now, when you said 'let him go.' You will live to know that some of these days, and that at no very distant time either. D—n you all, and your dog too!"

So saying, he dashed off among the trees, and in a few moments completely disappeared. Poor Mabel was glad to lean upon the arm of Charles Morton, for that was the youth's name, and what with the fright, and the tumult of her thoughts, joined to the exhaustion of more exercise than she had been accustomed to, she had only strength sufficient to reach the threshold of the farm-house, and then consciousness deserted her, and she fainted, to the great terror and grief of her young companion, who filled the hall with his loud lamentations.

———

## CHAPTER VIII.

A SCENE OF CONFUSION AT THE HALL.—
THE NARRATION OF MABEL.—A CON-
SULTATION AND ITS RESULTS. — THE
DECLARATION OF HENRY MORTON.

TOTALLY unused as was the young lad,
Charles Morton, to faintings and those
powerful mental emotions which produce
such results, no wonder he was both
amazed and terrified to see Mabel, now
that the danger to which she had been
exposed was completely over, so suddenly
lapse into a state of, to him, alarming
insensibility. It was, however, precisely
that very circumstance of the danger being
over which produced so sudden and complete a prostration of strength in Mabel.
While there was something to be done—
something to be contended against, she
had kept up resistingly; but now, when
she had reached the porch of that house
where she knew well there was ample
protection against all harm, her feelings

overcame her, and no longer making the
effort to be firm, which had hitherto
restrained her, she had, as we have
recorded, given way to it.

The cries of Charles very quickly
brought the active assistance of every
member of the household to the spot, and
from the nature of his lamentations, the
excess of his grief, and the frantic manner
in which he called aloud for aid, every one
feared that some dreadful and serious
calamity must have befallen her, who was
the beloved of all hearts, from the highest
to the lowest, in that pleasant and united
household.

The dog, too, and dogs will often do
such things, actually participated in his
master's grief, and when he heard Charles
calling out in such tones, he set up a howl
that was heard far and near, and added
greatly to the scene of confusion and
dismay that now ensued. Old women
don't often make very valuable discoveries;
but it was reserved for an ancient nurse
in the family, who came hobbling up
when Mabel had been raised from the
ground, to ascertain really what was the
matter.

"The dear child has only fainted," she
exclaimed. "Lord bless you, in my time,
when I was young, a matter of fifty years
ago, the young ladies never dreamt of

fainting. Bring her along — bring her along."

"Oh, Mabel—Mabel," sobbed Charles, "dear Mabel."

"Now, don't be a little fool, Charley," said the old woman. "You'll live to see a great deal of fainting, no doubt."

"But Mable might die."

"Fiddlestick! Mr. Henry, just get her carried in."

Henry Morton, who had, in common with every one else, heard the outcry which was made in the house by his brother and the dog, had rushed to the scene of action; nor was his wife far behind him, and taking the light form of Mabel tenderly in his arms, he carried her into the nearest apartment, and laid her on a couch which it contained.

"Poor Mabel," exclaimed his wife, "we will have medical assistance, Henry; I'll send some one."

"If you wish to do so, Alice, certainly; but if it be that she has only fainted, you can do as much for her as any medical man."

"Ah, and a great deal more, too," said the old nurse. "Why, I remember when I was young ——"

"Well, well, old Deb," cried Henry, "we know that was so long ago that we can't carry our minds so far back. Do your best to recover our dear Mabel, and we will give you credit for being an able physician."

The old woman laughed, for she loved Henry Morton, whom she had nursed, and she seemed so wonderfully tickled at the idea of her being a physician, that she nearly choked herself, and then brought tears into her eyes, and coughed and laughed again as she threw cold water into the face of Mabel.

"She does not recover," said Charles. "She is dead! Oh, my poor, dear Mabel, she is dead !"

"Now, drat the boy," said the old woman, "he talks just like a grown person, he does. Be quiet, Charley, will you."

"Brother," said Charles, addressing Henry, "let me get medical advice, will you? I can ride the bay mare over to the village and get the doctor."

Henry was upon the point of saying that he gave his full consent for Charles to go, when a voice, which our readers could not but have recognised, chimed into the conversation, saying—

"Don't, sir, now don't be after sending for those rogues of doctors, sir, to poor Miss Mabel; bless the lights of her two darlint eyes, sir, don't do it. It's always dangerous to send for a doctor, sir."

It was no other than our old friend Rafferty Brolickbones, who held, and had held ever since that memorable day when fate had thrown him and Mr. Morton, then the young wounded ensign, together on the field of Waterloo, a confidential place in the family of the Mortons.

"If so be, sir," he added, "you will have a doctor, let me go, sir, and not little Charley here, who is all of a shake, like an ould jelly bag, if you plase, sir."

"No, Rafferty, there is really no occasion."

"Thank you, sir. Bedad, I didn't think as there was. As for fainting, it's mighty genteel now-a-days, sir. More's the pity it was invented. But as for doctors, sir, I can tell you there's mighty great danger of having them. The old man, sir, my father, never had a doctor all the days of his life; but, at last, one day, he had two, and, sure, enough, that settled the business, and he went as dead as nothing, sir, before you could say pace to him."

"Indeed."

"Yes, sir, it's true for you, sir. That's how the family fell."

"Ah," chuckled the old nurse, "she is coming round again; dear, dear me, what has been the matter? You must help her to her own room, Mr. Henry, and then she can lie down and rest herself a little. See, she's opening her eyes."

Mabel was certainly recovering, for now she gave a faint sigh, and, opening her eyes, she gazed around her with looks of confused surprise. It is a common supposition, that when people recover from fainting they say, "Ah, where am I?" and in novels they almost invariably do; but we, who are the chroniclers of truths—truths which are infinitely stranger than fiction— are bound to declare that Mabel said no such thing, but when she saw around her those well-known familiar faces which were so dear to her, and which had ever beamed upon her with so much kindness, she burst into tears.

"Ah, now, that'll do her good," said the old nurse.

"Will it?" said Charles. "You are an old brute, Deb, that's what you are, and you don't care for dear Mabel at all."

"Eh, you jackanapes—you little villain !"

"Hush—hush," said Henry. "What has alarmed her? She seems evidently in a state of great nervous trepidation."

"A strange man," said Charles, "whom we met in the wilderness."

"A strange man?"

"Yes, Henry. I was out shooting. It

was late, but, you know, I wanted a bat for my museum, and I had just taken a shot at one, when Leo, who was with me, seemed to hear something he didn't approve of, so off he set, and I followed him. Sure enough he led me to where poor Mabel was trying to run away from a beggar-man, who looked one of the greatest ruffians I ever beheld."

"Indeed! and in the wilderness, too?"

"Yes, in the wilderness."

"This is insufferable. I have made great efforts to let it be known that I wish that place to be considered devoted solely to my own family. Did the man go away, Charles?"

"He did—he drew a knife."

"A knife!"

"Yes, and wanted to kill Leo with it; but I promised him a charge of small shot if he attempted it; so then he thought it was best to go."

"Rafferty," said Henry Morton, "take some one with you, and search the wilderness. If you find this fellow, take him to the cage, and, by fair means or foul, we'll convince him that we are not with impunity to be thus treated on our own grounds."

"Faith, sir, I'll have him if he's above ground, sir. Oh, the murthering villain; oh, the rapparee!"

"Charles can describe him to you."

"Yes, and go with you, too," cried Charles. "He was a tallish fellow, and in such a collection of old rags, that he looked as if he had robbed all the scare-crows for twenty miles round."

"Come along, my boy," cried Rafferty. "Bedad we'll find him, and, Charley, if he don't resist we'll make him, and have one of the most illegant rows in all the world."

"Is Mabel well now, Deb?" said Charles, in a whisper, to the old woman, before he left the room.

"Now, what's that to you?" she replied. "Boys now quite give themselves the airs of men, I do declare. It wasn't so when I was young."

"Oh, how cross you are, Deb. Mabel, dear Mabel!"

"Yes, yes."

"Are you better now, dear Mabel?"

"Oh, yes, yes; well now—quite well now."

Tears of joy gushed to the eyes of Charles, and he thought to himself—

"Oh, if I dared kiss her now as I used to do when she was a little thing some years ago! If I only dared.—Mabel, dear!"

"Yes, Charles, I am better. What is that?"

"Only Leo, dear Mabel, licking your hand. I'm going to find the fellow who frightened you—Rafferty and I will find him."

"No, no, do not; let him be—I implore you not to interfere with him. Never mind what has passed—I am not frightened now."

"Never mind him?" exclaimed Rafferty. "Oh, the murdering villain! The Connaught man, I'd wager my head any day. Never mind him?—Faith, then, we won't mind him, Miss Mabel; but he'd better be after minding himself, so he had."

"No, no, let him go, let him go."

"If it be your wish, Mabel," said Mr. Morton, "that the matter should not be pursued further, of course it shall not. Let him go."

"What an illegant piece of weakness!" sighed Rafferty "Charley, boy?"

"Yes, Rafferty?"

"Come along. Don't whisper a word to anybody; bedad, there will be one of the most illegant moons up in another hour as ever anybody saw. Let's be off to the meadows and the wilderness—who knows but we may light on the spalpeen, after all? Come along, Charley."

The young lad was nothing loth to follow Rafferty Brolickbones, who, the reader will perceive, was a privileged person, and was permitted just to say and do what he liked at Monckton Friars.

Charles Morton, too, was the more willing to go, since Mabel was on the point of being removed to her own room, whither he knew he could not intrude; and what was the house to him if he were not to see her until, most likely now, the following morning?

He watched with an anxious glance his brother assist Mabel from the parlour into which he had first carried her, and then, when the door had closed upon her, and she was fairly gone, he turned to Rafferty, with a sigh, and said—

"I'm ready; come Rafferty, I am quite ready."

"That's right, Mr. Charley. We can just ask the fellow, you know, in a civil way, how hard his head is, without troubling Miss Mabel any more about it, sweet young creature as she is."

"Ah, she is indeed."

"The quane o' beauty, the darlint of the whole world."

"You are an enthusiast, Rafferty."

"A what, sir?"

"An enthusiast."

"And what may that be, sir? Why don't you call be a spalpeen at once, and not be insulting me in French, sir—*voulez vous Frenchy*, sir? That's what I used to say on the Continent, when I came across anybody who hadn't an Irish tongue in his head, as he ought to have had; only nature can't be indulgent to all, you see, Charley."

"Certainly not."

"Well, sir, then don't call me a hen—thusi—hen—Bedad, I don't know what is was you took upon yourself to call me."

"Never mind it, Rafferty; I only meant that you very much admired Miss Mabel—bless her."

"Amin to that, Charley. She's as pleasant a little girl, sir, as ever stepped. I've known boys, sir, who would have gone mad after her."

"Indeed?"

"Ah, to be sure, and swing a shillelah for her. Many's the faction fight that's been got up all along of a pretty face like Miss Mabel's."

"Who would not fight for her—who would not die for her?"

"Better live for her, sir. These purty gals wouldn't give a pin for a dead man anyhow, I'm thinking."

Charles sighed, as he thought how he would fain live for her; but Rafferty Brolickbones was not exactly the sort of person to make a confidant in love matters, so he wisely made up his mind to change the subject.

But yet, with a natural acuteness that enabled him to draw correcter conclusions, perhaps, than many a one who was better informed than himself, Rafferty Brolickbones had for some time been in possession of the secret of young Morton's heart; and that the boy, for boy he still was, loved Mabel with far more than the affection of a brother for the dearest sister, and he had no doubt, although that was the class of affection which Charley professed to all but himself to feel for her.

Although Rafferty felt convinced of the fact, he had made up his mind never to mention it in downright tones, unless Charles made a confidant of him. Whether Rafferty can keep to so proper and so prudent a determination, remains to be seen.

When he, Rafferty, and the young ensign Morton, were, along with the child which had been placed in the care of the latter, taken from the field of battle, they were carried to different hospital, and there remained for a considerable time; and what was strange enough, Rafferty, although to all appearance much more con-siderably injured than the young officer, recovered much the soonest, and without the loss of any of his limbs, although the battle had cut him up severely.

Not unmindful of the great service which had been rendered to him on the field of Waterloo, Morton, as his own wounds healed, and convalescence began to approach, had made frequent inquiries after Rafferty, and sent him the means of procuring many indulgences he would else have never seen.

The consequence of all this was, that when Rafferty was able to move about, he got leave to visit the ensign, who received him with great cordiality and kindness, and from that day forthwith Rafferty installed himself as a sort of follower and confidential attendant to Morton.

We forget to add, when talking of his wounds, that he lost an eye, and that circumstance invalided him, so that he got his discharge and a pension, and might have gone back, had he wished it, to the emerald isle; but when Morton spoke to him on that subject after they both landed in England, he said—

"No, sir, I'll stay by you, sir, now. You've sould out now, sir, and I've had my eye poked out, sir, which has turned me out; so, by your lave, sir, I'll stay by you, if you can make me any way useful."

"I do not want to make you useful, Rafferty. If you like to reside at my estate in England,—I grieve to call it mine, since it has become so by the recent deaths of those who were dear to me,—you shall be welcome."

"An estate, sir?"

"Yes, Rafferty, in Cumberland."

"Oh, then, sir, I shall find abundant things to do; and plase, sir, whenever I may happen to be in the way, jist tell me, sir."

"I will, I will," said Morton. "But I should have thought you would have liked to go to Ireland."

"No, sir; the ould mother is dead, sir, and there's nobody else of all the family that I want to see particularly. To be sure, there's that vagabond, Dermot."

"You wish to see him?"

"I want to fight him, sir.—The thief of the word—och!"

"I would not advise you to go to Ireland with that object, Rafferty, and if you have no other, why, you had certainly better remain with me."

"So I will, sir; I'll make myself generally useful, like a maid-of-all-work, sir. I'll wring the pigs' necks, and scald the poultry, sir, dig up praties, and kiss the maids."

"We can dispense with the latter accomplishment, Rafferty."

"Very good, sir. I don't want to interfere with you, sir, in any little matter—very far from it, sir, I assure you, always."

With this understanding it was that Rafferty Brolickbones went with Captain Morton, as he was frequently called,—for, although he had left the army, he was gazetted a captain before he did so,—to Cumberland, and never was any human being more astonished and delighted than was Rafferty with Monckton Friars. And although having all the appearance of an idler about the house and grounds, Morton soon found him of inestimable value, from the fact of his being so thoroughly trustworthy and confidential —he was here, and there, and everywhere, and the greatest torment the world could have produced to any one who attempted any peculations at the farm, or who avoided, or attempted to avoid doing his duty. And yet he was a general favourite; and at any merry-making of the farm labourers and servants, Rafferty was in immense request, and the life and soul of the party—he could dance, sing, shout, jest, drink, and fight; in truth, Rafferty's accomplishments were of a very numerous nature, and he soon became as much at home at Monckton Friars as the most ancient of its inmates, and as much a part of the place as one of the wings of the building itself. His attachment to the whole of the family was immense, not that that family was a large one, for, until Henry Morton married, which he did not do until he had been nearly five years settled on his estate, it merely consisted of himself and Charles, and the little Mabel, who certainly made the house look much more cheerful and inhabited than it would have looked had she not been there to make a little bustle in it.

Morton had liberally remunerated the sergeant's wife, who, during his detention at the hospital in Brussels, had taken charge of the infant, and he had agreed with her that she should bring it to him in Cumberland, and which she did; and after experiencing the munificence of his recompense to her, she left the young child of the battle-field, and again rejoined the regiment in which her husband served.

Henry Morton considered with himself, and consulted with Rafferty what he should do.

"I don't know, Rafferty," he said, "which would be best—to bring up this child along with little Charley here, or send her to nurse somewhere."

"Let her stay, sir," was Rafferty's verdict. "Only think what a pleasant thing it will be to see the little thing running about the farm like a young kitten. It'll make the house look alive, sir."

"You think so?"

"Yes, in truth I do, sir; and, besides, the two children will be mighty fine company for each other, sir."

"They would, certainly."

"And there's the old woman, Mrs. Deb, to mind them, sir; a very good ould soul I daresay she is, in her way; so I advise you to let the little cratur stay where she is."

"I am not at all indisposed for her to stay her, Rafferty—nay, my wish is to do the best I can for her."

"And that is the best, sir. I'll look after her edication myself, sir."

"You, Rafferty?"

"Yes, sir; and why not?"

"Well, I think you ought not to put me on the proof of why not; but we will waive that branch of the subject, Rafferty, and consider it decided that Mabel shall remain here; and now to come to another consideration."

"Go on, sir, I am listening to you."

"I do not wish the mode in which I became possessed of Mabel to become the talk of the whole country."

"No, sir."

"Therefore, you will not tell any one of it, not even herself, when she is old enough to listen."

"Very good, sir."

"We will keep it to ourselves, and people will then not busy themselves with any conjectures concerning her."

"Oh, they don't now, sir. Everybody has made up everybody's mind, sir, about it in the whole neighbourhood."

"Indeed!"

"Oh, yes, sir."

"But how, Rafferty? What can they know of Mabel."

"Not a whit, sir; but it's known yer honour manes to keep the little darlint."

"Of course."

"Well, then, it's generally believed that no one has a better right to do so, for one and all declare it's as like yer honour as one pea is to another, and they give you great glory, sir, for your kindness in bringing it home, instead of sending it somewhere away from you."

"Why, you don't mean to tell me, Rafferty, there is an impression that the child a child of mine?"

"Mighty gineral, sir. That's just what I do mean to tell you, sir."

Morton was excessively annoyed, and paced the room in which this conversation had taken place for some minutes in silence. Then he spoke in a tone of wounded pride, saying—

"It is a hard case that a man cannot please himself by doing a kindly act, but the very worst construction must always be placed upon it."

"Worst construction, sir?"

"Yes; you tell me so."

"I told you they thought it was your child, sir."

"Well?"

"Bedad, then, I think it's a very good construction, sir."

"What! to be supposed to have brought home a poor thing so situated? No—no, Rafferty. It is a construction which mortifies me."

"Well, sir, you needn't care—you know it isn't so, yer honour. You know you have taken the little crature out of charity, and let them all say what they like about it—what need you care, sir?"

"True, Rafferty. I was foolish to allow myself to be annoyed about the opinions of such persons. I will act a father's part by that child, although I am none; and let the world be as censorious as it may, it shall not swerve me from my self-imposed duty. Still keep the secret, Rafferty; and if questioned upon the subject, say that you have my commands to refuse an answer."

"I will, sir, and if that won't do, I'll just try the strength of a stick on the boy's head who makes himself troublesome."

"But females may question you."

"Oh, thin, sir, I daresay they will have some he relation I can knock down the next time I meet him."

"Rafferty, that kind of thing won't do in England; you must keep out of broils."

"I will, sir—I will. Bedad, sir, I'm the most paceable man alive, if people will but interfere with me; if they let me alone, It's the devil. Then your honour won't send the child away?"

"I certainly will not."

"Hoorah—hoorah!"

Rafferty was delighted with this arrangement, and truly did he do his duty to the orphan girl; for a more attached and patient playfellow and escort about the grounds of Monckton Friars she could not have than Rafferty Brolickbones. He tended on her with the greatest affection, and carried her about for the first first years of her life as if she had been some curiosity, or exquisite piece of porcelain, which he was afraid of breaking by some unlucky chance.

Of course it became quite a settled thing in the neighbourhood that the child was Mr. Morton's, and some blamed him furiously for having it in his house, while others as vehemently praised him.

Still he kept his own counsel, and, with rare discretion, Rafferty kept his, so that no one was at all aware of the real facts of the case.

When Henry Morton married, however, surprise reached its climax, for everybody, of course, then supposed that the child would be sent off; but no such thing occurred; and, to the intense astonishment of everybody, Mrs. Morton was seen leading about the little Mabel, then five years old, with an air of the greatest fondness and affection for it.

Some were indignant; some pretended to look wise, and to shake their heads, as if they knew some solution of the mystery, which they meant to keep entirely to themselves; and some ladies of the neighbourhood went so far as to cut the acquaintance of Mrs. Morton for her want of spirit.

She ought, they contended, to have turned out of the house the little girl the moment she came home.

But the women are so dreadfully virtuous—especially when they reach a certain age — that they forget altogether to be charitable.

But Mrs. Morton and her husband lived together in the greatest harmony, and paid not the least attention to all these insinuations; so that in time the more sensible people ceased to speak or to think about it; and the orphan child, who had been so happy in finding kind friends, was called Mabel Morton as naturally as if she were one of the most acknowledged and well known members of the family.

And so she grew in years and beauty, and was the delight of both Mr. and Mrs. Morton, who had had but one child of their own, which they had lost at an early age. They never had another, and so the full tide of their affections were strangely enough cast upon those who, in one case, had no natural claim at all, and, in the other, only a collateral one.

Charles Morton and Mabel—the two happiest hearts that ever beat—were attached playmates, brought up together completely as brother and sister, and receiving all the care and attention from Mr. and Mrs. Morton, as if they had been their own children.

But although Morton would sooner have parted with all he possessed in the world besides than with Mabel Morton, as she was called, yet it must not be supposed that he had made no effort to discover who and what she was.

These efforts, though, he had made with great secrecy and caution. It was to gratify a natural curiosity he did so, and not to awaken any claimant for his young charge.

It will be recollected by the reader that all he knew of Mabel consisted in the very brief conversation he had had with the wounded French officer, and that he had said so little, in consequence of the dreadful state he was in, that even whether he was her father or not was a doubtful point. The young female whom he had called Marie, and who, to all appearance, lay dead by his side, Morton knew nothing further of than that such a form did lie there. Of her subsequent proceedings he was ignorant, although the reader has had some insight into them.

Around the neck of Mabel he had found the cross which the audacious and brutal beggar in the wilderness had alluded to, and which he had really described so readily and so truly; but beyond the letters at the back of it of M. R., it afforded no tangible clue.

He had likewise heard the name of Rouselli; but so confused had been his own perceptions, in consequence of the anguish of his wounds and the weakness incidental to them, that he could not tell to whom it had belonged, or in what manner it had been used.

Thus were Morton's means of inquiry most vague and small indeed: yet he did try to obtain some information on the subject.

He took a journey to Paris himself, and made cautious inquiries, but he could learn nothing satisfactory. The only shadow of intelligence he got was from an old soldier, who was in the Hotel d'Invalides, at Paris, and who told him that as he lay upon the field of Waterloo, badly wounded, a beautiful young female passed him, with an infant in her arms, uttering lamentations, and apparently looking for some one among the dead or the dying.

This was all he could learn. There was no officer of the name of Rouselli who had been at Waterloo, he was assured, and fearful of awakening surmises unfavourable to the peace of Mabel, he gave up further inquiry, and returned to England with a determination never again to revert to the subject, but to inform Mabel, when she should become of an age to understand the nature of the intelligence, of the means by which she had come into his possession and under his protection.

## CHAPTER IX.

MR. MORTON'S SUGGESTION.—THE TRIUMPH OF THE GOSSIPS OF MONCKTON.—THE DESPAIR OF CHARLES MORTON.

As may be naturally presumed, both Mr. and Mrs. Morton were extremely anxious to know the prime cause of the alarm which had ended in Mabel fainting. They knew that she was not of a timid disposition, because they had taken care, in the course of the very excellent education they had given to her, that she should not be made so. They knew that she was not one who gave way readily to alarm, or who would feel at all inclined to make "a scene" about nothing.

From Charles they hoped, after Mabel had been duly conveyed to her own room, and left in charge of old Deb, than whom no one was more capable of taking charge, to hear, at all events, an accurate description of the man who had terrified her; but, as we are aware, Charles had left the house with Rafferty, and, to tell the truth, Henry Morton did not feel very much displeased to hear that he had done so, for, notwithstanding he had given in to Mabel's feelings, and taken no energetic steps to have the daring and audacious beggar apprehended, yet in his heart he would have had no objection to have him lodged in the cage by Rafferty and Charles.

Foiled, therefore, in getting any information from any one else, Morton eagerly waited until Mabel should herself be sufficiently recovered to give him her version of the affair.

As the indisposition was of so very simple a character, and arose rather from the sudden revulsion of feeling on finding herself safe at home, than from any continued terror, it soon yielded, and a glass of wine restored her completely to herself, so that she was able to come down stairs again and join those whom she always called father and mother, and who, from the care they had taken of her, were eminently entitled to the distinction.

Morton kissed her, and so did his wife, and then they sat her down on a sofa between them, and he said,—

"Tell me, my dear Mabel, what is it that has so much terrified you, and I will take steps to prevent for the future such an occurrence as my darling Mabel being annoyed within sight of her own home."

"Ah," she said, "I will never go out without Leo with me."

"A wise resolution, dear Mabel."

"And yet, Henry," said his wife, "it is something quite new in our peaceful place and neighbourhood that any of the family should require protection—we have not an enemy."

"We ought to have none."

"I am sure we are at good will with all."

"I have ever striven to carry my conduct in such a manner as to be equally on kindly terms with rich and poor."

"And I am sure we are."

"This was some stranger," said Mabel. "I am certain, from the questions he asked, that he was quite strange to Monckton."

"Indeed!"

"Yes. He seemed like some wandering mendicant, who, when opportunity offered, would scruple not to enforce his demands, and convert an appeal for charity into a robbery."

"Did he rob you, my dear?"

"He has my purse."

"Now, really, this is too bad. This man must be apprehended. Mabel, why did you not mention this before? We cannot be trespassed upon, insulted, and robbed all at once with impunity."

"Let me tell you all that occurred before you come to any decision," said Mabel. "There is more in the affair than meets the eye."

"Indeed!"

"Yes, yes—at least I fear so."

"You fear so, Mabel?—what have you to fear?"

"Nothing. I know that your persevering love can protect me from harm, and yet am I full of fears."

"This is inexplicable."

"Tell us all, my dear," said Mrs. Morton. "We will hear you with patience, and then, as you say, decide."

"You know," said Mabel, "that it was some time ago that Mrs. Claxton, at the village, told me I was not your child."

"Confound her!" said Morton; "I heard as much. That woman is enough to breed contention and unhappiness among a regiment of angels."

"A regiment, Henry?" said his wife; "how can you talk of a regiment of angels?"

"Well, well—a troop, or a battalion, or anything you like. Hang her long tongue; what business was it of hers?"

"It was none, indeed," said Mabel; "but when I told you, you will remember that you said, 'Wait till the next anniversary of the battle of Waterloo, and you shall know all that it concerns you to know, that it is in my power to tell.'"

"I did—I did."

"To-day is the 18th of June, and no wonder that my mind was full to the overflowing of so interesting a subject to me. I knew from your answer that what Mrs. Claxton had said was so far true, however wrong it was of her to say it, and I became extremely anxious to know what I was, and how I came to be with such kind friends who were not related to me, and yet were all the world to me."

"But, my dear, what has this to do with your being alarmed in the wilderness by the too abrupt importunities of a mendicant, or the rougher wickedness of one we may call a highwayman?"

"You shall hear. It has to do with it, and it was solely on that account that I was so much terrified, and my spirits became so much depressed as to cause me to faint on the threshold of the hall."

Henry Morton and his wife exchanged a glance of alarm, and they were more anxious than ever to hear the full and particular account from Mabel of what had occurred in the wilderness. She then proceeded to relate to them with particularity everything that had occurred, and concluded by saying,—

"Dear, kind, good friends,—parents, as I may indeed call you,—can I now do otherwise than believe that this man, desperate as his demeanour was, and despicable as was his conduct, knows something of me which I would give worlds to hear from any other lips?"

Morton was silent for a few moments, and his wife hid her face in her handkerchief. The same dreadful idea had come over both of them, that in that interview which Mabel had had with the stranger, there was the commencement of some train of circumstances which might tear her from their arms, and so deprive them of their only great consolation for having no child of their own on whom they could lavish the fond affection which formed a principle of their nature.

Mabel was inexpressibly grieved at these symptoms of disquietude which her friends betrayed; she threw herself on Mrs. Morton's breast, and exclaimed,—

"I know it—I feel assured that there is some dreadful mystery attached to my birth, which you dread to disclose to me for fear of the great unhappiness it would give me. But do not keep it from me—let me know all; let me know the very worst, and in your love I will find a joyful recompense for any other evil, be it what it may."

"No, no; you are wrong, Mabel; you

are wrong," said Mr. Morton, with tenderness. "You do not guess aright the cause of this emotion which we feel. It is on your account, but not from the reason you fancy."

"Indeed!"

"No, dear Mabel; no."

"Then tell me all. Redeem the promise which you made to me, and tell me who and what I am."

The Mortons looked at each other distressfully, and Mrs. Morton said,—

"Mabel, will you leave us, and allow us to consult upon what is best to be done in this matter?"

"Oh, that you would trust me," said Mabel, as she rose to proceed to the door.

Henry Morton went after her, and took her hand tenderly in his before she could pass out of the room.

"My ever dear Mabel," he said, "believe us, it is not that we hesitate about trusting you—that we hesitate to tell you all we know; but there are many things to be considered."

"I meant not my words for a reproach," said Mabel, her eyes filling with tears as she spoke.

"I know you did not, dear Mabel—I am sure you did not; but be calm and patient. Believe—continue to believe, as I know you do, that we have your best happiness at heart."

"I do—I will."

"And you will be guided by us?"

"In all things."

"That is a solemn promise, Mabel?"

"It is meant as a solemn one, and so help me Heaven I will do my best to keep it sacred."

"Then leave us now. In an hour we will speak again upon the subject."

"In an hour?"

"One hour; for no longer shall you endure suspense."

"And may I then come to you?"

"Yes, do, dear Mabel, come to us. We shall be ready then to converse more freely; but, remember, let the determination to which we may come be what it may, it will be one indicated but by one motive, and that is, for the accomplishment of your happiness."

"I know it—I know it."

She passed from the room, and immediately Henry Morton turned the key in the lock of the door, so that no one could intrude upon them unawares; then turning to his wife, he said—

"Alice, Alice, it has come to this at last. My constant dream of apprehension has begun to assume an aspect of reality."

"It has—it has."

"This, I feel morally convinced, is the beginning of the train of evils which may destroy our happiness."

"By tearing from us her whom we love."

"True, true; most true."

"Oh, Henry, we cannot part with her; she is to us, and has ever been, all that a dear, devoted child should be. We cannot part with Mabel—we will not part with her, Henry. Say you will not."

"Not with my life will I part with her, Alice."

"'Tis bravely said. I breath again."

"Unless——"

"Oh, make no conditions—no exceptions."

"Unless she herself should wish to leave us."

"And that she never will."

"Never—never. She loves us too well for that, so we may safely make such an exception. But now let us consider; if this be indeed the commencement of events which may end in Mabel being claimed from us, how are we to defeat them?"

"We will hide somewhere with her, Henry; we will fly to some other land. We will not part from her."

"I tremble."

"Tremble, Henry?"

"Yes; for are we not even now setting up our affections against the immutable law of justice and of Heaven?"

"Oh, Henry—Henry."

"Suppose we had lost such a child; suppose we found where she was hidden from us——"

Mrs. Morton hid her face in her hands.

"Suppose," added Morton, "we were in such a position, and went to claim her, and found her gone, torn a second time from our wounded hearts?"

"No—no—no."

"Yes—we are endeavouring to compass such an injustice."

"Say what you will, Henry—reason as you will, I cannot part with Mabel. She is as dear to me as ever child of my own

could be. I cannot part with her, Henry. It would break my heart."

"But dare we——"

"Nay, you refine too much upon this abstract principle of justice, Henry."

"Is it possible to do so?"

"In such a case as this 'tis easy."

"I cannot see any way."

"And to me all is plain and clear. Listen, Henry, and your better judgment will be convinced, and furnish me with fresh argument to maintain the position that I take up."

"Speak—speak. I will listen, Alice, I will listen."

"Who, Henry, saved her from inevitable death but you—who looked to her welfare at a time when most men would have been selfish, and had every sympathy used up in a consideration of their own sufferings —who tenderly nurtured her, and saw to her welfare and her wants in the early years of childhood but yourself? Then who can love her as you love her? And for ten years too, which have seemed short because they have passed away happily, have not I been as a mother to her? Then who can love her as I love her, and as you love her?"

"I hear—I hear."

"What is she, what can she be to any one else? Is all this labour of affection to be thrown into another's cup of happiness? After we have made her what she is, is another to know the joy of loving her? 'Tis against nature, Henry—'tis against all justice; and, besides, those who have not tended her as we have, never can really love her as we love her."

"Alice—Alice! I know not what to do."

"Why, after all, Henry, he who died upon the battle-field, and consigned her to your care, may have been her father—nay, there is every reason to believe he was, and, in that case, you have a right to protect her."

"I have in such a case; but he did not say he was her father."

"Death alone prevented him."

"I know not that. Some other explanation may have lingered on his lips than that. I know not that he was about to make such a declaration, when the hand of death stopped his utterance."

"Husband—husband! do you want to break my heart? I cannot part from her —I will not part from her!"

"Oh, Alice! what would you have me do?"

"Adopt some line of policy which will enable you to resist every attempt to take her from us, until she is of age; and then tell her all, and leave her to her own judgment and her own affections."

"Ah! there is something in that suggestion."

"There is, Henry. You see," added Mrs. Morton, with eagerness, "that by so doing, we ensure the happiness, for some years longer, of ourselves, as well as of our dear, dear Mabel."

"She is happy with us."

"Most happy; she has often wept upon my breast, and blessed us both. Oh, she is very happy with us, indeed."

"That comes across my heart like a good reason."

"It is a good one. I knew, Henry, that you would soon see what was right in this matter. You would soon perceive that we were but struggling, as we have always done, for the happiness of the dear one whom Heaven had given into our hands."

"But how would you do it?"

"Firstly, you must still keep Mabel in ignorance of her real history; and Rafferty alone, of all our household, knows it as well as ourselves."

"He would not betray us."

"I know he would not—he is faithfulness itself; and unlike the generality of his countrymen, he is blessed with sufficient constancy of purpose to keep a secret well, Henry."

"I do believe he is."

"Then we are safe."

"But what shall we say to Mabel?"

"Tell her we are her nearest and natural protectors. Tell her that many reasons have combined to prevent you from letting her know so much before, but that she has no nearer friend but you, although there may be persons who will pretend they are so, and seek to induce her to leave us."

"It might be done, and so a feeling of resistance could be got up even in her mind against any one who should come to claim her of us."

"It would, of course."

"Alice, I yield. You have overcome me; I yield to you—let it be so; and at once, before I sleep to-night, I will make out a written statement of the whole of the circumstances under which I found her on the field of Waterloo. That shall be pinned to my will, so that should anything happen suddenly to me, it would be found there. When she is of age, and capable of saying of her own free will that she chooses to stay with us, she shall know all."

"Be it so, Henry; you have given me new life; be it so."

"It shall—it shall."

"And you will be firm. You will see something of this mysterious man, you may depend, Henry. He will not let the matter rest; you are sure to hear yet something of him; but you must be very firm, indeed—you must be extremely firm."

"I will—I will. Rafferty shall sign the paper I write out, containing the full particulars of how Mabel came into our hands, and then, although we may be doing a little wrong, I think we may seek for some excuse in the motive."

"Yes; and if the worst should arise—if some strong claimant should appear, who will not be put off, you can verify the popular rumour of the village, that Mabel is your own child, you know, Henry."

"As a last resource, I might set up such a claim, false though it be; but let us hope that we shall not be called to do aught positively false. Let us place ourselves merely in a negative position, if possible, and defy others to the proof that she is theirs, without too roundly asserting she is ours."

"Let it be so, then. Oh, Henry! if you had not consented, I think I should never have known happiness again."

"And Heaven can only know how much I love her," said Henry Morton. "I would not lose her for the accumulated wealth of worlds."

At this moment there was a gentle tap at the room door, and both Mr. and Mrs. Morton started at the sound.

"'Tis she—'tis Mabel," said Henry Morton.

"Yes—yes. Be cautious. Calm her fears, but tell her nothing, Henry. Be very cautious!"

"I will—I will."

He rose, and unlocking the door, found a servant instead of Mabel, who said—

"If you please, sir, there is a beggar at the front gate."

"A—a beggar?"

"Yes, sir," the man continued; "but he insists upon seeing you."

"Upon seeing me?"

"Yes, sir. He says he has not seen you since you were at the battle of Waterloo, fifteen years ago."

Morton staggered to a seat, as he said, in a faint voice—

"Show him into the library, and let no one see him—let no one see him."

## CHAPTER X.

THE INTERVIEW BETWEEN THE MYSTE-
RIOUS MENDICANT AND TOGGS, THE
LANDLORD OF THE MORTON ARMS.

WHEN the highly disagreeable man,
who had filled poor Mabel with so much
consternation in the wilderness, was compelled to fly before the attack of Leo, he
took his way towards the neighbouring
village, full of the most malignant feelings,
if one might judge from his looks, that
ever found a home in the heart of any
human being.

By the direct and undeviating route he
took, it would seem as if he were well acquainted with the way, after he had once
got clear of the wilderness belonging to
the estate. He muttered to himself as he
went, and now and then he would clench
his fist, and shake it in the air, as if he
wished to give potency to some threat
which arose from his hard heart.

"So—so," he said, "she defies me; she
is not quite the yielding creature I somehow expected to find her, and yet I don't
know why or wherefore I ought to have
had any such expectations. I came upon
the very estate unawares, and upon her
more unawares still. She is beautiful—
she is very beautiful."

He decreased his walk, as if some sudden thought had struck him; and, after a
time, then he burst into an exultant laugh,
as he cried—

"Yes—yes; who can say me nay? By
Heaven! a glorious plan—a most glorious
plan! Who can gainsay it? No one. The
grave—the grave is over them all. Ha,
ha! ha! Hilloa! who have we here? A
boy, and coming up to me, too!"

A lad was slowly approaching the
stranger. He was a country-looking
fellow, too. He dragged one foot after
the other, as if to walk was quite a trouble;
but still he seemed intent upon saying
something to the most uninviting personage who had been so much engrossed
until that moment with his own evil
thoughts and impulses.

"I say, old fellow," said the boy, "oh,
what a trouble."

"What's a trouble?"

"I—I had something—to—ask you."

"Well, what is it?"

"You don't look over bright. Is begging
a trouble?"

"Confound you! do you want to insult
me?"

"Now, don't get into a passion. I
shan't if you do. It is such a trouble."

"What on earth do you want?"

"I suppose, oh, dear, I must explain;
what a trouble! I'm the farrier's apprentice."

"And what is that to me, booby?"

"There you go again. I want to do
something that's no trouble, do you know.
Everything is a trouble that I've heard of.
Is begging a trouble?—that's what I want
to know."

"You are an odd fellow. Why do you
ask me?"

"Because shoeing horses is such a trouble."

"And you want to do something
else?"

"Yes, if it's no trouble. I'd have run
away a long while ago, only it's such a
trouble to me."

"You are an oddity; but I can tell you,
that through life you will find that everything has its troubles, my friend."

"Oh, lor!"

"As I tell you will you find it."

"Oh, I wonder if it's much trouble to
die some day? I like going to sleep; it's
no trouble. I don't waking up. There's
the trouble of dressing and the trouble of
taking one's breakfast. They call me
'Troubled Tom' in the village. Oh, lor!
what a trouble."

"Curse you!" said the mendicant, as
he walked on; "what do you trouble me
for?"

"Oh, that's the way," moaned Troubled
Tom. "Nobody really likes trouble,
though some people are hypocrites enough
to pretend that they don't mind it. Hoi!
hoi! hoi!"

"What now?—what now? Eh?"

"Nothing. I was going to say something; but it's such a trouble, I really
can't."

"If I come back to you I will give you
some real trouble," said the beggar,
angrily.

"There," said Troubled Tom. "He's
off in a rage, now. I can't get into a
passion—it's such a trouble. I sometimes
wish I could. There's some of the other
boys in the village, they bonnets me, and
all sorts of things, and I don't wop 'em, it
is such a trouble. Oh, lor!"

On the first raised bank he came to,
down sat Troubled Tom, and in the
course of a few minutes he was fast
asleep, muttering now and then in his
dreams,—

"What a trouble."

The mendicant pursued his way till he
came to the village, and then he walked
direct up to the Morton Arms, which was
the only place of entertainment for man or
beast that the place afforded. His ap-

pearance, as our readers may well imagine, was not one that was likely to be hailed with satisfaction by any publican; and as the landlord of the Morton Arms was himself at the door, he commenced, the moment he espied the approaching form of the stranger, shaking his head at such a rate, that it would seem as if he really never intended to leave off.

Still the mendicant advanced undauntedly, and when he came so near that the portly landlord felt himself compelled to get out of the way or say something, he cried,—

"My man, we are very sorry, but we really cannot afford to be charitable; times are hard, prices high, money scarce, and taxes horrid. You'd better go somewhere else."

"What do you mean?" said the mendicant.

"What do I mean?"

"Yes. Who asked you for anything, eh?"

"Why—a—a—I certainly cannot say —a-hem!—that you did; but, my friend, I had good reason to suppose so, surely— a-hem!"

"I will give you a word of advice, my friend. Don't estimate people by their looks, or you may make some odd mistakes, occasionally, I can tell you. A gentleman may strut about in the costume of a beggar."

"A gentleman? Did you say a gentleman, my friend?"

"Yes, I did, consume you. Stand out of the way, will you?"

"Now, really—really——"

"Look here."

The fellow took from a concealed pocket in his tattered apparel some silver, which he showed to the landlord, and which had such a mollifying effect upon mine host of the Morton Arms, that he did move out of the way, saying,—

"Well, my friend, if you really came to spend money, instead of begging money, which you must own I had every reason to believe, you will find the tap-room the first door on the right."

"Good. Let me have brandy and something to eat."

"Humph!" said the landlord, when his ragged guest had passed into the house; "brandy and something to eat. A very tidy order, truly, for a vagabond such as that. Upon my word, a very tidy order. Brandy and something to eat for a fellow like that. Howsomdever, one man's money is as good as another's any day in the week; so here goes. I'll serve him myself, though, and take care to have the

money before he takes any of the drinkable or the eatable."

With this prudent resolve, the landlord set about obeying the order of his mysterious guest.

The landlord's name was Toggs. He was not a bad fellow; but he certainly had, from sheer botheration with such people, contracted a tolerable horror of mendicants.

When first he had set up in the public line, his heart was fresh, and he thought poor people ought to be relieved a little somehow, and he gave accordingly; but, alas! he soon found that by so doing he was getting up a most profitable and unenviable reputation, and that one mendicant told another of him, so that he was thoroughly beset, and, in addition to finding himself eaten and drunk out of house and home, he had acquired among the begging fraternity the nickname of Thunderpated Toggs, which was really too bad.

Then he was advised to do the hardhearted for a time, and he did so; he would relieve nobody, and so, as always is the case, indiscriminate charity was forced to lapse into an indiscriminate refusal, and when once Toggs got into the habit of saying no, he was not likely again to lapse into the one of saying yes.

Toggs then himself took into the taproom the ardent liquid which had been ordered, along with some bread and cheese, which he translated something to eat to mean. He found his guest looking as much at home as any one well could. The tap-room of the Morton Arms at that time boasted of no other occupant—not that it was any great boast to have him who was there—and the fellow sat with his legs upon a chair he had drawn opposite to him, looking, for all the world, as Toggs said to himself, as if he were the sheriff of the county.

"Fifteen-pence," said Toggs, as he laid down the materials for refreshment he brought with him, but not so far out of his reach that he could not, should he see occasion so to do, lay hold of them again with sufficient rapidity.

"Good," said the stranger, as he threw down a shilling and a sixpence, which, after ascertaining they were both good, Toggs transferred to the canvas pocket in the apron he wore, and from the similar receptacle on the other side produced the change.

"Have you sprightly neighbours hereabouts?" said the mendicant.

"Sprightly neighbours?"

"Yes; people of standing and station."

"Oh! ah—yes."

"What sort of neighbourhood is it?"

'Why, a very good sort of neighbourhood in its way. Poor-rates are rather high."

"Are they, indeed! I suppose that's owing to so many wandering casual poor about?"

"Cool that," thought Toggs; but he supposed it was, and then the mendicant added,—

"I saw a large, handsome-looking house in the neighbourhood, close to the lake."

"Oh, that's Captain Morton's."

"Indeed! Then it was his daughter whom I saw, I suppose, in the grounds—a pretty, dark-haired girl, of about sixteen?"

"His daughter—well—but it's no business of mine."

"What, is there a mystery, my friend?"

"Why, perhaps there is, my friend."

"Oh, indeed! I suppose some matter of mere gossip, which may be well enough communicated to anybody. Come, let's have it. What is it?"

"Why, after all, I don't know that it's much of a secret; for everybody talks about it."

"Oh, so I thought."

"They do say that the young lady is a natural daughter of Captain Morton's, and the only wonder is, that his wife takes to her in the way she does."

"You may well say a wonder, master landlord. Women are not the most famous creatures for liberality in that respect."

"You are right enough there. However, they tell me that Captain Morton brought the child home to the hall all of a sudden, and nobody knew anything about it but himself and Rafferty Brollickbones."

"Who may he be?"

"An Irishman who was in the war with Captain Morton—not a bad fellow in the main, and about as good a customer as I've got hereabouts. A discreet man, too—never takes a drop too much; indeed, I have my doubts if any quantity at all that he would hold would be too much for him."

"Indeed! And this Captain Morton, has he children of his own?"

"He has not. There's Charles, his brother, lives with them, and Miss Mabel, as they call her, as sweet a young creature, too, she is, as ever the eyes of man looked on. Of course, she is no customer of mine, so I can't be prejudiced in her favour, you know; but she is quite a young angel, that she is."

"Oh!"

"You should see her galloping about on her favourite pony. You should hear her laugh. Oh, she is a rare creature!"

"I have seen her, I tell you. The girl is pretty; there can be no two opinions upon that head. Can I sleep here to-night?"

"Sleep? Oh, why—we have beds."

"Pho! bother your beds. Anything will do for me. A bundle of straw in an empty room I prefer."

"Then we can easily accommodate you with that," said Toggs, with a feeling of relief that so very unpromising a looking customer did not contemplate getting between the sheets of the beds of the Morton Arms.

"Be it so, then. I will remain here to-night; and remember, landlord, I am not what I seem."

"Are you not?"

"No. Now, what do you take me to be? Answer candidly; I shall not be offended. You don't know but what I am playing a part, and would like to be complimented upon my appearing in it. What do you take me to be?"

Toggs looked posed. To tell his guest what he took him to be, would be, if he spoke his genuine sentiments, very far from complimentary, and he neither liked to tell him that, or a thundering lie upon the subject.

"Why—a—really, you know, I'm no judge," said Toggs, trying to shirk the question. "I'm the worst in the world for judging of any one."

"Nonsense, man—nonsense. What do I seem?"

"Pray excuse me."

"No, no, no."

"Well then, my friend, if you will have it—mind, I don't say you are—but you seem to me, mind you, to be the dirtiest and most outrageous blackguard that ever I saw."

"Thank you."

"You would make me tell, you know."

"Very good—very good. That's just the character I wished to assume, I assure you."

"Well, then, you do it so well, that any one would swear it came quite naturally."

"Clever," said the stranger—"clever! You are a wag."

"A what?"

"A wag—quite a wag, I can assure you."

At this moment the sound of horses' feet pausing at the door of the public-house, met the landlord's ears, and he rushed out to the porch, in the hope of receiving under his roof a more engaging-looking customer than the mendicant in the tap-room, and with whom, for want of something better to do, he had been amusing himself in gossip.

"A customer worth having, I hope," said Toggs, as he flourished a white napkin, and rushed to the door.

---

## CHAPTER XI.

THE ROBBERY AND MURDER AT THE MORTON ARMS. — THE PACKET OF PAPERS.

THE person who had halted at the Morton Arms was a young man, who, from his general appearance, seemed to have ridden far. He was covered with dust, and his horse, as well as himself, looked jaded and anxious for a rest. As he reined in his steed, he looked anxiously up at the sign of the public-house, and, when the landlord made his appearance, he said,—

"And this, then, is the Morton Arms?"

"The Morton, sir," said the landlord, "as you remark, and very much indeed at your honour's service. This is the genuine, the original, the real, and the only Morton Arms, sir."

The young stranger dismounted, and said—

"Let my horse be well seen to, if you please; show me to a private room, and bring me some of the best wine you have."

"Certainly, sir—certainly—most certainly. God bless me! what do you get in people's way for?"

These last words were addressed to the mendicant, who had followed the landlord to the door, and was run against by him as he turned to enter the house.

"Look where you are going another time," said the beggar.

"Confound you!" muttered Toggs. "You might make yourself useful, and hold the gentleman's horse, till Jem, the hostler, comes, as you are here now."

"It's the very thing I was going to do," said the mendicant.

He placed his hand on the horse as he spoke. The young traveller was about to follow the landlord into the inn, but he suddenly paused, as if a new thought had struck him, and returning to his steed, he commenced unbuckling the saddle.

"Oh, sir, we'll manage all that in a minute or two," said Toggs; "pray don't trouble yourself."

"No trouble," said the stranger. "I have some matters in the pocket of the saddle, which I prefer having in my own room."

Any one who, at that moment, could have seen the countenance of the mendicant might well have started at the perfectly demoniac expression of rage it assumed. Fire seemed to flash from his eyes, and it was, evidently, only by a great effort that he succeeded in keeping himself from exhibiting some loud and violent ebullition of temper. Was that solely on account of the apparent unwillingness of the young stranger to trust his saddle and its contents, even for a few moments, in his custody, or had he some more stringent motive for the disappointment and malignity which his face exhibited? He had a far more powerful motive than mere passing anger. What it was we shall shortly see.

The traveller was too busy himself taking the saddle from his horse to take any notice of the countenance of the mendicant. By the time he had nearly finished that operation, Jim, the ostler, made his appearance, and lent his aid.

"Carry the saddle at once to my room," said the traveller to him.

"Yes," said Toggs. "No. 8, Jem. No. 8 will be the gentleman's private room. Your bedroom, sir, will adjoin it. I presume you intend to honour us with your company?"

"Yes. And, perhaps, for more than one night."

"Thank you, sir, thank you. Very much beholden to your honour. This way, sir, if you please."

"No. 8," muttered the mendicant— "humph! No. 8, and the bedroom adjoins that room. 'Tis well—'tis well."

He gave the horse a kick which set it rearing and shying, and then he walked into the house again, whither had gone Toggs, the ostler, and the traveller, whose steed, had it not been so weary as it was, might have started off after the rough usage it received from the beggar.

"A pretty fellow you are to mind a gentleman's horse," said the ostler, when he came back.

"Mind it yourself, and be d—d,' was the polite reply.

"You are a beauty."

"There's two of us then."

"How long are you going to stop here, I should like to know?"

"Should you?"

"Yes, I should. Because, if anything's missed, we shall know pretty well who's got it. You look so very honest!"

"Hark ye, friend," said the mendicant; "there's one of my looks that you have not translated. I'm a little dangerous now and then."

"Are you, indeed? There's an old muzzle in the stable that I'll pop on you in a moment, whenever I think you want it."

Feeling quite satisfied then that he had got the best of the encounter, Jem, the ostler, walked away, leading the horse, and whistling as he went.

"Fool that I was," muttered the mendicant, "to waste words upon such a man as that. When shall I be able to subdue this headstrong passion, which has caused me to fail in so many of my schemes and projects, and which will ruin this, the greatest and most important of them all, if I am not most especially careful? Let me consider—let me consider. I have done no harm as yet."

He threw himself into a seat, and for more than half an hour was lost in deep thought. No one came near him for the whole of that period, for the whole establishment was busy with the new guest, who seemed a man of wealth and substance, for everything he ordered was directed to be of the very best description, and he never asked the price of anything, so he was considered to be a guest well worth attending to, and just the sort which Master Toggs would have been glad to see come a little oftener to the Morton Arms than they did.

The night was a very dark one, for the moon, although somewhat advanced in her monthly pilgrimage, rose late, and, consequently, between sunset, or rather the end of twilight and the rising of our satellite, there was a period of very intense darkness over all things.

The air, though, was balmy, pleasant, and refreshing, and as the window of the room in which the young traveller was placed opened upon a well-kept garden, he had opened it, and there sat silently examining some papers which he had taken from a carefully secured pocket in the saddle he had been so particular about, and which lay on the ground close to his feet.

He had two candles upon the table, and the rest of the room, for it was a good sized one, was in that state of semi-darkness which the inefficient light of candles always produces.

There was upon his countenance a look of great anxiety as he appeared to be comparing some of the papers with others. Some, too, he read carefully through, and in his pocket-book he made various memoranda in pencil from time to time. Then he suddenly rose, and clasping his hands behind him, he paced the room to and fro for nearly a quarter of an hour, evidently in very deep thought, and then he, as suddenly as he had risen, sat down again, and carefully collecting all the papers, he replaced them in the pocket of the saddle from where he had taken them. Having done this, he immediately rung the bell.

Toggs himself waited upon a guest who promised to be so well worth the waiting on, and he was in a few moments in the room.

"You pleased to ring, sir?" he said.

"Yes—yes."

"What can I have the honour and the pleasure, sir, of bringing to you?"

"A bottle of your Madeira that you said you had good, and two glasses, Mr.—a—, I don't know your name."

"Toggs, sir."

"Oh, Toggs."

"Did you say two glasses, sir?"

"Yes. I hope to have the pleasure of your company, Mr. Toggs, in discussing the bottle."

"Oh, really, sir, you are too good, sir. Upon my word, sir, I'm extremely obliged. The—the—honour, sir."

"Oh, not at all—not at all. I am not fond of solitude. Get the wine."

"Directly, sir."

Toggs backed out of the room as he would have done out of the presence of royalty, and when he was gone, the stranger said—

"He surely, at all events, can give me some information, and to get it from him, I foresee, I shall be forced to endure a world of unmeaning gossip, which will dreadfully weary me; but it must be so, and I am resigned to the infliction. He must know something that will be useful on the mission I have come so far—so very far to fulfil. God send it may be a successful one. He comes."

Toggs, as may be well presumed, had lost no time in obeying the orders of the young traveller, especially considering the very satisfactory nature of them. Many a glass of ale was Toggs treated with at his own bar, and many a pint of porter was handed to him in the course of its round, by half friends, half customers, of the Morton Arms; but for a gentleman to come and order a bottle of the choicest Madeira for him, Mr. Toggs, to have a

share o', was something most unprece-
dented.

"Quite a gentleman," soliloquised Toggs;
"quite a gentleman, every inch— I'm a-
coming!—a very good-looking, well spoken young man, too; and the horse he
rides is quite unexceptionable.   Jem!
Jem!"

"What's the row?" said the ostler.

"What do you think o' that saddle-
horse, Jem?"

"A out-and-outer, sir."

"You don't say so?   Well, really, now,
if I didn't think so."

"A hundred guineas down on the nail
never bought him."

"Really—upon my word—quite a gentleman!   He's asked me to take a bottle
of Madeira with him, Jem.   'Mr. Toggs,'
says he, 'when I find united,' says he, 'in
one person, the landlord of an inn and
the gentleman,' says he, 'I'm proud of his
company.   Will you take a bottle of wine
with me?'   'Sir,' says I (you know, Jem,
that, when I like, I can speak like the
county member), 'I will;' and now I'm
a-going. It's a fact, upon my honour. Two
glasses and a bottle of Madeira!"

THE EXAMINATION OF THE MENDICANT BEFORE THE MAGISTRATE.

## CHAPTER XII.

THE LANDLORD'S SURPRISE.—THE STRAW
BED OF THE MENDICANT. — NIGHT AT
THE INN.—THE MURDERER'S FOOTSTEPS.

WHEN the landlord entered No. 8, with
the bottle of Madeira, and the two glasses,
it was with such a profusion of bows, that
he could hardly get them placed upon the
table.

"Pray sit down," said the traveller,
"and make yourself comfortable."

"Thank you, sir, thank you," said Toggs,
just sitting on the extreme edge of a chair,

so that the slightest knock in the world
to any of its legs must have precipitated
him on to the floor; "thank you, sir;" and
then, with a miraculous kind of speed, he
wiped out both the glasses, and held them
up to the candle to see if they were perfectly clean, after which he uncorked the
Madeira, and placed it before his guest.

"Help yourself, Toggs," said the
stranger, after he had poured out a glass.
"What sort of a neighbourhood is this?"

"Neighbourhood, sir— neighbourhood?
How odd!"

"Odd, is it?"

"Not at all— oh, sir, not at all; only I've been asked that before to-day, that's what made me say how odd."

"Oh, indeed."

"Yes, sir. As for the neighbourhood itself, it's a likely enough neighbourhood, sir. Do you think of settling hereabouts, sir?"

"No, no, I have no such intention; my home is far distant from here."

"Sorry to hear it, sir. An honour to the neighbourhood, sir, it would be, to have you in it. I'm sure I hope the wine is to your liking?"

"Very good. Have you any families of note residing about here?"

"We have, sir. There's the vicar; and there's the Dowager Lady Muddlebustle; and then, to my mind, the pleasantest people are the Mortons."

The stranger gave a slight start, and spilt a little of his wine, as he said,—

"Oh, the—the Mortons."

"Yes, sir; real good sort of old English people."

"Old?"

"Not they, sir. Old, I mean, as regards the—the manners, and the—the hospitality, and the—the—you understand, but not old themselves, sir."

"I comprehend you. You would say, they are, though young, full of ancestral virtues; rather acting up to the character of ancient English residents, than succumbing to modern frivolity."

"Exactly, sir; that's what they are exactly. If you'd know'd 'em a hundred years ago, you couldn't have said more about 'em to the purpose, sir. They are just what you say."

"A large family of them, I suppose?"

"No, sir. Captain Morton ——"

"Captain in the army?"

"As was, sir—as was. He was in a many fights, sir; and the battle of Waterloo, too, sir, I've heard. In course, I can't say on my own knowledge, 'cos I wasn't there to see him, but they do say as such was the case, sir. He's not very big, either, sir."

"Big? Why should he be big?"

"Why, sir, somehow, one expects a man who was at the whacking of the French at the battle of Waterloo, to be a whopper."

"I don't myself see the necessity for his being a whopper; but, however, that's a mere matter of opinion."

"Just so, sir—just so. He's a mild-looking man, enough, too, sir. He don't look as if he'd cut off lots of Frenchmen' heads, and arms, and legs, and pokeds cannons, and swords, and spikes, into their insides."

"Indeed. And his family?"

"Sir?"

"His family, I say."

"Oh, he's got no family—always excepting one."

The landlord here winked mysteriously, and the stranger said,—

"What do you mean? I really do not understand you."

"Oh, well, he's got one. A pity it's a gal, sir; a wonderful pity she's a gal. That's what I always do say. A wonderful pity, sir—a-hem! There's two sides to a blanket, sir."

"So I suppose."

"Well, captains, you know, will be captains. Miss Mabel ——"

"Ah!" cried the stranger.

"Good God, sir, what's the matter?"

"Nothing; a—a—nothing."

"But you called out 'ah!'"

"Yes, I—I—yes, I sometimes do. I'm subject — to — to it, sometimes. Never mind, fill your glass."

"Lor, sir! is it a family complaint, sir?"

"Yes—no; of course—nothing. Go on, Mr. Toggs, and never mind me. A sudden sort of spasm, you see, which comes over me, now and then—you understand; an affection of the pericardium."

"God bless me, I suppose that's some fashionable name for a card-table, sir?"

"Just so."

"Ah, young men will gamble. There's no keeping 'em from it. Dice is dice, say I. Oh, dear me."

The Madeira was having some effect upon mine host of the Morton Arms, and the young traveller saw that if he did not get the information he wanted quickly, he would run a chance of not getting it at all.

"You mentioned that a young girl named Mabel," he said, "formed one of the captain's family."

"I did. Oh, gracious providential Providence, she's lovely. When I think of her, I think as I never seed her equal; and I never shall, go where I will and come where I may."

"Is she beautiful?"

"A angel, sir—a angel."

"And her age?"

"About sixteen—may be yonger, may be older. Jem, the ostler, thinks she's 'rising' sixteen, but I don't."

"And she is known to be his daughter?"

"Not a bit—not a bit. Known, indeed!

Lor bless you, of course nobody says nothing to him about it. He's not the sort of man to ask questions of in an off-hand way, sir. He'd soon put anybody down, he would; only we know she isn't his wife's child, and we know she's nobody's; and when we put it all together, and take that from this, and this from that, and give it a turn in our minds, you see, sir, we comes to a conclusion, and we says, 'Miss Mabel is the captain's—of course, she's the captain's, and very much to his credit, too, that he will have her home in the way as he does.'"

"He has to exert his authority, then, upon that point?"

"Oh, no—oh, no—oh, no. They all like her, they do. I heard from Sarah, which is parlour-maid at the hall, that when the captain thought of sending Miss Mabel to a school somewhere to be finished off, Mrs. Morton cried for two days, till the captain had to say he wouldn't have her finished at all, and she should stay."

"It is strange that so much affection should subsist between the captain's wife and one so peculiarly situated as this girl."

"It is, sir. That's what I often say. It's wery extra amiable, it is, sir. A long way over proof, I should say, speaking in a spirituous sort of way."

The young stranger produced an elegant gold watch, and exclaimed, as he glanced at it—

"Past nine, I declare; I knew not that it was so late. I shall go early to bed to-night, Mr. Toggs, for I have ridden far to-day."

The bottle of Madeira was now exhausted, and as Toggs had sufficient rationality left him to understand that the consultation of the watch was a hint to be gone, he arose accordingly, saying—

"Sir, if there is anything else the house affords, I can only say you have but to signify your commands, sir, and it's yours."

"Thank you, thank you; in half an hour I shall retire for the night."

"Very good, sir."

"Do not let me be disturbed; and before I retire, I shall go and look at my horse, as I make it an invariable rule so to do before going to bed myself."

"Certainly, sir, certainly."

Toggs again bowed himself out, and off he ran to Jem, the ostler, to announce the intended visit to the horse.

"And quite right, too," said Jem. "How's he to know what sort of a conscience resides in my busem, eh? How's

he to know as the most conscientiousest ostler as never lived is me?'

"Certainly not."

"Sartinly not, do you say? Do you deny my being that same?"

"No, no—I mean, how should he know it?"

"Oh, I forgive you, I forgive you. He'll find the oss as right as a trivet, let him come when he will; I know he will. I've give him a hard rub down and a soft rub, a brush of the feet, and I've stopped his fore-feet as well as ever a fore-feet was stopped."

"Here he comes, Jem."

The young stranger came down stairs, and Jem, stepping up to him, said—

"Want to see the oss, sir?"

"Yes."

"This way, sir, please—this here's the way."

Holding his stable-lantern as high as he could, Jem led the way to the stables, where, to do him justice, he had done ample justice to the gentleman's horse.

"I have not visited the stable from any suspicion that you had not properly attended to my horse," said the young man; "but as I always proportion what I give an ostler to the state in which I find my steed, I always go myself and look at it."

"All right, sir."

A half-crown, placed into Jem's capacious hand, showed the estimation in which the stranger held him; and then they were both upon the point of leaving the stable, when they were confronted by the mendicant, who said, in an insolent tone—

"You seem mighty liberal, sir; perhaps you'll pay me for holding your horse."

"Who are you?"

"You may well ask, sir," said Jem. "He's a wagabone, sir, an out-and-out wagabone, sir, that's what he is, and you don't ought to give him a farden."

"Nor shall I."

"Then you may be d—d!" said the fellow, "and I tell you what it is—I did intend to sleep here, but I won't now; I'll walk on, if it's ten miles further, to the next inn."

"How dreadful!" said Jem. "Why, I'd a stood a pint at any time to get you into that mind, old fellow. He's disgusted with us, sir, and won't patronise us any more. Ain't it a dreadful pity?"

The traveller made no remark, but walked on, although he heard the mendicant say, in a loud voice—

"I shake the dust of this house off my shoes—I leave it never to return to it. Let me be cold, hungry, or weary, I will never again set foot beneath the roof of this house. I leave my malediction upon it and all its inmates."

## CHAPTER XIII.

THE GOOD RIDDANCE.—MIDNIGHT.—THE STEALTHY FORM.—THE WATCH-DOG.— TROUBLED TOM'S ADVENTURE.

THE young guest of the inn bade the landlord good night, and retired to his chamber. Jem then related how the mendicant had taken offence and left the house, which was declared to be an amazingly good riddance of bad rubbish by the landlord, who in proportion as he congratulated himself upon the departure of the beggar, was loud in his praises of the guest he still retained.

"What's his name?" said Jem.

"Well, that I don't know," said the landlord, "and so I can't tell you; but he's quite a gentleman, and I only hope he'll stay here some weeks, that's all."

"His horse wouldn't be the worse for a few days' rest at all events," said Jem. "It's done its work lately, I can see."

"I shouldn't at all wonder if he made quite a stay of it for his health."

"His health! What's the matter with him?"

"Oh, a family complaint. He can't help saying 'oh!' sometimes, and making you almost jump off your chair."

"You don't say os?"

"Yes I do. I nearly fell down when he said it."

"How very odd! Perhaps a cough-ball would do him good, or a cold mash as he goes to-bed."

"What a fool you are, Jem. You think that what does osses good is the same for human beings."

"Well, I don't know—why shouldn't it? When I get's a cold, I mixes up for myself a cold mash in a pail, and I drinks it up, and in the morning I can go on to my work again."

\*    \*    \*    \*    \*

All was still at the Morton Arms. It was midnight. For nearly an hour every one within the building had retired to rest. No guests were expected late at that country place, and, after eleven, the most profound repose generally reigned throughout the whole district. The distant bay of some house-dog, or now and then the low of cattle, or the crow of some more than commonly fidgetty fowl, were the only sounds that ever broke upon the profound stillness of the village.

It was not a high-road to anywhere that ran through the straggling collection of houses, so no coaches passed that way, excepting rarely; therefore, there was none of the bustle of the coming mail, or any of the long stages. Chance, and local passengers, and horsemen, only passed through the place.

And now the moon has risen, but not high in the heavens, so that there is abundance of shadow yet. The hour of midnight has solemnly pealed forth from the village church, which was situated in the centre of the grave-yard, where reposed the remains of many who had been born, had lived, and had died within the sound of the old church bells.

A conspicuous object in the churchyard, close to one of the windows of the sacred edifice itself, is the monument of the Mortons, which covers the entrance to the family vault, an excavation of considerable extent, stretching under the marble flag-stones that pave the church. This monument was a long square building, having few pretensions to anything in the shape of architectural beauty; it was more intended as a covering for the entrance of the vault than anything else.

The moon had risen in the sky on the other side of the church, so that the whole of the tomb was in darkness, owing to the broad, black shadow of the ancient building falling full upon it, and stretching far beyond it over many a humbler resting-place for the dead. We say humbler; but there was no feeling of ostentation about the Morton family in having the family vault. They would have been quite willing that any one should have had the same; but, because such a thing was not possible, they saw no reason why they who could should not.

It may suit a greedy and an eager class of politicians to decry the rich merely on account of their being so—to abuse them for having money, and to abuse them for spending it. Of course, these people who make such a senseless clamour, would be better pleased if the rich men were to hoard their money instead of expending it. They either do not, or they will not see that a rich man's extravagance is invariably a poor man's gain. But, to resume.

From among the tall rank grass which grew between the wall of the church and this monument of the Mortons—a space not above two feet in width—arose, as the midnight hour was struck, a human form.

With stealthy steps he walked out from that place of concealment, and stood for a moment listening among the tombs. It was the mendicant, who had so recently affected to take leave for ever of the Morton Arms. For more than five minutes he listened attentively, and then he felt satisfied that all was still.

"Silent as the grave!" he muttered. "Silent! and I am cramped up so that I can scarcely move. Curses on that queer place to work in! I have, however, made a hole in the brickwork now large enough to get through, so that at the very worst I could conceal myself in the vault. Some folks would not like such a place of refuge; but I have seen death and its victims in too many shapes to care how it is presented to me now. A vault indeed! what is a vault to me?"

He listened again, but all remained as before, and then he picked his way slowly among the tombs in a crouching attitude, for fear of being seen by any one who might by possibility be out, or who might be looking from one of the cottage windows of the surrounding picturesque-looking habitations.

"So," he muttered, as he walked nearly to the confines of the space allotted for the repose of the dead, "so, they fancy I have gone, and that they are rid of me, which, no doubt, pleased them much, as they have a richer guest at the Morton Arms; but they are most grievously mistaken, as yet they will find. I will go, truly, but not till I have left behind me some stronger remembrance than an empty curse."

The mode of entrance and of exit which was attached to the little rude churchyard, consisted of a wicket-gate without a fastening, so that any one, at any hour, could seek that place of holy and hallowed thoughts without having to apply to any official upon the subject. Through the wicket-gate passed the mendicant, and from there he gained the principal thoroughfare in the village. It was not, however, as may be well supposed, his intention to linger long there. Darting across the main street, with great rapidity, he was soon in the gloom of the large shadows cast by the moonlight on the hedgerows and gardens. He had taken care to note well the position of the inn, and now his object evidently was to gain the back part of the building, which was by no means difficult of access to any one who knew the route to take. It was necessary, to be secure, to pass over several gardens; but there was no danger to be apprehended from that, for every one in the village had a garden, and the idea of one robbing another of the produce of the land, never entered into their imaginations;

consequently, their fears were extremely slight. He had in his progress but one source of danger, and that arose from the likelihood of meeting some dog, whose suspicion might be awakened, and who, consequently, might challenge his right to be trespassing on land not his own.

"Curse all dogs," he muttered, as the distant howl of one, a mile off at least, came upon his ears, and put him in mind of them. "Curse all dogs, say I; they have always interfered with me in some way or another, and marred some of my projects and schemes. If I should meet with any one to-night, I will take good care to put him past all power of interfering with me twice."

As he spoke, he produced the knife that he had drawn when attacked by the hound that had saved Mabel from his ruffianly violence; and, setting his teeth, he, with a look of fiendish malice, pursued his route towards the inn.

"Let me consider," he said; "I cannot be wrong in my man. Young, rather tall, and inclined to be fair; gray eyes, and riding a valuable bay horse. Yes, he is my man; I must and will have those papers; let the acquisition of them cost me what amount of trouble it may, I will have them, I am resolved. With them, to achieve all I wish will be easy; without them, I can do surely but little, if anything. I will not be foiled. A man who has no scruples as to the means, can almost always accomplish what he determines upon, and no scruples have I—I have waded through blood enough not much to mind another murder."

By this time he had arrived at a farm, which divided a long strip of land, which was converted into a kitchen-garden, from an adjoining meadow. This kitchen-garden actually belonged to the inn; so that, when he crept under the fence, which he did, he was actually on the premises which it was his object to reach. He paused a moment now, to listen if any sound met his ear indicative of any one stirring in the inn; but all was as still as that lonely grave-yard in which he had concealed himself for several hours.

"All's safe," he muttered; "all's safe. Now, to think of what I have to encounter. There is no doubt about my effecting an entrance to the house. I wonder if that rascal, Jem, the ostler, lives at the inn, and sleeps in it. He have I most to fear. I don't seem to care for any one else, but I do for him."

The real fact was, that there were but three men in the house at all—one was the guest against whose papers the menddicant meditated his present attack; the second was the landlord, and the third was Jim, the ostler, whom the ruffian had the greatest fear of. To have asked any questions with regard to the chambers inhabited by any one in the inn, would have been, of course, to direct suspicion and pursuit to himself, and, therefore, he did not do so. All the information he had was, that the young stranger lodged in a room adjoining to one numbered eight, the abiding places of the others he knew not. He slunk along now very cautiously indeed, although he was in the full shadow of the house, for he feared that the least noise might disturb some one, and he laboured under the disadvantage of not knowing how near he might be to some of the sleeping places.

"It will be the worse," he muttered, "for any one who may come in my way. I am confident that this is the last opportunity I shall ever have of getting the papers, and I will have them. I say I will have them, or lose my own life in the attempt."

He came now upon some outbuildings belonging to the inn, and he felt that more caution than ever than before was necessary.

"I wonder," he muttered, "that the place is left so much exposed."

Scarcely had he spoken these words when he heard the low growl of a dog, and he was immediately as still as a rock. A short, sharp bark now proclaimed that the suspicions of a dog were thoroughly awakened, and it likewise enabled the mendicant to find in what quarter his danger lay.

"This hinderance," he muttered, "must, and shall, be put a stop to at once, even if I run some risk in so doing."

Instead, then, of, as might naturally have been supposed, taking some other and, perhaps, more circuitous route, to escape the dog, he turned towards the quarter from whence the sounds came. Upon looking over a low wooden fence he saw a mastiff dog chained up, but regarding him with hostile looks. The moment the dog saw him, it flew to the greatest length of his chain, and began a furious barking, which would soon have had the effect of rousing everybody in the inn, had it not been very suddenly and completely put an end to by the boldness of the mendicant. He did what ninety-nine men out of a hundred would have scrupled very much to do; that is, he sprang over the fence in a moment, and, with his knife in his hand, he closed with the dog, which, of course, laid hold of him in an instant.

His right hand, in which he had the knife, was, however, at liberty, and he plunged it as fast as he could do so, and withdrew it again, reeking with blood, into the side of the animal. So very unequal a contest could not last very long; and, after a few moments, the dog relaxed his hold, and sunk on to his side exhausted through loss of blood.

"So much for you, and be d—d to you," said the beggar, as he cut the poor animal's throat from ear to ear.

Then he rose, and commenced sucking the blood from the only bite he had himself received. He continued this operation for some minutes, spitting the blood he extrated from the wound repeatedly out of his mouth; and then, with an oath at the delay which the occurrence had occasioned him, he once again turned towards the inn, with stealthy steps. Scarcely had he left the place where he had had such a contest, so brief and yet so sanguinary, with the mastiff, than a human form rose up into a sitting posture, and some one, whom our readers will not fail at once to recognise, ejaculated,—

"What a trouble! That was that beggar fellow. I know him. I—I wonder what he's up to? What a trouble it is to wonder!"

Down lay "Troubled Tom" again upon a truss of straw, on which he had been now, for about six hours, fast asleep, and still muttering faintly,—

"Everything's a trouble," he again fell fast asleep.

It was well, no doubt, for Troubled Tom that he did consider it too much trouble to follow the mendicant, or, in the furious frame of mind that individual was, it is more than likely the poor fellow's troubles would have been all ended with the same knife that had taken the life of the mastiff dog. So deep, however, had been the sleep of Tom, that he only awakened at the end of the fray, and he went to sleep again without knowing that the dog was dead.

---

## CHAPTER XIV.

THE FALSE ACCUSATION.—THE PURSUIT, AND THE MYSTERIOUS DISAPPEARANCE OF THE MENDICANT.

THE mendicant, when now he reached, without further interruption—as the only dog Toggs kept was now dead—the back-door of the inn, found no difficulty in undoing the fastenings, and in a moment he was fairly in the house. He closed the door, but took care to leave it so that he should himself be able to open it any moment he pleased, and then he listened for a length of time sufficient to be quite convinced that no one was stirring in the inn. He now slipped off his shoes, and commenced his progress into the interior of the building.

The Morton Arms was one of those straggling built places, a sight of which at once convinces any one that it was not an object how much ground was occupied by it. It had in it a good number of passages, and no less than three staircases, so that a stranger might be considerably puzzled in finding out all the ins and outs of such a building. By, however, an accurate investigation, conducted as carefully as he could in the dark, of which way he went, the mendicant made sure he should be able, if any sudden movement were necessary, to find his way back again, and so on he went up the principal staircase towards the floor on which the best beds were situated.

Suddenly, when he least of all expected it, a light flashed across his eyes, and he had just time enough to throw himself down flat on the floor, when he heard a footstep coming up another staircase, which led to the floor on which he then was. Slowly came he who was approaching, and, to the surprise of the mendicant, he saw that it was no other than his enemy, Jem, the ostler, who was yawning, and carrying a candle all on one side as he went.

"The deuce," muttered the ostler; "how stupid of me to fall asleep in one of the stalls. I—I am as cold as an icicle, and I don't see why now I shouldn't turn into one of the spare beds; old Toggs will be none the wiser. I don't want any sheets, and I can easily put it up all straight and smooth in the morning. I'll—I'll,—ah! how sleep—y I am, to be sure. I'll turn in to No. 6. That's a nice enough room, is No. 6. Hilloa! what a goose I was, to be sure, to fall asleep in the stable. I haven't the least idea of what o'clock it is."

At this moment the village clock struck one.

"One!" exclaimed Jem. "The deuce, and I got to be up at five. Here goes for a snooze in No. 6."

So saying, and tumbling about from very sleepiness, he opened the door of a chamber and went in, closing it after him.

In a few moments the mendicant rose, and with the expression of a perfect fiend upon his face, he shook his clenched fist in the direction the unconscious ostler had taken, as he muttered, in a low growling tone,—

"You are a doomed man; but not by my hands shall you fall. I need not take that trouble. It will be done for me. It shall be done for me, if any violence is necessary to-night. You will be hanged or transported, my friend, as comfortably as ever anybody was. Your evil genius has delivered you into my hands."

He now gathered more boldness, for he reasoned with himself,—

"If he, the ostler, could carry a light here, and create no alarm, why may not I? I have the means of getting a light. Yet, stay; what a glorious thing it would be now to possess myself of his."

This idea once started, presented itself to the mendicant in such captivating colours, that he could not think of abandoning it, so he approached the door of the room into which the ostler had gone, to listen if he could hear if he were sleeping or waking. He could perceive that the light had been extinguished, and when he got close to the door he found that it was but imperfectly shut, and opened with a touch, although the lock made a click in so doing. This, however, which alarmed him at first, assured him in another moment that the ostler was fast asleep, as he took no notice of the accidental circumstance.

"He sleeps—he sleeps," whispered the villain, and he crept at once into the chamber of the unconscious man.

The slant rays of the moon came into this room, and he saw all within it with perfect clearness. The candle, with no extinguisher upon it, was upon a table. To secure it was the work of a moment, and the mendicant left the room again as noiselessly as he had entered it. By the aid of a phosphorus match he lit the candle, and looking about him, he saw the number 8 upon a door, and he at once opened it, and walked into the private apartment of the young traveller.

The first glance sufficed to convince him that the saddle which contained the papers he wished to appropriate to himself was not there. He knew from the position of the house that the next room must have the moonlight in it; therefore, he would not take the light with him, but he placed it in a corner of the room. He then slowly approached the inner door, which opened to the sleeping chamber of the traveller. He placed his ear against the panel of the door, and listened for a few moments; all was still, and then he slowly turned the handle of the lock. It resisted him, and, with a suppressed oath, he exclaimed,—

"Locked in the inside. Curses on his caution. I may be foiled yet, and by such an impediment as this. Has he left the key in the lock or not? that is the question. If he has, all labour is in vain —if not, it is no sort of impediment."

He went to the outer room again and got the light, which he held eagerly to the lock, in order to ascertain if the key was left in it or not. A smile of satisfaction crossed his face—it was in the lock, but so much of the end projected right through to the side on which was the mendicant, that, with some of the tools he had about him, he felt confident he should be able to turn it. Replacing, then, the candle from whence he had brought it, he produced a pair of small but powerful pincers, with which he took hold of the projecting end of the key. He turned it easily, and in another moment the door was unlocked, and the slumbering man at the mercy of one who had no atom of that quality in his composition.

As he had anticipated, the moonlight came into that room sufficiently to make every object in it plainly visible. By the foot of the bed he saw the saddle, in the pocket of which he doubted not were the documents which he had so much set his heart upon possessing. On the table, too, were various articles, one of which was a purse, which, from its weight, seemed to be tolerably well filled, and which the mendicant immediately possessed himself of.

He seemed to be fully convinced that rapidity of action now was of considerable importance, and, hastily laying hold of several small articles—not that he wanted them for their value, but that he intended to cast them into No. 6, where was sleeping the unconscious ostler, in order to throw suspicion upon him—he placed them in his pockets, and then he laid his hands upon the saddle, and with his knife commenced ripping it open in search of the secret packet that contained the papers.

Such a mode of search was certain, in a few moments, to obtain its object, and he, accordingly, found a small packet, tied round with a piece of green silk. He could hardly keep from expressing his satisfaction as he found it, and, in an instant, transferring it to his pocket, he rose to his feet, and was on the point of rushing to the door to escape with his prize, when he heard the bedstead creak, and casting his eyes upon the bed, he saw the young traveller looking him full in the face.

So little prepared was he for this sudden awakening of the man he had robbed, that for a moment fear paralysed him. During that moment the traveller placed his hand under the pillow on which he had slept, and drew forth a pocket pistol, which, without any further ceremony, he discharged full at the midnight robber's head. The report in a room, and at such a still hour of the night, was tremendous.

The mendicant thought he was hit, but a moment's reflection convinced him that although the bullet must have passed very near indeed to his face, it had missed him. Then, with a shout of rage, he rushed upon the young man before he could rise from the bed, in much the same manner as he had rushed upon the dog, and with the same knife he inflicted a deep stab in his breast. With a groan the traveller sank back, weltering in his blood, on to the bed. To leave the room was now the work of another instant; he knew that the pistol-shot must alarm every one in the inn, and that now his only chance of safety consisted in the rapidity with which he could leave it. Still he would not forsake his idea of revenge against the ostler, for the little dispute he had had with him, and as he passed the door of No. 6, he threw into the room the knife covered with blood, and several of the little articles he had taken from the sleeping chamber of the traveller. A man fully awake and up can do things with so much greater celerity and certainty than those who are suddenly aroused by a loud noise from sound sleep, that it was not to be wondered at that the mendicant, notwithstanding the report of the pistol that had been fired at him nearly awakened every one, reached the back door of the inn before anybody was fairly up. He opened it in a moment, and passed out into the open air, carrying his shoes with him. These he put on quickly, and then he took to flight with all the speed he could.

The shortest way is always the way one knows best, and he was fully alive to such a piece of philosophy—so with great precision, a precision which showed what accurate notice he had taken of his route as he came, the murderer took his way over the same fences he had crossed in coming, and passed the dead body of the dog he had killed in his progress. Thus, then, he reached the village High-street; but here he found that a new danger awaited him, for a number of men conducting horses to a cattle fair were passing through the place, and just as he appeared among them, some window of the inn was flung open, and the loud discordant spring ng of a rattle fell upon his ears.

"Some thief!" cried one of the men, as he made a dart at the mendicant. "There he goes."

The beggar eluded him, and dashed across the village in the direction of the church-yard, cursing his evil destiny that had exposed him to such a danger, when a few moments earlier, or a few moments later, would have altogether avoided it. There seems to be something exciting and pleasurable always to human nature about a chase, and, accordingly, as many men as could be spared from the care of the horses ran after the flying mendicant, without having the least idea of what he had done, or indeed being quite sure that he had anything to do with the circumstance that had induced the spring of the rattle.

They were swift runners those men, and they reached the wicket-gate of the church-yard a moment after he had passed through it. They saw him threading his way among the grave-stones. Then they saw

MABEL FAINTS FROM TERROR AFTER ESCAPING FROM THE MENDICANT.

him suddenly make, what appeared to them, a headlong dash at the very wall of the church, and from that moment he disappeared, and no trace of him could be found.

---

## CHAPTER XV.

### THE CONFUSION AT THE INN.—THE LAST WORDS OF THE YOUNG TRAVELLER.— THE CONSTABLE AND THE MAGISTRATE.

"WHAT a trouble," said Troubled Tom, as he awoke from being actually trodden upon by the mendicant, in his rapid flight from the inn, after committing the dreadful deed of blood he had done. "What a trouble—it is hard a poor fellow can't have a sleep without being bothered. There goes that fellow again, I do declare. I'd make a row, only it is such a trouble. I thought I heard a noise just now, but, really—ah, what a trouble."

Down lay Troubled Tom to sleep again, and in another few moments he was as sound in repose as before. The springing of the rattle was in front of the house, and although, despite that circumstance, it would easily have awakened any ordinary sleeper even at the back, it failed to do so in his case, although it might perchance give a current to some dream that was flitting through his brain—that is to say, if it were not really too much trouble to dream.

But he had seen the mendicant now twice, when that personage little suspected any human eye was upon him, and although, slow thinker as was Troubled Tom, he placed no importance upon the circumstance, yet he would soon be doomed to discover that it was of the greatest possible interest to some one. The report of the pistol simultaneously awakened every one in the inn. The landlord, Master Toggs, sprang out of bed with a bewildered look, and cried out aloud—

"Coming—coming—coming."

Jem, the ostler, awakened, and sat bolt upright with a half sleepy stare, as he said—

"What's the row now?"

At the moment that he did so, something fell on his bed, and this extra circumstance so bewildered him, that he began rubbing his eyes, and remarking to himself—

"I suppose I'm fast asleep still, and it's some odd dream; that's all I can say about it."

But Toggs felt convinced that his alarm was no dream, especially as he now heard the banging of doors, as some of the female part of the establishment were aroused.

"Is it a fire, or thieves?" he heard the cook exclaim, in a loud voice, and then came a scream from Susan, who was the "odd woman" of the establishment.

"It's something or another," said Toggs, and, accordingly, he rose, and opening his window, which was to the front of the house, he commenced springing the rattle which had caused so active a pursuit, and so nearly a capture of the mendicant.

The springing of the rattle at once convinced Jem, the ostler, that there was something more in it than a mere dream, and he at once rushed into the corridor.

In the state of drowsiness he was in when he had so surreptitiously taken possession of No. 6, he had not thought it necessary to divest himself of all his apparel, so that he was quite dressed sufficiently to be able to make an appearance.

"Hilloa, Toggs—Master Toggs," he cried, "what's the row? Who's got hold of you?"

"Nobody," cried Toggs. "What's the matter?"

"Can't say, on my life. You are making such an infernal riot with that rattle that I don't think we ever shall know."

"But something was the matter, Jem."

"Very likely."

"Didn't you hear a noise?"

"Yes, I did; but what it was I don't know or care, nor can I attempt a guess. Here comes somebody with a light. I suppose you are quite aware, Toggs, that the somebody who's a-coming is the cook or Susan. It's no business of mine, but you've forgot your breeches, and that shirt of yours isn't so long as it might be."

"God bless me!" said Toggs; "really, I did forget;" and he dashed into his room again to array himself more properly, just as Susan, the "odd woman," appeared with a candle.

"Oh, Jem, whatever is the matt    " she said, holding the candle at an angle of about twenty degrees, so that the grease came from it drop by drop on the floor. "What is the matter?"

"Don't know," said Jem. "Toggs is a making himself respectable, and when he comes out, perhaps he'll tell us. He sprang away at the rattle, and ought to know what for."

Toggs, now, having made the necessary addition to his toilette, came out, and the first words he said, were—

"What is it all about?"

"Don't you know, sir?" said Susan. "Cook's in *highstewricks*, sir, with the fright of it."

"Fright of what?"

"Ah, she don't know, sir; and that's what I thinks makes her so very bad."

"Then, does nobody know?" said Jem.

"Not I," said Toggs. "I only know there was a great noise; and I very much wonder that the gentleman in No. 8 has not been disturbed by it, as we all were."

"Hang it all! I forgot him," cried Jem. "Something's happened to him, or he must have been disturbed. It isn't in human nature to sleep in the middle of such a racket. Come, and let's have a look at him. My mind misgives me, Toggs, but something queer has happened to him."

"Good gracious!" said Toggs, "you don't mean that, Jem?"

"Yes, I do. Come on."

"Lor, shall I venture, too?" said Susan.

"Yes," cried Jem. "Let's have lots of witnesses. Come on both of you—come on. I feels, as sure as that we are alive, something's amiss with the gentleman in No. 8."

Had the ostler been guilty of the crime which was afterwards imputed to him, it is not at all likely he would have made these observations; but the fact of his having made them was used against him when the suspicion of his guilty participation in the murder did arise ; which was natural it should, in consequence of the rascally conduct of the mendicant in casting the ensanguined knife, with which he had committed the deed, as well as some of the articles he had taken from the chamber, into the room in which the ostler was sleeping.

Jem was looked upon at the Morton Arms as a sort of oracle, and, therefore, the words he indicative of a belief that something serious had happened to the gentleman in No. 8, filled both Toggs and the old woman with so much alarm that they both trembled as if they had had the ague as they followed Jem to that room.

"Lor, Jem," said Toggs, "what could have happened to him ?"

"I don't know," said Jem; "but we soon shall."

They passed through the outer room in which Toggs and the young traveller had discussed the bottle of Madeira, and there was nothing to excite any particular attention. The door of the bed-room was a little open, and with a feeling of certainty that something terrible was within, Jem pushed it wide open, and with the candle in his hand, which he had taken from the old woman, he entered the apartment, while the landlord and Susan lingered a moment at the door.

The traveller was sitting up in his bed, his face was ghastly pale, and both his hands, through the fingers of which blood was trickling, were pressed upon the wound which the mendicant had inflicted on his breast. There was no mistaking the look of agony which was upon his face. He was dying.

"Good God !" said Jem, as he actually reeled back a pace or two towards the door as this dreadful sight met his eyes. "Good God ! look here."

"Eh ?" said Toggs. Don't terrify me ; what is it ?"

"Come in, for Heaven's sake!" said Jem. "Here's murder done."

Susan gave a scream, and fainted off-hand at once in the outer room, while Toggs, to the full as pale as the wounded traveller, looked into the room with horror-stricken eyes.

"Help—oh help!" said the traveller faintly. "Oh, God! I bleed to death. Help—help—help !"

Jem recovered all his faculties in a moment.

"Toggs," he said, "stay here, and don't move for your life. I'll get Mr. Bland, the doctor, in a minute."

Without waiting for the reply of Toggs, Jem dashed out of the room down the staircase, and out into the village, like a madman.

The only medical man which the place afforded was he who had been named by Jem, Mr. Bland, a gentleman of considerable skill and professional acquirements, who had retired from a much larger practice with a comfortable independence, but who still did not entirely desert his profession.

To the house of this gentleman did Jem hasten, and he executed at his door such a knock that it was enough to awaken the very dead as well as the living. Mr. Bland's head was popped out of a window in the course of a few seconds.

"Who's there?"

"Jem, sir, the ostler at the Morton Arms. A gentleman has been murdered there; God knows by who. Will you come?"

"In a moment."

Down went the window, and then off set Jem again to the inn, quite satisfied, from his knowledge of the habits of Mr. Bland, that he would not be long behind him.

But while Jem was gone, a rather important, though very brief, conversation took place between Toggs and his bleeding guest ; a conversation which—the latter from increasing weakness, and the former from fright—was rendered very difficult to be carried on with any alacrity on either of their parts.

Toggs obeyed the injunction of Jem not to stir from the spot in its most literal sense, for he remained exactly as he was, about two inches within the doorway of the chamber, which, henceforward, was to possess so fearful a notoriety, glaring in the face of his murdered guest, with a mixed expression of compassion and fear.

"Help—help !" groaned the wounded traveller. "Help! Don't, oh don't let me die for want of help !"

"He—he—he's gone for the doctor sir," stammered Toggs. "I'm a fool, and can't do nothing. Jem's gone for the doctor, sir. Oh, Lord! what will become of us all?"

"My—my life-blood is ebbing fast."

"Is it, sir?"

"I—am getting fainter."

"Oh, don't say so, sir."

"And such anguish — oh, God—oh God! such anguish as I suffer. Help me Heaven !"

"Amen, sir! Oh, Lord—oh, Lord! Here's a horrrid go at the Morton Arms. Oh, dear—oh, dear."

"I—I cannot live long now! Hear what—what I have to say, ere I am—a corpse!"

"Yes, sir—yes, sir. God bless you, sir! I'll hear you."

"Heaven have mercy upon me, and give me leave to—to—speak—a moment witho ut—this anguish."

He paused a moment, and rocked himself gently to and fro. The perspiration fell from his brow on to the bed. Toggs saw it fall, and he trembled in every limb himself, expecting each moment that his strength would fail him, and he should faint away upon the spot, without hearing what the dying man wanted to say. The wounded traveller spoke again, but his voice was getting weaker and weaker.

"I—I want, before I die, to see—Captain Morton."

"And so you shall, sir," stammered Toggs. "You shall—you shall; oh, Lord! you shall, sir."

"Yes, yes; I must—I must see him."

"Yes, sir. But who did it, sir—who hurt you?"

"A man—came into the room. I fired a pistol at him—missed him, and he sprang upon me with a knife."

"Who was he, sir?"

"I—I cannot tell."

Slowly the wounded man sunk back on the pillow—a deep groan came from his breast, and Toggs jumped out into the outer room, just in time to run against Jem, who had returned, exclaiming—

"He's dead—he's dead!"

---

## CHAPTER XVI.

### THE DISTRESSING INTERVIEW.—THE PERPLEXITY OF CAPTAIN MORTON.

"You don't mean he's dead, Toggs?' said Jem.

"Yes, I do, though. All he seems to want is to see Captain Morton."

"Captain Morton, of the hall?"

"I suppose so."

"Then he shall see him. I've told Mr. Bland, and he's a-coming. I'm off again to the hall. You're sure he said Captain Morton, Toggs?"

"Am I alive?"

"Very good, then, he shall see him, if there's life in him to do so. And, at all events, if he's named the name of Captain Morton, he ought to know what's happened at once—so I'm off again."

Away went Jem on his new errand, and scarcely could he have got half way there when Mr. Bland arrived at the Morton Arms, and was let into the house by Susan, who had recovered from her fainting, and crept down stairs again.

"How is he?" said Mr. Bland, as he ascended the staircase.

"Oh, uncommonly dead, sir, I believe, now."

"Dead? Humph! The doctor, then, is not of much use. Where is he? Come, speak quick—where is he?"

"Number 8, sir."

"Very well."

Mr. Bland was in the outer room in another moment, and Toggs, the moment he saw him, exclaimed,—

"Oh, sir—oh, oh, oh! It's a comfort you've come; I'm afeard as he's died without you, sir."

"Are you? Hold the light for me. What are you trembling at? Don't be a fool, Toggs; hold the light for me."

Toggs, thus admonished, held the candle, which, however, he shook to and fro in an odd way as Mr. Bland walked into the sleeping chamber, which now, from the stillness that pervaded it, appeared to be the chamber of death.

"Go to the other side of the bed, Toggs," said the medical man, "and then you can light me without being in my way at all."

Toggs obeyed the order, and then Mr. Bland looked earnestly in the face of the wounded traveller. He took a small mirror from his pocket, and held it for a moment before the lips.

"He is not dead," he said. "We may rally him yet. Set down the candle, and get me some brandy."

"Yes, sir—yes, sir," said Toggs, who was the more disposed to obey this order with alacrity, inasmuch as it took him out of the room, which to him presented such a scene of horror.

Toggs had weak nerves, and he could not help it. He was not the kind of man to look on with apathy upon such a scene as the chamber of the traveller now presented. The bed appeared to be drenched with blood; and, although it is undoubtedly true that a little of that fluid makes a great show, yet was it quite evident that not a little only had flowed from the cruel wound which had been inflicted on the young traveller — whose only offence against him who had done so was, that he exercised the unalienable right of all men to defend himself and his property against any aggression.

The medical man bound the upper

sheet carefully round the wound which the traveller had received, before Toggs came up, after he had made a rapid investigation of it, and fully satisfied himself that nothing could really be done to save the life of the wounded man.

"He is a dead man within the hour," he said to himself. "The wound is mortal; but if the further effusion of blood can be prevented, he may live some hours yet, especially by the aid of stimulants carefully and in small quantities administered."

At this moment, Toggs, who, to do him justice, had, notwithstanding his dislike to the sight which that chamber presented, not at all lingered on his errand for the brandy, returned, and handed a glass of the liquor to the surgeon. Mr. Bland poured a very small quantity of it between the lips of the traveller, and then, sliding his hand under his head, he partially supported him in the bed, as he said—

"I cannot, Toggs, take upon myself to say that any good is to be accomplished by the partial restoration of this young traveller, now I am quite satisfied his wound is mortal."

"Captain Morton's been sent for, sir," said Toggs; "he said he wanted to see Captain Morton."

"Did he?"

"Yes, sir. Before he died, he said, he must see Captain Morton."

"Then I hope Captain Morton will come soon, or he will be too late to gratify the wish. No human means can keep this wounded man long alive."

"Lor, sir! Then there will be a death, after all, at the Morton Arms, and an inquest, and all that sort of thing?"

"You may make up your mind to that, friend Toggs."

"How dreadful!"

"Who is this gentleman?"

"Lord bless you, sir, I don't know!"

"You don't know?"

"No, sir. He only came a few hours ago on horseback, and put up here. I don't know at all who he is, sir."

"Who could have done this dreadful deed?"

"That I don't know, sir—no more than the babe unborn, sir. He told me as a man came into the room, and he fired a pistol at him and missed him; and then, that the man stuck a knife in him. It was the noise of the firing of the pistol, sir, as woke us all up, and then we found him all as you see him, sir, a-bleeding."

"It's very odd."

"It is, indeed, Mr. Bland. I'm a ruined man, of course. Nobody'll think of coming to the Morton Arms. I'm a done-up individual;—but I always was the most unlucky fellow as never was. I'm ruined—that's clear. There's a end of me, and all my *prospectusses* for the future. A deuced good thing it is, that I ain't a married man, with a mob of little Toggs a-calling out for breakfast, dinner, tea, and supper, and lots of bread and butter, atweenwhiles—isn't it, sir?"

"It is, indeed."

"Lor! He's a-breathing again, sir."

"Oh, he is sure to recover a little from the state he is in. The bleeding has stopped; although I am afraid, when the general system revives a little, it will have the effect of reproducing it."

"Do you think so, sir? Look, he's got one of his eyes open. Do you think he'll be sensible, sir?"

"I doubt it."

The wounded traveller groaned, and then, in a low, feeble voice, expressive of much pain, he said,—

"Dying—dying—dying!"

"Can you see?" said Mr. Bland.

"Who speaks to me—who speaks? I see around me a yellow ocean; all is yellow—yellow!"

"What a idea, Mr. Bland," said Toggs. "You sees as the curtains is green, sir. They ain't yellow a bit."

"Hush—hush!" said Mr. Bland.

"All yellow," moaned the wounded traveller.

"Who wounded you?" said the surgeon.

"I—I know not. Tall, dark——"

"Remember that, Toggs."

"Yes, sir."

"The knife—the dreadful knife! My life-blood followed it as he drew it forth from my heart."

"Was he dressed or undressed?"

"Dressed—dressed; tall and dark. He—he killed me—he killed me, and with me killed hopes which to-morrow might have realised. The saddle—the saddle. The papers—oh, the papers—where are they?"

"What does he mean, Toggs?"

"Why, Mr. Bland, he means——"

"Captain Morton is here," said Jem, popping his head into the room.

"Thank Heaven!" said the surgeon. "If he has anything of importance to communicate, he may do it now."

Captain Morton had been aroused by Jem, and, with his habits of military precision, he had been able to get from home and down to the Morton Arms much sooner than might have been expected, considering the distance he had to come.

Jem had ran on before, and had the door ready opened, so that there was no delay whatever in admitting the captain, who had proceeded straight to the chamber, conducted by Jem, who could tell him no more than that the wounded man had expressed an earnest desire to see him before he died. This, however, was quite enough to induce the captain to come at once; and now when he entered the chamber he looked anxiously towards the bed, fully expecting to see in the person of the sufferer some one whom he should recognise as an acquaintance.

Mr. Bland understood the look, and he said at once—

"Do you know him, Captain Morton?"

"I do not."

"That's odd. He wants to see you."

"I never, to my knowledge, saw him before."

Mr. Bland stooped over the stranger, and said, in a clear, distinct voice,—

"You wished to see Captain Morton. He is now here in the room, ready to hear anything you have to say to him."

A greater degree of animation appeared for a moment to come over the dying man, and he said at once,—

"Morton — Morton — yes; where is he?"

"Here," said Morton. "I am here."

"All yellow! all yellow!"

"He is dying," whispered Mr. Bland. "His very moments are numbered."

"I am here," added Morton, "willing to do you any service in my power. I do not know you, though."

"You—you never saw me," faintly ejaculated the dying traveller; "you never saw me before. Your hand—your hand!"

He waved his own hand to and fro, as if seeking for Captain Morton's, and the latter placed his hand in that of the unfortunate man, as he said, in a voice of deep compassion,—

"There is my hand. Speak, will you, and speak your wishes. God forbid that at such a time as this I should refuse to comply with anything you desire. Although I never saw you before, as you admit, you may know me."

The dying man grasped his hand as, in imploring accents, he said,—

"Thank God! I have lived long enough——"

He gasped for breath, and Mr. Bland raised him a little, and administered some more of the brandy. He appeared a little revived, and, after a moment, continued,—

"Long enough to—to tell you—you——"

"I attend; what, what?"

"Oh—oh! God—God!"

"Speak on—speak on; I am here; Captain Morton, remember, whom you wished to see."

A strange gurgling sound in the dying man's throat was the only response, and he was evidently making an effort to speak,

Mr. Bland shook his head.

"Gone?" said Captain Morton.

"Not quite, but nearly. He cannot tell you what he means now."

"How unfortunate. Speak, oh, speak, if you can; Captain Morton—Morton whom you wished to see, implores you to speak again. Summon energy, and speak your wishes."

A gasping sob came from the dying man. A gush of blood issued from his mouth, and in a clear, loud tone he cried—

"MABEL!"

The limbs relaxed; the eyes become glazed and fixed; the head sunk on one side. Then came a faint puff of breath which, for an instant, gave a roundness to the cheeks, and then they sunk for ever The stranger was dead!

## CHAPTER XVII.

THE INCOGNITO.—THE WARNING, AND THE STRANGE TALE OF THE PURSUIT TO THE CHURCHYARD.—MORE PERPLEXITY.

"HE is gone," said Mr. Bland.

"You are certain he is dead?" asked Captain Morton with a perplexed air.

"Quite. And I fear your interview with him has been far from satisfactory, Captain Morton."

"By Heaven! I can gain nothing from it. He has mentioned the name of a member of my family."

"Miss Mabel?"

"Yes; but nothing but the name. God only knows what he intended to say. How unfortunate that he should die so sudden as this. It is most vexatious. I would have given a hundred pounds a minute to have heard what more he had to say."

"Ah, captain, death will not be paid off in that way."

"Indeed, no. What was his name?"

"That nobody knows."

"Not know his name?"

"No; such has been the confusion

here, and such the anxiety to hear what he wished to say himself, that nobody knows who or what he is. Possibly, though, among his papers—he talked of having papers—some clue may be found to his name and connexions."

"He had some papers he was very careful of," said Jem, "in a private little pocket in the saddle of his horse."

"Had he?"

"Yes, Captain Morton; here's the saddle. Hilloa! the leather is cut to pieces. My life on it, whoever did the murder has stolen his papers, and who knows but it may have been done just for them?"

"More provoking still," said Captain Morton; "more provoking still. Those papers might have aided us in finding out who he was."

"If you please, sir, here is Master Spurgin," said Susan, suddenly appearing at the door of the chamber.

"The village constable," said Captain Morton. "Let him come in. It is his duty to take some cognizance of what has happened, although he may not bring the soundest judgment to bear upon the circumstances, or the most extended powers of research."

"Gentlemen," said the constable, walking in, "I'm your extreme dewoted, as we says. I heerd as there was a skrimmage, and here I is. Where's the malefactor? I suspect this will be some case of manslaughter, and misdemeanor at *nisi prices*, as we used to say in Westminster Hall. Ha! what has happened, Master Toggs?"

"If you look at the bed you'll see," said Toggs; "and, as nobody knows who did it, you may as well take me up, and have me hanged for it, as I'm a ruined man whether you do or not."

"The bed—what—oh, good thingumby! what is it—a dead man? Oh, I don't like to interfere—oh—oh! A glass of something warm and strong, Mr. Toggs, if you please. I'm putrified."

"You don't mean to say you are afraid?" said Mr. Bland.

"No—no—no—no—I—I'm only a little galwanised, that's all. I—I—oh, dear! I didn't—upon the honour of a sworn constable—I didn't think it was anythink in the sanguinary line. Oh, good gracious, here's a go! I shall be put in the papers, and called the active and enterprising Spurgin. I think I sees myself there."

"As you are the only man here in any authority," said Captain Morton, "you had better take what steps you think ne-cessary. There has been a murder committed, there can be no doubt."

"Shall I take up Toggs—shall I take up Toggs? Didn't he confess as he did it?"

"I don't think he did exactly."

"Oh, yes," said Toggs; "take me up—take me up. No matter what becomes of me. Take me up."

"I must take somebody up," answered Spurgin; "and all I can say is, Master Toggs, that if I can't find anybody else, I'll take you up."

"I thank you."

"But who does anybody strongly suspect?"

Mr. Spurgin laid his finger on the side of his nose as he said this, and when he was told that no one was strongly suspected at all, but that the whole affair was involved in profound mystery, all he could say upon the subject was,—

"Oh!"

"The proper way," said Captain Morton, "will be, as I have declined being in the commission of the peace, to send to some one who is, and I should suggest that a messenger be instantly despatched to Mr. Ormonde, at Ormonde Lodge, asking him to come here as soon as possible."

Jem was again in request as the messenger, and, as Ormonde Lodge was nearer to the Morton Arms than was Morton Hall, he soon returned with Mr. Ormonde, its proprietor, who, after exchanging civilities with Captain Morton, heard with unfeigned surprise the particulars, as far as they were known, of what had occurred.

"This is a most dreadful circumstance," he said.

"Dreadful, indeed," said Captain Morton. "What can be done?"

"My first duty is to search the house."

"Search away," said Toggs, who had quite lapsed into a state of melancholy. "You'd better take me up and hang me off-hand at my own sign outside the door."

"Why, my friend?" said Mr. Ormonde.

"Because I'm a ruined man."

"Ruined? How?"

"Who'll come here now, after a murder has been committed in the house, do you think?"

"Plenty. Do you imagine, dreadful as this circumstance is, it will do your house any harm?"

"Yes, I do, sir."

"Far from it; you will have plenty of

custom now, you may depend upon it. Curiosity will bring you people from all quarters."

"Well, I didn't think of that."

"I daresay you did not; but you will find it so, whether you thought of it or not. Far from being ruined, Toggs, I lament to say that a morbid curiosity is always got up for places were murders are committed, and I should not be at all surprised that you made your fortune, Toggs, so don't be in a hurry to be hanged yet."

"No, I won't, sir—I won't. I'll see how it turns out yet."

"Do so. And now, what other guests had you besides this unfortunate murdered gentleman?"

"None, sir."

"Then, Spurgin, you will come with me, and we will search the house first ; and then, as I see the daylight is momentarily increasing, you will look to all the out-buildings, and see if we can discover any suspicious circumstance, or the weapon with which this dreadful deed has been committed."

The chamber of the traveller was first thoroughly looked over, but nothing was there found having any further connection with the murder. Then the outer room underwent the same scrutiny, and the landlord at once said, in a tone of astonishment,—

"Why, here's a kitchen candlestick here, such as is never brought up-stairs into these rooms."

"I can account for that," said Jem.

"You ?"

"Yes, I brought it up."

"Oh, when the alarm was given ?"

"No—yes—no—yes ! How came it there ?—let me think."

"What do you mean?" said Mr. Ormonde, fixing a keen glance on the countenance of Jem.

"I can tell you, sir. I fell asleep in the stable last night, without thinking of it, and I woke up cold and stiff through lying half on the stones. I went into the kitchen, and by the nearly dying embers of the fire, lit a kitchen candle, and came upstairs with it. I was half asleep, and blundered up the wrong staircase, so I went into No. 6, and threw myself on the bed, and went to sleep there."

"Ineeed!"

"Tnat's all I know about it. But I heard a great noise, and then sprung out of the bed again."

"But this is not No. 6."

"No, sir, this is No. 8."

"Then how came your candle here?"

"I cannot tell you."

"My friend, you must yourself feel at this moment that the circumstance is a suspicious one."

"It is, sir. But how it came there I cannot tell any more than you can. All I know I have told you just as it happened. I had no business to sleep in No. 6, but I thought no harm of it at the time. Indeed, I was too sleepy almost to think of it at all. I remember, though, putting the light carefully out, and leaving it on the table."

"At what hour did you come up stairs from the stable?"

"I heard it strike one as I stood on the landing."

"You saw no one, and heard no noise ?"

"Nothing whatever. I went into No. 6, and shut the door, as I thought, and threw myself on the bed. I believe I was fast asleep in a moment."

"We will go now at once to No. 6," said the magistrate, calmly. "Perhaps you will have no objection to accompany us?"

"I objection, sir?" said Jem; "none in the least."

Jem followed the magistrate into the room he had certainly been foolish enough to obtrude into overnight. The first object almost that met the eyes of Mr. Ormonde upon walking in, was, lying close to the foot of the bed, a long knife covered with blood.

"Good God !" he said, as he picked it up.

"What is that?" said Captain Morton.

"A knife."

Mr. Ormonde turned to Jem, and showed it to him silently. The ostler looked at it, as any innocent man would at such an object, with a shudder.

"What do you say to that?" was the question of Mr. Ormonde, in a voice of calmness.

"What can I say?"

"It is found here."

"As I see, sir."

"But how came in here?"

"As God hears me, sir, I cannot tell you. It appears as if within the last five minutes circumstances were accumulating to fix the guilt of this dreadful murder upon me. I can only say that Heaven knows I am as innocent as you are of it, sir. May God's vengeance for both crime and impiety both strike me dead upon this spot, if I did the deed, or had any knowledge in any way of its doing."

There was a bold sincerity about the manner of Jem, which staggered all who heard him. Suddenly, then, Mr. Spurgin, the constable, cried out, as he held something in his hand—

"Here's a ring."

"Let me see it," said Toggs, faintly.

"Do you know it?" cried Mr. Ormonde.

"Yes, yes."

"Whose was it?"

"The murdered traveller's. Oh, Jem, Jem! who'd have thought this of you? I'd have trusted my life with you a dozen times over, if my pockets had had the *waley* o' the national debt in 'em."

"And so you might," said Jem. "God only knows how these things came here. I am innocent."

Mr. Ormonde shook his head.

"I grieve very much," he said, "that I cannot, consistently with my duty, do otherwise than give you into custody."

"Were I you, sir," said Jem, and he turned very pale as he spoke, "and were you me, I should do as you are now doing. I am innocent, sir. God help me, for God knows I am innocent, and that is all I can say."

"Remember, no one asks you now to

THE DOCTOR EXAMINING THE WOUND OF THE YOUNG TRAVELLER.

say anything, but all you do say will be sworn to by those who now hear you."

"An innocent man need be afraid of nothing. I am willing to answer any question. I cannot invent a lie about how that knife came here, but on my soul I never had it in my hand. I am willing now to lay my hand upon the heart of him who is cold and dead in the adjoining chamber but one, and call down upon my head Heaven's most exemplary vengeance, if I raised a hand against him."

"We do not want those kind of ordeals," said Mr. Ormonde.

"And yet it shall be done," said Jem

As he spoke, he rushed past Spurgin, who, in the vain effort he made to catch him, fell flat on his face.

"This may be a plan of escape," cried Mr. Ormonde, and he ran after Jem, closely followed by Captain Morton and Toggs, whose surprise at what was occurring knew no bounds.

Mr. Ormonde, however, found that he was wrong in his conjecture; for, in the excitement of the moment, Jem did betake himself to the chamber where lay the dead body, and did what no one else there present, but the surgeon, would have done, that is, he placed his hand flat upon the breast of the corpse.

"Now," he cried, "pitying, as I do, from my soul, this gentleman's sad fate, and execrating his murderer, be he whom he may, I declare my own entire innocence of the deed, and call upon Heaven to defend truth by some signal act of its justice, if I am guilty."

"Lor!" said Mr. Spurgin.

Toggs looked aghast, and Captain Morton betrayed much interest in what was proceeding.

"Such a scene as this," said Mr. Ormonde, "can have no effect in inducing me to swerve from what I consider to be my strict line of duty; you will consider yourself to be in custody."

"Lor! it's dreadful," muttered Spurgin, as he produced his staff as a signal of his authority, "that ever I should live to take up a real out-and-out murderer. Oh! Spurgin, your grandmother always said you would be a great man, and now the old lady is quite correct."

"I did expect, Mr. Ormonde," said Jem, as he took his hand from the breast of the corpse, "that, upon such a circumstance as this, you could possibly be convinced of my innocence. I came here to say what I have said on the impulse of a moment."

"Oh! Jem—Jem," cried Toggs, coming towards him, and holding out his hand, "upon my soul I don't believe you did it."

"Thank—thank you, Toggs," said Jem, as the tears rushed to his eyes, and he clasped his master's hand, "thank you; that's like you now. God bless you for those words, Toggs; I'm a fool, but not a murderer."

"I know you ain't, Jem, and I'll sell the very pewter pots of the old Morton Arms to see you through it."

"There need be no such sacrifice made," said Captain Morton; "I will take care that no injustice be done him. There are circumstances of very grave suspicion; but he shall want for no advice or assistance that money can procure."

"God forbid," said Mr. Ormonde, "that any injustice should be done to the poorest, or the most friendless; no one would rejoice more than I should myself at these circumstances being all cleared up in a manner compatible with a perfect conviction of your innocence, Jem."

"Thank you all—thank you."

"But you, I am sure, would rather yourself that a full investigation took place, than that you should labour under a load of suspicion which otherwise might never be removed from your name."

"I'd rather die, sir, a hundred times over."

"Very well; then you have no objection to accompany Spurgin?"

"None in the least, sir; I'll go with him. Do with me what you will, but don't think me such a dastardly villain as to take a fellow-creature's life, as this poor gentleman's has been taken."

"It is the duty of all entrusted with the administration of justice," said Mr. Ormonde, "to consider every one innocent until proved to be guilty."

"Carry the feeling a little further, sir," said Jem. "A poor fellow may be found guilty, as—God only knows—I may be, and yet be innocent after all. Don't condemn me, then, for I am innocent, and nothing can make me guilty. I did not do the deed, although the knife that, no doubt, inflicted the wound was found where I slept. It couldn't come there without hands to bring it, and he who did the murder must, of course, have placed it there. Heaven only knows who he may be, for I did not think I had an enemy in all the world."

---

## CHAPTER XVIII.

THE ANXIETIES OF THE MORTONS.—THE CONSULTATION.—THE SEARCH IN THE CHURCHYARD.

A LONG stream of daylight suddenly came in at the window of the chamber of death, and Spurgin, flourishing his staff, exclaimed to Jem—

"You are my prisoner; don't resist now, or else I shall be compelled to run away—I mean, knock you down."

"I am not disposed to resist you."

"Are you sure of that?"

"Quite—quite."

"Oh, then, it's an uncommon good thing for you as you have come to such a determination, for I tells you I should have had to have done something as was desperate."

After this, Jem said nothing. He appeared to consider that it was beneath him as an innocent man to be continually asserting that fact, and having proclaimed it to all present, and to all whose opinions he cared for, he let fate take its course, and quietly resigned himself to circumstances, to oppose which would only be to aggravate the perils of his present painful and harassing position.

The mind, perhaps, is scarcely ever in so painful a position as when it is compelled, by the sheer force of apparently irresistible evidence, to receive some proposition which is strikingly at variance with all its previous opinions and rooted predilections.

As, in the acquisition of any branch of knowledge, we come to it with a much better chance of rapidity of acquisition and correctness if we have no previous erroneous impressions to unlearn, so it is with regard to opinions upon the moral turpitude of individuals. The mind at once yields to impressions with reference to people of whom it knows nothing; but when one in whose honesty and humanity we have had abundance of faith is accused of a crime, which shows in its nature and in the manner of its commission a total absence of those high qualities, we naturally shrink, even from the most abundant evidence, and are tempted to tell ourselves that such things cannot be.

Mr. Morton, as he went homewards, was sorely perplexed by conflicting emotions. The whole circumstance of the murder of the young man at the inn was involved in the most profound obscurity.

Under ordinary circumstances it would have been a matter to have called forth his sympathies most abundantly; but there were peculiarities in the case, of which the reader is aware, and which, to his mind, naturally enough invested it with a fearful interest.

The enunciation with his last breath of the name of Mabel by the murdered man was to Morton a most incomprehensible circumstance, and one of which he knew not what to think. Naturally enough, now that his fears had once been awakened to the possiblility of some claimant starting up to drag from him the beautiful girl whom he loved to the full as tenderly as if she had been a child of his own, made him nervous as regarded every trivial circumstance that had such a tendency. That the young murdered traveller at the inn would in the morning have sought his, Morton's, house, and entered into some revelations connected with Mabel, appeared now to Morton's mind a proposition of positive certainty. But death had stepped in at once, and, with the young traveller's life, put an end to his visit.

"Who and what can he be?" thought Morton. "What am I to think now of these most mysterious affairs? He seems a gentleman. He had about his face and his general aspect and manner that indescribable look of a well-kept man. He seemed like one well accustomed to the elegancies of life, and the landlord assures me that the horse he rode is one of considerable value."

So absorbed in these reflections that he noticed nothing of his route homewards, Morton sought the hall.

His wife was anxiously expecting him, and he could hardly find breath to answer the multitude of eager inquires she put to him immediately upon his appearance.

"What is all this?" she cried. "Tell me at once, Henry, how it affects our dear Mabel, or, rather, tell me that it affects not her at all."

"Hush! be calm—be calm!"

"Then tell me, Henry?"

"I will. What has happened does not immediately, that I can perceive, affect Mabel, but it is sufficient to afford us, in our great anxiety concerning her, abundant food for painful conjecture."

"Indeed!"

"Yes, indeed; but hear what I have to relate, and then you will be able to judge for yourself."

He then related to her all that had occurred, not omitting the minutest of the particulars, and when he had concluded the distinct facts of his narration, he observed,—

"And now, dear Alice, what do you deduce from all that? Your judgment upon the subject is more likely to be cool and dispassionate than mine, for the sight of the dying young man at the inn, and the general confusion and bustle incidental to the whole scene, have, I fear, thrown me into a state of too much excitment to enable me to come to any very calm decision."

"Alas! Henry, I know not what to think. I have but one very strong impression, and that regards the innocence of the ostler."

"That is my own view."

"It is strange, and may be incorrect; but, from first to last, I have connected with this dreadful outrage at the inn the mysterious beggar who attacked our dear Mabel in the wilderness."

"And I, too."

"You have had the same feelings?"

"I have, indeed, most strongly."

"In that quarter, then, I am inclined to think will be found the criminal, and I confess I dread to reflect upon a part of the subject which comes across me with terror."

"What is that?"

"All regarding the birth of our dear Mabel is involed in mystery. Oh, what a shock it would be to such a mind as hers to find herself closely connected by ties of kindred to him who has done this deed, instead of to him who has suffered from it."

"I will not encourage such a thought.'

"Nor I; but those thoughts we wish the

least to encourage will sometimes the oftenest obtrude themselvs upon us."

"Still, it is much more probable that he who has met with so sad a death, and who expired with the name of Mabel on his lips, may have been in some manner connected with her. Despite, too, of the pangs of death, there was a tenderness in the pronunciation of the name, which showed that, even at such a moment, it was in his mind associated with his best feelings."

"You noted that?"

"Indeed I did, with mingled feelings."

"Oh, if he had but lived—if he had but lived. Then what now remains a painful mystery might have been cleared up to the joy of all of us."

"Our dear Mabel might have been taken from us."

"No, Henry, I do not think so. What we have to dread is, not that she should find friends among people of feeling, but that she should be harassed by some one claiming such kindred with her as we should find it difficult to resist, in a class of society of the habits and manners of which she can now have no conception."

"You think the former class of people would leave her with us?"

"I am inclined to think they would study her happiness, sufficiently, at all events, to spare us very much of her company."

"It might be so."

"And besides, husband, there is another view of this subject which we ought always to consider."

"What is that?"

"In the natural course of events, Mabel will far outlive us."

"True—true."

"And then it would be a sad thing to leave her friendless, for, although we might, and will, of course, guard her against the possibility of want, we cannot bequeath to her kind friends and near ties."

"True, we cannot; but, in connection with that part of the subject, I have always had another conviction."

"I can guess what you mean; you allude to Charles."

"I do. My brother, although yet little more than a boy, is, I am sure, possessed of strong feelings of attachment. He loves Mabel."

"And thank Heaven he does!"

"In becoming his wife she may not feel the loss of those natural ties, which, even where they exist in abundance, generally occupy but a second place in the feelings of a wife."

"They do, indeed, Henry. There is something far stronger in that tie which is created by ourselves, than in any of those which are accidental."

"Hence, then, I do not conclude that Mabel will suffer much, even when she comes to know, as sooner or later she must, that she is not our child, as she now fancies herself."

"Thank Heaven we did not impart to her her history before these circumstances occurred, for what an abundant source of misery they would then have been to her; when now they can but excite her natural curiosity in common with others who have no manner of concern with them."

"That is a subject of congratulation, indeed. But now retire to rest, for I know you are unaccustomed to these early hours. I will myself go back to the village, and make what inquiries I can with regard to the events of the night."

"I could not sleep, Henry, now," replied Alice, "so I will, being up, remain so, and do you bring me what news you can, and that as soon as you can."

"I will—I will."

Morton now, at once, left his home again, and proceeded, as fast as he could walk, once more to the village, with the hope of at least picking up some more information regarding the proceedings of the night. So little had been said by the landlord of the Morton Arms of his guest, the mendicant, that it had not made much impression upon anybody; but from the few words he had dropped, to the effect that there had been another person at the inn, Morton imagined that it was worth more minute inquiry. He accordingly went first to the inn, which was still in a state of very great confusion, for the news that a murder had been committed there had spread like wildfire over the entre neighbourhood, and produced an immense amount of general excitement.

The house, indeed, was now literally besieged, and the state of gossiping frenzy into which the good folks got, produced so much drought, that the prophecy of the landlord that, in consequence of what had happened, he should be ruined, proved to be a wonderfully mistaken one, inasmuch as now it looked much more probable that he would be literally drunk up, and, before many hours had elapsed, not have enough beer and other commodities with which to supply his fast thronging in customers.

"There's always some trouble or another," he now exclaimed. "When I had lots of beer I had no customers, anp now that I have lots of customers I have no beer."

"But you had," said one.

"Ah, but what's the use of what a man had? It's what he has that's of importance."

The gentleman who had made the previous remark could not very well get over the landlord's philosophy; but he was not convinced, nevertheless, so, like most people in a similar predicament, he retained his own opinion, in spite of the argumentative powers of mine host of the Morton Arms.

When Captain Morton arrived now, he found it no easy job to get into the house at all, so thronged was it with visitors. He, however, had the good fortune to catch the eye of the landlord, who, by dint of pushing and persuasion, made a passage for him, exclaiming, when Morton got near enough to hear what he said,—

'Here's a pretty state of things, sir, to be in."

"What's the matter now?"

"Why, sir, to tell the honest truth, I don't think there's a dozen gallons of beer in the house."

"You don't say so?"

"Yes, sir, I do, with my own voice, sir."

"Well, certainly, I did not expect you to say so with any one else's."

"No, sir, in course—in course; but isn't it dreadful? and atween you and me, Captain Morton, and the post, there was a cask as was *werges* itself, sir, as I'm a Christian."

"Was what?"

"Sour, sir, sour."

"Oh!"

"Positive *winegar* — positive *winegar*; and, hang me, if they haven't drunk every mortal drop of it."

"A good thing for you."

"No, no, no."

"How do you make that out?"

"I sees into the future right slap bang."

"Do you? And what may be the result of your power of divination?"

"Just this, sir; the whole of them as has taken the sour cask will be reg'lar bad to-morrow, and then I shall be abused, as a matter o' course, and my beer will have a bad character."

"You should not have brouched the sour cask."

"Oh, sir, that's where it is. I knows I shouldn't."

"Then why did you?"

"'Cos I'm one o' those unfortunate individuals as is always doing what they shouldn't, and never doing what they

should. I always is a doing somethink, and always a repenting of it. I'm born to bad luck: and what would be the fortune of anybody else is a out-and-out, reg'lar, right down, killing flummoxer to me."

"Well, no one can aid you in such a case; but, pray tell me who it was you had in the house at the same time as this young gentleman, who has been murdered, arrived?"

"Oh, a rascal, a beggar, and yet one of the most insolent fellows that ever stepped."

"What kind of man?"

"A ragged rascal."

"Tall?"

"No; about the middle size. I suppose some time or another he must have had a complexion."

"What do you mean?"

"I mean as that couldn't have been very lately, for what with dirt, and what with whiskers, I'll be hanged up at my own sign if he wasn't a million times more like a baboon than a Christian."

"Did he beg of you?"

"No; he had money."

"Should you know him again, do you think?"

"In course I should. That's to say, always if so be as he don't shave himself. If he was to do so, I won't take upon myself to say as I should know him in the least."

"Do you know, I am inclined much more to suspect that very man of the murder than your ostler."

"Lor!"

"Yes. Everything that we know of Jem, leads us to a conviction of his innocence of the deed."

"But the beggar fellow left here, captain. Not but what I believe as Jem is as innocent as a baby."

"I think him incapable of the act."

"And so do I, sir—so do I. He's the *humanestest* ostler as ever I come near, and he's too independent and John Blunt a sort of fellow to go sneaking into anybody's bedroom to steal anything. You may depend, sir, whoever did it, he didn't."

"I am quite of your opinion, and I shall institute the most vigorous search in the village."

"Do so, sir. Folks will tell you things as they wouldn't tell anybody else, 'cos they knows as you are safe. Now, there's old Morris."

"What of him?"

"I know well enough he knows something."

"Indeed!"

"Yes, but he won't tell me. I seed him a brushing his Sunday coat, though he didn't think I did."

"But what can that have to do with it?"

"That's what I asked his missus. Now, she is a reasonable woman as you can get anything out of."

"Oh, indeed. And what did she say?"

"Why, sir, she said as he was a brushing his Sunday coat, because he was a going afore the justice to say what he'd seen, and she says, 'Don't you let it go no further;' and I says, 'In course not.' Then I asks her what it was, and then she says, 'That's the *prowokingest* thing about it all. Morris,' she says, 'won't tell me a word about it, and he says as the only way in all the world to make a woman keep a secret, is not to tell one to her.'"

"I will go to him at once," said Captain Morton. "He may tell me what he very properly refuses to entrust to the garrulity of his wife."

So saying, and after enjoining the landlord in a few words to be extremely cautious not to let any one whatever into the chamber of death, Captain Morton walked from the inn into the main street of the village, to seek the old man who had been mentioned as possessing some piece of evidence, which, in his opinion, was of sufficient importance to warrant him in going before the justice.

In a little country village everybody knows everybody, and although Morton was not precisely aware which cottage was occupied by old Morris and his wife, he was directed to it by the first vagrant urchin he demanded the information of. He found the old man at his own door, fully equipped for starting to the justice's, whenever the morning should be sufficiently advanced to warrant a reasonable expectation that the case of the murder would receive judicial cognizance.

The old man seemed, when he saw Captain Morton approaching him, to guess the nature of his errand. Advancing to meet him, he said,—

"Good morning, sir; I am right glad to see you, because you can tell me, sir, whether what I have got to say about last night's business is worth the saying or not."

"I will give you what advice I can."

"Well, sir, after all the bustle was over, and there was a little quiet, I was standing in my bit of a garden, which you may see, sir, commands a sort of view of the churchyard."

"Yes, of course it does."

"And, consequently, sir, of the church, too, as you will perceive."

"Yes, yes."

"Well, then, I chanced to look in that direction, and I all at once saw something dark and odd-looking at one of the windows. I looked and looked, for I didn't want to make a fuss if I could help it, and then I saw the window opened, and a man leaped out."

"Indeed!"

"Yes, sir; and when I felt quite sure, I got over the palings of my garden as quick as I could, and ran towards the churchyard."

"You did right."

"I hope so, sir. I made direct to the window; and what's more, I kept the exact spot where the fellow must have jumped to so completely in sight, for I never for one moment took my eyes from it, that I knew he could not get away from it without my seeing."

"How was it situated?"

"There's a big square stone-work covering one of the vaults; it is but a short way from the window; and where he jumped was between that stone tomb and the wall. Of course, there he must remain, or come out from behind it on one side or the other."

"Certainly."

"Well, sir, from my window even, far more from my garden, you can see both sides, and it was quite light enough for me to see well enough if any one had come out from behind the tomb."

"And saw you no one?"

"No one whatever."

"That is strange."

"It is strange. I cannot make it out. I never took my eyes off the spot, but clambered over my own garden fence without looking, and then went direct to the churchyard, and never stopped or glanced right or left till I got to the exact place."

"Well?"

"There was nothing there. I fully expected to find somebody hiding behind the tomb, in the narrow space between it and the church wall; but I was disappointed."

"This is certainly singular."

"It is, sir, and I don't know what to make of it. If I had taken my eyes off for a moment I should have said that it was just then he came out, but I can take my oath I didn't, and that's what puzzles me."

"It is enough to puzzle you. There is a good hour to spare. Have you any objection to showing me whereabouts exactly this occurred?"

"None in the least."

"I should like first to look at the spot from your garden, where you first observed the figure."

"Certainly, sir; pray walk in."

Morton walked into the cottage, and passing through it, emerged into the little garden in the rear, where, as the old man had said, could be obtained a clear and perfect view of the church and churchyard.

"There is the window, sir," he said, "and there is the tomb; and, you see, situated as we are, it's just before us, so that you need never for half a moment lose sight of the spot."

"I would rather go, then, that way, if you please," said Captain Morton.

"Very good, sir."

The plan was carried into effect; keeping his eyes upon the tomb, Morton surmounted the fence of the old man's garden, followed by him, and in a few moments they were both in the churchyard, having kept the tomb fully and easily in view the whole of the way.

"Here we are, sir," said Morris, "just at the spot, and we have come every bit of the way as I came."

"No doubt; no doubt."

Morton stepped behind the tomb, but there was nothing to be seen—not the least indication of any one, indeed, having been there lately was at all observable.

"It is a very mysterious piece of business," said Morton. "If you feel so sure that you saw a man jump from this window as to be able to take your oath of it, I certainly advise you to do so; for although just at present that circumstance of itself has no clear connection with the murder at the inn, it may in the course of time come to be important."

"I can safely, sir, take my oath to what I saw."

"Of course. I shall meet you before the justice's, and can corroborate your statement so far as regards the ease of getting from your cottage garden to this spot, and still keeping the tomb and the wall on each side of it in such perfect view that no one could possibly move away without being instantly and easily observed."

"I will be there, sir. Something comes over me with a strange feeling that the man I saw here was the murderer of the gentleman at the inn last night."

"It may be so."

"I don't believe for a moment that Jem did it."

"A belief in his innocence appears prevalent."

"Of course it is, sir. We all know him too well. Why, sir, there ain't a dog, or a cat, or a child in the village that don't love him; and that ain't the sort of man to commit a murder."

"You are right."

"Do what you can, then, for him, Captain Morton, and you may depend, as sure as that the sun shines, some day or another the real murderer will be found; for murder will out, if it should be a hundred years first."

There was a solemnity of manner about the old man, and a stern kind of truthfulness about the way in which he spoke, that made a strong impression upon Captain Morton, and he replied—

"My friend, you may depend that justice shall be done to the accused man. No one shall—indeed, no one, that I am aware of, feels any inclination that may oppress him."

"Jem wouldn't hurt a fly," added the old cottager. "It's a disgrace to the village to have him even suspected. What will the world say now, I wonder, to us, when it gets spread about?"

Captain Morton could not but smile at the idea of the world saying anything at all upon the subject; but he would not offend the old man by telling him how insignificant a place in the world's thoughts that little village, with its hundred or so inhabitants, was likely to occupy.

"Well—well," he said, "make yourself easy. I dare say, before long, something will turn up as regards the murder, which will entirely exculpate Jem from all share in the transaction."

"I hope to God it may, sir."

Morton slightly inclined his head, and then walked back to the inn, with the hope that, even during the short half-hour he had been away, something might possibly have occurred to throw some new light upon the mysterious transaction. But this hope was soon disappointed. He still found the eager gossiping crowd, and the landlord in a greater perplexity than ever, for now he had to count his remaining stock of beer by quarts instead of by gallons.

Indeed, before Captain Morton got fairly into the house it was all gone, and the landlord had mounted on the top of an empty cask to make a deprecatory speech to his customers. It is a peculiarity of Englishmen that anything in the shape of a speech is always welcome. In no country on the face of the earth is speech-making so popular; and, probably, as a consequence, in no country are there so many abominably bad speeches. After-dinner speeches, and supper speeches, and speeches of all kinds, and sorts, and descriptions, are the curse of social life.

It has been said that 'nothing can be done in England without a dinner; but the dinner is nothing but a preface to the speeches—a mere shadow compared to them—a sort of excuse to get men together to make bad speeches. And, oh, the nonsense that men utter when they are "upon their legs." The stammering and the hammering for words—the tautologies and the mal-pronunciations. If men of limited education did but know how fearfully they expose the barrenness of their head-pieces when they get up to make a speech, they would as soon sit still and consent, like the immortal Dogberry, to be written down an ass.

The ejaculation of—"Oh, that mine enemy would write a book!" might well be equalled by a cry of—"Oh, that mine enemy would make a speech!" for it would most likely answer the same end—namely, of making the aforesaid enemy look like a consummate donkey.

The mere sight of the landlord on the top of a cask, in an oratorical attitude, was sufficient to excite attention. The jar of discord ceased. People left off gossiping. Those who had something to drink left off drinking it, and all eyes were turned upon the orator, who, after waving his arms for some moments about like the sails of a windmill, commenced:—

"Ladies and gentlemen——"

Then everybody moved a little, and several cried, "Hear! hear!"

An amazingly fat woman, who had never heard herself called a lady in all her life, cried out—

"Thanks to ye, master; you're a polite man, let you be never so ugly, and that you are."

"Silence! silence!" shouted a dozen voices, and then the landlord gathered breath ... ence anew.

"Ladies and gentlemen——"

"Ye said that before," growled one fellow.

"Knock him down—turn him out—turn him out!"

"Hear, hear, hear!"

"Ladies and gentlemen, unaccustomed as I am——

"Go it—go it! Hear, hear, hear!"

"Unaccustomed as I am——"

Here a little supplementary fight was got up among some who were so near to the door that they despaired of hearing what was said, and believing that it must be some important information concerning the murder, became nearly frantic at the idea of not being permitted to share in it as quickly as any one else.

This interruption seemed likely to be a serious one, for it occupied some time, and most probably, had not Captain Morton interfered, would have ended in a general riot, but he was well known to them all, and the moral effect of his presence kept some of the most unruly in awe.

Guessing that the announcement of the landlord was going to be to the effect that he had no more beer, Morton was inclined to believe it was better to let him make it, than interrupt him in it.

"When they hear that, some of them will go away," he thought; and, doubtless, such would have been the case, but the speech was not yet made.

Comparative order being restored, the landlord again essayed to begin his oration; and as he had once heard a country member commence a speech in the words he had himself begun with, he tried back again upon them—

"Ladies and gentlemen, unaccustomed as——"

He got thus far, when some malicious wag gave the cask a tremendous kick, and down went the landlord among those of his admirers who happened to be immediately close to him. Captain Morton now thought it high time to interfere more actively, and accordingly, having happened to have his eye fixed on the fellow who had kicked the cask, he made his way towards him, and at once collaring him, hurled him into the street. Morton was a man of considerable physical power, and not one whom many men would like a personal encounter with. As for the big bully, for such he was, whom he had just turned out of the inn, he was a rank coward at heart, as all big bullies are, so he made not the least attempt at resistance, but, pretending he was hurt, and that it was very hard for a poor man to be knocked about for nothing, adopted the most prudent course he could, which was most certainly to take himself off at once. Morten, then, in a loud voice, cried—

"I am ashamed of you, friends and neighbours, to make a disturbance of this character at a house in one of the chambers of which you know now lies so terrible a spectacle. Respect for the dead, if you have none for the living, ought to teach you better."

"Oh, it's all very well," said a brawling, wide-mouthed fellow; "it's all very well for you to talk; you are one of the grinding aristocracy that feeds upon the vitals of the poor."

"Hear, hear, hear," cried several. "Let's hear John Snobbins; he's an advocate for the poor man, he is."

"I can perceive," said Morton, "that when I spoke to you as friends and neighbours, I made a mistake; the most of you here present, now I come to look at you, are from the market-town, and, having heard of this murder here, have come to make holiday over the remains of a fellow-creature."

"Englishmen! Britons!" cried John Snobbins, "are we to be abused by a grinding aristocracy? are we to have our birth-rights torn away from us?"

"No—no—no."

"Are we to he poor men always?"

"No—no—no."

"Are we never to be men of property, as we ought to be?"

"Yes, yes; we are—we are."

"Englishmen, I am for everybody."

"Then why do you beat your poor, hard-working wife," said one, "who keeps you in drunkenness and idleness?"

"You are an enemy of the people,"

THE UNKNOWN ENTERING THE CHURCH BY THE WINDOW.

shouted Snobbins; "I know what you are; you are a spy employed by the grinding aristocracy."

"You are a fool."

"Ah! am I to be insulted among Englishmen? I am for equal rights, and a complete change of property; I am for all who have anything to have it at once distributed among those who have nothing."

This sentiment was received with vociferous cheers.

The fact was, that, in the neighbouring market-town, a number of idle, disorderly ruffians had, what they call, "stuck up for themselves," which consisted in doing no work at all; and, upon the news that a murder had been committed at the Morton Arms, they had repaired thither in a body, to drink beer and discuss the point.

John Snobbins was one of those popular demagogues, of whom, alas! there are so many, and who have already done such a world of mischief to the honest working men of this country. Vain, self-sufficient, ignorant, and abusive, these men exist in all countries; but England is the hot-bed of them. Here they luxuriate, and they are the worst foes of liberty, equality of rights, and good feeling.

"Three cheers," cried John Snobbins, "for a destruction to the grinding aristocracy, who keep all the good things from the poor man, who is the right arm of the state, and only ought to have them."

"Hold!" said Captain Morton; "my good friends, you are fond of beer; you like a bit of amusement, too. Now, there is no more beer at the Morton Arms."

"No beer?"

"Not a drop; the landlord wanted to tell you so, but you would not let him; but there is amusement here."

"Hear him—hear him—hear, hear," cried a number.

"Now, I propose that you duck John Snobbins in the horse-trough, opposite the door here; for, if it were not for him, you may depend you would have loads of beer."

Alas, for popular applause! Alas, for the idol of the people! Some laughed—some cheered—some cried, "No, no," and John Snobbins had the impudence to give one man a blow on the mouth who laughed, and this settled the business. He was dragged out, and ducked within an inch of his very life.

## CHAPTER XIX.

MABEL'S SUSPICIONS.—HER PRAYER.—
THE MIND'S RELIEF.

WHILE all these matters were proceeding, Mabel could not be without some painful feelings and suspicions that after all there was really some fearful secret connected with herself, weighing upon the minds of those who had ever shown to her a tenderness such as only the most affectionate of parents could show to a child. She could tell by the glances of alarm that passed between Morton and Mrs. Morton, that something was amiss; but far, very far, was she from suspecting the real facts of the case.

The mere idea, had it once entered her mind, that she was not the near relative of those whom she looked upon as the kindest of parents, would have given her a pang of the most intense affliction; but as yet she was spared it, and in all her misgivings of what might be the hidden causes of the apparent distress and indecision which the manner of Captain Morton had exhibited, she did not dream that it was the dread of having to give her up to some better claimant. Still, that there was a something which she was not permitted to know, she felt convinced.

To such a mind as Mabel's the conviction that any one whom she loved wished to keep any matter a secret from her, was at once to lead likewise to the consideration that they knew it would be painful to her to know it. Therefore was it, that her fear for the peace of mind and the happiness of those about her, exceeded any feeling of awakened curiosity on her own account in her bosom.

After torturing herself for a considerable period of time mentally, without being able to come to any conclusion of a satisfactory nature, she had recourse to an expedient which always sufficed to calm her mind when under sickness of the body, and therefore was more likely, inasmuch as it itself partook of a strong mental emotion, to induce peace in her bewildered imagination. That expedient consisted in the repetition of a simple, but beautiful prayer, which had been taught to her by her old nurse years since. And now she knelt in the solitude of her own chamber, and uttered fervently those same words which had been often lisped by the half-formed voice of the child.

They say faith in any remedial matter goes a long way, and no doubt it does. Mabel always believed that the repetition of that prayer calmed her spirit, and, therefore, it was sure to do so. The effect was produced in this instance. She was singularly happy, in comparison to what she had been, and although her thoughts did certainly revert back to painful impressions and feelings, they were not of that agonising description they had been, and she found she could mingle with her reflections far happier matters.

"All may yet be well," she said. "I may be tormenting myself about what, after all, may not materially affect me or those whom I love; and yet, what a strange boldness of manner there was about the manner of that mendicant, as if he had possession of some secret which made him know he might, if he liked, be bold."

Then she thought she would summon courage to ask— nay, to implore Mrs. Morton to tell her what it was that made them both look so anxious when she had stated what the mendicant had said to her. But another moment's reflection made her shrink again from this course, and she said,—

"No, no. I will ask no questions. If I am not told, I know that what is withheld from me is so withheld from some just, and proper, and affectionate motive. I will not give them pain by asking questions they do not like to answer. I will be patient."

Mabel wished now to distract her mind as much as possible from the subject of the meeting with the mysterious man in the wilderness. It was early dawn only, and she strove to sleep, but that she found not possible, so she engaged herself for a time in tending her flowers, a large collection of which she always kept at her window.

The love of flowers appears to be one of those amenities of human nature which are incidental to the young and the beautiful. It exists never in vitiated or degraded minds, but always in those of a better and more pure order. We must not have instanced to us that degraded, ignorant, and brutalised intellects have been found to tend flowers carefully, because such conduct will frequently arise in such persons from mere vulgar ostentation, and vanity of having a better article of its kind, be it what it may—a pig or a dahlia—than anybody else.

But the love of flowers in such a mind as Mabel's was a love of them in its purest sense. She tended them because she loved them, and not that they might become specimens of their class or kind. And when she had done this grateful office, she was still resolved that she would not let her mind go back again to sad thoughts and feelings, and she had the reflection to know that occupation could alone prevent such a result.

Perhaps the surest and the best way to get rid of the agony of real troubles, is to contrast them with imaginary ones, and hence the delight which the pages of fiction generally afford to the sick and the weary-minded. We escape for a time into a new region; we become, as it were, acquainted with a number of new people, and with this advantage, that we can cut the acquaintance whenever we like, without giving them any offence.

This feeling Mabel had ever had since she could read at all, and now until she should be sought, which she knew she would be soon by Mrs. Morton, she took one of her friendly books from a shelf in her bedroom, and commenced reading to while away what might otherwise have been weary minutes.

The following anecdote met her eyes :—

One fine summer's morning I determined to visit some little suburban retreat, to wear off the sense of fatigue and weariness caused by a too close and arduous pursuit of that dross that everybody abuses, yet seeks with the utmost vivacity and perseverance—I mean gold. I scarce knew which way to go, but at length determined upon going down as far as Greenwich, and look over that splendid building, the hospital, which, to my mind, is one of the finest in or near our great metropolis.

I sailed down to this place, and the breeze from off the river seemed to do me good, and I felt somewhat revived and invigorated. I am a man of some weight in society, for I weigh something over fourteen stone, and am not all great in pedestrianism. I was once a stripling that could almost outrun a deer ; but now a few hundred yards, at a slow pace, winds me ; so much for age and grossness ! I had walked about as much as suited my condition, and had a good appetite, the cravings of which I found means to appease, and after that I called for my glass, and sat quietly sipping that, and performing the tiresome operation of skinning some shrimps, for the purpose of mastication. I have often thought they never would have had any but for the express purpose of throwing difficulties in the way ; I was somewhat angry, and couldn't divine the reason they hadn't been created without them, when the door opened, and somebody entered the room.

My back was towards the door, and my face towards the window. I was in the act of gazing on the river, watching a stately vessel slowly sailing past, and was endeavouring to extract one of the aforementioned shrimps from its skin, and, therefore, being doubly engaged, I took no notice of the new comer. He ordered something—I did not exactly hear what ; and, when it was brought him, we were both left to ourselves.

After a time, I saw the individual. He was dressed in what I call a half-military style, and wore a cap. He, too, was gazing upon the river, and watching the shipping. He sighed once or twice, and this attracted my attention towards him. At length, he turned and saw me looking at him.

"Fine day, sir," he said. "The beauty of the scene before us is much enhanced by the calmness of the air and the river."

There was something in his voice that sounded familiar to me.

"Yes," I replied, "it is a treat to get so far to see and enjoy the sight."

"So it is—so it is. But, excuse me," he said, "I fancy I have seen you before."

"Very likely," I replied. "Your voice appears to be familiar to my ear, though my eye receives no such similar indication of recognition."

"Is your name Wooly ?"

"It is."

"Charles Zenas Wooly ?"

"Yes, it is. But how on earth did you learn my name, for the second is one I never use, though I was christened such ?"

"I learned of yourself."

"Of me?"

"Ay."

"But what can be your name?"

"John Buckthorn."

"No! Good Heavens!"

"It is!"

"What, my fellow apprentice?"

"The same."

"Who ran away?"

"About five-and-twenty years ago."

"Well—Good Heavens! Can it be?—no, it cannot! Impossible!"

"It is both true and possible. But perhaps you are not desirous it should be possible—I have heard of such things."

"Nay, you are too fast, sir. But, take off your cap, and let me see for a mark a little above your left ear."

"Oh, you hav'n't forgot the mark you gave me when I was a boy."

"No, indeed," I cried, examining the spot. "I can well remember it, and the licking you got me for my trouble."

"Ah! ah! ah!"

"But there it is as clear as if it were but just done. Ah, you are indeed the same —the same. Well, I never expected to see you again. I thought our acquaintance had been severed entirely in this life; but, Heaven knows, it gives me great pleasure to see you again—I know nothing that gives me greater."

"And none that I could name would give me more unfeigned pleasure. My life has been spent in hardships, and, at the end of it, to find our first acquaintance is indeed a pleasure, that recals the early days of one's youth to one's mind so strongly and so vividly, that I can almost fancy that I am young again."

"Yes, I can fancy that I see the consternation of the whole house, when it was ascertained that you had run away."

"I dare say—I dare say."

"The master was desperately angry at first, and then he cried like a child."

"Cried?"

"Yes, absolutely shed tears, and thought you were sure to come to an unhappy or violent death, and because he had acted too harshly and had given you some cause for offence."

"Does he live?"

"No, he's been dead these ten years."

"Poor man; I am sorry I gave him any cause for uneasiness, but we must all come to that situation at last."

"We must—we must," I said; "and we are verging on to that bourne we all endeavour so unsuccessfully to avoid."

"That's true; and how have you been since we last saw each other?"

"It would take months to tell you; but there have been the usual ups and downs, and the variations in human affairs. I got into business when I was out of my time."

"That was good."

"Then, as a matter of course, I got married, as men, who have just incurred one responsibility, are always willing to increase it, by taking another by way of recklessness."

"I see—exactly—may I say that was good too, eh?" inquired the other.

"Well, I suppose you may, though the married life is no exception to any other. It has its vicissitudes and its crosses, as well as any other; and yet, upon the whole, I can't say I have done badly even in getting married."

"Well, that is good, then, though maybe you think you would have done better had you left that speculation alone."

"That may be very true, but it is a speculation scarce worth entering into."

"Then, worldly affairs."

"Have been pretty prosperous—pretty prosperous. I can leave business when I like. I need not open my books again."

"And why don't you retire?"

"What could I do? I have been brought up to business, and have been in some kind of labour and industry ever since, and to have nothing to do now, would be as great a calamity as if I never had had anything to do."

"Well, well, there is reason in that, but how different are we. You are as plethoric in person as purse, and here am I the reverse in both. I can run and jump as heartily as a roebuck, but not so pleasantly burdened as you are with the pleasures of life."

"I don't know," said I, "about that; but how have you spent your time?"

"Oh, strangely enough, and as diversified as it could well be spent. I have seen some strange things during my career."

"Have you?"

"I have, I assure you."

"What made you run away?"

"I believe nothing but caprice, and an inclination to try my fortune over the world, and a desire to see some change for I had nothing to complain of that I remember."

"Nor I.'

"Well; I enlisted a common soldier."

"Good Heavens!"

"It was a strange freak, I'll admit, and one that did not show much discernment, and I soon found out I had gained nothing in ease or comfort by the choice I had made."

"Indeed!"

"No; I had a strict officer, and, for fear of the disgrace of the lash, I soon became very attentive to my drill, and soon knew enough to make me an efficient soldier. I was tolerably well schooled; I was by no means a bad or inapt scholar."

"You were not; you were famous for your book, I recollect very well."

"This was soon discovered, and I obtained promotion, and then we were sent on foreign service, and on active service."

"That was still harder, and more distasteful to you, I should imagine."

"No; for the constant change suited me very well, and I was well pleased with an active life; we marched, and countermarched, and were first in one battle, and then in another, until I had become a thorough soldier in body and in mind, and felt pleasure in the strict observance of the military character. I had received more than once praise in the ranks for good conduct in the regiment and in the field of battle, and was a general favorite with my superior officers, and also beloved by my men. But this active and arduous life cannot for ever last; and I received a wound that laid me by for some months, and it was deemed very likely that I should never recover from my unfortunate condition. Well, I did recover — or you would scarce have seen me here."

"No, no."

"Well, I recovered, and served for some time longer during the war, until at length I came to England, where our complement was made up (for we had suffered many casualties), and then we were drafted for India."

"Did you not try to find out some of your old friends before you left again?"

"I had no time, and I was stationed in a part of the country that was entirely strange to me, and in a very few weeks we were ordered to India, where I spent about eighteen years."

"It was a long period, and about the time I got married."

"Indeed. Well, I was invalided. I had suffered much, and obtained a brevet rank of major, upon which I have retired from the army."

"And how long have you given up the sword?" inquired I.

"About two years and a half. I had a very decent time of it. I have earned the right to lay by and enjoy the fruits of my labour and successful daring of every danger."

"You have indeed. Your health is much cut up, I dare say," said I.

"No," he replied; "I can walk and ride well, and for several hours a day. I have been well inured to exercise, but I do not task myself. I allow nature to be my monitor."

"That's well," I said; "but I envy your capability of exercise. But you have nothing down here, I suppose, that will prevent your returning to town with me, and staying a week or two at my house, and allowing me to introduce you to my wife and family?"

"Nothing, I assure you. I came merely to see an old man who is in the hospital, and who saved my life when I was going out to India."

"Does he live?"

"Yes, and is likely to do so."

We chatted for nearly two hours more, and then we arose to return to town, and proceeded by water to London.

I had some misgivings about the propriety of taking a stranger home without my wife's being privy to, and a party to the invitation; but there was no time to lose; I trusted to the chapter of accidents, and all went off as smoothly as I could have wished.

---

## CHAPTER XX.

THE EXAMINATION AND RELEASE OF THE ACCUSED.—AMPLE EVIDENCE, AND ITS RESULTS.

THE rapidity with which news of any strange and marvellous, or horrifying character travels, is truly wonderful. It is no exaggeration to say, that for twenty or thirty miles around the Morton Arms, at which so sanguinary a scene had been enacted, there was scarcely a man, woman, or child who did not, before the day was two hours old, hear something of the murder. And that something, having for its nucleus the fact itself, was variously coloured, according to the feelings and the habits of the parties who carried the tale from ear to ear.

Let us, however, in common justice, aver that in no case whatever did the affair lose anything by travelling; but it was added to with as many exaggerating circumstances as the fertile imaginations of those who were interested in such matters could possibly invent. Some declared that not only had a traveller been murdered at the Morton Arms Inn, but that the landlord, for interfering in the matter, was shot dead upon the spot. Others improved upon this again, while they admitted it, by adding, that after the landlord was shot, the murderer set fire to the inn, and not only reduced it to ashes, but burnt everybody to death who happened to be in it at that unfortunate juncture.

There were, too, the most wonderful discrepancies with regard to who the murderer was. Some declared he was killed in the affray that followed. Others, that he was still at large ; and others, that he was in custody.

One of these three suppositions was extremely probable, so no one attempted to set up a fourth, which must have been very far-fetched indeed, and could not be expected to compete with those that presented much more reasonable features.

There certainly was one ingenious man who declared that the young man who was murdered at the inn, had turned out to be a young woman, and that the cause of her death was, that upon the evening before her marriage she had eloped with her former lover, and that the enraged bridegroom had followed her to the Morton Arms, and executed summary vengeance upon her for so cruelly deceiving him.

This ingenious individual, however, got very few supporters indeed, so that his version of the story was in great disrepute. All, however, who had sufficient idleness and leisure upon their hands made what speed they could towards the Morton Arms, and our friend Toggs had, for hours after the francas at the inn, in which Captain Morton took part, to lament that his beer barrels were empty, so very thirsty, and so very clamorous, were his numerous visitors.

"It's always the way with me," he exclaimed, as he gave a kick to the last empty barrel. "I was born under the most unluckiest of the blessed stars, that's clear. When I've got lots of beer, and don't know what to do with it, nobody comes to drink it ; and now, when people comes a matter of a dozen miles or more all for to drink it, I haven't got a blessed drop."

Like most miserable philosophers, who make the worst of everything, Toggs completely put out of the question the fact that the reason why he had not a blessed drop of beer, was simply because it had all been drunk up by his friends and admirers. He contented himself with the now pet misery of being without beer to sell, and he blinked altogether the question that such a state of things arose from his having sold it all, the celebrated cask of sour, which he had made mention of to Captain Morton, included.

But Toggs did not stand alone as regarded that little peculiarity in making the worst of everything. It is an inherent principle of human nature. There are thousands of people who always like to have something to complain about, and who, in fact, are never happy unless they have. If all things were going comfortable and square with them, they anticipate some evil, and, in some cases, they invent one. Human nature likes to have complaints, but then they must be of a comfortable character.

A man likes to astonish his hearers by saying, "Well, I have lost ten thousand pounds by such and such a speculation;" but the same individual would make no call upon the sympathies of his kind friends if he had been well kicked.

It is, then, in the cause of the complaint that people find such intense satisfaction. And more particularly in London, from some strange notion that it is very great and grand, somehow, do people congratulate themselves upon the loss of their money. Some fellow, who, by his own vices and extravagances, has brought himself to ruin, will discourse by the hour with evident satisfaction, although with affected regret, about his losses.

We remember an instance when one of this class was monopolising the ear of a company at a tavern, by an account of what wonderful sums of money he had lost by this thing and by that thing, until another, who had in vain tried to get some of the attention of the company to himself, suddenly rose and exclaimed—

"Confound you ! do you think nobody ever lost anything but you ? I lost all the money in the world before I had it."

And so Toggs went about with his hands in the pockets of his little apron lamenting.

But the day was now getting on, and it is our duty to conduct the reader to the magistrate's, where the examination of Jem, the ostler, who had been charged with the murder, was to take place. There were, unhappily, some corroborative circumstances connected with the suspicion that he had done the deed, which pressed fearfully upon the minds of his best friends.

It is a hard case when one has nothing to set up against strong presumptive evidence of the guilt of any individual, but one's preconceived opinion that he was not a likely man to have committed the deed of which he stands accused. The mind is then placed in the most painful of all possible conditions. A mass of previously conceived impressions is attacked by a few new and most unexpected circumstances, and we tremble between doubt and certainty, not liking to sacrifice our judgment to prejudice, or our own strong opinion to even the facts which are arrayed against it.

The evidence, to be sure, against Jem, was but circumstantial; but then circumstantial evidence may be so strong as to run into the actual, and here were two or three little matters which were quite sufficient to hang a man. There can be no doubt in the world, but that, taking Jem's case as it stood before the examination at the magistrate's, he must have been committed for trial, and the probability is that a jury would have pronounced him guilty.

In what are called the good old days of George the Third, by fools who have not awakened to a perception of the real character of that blood-thirsty, idiotic bigot, Jem would have been hung as sure as fate; but we, certainly, do manage these things better now; and if, as in a shocking instance of the poisoning a wife by her husband a short time since, a real criminal does sometimes escape, it is now next to impossible that an innocent man should suffer.

The magistrate to whom it had been proposed to convey Jem for examination, was a very old man, and when he was told of the nature of the charge, and that it involved the most serious considerations, he had the candour to say that he would rather the matter was taken to some younger and more active member of the county magistracy. In consequence of this, it was determined that a Sir Francis Knightley should be the magistrate before whom Jem should be taken; and as that gentleman's seat was nearly four miles from the Morton Arms, it became nearly twelve o'clock on the morning succeeding the murder at the inn, before the parties were all assembled.

Knightley Hall was one of those ancient, Tudor-looking mansions which irresistibly attract the tourist, and which find a place in all picturesque books of the country. It had been in the hands of the family, the representative of which now inhabited it, since it was built; and well he might be, as indeed he was, proud of his ancient house. Sir Francis Knightley was a man who had travelled much, and he had not travelled, as many young men with more money than brains do, in vain. He had studied men and manners wherever he went, and when summoned home, on the sudden death of his elder brother, to assume the title, and with it the estates of the family, he returned vigorous in intel-

lect and of a liberal and candid disposition.

Such was the man, perfectly unbiassed and unbigoted, before whom Jem had now the good fortune to be taken. We say good fortune so far as regards the magistrate, and, of course, not with any reference to the charge which hung over him.

The great hall of Sir Francis's mansion was thrown open to admit the throng of persons who came to witness the examination; for he was not one who thought that any of the proceedings of justice should be conducted in secret. The hall was capable of holding five hundred persons, so that there was ample room, and to spare, for any one who chose to come and take a place in it during the examination of the prisoner.

At about a quarter past twelve Sir Francis himself came in, and bowing, in the most ostentatious manner to the assembled throng of his friends and neighbours, he said—

"I regret that I cannot accommodate you all with seats, but such facilities as I can offer to any one who wishes it, to become acquainted with what transpires, I shall gladly avail myself of. If, however, friends, during the course of this preliminary inquiry, anything should appear to be on the point of transpiring the common knowledge of which would go towards the subversion of public justice, I trust that you will give me credit for keeping it a secret for that reason, and that reason alone."

A murmur of applause ran through the hall, for Sir Francis was generally esteemed; moreover, his mild, gentlemanly, and unaffected mode of speech was especially captivating.

The constable was a great man that day. The perspiration stood upon his brow, and some of it rolled to the very tip of his nose. He was here, there, and everywhere, as somebody said, like a small dog in a fair. His staff was visible continually, and at length, when the magistrate said,—

"Bring in the prisoner," he made such a wild rush to do so, that there was quite a commotion.

Poor Jem had not the least intention to escape, so that all the precautions and all the valour of the constable were thrown away, although that redoubtable individual himself was very far from thinking so. He was continually exhorting Jem not to resist, and so place him, the valorous constable, under the awful necessity of doing something desperate and dreadful.

What that something would have been, Jem, as well as everybody else, had a shrewd suspicion, namely, the running away of the constable, had he shown the least indication of showing fight for his chase. Luckily, however, for our friend, the constable, he had a man for his prisoner who had everything to gain by an active investigation into the circumstances of the murder, and nothing to lose. All that could possibly be adduced against him had been done. There were the two or three little circumstances that seemed to connect him with the deed, and they were all. If anything else arose at all, it must be to his benefit, and in contradiction to the obvious deductions which any one who knew him not might well be supposed to draw from those apparently suspicious and guilty appearances.

Therefore was it, that Jem, had he been left alone completely, would have walked of his own accord to Sir Francis Knightley's. But when some one intimated as much as this to the constable, that noble-minded individual got uncommonly angry, and declared, with many oaths and asseverations, that, but for his determined looks, and known, or at least strongly suspected, indomitable courage, the prisoner would have made some dreadful attempt to escape.

"Look at the perspiration I'm in," he said, "that ought to convince you. Look at me—there's proof."

When Jem was brought into the hall before the justice, all eyes were upon him, and no wonder that a slight accession of colour visited his cheeks for a moment, and then left them, to all appearance, paler than they were before.

It is always hard for an accused person to be judged of by their looks, and yet, by the unthinking multitude, how often this is done. There are many men of perfect innocence as regards any criminality, who are of so excitable and nervous a temperament, that, were they suddenly accused of any crime whatever, they would turn pale and red by turns, and tremble.

But, with many persons, the looks of an accused person go a long way; and these foolish individuals quite forget that it is the guilty man, and not the innocent, who is likely to put a good face on the matter, because he is prepared for such a contingency; and the mere fact of his criminality at all, betrays a kind of mind which is likely not to be so much affected by the accusation, as one who with horror shrinks from anything at all in the shape of wrong doing.

"Look at him," said one; "he begins to feel it now."

"Ah, to be sure he does," said another; "I saw him turn red."

"And I pale."

"Then you may depend he did it. An innocent man would not think of changing colour."

"Oh, of course not."

"Take my word for it, he will be hanged. I can see it in his face. There, he changes colour again."

"Ah, that's because he sees somebody he knows."

"Bless me, it's the captain."

"Captain Morton?"

"Yes. Ah, he is like all rogues, ashamed to look an honest man in the face. He did it, you may depend."

And thus, upon such lamentably insufficient reasoning, was Jem's guilt settled in the minds of some of those spectators. Well it was for the accused man, that he had men of profounder intellect and judgment to judge him.

Sir Francis Knightley's clerk busied himself in procuring silence, and then, after a few preliminaries, with which we need not trouble the reader, the landlord of the Morton Arms was first called.

He deposed to the stranger coming on horseback to his house; to his making inquiries about the neighbourhood, and finally, his retiring to rest. Finally Toggs concluded by saying—

"And that's all I knows about it, only excepting as I feels quite clear as Jem didn't do it; and as far as trusting him went, I'd sleep in the same room with him, if so be as my pillow was stuffed with gold-dust, and there was a diamond sticking in my throat."

Captain Morton was standing close to the magistrate, to whom he now said something, upon which Sir Francis Knightley nodded, and then addressing Toggs, he said—

"Had you any other visitor at the inn?"

"Yes, your worship."

"Who was he?"

"A beggarman. He wanted to mind the gentleman's horse, but he would not let him, till he'd taken off the saddle, and that seemed to offend him, so off he went at once."

"Have you seen him since?"

"I have not."

"Should you know him again?"

"Oh, dear, yes."

"Describe him."

"A middle-sized man, dressed very much in rags, with a cloth cap, and very black hair."

Toggs was asked no more questions.

and then the cook at the inn was examined, who deposed to the fact concerning the candle, with which the reader is already acquainted, and which, therefore, we need not repeat at all. She, too, had seen the mendicant, of whose personal appearance she gave a similar description to that which Toggs had given.

No questions were asked either of these witnesses by Jem.

The flight of some man across the village, and into the churchyard, was now proved, and the man who had from his garden seen a stranger leap from one of the windows of the church, and who, it will be recollected, detailed that fact to Captain Morton, was examined. It was a most puzzling case, for while there was quite enough to warrant any magistrate in committing Jem for the murder, yet there were circumstances connected with the affair, which threw a great air of doubt and mystery over it.

"There will be an inquest upon the body of the murdered traveller," said Sir Francis, "and I feel strongly inclined to

THE OLD SEXTONESS READING THE PAPERS.

take no step beyond remanding the prisoner for a few days now. Have you anything to say, prisoner, in opposition to such a course, in explanation of anything which has been said against you? You have no occasion to make any statement unless you like, and I must warn you that every word you do say will be taken down."

"I have little to say," said Jem, "but that I am entirely innocent of the deed. I was foolish enough to go and sleep in a bed where I had no business, and beyond that I know nothing of it."

"That is all you wish to say?"

"That is all, sir."

"Then I shall feel it, at all events, my duty to remand you till this day week, and during that period of time every attemp shall be made to capture this beggarman, who seems in some way connected with these most disastrous proceedings."

"It's of no use me accusing anybody, of course," said Jem; "but if he did not do the deed, I will consent to be hung."

"What is the matter?" said Sir Francis. "There has been nothing but tumult for the last five minutes at the lower part of the hall."

"Please your worship he won't wake up," cried one.

"What is it ?"

"Troubled Tom, your worship."

"I want to be quiet," said a voice. "They won't let me. Oh, what a trouble. What's it all about ? How's the dog?"

"What does he mean ?"

"What do you mean?" cried Toggs, who was near to Troubled Tom, and now effectually awakened him by a tweak of the nose.

"Sir," said Tom, "what a trouble—you won't have to get any more tripe for Pincher. I see the fellow put a knife in him. Sir—what a trouble—it was that beggar fellow. What a trouble, to be sure. Well, there's nothing but trouble."

---

## CHAPTER XXI.

TROUBLED TOM'S EVIDENCE.—SIR FRAN-
CIS KNIGHTLEY'S OPINION.—THE END
OF THE EXAMINATION.

"Do you mean my dog Pincher?" said Toggs.

"In course I does. The beggar fellow did his business. Oh, I seed it with my own eyes. It was a trouble, but I did see it."

"Come forward," cried Sir Francis Knightley. "What's that he says about a beggarman? Bring that boy here."

"Sir," said Tom, as he was brought forward, "here's going to be a trouble. Oh, dear, oh, dear."

"Who are you?" said the magistrate.

"Who is me ?"

"Yes ; who are you ?"

"I often wishes—oh, don't I—that I was Farmer Jackson's prize pig as he's a fattening up quite to a pitch o' wengeance. Nothing to do, and lots to eat, he has. Oh sir, he's got no trouble."

"Is he idiotic ?" said the magistrate.

"Not a bit of it your worship," said Toggs. "I know him. He's as cunning as blazes, only he thinks anything is a trouble."

"You must tell me your name," said Sir Francis.

"Oh, dear—Tom Sharp."

"Sharp?"

"Yes. What a trouble !"

"Do you know the nature of an oath?"

"Ah, all sorts o' natures. If you tells the blessed truth, you goes to Heaven without any trouble. If you don't, you goes to blazes."

"I am bound to consider that answer sufficient," said Sir Francis. "It is considered so in the courts, therefore swear him."

Tom was sworn, and then Sir Francis said—

"Now, what have you to say about a beggarman ?"

"Oh, nothink."

"Nothing?"

"Oh, dear me. Well, well—what a trouble. I went to sleep in one of Toggs' barns, close by Pincher. He knows me, and only says a sort of 'how are you, Troubled Tom ?' when I comes and lays down among the straw. Well, in course I forgets my troubles, and goes to sleep ; but there's always a something."

"What do you mean by that?"

"Oh, I means there's always a something to wake one up."

"Indeed. Go on."

"Well, I heard a row, and it *waked* me, and then I sees that very beggar fellow as ought to have been asleep, and troubling nobody, a having such a row with Pincher as never was. At last it was all quiet, and I thought as how they had made it up again. Leastways there wasn't any more trouble, so I goes to sleep again."

"Is that all you know?"

"Won't that do ? Lor, ain't that enough all at once?"

"Not if you have any more to say."

"Oh, dear—oh, dear ! There's nothing but trouble in this here world."

"At what hour was it this happened?"

"I heard it a striking one."

"And the dog, you say, was killed by the beggarman you had before seen at the inn?"

"I didn't know. There was more trouble. All on a sudden I was *waked* up agin, and what do you think that was ?"

Sir Francis Knightley saw that if any evidence was to be got from Trouble Tom, he must be allowed to give it in his own way, so he humoured him, and merely said—

"I really cannot say."

"No, in course you can't. It's a trouble, but I'll tell you now. I was waked up agin by somebody actually a standing slap on my inside—the outside of my inside, I means—and when I looked up, natural in consequence o' that ere, I seed him agin."

"The mendicant ?

"The who ?"

"The beggarman."

"Ah, that was him. I didn't see no *medcant*. I doesn't want to have the trouble of going to blazes all through a swearing as I seed what I didn't. No, no—catch me at it. I seed the beggar, but I didn't see nobody else. He was all over blood it looked like, and he looked as scared as if he had been doing a something as he oughtn't. Then there was such a noise, and I heard a rattle a springing, as if somebody didn't mind the trouble a bit."

"And what did you do then?"

"I went to sleep again."

"You are a very extraordinary fellow. And when did you find the dog was killed?"

"When I was hungry."

"When you were hungry?"

"Yes; I always wakes up when I'm hungry, and never afore—leastways, unless somebody treads on the outside of my inside; then I does wake up as a *reglar* thing, and so would you."

"And that is all you have to say?"

"Very happy to say it is," said Tom. "Somebody almost pulled me over here, or else I shouldn't have took the trouble."

"I shall bind you over to appear as a witness whenever you are called upon in this matter, or else you may think it's too great a trouble to do so."

"Bind me over? Oh, dear—oh, dear. When will you undo me agin?"

"Be quiet, will you!" said the constable, "or else I shall have to *exart* my blessed authority, I tells you."

"The evidence of this lad alters very much the aspect of the case," said Sir Francis Knightley. "The weight of probability is strongly in favour of the supposition that the mendicant, who has been so frequently mentioned, is the author of the frightful crime we are called upon to investigate.

"It will be readily perceived that, although he appeared to have left the Morton Arms, there is abundant evidence to the fact that he came back to it again, for he has been seen by numerous witnesses.

"The prisoner before me was not intoxicated when he was taken, nor is there anything in his behaviour to induce a belief that he is mad. None but a drunken man, or a madman, would have committed a murder and then gone to sleep so close to his victim, and left about, as if purposely, abundant evidence of his guilt.

"I am disposed to think that by the back of the house this mendicant made an entrance, and then committed the deed, and that, in order to throw suspicion from himself, he purposely cast into the other's room the property there found, and took out the candle.'

These words of the justice brought conviction to the minds of all present, and Jem said aloud,—

"Do not release me, sir, if a shadow of suspicion is still upon me. I did not, as God knows, do the deed ; but I could not walk about among those who know me if I am suspected."

"I do not suspect you," said Sir Faancis, "and I shall discharge you, if you can procure moderate sureties for your appearance before me again if called upon."

"I'll be his security," said Toggs.

"And I," said Captain Morton.

Jem had kept up his resolution well till now ; but the severest trial he had endured was to find that the magistrate acquitted him, and that his master and Captain Morton thought so well of him as to become sureties for him. He strove in vain to hide the emotion that was visible in his countenance.

"Do your utmost," said Sir Francis Knightley, "to discover the real perpetrator of this offence. Spare no pains, and spare no expense. If money is wanted, come to me, and I will supply you. You are free now ; but you must feel how very gratifying a circumstance it would be to yourself and to all your friends that the real criminal should be found."

"He shall be found, sir," said Jem, "if he is above ground. I devote myself to the task. I will find him, let him be hidden where he may. He is a double villain who would do such a deed, and then seek to destroy an innocent man by making the guilt appear to be his. Let him beware of me, for never hound hunted its prey more keenly than I will hunt for him. I will have him, dead or alive—I will have him yet."

"Every one here, no doubt, as I do, wishes you success in your endeavours," said the magistrate. "Of course you will attend the inquest, as I shall do, and I make no doubt but that the verdict of the jury will again exonerate you from the suspicions that have been raised against you."

"I hope and trust it may, sir. But God's blessing on your head and heart, that have acted to me so nobly this day."

"I have but, according to my own perceptions, endeavoured to do my duty. I shall order the constables to give you all the facilities you may require in finding out the mendicant."

"Your washup," cried our friend, the village constable, "am I to take nobody up now?"

"There is no prisoner at present."

"Oh, gracious, I must take somebody

up, you know. Toggs, I promised to take you up if there was nobody else."

"I'm very much obliged to you," said Toggs, "but I have completely altered my mind on that little point."

"You have? Then I must take up somebody else. It won't do, I tell you; I must take up somebody. Your washup?"

"What now?" said Sir Francis, who had been conversing aside with Captain Morton ; "what now?"

"Is there nobody I can take up?"

"If you make yourself so troublesome, I shall commit you for a week to the county gaol for impeding the business of the court."

The constable fell back among the crowd in such a state of amazement that it was half-an-hour before he uttered a word. Then, as he walked home with a neighbour, he said,—

"I say this. There will be a revolution."

"A what?"

"A revolution in this here country afore long. Society at large is broke up. Quite broke up."

"You don't say so ?"

"Yes, I does ; I notes the signs o' the times, doesn't you?"

"I notes the signs o' the public-houses."

"Pho—pho !"

"Well, what do you mean, then? I'll be hanged if I understands you, you are so very larned."

"I means just this, and no more. When magistrates talks of sending constables to prison for a week, I does consider as a revolution is close a coming, and that that ere is a sign o' the times."

"Well, you know best. He didn't, you know, commit you."

"Very true, he didn't, and that fact may put off the revolution a little; but, come it must, neighbour. You may take my word for that. I knows what I knows, and that ought to convince you."

"Well, I daresay you are right."

"You needn't mention it to anybody, but I happen to know as I'm right. Society is being gradually pulled up slap by the roots."

"Indeed !"

"Yes. And all as is won't be, and all as isn't, will. There's going to be a horrid state of things. I feels it here."

The constable gave a slight blow at the region of his stomach, and his friend did the same, remarking that he, too, felt it there ; and, as they were near a road-side house, called the "Farmer's Friend," he thought it would be just as well to turn in and take some comfort in the shape of strong ale. This motion was not objected to, and the constable and his friend were rather in states of mind bordering on what, in the expressive phraseology of the constable himself, might be called "muzzy."

When the justice hall had been cleared of the motley assemblage that had found their way into it, the magistrate sent for Jem into a private room, where only he, and his clerk, and Captain Morton were, and he said to him,—

"Both Captain Morton and myself are of opinion that this mendicant, whom we believe to be the real author of the crime which you were charged with, is still in the neighbourhood."

"That he is, sir."

"We think so, not only on account of his having been seen recently, but because, if he has found out any hiding-place hereabouts, it is the safest thing he can do for a while."

"Think you so, sir?"

"Assuredly. He would be easily traced if he were to leave the neighbourhood. Some one must have seen him. He must get food by fair means or by foul, so that we should hear news of him."

"I will leave no spot unsearched."

"And particularly about the church," said Morton. "There appears to be some mystery about his disappearance there."

"It's impossible to say what hiding-places may be thereabouts," said the justice. "It sometimes does happen that in very old churches, such as the one in that village, there are strange hidden passages and hiding-places that are only found out by accident, or the most careful research."

"You give me new hopes, sir," said Jem.

"Captain Morton and I throw out these matters as hints to you," said Sir Francis Knightley; "because, to tell the truth, we have more hopes of finding out this mendicant from your exertion than from those of the constables."

"I am, of course, deeply interested in the discovery."

"So we conceive you to be. Think over what plan you imagine will present you the best chances of success, and rely upon every facility being at once thrown in your way to carry it out."

"I cannot be too grateful."

"Never mind about that. We are quite convinced of your innocence ; but you know, from your language and demeanour, quite enough of the world to be convinced that a man must not only be innocent, but, if he would escape censure, he must avoid even being suspected."

"I know well, gentlemen," said Jem, mournfully, "that unless the real murderer of the unfortunate gentlemen who lost his life at the inn be found, I shall, in the minds of many, always be associated with the deed."

"That is a fact which to you it would be a folly to deny. Go, now, and do your e st to clear up the affair."

"I will ; and with Heaven's help, I will clear it up, if it cost me my life to do so."

Jem left Knightley Hall, and proceeded towards the Morton Arms at a brisk pace, which brought him there within the hour.

It might have been his imagination, or it might have been real, but he thought that those of the villagers whom he overtook on the road looked coldly at him, and replied to his passing words of salutation as if he were a man to be shunned, as one more than suspected of a great crime, which, although it could not be brought directly home to him, there was a great presumption he had committed. For a time Jem strove to do his utmost to fight up against such a painful idea as this, but each moment it grew upon him. Then he tried to treat it with the contempt it deserved, and by telling himself that he was an innocent man, and that he was right, while they who treated him with such chilling courtesy were wrong, to consider himself as above being touched by such a circumstance.

This was, however, a struggle which he could not long maintain, and by the time he reached the Morton Arms he was fairly spirit-broken.

"They had better have kept me in prison," he said to himself, bitterly; "far better have kept me in prison than exposed me to such risks as these. I am innocent, and why, then, should I be looked coldly upon, because I have had the misfortune of being wrongfully accused ?"

Jem had all the reason upon his side, and yet he felt almost broken-hearted at the state of things. He went by the back way of the inn to the stable, and in one of the stalls of the horses he wept bitterly. Then he was better. Suddenly arousing himself, he exclaimed,—

"Now this is d—d cowardly, and I ought to be ashamed of myself. This won't happen again. I shall be ashamed ever to look that horse in the face."

He went to the pump, and washed away all traces of his tears ; and while he was engaged in that occupation, Toggs came up to him.

"Hilloa! Jem," he said, "I didn't see you come in."

"All right, master," said Jem, "all right. I came in by the back way. I didn't see poor Pincher."

"Oh, I passed him stiff and dead."

"Indeed!"

"Yes; just where Troubled Tom said he was, so we dug a hole and put him in at once."

"Poor fellow."

"Yes. I had no idea he was killed, Jem. What with the fright and the hurry of what has occurred, and the man in the house, and the crowds of people, and the having no beer, I really forgot Pincher altogether, till Troubled Tom mentioned him. I haven't been home above ten minutes, but of course I went out at once to look, and there, sure enough, he was, poor fellow, half cut to pieces; so, as I couldn't bear to look at him, I had him buried."

"Yes, master."

"Why, Jem, you will never be done washing your face."

"I'm done now," said Jem, rising, and wringing the water out of his hair, "I am done now, master."

"Well, I'm as glad, Jem, as if anybody had given me a twenty-pound-note," said Toggs, "that you have got rid of this troublesome affair."

"Got rid of it, master?" said Jem.

"Yes, to be sure."

"No, I haven't got rid of it quite, and perhaps sha'n't as long as I live."

"Indeed! how's that?"

"I'm going to leave you."

"Leave me, Jem? Leave me and the osses and the Morton Arms? Oh, no, you don't mean that, I know. Now, you're a-joking."

"I don't ever joke again, master. I'm going to turn all my attention to finding out who really did the murder; so, you see, when anybody comes here, I might be off and away Heaven knows where, instead of being ready to attend to my duty as regards you."

"You don't say so, Jem?"

"I'm fixed as fate, master; I've made up my mind to it. As long as I live, I'll hunt up that fellow, you may depend. Captain Morton and Sir Francis Knightley both encourage me to it."

"Well, if that's the case, I can't say anything agin it."

"You know, I may find him, and then I'll come back."

"Do, Jem. Mind you do."

"You may depend upon that, master I've been here long enough to love the place; I did love the people, too, but e sha'n't do that again in a hurry, you ma<sup>I</sup>

depend. However, that's neither here nor there. If you won't mention it to anybody, I'll tell you what I'm going to do to-night."

"Mum's the word, Jem; mum's the word with me. I won't mention it, you may depend. What are you a-going to do? I long to hear. What is it?"

"I'm going to keep watch all night in the church."

"In the church, Jem? the old, dark, dismal church? You don't mean that, and all night, too, and all alone?"

"All alone, and all night. I have some hopes that the beggar hides somewhere there. Only let me once get a sight of him, that's all."

"I wish you may, as far as I am concerned. I wouldn't stay all night in that old church; no, not for ever so much, I wouldn't. Only consider—who knows what may happen? What a horrid idea. It's enough to make one's hair stand on end, and walk about of itself, to hear talk of doing such a thing."

"Why, what is there to fear?"

"Oh, lots, lots."

"Lots of what?"

"Why, ghosteses, to be sure. Isn't there the churchyard close at hand, and the ghosts and all that sort of thing have nothing in the world to do but to get up and walk into the church."

"Well, it's a great pity they have not anything else to do."

"Jem, Jem, don't be a fool."

"I won't if I can help it, master. I never saw much worse than myself, and perhaps the ghosts, when they see me there before them, will have the goodness to leave me alone."

"There you go again, Jem. Oh, I wouldn't be in your highlows for a trifle."

"Wouldn't you, indeed. Well, well, master, all I ask of you is, to be so good as not to mention it to anybody, that's all. I shall go a little after dark."

"How will you get in?"

"I'll manage that by one of the windows; or, for the matter of that, I daresay old Dame Strangeways, the sextoness, would lend me the key."

"Well, she might. She's a rum'un, and you never know what sort of humour she's in; though, if you was laying a wager about her, the safest thing, in course, would be to bet she was in a bad one."

"So I believe; but I will try her."

"A wilful man, Jem, must have his way. I suppose we shall see you in the morning?"

"Yes, if I'm alive."

"Alive! Good gracious! don't talk in that sort of way. You give one the horrors to hear you. Of course you'll be alive, if you are frightened out of your wits, so mind you come in the morning, and let us hear what you have to say."

"Depend upon me, master; depend upon me. I feel a sort of confidence that I shall find out the villain who did that dreadful deed here. I suppose the poor gentleman lies as he did?"

"Yes; I locked up the door."

"Will it be any more satisfaction to you, master, if I lay my hand on his heart, and declare my innocence?"

"Not a bit—not a bit; I wouldn't see it done for ever so much. No, no, no—Jem, I'm quite satisfied you didn't do it."

Fearful that Jem might renew and perhaps insist upon his proposal, the landlord affected to hear some bell ring, and hurried away into the house to serve the imaginary customer.

------

## CHAPTER XXII.

THE LONELY WATCH IN THE OLD CHURCH.
—THE STRANGE APPEARANCE.—THE
OLD BELFRY, AND THE FEARFUL LEAP.

THE sun had sunk upon the village, and the dim uncertain light of twilight was slowly fading away, when Jem sought a lonely-looking cottage standing not far from the side of the old church, that was farthest from the cluster of houses composing the village. This cottage was that of Dame Strangeways, the sextoness; and Jem's errand to her was to endeavour to persuade her to lend him the keys of the church for one night, in order that he might keep watch there, in case the mendicant should be hiding anywhere about the sacred pile.

Dame Strangeways was rather a singular character. She was very retired in her mode of life, and if any of the villagers sought to intrude upon her privacy, they generally got repulsed with bitterness.

It did not seem, therefore, the likeliest thing in the world that she would grant the request of Jem; but, at all events, he determined to make it rather than effect any clandestine entry into the church, which he told himself he could still do in the event of her refusal.

He tapped at the cottage door, and was answered from within in the loud tones of the sextoness.

"Well—what now—what now?" she screamed.

"I want to speak to you, Dame Strangeways," said Jem.

She opened the door immediately, as she said, in a lower tone,—

"Well, and what do you want, murderer of poor travellers in their beds—what do you want, Judas ?"

"Since you are inclined to be so abusive, Dame Strangeways, I will go my ways."

"Hold ! What is the use of your coming here, if you don't say what you want ?—Come in."

"Never across the threshold of one who can suspect me to be guilty of the crime of which God and my conscience acquit me."

"You are a fool !" she said, as she seized him by the collar and dragged him in. "Now, what do you want ?"

"I will not say. Good night—good night !"

"Now, was ever such an angry blockhead ! Will it please thee if I say I believe you innocent ?"

"It is the simple truth, that I am innocent ; and of course, being so, it cannot please me to be called guilty. What right have you to assume my guilt ?"

"Because I please."

"Then you are behaving very unjustly towards me. I might as well accuse you of ——"

"Of what ?" she screamed. "Speak—of what do you accuse me ?"

"Of murdering the traveller at the Morton Arms. Why, how dreadfully agitated you are."

"Oh. That is all. That is what you meant to say. Oh—I agitated ?—pho—pho ! I am never agitated now. I agitated, indeed ! A foolish thought. What could make you think that I was agitated ?"

"Your own conduct."

"My own conduct ?"

"Yes, you suddenly looked as if you were a maniac ; but that is no business of mine. Dame Strangeways, I have come to ask yon a favour."

"Who asks ever a favour of me with a thought that he will ever be awarded to his asking ?"

"It may be hopeless ; but hear me, dame. I am innocent of the murder of the young traveller at the inn ; but there were circumstances which made me seem guilty, and those circumstances were, of course, contrived by the real criminal in order to shift the burthen of his crime from his own shoulders on to mine. Of that I have no doubt."

"Well, what then ?"

"It is believed that he is lurking somewhere in the neighbourhood, and more particularly is it believed that he has found a hiding-place about the old church."

"About the church ? There are no hiding-places about the church."

"None that you or I know of, I daresay ; but he may have found one, and what I want of you is the key for to-night, in order that I may keep watch there till the morning in silence and in secrecy."

"You are innocent, or you could never wish for a moment to be the long night in a church alone."

"I have no terrors."

"None at all ? Do you not fear the dead ?"

"No, as Heaven is my judge, I do not."

"Fancy yourself there at the still hour of midnight, when all human sounds are hushed. At that moment, when the popular belief of countless ages has sanctioned the appearance of things unearthly. Fancy yourself then in such a place, cut off completely from all human companionship, or human succour, and there and then condemned to hear hideous sounds, and see such sights as may well make your blood curdle in your veins, and haunt your imagination while you live. Fancy all that, and ask yourself if you can endure so much, even in such a cause ?"

"Not believing," said Jem, "in the superstitious fancies you would instil into my mind, dame, I have no such fears. Before I sunk to what I now am, I was better educated for better prospects in life. Villany contrived to rob me of all but that knowledge, which with no sparing hand had been given to me by one who loved me."

"Indeed ?"

"Yes. It may be, that at times, ay, most commonly, I adopt the language, and the manners, and the habits of the class to which I have fallen ; but glances of what I was will now and then break through what I am, and help me to despise those thoughts and feelings which are, and should ever be, the sole property of the most ignorant."

The old woman was silent for some moments, and then she said, in a tone of inquiry,—

"It is said in the village that no one knows your real name ; is such a statement true ?"

"It is true."

"You much surprise me. May I know it ?"

"I have made a determination to utter it to no one. You will, therefore, now excuse me, that I do not make you an exception merely because I come to ask a trifling favour of you."

"I should despise you were you to tell me for such a reason."

"I thank you for those words, and they give me some hope that you will lend me the key."

"You shall have it."

"Thanks, dame, thanks."

"Nay, 'tis not worth thanking me so earnestly for. You must return it to me early in the morning. Be cautious, and I hope you will make some discovery that will enable you to be an eaiser man."

"I pray to Heaven I may."

"Go you armed?"

"I had not thought of that."

"I can supply you, then. But not a word of this to any one."

She unlocked an old oaken cupboard that was fastened against the wall of her cottage, and she took from it an ancient-looking pistol with two barrels. The weapon was heavily inlaid with silver, a mass of which material nearly formed the whole of the stock of it.

"This is an odd weapon for a woman to have," said Jem, as he looked curiously and admiringly at the pistol.

"Not at all, for a lone woman like myself."

"Well, if it be your fancy, it is a rare one and a tasteful one. The weapon is as handsome of its kind, although antique, as ever I saw."

"And what is that to you?" she cried, angrily; as if, by merely praising the pistol, he had touched upon some subject that was most distasteful to her.

"I did not intend to offend you, Dame Strangeways. I only praised the old pistol."

"Then do not praise it: I do not want to hear it praised. Take it away. I have not looked upon it for a year or more, now, and I am sorry I lent it to you."

"Nay, then, take it back again. I do not wish to take it accompanied by your regrets."

No, no; 'tis done now. I have lent it to you, and you have made your remarks upon it ; so take it, and say no more to me about it."

"I will take every care of it, you may depend, dame, and return it to you along with the key of the church."

"Ay, the key—the key," she said, as if suddenly recollecting she had not given it to him.

She proceeded to the same cupboard from which she had taken the ancient pistol, and took from it the massive church key, which, with its curiously ornamented handle, and complicated wards, most of which were far more for ornament than use, was quite in itself a curiosity.

"There !" she said ; "now go away,—

now go away. You are satisfied. The pistol was loaded when put away."

"Indeed ! I'm glad you told me, though, I dare to say, that by this time the charge is useless."

"Go away—go away ! You have that which you required. Why do you linger here ?"

"I am going. Thank you, dame— thank you."

"Will you go ?"

"Well, well. There—I am gone."

Jem found that Dame Strangeways was getting into one of those desperate ill-humours for which she was so very celebrated all over the village, so he thought it better to go at once, than protract a conversation with her which, for all he knew, might end in her demanding from him again the key of the church.

"I wonder she lent it to me so readily," he said to himself, as he walked from her cottage door. "There were many chances to one against it truly, and I only have had the rare good fortune of finding her in the humour to do so, or I should have had nothing but abuse for my pains."

This was true enough ; but the people about her knew not very well how to manage Dame Strangeways. That she had something upon her mind of an uncomfortable character, which she never forgot, except for a few minutes at a time, seemed pretty evident from her sudden gusts of passion, without any assignable or adequate cause for them. However, it was with her as it is with a great number of very odd-tempered, obstinate people ; they are always the more civil the more they are opposed.

Probably Jem, the ostler, owed all his success in getting the loan of the key, to the fact that he showed a disposition to be angry with her for so quickly, upon recognising his voice, accusing him of the murder of the traveller at the Morton Arms. Whatever it was, though, that had produced his success, he was pleased at it ; for although he had quite made up his mind that he would that night, despite any and every obstacle that could be thrown in his path, keep watch and ward for the mendicant in the old village church, he yet felt how much better it was to go as he was going, than to be compelled to effect some clandestine mode of entrance into the sacred building.

He did not wish to go until it was quite dark, but that period now was very close at hand ; indeed, when he left the cottage of the sextoness, he was surprised to see what a rapid stride the coming night had made during only the period of his very

JEM, THE OSTLER, SHOOTS AT THE MENDICANT IN THE OLD CHURCH.

brief conference with her. He had walked some distance towards the inn, when he paused, and said to himself—

"Why should I not go at once ?"

There was only one objection to this, and that was, that, although loaded, the pistol that he had was in all probability useless, from the length of time the charge had been in it. He carefully examined the priming, however, and finding the powder perfectly clean and dry, he contented himself by poking the touchhole with a pin, and ascertaining by means of the ramrod that there was a charge it.

"I did not ask her," he said, "if it was loaded with ball ; but I presume it is, so I, therefore, will waste no further time, but go to the church as once. Toggs will know what has become of me when he finds I don't come back at once."

Jem now retraced his steps, and passing again the cottage of the sextoness, he, without the observation of any one, reached the low fence which skirted the old churchyard, and springing over it, was in the precincts of the consecrated ground.

What an uncommonly dark night that was. The moon would not rise until much later, and there was not a star to be seen. It was even a matter of some difficulty to separate with the eye the old chruch tower from the dense black clouds which formed a back-ground to it, and even the white grave-stones, bleached as they were by many a year of rain and sun, showed but dimly to the eyes of him who now, softly and gently, glided among them.

## CHAPTER XXIII.

THE MIDNIGHT WATCH.—THE ALARM.— THE SANCTUARY OF THE DEAD.

WELL acquainted as was the ostler with the localities of the churchyard, whether it was from the novelty of the circumstances in which he was placed, or the darkness of the night, certain it was h found great difficulty in making his way to the low, arched doorway of the church ; and then he forgot that, to get to it, there was a steep step to descend, and he met with a severe fall in consequence.

"Now, what is this?" he said. "Am I indeed so foolish as to allow my imagination to be overcome even to the extend that Dame Strangeways predicted, and which I was so bold as so unhesitatingly to deny? Courage—courage—courage!"

He took the old gothic-looking key from his pocket, but so intensely dark was the deep hollow of the doorway, that it was only by feeling carefully over the surface of the old indented oak, that he could at all find the keyhole into which he was to place the massive key.

"It is wondrous dark," he said. "If the moon would now but rise, were it ever so cloudy, it would afford me some means of seeing my way. This is, indeed, a most unpropitious night for my purpose; but I have too heavy a stake upon the issue to desert my enterprise. I have said I would devote my life to the discovery of the murderer of the traveller, and I will keep my word, let what will occur to appal me, or to draw me back from my fixed resolve."

When once he found the keyhole, strength was all that was required to open the massive door, for the complexity of the lock was not at all to be judged from the curious arrangement of the wards of the key. It was rather massive than artful in its construction, and soon it shot back with a sullen sound that produced a dreamy sort of echo within the ancient church, and then the low but heavy door creaked on its hinges, as if questioning the right of him who opened it at that unhallowed hour to enter the sacred edifice.

A rush of cold air came from the interior of the church, so cold indeed, in consequence of its contact with the ancient stone walls and numerous marble slabs, that the ostler recoiled again with a shiver before he could cross the time-worn threshold.

Recovering himself then, he entered the silent precincts of the place, and he closed the large door behind him, and from the interior securely fastened it.

Depositing then the key securely in his pocket, he felt for the silver-mounted pistol which the sextoness had lent him, and then, carrying that weapon in his hand, ready for immediate service, he crept slowly up the dark and solemn aisle.

The silence as of the very grave was in that place; so dim, and so obscure, and so death-like did it seem, that not all the courage that the most courageous men were endowed with could have prevented some feeling of awe, if not of terror, creeping over the soul. Our friend was quite sufficiently imaginative to feel all that could be felt in such a situation, and but for the strong purpose that urged him on, he might even have slunk back, and been scarce ashamed to own to himself that such a place had terrors sufficient to warn him from remaining longer within its walls. But he would not be appalled; true, he had been virtually exonerated from the charge which, with its blighting influence, had only for a few short hours hung over him, but he remembered the cold salutations of his neighbours as he returned from Sir Francis Knightley's, and he longed to shame them from their suspicions by being able clearly to point to them who really did the deed of blood.

And now the question of where he was to hide came strong across him, and after some consideration he thought he would get into one of the large, roomy old family pews, which were in the best position in the church.

There he knew he could even lie down at full length, if need should be, and listen to every sound that might occur to disturb the sacred stillness of that place.

This thought no sooner entered his mind, than he proceeded to act upon it. His eyes were getting a little familiarised with the darkness of the place, and he could see dimly the outlines of the blackened oak, as it slightly contrasted with the whitened walls of the building.

Noiselessly he got into one of these pews, and sitting down upon the floor of it with his back supported by one of its angles, he prepared himself to wait for whatever time or chance might bring before him.

He heard the wind whistling from without, and careering around the ancient pile, as if seeking from window to window some means of entrance; he felt the chilling, benumbing influence of the place, in the decreased circulation of his blood; and the impossibility of taking exercise made him fear, if an alarm should occur, he would be far from ready for immediate action.

But these were all passing considerations, or rather merely curious reflections, that turned him not from the stern purpose he had in view. They might make the carrying out of that purpose more difficult and more uncomfortable, but they could have no effect in inducing him to abandon it.

And now the old church clock suddenly awoke, and the whole building became vocal with the sound it made. It struck eleven. He counted them stroke by stroke; the dull, sighing echoes of the stroke appeared to be to him endless, but at last they died away, and all was still and lonely as before.

Then, at such an hour, and in such a place, did that lonely man give more thought to some most sad circumstances of his early life, than ever before he should have thought it worth his while to do.

This false accusation of murder which had been made against him seemed to have awakened in him a new nature, or, perhaps, more properly speaking, to have enabled him to have shaken off a number of acquired habits, which, like the rust upon the polished steel, dims its lustre without taking much from its integrity.

He was no longer the man we first presented him to the reader, and it was unlikely he would ever be again such a one; he felt himself that henceforward he was unfitted for those menial duties he had so long chosen to execute.

Truly, those hours of reflection in the old village church might be said to be the most important in his life.

He thought of how old the building was, of how many persons, who perchance had sat in that very pew, were now lying in the calmness of death in the churchyard that adjoined the sacred structure. He remembered to have heard some one say it was twelve hundred years ago since the old flint stones were piled one above another, to compose that old building.

It was irregular inside, though outside it took the form of a cross; it was simple in its structure, and this simplicity recalled more strongly those ancient times when its structure was raised by the pious founders.

The old walls here and there exhibited rude monuments and slabs that bore inscriptions, now effaced, or partly so, by the unsparing hand of time; the old windows, too, bore all the marks of being of the same age, large, and composed of innumerable panes, secured at intervals to long iron bars, that traversed in different directions the lattice or lead work.

The communion, too, was without ornament, and the inscriptions were of the rudest and plainest characters; they had been preserved carefully as though to perpetuate the memory of those who knelt there and worshipped hundreds of years before that time ; the rails and table were of oak, and the material lasted, while man perished and returned to the earth.

The pulpit, too, was rude, a simple structure, and that too was oak, covered for the use of the preacher, but which had been removed until another sabbath should require its replacement for the minister.

Such was the old church and its rude construction, but revered and admired by its frequenters. And it was astonishing to consider how, knowing this place so well as he did, and every nook and angle of it, the man who now kept his lonely watch within its walls should feel such strange sensations creeping over him, minute by minute, as the hours progressed. But so it was. Each moment added to the gloom that oppressed his mind, and he could not help saying to himself—

"It will seem an age to me before the morning comes in this place."

And now an hour passed away, and nothing occurred to break the dull monotony of his lonely watch. By that time, however, the moon began to show indications of performing its beautiful office—of lending sweetness and sublimity to that period of time when, in consequence of the absence of the sun, we can look upon nothing on the face of nature but cheerlessness and gloom.

A soft and beautiful light began to diffuse itself around, and object after object became plainly visible. And what a beautiful magic there is in light of any kind or description. The gloomy thoughts and feelings which had held triumphant possession of the brain of him who sat in the old-fashioned pew became completely changed. A holy calm crept over his mind in lieu of those strange sensations of dread that possessed it, and he felt that to pass a night in that ancient church was not the frightful thing it had seemed to be to his imagination so short a time before. A far better spirit animated him now by the time the moon had climbed so high as to shed some of its brightest and most beautiful beams in at the old windows, and he felt that he was a different man to what he was a short hour since.

"This is strange," he said, "this revulsion of feeling. I am not that which I was; the blood circulates more freely through my veins. I am ready for immediate action, come what may; and instead of this place investing any object that may appear to me with false alarm, it will rob it of some of its terrors by the very holiness and sanctity it breathes around it."

These were thoughts from which he was not likely to stray: if they were produced by the light, they were likely to increase, for the light was increasing, and by the time the church was brilliantly illuminated as it could be at mid-day, the singular man who was ostler at the Morton Arms began to hope that he should not have the mortification to say that he kept his watch in vain. He strained his ears to catch the slightest sound that broke the stillness that reigned around him. And now another hour had passed away, and the small hours of the night were creeping on.

The moon in its career had now shifted round so far, that it was opposite to one of the angles of the building, so that but very few of its beams came through its ancient windows,. But still there was a diffused light, and there could be no difficulty in seeing any object which might move within the venerable pile.

Twice now the ostler thought he heard a strange scratching noise in the direction of one of the windows; but as it was followed by nothing more for some time, he began to think it but the effect of imagination, or possibly it might be some rats or mice that infested the place.

Suddenly, however, when he had nearly made up his mind to this conclusion, the noise increased, and turning his eyes in the direction whence it came, he saw some strange, dark object moving either inside or outside one of the windows, he could not tell which. It provokingly happened that that window was in the greatest gloom of all, so that, although he felt certain there was something like a human form attempting to get out of the church by means of the window, or to get in, he could not determine with any degree of certainty its size, aspect, or general appearance.

His first impulse was to rise and rush towards the spot, but he controlled that by a more prudent one, which was, to remain where he was and watch attentively what was about to ensue, for he felt almost certain, although he could not have sworn positively to the fact, that the figure was trying to effect an entrance into the church by means of the window, instead of trying to leave it. Such being his impression, it was obviously his best course to allow the entrance to be effected, after which, he would have a far better opportunity of making prisoner the man, whoever he was, who was making so nefarious an attempt upon the sacred building.

Jem's heart told him that this man must be the murderer, and he could scarcely keep his joy within anything like reasonable bounds at the prospect of so soon and so easily capturing one who had endeavoured to do him so deadly an injury as to draw down upon his head the consequences of a crime of which he was so entirely guiltless. The idea that it might be some supernatural being never once entered his head. He was completely possessed with the notion that it must be the murderer, and again and again he found it difficult to repress his impatience, which goaded him to rush forward and attempt to seize him, before such an act could be effected with the greatest chances of success.

The more he looked the more he felt that the figure was outside the window; and a circumstance occurred that added the full force of truth to that supposition, for the fastening of the window was undone, and it was thrown open, evidently from the outside, because opening inwards, as it did, the figure must have moved down from the sill, instead of remaining where it was, had it been on the interior, instead of, as it was, on the exterior of the building.

Now that the old fashioned glass-work was removed from before his eyes, Jem could see much better than before, and he at once discovered the party who was endeavouring to effect an entrance was a man of about the middle height, and apparently attired in very dark apparel.

"Let him but get in—let him but get in," thought the ostler to himslf, "and if he succeed then in eluding my vigilance, he will be a wonderfully deal cleverer fellow than I take him to be."

But this was a step which the figure did not seem inclined to take in a very great hurry. Be he who or what he may, he was sufficiently cautious, and took a long and anxious survey of the church before he would trust himself within it. Jem's impatience increased each moment. He might easily have shot him where he stood, always provided old Dame Strangeways' pistol would have gone off, which, after all, was, perhaps, a doubtful point, but he never once thought of that. To fairly apprehend him, and have him convicted of the murder, was what he wished, and so to show him, ruffian as he was, that he had failed to fix the guilt of his own misdeeds on an innocent man. The window was not above four feet from the ground, but the fellow stooped very low upon the sill before he would venture to leap in, and then he might be said rather to drop, than to leap into the aisle.

"I have him now," thought Jem, and he sprang over the side of the pew with the rapidity of thought.

It would have been better had he waited a few minutes longer, for doubtless the fellow would then have been more advanced in the church. As it was, however, he seemed so confounded at Jem's sudden appearance, that for about one half instant he was unable to fly. He must have inevitably have been caught, had it not been that Jem struck his foot against something in his progress, and nearly fell, at least he had to take one of those formidable springs forward which people do to save themselves from falling, and then, as always follows any sudden and violent action, there was a slight pause.

The man who had introduced himself into the church now took a run into the body of the building, as if he were intent, upon attacking the ostler, instead of escaping from him, then suddenly turning with the rapidity of lightning, he took a short run again towards the window, and sprang through it again as cleanly as an accomplished harlequin could have accomplished the feat.

These kind of actions take far longer to tell than to execute, and the affair was all done and over with such rapidity, that it is no exaggeration of the fact to say, that not half a minute had elapsed from the period of Jem's springing from the pew and the disappearance of the supposed murderer through the open window.

---

## CHAPTER XXIV.

### THE CHASE THROUGH THE VILLAGE.—— THE RETURN TO THE CHURCH, AND THE MYSTERIOUS DISAPPEARANCE.

THE sudden dash at the open window by the intruder, was so unexpected and so instantaneous, that Jem was taken by surprise, and though he was very close upon the heels of the man, yet he was not close enough to seize him ; and just as he reached the window-sill, which he did by stumbling against it with some force, for he had thrown himself forward in the hope of seizing his enemy by the legs as he drew himself up, he felt the heel of the boot strike against his fingers; but he had the pistol in his hand, and that prevented him making a grasp, and he saw the man reach the window, and just as he was about to disappear, he levelled old Dame Strangeway's pistol and pulled the triggers, when both barrels went off. The church echoed and re-echoed with the sound of the report, so loud and so stunning, that even Jem himself was amazed for the moment.

The stillness of the night, and the bare walls of that ancient building, with all the windows, save one, closed, caused the report to be so stunning, that few would have believed it, and the ostler for a moment paused. In another moment he too had leaped up into the window-sill, and was in the old churchyard. He felt his feet come in contact with the old flat tombstone that lay so short a distance from the wall beneath. So rapidly did all these events pass, that the man who had so narrowly escaped being captured, was scarcely a dozen yards in advance.

His form no sooner met the eye of the ostler, for in the hurry of getting out, and the smoke of the pistol, he had lost it, than he rushed forward to follow the midnight intruder upon a scene so sacred. The man seemed to be well acquainted with the place, for he never halted or hesitated. He ran against none of the numerous impediments that existed, and which would have caused any one less acquainted with the place to be thrown down and captured. Not one of the many mounds and gravestones did he run against, but straight onward he ran, sometimes turning to the right, and now again to the left, to avoid what would otherwise have stayed him. Jem, too, avoided the same impediments, but he did it by instinctively following the man and avoiding what he avoided, and turning when he saw him turn.

Thus it was—they kept pretty well at the same distance from each other, and it was evident that nothing but an accident could give either the advantage. They were both fleet and fast, sure footed and deep breathed. The race was such a one as had never before been run in such a vicinity, and the living never saw such a scene among the tombs of the dead. The prize to one was life, and the other justice. Each strained his utmost, and exerted every nerve and sinew to the extreme.

The moonlight lit up the old churchyard, and the two dark human figures, rushing with the speed of wind among the old tombstones, gave the place an awful and mysterious appearance. Indeed, had any of the simple-minded peasantry of the neighbourhood seen their gambols among the dead, they would have believed they were beings of another world, and never again would the old churchyard be visited by man—it would never have been believed that such men were actually living beings. The murderer still maintained the distance between himself and Jem, and the latter endeavoured to lessen it, but they were well matched.

"Now," thought Jem, "had I not discharged my pistol, I could have shot him, and have secured the villain."

But the slightest accident oftentimes bars the best made and easiest executed schemes that man can devise; and so it was now, for, had not Jem discharged the pistol, he would now have secured the man who fled before him. As they neared the wicket-gate, the man rushed through; but he was impeded for a moment, and this enabled Jem to reach him, and he could with another stride have seized him. But at that moment he himself met with the same impediment, and the man, having released himself, was again enabled to secure the same distance between them as before existed, for Jem had to pass through the same wicket.

"Murderer! villain! you shall not escape me; you shall answer with your life for the bloody deed you have committed."

The man answered not; he still fled onwards, with the same rapidity, the same firm struggle for the mastery in speed—for the security of life, and the attainment of justice. On—on—on they went, with a bounding step; the sound of their feet was dull and heavy, but quick; the heavy beats sounded in startlingly rapid succession, and the wind almost whistled through their clothes. There was, indeed, that rustle and sound of their feet that could have been distinctly heard by any one near at hand; but which, from its lowness in scale, could scarce be heard to a short distance. The man seemed inclined to make towards a wood that lay at no great distance; but Jem, seeming to anticipate that, contrived to keep on that side of him; so that, should he attempt to do so, he must make an angle, and then he would cross it, and come close upon him. The moon threw a broad and bright light upon the earth—not a cloud now was to be seen in any part of the heavens—on the contrary, they were cloudless, and the earth was illuminated by her silvery light. Broad shadows reached the plain, and the trees at a short distance looked, by the strength of the shadow, as if they were double, and impenetrable; and could the man have reached any of these, no doubt he would have attempted a deviation of course; but he seemed fearful of attempting such a manoeuvre with an enemy so close upon his heels, and when the lose of a single stride might cost him his life. Desperate was the struggle of those two men, the one to escape, and the other to overtake, and yet neither could succeed. At one moment, indeed, there was almost the certainty of the chase being ended in a mortal struggle; for the stranger missed his way, as he made for a gap in a hedge; he had to make a bend to get to it, and this gave the ostler the opportunity of reaching him on the bank. Just at that moment, as the man was about to spring, and Jem's hand was about to close upon his shoulder, he fell, and rolled down on the other side of the ditch. This accident released him

from Jem's intended grasp, who was unlucky enough to stumble against a stake, which threw him into the gap, while the other scrambled out of the ditch. With a sudden spring Jem rose, and cleared the ditch.

Then again commenced the desperate chase, which for a moment only had been disturbed by this slight accident, which had, indeed, been nearly fatal to the fugitive. Onward they dashed, and Jem now saw, with pleasure, the stranger took towards the village.

"Now," he thought, "should any one be, by accident, about, he will be stopped, and close to a spot where he can be secured."

On they went, and were soon on the confines of the village. The houses were all quiet; not a light streamed from any of the windows—not a soul could be seen, not a sound heard, save such as proceeded from themselves. Into the village the stranger dashed, and seemed determined to make a desperate effort to shake off his pursuer by speed, and he rushed over the hard road with increased speed. But here he found he was followed by a like struggle on the part of the ostler to make a desperate effort to overtake him, and this effort was, therefore, only so much increase of exertion as must materially diminish their mutual strength, without gaining any advantage. The ostler could hear his enemy's breathing—it was hard and rapid; and he could not, he thought, hold out much longer. But Jem became aware, too, that he was much distressed by this unwonted exertion; and, but for the excitement and the hopes that drove him onward, he could scarce have held out so long in the desperate struggle as he had done. Notwithstanding the readiness with which the man leaped from the window, and started off, Jem had hoped he might have been wounded, and then loss of blood would have weakened him so that he must have fallen into his hands; but no such hope could be entertained now. They passed through the village, and its peaceful dwellings; once, indeed, a dog barked, and sprang out into the road; but neither took any notice of him, and he slunk back to his kennel, and in a few moments they were past, and out of sight—the village was behind.

To the left of the village was a wood that ran some distance at the back of the village church; part lay in a hollow, and part lay by a hill-side. The stranger turned to the left, and made towards the wood. Here another struggle commenced, and Jem made his utmost speed to overtake the murderer, thinking that if he got into the covers he would have every probability of escape. Indeed, he did gain slightly upon him; but it was so slightly, and the wood was so close at hand, that Jem feared he should not gain enough upon him to seize him before he got to the wood. However, he could not hold out much longer; he must be even more distressed than himself. Still, he had no thought of giving up the chase; his heart and soul were in the successful conclusion of it, and not for worlds would he have stopped while he could move a limb.

Jem's fears were realised; the man did gain the wood, and rushed into it as though he felt himself somewhat secure. He bounded on through the dark walks, heedless of the briars that grew across the path, which came with force against the ostler, who came after him with a steady pace; and the rapid strides they both took were timed, and it seemed as though it were but one man, and one step that bounded through the wood. The wood was dark, and the boughs were so thick and tangled, that the moon's rays could ill penetrate, and Jem could only see the dark moving body of the man who yet remained but a few paces in advance.

The cover and shelter the wood afforded seemed but ill calculated to be seized upon by the fugitive, for his pursuer being so close on his track, that any spot or brake he could have rushed into would have been no hiding-place, for the ostler was close behind him, and what gave way to one could be entered by the other.

Had the place been large, and a vast quantity of brushwood about, and he had a start of a hundred yards, he might have had time to dive into the recesses of the wood; but to attempt such a thing would be to slaken his pace, and doing so but for a second would be to place his adversary's hand to his throat.

He could not stop—he could not turn; to rush in among the tall trees at full speed might be successful, but it might also be unsuccessful, and there was the chance. To turn unsuccessfully, was to give up; and if he turned at the speed he was running, among the trees, he knew not how soon he might run against one of the huge trunks, and thus prostrate himself.

These considerations, no doubt, actuated the man to keep the open cleared paths, that gave no obstruction to his flight. Whatever stopped his pursuer, he knew would stop him first, save some slight fall, or slip of the foot, and such accidents were not to be reckoned upon as means of escape.

They now emerged from the deepest and most gloomy part of the wood to a part where the moon's rays penetrated, and relieved the dull gloom, nay, almost darkness, of the former part, and the diffused light that reigned served to show the ostler of the Morton Arms that his enemy had maintained his distance.

The two men who thus acted the parts of the pursuer and the pursued in so desperate a chase, had now nearly exhausted themselves, and could not now maintain their former pace; they both slackened—nature could not support for any unlimited period such tremendous efforts of strength and endurance. They slackened slightly their pace, but this did not alter the relative position of either; they still remained as they were, the one to fly, and the other to chase.

They neared the confines of the wood, and in another moment they both emerged into the open moonlight.

"Murderer! villain!" shouted the ostler, "you are a doomed man."

No answer was returned, but, crossing a small field, the man swept up this, skirting a hedge, and again made the churchyard whence he had started.

Jem now thought he should at least chase him to his lair; he followed stoutly on, determined that while he could follow on—while life remained, he would never lose sight of him. At a bound the man cleared the wicket; Jem followed through the gate, which gave him a moment's advantage, and away he sped for the very window he he jumped out of. The ostler followed through the yard and among the tombstones as nimbly as the fugitive; but the latter tripped and fell, and Jem would have seized him, but he overshot his prey, and had to turn back, which he could not do for several paces.

Again had his foe eluded his grasp, hurrying through the churchyard, in a contrary direction, and again did the ostler, with almost unabated vigour, and unimpaired determination, rush after him. Now, however, he was rather more in advance, and the manner in which he rushed among the tombstones gave him a slight advantage.

At one moment he turned a large monument, and Jem rushed round the other side, intending to have caught him sideways; but here he was foiled, for the fellow made straight onwards towards a tree, which he turned, and ten again made for the open window.

There could be no mistaking his intention, and Jem thought he was quite sure of his victim. The moon shone on the other side of the church, and this side was in gloom, save the diffused light of the moon that was shed around. He rushed to the window, and then disappeared ; in another moment Jem was under the open window. He paused a second, and became convinced the man was not hidden in the obscurity of the shadows cast by the church. It was a blank wall beneath —a narrow strip of earth lay between the tomb on which he stood—and he became convinced the murder was in the church, and in another moment he stood again in the sacred edifice.

## CHAPTER XXV.

THE SEARCH IN THE OLD CHURCH.—
JEM'S RETURN TO DAME STRANGE-
WAYS' COTTAGE.—THE QUARREL.

CONVINCED that the man who had taken refuge in the church could not escape—for all the doors were locked, and he himself had the key—he paused a moment or two to gain breath. Jem's heart beat violently, and the sweat stood in large globules on his forehead, and ran in streams from various parts of his body ; he was bathed in moisture. He could feel the pulsation of his heart beat with tremendous violence, and his breast heaved quickly, while the blood flowed at such an increased rate through his whole body, that he felt dizzy and sick.

For a minute he reeled, and could scarcely stand; but it was only for a minute, and then he turned to the work of examination for the man whom he made no doubt was secreted somewhere in the church, among the pews or seats, and he determined he would have him out.

"Now," said the ostler to himself, "shall justice be done, and it shall be acknowledged by all men, within their own minds, that I am innocent of the foul deed."

Jem had carefully listened, but yet he heard not the slightest sound to indicate the whereabouts of the fugitive.

"He surely came in," thought the ostler. "Yes, of that there could be no doubt; he had not time to slip either to the right or to the left. I must have seen it instantly, and had he crouched in the shadow of the wall, then I should have discovered him as I stood upon the grave-stone beneath the window."

To secure the window was the work of a moment; and though it could offer little or no impediment to the escape of the sup-posed murderer, if he were again to make for that place, yet it would be a hindrance for a second or two, and that would give him the opportunity of overtaking him before he could get clear off. Then going up to the communion-table, he looked carefully around the place—he looked down both aisles, and could see nothing. He then carefully walked down on one side—that which was the darkest, for the moon's rays fell upon one side, and down the darkest side Jem walked, examining every little nook and corner, and looking into every pew, which were not many, and every shadow that was thrown across the aisles; and then he looked round on every side, so that no movement could take place in the body of the church without his being perfectly cognizant of it, so still and quiet was the place.

Jem scarcely breathed ; his footsteps were slow and stealthy, because he would not disturb the wrapt stillness of the scene; he had eyes and he had ears, and both faculties did he carefully make use of. The ostler had examined one side, and he crossed at the end of the aisle to that on the other side, and then commenced as careful an examination on that side as he had made on the other. This, however, was fruitless, also; and the ostler began to fear that, after all, he had been defeated, and the supposed murderer had contrived to elude his search, and had securely concealed himself.

"Surely, surely," he exclaimed mentally, "he never could have escaped from me. I saw him come in—his shadow was on the wall. I saw him leap, and he must have come in. Ay ; but where is he? He cannot escape my search; the place is too simple and unadorned, and presents too few hiding-places to enable such a man to lie without discovery. No, no," he said, "he cannot be here."

Again he went through every nook, every pew, and walked into every shadow, where not even a cat could hide itself ; still he was not there, and no sound met his ear. It was then, as the conviction that the supposed murderer had escaped, stole over him, that he felt an almost overpowering sense of fatigue, from the toil he had gone through, for the first time steal over him.

He staggered, but he would not sit down; he would not even give his enemy a chance, if he were there, of suddenly overcoming him, and thus securing impunity for himself ; he determined to walk up into the pulpit, and there watch the body of the church, and listen to the smallest sound that might reach his

He walked up and sat down ; he leaned his head on his hands, and gazed wistfully up and down the body of the church, and listening intently the while.

The church was nearly enveloped in gloom now, and nothing but the dark outlines of the pews and the monuments were seen or distinguished—the moon was fast waning, and morning was approaching. He sat there and trembled ; he felt he had done much—he had strained every sinew, and had yet scarcely recovered his breath ; he yet panted, and the disagreeable effects were, even now, felt incidental to the race.

"He is gone—he is gone," he muttered ; "Heaven's own will be done, but he's gone."

It was strange to see that singular man, he of the Morton Arms, the ostler, too, seated there, and thinking on his past life, and contemplating his present painful position.

"Yes," he muttered, "the murderer is now safe for a time. There was a deep-laid plan, and part has been defeated, and the old church will no longer be a hiding-place for the concealment of such a desperate criminal as a murderer. It would

THE PURSUIT OF THE MENDICANT BY JEM, THE OSTLER.

make me doubt Heaven's wisdom and goodness ; but some more signal punishment will follow this man's escape. Time—ay, time, will reveal that and many things."

\*   \*   \*   \*   \*

The gray dawn of morning was fast breaking in the east, the moon was fast losing her influence, and her pale face was shining among the clouds, or dying away, and becoming obscure because of the presence of a superior luminary ; the night clouds were fast deserting the sky, and here and there the lark might be seen just

flitting over a field or two, and then dropping peaceably to the earth, as if it had mistaken the morning, and retired for more rest, when the ostler of the Morton Arms descended from his watch-place in the pulpit of the old church. Taking once more a careful survey of the church, he approached the door he had entered by means of the key that Dame Strangeways had lent him.

He opened the door cautiously and looked around, but all was still, and he reversed the key, and secured the door behind him. Once again he stood in the open air, and felt refreshed, and the drowsiness that had overtaken him seemed to vanish before the pure air of Heaven.

He looked round the old graveyard—he walked round, and looked at the spot where he had last seen the supposed murderer, and yet still he could not believe he could nave escaped any other way—he must have seen it. There was nothing that could have hidden him from his view for one moment.

"It is strange," he muttered, "very strange. Here I saw him, and I believe I could swear I saw him enter; indeed, I can see no means of escape; I can see nothing that would have hidden him for a second, and yet he was not inside, that is equally true. It is strange, very strange," he muttered, and he turned his back upon the church, and passing through the churchyard, he made for the cottage of old Dame Strangeways. "I will, however, make all this known," he muttered, "and he shall have no safe abode there. What could induce him to hide in this neighbourhood. Has he not finished his work here? Are there more to fall beneath his knife, and others suffer in reputation for the deed?"

Absorbed in these and other thoughts of a strange unusual import, he arrived at the cottage of the dame, and tapped at the door.

"Who is there?" inquired a voice from within, which he knew to be the dame's; he said,—

"'Tis I, Jem the ostler."

No answer was made; his voice was well known, and she straight undid the door.

"Come in," she said.

The ostler walked in, and taking out the key of the church door which she had lent to him, he threw it on the table, and the pistol also, with the air of a man sorely vexed and fatigued. He threw himself into a chair, and sat gazing upon them both with an air of abstraction, when the dame said,—

"Well, Jem, did I not speak aright? You have got heartily tired of your watch?"

"I am of its results," he replied.

"Have you seen anything?"

"Look at the pistol," said the ostler, sententiously; "look at the pistol, and then tell me what it says, and if it is not as it was."

The old woman took the pistol in her hand, and seeing the pan open and the hammer down, said,—

"Ah! you have used it. What news? Tell me what has happened to you."

"Disappointment, disappointment," said Jem.

"Indeed! and wherefore did you use the pistol? Tell me all that happened during your watch at the old church. Were the lonely hours broken in upon by any human or superhuman being?"

"By flesh and blood, like myself, I believe; and it disappeared most unaccountably, at a moment when I deemed him safe, and when I believed escape was impossible."

"And you believe——"

"He was a man like myself. I will tell you how it was done. Sit down, and I will tell you from the beginning to the end."

"Do so, and then I will tell you what I think of this strange business."

"Well, then, I got into the church by means of the key you lent me, and then it was all pitch dark; you could not see your hand, but I went into one of the old-fashioned pews, and sat upon the flooring in the obscurity of the place.

"It was an hour ere the moon rose, and then I had light enough, and I sat long in anxious expectation of something occurring; but no sound was heard, and nothing to be seen beyond what was proper to the time and place. I waited with some degree of impatience, when my lonely watch was relieved in its monotony by some slight sound at the window. This was repeated, but I could see nothing for some time, until at length a human being stood at one of the windows between me and the moonlight. I knew not by that uncertain light whether it was inside or out of the church. However, I soon discovered that it was on the outside of the church, for he flung the window open, and, after some hesitation, and carefully scrutinizing the place, he jumped in. His foot was no sooner in the church than I leaped over the pew, and rushed at him, but he contrived to rush into the church and then back again, cleared the window, and was in the act of descending, when I, fearing to lose the man, fired; but I must have missed my aim."

"If he got off, you did only slightly wound him," said Dame Strangeways.

"Listen to what follows, and you will soon be convinced that he was wholly unhurt. I, too, leaped through the window, and followed close on his heals; I was scarce five or six paces behind him, and did all man could do to overtake him."

"But you could not, and he so close to you?"

"No, I could not. He passed through the churchyard, and made for the village.

It was desperate running, and no other motive could induce me ever again to share in so desperate a race. Onward we ran, still keeping the same pace, and we reached the village. Every human soul was asleep; no stray man was there to impede his flight, and not one to look upon the chase. We were alone in the pale moonlight, and, save the eye of Heaven, were unobserved. He made for the wood. I feared his reaching that place, believing he could hide himself, and thus baffle my pursuit, and I made another desperate effort to overtake him; but he must have been conscious of my attempt, for he met it by a corresponding effort. Notwithstanding all I could do, he gained the wood, and, almost at the same instant, I did so too, and a desperate pursuit was kept up there. He ran through the open paths—had it been otherwise, I should have secured him—one moment's delay, and he would have had my hand at his throat. But he could not find time to seek the covert of the wood, and again made for the churchyard, and here, making one or two sudden turnings, I was thrown out, and he gained a few yards, and rushing to the window, I believe cleared it, and got into the body of the church. I paused a moment, believing him secure, and became certain he must have gone in. There was no escape but such as I saw. I leaped into the church also, but found him not. I searched every nook and corner, but to no purpose—he was gone."

"And what do you intend to do next?" inquired Dame Strangeways.

"Why, give information concerning the man whom I have seen, and relate what I have told you to the justice, and see if he cannot be secured."

"And who, think you, will believe your relation, so strange as it appears?"

"I care not. I know it to be the truth, and nothing more than the truth, and it will go far towards proving my innocence."

"What no one will believe will prove nothing that you wish to prove, but may engender suspicion. Take my advice—say nothing of what has happened to anybody."

"Ay, but I shall; and by their means this man may be secured."

"It is useless. But, Jem—if Jem is your name—you must have another; surely you have no motive in concealing it from me?"

"I will conceal it. I shall never be known by any other, and do not intend to reveal to any one what I deem fitting to conceal."

"Are you ashamed of it?"

"I may rather be ashamed of my present condition; but I have said all I shall say about that subject; do not, therefore, ask me questions."

"Ask no questions!" said the dame, in an irritable manner. "Go where none will be asked of you; since you cannot even trust me with your name, nor be guided by my advice, seek some other place: my cottage is no place for you."

As she spoke, she threw the pistol and key into a cupboard, which she locked in great anger, and the ostler, without any apparent emotion, rose and quitted the cottage.

Dame Strangeways paused a moment or two, and muttering some incoherent expressions, evidently in anger, she walked to another cupboard, which she unlocked, and took therefrom a bundle of papers carefully tied up. Then arranging her chair, she sat down in the most convenient position to catch the light and sit at ease. She was soon immersed in the papers before her, and heeded nor thought of aught else. It was strange to see the eagerness and avidity with which she perused the papers she held in her hands. The sharp features of the old woman were concentrated upon one point, and she felt but one sensation. She sat in her chair as though she had been a piece of curious carved work, so still and motionless was she.

---

## CHAPTER XXVI.

THE COFFIN BENEATH THE FLOOR.—THE DEAD CHILD.—THE NARRATION.

AFTER some moments spent thus, Dame Strangeways rose from her chair. Her passion had cooled, and she seemed actuated by other feelings, of as strong a character, but of a different aspect; they were of grief and melancholy, so long and so often indulged in, that they appeared to become nearer allied to insanity than the expression of grief and woe of a sorrow-stricken woman, fully informed of all she most feared or most desired should not be true. The papers were flung upon the table, and she buried her face in her hands, as if in an agony of doubt and grief.

"No, no, no!" at length she said, with convulsive energy—"no, no—it cannot be—I cannot see it—I cannot!"

Another pause, and then she traversed the floor of her cottage. All was silent; not a sound came upon her ear, save that of her own feet, as she traversed the low, sanded floor of the room.

"Yes," she muttered; "I will once more look upon those sad last remains. Oh, how dreadful! and yet I cannot refrain. I am fascinated—and yet, why? But—ah, no! I cannot part with them—I will not."

She went to the cupboard, and taking out a long turnscrew, she slowly walked towards a portion of the flooring, in a chink of which she put the tool, and, with but a slight effort, she lifted up a portion of boarding evidently made to do so. Beneath the boards was the coffin of a child. The woman paused as she gazed upon it. It was the coffin of a tolerably sized child. She carefully laid the boards on one side, and, after examining the lid carefully, she paused before it some moments.

The coffin was worn; there was dirt and dust upon it, though there was an attempt made to keep it otherwise. There had been some years elapsed since the time that coffin was made, and that in which the old woman gazed at it. She took off the lid, and displayed the form and decaying body of a child; but it had long since ceased to be offensive. Indeed, there was but little more than the mere bones and tougher integuments that held them together; what did remain was like skin or parchment drawn over the bones.

It was a ghastly and horrifying spectacle. The grave-clothes were yet entire, the cap was still on the head, and its whiteness was a strong contrast to the deep, brown-like hue which the body had taken. The contrast was strong, and the sunken, eyeless sockets—the noseless face, altogether presented a truly terrifying spectacle. And yet Dame Strangeways felt, or seemed to feel, no repugnance to gaze and even touch the mouldering body. Indeed, to her it seemed no new sight, but such as she had been accustomed to.

Her head shook several times as she looked at the body, and then slowly replacing the lid of the coffin, and then the boards of the flooring, and then replacing the turnscrew, she once more paced the cottage flooring. She shook her head and heaved a deep sigh, and again sought the papers and began to read. She, however, once or twice removed her eyes to the flooring, and not being satisfied that all was right, she walked on the spot where the coffin lay, and trod down the boards surely. Then, returning to her chair, she took the papers yet once again, and, in a mumbling voice, she read out the following narration, as though she were by no means certain of its import:—

There was a light in the chamber; the lamp was placed on a niche, whence it threw a dull and feeble light upon the panels and floor of the apartment, and—there was absolutely nothing in the place, save a wooden cross that was placed between the two windows.

The night was dark without, and the dim light of the lamp was scarce able to penetrate the darkness of the apartment—it could not reach to the farther end. No sound was heard, till a slow measured pace neared the door, and a man, with a sinister and ferocious looking countenance, entered the room and gazed around.

"Not come yet—not come yet."

He left the room, and then returned. It was a lone room in a deserted mansion—one that had been some ages before a place of strength, and, moreover, it had withstood many a storm and hostile assault.

In about half-an-hour, another individual entered the room, and walked towards the middle; he gazed around him in mute surprise, and said, in low tone,—

"No one here! All alone. Well, it is only a trick, after all. I might have known it; and yet the man told me of so much that was true, and which none could know that I knew of, save they knew more; and to learn more is the object of my present adventure," he added, gazing on the bare walls.

At that moment, the same heavy, but slow and measured tread, was heard approaching the door.

"It is he, I suppose," said the stranger, who put his hand to his belt and felt that his sword was by his side. "What a curious step he has. He is a strange man, and a fearful one too. I am familiar with his countenance, and yet I cannot recollect where I have seen him, or anybody like him."

At that moment, the door opened, and the same man entered and stood face to face with the stranger.

"You are here!" said the man.

"I am."

"You are late."

"I could not well leave the hall unnoticed, and I did not wish my absence observed even by the servants."

"'Tis well."

"What?"

"Your presence."

"And now I am here, let me be informed of the knowledge that you possess respecting my brother, whom I believed dead."

"Murdered!" said the man, slow and solemnly.

The first stranger started.

"Know you the meaning of the word murder, Sir John Foster?"

"Yes."

"Do you know what is meant by fratricide?"

"I do."

"What?"

"It is useless to answer such questions."

"Well, I will tell you. It is the dyeing of one brother's hands in the blood of another!"

"Well, go on."

"Have you no feelings of compunction?"

"Ha, ha, ha! My good friend, you deserve a warmer reward for bringing me here on a fool's errand than any I can bestow upon you."

"'Tis well; you have no recollection—but recollection you must have: compunction and regret for the past, you have not."

"Nor any reason."

"Indeed! And yet you had a brother?"

"I had."

"He died?"

"He did."

"And by your hand."

"Liar!"

"Dare you say so? Did he not fall beneath the perfidious hand of his brother—did not your dagger drink his blood?"

"No,"

"Audacious criminal that you are, listen to me! and then I will tell you how you can commit a murder."

"I want not the information," replied Sir John Foster, "and, as you have nothing else to say, I shall leave this place."

"You will not, till I have said all I have to say."

"We will try the experiment—for I may as well go to extremes, before we do anything else."

The man returned to the door, which he closed and walked away.

"What is the meaning of this?"

"Simply that you are my prisoner, until you have heard all I wish to say."

"Oh, your prisoner! What mean you? If this be any trap, you are at least within my reach."

He rushed to the door, and endeavoured to open it, but could not; he then turned upon the other, and drew his sword.

"Put up your sword, and listen."

"Open the door."

"I will not."

"You are unarmed, and I will take your life if you do not."

"Be cautious what you do. If you take my life, you will remain here, and die a slow death; you will stay here and starve, with my stinking carcase—you will live while that corrupts—you will be able to watch its decay, while you are sinking yourself."

"Horrible!"

"The place is strongly guarded with iron bars, and the doors are well secured; the vicinity is unfrequented, and, by the time you were dead, your friends might by chance pass this building, and yet not enter it."

Sir John Foster looked aghast, but said—

"Well, and what is it you desire of me —is it money? If so, name your demand.'

"Listen to what I have to say."

"Proceed."

"You once had a brother."

"I had."

"An elder brother."

"Yes."

"And while he lived you could not enjoy the lands you now hold."

"Exactly."

"Then it was to your interest that that brother should die?"

"No—no."

"Yes; and moreover, you wished him dead, and plotted for his death."

"I did not."

"Well, listen."

"Proceed."

"Your brother—— But stay: suppose you had been that elder brother, and I the younger. Well, then, you depart on a journey, and leave me in charge of all you possess—of a wife, of children, and of all, in fact, a man could leave in the care of a brother. Well, I accompany you on the road for some leagues, and then, when in a lonely part of the road, and when you least expected it, suppose I were to draw my dagger and plunge it into your back. What would you say to the perpetrator of such an act as that?— Answer me!"

"I did no such act. This is mere madness. Who, and what are you, man?"

"You did no such act! Well, so much the better for the salvation of your soul. But suppose, further, his wife and children were seized and imprisoned, and retained there for years in a place of concealment."

"No—no, I tell you."

"'Tis well. But think you I can believe all you say?"

"Who and what are you?"

"A friend of that brother."

"Ha! ha! A friend of the dead,"

"Yes," said the stranger. "All this I know from a communication with the other world."

"You?"

"I have seen and conversed with your

brother's spirit. Would you see him? If you have the nerve you shall see him."

"No—I'll have none of this jugglery—open the door or I'll pass you through the body,"

"Ha! ha! ha!" shouted the stranger, in loud and unearthly laughter, that rang through the room with an appalling sound. "You have the wife of your brother secured in a loathsome dungeon under your own habitation, which is theirs also. Your brother's son is now a fine lad, despite the poison and miserable food that is given him daily by his uncle."

"Hell and fury!" exclaimed Sir John, in a rage: "you know too much—you must die!" and he drew his sword and rushed upon the stranger, who, with a loud and strange laugh avoided him, and stamping upon the floor, which opened at his feet, disappeared before his eyes, leaving him alone.

Sir John cursed and swore, he walked over the room and stamped, but no like result proceeded from the act, and he was alone, and, to add to his misfortune, the light went out suddenly.

Strange and unearthly music floated in the air—wild bursts of demon-like laughter filled up the intervals, and Sir John began to be overawed by the position he was in, and the singularity of the circumstances around him. The sudden disappearance of the stranger, and the knowledge he possessed, strengthened him each moment in the rapidly strengthening opinion that he was himself a being of more than ordinary power and means of obtaining it. He turned round and walked to and fro in the apartment—but what a sight met his gaze.

On the walls where these words, traced in an unearthly fire,—  .

"Sir John Foster, the murderer of his brother, and the despoiler of the orphan and the widow."

Sir John started, and tremblingly gazed upon the terrible words that burned so brightly and shone so luminously upon the wall—he could not bear to look at it, and he buried his face in his hands.

A few moments after, the scene was changed, and instead of the words he saw represented two men on horseback—he could recognize his own likeness and that of his brother. He shuddered. He drew his dagger and plunged it into his brother's back, and he fell dead at his feet—he then galloped away. Sir John groaned, and sunk on the floor in a swoon.

It was broad day when he awoke, and he arose from the floor—he had lain insensible for some hours. He shivered from cold and fear as if he had the ague—he looked around, but could see nothing but the bare walls, and then rising, he went to the door. It was closed, but it opened when he turned the lock, and Sir John gladly quitted the place to make the best of his way back to his own abode—that abode which he had so ruthlessly seized and deprived his brother's widow of and his children after having made them orphans.

Sir John was ill—he had received a great mental shock, he had become well aware that his crimes were known to others besides himself. This was what alarmed him most—he could not believe that the man with whom he had had that terrible interview was a supernatural being—no, he thought and believed that he had dealings with the spirit of darkness—that he was endowed with more than usual power —that he could obtain information by these means, and then become rich by fleecing his victims of money.

Sir John hesitated in his course—he knew not what to do, whether he would become the victim of this man, who, doubtless, would now attempt his ruin, or should he make his peace with his brother's widow. These thoughts passed rapidly through his mind, but as he felt the first impressions fade and become less urgent, he thought less of their cost, but determined to await the next thing that occurred.

The night came, and with it new horrors, for whenever he was alone and the room darkened, the following words were visible:—

"Sir John Foster, the murderer of his brother, and the despoiler of the orphan. Repent, for your day is at hand."

Much terrified at these words, he called for lights, and these seemed to charm away the demon's letters which he saw traced upon the wall.

In the middle of the night Sir John Foster awoke, and saw before him those terrible words that so much distressed him, and he began to think that a day of retribution was still at hand, and that it was even now begun. Suddenly he turned his face toward one side of the bed. He thought he observed something dark; he looked again, and became convinced that there was some one standing in the shadow of the curtains.

The curtains were drawn on one side, and he beheld a form that caused him to shrink with horror and fear. It was his own brother;—his pale and ghastly form standing by his bedside. He was pale and thin, his cheeks hollow, and his eyes sunken, his teeth closed, as in death, and his lips parted and drawn tightly over the jaw.

He gazed with his large glaring eyes upon the trembling man, and pointed to his blood-stained garments, and, placing his hand upon a ghastly wound, he withdrew a dagger that had been left in it. The blood flowed afresh, and as the figure slowly moved away, it threw the dagger upon the coverlid of the bed.

Sir John fainted, but the next day when he awoke, he saw the bloody dagger still on his bed; it had been his own, and the very weapon which he had used in the murder of his brother.

This discovery caused his death; he took ill, and kept his bed until he died; but he released his brother's widow and restored her to her proper station, and restored to his nephew his father's estates and valuables,

When this was done, and he had asked forgiveness of the church and of those whom he had injured so greatly, he resigned himself to his fate, and died from the effects of remorse and terror.

---

## CHAPTER XXVII.

### THE MEETING BETWEEN THE OSTLER AND TROUBLED TOM.—AN UNWILLING WITNESS.

WHEN Dame Strangeways had finished the perusal of the papers which we have laid before the reader, she dropped them from her hand upon the floor, and sat for some moments in a fixed attitude, as if to move ever so slight would be to disturb the current of thought by whish she strove to connect that narrative with some of the particulars of her past career.

"It is very strange," she said, "over and over again have I perused these papers, but even yet I cannot well trace the precise manner in which they bear upon other incidents, that seem to contradict them; a feeling as of madness overpowers me, and all thought becomes vague and unsatisfactory. I must banish it, for, if I do not, there can be but one result, and that is too terrible to think of—it is the cell of a maniac—the cell of a maniac!"

She pronounced these words with terrific energy, and then springing to her feet, she exclaimed,—

"The old resource and the only one — the only one."

She went to the cupboard from whence she had taken the pistol which had been lent to the ostler, and laying her hand upon a small phial, she held it up to the light.

The words, "Laudanum, poison," were upon the phial, and she smiled as they caught her eye.

"Potent drug to others," she said, "long habit has made you familiar to me. I fear you not, you cannot injure me. Poison, you have been to me a friend; for by your aid alone have I succeeded in stilling those pangs, which else must have driven me to despair; and long ere this to death. Welcome, welcome, most welcome."

The old woman placed the bottle to her lips, and took enough of the deadly drug that must have insured the destruction of any one else not largely used to indulge in it.

It soon had its effect; reflection for the time was stilled, the agony of memory or remorse was felt no more. She laid herself upon the couch which was in the further corner of the apartment, and sunk into a deep and dreamless repose: and thus we will leave her to follow the footsteps of him in whose fate we cannot but feel greatly interested, were it only that he has been made the victim of so much falsehood and calumny.

With a heavy heart Jem made his way from the cottage of Dame Strangeways to the Morton Arms. The words of the old woman repeatedly occurred to him, namely, that no one would believe the account he gave of what he had seen in the church, because he was considered by far too interested a party in the proceedings to be trusted in the evidence he might give concerning them.

"But that shall not deter me, even that shall not deter me. I will speak the truth, although there shall not be found one who may believe it. I will relate that which has occurred fully and distinctly, and more than ever has it convinced me that the mendicant with whom I had some words at the inn, was the real murderer. I must and will discover him."

"Oh, dear me!" said a voice, as if coming from some person a few paces behind him, "what a trouble everything is to be sure: it's a trouble to live, and I wouldn't mind dying but for the trouble of that."

There could be no doubt in the world from whom these words proceeded Troubled Tom, of course, gave utterance to them, and as Jem now paused he was soon by his side.

"Why, Tom," said Jem, "it's an odd thing to see you up and stirring at such an hour as this."

"Oh, you may say that; it's a dreadful trouble and no mistake; but somehow or another nobody will let anybody rest anywhere."

"Indeed, how is that?"

"Now, how can you ask? You know I tried to go to sleep last night in Togg's pig-stye, and just as I got comfortably off, somebody comes and treads slap on my stomach, There's a trouble."

"Oh," said Jem, "and a very good thing they did, too, for it put suspicion into the right channel, and cleared one of the false charge of murdering the gentleman at the inn."

"Oh, did it? It's a very great trouble for all that, though. Well, to-day, Jem, you know, I turns the matter over in my own mind, and, after a good deal of trouble, I recollected the churchyard was called the place of rest, and was sacred to ever so many people's repose, and so there I went."

"Indeed?"

"Oh, to be sure, anything for a quiet life, you know; so down I lay, as comfortable as possible, atween Mrs. Meggs and Squire Mutton's family graves. ' She sleeps in peace,' was on one blessed tombstone, and ' Lightly tread the hallowed ground,' was on the other. Now, wouldn't you have thought one was safe to be quiet there for a few hours?"

"I certainly should, Tom."

"Ah, so did I; there was the trouble on it, it wasn't a go at all. I tell you what it is, there's somebody going about as don't mind the trouble, and making it their business to tread slap upon the outside of my inside whenever I'm going to sleep."

"You don't mean that, Tom?"

"Don't I? I just got comfortably off again, when whack somebody comes, and blessed if I didn't think I was smashed, and away they goes again like a bumshell; but in course I was waked up—there's the trouble."

"What, in the churchyard, Tom?"

"Ah, to be sure, atween the graves of Mrs. ——"

"Well, well, never mind the graves. Are you quite sure you were sleeping in the churchyard and trodden upon by some one?"

"Ask my blessed inside that has been in a blessed state of trouble ever since."

"You much surprise me; but this may be important. You can swear to this fact, Tom, I presume?"

"Oh, dear no, oh, no. More trouble — more trouble!"

"A trouble? Surely, surely, Tom, you cannot think it a trouble to give any evidence in your power that may go towards thoroughly clearing me of an imputation that otherwise would, perhaps, in some people's opinions, stick to me for life. I did not expect this of you, Tom."

"I didn't say I wouldn't do it," said Tom. "What are you a growling about? I didn't say I wouldn't."

"But you complained of the trouble."

"Well, now, I think the least you can do is to let a fellow growl and grumble as long as he likes. It is a trouble. There's no mistake about that—it is a trouble. There's nothing but trouble in all the world, only, of course, we must do things, and ——"

"And what?"

"I don't know. I was a-going to say something, but it's such a trouble, that's the fact, that I can't. Oh dear, how I should like a fellow as didn't mind trouble, to take me about where I was forced to go, in a wheelbarrow, always with a lot of straw in it. Oh dear!"

"Would you indeed? And where would you sleep, Tom."

"Oh, when night comed, or I got sleepy, I'd tell him to shoot me down in some place where I shouldn't be disturbed, you know; but there's no peace anywhere, not even in the blessed churchyard, where I thought nobody would have interfered with me."

Certainly one would have imagined you were safe there, Tom."

"Ah, to be sure."

"But I am glad you were not, because it convinces me that he whom I have seen was no creation of the imagination, but a being of flesh and blood like ourselves."

"Yes; and bones too," groaned Tom.

"Bones?"

"Ah, to be sure. Flesh and blood only could never have gived me that dig in the stomach as I had. There was lots o' bones too, you may depend, or else I shouldn't have had it. I feels it now: Lots of trouble. Dollops o' inconwenience.

Despite his mind being so seriously full of those events which had placed him in so strange and anomalous a position, Jem could not forbear laughing at the extent to which Troubled Tom carried his notions of laziness.

"Well, Tom," he said, "by some strange chance you seem to be always at hand to confirm something that I want confirmed. It has been jeeringly said to me that what I have to tell of my adventures in the church to-night would not be believed because my own word only could be given in support of the narration."

"Lor! Adventures in a church?"

"Yes. Strange ones too."

"Much trouble?"

"I did not think of that."

"Ah, well; that shows the difference there is between people; I think o'nothink ese. Howsomdever, don't tell me, for I'm deadful tired, and don't want the trouble of listening at all to nothink."

"I have no wish to tell you. All I want of you is, that you will tell me where to find you when I want you to confirm by your evidence the statement which I shall now fully make."

"Where shall I be. Oh, let me see : I shall be in Farmer Lake's pea-field fast asleep, I hope. You'll find me there."

"But a pea-field is rather an awkward place to find you in, Tom."

"Well, then, I'll get down by old Jacob

THE DISAPPEARANCE OF THE UNKNOWN FROM SIR JOHN FORSTER.

Green's three new hay-stacks. You'll find me somewhere thereabouts, and no mistake."

"Very good.',

"Oh, dear me! Oh, for that blessed wheelbarrow as I mentioned and some fellow as didn't mind trouble, now, to wheel me about continually wherever I wanted all for to go to."

Tom left Jem with a lounging pace, which the latter looked after with some such feelings of curiosity as a man would look at some curious specimen of natural history with which he was tolerably familiar, but yet which could never cease to interest him.

"Well," he said; "I wonder that fellow don't find it a deal too much trouble to live. Eating and drinking must be quite a toil to him. I suppose, some day or other, he will lay himself down and starve, because it will be too much trouble to get up again. Well, well; we are not all made alike, and Troubled Tom, I dare say, thinks people who take a deal of trouble are very great fools indeed for their pains."

Upon the whole, though, Jem was well enough pleased with his night's adventure, although it had come to no practical result. It, howerer, proved several things: first, it unquestionably proved to his own mind that the individual who had behaved with so much audacity was the murderer of the young traveller. Secondly, it went far to prove that that unprincipled scoundrel lingered in the neighbourhood for some object or another which was concealed in mystery; but by doing so he of course afforded a much better chance of his capture.

Then it occurred to Jem, as it certainly would to one of so acute a mind as he possessed, that the murderer must have some place of concealment about the churchyard somewhere, or he never could have disappeared with such marvellous activity as he had done.

"In broad daylight," said Jem, "I will have a thorough hunt about that spot, and I feel as if to a certainty I should make now some important discovery. I know my man, and I know the spot about which he hides, so that now I shall go to the search with a much greater prospect of success then before."

Thus did Jem strive to hearten himself up to a continual prosecution of that inquiry which was to be in its results of so much importance to him, and every new fact concerning which was sure to place his innocence in a still stronger light than before.

Being innocent, anything that came forward in the shape of truthful evidence was certain to tell for him, and hence the undertaking he had commenced promised to become eventually gratifying in its results.

The morning was now beginning to show itself in all its beauty, and a glorious one it was—a morning which seemed as if it came on purpose to cheer the heart of that wrongfully suspected man, and to convince him that there was a Heaven of light, and beauty, and goodness above, that would yet make his guiltlessness apparent to all beholders.

The warm sun now rose and showed itself in the east, and floods of light were beaming upon the green fields, and upon the gracefully waving corn-fields, or upon the stubble that yet remained to be turned over by the plough. The white mists were curling up before the influence of his beams, and the trees, here and there, shone above the moving sea of vapour.

Each moment, however, lightened the load, and the vapour began to ascend and become invisible, and waft in the ambient air the sweets it had gathered from the fields. At that time the harvest field had a beautiful and joyous appearance, because it was a time of abundance and plenty, when there were more beauties to be seen than at any other.

It is plesant to walk in the fields before the sun has risen long enough to deprive the flowers and leaves of the pendant drops that glisten from their boughs, and add a new and lovely feature to the landscape. At that hour of the morning, too, :he blossoms in the hedge-rows look more beautiful and more lovely than at any other. The senses are fresh, and the day is new, and the capacity for enjoyment is greater.

The bird's cheerful note is heard from bush to bush, and from spray to spray. The lark soars high, and not a sound can fill the air equal to the outpouring flood of music with which he makes the welkin ring for a great distance. Innumerable are the points from which descends this sweet melody; from each field, each spot you tread on, start some of the songsters on the alert, and each one adds his song to the general harmony that rings out wherever you go.

Such was the morning, one of beauty and joy, though joy reigned not in the hearts of all below. Some where sad, and complained of their fate, and the evil they were compelled to endure amid so much cause for general rejoicing. The skies shone with the full lustre of the celestial beauties that are sometimes noticed before the night clouds have entirely disappeared, and the sun risen high in the heavens themselves.

## CHAPTER XXVIII.

THE INTERVIEW WHICH THE MENDICANT HAD HAD WITH CAPTAIN MORTON.—THE DEMAND AND THE EVASION OF IT.—THE THREAT.

The reader will probably recollect that, at a time when Captain Morton and his lady were in the midst of their great anxiety for fear some claimant was about to arise for the possession of Mabel, who had become so dear to them, both on account of her many excellent qualities, and the friendless position in which she was placed, the mendicant upon whose shoulders popular opinion was correctly enough fastening the odium of the dreadful crime of murder which had been committed at the inn, had had the insolence to come to the Hall and demand to see Captain Morton.

We now propose to lay before our readers what occurred at that interview which Captain Morton's fears, rather by far than his inclination, prompted him to afford the ruffian. When we say fears, of course, we do not mean for one moment to impute anything in the shape of personal cowardice to such a man as Morton, whose courage stood on too high a pinnacle to be assailed; but his anxieties, intense as they were concerning Mabel, made him fear that if, without knowing the extent of the information, and the power possessed over her destiny by this mendicant, he refused to see him, he might at once take some steps highly inimical to the peace of the whole family.

After, therefore, a very slight hesitation, indeed, he determined upon seeing this man, and endeavouring, by fair means or by foul, to discover who and what he was. He ordered him to be shown into a small room on the ground floor, leading from which was another apartment, from which there was no outlet, at all events in the shape of a door. When Captain Morton entered the apartment in which the mendicant was, he found him standing near to the door of this inner room, and apparently in as free an attitude as he could assume, as if he knew not how quickly he might be called upon for some vigorous action in the shape of self-defence.

"This is," said Captain Morton, who spoke first, "a piece of the most unparalleled audacity."

"Indeed !" was the reply in tones halfsubdued, and half-insolent. "Indeed ! And yet you come at my demand to see you, because you do not know but I may have abundant power to touch you nearly."

"It is useless to disguise from you," said Morton, "that I consider you a scoundrel, capable of inventing any tale to the prejudice of anybody. Sometimes we feel inclined to put up with an evil merely of a pecuniary character rather than encounter others of a different tendency. I presume your errand here is for money ?"

"Indeed, Captain Morton," said the mendicant, "you have a ready wit. A young girl, named Mabel, resides under your roof."

"Well ?"

"It is well, so far as it has gone, I have no doubt; but it remains to be seen if it continues well. She is not your child."

"Not my child ?"

"Come, come, this is useless prevarication. It can do no good between us whatever. We shall come to an agreement, or we shall not ; but concerning the facts there can and need be no dispute. You remember the battle of Waterloo ?"

"All who look back on that great struggle cannot forget it."

"True. You and I were both there, and when the fight was done, or nearly so, you lay wounded on the field."

"Well, well."

"Yes, you got well."

"Do not quibble upon my words. If you have aught to tell, tell it at once, or let this interview terminate."

"Don't be too hasty, captain, By-theby, you were only lieutenant then. I am coming to the point. A wounded officer placed the child in your care, who you now call Mabel, and would fain pass off as your own. It is of no use your denying these facts. I was an eye-witness. Let that suffice."

"Be you whom you may, I have neither desire nor skill to deny what is true; but, after all this, I would just say, what then ?"

"Indeed ! That is your only remark.— What then ?—I will tell you. A claimant may come for the child."

"Well ?"

"Oh, you think that well, do you ? but I can see through the disguise of calmness. You are troubled, Captain Morton. You shrink and tremble. You have wound your affections round the girl. You dread even that she should know she has no right to call you by the name of father. Now, you see, from what I have told you, that I can, if it so please me, blazon this story over the whole of England ; ay, over the whole of Europe. You cannot prevent me, and then what situation will you find yourself in, if some worthy claimant should come and say, 'That child is mine ?'"

"If this is all you have to say," replied Captain Morton, "you might have spared yourself the trouble, as well as the risk of this interview."

"Risk ? But no matter. Let that pass. What if some one were to step forward at once and claim her, who was so poor, so criminal, so despicable, that it would break her heart, and yours, too, to find that she had such a father ? Ha ! that touches you, and why may it not happen ? Such a fellow as would terrify her to look at : and who shall say I may not find such a one for her, Captain Morton ?"

"Come to your errand," said Morton. "You have still something to say, about which you hesitate, and to which this is merely an exordium. Come to your errand at once. I do not wish to disguise from you that your presence here is anything but welcome."

No, ' said the fellow, with a bitter

laugh, "I am aware of that. I come with unwelcome truths in my mouth."

"You speak as if you were one who came here armed with some accusation against me. What could even a parent of the girl you mention say, but that I had done almost more than a parent's duty by her?"

"Nobody disputes that. I don't come here to find fault about your conduct to the girl; my business is of another nature. I want money."

"Now, indeed, you have come to the point."

"Well, it's point we all come to, from the king to the beggar. How much a-year will you give me to let this matter rest, and leave you in undisturbed possession of Mabel?"

"How much a-year!"

"Yes, to be sure. I'd rather have a handsome annuity than a large sum down at once. I know my own failings, and one of them consists of a facility in getting through money; so, I have considered the matter, and think it better to have it by degrees, and, consequently, I prefer an annuity to anything else."

This was said with so much coolness and *sang froid*, that for a moment or two Captain Morton was silent from downright astonishment at the insolence of the fellow. This silence the individual either mistook, or affected to do so, for some sort of acquiescence in his demand, and he said,—

"Well, as we have got thus far comfortably, and without any disputing, suppose, now, we go to the more important consideration of settling what the actual amount shall be."

"Hold!" said the captain; "we have not got so far without dispute. You say, or rather, you insinuate, that you know the parents of Mabel:—I do not, but if you really do, and will impart to me that information, I will give you a reward of twenty pounds."

"Twenty what?"

"Twenty pounds."

"D—n your assurance! Twenty pounds! Why, how long do you suppose twenty pounds would last a man like me? I tell you what it is, Captain Morton—you either do, or you do not, wish to keep Miss Mabel all to yourself. If you do, I am the only man in existence who can enable you to do so, and I will be well paid. If you do not, say so at once, and leave me to adopt my own course."

"Candidly, I do," said Morton; "but, if the parents of Mabel are in a rank of life such as would enable her to associate pleasurably with them, God forbid that I shall

step between a parent and a child, however much my heart would be grieved at her loss. Besides, under such circumstances it would not be a loss, for such people would consult her happiness by leaving her with those who had so long stood to her in the place of natural protectors."

"Ah, that's all very well, captain, if such were the case. Under those circumstances you would have seen nothing of me; but it is because the friends of Mabel, who can claim her, are not such as she or you would much admire, that I think you will consider it worth your while to come down handsomely to me for the sake of keeping them separate."

"This you must prove to me."

"Prove! D—n it, I'll swear it."

"I would not take your oath. If you can give me such particulars and such references as shall convince me beyond the shadow of a doubt that this child of the battle-field—whom I swore to protect, and whom, Heaven knows, I have done my duty by—has parents, or a parent, who may be in such a position of life, not through poverty, for that can be amended, but through character, that her heart would be shocked to own them, I will pay you for keeping her from them, or rather, them from her, till she is of age, and can act for herself, legally as well as precisely."

"Well," said the fellow, with rather a look of discomfiture, "you take tolerably high ground in this affair."

"Why should I not?"

"Please yourself; please yourself."

"Be assured that I mean to do so."

"Good; but that is a game which too can play at. Now, I tell you, Captain Morton, that you must, if you deal with me at all, take my word for what I state; and then you must deal tolerably handsomely."

"Your word?—the word of a ruffian such as you are?"

"Yes. Ain't my word as good as another's because my coat is not?"

"I promise that our conference is not likely to lead to any satisfactory result, and, therefore, I shall apprehend you at once, and have you lodged in gaol."

As he spoke, Morton darted forward with the hope of seizing the fellow; but it would appear as if he had had a remote suspicion that such might be the termination of the conference, for he eluded the captain, and made his way into the inner room in an instant, closing the door of communication so quickly and so adroitly, that he struck Morton in the face with it, and caused him to recoil a step or two.

It was only for a moment, however, that Morton was thus foiled, and darting forward again, he quickly had the door open; but when he entered the room, he saw by the wide open window that such must have been the way by which the fellow had escaped, and to conclude which way he had gone was a matter of impossibility.

The first thought of the captain was to alarm the servants, and endeavour to find the fellow before he left the grounds; but, upon second consideration, he made up his mind to let him go, considering it probable, that now he was disappointed, he should hear of him no more.

----

## CHAPTER XXIX.

THE ADVENTURE OF THE MURDERER WITH THE CUNNING OFFICER FROM LONDON.— THE CAPTURE AND THE AGREEMENT.

THE country magistrates, after being convinced of the innocence of Jem the ostler, and having discharged him, in consequence of feeling very dissatisfied with the state of the case, and the useless efforts of their own rural police in tracing the murderer, had resolved upon sending a report of the case to the head police-office, London, with a request that they would send down some instruction as to how they had better proceed, and also for some one who was well qualified to act under such emergencies. This application was answered promptly by the chief magistrate sending down an officer on whom they could reply, and whose reputation for sagacity was great, with orders to act as he should see occasion in the affair.

Mr. Samuel Lewis, more familiarly as he was wont to be called at the office, Sam Lewis, was an artful card in his way. Sagacity or cunning sat beneath his hat when he had it on, and no raven looking into a gutter could look with greater gravity and silence than Mr. Samuel Lewis. He was very stout—he had been a strong-made man, about the middle height, but now he had grown fat, and his scarlet waistcoat served as a sort of shelter beneath which his broad ribbed smalls took refuge, and were seldom seen by their owner, save when he had occasion to dust his top boots.

His coat was blue, with a velvet collar, and he was evidently in the habit of tucking his cuffs up, for they would scarce keep down, and they were never buttoned. His neck was guarded by a belcher handkerchief, and his hat was a broad topped beaver of the old school, what used to be vulgarly termed a "bell nobbed un." His great, or over-coat, was what is called snuff-colour, which is rather indefinite, seeing that snuff is of divers colours, and so any one might be the colour alluded to. It was a respectable brown, with buttons on the hips behind, intimating in the tailor's opinion, that the waist ought to be there, and nature was a fool for not putting it there.

Thus dressed, Mr. Sam Lewis was a cunning and a clever man in his own opinion. He could scarce say or do more than other people, and by way of attaining a character for cunning sagacity, which he had discernment enough to see he could never earn, he said less, and did less than other people. This was one way of obtaining a character, and few could have succeeded it; but Sam Lewis looked grave, screwed up his mouth, cocked his eye, and looked so earnest, that it made a deep impression upon everybody.

Good fortune often attends those who may certainly be deserving it, yet who would never have achieved anything by their own sagacity; and it did attend upon Sam Lewis, and on one or two occasions he disappointed men, business men, who declared he was a fool, and would fail, for he did succeed in doing one or two clever and acceptable things to the magistracy. Any blunder he might make would pass now as an instance of unavoidable failure, when if he failed, nobody else could, and therefore he could not be blamed. In truth, he was one whom, some of the more steady and elderly magistrates pronounced to be the model of an officer.

However, down came Mr. Samuel Lewis, and he introduced himself to the chief magistrate, that is to say, he who had taken the greatest interest, and had busied himself in the affair the most. He presented a letter of introduction, which the learned magistrate read, and then turning his gaze upon Mr. Lewis, he said—

"You are from London, I see?"

Mr. Lewis nodded, gave a suppressed laugh, and said—

"I am."

"From Bow-street?"

"Yes."

"You are an officer of some experience in your business, I believe?"

"I have been an officer for some years, and have had some difficult jobs, and I have succeeded in a good many."

"In others failed?"

"In the same way as a man would fall through a bridge when it broke under him."

"Because it wasn't strong enough to bear him ?"

"No," said the cunning Mr. Lewis, slowly ; "because my information was too rotten to bear me forward."

"Well, well," said the magistrate, looking hard at the officer, and scarce knowing what to make of the man, though he thought he would not have been posted from London if he had not been capable, and he proceeded.—"You have heard of the particulars of this affair, I daresay ?"

"I have."

"Then you know all I can tell you ?"

The officer paused, and, after shaking his hat too and fro upon his head for some time, at length he said—

"The man was pursued—was he not ?"

"Yes."

"And lost ?"

"He was, else you had not been sent for."

"I can understand," said Mr. Lewis; "we don't do things in so great a hurry in London. Have the goodness to give me all the information I want, and in the order I ask it."

The magistrate leaned back in his chair, and looked at Lewis, as much as to say—

"You be d—d !" but he abstained, and thought the officer must be a clever man, as he had such assurance, and said—

"Go on."

"Where was he missed ?"

"Somewhere in the churchyard."

"Indeed; and has the churchyard not been watched by any one ?"

"No."

"Ah! we do these things different in London."

"Very likely."

"That is the last that has been heard or seen of the supposed culprit ?"

"Yes, it is."

"Very well. The scent is cold, and I have the greatest disadvantages to struggle with ; but I must take it up where it was last lost, and try back. You see ?"

"Yes."

"I may pick up a trace that may enable me to carry out my views of the subject, and probably secure the gentleman."

"Indeed."

"I am not sure. I can't tell. Time alone shows these things; they ain't as easy to do as signing peace-warrants."

"Well, do as you will," said the magistrate. "You see how the case stands, and how we are at a loss to find the man who is supposed to have committed the murder."

"There has been one man take up upon suspicion—has there not ?"

"There has, but been discharged, as being quit innocent."

"Of that you are satisfied ?"

"I am satisfied of that."

"Then I shall not trouble my mind about that affair," said the officer.

"Exactly."

"Then I shall bid you good afternoon, and set about my plans at once."

"The sooner the better."

"I wish I had been here on the occasion ; that would have been the best by far."

"It would so ; but we have now to make the best of a bad job, and in doing so you will exert your skill and sagacity for which you are known."

They parted. Mr. Samuel Lewis walked from the abode of justice, and putting his hand into the pocket of his greatcoat, in which he felt the favourite of his walks— his staff—he twined his fingers around it, and muttered, as he came in sight of the churchyard—

"They should have kept watch there for some time ; these old places have plenty of hiding holes about. I'll show them what one of the London officers can do when they are done up."

With these self-congratulatory thoughts, Mr. Sam Lewis entered the churchyard. As he entered, the sun's rays were glaring across the churchyard, and shone upon the windows with strength and intensity. The windows seemed all on fire, and reflected back the setting rays.

"Ah," said Lewis, as he looked round the yard, "there ain't much here, but there's no knowing what may or what may not be ; I'll occupy a post that will at least give me time for reflection, and conceal myself from the observation of any one who may come."

Having looked about for some time for the best place to screen himself, he found two graves that were raised tolerably high with others at either end, so as to effectually screen him, and yet he could be perfectly cognizant of all that occurred in the churchyard.

"Here's room for meditation," said Sam, as he sat down between the gravestones, carefully doubling the tails of his great coat to save himself from the effects of the damp.

He sat down, and began to watch, but whether it was that he had partaken of anything calculated to keep up the circulation under difficulties, or not, it would he difficult to say, but the vigilant officer fell asleep.

Just at that moment, a man entered the churchyard. With a rapid, but cautious glance, he looked around, and then made a hasty stride or two, and suddenly stopped as his eye lighted on the sleeping officer. Lashing a coil of cord which he had around him, he made a running noose, which he carefully slipped over the officer's head, and then going to a distance, and drawing the cord over the chink of a stone so as to serve as a pulley, he gave it a sudden jerk to awaken the officer.

"Hilloa! hilloa!" said the officer; "I'll take (a jerk)—you into (jerk)—custody (jerk). I'm (jerk)—officer (jerk)! I'm choking (jerk)! Mer—(jerk) cy!"

"Be still, and lay quiet," said a voice.

"You rascal, I'll take you into (jerk)—"

The officer flourished his staff of office, but found himself unable to speak, and was choking in earnest; he accordingly gave in.

The mendicant came up and secured him, saying, that if he moved or stirred, he was a dead man, and then he began to strip, and dress him in the officer's clothes.

"When they send you from London again," said the mendicant, when he had put on every article of dress the officer had, save his breeches, stockings, and shirt, "they should send an easy chair and a nurse."

The officer boiled with anger, but he couldn't help himself. There was he, who had been sent from London a specimen of superior intelligence and vigilance, at the mercy of the man he was intent upon taking. He was to be an example to them, and a pretty example he was, too.

When the mendicant had finished his toilet, he took the staff, and, flourishing it, he said—

"Now, I'll take you into custody."

At the same time he turned the officer over, and seized his hands, and then dragged him to the tombstone beneath the window of the church, where Jem, the ostler at the Morton Arms, had suddenly missed him. Here he thrust some loose rubbish on one side, and put him in head first.

"For the love of Heaven, don't put me here, I shall starve to death among dead men's bones."

The mendicant made no reply, but, dealing him a blow on the only part within reach, he covered the place over again, and left the officer to his fate, and immediately quitted the churchyard.

Suddenly there came the cry of "Stop him! stop him!" and, on looking, he saw several men who were pursuing another, more out of wantonness than aught else. He drew his staff, and ran towards the man, but, when they met, the recognition was mutual.

"What, is it you?" was the cry of both.

"For God's sake, save me!"

"This way," said the mendicant, jumping a ditch that was out of sight of the people behind, and in another moment they were safe in the wildness of a wood.

"Have you turned Bow-street?"

"Ha, ha! have you a mind to help me? I was going to London for a pal."

"I'll do anything for drink and money."

"Then come this way."

They both walked further into the wood, and after earestly conversing for about an hour, the confederates shook hands, saying—

"It is an agreement then?"

"Yes, I promise."

---

## CHAPTER XXX.

THE LETTER TO MABEL.—RAFFERTY BROLICKBONES BECOMES TOO INGENI-OUS.—THE MEETING IN THE WILDER-NESS.

THESE two very questionable characters now having settled in their own minds some diabolical plan, no doubt inimical to the peace of persons who were, compared to them, as angels to devils, began to look cautiously from the covert they had chosen for the purpose of ascertaining if it would be safe to emerge therefrom.

"All's right," said he, whom we have called the mendicant, but who was named by his companion Solme, and, therefore, whom we may as well call by that name, whether it be or not his correct one—"all's right, Ned; there's no one near now, and if there were, this costume that I am in would be amply sufficient disguise to pro-tect me and enable me to protect you."

"Well, mind you stick by me, Solme. I don't want, if I can help it, to get into the hands of these infernal rustics. When once they catch a fellow, they father upon him all the horse-stealing, and hen-roost robbing, and burglaries that have happened for the last twelve months."

"And perhaps they would be right enough in your case, Ned," said Solme.

"No, d—n me, no. London got too hot, you see, to hold me, that was the fact, and I came down here to rusticate a little, that was all, and more for the benefit of the change of air than anything else, I can assure you."

"Why could you not keep yourself quiet then?"

"Oh, you know what's bred in the bone will not come out of the flesh. Keep myself quiet, indeed!—stuff! I only took from a farmer's wife the proceeds of her poultry and eggs as she was coming from market, when the old dame set up such a yelping, as if she were not sensible of the honour of being robbed by me, Dashing Ned of Newington."

"Do you still, then, retain your old name?"

"I do."

"And I daresay deserve it. Now, go to the village, and just on the outskirts of it, on this side, you will see a little huckster's shop, where they sell everything; get there a sheet of paper, a bottle of ink, and a pen."

"Do you think I shall be safe?"

"Quite. The pursuit has gone the other way altogether, and died off in the distance, as you are aware."

"But you haven't told me why you can't go yourself."

"There is a special reason. An accident has happened in the village, and they seem inclined to blame me for it."

"Whew! A bad accident?"

"The worst."

"Oh, I understand. Well, these things will happen. It isn't the first throat you have cut by a good many, if you did it that way. Ah, this puts me now in mind of old times and scenes. Don't you remember——"

"Silence! What the devil is there in my past career that I want to be reminded of by you?"

"Not much, I daresay. A shilling?"

"What?"

"A shilling to get the learned utensils for writing. Do you think I walk about with money jingling in my pockets to go of everybody's errands, and pay besides?"

"Pshaw! You are the same reckless man you ever were. You will joke when you come to the gallows."

"Which you won't live to see, old friend; for the hangman will be cheated if you don't go first. I always give way to my betters. I wouldn't be hung before you, no, not on any account, I wouldn't."

With a half swaggering, half crouching gait, the fellow now walked towards the village on the errand which the other had specified to him.

For some moments Solme stood, with his arms folded, looking after the brutal companion of his former iniquities, and then, in a suppressed voice, he said—

"This is fortunate so far. This fellow I know well. He is perfectly safe and unscrupulous. He cares not what he does, provided there be no appearance of personal danger: if there be, he is the veriest cur that ever stepped. I hate him. He shall not live very long; but while he does exist, he may as well, as indeed he shall, be useful to me. I could not, single-handed, with any chance of safety, have carried on the game I wish here."

The evening was very rapidly darkening now, and it was scarcely requisite for Solme to seek the refuge of the wilderness, and, accordingly, he walked out to where he could command equally a view of the village and of the mansion of Captain Morton in the distance. There were lights at some of the windows of the house, and as he listened attentively, and the night was very still, he could just hear the tinkling sounds of a pianoforte, which was being played in the house. A dark malicious expression came across his face, and he raised his hand threateningly, as he said—

"Soon will I take care that those sounds of mirth and music shall be exchanged for those of lamentation in that house. Not for long shall any one smile within its precincts, for I will take her away who seems to be the life and the soul of that household, and none shall know whither she has gone. Then, at length, shall I have fulfilled some portion of a vow I made years since, when I scarcely expected such an opportunity as now seems would arise to enable me to keep it."

He was silent for some moments, and then he added—

"That proud soldier, Captain Morton, might have bought me off for a time, but he would not. I want money, and I must and will have it. He shall yet find that he must disburse to me, and not so pleasantly as he might have done. Mabel—Mabel! so they call you, Mabel, do they, child of fate, as you are? Minion of destiny! you have been fortunate, but the day of your prosperity is near its close. You shall yet, as I have sworn, pay the penalty of those indignities that have been heaped upon me by her who is no more, and by him who is no more—by him for whose sake I hate a whole nation, and for whose offences towards me I have declared war against a whole nation."

He waved his hand impetuously as he spoke, and evidently became so wild and so excited from the recollection of bygone events, that he forgot all the caution of his disposition, and began to speak in a tone of voice loud enough to have reached the ears of any one tolerably near to him.

"I will yet keep my oath of vengeance," he said; "I swore it thrice. I swore it

once at the foot of the altar—I swore it once when lying helpless from injuries inflicted by the hand of him whom I hated most off all men—once on the blood red battle field, and now I will keep that oath so sworn. For the fourth time I swear it now—vengeance on——"

"Lord bless me! what's the row now?" interposed Ned, as he suddenly made his appearance.

Solme gave a cry of alarm, and crouched down among the trees, as he said in a startled voice—

"Who goes there?"

"Why, it's me, to be sure, Dashing Ned, of Newington. What are you blazing away about now? Why, I could hear your voice half-a-mile off."

"I—I know not what induced me to be so indiscreet. But I am glad you have come. At times the thoughts and the impulses of the past get the better of all judgment."

"Do they, indeed? D—d if you ain't a greater fool than I thought you."

"Hold! Do not provoke me. I am in no mood to be annoyed, and can take no jests."

"Indeed! What an infernal tail our cat has got."

"Peace, fool, peace! Have you the writing materials?"

"Yes, donkey; I have."

"Ned, if you persist in this strain, we had better part at once friends while we may. I cannot endure it."

"You called me a fool; and if you give bowls you must expect rubbers, you know. You be civil, and I'll be polite."

"Well—well, I was wrong. I know I was wrong. But you ought by this time to be aware of my hasty temperament."

"That's no excuse. A fellow can't go through the world abusing and snarling at everybody and everything, on the ground of having a hasty temperament, although a good many try it on, but it won't do with me. If you have a bad temper, you must do the best you can to control it, for I won't put up with it, I can tell you; so as we have a little piece of business to settle in this neighbourhood, it's just as well to settle it at first as at last how we mean to agree."

These words were uttered with considerable carelessness, if they wanted the more dignified character of business, and they had upon him to whom they were addressed all the effect which a stern resistance generally has upon those persons who want to abuse everybody, and to say what they please without a reply, on the ground of having a hasty temper.

Solme was for once civil, and we recommend our readers, when they come across a character of that irascible description, to give him a good setting down, and not to put up with it for a moment. In nine cases out of ten, such men are subdued with the greatest possible ease, and at once succumb to any one who has the firmness to make the attempt.

"Peace, peace," said Solme. "No more of this. Let us now proceed to business at once, if you please. Have you the means of procuring a light?"

"Yes. Never without."

"That will do, then. The few words I want to write can be easily done behind one of the old trees, and if the glimmer of the light is seen, it can be extinguished too quickly to cause us any danger."

"But I say, Solme."

"What, what?"

"How the deuce are we to get something to eat and drink?"

"You can go to the village and buy something, as you have these writing materials."

"I beg your pardon there, I didn't buy 'em."

"Not buy them?"

"No. The old woman placed 'em all before me on the counter, and then I thought it would be a thousand pities to pay for them, so I just took up a mop that was close at hand, and knocked her down, but I forgot at the moment how difficult it was to stun an old woman, and so I very nearly had the whole village after me on the instant."

"What folly, for the sake of a few pence."

"It wasn't for the sake of the few pence."

"What then?"

"Principle, principle. D—n the pence, but sheer principle forbade me to pay for anything, when I could manage to prig it."

"You are a fool, as you always were, and will bring your own neck into jeopardy. As for now, where and how you are to get food I cannot tell you, unless you feel disposed to go to the next village or market town to this one for it, since you have deprived yourself of the advantage of going so near. But I cannot waste time now upon you. Be quiet for a short time while I write the letter, of which I wish you to be the messenger."

A light was soon procured, and with some difficulty, on account of the awkward situation he was placed in for any such employment, Solme succeeded in writing the following epistle:—

"To her who is commonly named Mabel Morton.

"Mabel, you are not the child of him who would fain, because he has done much injury to your parents, make you think so You, of course, wish to know to whom you owe your being. You shall know so from the only person who now will tell you, or who really feels a disinterested interest in your welfare. If to-morrow evening at dusk you will be on the margin of the lake, at a spot where a cluster of trees come so near to the water that one, a fir, has loosened itself from the bank, and seems ready each moment to fall into the lake, you shall know all. If you doubt that there be any truth in this, ask Rafferty Brolickbones, the servant to Captain Morton, who knows well that you are not a child of Morton's, although he knows not who you really are."

Having written this note as carefully as he could, under existing circumstances, he folded it, and turning to his companion, he said—

"Now, Ned, you see yon house, many of the windows of which are lit up from within?"

"Yes."

"I want you to take this note there, and endeavour to bribe one of the servants to place it in the hands of her to whom it is addressed."

"Bribe one of them? What am I to give him?"

"Anything. Here is gold."

"The deuce there is! You are mighty generous all of a sudden."

"The stake I play for now is a heavy one, and I will not risk the losing it for the sake of some of the petty contingent expenses. I daresay one of the gold pieces will suffice, but if one will not, you must try two."

"You won't spend three?"

"Yes, or three."

"Very good. You are the man for my money. That's the way to do business. I'm off. Never fear but your letter will find its way to its place of destination. You have supplied me with golden arguments to use to John the footman or Sally the maid. It will be all right, you may depend."

"I hope it may. Remember I shall await your return on this spot with some impatience. Now go at once."

Ned, or Dashing Ned of Newington, as he appeared to be pleased to call himself, at once started on his errand, and the reader, from what he already knows of that gentleman's character, can easily imagine that he made up his mind none of the gold which he had received from Solme should find its way back into that very enterprising individual's pocket again.

Several times, while he waited the return of his companion, the man who was thus plotting against the peace of mind of the beautiful and accomplished girl who was so happy in her present situation, seemed inclined, as the full gush of memory came over him, to indulge in those strange violent speeches and invectives, which he had been interrupted in by his companion in crime. There was no feeling of remorse in any of the feelings that came over him; on the contrary, the state of mental excitement and exultation which he appeared to be in, arose evidently from what he considered the near consummation of a vengence which for so many years he had cherished in his heart without having the means of carrying out.

What the circumstances were exactly which had produced such a feeling of bitterness in the mind of that man, we shall eventually know. The story is a dark and fearful one—one in which, perhaps, he justly had some cause of complaint, but not one which for one moment could justify the vitiation of intellect that induced him now to carry his revenge beyond the grave, and seek to recompense himself for injuries he had received, or supposed to have received, from the dead, by a persecution as unjust as it was cowardly, when we consider its object, of the living. But men of such malignant passions do not reason thus: they only consult the dictates of a heart that is at war with every one nearly or intimately connected with whatever gives them uneasiness, and they can find no delight but in the infliction of misery and pain upon some one, however innocent that one may be of the causes of their mental uneasiness.

What his precise line of conduct, as regarded Mabel, was to be, we shall soon preceive, for evil fortune is hurrying that innocent and unsuspecting creature to a sad condition, such as, in her wildest dreams of fortune's vicissitudes, she could never have pictured to herself. It appeared now

that every circumstance was combining to deprive poor Mabel of that efficient protection she had hitherto enjoyed.

When Dashing Ned of Newington reached the house of Captain Morton, he found that the captain was from home, by an inquiry which he made of a stupid servant who answered him.

"Oh, then," said Ned, "here's a note that the captain wants Miss Mabel to have at once, that's all. Can you give it her?"

"To be sure I can. What's to hinder me?"

"Very good ; I can see that you are a clever fellow."

Away went Ned quite satisfied that he had done his errand, and the note was duly taken to Mabel, who, as may well be supposed, was both surprised and affected at its contents.

And now she committed the greatest error of judgment she could, under the existing circumstances, at all commit. Instead of waiting patiently until Captain Morton came home, and at once showing him the note she had received, and leaving the matter in his hands, she at once caught at the suggestion it contained, and, in her anxiety and impatience to ascertain the truth, she sought out Rafferty Brolickbones. This individual was in a room which contained various fire-arms, and a unique collection of weapons of the chase, which it had been a hobby of Captain Morton for some time to collect, and which were all placed under the care of Rofferty, who derived much pleasure from keeping them in order.

He was now solacing himself with a song and a jug of ale, while he was freeing from the accumulated rust that hung about it some ancient weapon, which had been probably in active use in those days when man made war with the brute inhabitants of the forest and the wilderness for his daily bread.

"Troth, Miss Mabel," he said, "and is that you ? It's good for bad eyes is the sight of you."

"Rafferty, I have come to ask you a question."

"A question, Miss Mabel? And it's me would like to hear the question the likes of you would put to Rafferty Brolickbones he would not answer."

"Rafferty, am I not Captain Morton's child ?"

The old rusty piece of iron dropped from the old sergent's hand, and he screwed up his mouth to a most portentous whistle, as he looked askance at the beautiful but anxious countenance of Mabel.

"Oh, Rafferty," she added, "tell me,

tell me truely, if such be the case or not: am I the child of Captain Morton, or am I not? Tell me at once, and truely. To doubt on such a point is too terrible."

Rafferty looked up to the ceiling, and then down to the floor, in great perplexity. Indeed, to any one but Mabel is hesitation would have been a sufficient answer; but poor Mabel had not the art to read any one's countenance, and she only waited with clasped hands and a most anxious expression of face, for what reply Rafferty would make to her.

"Why, you see, Miss Mabel—why, you see," answered Rafferty, "taking all things, you understand, Miss Mabel, into consideration—a-hem! you see, that's it, you see, Miss Mabel."

"But, Rafferty?"

"Darling, what is it?"

"Answer my question, and answer it truely. Am I, or am I not, the child of Captain Morton? Oh, tell me at once!"

"Who said you wasn't, Miss Mabel?"

"Read this."

"Is it read this? Mabel, what thief o' the world wrote this same, if it's in here you find who you ain't, Miss Mabel? Just let me drop across him, that's all, and no sort of mistake in all the world, my darling. Oh, the rapparree."

Rafferty Brolickbones was rather a slow reader of writing, but he contrived to make out the general purport of what was said in the note to Mabel, and when he had done so, he gave it back to her, saying,—

"Sorrow to the hand that wrote that, and sorrow will be to the side of the top of his head, Miss Mabel, if he comes across me."

"Is it true?"

"True! Oh, is it true? You want to know is it true? Oh, that's it—is it true, you want to know? Of course you want to know. It's mighty natural that you should want to know."

"Rafferty, are you determined upon driving me distracted? If you are, you need but pursue the course you are now adopting, and you will succeed in your object. I ever considered you as a kind and indulgent friend, one to whom I would never appeal in vain, but now I see my error."

"Error, Miss Mabel? Ha, bedad, and the holy poker, and all the holy fire-irons, you are wrong there. Just show me the mighty illigent fire, and the great sheet of water I wouldn't go through any day of the week, Miss Mabel, to do you some service."

"Then why refuse me the simple request I now make?"

"Simple?"

"Yes; surely nothing can be more simple than telling me if I am, to your knowledge, the child of Captain Morton, or not?"

"By the holy, hasn't he done a father's duty by you?"

"He has. God knows he has, but yet my heart yearns to know the truth."

"Miss Mabel, will you give a poor fellow half an hour to gather his wits about him, and think a little before he gives an answer?"

"Yes, yes."

"Then come to me, or I will come to you, Miss Mabel, at the end of that time, and in the meantime I ll think."

"I will come to you, Rafferty, and let me implore you to keep this affair a profound secret from every one."

"You needn't be after telling me that," said Rafferty. "I wouldn't tell it to the Pope himself."

## CHAPTER XXXI.

RAFFERTY'S SCHEME.—THE DETERMINATION TO KEEP THE APPOINTMENT BY THE LAKE.

"Oh, murder," said Rafferty, when he found himself alone. "Oh, murder and turf, here's a pretty piece of business. Miss Mabel will be after finding out that she isn't Miss Mabel at all, at all."

Poor Rafferty was so cut up at the prospect of what might occur, that probably he made a more serious face upon the occasion than he had ever done since the memorable morning on the field of Waterloo, when he had that, as he called it, "mighty illigant" cut on the head that disabled him from action.

"What's to be done? That's the question, as the fellow with the mullygrubs in the play says. Oh, murder, here's a mighty large kettle of fish. I shall be finding out, some day, who knows, bad luck to me, that I ain't Rafferty Brolickbones at all, at all, but somebody else, and no mistake."

Accustomed, however, to prompt action as was Rafferty, from his early military habits, he was not likely to remain long lamenting without endeavouring, at all events, to adopt some means of overcoming the difficulties which presented themselves, so now he set to work enumerating them.

"Let's see," he said; "first and foremost, if I don't do anything in this affair, she'll be going to the captain, and then he will have the vexation of having to tell her all about it, which will be the death of him; and then she won't be satisfied till she sees the fellow who wrote the note to her. If she don't go and meet him, he'll be bothering her again, and who knows but he's the same thief of the world who has given us all some trouble before now? Rafferty, my boy, you must take him prisoner; and, by the holy, so I will—so I will."

When once this idea got fair possession of Rafferty's mind, it grew, each moment, into stronger plausibility, and at length he said—

"She shall go, just to decoy the fellow to the place, and I'll take good care to be there, and be down upon him mighty convenient—that'll do. She may as well hear what he's got to say, and so may I; she'll be satisfied, I can tell the captain, and we can send the thief of the world to prison. Murder! Here she comes."

The impatience of Mabel had induced her to make a very short half-hour of it, and now, with anxiety depicted on every feature of her countenance, she again sought Rafferty in his room of curiosities, to learn what determination he had come to, on a subject which, to her, was of such paramount importance.

"Well, Rafferty," she said, "what have you to tell me?"

"Why, Miss Mabel, say nothing to nobody, but keep the appointment named in the letter, and depend upon it Miss Mabel, I won't be far off.'

"You will accompany me?"

"Not exactly that, darling; but I'll be near enough, that woe be to him who gives a cross look to you, or endeavours to hurt a hair of your head. Trust me for that, Miss Mabel."

"I know well that I may, Rafferty; I am glad that such is your determination, and I will act in accordance with it."

The time had come, and Mabel, with timid steps, sought the spot where she was to meet the individual who had written her the mysterious letter. Her agitation did not arise from personal fear, for she relied upon the promise of protection that Brolickbones had made her—that he would be at hand to secure her against any violence. Her feelings arose rather from another source— her agitation and timidity were caused by the fear of what might be disclosed to her by the stranger whom she was to meet.

The sun had sunk an hour, and the shades of evening had become too thick to throw a shadow upon the earth, and nothing could be discerned distinctly as she walked along, at any distance from her, save the deep gloom of the trees and hedges, which, at a distance, seemed palpable shadows, and could not be traced to their various ramifications as in day-light.

There was yet a white light running along the western horizon, and yet it was not light enough to have any effect where she was—the light might be seen, but not felt.

The sombre, quiet hour that merges into the darkness of night, is one that can be enjoyed by those whose minds are at ease, and have no agitating thought, no fears, to disturb the equanimity of the soul; but such was not Mabel's case; she had an internal fear of the consequences of the interview, that she would hear something that would disturb her peace of mind. And yet she felt herself urged on to meet the mysterious unknown, and learn what, perhaps, she would not otherwise know.

She came within sight of the place; there was the clump of trees all plain and palpable—the lake beyond them, against which they stood in strong relief. And there, too, stood, or rather leaned over the waters, the old fir tree, whose domain had been encroached upon by the waters; its roots were loosened, and it hung bending over the destroying element, as if even resisting, with all its force, the irresistible power that was drawing it downwards, and which would ere long swallow it up.

All was hushed and quiet, no sound met her ear, the stillness of death reigned around; she paused for a moment or two —and then slowly advanced towards the appointed spot. As she slowly paced the short distance that lay between her and the old fir tree, she listened for any sound, but not so much as a falling leaf disturbed the quietude of the scene; all was calm and silent, not even the sighing of the evening breeze met her ears. She would have given anything for a sound of any kind—silence seemed, then, to her, irksome and fearful.

She now approached the tree; it was a large one, and must have stood there many years—and the wonder was, how it had contrived to resist the inclination to fall into the lake, for its weight must have been enormous, and the loosened fibres and roots must have lost much of their hold and strength in the earth. But there was the tree, and there it hung.

Mabel looked around carefully, but she could not see any one near—she felt uneasy, and again looked around with much anxiety.

"Oh, if he should not come," she muttered to herself, "and I have been brought here to endure all this misery and anxiety —but, see! what is this moving? it must be him."

She stooped low, so as to catch the figure against the water, to enable her to distinguish whether it were human or not. After a careful examination she could make out the figure of a man, who was creeping low by the bank, and coming cautiously towards her, at a slow pace. She trembled excessively, and looked around, as if to ascertain where her promised protection could come from, and clasped her hands—

"Heaven and my innocence protect and guard me !" she uttered, aloud.

"Don't yer be alarmed, Miss Mabel, dear—it's only I—Brolickbones—you know. Here am I—oh, it's a nice little place that I have got here—bedad, it was made to fit me, I think."

"You, Brolickbones ! where are you?" exclaimed Mabel, looking up, for the sounds seemed to come from the air above rather than anywhere else.

"Yes, Miss Mabel, dear ; here am I in the tree sure. Bedad, where would you find sich a place as this to hide in, eh?"

"In the tree ! Oh, you are near, then."

"Yes, I am, dear Miss Mabel. Don't yer be frightened at the ugly brute, but hear what he has to say. I thought I'd conceal myself here, and hear all about it myself, and then I'd be down upon the wagabone like a hawk upon a wagtail."

As he spoke, Brolickbones drew himself up out of the hollow of the tree, and looked out upon Mabel, who was now aware of her protector's place of concealment, and felt reassured.

"I am glad you are there," she said. "The place is lonely, and I know not who comes."

"Bedad, that's what I said to myself, and, therefore, ye see, I got here in time to distrain upon the tenants, and turn 'em adrift, sure. It's the first time I ever turned process-server, bedad !"

"Tenants, Brolickbones—what tenants?"

"The owls."

"Owls !"

"Yes ; there was more than one individual, sure—it was a whole family of 'em; and it was a fight for possession, and I thought sure, I should have had to give in. They are real born devils, I assure you, Miss Mabel, dear."

"Are you sure you have not been observed when you came here?"

"The devil a bit, for I came here in the broad daylight, and there was nobody stirring, save the fish. But whist—whist, darlint; do you hear anything?"

"Nothing; but I can see a man coming this way, very cautiously; he's creeping yonder by the bank. Take care he don't hear you."

"He can't do that, dear; he is a thief of the world, but he can't hear all that way; and if he should ax ye, all ye have to say is, that you thought it a good time to say yer prayers."

"Well, but it will be better not to let him have any suspicion at all, Brolickbones; for if he have any reason to fear detection, he will not come near, thinking he may be secured."

"Secured, bedad ! Ay—ay, I've made prisoners before to-day, anyhow; but it is as well not to let other people know all we know. I'll be quiet and safe enough, anyhow."

"Do so, Brolickbones. I am glad you are there; and yet I cannot help feeling a dreadful palpitation at my breast, and I could sink."

"Sit down on the stump of the tree," said her faithful ally, "and just, for the love of Heaven, keep your eyes on the ugly thief; and when he's within fifty yards, do not miss him for the love of Heaven, or we shall lose all the sport."

"Well—well, I will watch; but do not speak so loud, nor shake the tree, or that will be remarked also, and then all precautions would be useless."

"Then I'll take care; but there's no more fear of my shaking the tree than there is of the tree's walking away to the church-yard. It was a good thought of mine to get in here."

"It was."

"Is he coming?"

"Yes, but very slow. He is looking and peering about in every direction, as if he were suspicious; and now he is listening and kneeling down."

"What's he afraid of, I wonder?" said Brolickbones. "He must have done something that he's afraid of being seen about."

"Perhaps he contemplates doing some deed of wickedness," said Mabel.

"Bedad, and if he does, he'll have an old Waterloo man a top of him in no time at all, at all. I haven't lost my old tricks of fence yet, Miss Mabel; and I'll warrant he'll be a good man an he once escape from me, anyhow, at all."

The man during this time had come from the wood, but had chosen the path by the margin of the lake and below the bank. He had crept slowly and cautiously, watching the wood and the pathway alternately, to prevent any surprise, and as though he were fearful of an ambuscade or an attempt to surprise him.

From the spot whence he came, indeed along the whole line of pathway, he had the old fir-tree in view, and could see all around it as he came towards her; he could see Mabel very distinctly because of the tree, and the fact that as she stood there was no water to be seen, and, therefore, the tree stood like a dusky bush.

Thus the man crept slowly forward, suspicious of everything he saw, and cautious to a degree of anything that stood out and appeared a dark mass, that he couldn't very well discover in the distance.

"Och, bedad," said Brolickbones, "but the thief of the world is afraid of somebody's catching him; if he knew I was here, I expect he'd take the water and swim on t'other side like a stoat."

"He comes very slowly."

"Slowly— by Jasus, I think the tree would grow as fast, and by the time he gets here I shall have become grown into the tree."

"Hush—not so loud, Brolickbones."

The evening was dark and dusky; and nothing could well be seen as yet, and a slight mist now began to collect, such as usually rises in the fall of the year, the lake itself aiding materially in this. This mist now began to obscure everything, and that which could have been seen distinctly from the spot where they were now standing, was now very indistinct, and sometimes wholly obscured.

"I'm like patience on a monument, smiling at grief, Miss Mabel; or, maybe, an owl in an ivy bush—but, lord, some of the owls might return and try and turn me out."

"Hush! hush! here he comes; for mercy's sake, conceal yourself, or all is lost."

"I'm dumb as an angel in effigy," said Brolickbones, as he drew himself in, and got quite out of sight in the interior of the fir-tree.

He had scarcely assumed that position when Mabel saw the man approaching towards her; she rose up, and in another moment the man made a rush and stood up before her. There was a strange emotion playing around the heart of Mabel when she saw that mysterious man standing erect before her. Her power of speech was gone, and though she was anxious, most anxious to ascertain the secret of her birth, yet she found the courage that buoyed her up now fled, and a feeling of terror and even despair sat at her heart.

She felt that what she was about to learn might probably be something that would for ever blight those moments of happiness and innocence she enjoyed. How could she tell but that some dreadful secret might not be communicated to her which would cause her heart to feel more and more the loneliness she now felt—a secret that might weigh upon her mind like some crime—that might cast a shadow upon the sunniest passages of that life she might be reasonably supposed to long and hope for —such life as she was formed to enjoy might be turned to a perpetual gloom into which could creep no sunny moments.

These thoughts passed with vividness and rapidity before her, and now she could see, more than ever, with clearness, what might or might not be the result of the very occurrence she so much desired should take place. The pause that ensued lasted some moments, and the man who thus strangly appeared before her stood examining her features with a scrutinizing glance, as if he were making some observations from which he might gather some kind of intimation of the nature of the character he had to encounter.

---

## CHAPTER XXXII.

THE DREADFUL DISCLOSURE.—THE ATTEMPTED FLIGHT.—THE FATE OF RAFFERTY, AND THE CAPTURE OF MABEL.

MABEL trembled, despite the assurance she had of Rafferty's protection, as the stranger gazed upon her, and she recognised in him the same man who had before alarmed her so much in the wilderness, when the faithful dog had probably been the means of saving her from his violence. But the alarm she now felt was only of a momentary character. She had made up her mind that she would give the man this meeting. It was upon a subject of by far too anxious a character for her to shrink from. She only wished that in whatever revelation he made to her, he would be quick, in order that she might the sooner free herself from the terror of his presence.

"You are punctual," he said, in a low voice.

"I want no compliments," she said. "I want no words whatever with you, but upon the subject mentioned in your note to me, for I presume it came from you. You invite me to this spot under promise of making to me a certain statement. Make it, and let me go."

"Indeed. You are peremptory."

"Once, and for all, I will tell you I will not engage in conversation with you."

"Girl, you know not what you say."

"I begin to fear I was wrong in coming here."

"If you had not come, you would have had cause to regret the not coming, the longest day you had to live."

"Wherefore?"

"Ay, that is the question. Do you fancy, now, that I have taken some trouble, and more danger, to meet you here to tell you something, unless I expected something in return for the information?"

"I did not think of this," said Mabel, despairingly, "or I would not have come upon such an errand. I have no reward to give you, and, therefore, will now return as I came, without the information you have promised me."

"Do you mean to say you are kept so close by the captain, that you have no money at all? Come, come, girl, don't tell me. You can lay your hands on some pounds, I daresay. Go back to the house, and get me what money you can. When you return, I undertake to receive it, let its amount be what it may, as a payment for the secret I—and I alone—con disclose to you."

"No," said Mabel, "no; that is a course which I cannot adopt. It is sufficient for me that you want money, and that I have none to give you. Here let our conference end at once."

"No—not so. If it's the real fact that you have no money, why, of course, I can't have it of you, and so I must tell you, and you shall owe me whatever reward, at a future time, you feel inclined to give me, for the information, which you cannot estimate too highly. Come now, Mabel Morton, as you call yourself, I am able, from a little knowledge of your early history, to surprise you a little. You don't like me, but I am not so bad a fellow as I look, and we shall be good friends, I know, in due time."

Mabel did not think it necessary to make any reply to this speech, either in assent or in contradiction to it, although she could not but feel insulted that that man should talk of ever becoming better acquainted with her—he, a man whom she despised—a man whom she looked upon as so far beneath her in rank, that nothing but the most urgent circumstances could have induced her to associate herself for a moment in conversation with him.

"You do not answer," he said.

"I came here to listen," said Mabel. "I have nothing to say."

"I cannot help thinking that you must have been tutored by some one, or you would not exhibit this indifference of manner. Still no answer! Mabel, you will live to repent of this indifference."

"I repent already," she said, "leaving my home to meet one who has nothing to tell me. If you will not commence the narrative you promised, I will return again, and forget the delusive promise which lured me here."

The man now seemed to be quite convinced that as yet there was no chance whatever of getting her into anything like a familiar conversation, so he gave up the attempt at once, saying, in an off-hand manner, as if, after all, it mattered not to him,—

"Well, well—be it so. I will now proceed to tell you the circumstances connected with your coming into the possession of Captain Morton."

By the reflected light from the surface of the lake, he could just see sufficient of the beautiful features of Mabel to be well aware that her interest was painfully excited, even if her attitude had not convinced him of that fact. In a voice to which he now evidently tried to impart solemnity and importance, he said,—

"Captain Morton was lying wounded on the field of Waterloo. The fight was over, and he had no prospect but to die a lingering death on that plain of carnage, when one, who to all appearance was worse hurt than he, contrived to crawl close to him, and in agonised accents to speak."

Poor Mabel breathed thickly, and a faintness came over her, as she strove to say, without being able,—

"And—and that was my father?"

The sound she uttered was too inarticulate to be understood, and Solme continued his story, the truth from the falsehood of which the reader, from his pre-knowledge of the circumstances, will be easily able to detect.

"This wounded man had in his arms a young child, in fact, a mere infant, and believing himself, in consequence of the severe nature of his wounds, to be at the point of death, he sought to place that infant in the first apparently kind and friendly hands he could find. He spoke to Captain Morton; he implored him by every tie of humanity, human and divine, to save the child from death on that blood-stained field."

"And—and he promised?"

THE ASSAULT UPON MABEL BY THE MENDICANT.

"To nobly perform that promise!" ejaculated Mabel, as tears gushed from her eyes. "To nobly perform it!"

"No one doubts that much," added the mendicant. "You are, of course, too good a judge of that yourself for any one to venture to contradict you. The wounded Captain Morton accepted the trust."

"Yes, yes; and he who gave it him?"

"Dropped insensible upon the field of carnage, satisfied that he had done what he could under the circumstances for that child, who was his only care. Captain Morton was taken up by the British forces and carefully attended to at Brussels. He brought the child to England with him, and from that time forthwith he has, by all means in his power, sought to prevent those who had a right to know, from hearing if she were alive or dead. I need not say, Mabel, that you are the child."

"But tell me——"

"What?"

"Did he who gave the charge to Captain Morton expire on the field? Did he live not to know how nobly Morton had fulfilled his trust? Tell me that, and I will thank you from my soul."

"That is your question?"

"It is. Oh, tell me—tell me."

"That person, who consigned all that was dear to him in charge to the English officer, Captain Morton, I have told you, sank down exhausted on the field of battle."

"Yes, yes; but did he live?"

"Mabel, what matters it to thee?"

"What matters it! Oh, God! can any one suppose me to be so insensible to those most sacred ties which bind a parent to a child, and a child to a parent, as to be indifferent on such a subject?"

"He was your father."

"My heart told me so. Oh, tell me, lives he now? Tell me that. Having told me so much, it would be fiendlike to tell me no more. Yet stay, why do I implore so much of you? Captain Morton, finding what I know, will now tell me all. Yes, he, my second parent—he who has so nobly filled the place of father in my heart, he will now tell me all."

"Hold ! There is one difficulty in the way of Captain Morton telling you more than I have now told you."

"Difficulty !"

"Yes. He does not know more, although he dreads more. I am the only living soul in the world who can give you the information you require. I am the only human being who can bring forward proofs that what I assert is no fable. I tell you, Mabel, that from my lips you must hear all, or never hear it."

Bewildered by what she had heard already, and not knowing what to do or what to think, poor Mabel found herself enduring the most cruel tortures of suspense, and yet totally unable to find a means of ending them. It was impossible but what, at some chance periods of her life, something should occur to induce the belief in her mind that there was considerable mystery attached to her birth ; and the tale she now had heard but imperfectly, seemed, in its details, but too probable a one.

Besides, what he who had told her so much already now insisted on, might, indeed, be true, namely, that from him, and him only, could she hope to learn the particulars of her birth, and what name she was really entitled to bear. The idea of leaving him, and so foregoing such valuable information now to her peace, she could not entertain, and she now made to him an appeal which would have melted any heart less stubborn than that of that desperate and vicious man.

"Can you," she said, "withhold such information from a daughter who longs to know if her father lives? Oh, if you have a heart susceptible of feeling, think what must be the anxiety I am now enduring. I have for many years been anxious to learn the fate of my father—that father whom I have not known or seen since I was able to distinguish form or feature ; tell me if he lives ; my heart yearns for the knowledge, though it should cost me the severest pang to learn what I would fain not know. Tell me, I implore, —I entreat of you, tell me, does he yet live?"

"He did live."

"Did? Does he do so now—does he live now? That is what I most desire to know. Oh, in the name of all that is holy, tell me, oh, tell me, does he live?"

"And why should I tell you? wherefore would you know? Can you desire to see one who is unknown to you, save in name?—nay, you cannot surely desire so much?"

"I do, I do ; indeed I do. My very heart pants to know if he who gave me life lives. Yes, nature cannot be dead. You, too, must at one time have felt love for those who called you son—you must have loved them ; then tell me, by all you hold dear and holy, by all you ever held sacred—tell me, I beseech you, if he lives; on my knees I beg of you to tell me this."

The man seemed moved ; at least a sigh escaped him, and he seemed to feel the appeal. Mabel seized the favourable impression, and proceeded—

"Oh, do not let your heart be hardened; let it feel some of those tender sympathies which it must at one time, at least, have felt, and which it will again. Tell me, oh, tell me, does my father yet live?"

There was a pause, and the man, who had listened to her with downcast look, suddenly raised his eyes to her face, and in low accents, he said—

"He does live."

"He does live!" exclaimed Mabel clasping her hands; a flash of joy for the moment illumined her countenance, but she was unable to say more then.

"Yes, he lives."

"Thank Heaven, he lives!" murmured Mabel. "Yes, yes, he lives. I could almost die now without a murmur. Oh, tell me where he is. Where can I find him? Let me throw myself into his arms, and say, 'My father.' To hear him say —'daughter,' would be happiness indeed."

"Happiness !"

"Yes, happiness. Have I not for years mourned him as one whom I might never know—as one whom I ought to love and revere, and yet the object of my love and affection might never be present to me?"

"It never may."

"But surely you, who know so much, must know where is, and where I can find him. Amply shall you be rewarded; he would reward you, and I should be in your debt for my whole life."

"But he might not be able, or he might not be willing to do so."

"He could not—he would not. Tell me, I again implore you; do not leave me in this state of suspense. Complete the information you have given—tell me who my father is—tell me where he is, and I shall for ever bless and pray for you."

"Ah !" said the man, "you know not what you ask; you know not the consequences of such knowledge."

"I care not; all I wish is for my father; my own, my dear father."

"I say again, you know not what you ask; the knowledge may bring with it pain and sorrow. Your father, though still living, may be poor—he may be too proud to work—he may be—in short, he may be sought by hungry creditors, who seek him with the avidity of a wolf seeking its prey."

"I would stand between him and them."

"You?"

"I would; they should not touch my father. I would love and revere him, despite all the world. He would be my father, and what more could I think."

"But suppose he should be stained with crime. Suppose——"

"Hold; he could not be, I am sure. I feel a moral presentiment that such a man is not my father."

"Then you know your father?"

"I know his heart. It must be good—it must be honourable."

"Again I tell you, Mabel, that there are difficulties; you know not of difficulties you cannot foresee, and you may regret the knowledge you now seek to become possessed of."

"Oh, do not tear my heart. Surely you cannot feel satisfaction in seeing my misery. You cannot mean to harrow up my feelings by contemplating things that can never occur. Again and again I implore you to tell me who is my father, and where I may see him."

"And would you really know all this, in despite of all I have said—all the warnings I have uttered upon this subject?"

"For what came I here but to learn all this—to know what he his—to find, indeed, to find my parent?"

"Well, then, Mabel, you shall know it; you shall learn this secret, though I would have spared you the knowledge. Look up, Mabel, look up; behold me—I am your father!"

"You!" screamed Mabel, tottering back a few paces; "you my father!"

"Yes, I am he. I told you you might be sorry to find him—am I right? I told you the consequences of this knowledge might be unexpected—they are. You must now come with me; you are my child, and now you know your parent, you must not, shall not be separated from me."

"Oh! no, no; I cannot—cannot——"

"What!"

"Leave Mr. Morton thus. I must go and inform him. He must know all, too."

"You must come now," and he seized her arm; Mabel fell to the earth.

"Tunder and smoke," bawled Brolickbones from the tree; "be aisy—be aisy till I'm among you, and be after laving Miss Mabel alone, or I'll be among you in no time at all."

The mendicant started and looked up in the tree. He immediately guessed the cause, for he saw the Irishman struggling to free himself, and had nearly done so, swearing all the while, to keep Mabel in heart. Quick as thought, the mendicant placed his foot on the trunk of the tree, and then giving it a jerk with his whole might, the already tottering trunk came with a loud plash into the water, with Brolickbones and all. Then turning to the wood, he called aloud to some one, saying—

"Ho, there! now is the time, if you intend to lend a hand at all. Come, be quick, there is no one near, all is right."

In another moment a man came forward towards him, and both stood by the form of Mabel as she sat near where the tree so lately stood.

---

## CHAPTER XXXIII.

THE DISCOVERY BY JEM AND TROUBLED TOM OF THE CUNNING OFFICER IN THE VAULT.

TROUBLED TOM, always in difficulties, always disturbed, and invariably troubled to the last degree, slowly wended his way towards the village churchyard, there to seek the repose that so many were laid there to enjoy without any trouble.

"Here, at least," he said, "I ought to have quiet. I don't think I ever passed a quiet night in my life, and yet I have been at much trouble to find a place where I could lie without any disturbance; but it seems as though all the world stepped out of their way to annoy me. I tried this place once before, and then I had my stomach forced into my throat by some one who trod purposely upon me. I could almost have taken the trouble to have seized him, if he had not been in such a hurry. I am in no hurry, and never shall be, I hope."

He entered the churchyard, and began to look about for a convenient and out-of-the-way place, where he could lie without any disturbance whatever; and just as he got what he thought was a nice place, he thought he heard a groan. Tom listened, but not hearing it repeated, he said,—

"Oh, 'tis just the way with them. I

daresay I shall be disturbed, no doubt of it. Well, here goes; I'll lie down by this tomb. The old lady was dumb, and she, therefore, made no noise; and the infant under the other is said to slumber sweetly. Let me see if in such company I can sleep awhile without any more disturbance. Once in a night is enough to be disturbed; but that's less than my share. Oh, dear, what a place of trouble this world is, surely—it's a trouble to come in, a trouble to go out, and a trouble, a long trouble, to stay in. Well, for my part, I can't see the use of being born, if it's only to be troubled in this manner; but they know most about it, and it's too much trouble to think any more. I shall lie down once more, and sleep if I can."

Troubled Tom had scarce laid down before he heard again the same hollow groan which he heard before, and which was this time much louder than before.

"I thought as much," thought Tom. "No peace even in the grave; there's somebody moaning and groaning. Well, what's to come to us if we can't even sleep here in quiet? Why, even the grave stones tell lies."

Another groan came full upon his ear, and Troubled Tom rose up and listened, when it was repeated several times.

"Oh," said Tom, "somebody else is in trouble. I dare say nobody's without their troubles. Well, let's see what it is, for I can't sleep here with that groaning in my ears."

He rose, and going to the spot where he thought the sounds came from, he came to the rubbish that had been hastily kicked before the secret entrance to the vault by the mendicant before he left the church-yard in the officer's apparel.

The groans came fast, and there were some other noises, too, below, indicative that there was a living human being down there.

"Oh," thought Troubled Tom, "I never knew of this place before. Here's where the gentleman is lodged, eh? Won't Jem be glad—he'll be pleased enough. This is the gentleman who gave him so much trouble, and who nearly smashed my stomach. Oh—oh! very well—for poor Jem's sake, I must take some trouble in this affair, which will not end for months. I would I could only give a guess when it will be all over. Oh, it's a terrible trouble to do anybody a good turn."

Tom, to make sure that he was quite right, listened yet longer at the hole, and being perfectly convinced, rose up, and after scanning the churchyard, moved off, saying—

"Oh, who would think it?—it looks a nice little quiet place enough, and yet the disturbances that I have met with there would be enough to disgust a corpse, if it could only hear it."

Tom now left the churchyard by the wicket-gate, and slowly wended his way towards the Morton Arms, there to seek Jem, the ostler, and relate to him all he had heard.

Jem, who had not been idle all this while, but who had been unsuccessful in his whishes, was sitting alone, thinking over the many different occurrences that had taken place, and of the best means of capturing the man who committed the foul deed of which he had been accused.

When Troubled Tom entered the place, he looked up and saw there was something amiss, and he could not forbear say-ing—

"Well, Tom, what new trouble has be-set you now—won't they let you rest?"

"Rest, indeed! No, there's no rest on this side of the grave nor the other. No rest now, and no rest hereafter. What's to be done?"

"I can't tell you."

"Well, now, you may think it all sham in me, but, go where I will, there's always somebody or something to disturb me."

"Well?"

"But it isn't well, Jem. Now, look here—when I went to Farmer Carter's farm-yard I walked into the cow-house. I knew the cows had been in the field for some time past, and the cow-house was quite empty, and I said to myself, 'Surely nobody will come here; it's an out-of-the-way place, and always very quiet. The family are all abed; there is a chance.' Well, I went in, and what do you think?"

"I don't know what to think, Tom.

"Why, the farmer had turned a goose into the cow-house to roost."

"Indeed! It was a stray one, perhaps."

"I dare say, and had quarrelled with the rest. I didn't find it out until I had lain down, and then the brute set up a hideous noise. Well, I put it at the other end of the cow-house; but no, nothing would do, it must come back to me, and began to hiss and hiss with all its might and main. I couldn't remain there all night in that state, you know."

"Certainly not. And so you've come back to the yard to sleep."

"Yes, but not to sleep."

"What then?"

"I'd tell you, only it's a trouble. Well, I went to the churchyard again, hoping I should obtain some rest there."

"And did you?"

"Lord bless you, Jem, do you think it likely rest is to be had where something or the other is always a going on?"

"But what saw you in the churchyard, Tom?" inquired the other, with some interest.

"Nothing."

"Nothing? What made you come back here, then, if you were not disturbed?"

"I was disturbed. Just as I lay down—indeed, before I laid down—I thought I heard a groan, and began to suspect I should have an unquiet time of it, however the gravestones may speak of rest and retirement. However, I heard no more till I lay down, and fitted myself to a place quite snug and comfortable, when I heard a another groan."

"Indeed!"

"Yes, there was the groan this time plain enough, and it was followed by others as loud and distinct as you could wish. Well, do you think I could rest there?"

"Not very well; but you searched for the cause of the disturbance, surely?"

"I searched about, and at last came to a hole beneath the window, and there was some rubbish thrown loosely against a hole that led into some vaults below."

"Ay?"

"And from this place proceeded groans. I stooped and heard them distinctly; and I could hear a man move; he might be in pain, or starving, but I thought I would tell you, as it might be the person you are looking for."

"It might, indeed, Tom. It must be him. He must have got shot on the occasion I fired at him, and now he's feeling the effects of the wound. Nobody else could be there."

"No, I should think not," said Tom; "and I shouldn't have heard it at all, but I was in search of quiet, and went to the graveyard for it; but it wasn't to be had there."

"Well—well, you'll come back with me and some more to the churchyard, and show us the precise spot, Tom?"

"There," said Tom, "there's the worst of all these things; if I had said nothing about it, I shouldn't have had all this trouble. Oh, Lord—oh, Lord! where will all this end?"

"You know the interest I have in this affair, Tom," said the ostler, "and will not refuse to help an innocent man to clear himself in every man's eyes of a crime he never committed."

"There you go, you see. Well—well, it must be done, I suppose, and the sooner

it's done the better, and the sooner I shall go to bed."

"I tell you what, Tom, I'll go and get plenty of assistance, and we'll take some torches with us; the light will show us the way into the vault, and enable us to see who and what this man is."

"Very good; but there ain't any need of so many to one man."

"You don't know how little they like going to the churchyard at midnight; really, though a dozen might come very bravely, yet half that number would scarcely find courage to come."

Jem instantly set about getting together a few stout hands, and then some cords; the constable was sent for, and the sexton, in all making a company of nine or ten men. They were all ready, and set out in about ten or fifteen minutes after Troubled Tom returned to the Moreton Arm's with the information respecting the churchyard disturbance.

"We shall have him now," said the constable. "Yes; I shall take him into custody, and that will show the folly of our magistrates in sending to London for a Bow-street officer, while there were the rural police; he'll have to go back again."

"At all events," said Tom, "nobody would have found it out had it not been for me."

"And you wouldn't take more trouble about it than you could help."

"Who would take trouble?" said Tom. "I would sooner die a great deal, and yet there's much trouble in that."

By this time they came to the churchyard, and the party became silent and grave; there was a kind of awe creeping over them, and Jem and Tom were the first to enter the churchyard, and then the rest followed. They had scarcely gone a dozen steps when their ears were saluted by a loud groan; they started, and some of them looked pale.

"That's him," said Tom.

"Where—where?"

"Don't you hear him?"

"I heard a groan."

"Well, that's him," persisted Tom; "this way—here, beneath this window."

"Why, that's the very spot," muttered Jem to himself, "where I saw him disappear, and couldn't tell what had become of him."

"And here's the hole," said Tom, pointing to the ill-concealed aperture down which Sam Lewis, the cunning Bow-street officer, had been trust with such unceremoniousness.

They immediately set about clearing

the aperture, and then it was seen a man could dash down with ease and safety.

"This, then," thought Jem, "is the secret of the sudden disappearance; but now we shall have the man himself."

"Who's to go down first?" said Tom.

"You," said the constable.

"Oh, dear, no," said Tom; "I ain't a-going to give myself so much trouble."

"It's the sexton's place," said the constable.

"I know my place better," growled the sexton, "than to turn thief-catcher. Come, come, master constable, you who have the strong arm of the law to help you, you go down and take your man."

"I'm afraid there's no respect to person, or the strong arm of the law."

"Give me a torch," said Jem. He took one. "Now, follow me." And in another moment he stood in the vault beneath.

However, in going down, he jumped on the prostrate body of a man, who uttered a wild shout with the breath that was suddenly forced out of his body.

"Murder! help!" shouted the officer; "help me! help me; murder!"

"What's the matter?" shouted the constable without.

"Come down," said Jem.

Some who stood behind gave him a push, and in another moment he too had put his weight on the body of the Bow-street officer.

Tom followed, and the others too, and when they stood in the vault, Jem seized hold of the officer, and turned him over and over, and then said,—

"Why, who have we here? This fat man isn't the man. How came you here?"

"Who are you?" inquired the officer.

"Come, come, my fine fellow," said the constable, "we'll hang you on the old elm trees outside here if you resist or are insolent."

"I'm not going to resist. For God's sake, tell me who you all are."

"That would be a long catalogue; but I'm a constable, and intend to secure you."

"Constable?"

"Yes."

"Well—there, there—I'm a Bow-street officer, and I command you, in the king's name, to aid and assist me."

"Well, I'm darned!" said the constable, bursting out into a loud roar, in which he was joined by all present, "if this ain't the clever man that's come all the way from London to find out a hole in the churchyard; well I'm darned! But cheer up, old cock, it's well there's other people in

the world besides yourself, or you'd have been left to starve on old bones."

"How came you here?" said Jem.

"I'm hanged if I know; but I didn't come here of myself, you may depend upon it."

"Somebody got the better on you," said the the rural constable.

"Yes."

"And then, to secure you, put you down here?"

"Yes; and took all my clothes—save such as you see—and my staff."

"Well, that's the effect of catching a tartar—eh? But, come, let's undo him, lads; he's been long enough here, poor devil; he ain't used to our ways here. A—a officer must have his eyes open to take care of himself here, much less to make a prisoner."

The officer made no reply, he was conscious he looked very ridiculous, and merely availed himself of the rough but honest courtesy of the rustics.

Thus they all left the yard together, amid much wonder and merriment, and made their way towards the Morton Arms, promising the discomfited officer a glass of something so hot and strong that he would forget all his troubles in drinking it.

---

## CHAPTER XXXIV.

BROLICKBONES AFLOAT ON THE TREE.—RENCONTRE WITH THE WATCHERS.—THE SWIM ACROSS THE LAKE.

The sudden immersion of Rafferty Brolickbones in the water was an event that had not entered into the calculations of that individual; indeed, such a contingency had not found place in the remotest corner of his pericranium; in truth, if it had been hinted to him that such an occurence was possible, he would have doubted it, and then, as for the probability, he would have scouted it.

However, such was the fact—there was the tree and there was the water, and a strong arm had plunged both him and the tree into the stream, and it so happened that the stream which flowed through the piece of ornamental water, or lake, came away close to that side, and beneath where the grass grew it was very deep, and the stream was very strong, and hence it had worn away the bank.

When Brolickbones felt himself suddenly plunged by the force of the fall into the water, he came up with a great "Ah!" and much spluttering, and it was some minutes before he could ascertain where he was.

During this time the mendicant, as we have already described to the reader, had sufficient time to effect his purpose—that of carrying off Mabel, by the aid of his companion, Newington Ned.

It was some time before Brolickbones could so far free his head from the branches of the tree and the water to look around him, or before he could recognise the spot where he had been thrown, for the tree which had so strongly marked the spot was gone, and he scarce knew how to recognise it; but when he did, he saw that no one was near it.

"Ochone !" he exclaimed, in tones of regret and lamentation ; " och, murder ; I'll be kilt entirely ; and poor Miss Mabel, the ugly thief of a mendicant has stolen her away. Oh, by Jasus, but I'm a pretty defender and protector, sure enough ; and how did I then come to let myself be circumvented in this manner? Sure, the French never came over me in this manner; sure enough the battle had gone wrong, any how, if that had been the case."

Rafferty Brolickbones struggled against difficulties of more than one character ; the fact was, he had not entirely got clear of the trunk of the tree, and it was only with great difficulty that he got his head free of the mass, and to keep it above the water.

"Och, murder !" he exclaimed more than once, "and am I caught in this manner, to be drowned like a rat in a trap? Was it for this, faith, I came here to take care of Miss Mabel? It was a mistake altogether ; I'll never be caught in the like trap again. Where's Miss Mabel?—Oh, the ugly thief that upset the tree and me in it—sure he's no manners. I wonder where they have got to? Och, now, here's my leg stuck fast in the trunk, bad manners to it. What it does there except to keep one here, I can't say. Holy virgin ! I wish I could get my leg out and I would do——"

By dint of much thrusting he did at length get his leg free from the position in which it had been so securely held, and then he had a labour of time to remount the trunk of tree after many vain attempts to mount the branches that stood out of the water.

"Blather an ouns !" he exclaimed, "w.. the like of this ever seen ? What will become of Miss Mabel ? Oh, yer twirlegig wretch of the salt sea, which is the right side o' ye, or are ye all round alike, with neither top nor bottom ? I have tried ye, sure, all round alike."

This was said when Brolickbones found he had been immersed some six or eight times by endeavouring to sit on the branches that stood up, but which, when acted upon by his weight, turned the tree round in the water, burying that part upon which he sat to the lowest possible position, and after many attempts he found that it was perfectly impracticable.

"Well," he muttered, as he seated himself upon the trunk of the tree, "it wouldn't do to wear leathern coverables on such an excursion as this, or, by the holy mother, they'd never get them clean off again—they'd fit too tight. One sits like a goose hatching her eggs on the water, only it's a cold and moist seat, and one's legs hanging, look on either side like two saddle-bags."

The stream had carried him some distance down, and he was near the middle, and was fast going to the other side, for it ran not in a straight line through the water, but from side to side, as the nature of the bed, in fact, caused it, it being uneven.

There was Rafferty Brolickbones steering his tree across the stream with his legs as well as he was able. It was fortunate the stream did carry him to the other side, for had it not, despite all his steering with his legs, he would have long occupied a middle situation, and kept possession of the middle passage ; for though he endeavoured to use his legs as paddles, yet they had no effect, notwithstanding the fact that he did splash the water ; this was, as he afterwards expressed it, throwing dust into his own eyes, as to the facts of the case. However, he got to the other side, and after some trouble he contrived to get on land, and then he began to squeeze some of the water out of his clothes.

"The devil quench this fire," he muttered, "and brown ye with the smoke ; but little did I think of being thus caught. Oh ! Miss Mabel—Miss Mabel, what will become of ye ?"

He looked around him, and was about to rush from the spot, and had gone some yards, when he found that he had got on the wrong side of the stream.

"Ah, botheration, what a hass I am ! what do I do here ? But I'll run round, and if I should go the same way they are coming, why, sure, we shall meet. Oh, the thief of the world ; and here's a pretty pickle I'm in—spoilt my clothes. Why, if Miss Mabel ever gets over this job, she'll think what a pretty man I am for a protector ; i'faith, but I must look mighty foolish, anyhow."

Away went Rafferty Brolickbones to a place where he knew he could cross the stream, as there was a bridge; but he had some distance to go, and had many impediments to overcome before he reached that place; hedges and ditches and difficult places to make through; and there was another that he had not reckoned on at all, and that was trespassing on another man's property, and the individual was one who strictly preserved the game upon it.

Of late, poachers had been sent about the estate, and a strict watch had been kept in various places, with the hope of detecting the intruders, and two watchers were placed on the margin of the wood, where they could observe what took place for some distance, and, much to their amazement, they perceived what they concluded must be a boat, coming across the water, and one man get out of it, and begin to prowl about. This amazed the watchers, who could hardly believe their eyes; a boat they had never seen before employed for such a purpose.

"We have him now," said one; "he cannot escape. See, he's coming this way."

"Well, who would have thought it?"

"Nobody."

"This shows the necessity of having plenty of hands on the grounds."

"You are right."

"See how he runs."

"He's going to some favourite spot—the pheasant preserve, I'll be sworn."

"No doubt—the big rascal."

"There'll be a pretty capture; and won't it show how vigilant we are?"

"Won't it!"

"It will; but here he comes."

"Hist! Be quiet, or you'll alarm him."

On came Brolickbones at a round trot, little suspecting the encounter he was about to experience; on he came with a hearty good will, and was brought to a sudden stand still by a hilloa from the men.

"What now?" thought Rafferty.

"Hilloa!" shouted the men.

"Hilloa!" returned Rafferty Brolickbones to this second challenge.

"What do you do here?"

"Walking, faith."

"Then you'll walk off."

"And ain't I doing that as fast as I can?" said Brolickbones, "only you interrupted me, you bogtrotters. I was stepping out like a journeyman soap-boiler."

"But you must do that with us."

"Bedad, I've no objection to accompany you, if you are going my road."

"You must come our road," replied the game-keeper.

"Jajus, but I must attend to me own business before I can wait up you, my darling. Business before pleasure, you see, so don't be after bothering me with any more questions."

"That's cool; but you must come with us."

"That is as much as to say I mustn't attend to my own business."

"Ours is to attend upon you."

"Very well," said Rafferty, "come with me, then," and off he set at a good round pace, but he was soon seized upon by the gamekeeper, who crossed him.

"Now then," said the man, laying hold of the Irishman.

"Now then," said Brolickbones, "what do you want with me?"

"You shall see, you poaching warmint. You'll have a turn or two in the county gaol: you've been there before, I dare say."

"May be I have, and may be I haven't; but what's that to you, either way?—it's my business, and not yours."

"Oh, certainly; but you are our prisoner," said the man, and one came on one side and the other on the other.

"Very good," said Brolickbones; "but where's the coach?"

"The coach?"

"Yes, the coach."

"What coach?"

"What coach, indeed—the coach for me to ride in; for I am not going to walk upon other people's business."

"You want a cart, may be, and perhaps some time or other you'll have a cart, and that'll carry you to a dance that'll be performed from the end of a rope, and nothing to stand upon."

"You'll not find me at such an entertainment, save as a spectator, and then you will be the principal performer."

"Shall I?" said the man; "come along."

"Oh, dear, no."

"You won't come, ay?"

"Not by no means."

"Then we must make you, and that's all about it; so come along, mate; if he won't come quietly and orderly, we'll have a drag at him."

Before, however, he could well seize upon Rafferty, that individual planted such a heavy blow beneath the gamekeeper's ear, that he fell down insensible, and the assistant came in for a share of the same punishment, and he, too, was dropped on the grass as if he had been shot.

"There," said Brolickbones, "there

THE ENCOUNTER IN THE CHURCHYARD WITH THE MENDICANT.

you are both ; and now my own affairs require my presence elsewhere, so good evening."

Away went Brolickbones, but he had not gone far before he heard the game-keepers halloing after him.

"Ah, botheration," said he, "I cannot go on this way. I must go clean across again, and then they can't follow me. I can swim like a duck, and a precious goose I must have been to have been canted into the water in the way I have been ducked."

He turned on one side, and made for the stream, hard pressed by the game-keeper and his assistant, who made sure that they would now seize their man.

"Ah," thought Rafferty, "poor things, they'll only have the satisfaction of look-ing after me. They won't like to wet their skins."

Brolickbones paused a moment or two, and then, when the men were within a few yards of him, muttering in their own minds upon the capture they had made, he made a sudden plunge, and in he went.

"Well, I'm cussed," said the game-keeper, "these poachers is the hardiest set of people I ever seed ; they do anything, really anything ; but never mind, he may get drowned before he gets to the other side, and that would be one consolation."

"Yes, but I would sooner have cotched him alive; it's always best to seize such game alive, and then we can secure the reward, and show that we are of some use."

"Ay, to be sure."

In the meantime, Brolickbones breasted the stream bravely. He was a good and powerful swimmer, and he could swim with ease for a long distance; but it did require power and courage to swim across the lake; but Rafferty thought not of this, he plunged in, and soon got to mid-stream.

The stream itself carried him away a bit, but he soon recovered his place, and then, in a short while, he reached the opposite bank in safety, and when he got out on the bank, he squeezed the water out of his hair, and said,—

"Well, I have made a pretty night of it. What's to be done next?"

## CHAPTER XXXV.

THE MENDICANT AND DASHING NED CARRY OFF MABEL.—AN UNEXPECTED INCIDEN ON THE ROAD.

WHEN the mendicant, aided by Dashing Ned of Newington, had placed Mabel on horseback, they soon served themselves with the like means of flight, which they had taken care to provide themselves with, and in waiting but a short distance from the spot where the meeting was to take place.

It was not long before they quitted the spot; indeed, they were soon buried amongst the trees, for the mendicant led them through a path that was just practicable for them, though not without difficulty and disagreeables; but then it had this advantage, it led immediately from the spot through a covered and hidden track to a cross-road—one that would lead them clear of the neighbourhood, without any risk of meeting with anybody. Thus it was that Rafferty Brolickbones missed them as soon as he disentangled his head from the branches of the tree, which kept him under water and nearly choked him.

For some time Mabel was in a state of stupefaction and insensibility. Her feelings had received a severe shock, and she was almost stunned; in fact, she was not cognizant of what was going on around her. Without being perfectly in a trance or fainting fit, she was perfectly passive, and seemed incapable of thought or action.

It took her some time to recover from the stunning shock she had received, and before she had completely done so she had been carried some five miles from the place where the scene took place near the ake. In the meanwhile, the mendicant and his companion rode by her side, and urged their horses over every obstacle that came in their way, and exchanging every now and then a few sentences, whenever their position required it, or there seemed leisure to indulge in conversation.

"Well," said Ned, "you have done it, at all events; this will be a good haul for you. I wish I had been in your shoes when you came to think of this job."

"I dare say; but you know—and we are not all alike—if I have my lucky moment now, you have had yours, and if not, you may have. I have had more than ordinary risk in this affair, and it ought to pay well."

"So it ought; it ought, certainly, to turn out a lucky spec."

"If properly managed, I have hopes."

"Where will you stop to-night?"

"Upon the common."

"I see—a very good place that; it's one of the right sort of cribs, that."

"Yes; speak lower—there may be some of those d—d gamekeepers about and they may recollect such a thing as a whisper."

"Ay, but there are none about here; I have ascertained that."

"But there may be poachers, and they would have no objection to securing a good reward; and, as they know so much of the places we know, it would be bad policy if they knew anything we can say, or over-hear us."

"That's very true; but we shall soon be on the road, and then we shall hear the sound of our horses' hoofs, as they clatter over the hard roads. I hate riding in such a d—d place as this, where you are every moment in danger of being knocked off your horse by some branch of a tree; and there is no escaping bumps and contusions—my face is one mass of scratches. Couldn't you have picked out a place where we couldn't go through at all?"

"I might have done so, but I considered that was bad policy, as we might have been in more uncomfortable, though safer, quarters."

"Don't mention it," said Ned, "if you mean anything with iron bars to it."

"In truth, I do."

"That's enough; such quarters make my blood run cold. I had a very narrow escape lately, and I should be more welcome than I like, and that is saying something."

"So it is; but here we are at the end of the wood. Now, take care how you get down this bank, and across the ditch."

"A bank and a ditch, eh? That's no great comfort to an equestrian, in the dark, and enveloped in a mist. I wonder how a fox-hunt would be at night, and in the mists of autumn? I think the village doctors would pick up a twelvemonth's pay from a single hunt."

"I expect so; and, therefore, do you be careful, or you'll be in a fit state to come on with the baggage."

"Ah, d—n that, you know; it wouldn't do at all. Break my neck, but not my legs."

"Ah—ah !"

"What are you laughing at? I can't see anything very funny, if you can."

"Ah—ah—ah !"

"Well, what is it?"

"Why, the idea of your prefering a broken neck. Why, man, if you go to a certain place, you are sure to have one."

"I dare say; you think, then, they would accommodate me with a mysterious extinguisher, eh, is it not so?"

"Yes, they would oblige you with a hempen garment; so don't be melancholy, because you see it is useless. You have too many friends."

"And be cursed to them."

"So say I."

They now came to the bank, and down which they descended with much care and caution ; they succeeded in getting through the ditch also, and then they were all three on the hard, firm roadway—a cross road, to be sure, but then in half an hour's riding, at the most, they would enter the main road.

The night was perfectly fine, but there was but little moon, and that had not made its appearance. There was a white mist that hung low on the ground—heavy and wet, and made everything look gloomy and dark. Now and then, as they came to a little rising ground, they would rise above the mist, and could then see across the ocean of white vapour that lay on the earth. The tree-tops could be seen plainly, while their lower halves were completely and entirely lost to the eye ; even the road itself could not be well distinguished.

"This is a pleasant night," said Ned, "and has but one drawback."

"And what is that?"

"Why, the fog is so thick you can cut it with a knife."

"It is none the worse for that."

"I think it none the better, I assure you ; besides, my hair and whiskers are all as heavily laden as if they had been soaked in suds."

"You'll have a wash."

"That is all very well, you know, in it's way ; but you are very unsociable to-night. What is the matter with you?"

"I have serious matters to attend to."

"And are we not attending to them ? I wonder how that fool in the tree feels himself by this time ; if he ain't drowned, which I think is very likely, he will find his things will fit him before he gets home."

"Ah ! ah ! ah ! I cannot help laughing at the ease with which he went in. I had no notion the tree would have gone over so easily, and only tried it as the last and readiest thing I could do."

"His weight at the other end, you see, helped you very greatly. By George ! it was a splash, and it must have astonished him."

"Yes, his nerves were in a state of excitement, I dare say ; if he has got entangled with the tree, which is more than probable, he will be drowned."

"And a good job, too. What did he want there? It served him right."

"So it did ; but ride close on the other side. I expect the girl will be coming to now, and then there will perhaps be some little care wanted. She may not be so quiet ; but I can hardly think she will act with any great opposition."

"That will make our ride decidedly unpleasant," said Ned.

"Psha ! what are you afraid of?—You recollect the bargain, I suppose?"

"Oh, yes, I recollect all that ; but at the same time one can speak one's mind, you know—there's no tax upon words."

"There is not; though if there, were there would be very little chance of our paying the tax, would there?"

"There would be a difficulty, certainly, in the collection ; and I can't see how they could very well ascertain how much was due."

"They might compound for them, or fix such a machine as a gasometer, or something of the sort, to a man's face, and thus have a self-registering account—very pleasant."

They had come very near the high road, and Mabel, who had hitherto been passive and silent, now somewhat recovered the shock her nerves and mind had received. Thought once more was active, and her brain seemed to recover from a pressure that had been depriving her of the power of reflection, and of receiving any impressions from objects around her. By degrees, however, she began to reflect upon her situation. The speed, mysterious manner, and everything else connected with the journey, made her shudder, and more than once caused her to put the question to herself of,—

"Am I right in thus obeying a man

who tells me he is my father, and hurries me off against my will thus?"

She considered awhile; she began to reflect on the possible change that would take place in her home. What could such a man as that desire of her than to make some use of her—to serve some bad purpose, and to gain some evil object or other?

There can be but little doubt all these things made a strange and strong impression on her mind; the idea, too, of being forced away from those whom she supposed, with good reason, to regard her with kindness and affection. She now thought over the matter more coolly, and the words uttered by the mendicant to his companion were heard by her, and listened to, when they thought she was insensible, and she could not help saying to herself,—

"Such a man can never be my father; and yet he seems to be so—he is able to tell me many things that I could not otherwise know. I have no witnesses to say he is not my father, and yet, his having the means of knowing what Captain Morton knows, seems to argue that more knowledge is possessed by him. He is seemingly a criminal, and would make me the instrument of new crimes for aught I can tell. Oh, God! my knowledge, my long-desired and prayed for knowledge, is come at last; and I am likely to reap all the bitter fruits of it. I would I had never known it; though I had died of grief, I should have at least the satisfaction of painting to myself a father, whose grief would be as great as my own at our separation, and upon whom I would have thought and believed in dying, that he was the soul of honour, that his heart was tender and kind. But, no; the pleasing vision is lost—quite lost; and yet I have no other proof than this man's word for the fact. I will not believe it; and yet if it were, what love or affection can he feel when he tears me away from such friends as Captain Morton? No, no; I will not submit—I will resist. I may fail, but I shall have the satisfaction of knowing I have given no consent to this proceeding, tacit or otherwise."

They entered the main road, and put their horses to a good canter, and as the night was yet dark and misty they could see nothing; but suddenly they were startled by the sound of the horn of the guard of a coach that was evidently coming towards them.

"D—n them!" muttered the mendicant. "Keep close, Ned," he added.

"I'm here; keep on the right side, and ride on, else we may get a scrape with the coach wheels."

The horn again sounded, and the coach wheels now could be heard close at hand, and the lamps gave out a dim light.

"Now," thought Mabel, "this may be my only chance; they cannot disregard my cries, and these men will not attempt to keep me by force. Help! help! for mercy sake help! and save me from these men."

"D—n!" said Ned of Newington, "who would have thought of this? Be quiet, will you, or I'll stun you with my stick."

"Help! help! in mercy help!"

"Hilloa!" said the coachman, in a gruff voice; "stop them. What's the matter?"

"Go on, my fire-fly, with red wings; you are a pretty fellow to stop when you have his majesty's mails about you."

"Save me—save me from these men, who are dragging me I know not whither."

"Come, come, there," said the guard; "if you don't halt and give me less of your gammon, I'll put a bullet through you."

"Hold hard, Ned," said the mendicant, "let the man in red get down; I can satisfy him."

"Help!—do not leave me here with these men, who have seized me against my will, and are taking me away from my friends."

"What are they doing with you?" inquired an outside passenger.

"They have torn me from my friends, by main force, and are now carrying me away, I cannot tell where. Save me, in pity sake. Captain Morton will reward you well, I am sure."

"Come, just give up the young lady, you rascals, or I must make you," said the guard, getting down, with a pistol in one hand, and a lantern in the other.

"Not if I know it," said the mendicant.

"You won't?"

"I have had too much trouble to catch her to think of it."

"What do you mean?"

"That she's an escaped lunatic—very dangerous indeed at times, and never safe with any implement she can do mischief with; she has killed two children by putting pins in their eyes."

"Good God!" exclaimed the guard; "but where's your authority? You seem in a queer plight; you look like a beggar on horseback."

"And so would you if you had been as roughly handled as I have been; and as for my authority, why, here it is."

As he spoke he pulled out the staff he had taken from the cunning officer, and thrust it into the guard's mouth.

"Well," exclaimed the irritated guard, "you needn't cram it down my throat. I didn't ask you for anything to eat."

"Well, but here's my authority."

"You be d—d, and your authority. I don't wonder at the poor thing being sorry to go back, if this is the kind of usage she gets."

"What's the matter, Joe?" inquired the coachman of the guard.

"Oh, it's a female—a nice young woman to look at, but she's mischievous."

"Oh!"

"I assure you," said Mabel, who had been completely thrown off her guard by the cool and ready assurance of these ruffians, for she felt convinced that she had but to make such an appeal as this, and they would fly,—"I can assure you," said Mabel, "that all they have said is utterly false. These men are two criminals, and have seized me, and are bearing me away against my will. Save me, for pity's sake. As you are men, lodge me in any place of safety till the morning, and let inquiries be made."

"Our time won't allow us to do that," said the guard.

"Of course," said Ned, "she's got her tale, but we are responsible for her safe custody until we deliver her up into proper hands."

"What has she done, young man?" said a female voice inside the coach.

"She's a dangerous lunatic, ma'am," said Ned; "she has got a horrid propensity for pushing out children's and babbies' eyes with the handles of tea-spoons, and putting bulls'-eyes instead, and then telling them not to cry."

"Oh, poor things, poor things, poor things," said the guard, in a tone of mock condolence. "Push along, George—all right. We can't do any good."

And again went the horn with its sonorous sounds.

"Chip, chip," said the coachman, and smack went the whip, and they started off in the same direction as before. The wheels grated over the hard road, and the whole machine was out of sight in a very few minutes.

---

## CHAPTER XXXVI.

THE PARTY OF HORSEMEN. — ANOTHER FAILURE.—THE NIGHT RIDE.

MABEL's heart sunk within her when she saw the entire failure of her attempt to escape from the presence of those men She heard the sounds of the wheels, and the tramp of the horses' feet, and the sound of the horn, all decreasing with a melancholy and dejected air. She could not but look upon this as the most complete and entire proof of the power those men held over her.

"There," said Dashing Ned, "you see it's no use your kicking and squealing like an eel that's going to be skin'd, and would much rather not."

"What motive can you have for tearing me away from those who have been friends —nay, parents to me, and are, indeed, the only ones that I know of?"

"But I can tell you more than you already know, if I chose; but I have my reasons for doing what I do, and am not inclined to argue that matter with you; but I must say, I was not prepared to expect this kind of treatment from you. You know me now, after years of crimes and misfortunes, but that gives you no justification for your conduct. You are, to say the least of it, a very good judge of comfortable quarters, and have no relish for the society of a father who is indigent."

"It matters nothing—but there is too much of the man of violence and crime in your form, air, and appearance, to permit me to believe all you say respecting your being my parent."

"'Tis well. I shall have, however, the opportunity of teaching you somewhat differently. You cannot be wilfully unbelieving, and despite all things, I am still your father."

"Allow me to go back."

"Ay, indeed."

"I can do you no good, I can be of no help, therefore, do not involve me in misery. I have never known, nor should I ever know, any other state than that in which Captain Morton's daughter should know."

"That will do for the present. You are my child, and I have power over you, and will exert that power. Rest satisfied, for nothing more will I now say to you. Another time and place, and I may argue this question with you, but not now, and here. Ned, push on."

"With all my heart," said Ned, "for to tell you the truth, I am very tired of sitting here, and my whiskers all dripping wet; and, moreover, it isn't the pleasantest prospect, you know."

They put their horses into a round canter, and rode for some distance without meeting with any obstacle to impede them in their progress, or give them any uneasiness. Dashing Ned of Newington rode close by the side of Mabel, or a little behind, and the mendicant rode close by her, with her bridle in his hand, so that her horse was entirely under his control, and she could make no effort to escape.

"We shall not be very long," he said, to the mendicant, "before we get to the Moonrakers, and a good job, too."

"Yes, in about another mile and a-half we shall come to the road that leads across the common, and then we are safe."

"Bravo—I have many misgivings."

"What about, you fool?"

"Why, if we were to meet with any one more inclined to trouble us, we should have to cut it."

"No, no, you would never be such an arrant cur to ride off at the first sounds of danger."

"Did I?"

"You had not the means of instant escape from the coach, or I suspect you would have been off."

"If there had been any intention to hold me, or there had been too many, you would not stop yourself long, I'll bet a sovereign to a penny, talk as you will."

"Hold your clatter, will you? Listen a-head—something is coming."

Dashing Ned listened, and they could plainly distinguish the sounds of horses, and the voices of men. These sounds came clear and distinct on the night-air; though they could not see them, they could hear; but their eyes could not pierce the darkness and mist that floated around them. Everything was dim and doubtful beyond the hedge-rows, as they passed them, and the tall trees when they appeared.

The two men listened intently, and they heard the sounds increasing, and so did Mabel, but with different feelings; she failed in being able to secure the active interference or protection of the passengers of the mail-coach, and the guard and coachman, probably afraid of interfering in a matter that was of a doubtful nature. However, she determined to make another attempt, and she was, moreover, in hopes that this was some other kind of travellers, who might know Captain Morton by name and reputation, and think it worth their while to interfere actively in her behalf.

"Keep close, and say what I say," said the mendicant, "we shall have no difficulty in passing, if she screams ever so."

"Hadn't we better secure her from that noise by gagging and binding her?"

"No; I'll try her this time."

"You are wrong," said Ned; "but do what you will."

"If you make any attempt like the last to escape, it will end as the last. I shall have sufficient power to compel your obedience to me; I will use yet severer methods. I can prevent your making even a noise, or even asking assistance. Now, mark me! should you do what I tell you, it will be better for you—if not, I tell you, you will be roughly treated, and I will do the best I can to maintain my right."

They contrived to ride through the mist, and trotted onwards at a rapid pace.

"Here they come," said Ned.

"And let them come," returned his companion; "I have no need to fear them; they dare not stay me on this errand."

At that moment the voices of men, and the sounds of horses at a short distance, came full upon their ears, and they could not be twenty or thirty yards from the spot.

"Help! murder! help!"

"Hold your d—d tongue!" said Dashing Ned, "or by God I'll beat your brains in myself!"

"Hush! be quiet!"

"Help! help!"

"D——n!" muttered the mendicant; "but my turn will come by and by; filial affection, they say, is natural and inborn by you, Mabel; if that be true, you must be the most unnatural of children. Well, well, you will not be the first child that has caused the death of a parent, and I shall not be the first that has suffered from such a cause; but you may do what you will."

"In mercy, if you be men, rescue me from this situation. Help! help! help!"

The party who came up at that moment pulled up; they were a party of horsemen who were bent upon a long ride.

"Who's there?" said one of the horsemen.

"One who needs your help. In mercy protect me from these men, who are conveying me away from my friends by violence."

"Hilloa!" said one.

"What's the matter here? Some one cried for help," said another.

"Yes; 'twas a female voice."

"I cried for help. For God's sake, gentlemen, let me implore you to rescue me from the hands of these two ruffians."

The horsemen came slowly round the spot, to ascertain what was the matter; while Mabel, by a sudden movement, slipped off the horse she was on, and escaped entirely from their hands.

"D——n!" said the mendicant; "she has slipped away; lay hold of her; we shall never get her away to the asylum."

"Come, come, my good fellows, this will never do; you must not ill-use the young woman; you'll get into the county gaol."

"I have got her again," said Ned.

The fact was, Mabel, when she slipped off, went, as she believed, towards the horsemen who were near her; but Dashing Ned of Newington interposed.

"Help! murder! Save me from these ruffians! Save me! save me!"

"Leave go your hold of the women," said a gruff voice.

"Yes; when you can show a better title to compel us to do so than we can for detaining her," said the mendicant. And then he added, in a stern, authoritative voice,—"Hold her tight, Ned, and bring her back."

"Help me! help me!"

"I'm d—d!" said one of the horseman, "if these fellows don't mean murder. Let us bind them, and convey them to the next town; it is not far hence."

"Yes—yes."

"Help! for mercy's sake, help!"

The horsemen now closed in upon the whole party; and, when one of them attempted to interpose between Mabel and Ned, the mendicant jumped from his horse, and, catching her round the waist, he lifted her up, despite her cries and struggles, and placed her on the saddle.

"There," he exclaimed, "you do not get away again. I don't often have an escape."

"Save me, gentlemen, save me," she exclaimed, in piteous accents.

"What from, my good creature?" said one of the gentlemen, riding up.

"From that bad man."

"What does he want to do?"

"To convey me away."

"Where to?"

"I don't know."

"What to do?"

"I don't know; but this I know well—he is a bad man, and, therefore, capable of anything. I only wish to get back to my friends."

"A very reasonable desire, certainly."

"And who and what are you, that you would interfere and force this young creature away?"

"Ay," said Ned, "there's too much gammon in what she says, and yet there are people who are fools enough to believe anything."

"Who are you, and what do you want with her? You will get rough treatment unless you answer satisfactorily."

"Come," said the mendicant, "not too much of this, if you please; I will tell you this, I am an officer of a lunatic asylum, and this is my assistant; now, we are conveying her to the next market-town or public-house that we can find, where we can lodge her for safety during the night, and then in the morning we can adopt some other means of carrying her back again."

"She a lunatic!"

"Ay, a very determined one, too, as you would see by my clothes, if you could see me."

"God bless——"

"Who would have thought——"

"Poor young thing."

"Do not believe, gentlemen, this base fabrication—it is quite untrue."

"Indeed!"

"She'll tell you lots of other things, too, if you stay and listen."

"Where do you come from?"

"From about a dozen miles down the road," replied the mendicant.

"Was she doing mischief?"

"Not this time—we were too quick after her, and her bad—her furiously bad fit hadn't come on then, else somebody would have suffered for it, I can tell you."

"God bless me!"

"For Heaven's sake, gentlemen, do not be led away by this man who has the impudence to call me his child, and say he's my father. I do not ask for anything unreasonable. I can prove all I say —lodge me in any place of safety, until the morning, and then you'll see these cowardly fellows will not stay to claim me. Save me, gentlemen, and stop them."

"Well, that's reasonable enough, and it would be some satisfaction to all parties."

"But not to me," said the mendicant; "I should have to account for my expenses, and I can't give the time; I must be on the road early in the morning."

"But suppose we don't choose you to do so?" said one of the party.

"Then he who stops me must take the consequences upon his own head."

"And they will be visited upon your head with the haft of a riding whip."

"I give you fair notice," said the mendicant, "that if any of you attempt to stay me, or endeavour to rescue the prisoner from me, I will take that man into custody."

"Into custody?"

"Yes."

"Who are you?"

"A sworn officer—here's my staff," and at the same time he thrust the staff into the face of the individual.

"He has already made use of that staff sir," said Mabel; "but, instead of being, an offier, he's a criminal, and is going to take me away from my friends."

"Of course they are as cunning as sane people," said the mendicant, "but she has already made several attempts to escape. Look at my clothes, and see how I have been used, and look at his, and that will show you how I, therefore, have to punish her, and have received plenty myself. Look to her, Ned, else she'll be off again. I shall never be able to show myself by daylight."

"Well, well," said the gentlemen, "it is a sad thing, but it can't be helped—be humane to her."

"I will."

The party rode off.

---

### CHAPTER XXXVII.

MABEL'S REFLECTIONS DURING HER RIDE.
—A FEW WORDS, AND THE ARRIVAL
AT THE MOONRAKERS.

FEELING certain among themselves that this was no case for interference, the party considered that they had done all that humanity could require, and all that could be expected of them. Indeed, there is so much disinclination to interfere with an officer or person in authority, that they can commit any crime short of murder without being called to account. The fact is, things appear so different when coolly related in a court of justice to what they do when they are being enacted; the tone, manner, and many causes of irritation that these men have a particular felicity in producing, often betray those who do, for humanity's sake, interfere, into saying and doing what they would not say or do, but for nameless little incidents that are numerous, and singly too contemptible to be related, though at the time they were not without their effect. The insolence of tone and manner cannot be enacted before a bench. The reality never comes into their presence, and the individual who is thus betrayed, in the first place, from humanity to interfere, is betrayed also into saying or doing something that is not the proper thing, and then finds, to his annoyance, that his interference has been useless, and that he has either caused some damage to the party he would have benefitted, or he had damaged himself, or got into some troublesome scrape or other. Thus it is that no one likes interfering in any case in which an officer armed with authority is concerned, lest they should suffer, and this is reasonable enough.

The party seeing that there was an officer—for they believed him to be one, and being persuaded that the unfortunate Mabel was a lunatic, and her tale forestalled, they did not entertain a shadow of a doubt but that the account given was the correct one. The fact of not liking to go back again was easily accounted for by the dislike any lunatic has in being confined, and they saw nothing at all incompatible with the mendicant's version.

When Mabel saw them turn away their horses' heads, she gave a look full of despair and grief as she said—

"Alas! will no one befriend me? Am I, indeed, so far in that man's power that no one will stand between me and misery?"

"None, Mabel, none," whispered the mendicant, as he turned his horse's head, and again placed himself beside her.

Mabel had no power; she felt there was a mystery hanging about her and her destiny, and she thought there was no help; she could not escape. Dejected and dispirited, she sat on the horse, held on one side by the mendicant, and on the other side by his companion, Dashing Ned. She listened to the retreating footsteps of the horsemen in silence, and when they ceased to sound, she shuddered.

"Now," said Ned, "we ought to gag her."

"No," said the mendicant, "we have no need; this little staff, with the brass handle at the top, is a perfect treasure, a complete talisman. There's no need of gaging her; this will gag anybody."

"It's a rare piece of gag altogether,' said Ned.

"So it is. They may as well have it, they are so fond of it."

"Well, we come on very well, indeed; and our charge hasn't given us the slip, though she thought to do so."

"Yes, she did her best; but you see we had the good luck to keep her, and it will be very hard to me if we don't do so."

"To be sure; when shall we be at the Moonrakers? I'm hanged if I can tell where we are."

"Not far from the road that leads to the right on to the open common."

"And a pretty state of fog and mist that will be in, I'll warrant."

"It may."

"It will, you mean."

"Never mind. Push on, we needn't trouble ourselves about that; we must go through with it, and I have seen nothing to cause us to shrink, and, by Heaven, I will not"

"Bravo! You always were an out-an'-outer; you'll prosper."

"Well, time will show, Ned. I have seen a few things, and we musn't expect too long a lease.—'There's a sweet little cherub that sits up aloft to keep watch.'"

"Oh, yes, Newgate and eight o'clock. Monday morning,—how pleasant. That will do; you have become jolly all of a sudden, jolly disagreeable, I mean; but is this the place?"

"Yes, turn up here, Ned; and now we have an open road, let us push on. I am anxious to get to the Moonrakers as quickly as I can, as I wish no traces to be found of our having taken this road."

"All right."

The moon now rose and cast a gentle light upon the scene; the deep blue vault of heaven was studded with stars; the whole firmament was spangled with these transparent and sparkling luminaries. All was quiet and still. Not a sound disturbed the scene, and the chill night air now and then disturbed the calmness of the evening.

Mabel began to think of the house she

THE HALT AT THE MOONRAKERS.

had been forced to leave, and could not but paint to herself in glowing colours the alarm and the consternation of those at the Hall when they should become acquainted with the fact of her disappearance.

"They will be as unhappy about me as I am at my own misfortune. Oh! that this desire to ascertain who my parents were had never led me to keep such an appointment as this fatal night's without his being aware of it. I was ungrateful in acting clandestinely, and now I have met with a reward. And yet this is too severe;

this man can never mean to hurt me; he has rather some vile purpose to achieve, and which only can be completed by my absence from one place, or my presence in another."

She paused in her reflection, and asked herself this question,—

"But if he really be my father, ought I not to obey and love him? Alas! I have been brought up and educated for different purposes. I cannot obey and revere a criminal; were I sure he was my father, I would die for him to save him from harm;

but I could not, contrary to what has been taught me. I may be brought up above my birth; but never, oh, never, will I disgrace my benefactors by rendering their precepts and examples perfectly useless. They will think me ungrateful, and that nothing ought to have tempted me to hold a clandestine meeting with a man of such a desperate character as this appears to be."

Many and various ideas passed through her mind as she thought on what had been, up to this time, her home, and he who had been, in fact, to her a parent. She confessed that she could not, with any degree of pleasure, accept of such a change, far from it; indeed, the change was to her dreadful.

This man was strange and fearful, of an altogether desperate fortune; sunk in infamy and crime, and of what nature they might be she knew not, and dared not trust herself with surmising. She shuddered when she thought of them, for they might be so deep as to affect his life.

While she was thus busy in her own mind, while thoughts of a various and saddened character passed rapidly through her mind, her conductors were also busied with their own thoughts; and while they rode, each had some peculiar hope, fear, and object in view, the fulfilment, or the escape and attainment of which filled their minds with many dark thoughts.

"D—n it all," said Ned, suddenly, "the air is cold, and the way is not the most lively I have travelled."

"It need not be."

"That is true enough. Company is not desirable now, at all events, whatever it might be on another occasion, you know."

"Exactly."

"There's room enough here for a run if need be, is there not?"

"There is. We have nearly run the end of our race for the night. Ned, yonder fir tree marks a spot well known."

"I have heard so; I am always glad when I come here; I know then I am not far from the Moonrakers—about three hundred yards from this spot, ain't it?"

"Rather more."

"Is it?—but not much."

"There it was that poor Ned Huntley was shot through the head."

"Ay—ay?"

"Yes."

"How was that?"

"I'll tell you. He had a girl of his somewhere down the road, and he came to visit her: by some means or other he got recognised by somebody, and a trap

was laid for him, and no mercy was to be shown him.

"He came, as usual, to this place, when he saw a fat old gentleman, who came riding quietly on his cob. Well, Ned could not resist the opportunity, so he pulled out his bull-dogs, and began to coax the old gentleman out of his rhino."

"Ay—ay, he used to have a peculiar way—he put them in fear of their skin."

"Yes."

"Admirable plan."

"Well, but the old gentleman was a rum one; but he said nothing, but quietly putting his hand in his pocket he pulled out a pistol, and shot Ned through the head."

"I heard that much."

"Yes, that was the spot."

"I was good for the trick, and I know none who could have missed the opportunity; it was very tempting—I couldn't have lost the chance."

"Indeed."

"No I couldn't."

"Well, no more could Ned:—but here we are at the Moonrakers."

"I am very glad of it—ay, there's the jolly old sign-board."

"Yes."

"How still and quiet!"

"To be sure, they are not such flats as to tell where they are, like a flock of geese."

The Moonrakers public-house was a strange old house, of a rambling and indiscriminate kind of architecture; indeed, it occupied a vast extent of ground for such a building—it was extremely rambling, apparently composed of three or four odd houses, different in height, size, and make, so that it was sometimes difficult to tell which was the one end from the other. Some of it was brick, and some old flint-stone, of which there was plenty in the immediate vicinity. Some parts were tiled, while others were thatched, and then some parts were larger than others, more spread out, and some much higher; so, at a distance, it seemed like so many houses built together for security sake. The house was surrounded by a large quanity of out-houses, pig-styes, stables, and sheds, and then a large yard, pound, and fencings. The house was admirably well adapted to its use, and that was but very little known or understood, save among the initiated.

"Hilloa—hilloa—hilloa!" cried Dashing Ned of Newington.

"How's the moon?" cried a deep, gruff voice, as the door opened, and a big burly looking man came out.

"She's not in a well," was the reply,

"Some of the brothers——"

"That's the time of night. How are the lads of the moon?"

"Out an' outers — quite men in the moon."

"That's your sort; there never was a time when I felt more pleased to see your door open. Is there always a white fog kept on hand in this part of the country?"

"It's pretty stiff to-night; but never mind, Ned, you can make it all right by the fire, and your whiskers will curl again."

"D—d if I think they will. However, bear a hand, and see after the nags; we have somebody to take care of, and shall want your assistance to keep all right and tight till we can move on again, and nobody must see nobody; do you understand, you man in the moon?"

"Yes, I comprehend your hieroglyphs. Come in, or the patrol will be by soon, and he will be asking questions."

"Very good—as quick as you like."

They all dismounted and stood in the yard. The landlord took the horses by their bridles and led them to a small and private stable, which they were turned into—a whisp of straw was rubbed over them, and then, securing them for the night, he gave them some good hard food, and left the stable to return to the house.

"Now," said the mendicant, as he took Mabel and forcibly led her towards the house, "from this place it is very unlikely you can escape; however, I will sit and talk a little with you, and I have much to say, but not at this moment. In the meantime, of course, there's no harm intended you."

"Alas! I know not what to think," said Mabel. "Why do you wish to take me away from my friends? I would be with them, and nowhere else—this is truly distressing."

"It ought to be otherwise—you have your father with you; but you will find a finer home than the one I can offer you; but, it matters not—it matters not now. I have been hunted by my fellow men, and I have been long in the habit of consulting myself upon my own deeds, and consoling myself also."

"But——"

"Cease now, I will say more by-and-by. Come in, and you shall have a good fire and refreshments; if you cannot make yourself comfortable here for a short time, you are much better fed than I have the good fortune to be."

Mabel ceased to speak; and Ned turning to the mendicant, said—

"You are not going to stay outside, are you? Besides, I hear the sounds of horses' feet at a distance. We are better inside a great deal. Come—come in."

The mendicant compelled Mabel to follow Dashing Ned, while he himself followed Mabel, not leaving her for a moment.

---

## CHAPTER XXXVIII.

THE MOONRAKERS: ITS CONVENIENCES AND COMPANY.—A HALT.

THE house into which they now entered could not have been understood by any one under something near a twelvemonth's residence to qualify you to understand its various ins and outs, and in this consisted its great utility to the owners.

They entered a passage, and walked but a few yards down, when Dashing Ned of Newington opened a door and entered a sitting-room, a kind of kitchen, in which was a large fire-place and fire that shed a genial warmth over the apartment, while they could hear the huge logs crackle on the hearth, and the roar of the flames as they rushed up the huge chimney. Ned closed the door, while the mendicant wondered where he was till the landlord came with a light, and then he said—

"Now, then, let me have a safe crib to stow my prize in, who is a little refractory, and safe keeping is an object."

"You shall be accommodated," said the landlord, in a deep, gruff voice, "come along."

They followed him further back into the house, and then they came to a curiously-fitted door, which, in fact, seemed but an artifical opening, that would have escaped the most careful scrutiny of any one, so carefully was it done, and so well-favoured by the peculiar position of the place as regarded light.

"Go in," said the landlord.

"Come, Mabel, 'tis useless to question the landlord; he will tell you he cannot interfere in matters that don't concern him."

"Yes," said the landlord, "I never interfere in another person's business, so tumble in, Miss What's-your-name. The place is snug enough, and only wants a contented mind to make any one perfectly happy and at home in it."

"God help me," sighed Mabel, "for man will not—I am helpless."

She accordingly walked through the opening, for she could not resist; she would have suffered violence, and they would have carried her through, and she could not bear the idea of even being touched by these men. The tears trickled down her cheeks, as she walked up the stairs, followed closely by the landlord and that mysterious and fearful man, the mendicant.

She went up two pair of stairs, and at the landing of either was a strong door that was painted over the same as the wall, to prevent the ascent of any one they did not wish to enter. Besides, the second door on each landing was so much like the wall, that it would be difficult to distinguish it. This prevented either the ascent or descent of sounds; so, if a refractory person were hidden here, and the officers were below searching, they would be deceived, and believe they were on the wrong scent. After the second landing, he went along a little passage, and then opening a door, he entered the apartment, saying—

"You must make yourself easy here for a time; you shall have a fire, and that will give you light and warmth."

She entered a small apartment, at one end of which was a stone fire-place, and in it placed sufficient fuel, to which the landlord set a light, and in a few moments it began to roar up the chimney.

"Here," said the mendicant, "you must remain; and let me tell you, you had better take things kindly as not, because you will only compel me to act harshly, when I would not do so but for the necessity."

"There can be no necessity to carry me away forcibly from those who have befriended me from infancy; this can only be done from some bad, selfish motive."

"Be that as it may, it is my motive—your parent's motive—and it becomes not you to question it."

"God!" exclaimed Mabel, "into what hands have I fallen? And why should I be thus persecuted by one whom I have never injured in word or deed, but whom a malignant fate has made my persecutor."

"Your father."

"Alas! my father."

"Yes, alas! indeed, since it is thus you treat him; but it matters not, you will remain here till I think proper to remove you."

He left the room as the landlord entered with some few refreshments, which he spread upon the table, saying—

"Eat, drink, and be merry, my pretty bird; it will do you good, and thou art not overburthened with too many good things."

"Tell me, in mercy's sake, who that strange and mysterious man is."

"Who?"

"He who has forced me here."

"What, the gentleman who just went out, my dear, as I came in?" laying an emphasis on the word gentleman.

"Yes, the man who brought me here."

"I don't know, I am sure," replied the landlord, confidently.

"Not know! In pity tell me."

"Lord love you, miss, we know nobody, you know; we none of us know one another in this wally of tears; we never axes any questions, and nobody's nuffin to anybody else."

"But surely a man who knows the place and you so well, must be known in return; if you have a particle of humanity in your nature, tell me, I beseech you."

"I see you don't understand me," said the landlord; "I know nothing of the person you speak of; I never had occasion to ask him his name; we give no trust here, and, therefore, he may have a name as long as an endless chain, and I should know nothing about it."

Mabel sank into a chair when the landlord said this, and burst into a flood of tears. She was unable to control them, and they flowed plenteously.

"Come, come," said the landlord, "you need be under no apprehension; no harm is intended you; therefore, cheer up."

Mabel heard the words of the landlord, but they fell dead upon her ears. She could not but think the world was leagued against her, and that no kindly or sympathetic soul would stand between her and destruction.

The landlord once more exhorted her to partake of the food he had brought and placed before her; but she made him no reply, and he quitted the room, leaving her to herself.

The landlord and the mendicant then returned the way they came, and then entered the room in which were assembled a large concourse of guests, much greater than would have been generally supposed at all likely to have come together in such an out-of-the-way place. Indeed, there was a motley assemblage, and collected together from where nobody knew, and whither they were going nobody knew but themselves.

The kitchen was large; there was a solid deal table running down its whole length, and seats and benches were put in the most comfortable places. A large fire shed its genial influence, in both light and warmth, over the entire apartment. The floor was red brick and well sanded; the walls were white, and from the ceiling was suspended an enormous rack, on which were placed several sides of bacon and hams. The chimney of the fire-place was similarly ornamented, and it was a large place, for seven persons could sit in the seats around and beneath the ample shelter of its spreading funnel-shaped aperture. The fire-place itself was on a level, or nearly so, with the brick flooring. It was raised, however, a few inches above that, on which was placed a small iron fencing, of a primitive construction, to keep the fire within bounds, and to rest the logs edgeways upon it when they were placed on it. The fire roared and crackled, and not another sound was to be heard, though there were so many persons present, when the door was opened by Dashing Ned. He was known, but on making a sign that conveyed to them an intimation that somebody else was outside, all were silent. However, the return of the mendicant and the landlord soon broke the chains that held their tongues in bondage.

"Welcome," said the landlord, "my jolly crack; if you are out of luck, why, skewer me into a roasting joint if you don't know how to get into good luck again."

"It's a queer case," said the mendicant; "but there is more where this one came from."

"Of the same sort?"

"I shouldn't choose the same livery, useful as it has been to me."

"You are ungrateful."

"By no means; they have done their share of the hard work of keeping the weather out; why should they not be provided for, and another made to do duty instead?"

"Very good; and now, how do you find your precious self?"

"As commonly I do when inquired after so kindly; so much the better for your countenance, that I begin to get stiff about the neck."

"Ha! ha! Why, Joliff Rawbones does look a little hempen, to say the least of it; but, notwithstanding his extreme beauty, he will last his time out."

"No doubt, as many good men do," said another of the group.

"What have you been up to?"

"Something in the particular line."

"You do nothing in poaching, I suppose?"

"I should think not," said the mendicant, with extreme disgust.

"I should think many worse things might be done than poaching, especially when you come to think of the frequent dangers you are subject to, the rough fights, and all that kind of thing, which are so much salt to the entertainment."

"To my mind, it seems all salt and no meat; it don't suit my palate at all events."

"How's the road, lately?"

"I saw to-night a party of several; there would have been a good haul, but there was nobody there to do it."

"I saw them, and thought they looked like money-bearers, and should like to have had a dip into their pockets."

"Would you?"

"I believe you; but then, you see, one pair of hands ain't six; there's no help, and we can't all on us do impossibilities."

"I should think not."

"What have you been up to, Ned—eh? You dashing cove of Newington, have you run away from anybody of late?"

"By all that's lucky, you are right, my boy, for once, I have been running like wildfire. I think I stand to be shorn like a lamb by a dozen or more people. Thank ye for nothing. I don't do business that way, to say the least of it."

"Come, here's luck to the new comers," said a fat man in the corner, but who was half-hidden by the chimney, and he raised a hugh can up to his mouth as he spoke.

"Ah, Broadnose, are you there?—why, what mortal engine has carried you?—no single horse or even a one-horse shay."

"You are right. I rode here in an undertaker's cart, in the hole they pops the coffins in."

"Did you?"

"I did, and very comfortable riding it was. Why, bless you, they takes more care of corpses than they do of living 'uns."

"Ah! they think the last trouble the least."

"I prefers burying brandy and water to anything else. However, every one to their taste, as the old woman said when they tried to persuade her that milk from a black cow was as good as that from a white one."

"Ah!" said Ned, "I have an opportunity of ascertaining that lately; there's no knowing the shifts you are put to while ruralizing."

"What's the matter with you, Ned?"

"Very little."

"You've got something to say, I know, Ned; out with it; I hope it's worth listening to."

"I won't promise anything of the kind; but it is this:—I have been lying out a night or two, because I hadn't better lodgings. Well, as you may easily reckon, there ain't a moonraker everywhere, and I might have died of hunger and thirst, unless I could, like King Nebuchadnezzar, satisfy my hunger by eating grass, and quenching my thirst at the brook that was near at hand."

"I could never forgive you," said the landlord, "if you had done such a thing."

"I shouldn't have been a true moon-raker if I did such a thing," said Ned.

"You would be a disgrace."

"So he would."

"Well," said the landlord, "go on."

"I didn't know what to do," said Ned; "I was getting uncommon thirsty, and the idea came into my head that I had heard tales about hedgehogs being fond of sucking the cows—I thought I would try if I couldn't do so."

"Ha! ha! ha!" roared the landlord.

"Ho! ho! ho!—he! he! he!" laughed the guests, in all the variety of notes common to the exercise. It was some minutes before anything like silence could be restored; and when it was, each man wiped his mouth as if he had been engaged in the operation about to be described.

After a deep draught, Dashing Ned proceeded,—

"Well, I was some time before I could make up my mind to do so, but necessity knows no law, and I was determined I would try. I must confess I made several odd faces, and screwed my mouth up in shape. I had some difficulty in getting into position, and when I did, the cow upset me. I tried again, but I couldn't draw the milk, and, for the life of me, the whole affair seemed so funny, and the feel of the cow's dugs in my mouth was so dreadfully strange and queer, that I could not do it."

"You gave in?"

"I did."

"What did you do?"

"Why, I searched about, and found a mug, and milked her into that; it did me a great deal of good. I got on, and my hunger and thirst were somewhat appeased, and I did very well—and that was a black cow."

---

## CHAPTER XXXIX.

ODD INCIDENTS IN THE LIFE OF A MOON-RAKER. — THE DISTURBANCES, AND MABEL'S ATTEMT TO ESCAPE.

THERE was a good deal of merriment about the confession of Dashing Ned, and many questions and answers made that kept up a roar for half an hour. At length, one of the company said, when it had somewhat subsided—

"That almost reminds me of the trip I made down to Yorkshire, and the difficulties we were put to on the road."

"Were you ever in York?"

"I was in Yorkshire."

"Ay, what did you go after?"

"A tidy swag of plate, to be sure."

"Oh!"

"Well, we went down in a very private way; we had no outriders, and people to tell other people that we were coming."

"Exactly."

"We went on the tramp; we had a strong suspicion that we couldn't take it all at once, but should be compelled to make two bites at the cherry. Well, we thought we could do it, and, at all events we would try—there was no harm in that."

"I should think not."

"Well, we got to the place; it was a large house, at the end or beginning—it was difficult to tell which—of a village, and it would not have done to have lodged there—we should have been known, and we should have been so watched, that it was out of the question. Well, we determined to remain in the woods and plantations in the neighbourhood; they were preserved, and that made it the more difficult to do so, because the gamekeepers were vigilant, and poaching was common."

"Ay, common enough, everywhere!"

"Well, then, how were we to get our grub? — that was another thing. We determined upon a bold plan of operations."

"Very good—always do so when you can."

"We went to the only inn in the place, and every blessed night did we help ourselves to something or other that was good."

"There," said the landlord, "I wonder you ain't ashamed to look me in the face!"

"Ay."

"Lord love you! I could do that and rob you at the same time. What d'ye think of that for candour?" said the housebreaker.

"I admire you," said the landlord, "at a distance—a very great distance."

"I dare say," resumed the man, "the landlord wondered what the devil was the matter with the place, because we used always to leave things in their proper order, and nothing could be noticed save the decrease in the contents of the larder, and now and then a bottle of spirits and wine, as they came to hand. The place used to be frequented by the poachers a good deal and there was always some cold game in the pantry, or meat, and we helped ourselves gloriously. This lasted near a week."

"A week !"

"Yes."

"How could that be?"

"We couldn't effect our object so soon as we expected."

"Yes ; but how came it the people never laid any trap for the thieves ?"

"They did."

"Ay ay !"

"And we nicked them."

"How ?"

"I will tell you. There were bells placed on the doors and shutters, and every contrivance the yokels could think of for defeating and detecting us, but all to no purpose. We got through a small hole in the door, which, I think, none of them could have been aware of. There were a couple of boards that lifted up and allowed any one to enter that chose, and these we always secured afterwards, and then we left no trace. Their locks inside we picked with ease, though they put on several new ones.

"Ha ! ha ! ha !" laughed Ned.

"Well, we still continued the same game, and the last time we were there, we secured every lock they had, by putting pebbles in them, and old nails ; we secured the door that led up-stairs, locked the door, and threw the key in the pond, turned the water on, opened the pig-styes and hen-houses, and the garden-gate. Well, we did laugh surely at this, when it was all over, and we were on the road home ; didn't they curse and swear ! Only fancy the old boy stumping about in his knees and shorts, and white stockings and apron."

"Ha ! ha ! ha !"

"Well, it was funny ; but we got off, and our booty with us."

"Was it good?"

"Out and out."

"That repaid you for your trouble of procuring your provisions, and eating cold meat for a whole week at a time."

"Yes, it did ; though the fun of the thing almost repaid one for the trouble we had been at. I never felt better satisfied."

"That's saying something."

"There's many odd things that happen in our times ; but they don't happen very often, though almost every one has one or two instances to relate, and I have had one or two myself ; but I shall never forget the case of a young fellow I once knew."

"Who was he?"

"Oh ! Tomkins."

"What, broad-tailed Tomkins?"

"Yes ; the same."

"I didn't know you knew him."

"Yes, I did ; he was out upon the prowl, and one night he was in London, and, meeting with a gentleman about his own size and make, who, being very drunk, was not quite a match for him, they got up a fight. The gentleman undressed, and so did he ; and at length, having dressed himself in the gentleman's clothes, he gave him into custody, and walked away.

"In the pocket of his coat he found a card of address, and he determined to go there, and see if he could pick up something. He did go, and was admitted into a large house, and was attended upon by the servants. He, however, dismissed them all to bed. They had scarcely gone, when the lady descended to the drawing-room where he was seated, and began to upbraid him with keeping bad hours, and entreated him to come to bed. This was very awkward, and Tomkins's didn't know what to do, for he feared a discovery, and kept in the dark as much as possible. At length the lady gently kissed his forehead, and took his hand, which he held, with a handkerchief to his head, as though he were unwell. She jumped up, and staggered back, and, with a faint scream, sank insensible to the floor.

"'Now,' thought Tomkins, ' is my time, now or never.' Seizing her, he placed her in a small closet, which he locked, and then he ran up to the best bed-room, where he found a handsome amount in jewellery, and a very handsome sum in cash also. With this he walked away."

"Did he never hear what was said about the occurrence in the house ?"

"No ; he only saw the offer of a reward, and some general assertions about the house being robbed ; but I expect the unfortunate husband got rather suspicious, and entertained disagreeable thoughts about the affair. He must have known well that it was only himself that had been the cause of all."

"What the devil's that ?" exclaimed some one, as the sound of some heavy body fell outside the window, or near it, accompanied by a few tiles. "What's that ? Something's wrong."

The guests all looked at each other, and one or two were observed to turn pale, and rose to move away. The mendicant and Ned instantly arose.

"Be quiet," said the landlord, "don't be in a hurry. I'll give you warning enough ; you shall hear me speak ; I will go and see what is the matter, and who comes to my place in this manner ; it's a stranger, at all events."

"They know nothing of this place, that's certain, otherwise they would have given the hilloa, and so cleared up all doubts."

The landlord quitted the kitchen, and closed the doors after him. Taking a lantern, he took a turn round the house.

\* \* \* \* \* \*

While these scenes were enacted down stairs, a very different scene contrasted with this up stairs. Mabel had wept some time in silence before her thoughts once more flowed in an even current, and enabled her to think upon the peculiar situation in which she had been so unfortunately placed. A strange and singular series of circumstances had of late come about, and now she was placed in the presence of a bold, bad man, who would not hesitate to use any means to detain her. He said he was her father; but could such be? She felt none of those yearnings that she believed she must feel; but those dreams of relationship seemed suddenly to have vanished, and the reality appeared not in the glowing colours that her imagination had pictured it. How could she tell that this man was her father? He was a bad man, and he who will do one bad act, will do another; and, if he had a purpose to serve, or an object to obtain, as he certainly had, would he not be likely to use a falsehood, and usurp a character he had not any title to? Yes, he would. There could be no doubt about it; he would most surely do so. And then, those who had been so kind, so good, who had been more than parents—better than parents—who brought her up from childhood, bestowed every tender care that could be given or received—watched over her through childhood, and had made her what she was—how would they feel at this sudden disappearance from their roof? They would be alarmed, and their fears excited; for she believed they could not have done so much for her had she really not been loved.

"And shall I," she exclaimed "sit here, and not make an attempt to escape from this hateful bondage? Yes, yes; I will make the attempt, come what may. I will make the attempt; if I fail, I care not what becomes of me. Any harshness or severity is welcome; but, while there is a prospect of escape, I will use it, come what may. Thus, then, I will make the attempt."

She arose, and examined the room thoroughly, but she saw no prospect of finding an outlet, save that by which she had entered, the door. She turned away disappointed, for that was locked; but her eye lit upon the window, and she immediately walked towards it. The window was one of those old-fashioned windows, latticed, but it opened outwards, and she found she could squeeze herself through it. However, there was a great depth beneath, before her foot touched anything—perhaps some ten or fourteen feet.

True, there was another building at that depth, between her and the earth, but Heaven only knew what that was—it was tiles, it is certain, but they might be only a cover to a pig-sty, or a hen-house, or some frail thing that would let her through into she knew not what place. However, she was resolved that she would make the attempt, and to do that, she tied her shawl to the stanchions, and then with some difficulty she drew herself through the window.

The moon was now up, and there was enough light to have enabled her to see everything, and to have betrayed her, had any one been watching on the outside. She slid down to the end of the shawl, and then she could not touch the tiles; she feared to leave go, from a dread of falling with too much force, and causing some alarm. However, the shawl gave way, or became untied, most probably, and she found she had but a few inches to fall. She fell with force, notwithstanding, and she slid along the tiles on to a yet lower place, and in her progress several of the tiles, which were loose, came clattering down after her, and then she herself was suddenly precipitated to the earth. This was the disturbance that had alarmed the guests of the Moonrakers, and caused the landlord to come out to see what it was all about.

---

## CHAPTER XL.

### THE RECAPTURE.—THE INTERVIEW, AND ITS RESULTS.

WHEN Mabel had recovered herself from the first shock of the fall, she arose, and though she felt herself shaken and terrified, she soon recovered her presence of mind sufficiently to ascertain that she was not injured, and attempted to escape. Immediately she felt she could move, she hastened across the yard, heedless, or rather not knowing whither she was going; but by hastening from the house, she hoped to escape from the search she feared too well would most likely be set afoot.

In this hope she was mistaken, for the quick eye of the landlord instantly suspected that something had gone wrong, and when he perceived where the tile had fallen from, he cast his eyes up to the window, and there beheld it swinging open.

"Ah, ah !" he muttered ; "the bird's flown ; but she cannot have gone far."

He was right, for on looking carefully around, he could see the form of Mabel crouching behind, or in the shadow of the projecting end of one of the outhouses.

"Oh, this is the dodge," he muttered ; "what's the use of that ? when the landlord of the Moonrakers is out, he can see as well as a rat. We mustn't let you stand there in the cold."

So saying, he walked leisurely across the yard to where Mabel stood, who, seeing him approach, saw she was not concealed, and, therefore, left her hiding-place, and ran as quickly as she could towards the gate.

"'Tain't not the smallest possible ghost of a chance of a go, my dear, so you needn't flutter so much ; you'll tire yourself to death."

"For mercy sake, save me."

"So I will—you'll catch cold here. Come with me, else I'll carry you."

"Have you no mercy ?"

"Lots, my dear."

"But my friends will reward you, if you will aid me to get to them. Say you

MABEL ESCAPING BY THE WINDOW FROM THE MOONRAKER'S INN.

will help me to leave this place, and I will for ever bless your name. You shall be no loser."

"No—no—my pretty maid ; I should be no loser, as you say ; but I never act the sneak ; I never interfere in family matters. The landlord of the Moonrakers couldn't do such a thing as that, no, not until he's born again."

So saying, he took her by her arm and led her towards the door, and then he put his head in, saying—

"All is right ; it's only your bird that got out of her cage."

"Oh !" said the mendicant, "I thought as much when I left the room ; but I didn't think she would have thought of it."

"Oh, there's no knowing what women, young or old, will not think of."

"Let me have another room for her."

"Yes, there is another—there is a fire in that now, for I knew that would not be safe for the night when all was quiet."

The landlord then left them together in the room, and when the mendicant, after having walked up and down the room a turn or two, turned suddenly upon her, and giving her a peculiar look that he could put on, he said—

"And so, Mabel, you have attempted to escape from me a third time—have you not?"

Mabel answered not.

"It matters not," he said ; "the fact is certain, I may say you are not the most dutiful and loving child a father could well have. I have heard of dutiful and loving daughters, and yet I don't find you one."

"I am so to my friends."

"To your friends !—and what, do you reckon me less than your friends?"

"You are a stranger."

"It seems you would have me continue such ; but your sordid and avaricious disposition must surely be the index of a bad heart."

"I never was yet. Why do you detain me—why not let me go?"

"I do not choose."

"You cannot keep me ; why should you be so selfish as to desire to deprive me of the aid and countenance of friends who have loved me and supported me through childhood?"

"You have harped upon this subject before, and I must tell you it has no weight with me, for I have a fixed and definite object in view, and your presence is necessary with me, and that ought of itself to be a sufficient motive for you to obey my wishes."

"Can no good motive actuate you, nothing but some self-interested intention that you have to pursue?—what it can be, Heaven alone knows ; but this I know, that as far as I have the power of preventing it, I will never become the means of either inflicting wrong or committing injustice."

"You are strangely perverse, and must have been taught to disregard all filial ties ; affection and duty to parents have formed no part of your studies, I fear."

"They have taught me to eschew wrong and love that which is right ; and a crime is a crime, committed by whom it may."

"I don't deny that I have committed crimes, and hence it is I travel thus and carry you by force. I have, however, a legal right over you, and that right, if I cannot exert one way, I will another, and in so doing I am perfectly justified."

"But what can it benefit you to drag me about, carry me from place to place, and confine me? This surely cannot be any gratification to you, and you cannot be a gainer by it."

"You know not what I know. You have just become acquainted with one member of your family, and you do not seem gratified by the restoration of a father who happens to be unfortunate and poor."

"Such qualities or misfortunes," said Mabel, "would be no bar to my love and affection, if they were the misfortunes of an honest man ; but you cannot boast of being such."

"And, therefore, you will make every endeavour to escape from me."

"And why should I not ? You have neither love nor affection for me."

"Be it so; but, I tell you, you know nothing of my intentions, or what they may be, you know nothing, moreover, of your family's circumstances, you know nothing of my wants and intentions ; do not trouble yourself, therefore, about my motives. I have hopes, and fears, and feelings, to which you are a stranger—therefore, submit in silence."

"Never."

"Well, we shall know each other."

"You can have none of the feelings of a father for me, or your usage would be different to what it is."

"'Tis well—I know you will take every opportunity to escape from my keeping."

"I wish to return to those who have been my friends, and who would even reward you were you to convey be back."

"There is little policy in that."

"You cannot say I am ungrateful in wishing to return to those who have been all that a parent could be to me."

"And which I am not, you will say ; but no matter, I have been used to misfortunes and misconstruction. However, you will escape if you can, and I will, if I can, prevent you."

"You have."

"And will again ; but, mind, you may escape, and you may not, and in case you do escape, you will bring to, perhaps, an ignominious end your father. It will be a comfortable reflection in after life to know that you have destroyed the life of him who gave you life."

"It will be no act of mine."

"It will be caused by you. As well might the man who shoots another say, 'I took not his life, 'twas the gun.' "

"But if you have done that deserving an ignominious end, I can have no control over your fate ; you, in the commission of other crimes, are taken, and you receive your doom."

"Very philosophical and cool from a young lady to her father; however, there is another matter that I can press upon."

"What is that?"

"Some other secret of your birth, that you at present know nothing about."

"A secret?"

"Yes."

"And why?"

"Because it is unknown to all yet. But if you escape, I will at once proclaim to the world that you are the child of a criminal."

"Will the world say that it is my fault?"

"No; but every one shrinks from coming in contact with such people."

"They may."

"And, moreover, there is yet another circumstance connected with your birth that I could have spared you, if you had not forced me to this admission."

"And what is that?"

"That you are the child of infamy as well as disgrace — do you hear that, Mabel?"

"My God—my God! what am I reserved for?"

"For what you know not, if you oppose my will. Remember, if you escape, it may cost me my life—your father's life—it may be nothing, or a trifle, in your estimation; but understand it clearly; then, if I am thus thwarted, I will proclaim to the whole world who and what you are, and the hand you have had in your father's death—your near relationship to a felon, and your infamy of birth. Now," he added, "think of all this calmly, and then if you can act as you threaten, do so; but I will, in the first place, prevent it, if I can."

So saying, he left the room, and closed the door after him.

Mabel seemed stunned, she scarce moved, her heart would have burst but for the plentiful flow of tears that came to her relief, and she sat down and buried her head in her hands. She remained in this posture for some time, and when she looked up she saw nothing but the bare walls and dim light of that room, in which was nothing more than the merest necessities. Her breast heaved with the deep, long-drawn sighs, and she clasped her hands in prayer. She prayed for strength and firmness to go through the trials that were awaiting her.

## CHAPTER XLI.

THE PALOUR AT MORTON HALL.—THE GROWING ALARM, AND THE AGONY OF CAPTAIN MORTON.

ASSEMBLED in the parlour at Morton Hall, on that sad and eventful evening when poor Mabel went to keep the appointment with him who now held her in such a fearful state of thraldom, were Captain Morton and his wife, Henry, and a young friend of his.

This young friend had been in some of the Peninsular campaigns—a fact which made him all the more welcome to Morton Hall; for certain it is, that any one who has once been in the trade of war, whatever his philosophical thoughts may be, and his real reasonable convictions upon that subject, he will never divest himself of a yearning after the romance of a military life, and a love of the companionship of military men.

Such was precisely the case with Captain Morton. Although, from firm convictions, he had forsaken what is called the path of glory, yet his house was always open to any military officer, and he was always more glad to see such at his table somehow than he was to receive the visits of civilians.

It was usual with the Mortons to spend the evenings together in a large, comfortable, lofty room, which, from its situation in the house, was called the parlour.

Such, however, had been the disturbing events that had lately occurred, that this happened to be the first evening upon which Captain Morton determined that he would revive the said habit of assembling in that room.

He was glad when Henry introduced Mr. Vere, the young stranger to whom we have alluded, because the presence of one not belonging to the family, he felt, would have a tendency to hold them all together on that evening, as well as to prevent the conversation from merging into any unpleasant subjects, of which there were quite enough.

The only one absent was Mabel, but, for some time, no remark was made about that absence, because Morton Hall was Liberty Hall in the full sense of the word.

No one member of the family was in any way invited to attend the evening meeting, and it was not until Mabel's non-appearance—a very unusual thing for her—had attracted the attention of Mrs. Morton twice, that she at length said, with some surprise—

"Where can Mabel be?"

"Ay," said the captain, "where is she?"

"I don't know," said Henry, to whom Morton seemed to address the words; "I dare say she is in her own room, or the conservatory, which she now visits so often in the evening since it has been lighted."

"Go and look there for her, my dear," said Mrs. Morton.

It needed no second bidding on the part of Mrs. Morton to send Henry on such an errand as this. He was off in a moment.

Captain Morton just glanced at his wife, and she returned his glance. They each read the other's thoughts well and easily.

The presence of Mr. Vere prevented anything from being said; and now, of course, in all courtesy, they turned their attention to him.

"And so, Mr Vere," said Captain Morton, "you were in some of the Spanish campaigns?"

"I was, sir."

"With Moore, were you?"

"Yes, sir, I was with the Scotch general, whose sole merit appears to me to consist in his being killed at Corunna."

"I agree with you there. There was great incapacity in that man; and if he had not, luckily for his fame, died as he did, he would have sunk into utter insignificance and contempt in this country, even if he had escaped a court-martial and degradation."

"I have found many, sir, of the same opinion."

"Everybody is of the same opinion who has taken the trouble to investigate the matter at all. But General Sir John Moore was a Scotchman, and that accounts for how he was bepraised and bespattered by the press with fulsome adulation when he was dead. By some means or another, the press is in the Scotch interest always."

"I have often remarked it, sir."

"Hence, then, is it that such men as Moore get on. A Scotch author, a Scotch cadet, or a Scotch general, is sure to have advantages which an Englishman has not. The inordinate vanity of that dirty and grasping people enables them to make head almost against anything. But, to quit so ungracious a theme, I suppose your Spanish campaigns afford you abundance of anecdote?"

"They do indeed, sir."

"It is a sad country for the operations of war. I traversed part of it with Sir David Baird."

"Did you, indeed? I was in Falkland's division at the same time that Baird was making his demonstrations in Valencia."

"Then we were fighting on almost the same field?"

"We were, really. I heard, during my Spanish campaigns, many romantic little bits of adventure, which would be eagerly caught at by the London booksellers did they but know them."

"Can you amuse us, Mr. Vere," said Mrs. Morton, "by a recital of any of them?"

"I have a treacherous memory, madam," said Vere, "but I will endeavour to do my best. A little anecdote has just come into my mind which is more illustrative of Spanish manners than anything else; and if you do not mind putting up with a dull narrator, I shall have great pleasure in relating it to you, and shall feel myself complimented by your polite attention."

Vere then commenced as follows:—

During the Spanish wars many deeds of vengeance were perpetrated, such as would scarce be deemed at all compatible with civilization; but civil war creates additional horrors, even to those that are derivable from the fierce and vengeful disposition of the natives.

The family of Don Amarillac and that of Don Jose de Xavilla were united in the closest bonds of intimacy and friendship. They were as brothers, and their families, also, were upon the most friendly and pleasing terms. They saw each other often, accepted and gave each other invitations, spent days and nights at each other's chateaus, and performed all the kindly offices of the closest relationship.

"Their families were numerous, and they were such as they might well be proud of. Several sons and daughters were in either family, who looked upon each other all as brothers and sisters. The young men were sent to the same universities, and they returned to their families at the same time.

As may be imagined, it was not possible for them all to be equally endowed with good qualities; indeed, to the great misfortune of both families, the eldest son of Amarillac was not what his father would desire; indeed, he was wild and dissolute to a degree. The university had, indeed, educated him, and turned him out a complete Spanish gentleman, but of the most unprincipled and dissolute character, accompanied by a degree of *finesse* and speciousness, that for a while enabled him to defy detection, and to execute several diabolical plans.

The first of these was the seduction and ruin of the daughter of Don Xavilla. This was a great blow to that family, and was not discovered till he was far away from the paternal residence. As may be supposed, Don Xavilla could not, and would not, take the ruin of his daughter in good part. He was passionately fond of her, and felt all the sorrow and grief a father only could feel.

He wrote to Amarillac, and demanded vengeance upon his son, that he should not only marry her, but he should atone for the evil he had done in the most ample manner. Amarillac expressed his sorrow and regret at the occurrence; but said his son was beyond his reach and control. He had gone from home upon some expedition of his own.

Xavilla could not, or would not, take these excuses, and the families became as severed as once they had been united; indeed, the whole of the brothers and sisters felt the disgrace and injury inflicted. The young men all swore vengeance, and declared they would die before they would suffer so monstrous an act of injustice, and so great an injury and disgrace, to go unpunished.

They sought the enemy of their house all over Spain; they divided, and took separate routes, and one found him. A challenge was given and accepted, and they both met and fought with swords for some time, until they were both fatigued; but the brother of the unfortunate young lady was killed by his adversary's sword being run through his heart. This was another blow they had to lament, and sufficed to eradicate any good feelings that might have remained at their hearts, and prevented them from taking active measures against the whole family. Now, however, that feeling was at an end, and their hatred was as strong as their friendship had formerly been.

They had formed some plan to surprise and destroy them all; but the breaking out of the French war disconcerted all their plans of operation, and, for the present, they were deferred. Don Amarillac joined the French movement, and his wealth, in part, became a prey to the invaders and the natives.

Don Xavilla, on the other hand, took the side of his countrymen, and determined to make a stand against the enemies of his race. The first movements were in favour of the French, who entered Spain at different places, and had a large force.

The country was soon in arms, and all Spain was a complete battle-field. Every man that could bear arms was seen with a musket on his shoulder, and they hid themselves in the passes, and among the mountains in the vicinity, and then woe betide the stragglers of the French army.

Don Xavilla was filled with vengeance, and he joined the ranks of the defenders of the country. His enemy, who had done him so much injury, was with those who had invaded the country. He had passed much of his time in France, had become much infected with a prestige in favour of French interests, and now drew his sword, that sword already stained with the blood of a Spaniard, against his native country.

Often did Don Xavilla descend from his fastnesss into the plain, and oppose the French troops who came there, and defeated them repeatedly, and without loss. Indeed, in that part of the neighbourhood there were few Frenchmen who would trust themselves, unless in great force, and thus it was all over Spain. The French occupied the ground they stood and fought upon, and no more.

It was now that Don Xavilla determined to inflict the vengeance he had so long meditated upon, and for that purpose he had several spies placed around the residence of Don Amarillac, for he knew well the son would visit the father, for the purpose of seizing him at such a moment, and to deliver him to the vengeance of his men, who hated worse than ever those who joined the invaders of their own country. One night, as he lay near a watch fire, in readiness for an attack, for the French were in the neighbourhood, a man came softly up to him, and then said, in a low voice—

" It is time."

" Time for vengeance ?"

" Yes."

" Where are the French ?"

" In straggling parties—lying about in all directions, and one near the house of Amarillac ; and he who commands there is your enemy."

" Is it so ?"

" Ay, it is."

" And is he in the house ?"

" He is ; and unsuspecting."

" Then we will make an attack upon the whole party, and exterminate them."

Don Xavilla then rose, and ordered the party whom he commanded to prepare for an instant departure and an attack. There were near two hundred men, all of approved courage and determination, and who hated French dominion. They marched in silence for several long miles, and had even surrounded the house without any discovery taking place. Then, demanding admittance, the door was opened without any suspicion, and at the head of a chosen party, Xavilla entered the house.

Great consternation was felt when he entered with his drawn sword.

"What does your presence indicate?" inquired the guilty youth.

"Vengeance, demanded against the wrong doer—the traitor to his country, and the murderer and seducer. I come for a father's vengeance!"

"Stand apart—you shall have it—draw your sword."

"No ; I do not cross my sword—the sword of an honourable man—with you ; a rope is the fate that awaits you !"

"Not while I wear a sword."

"Nor I," said the father.

A desperate conflict ensued, in which the father was killed, but the son taken prisoner, and bleeding, as he was, from every wound, Don Xavilla said to him,—

"I have long sought this vengeance, and now I will take it. You dishonoured my daughter, and you took the life of my son ; for this you shall hang on a bough of the highest tree of your estate."

The old Spaniard was as good as his word, and the young man was so found the next day by his comrades, who were enraged and horrified at the event.

\*      \*      \*      \*      \*      \*

During the last few words of this recital, Henry Morton had glided into the room ; but perceiving that his friend, Mr. Vere, was talking, he had forborne saying anything that was likely to interrupt him. Seeing, however, that he had finished, he stepped forward with anxiety depicted upon his countenance, and said,—

"I do not know that there is any cause for alarm, but we cannot find Mabel."

A sudden pang shot across the heart of Captain Morton ; he seemed to feel instantly that something dreadful must have occurred ; he had no special reason to think so, and yet he could have sworn that such was the fact. A strong presumption which no reasoning powers can shake frequently comes over the human mind, which, although we have no direct evidence of, we yet feel with all the force of conviction. Captain Morton said nothing, but he looked the alarm which was crowding round his heart.

"Mabel not to be found !" exclaimed Mrs. Morton ; "oh, she must be in the house somewhere."

Henry Morton was far more alarmed, probably, than he chose any one should see, and he might have given more expression to that alarm, but for the accidental presence of a stranger, He looked, however, imploringly at Captain Morton, as if he would have said—"for Heaven's sake do something it this emergency."

The period of inaction in Captain Morton's mind, he knew, would not last long. He was too accustomed to the promptness of military habits to be vacillating, and now at once he sprang to his feet as he said,—

"Repress all hurry and excitement—let there be no confusion—let some of the servants instantly know, that we may get a systematic search. No doubt a short time will discover her ; there need be no alarm—not the least—not the least."

Of course, everybody would feel inclined to give Captain Morton the credit of the coolness which he assumed ; but while they did so, not one could possibly avoid seeing that it was an assumed coolness. His hand trembled, and he looked ghastly pale. It was quite clear that whether or not any calamity had happened to Mabel, he, Captain Morton, dreaded the very worst.

Mrs. Morton sat and trembled, and knew not what to do or say. Mr. Vere offered his services in any way that might be useful, but no one seemed very well able to tell him what to do.

Harry Morton, after the captain had spoken, rushed from the apartment in order to carry his orders into effect, and, despite the wise injunction to create no alarm and to show no flurry upon the occasion, the whole household was soon in a state of great excitement, and the servants were running hither and thither in that sort of confusion which ensues among people when they wish to do something very energetic, and have not the least idea where to begin. Harry, himself, soon succeeded in searching the entire mansion, and convincing himself that Mabel was in none of its apartments. The men servants were dispatched in different directions with lights through the grounds, and any one who, from a distance, could have seen the hurry and confusion in that mansion and its pretty pleasure-gardens would have wondered what calamity had so disturbed its inmates.

Each moment that passed without finding Mabel, added worlds to Captain Morton's anxiety ; indeed, such a search was then instituted as must have immediately discovered her had she at all been in the house, so that after a few minutes had elapsed, there could be no doubt whatever that something had happened. What that something was, was now the only question.

Captain Morton stood within the porch of the Hall, with his hat in his hand, pale and agitated ; his eagerness to do something towards the discovery of Mabel would have tempted himself to traverse the grounds ; but his reason told him this could be better and easier done by those who were about than by him.

If he himself had rushed with the frantic eagerness of excitement from place to place, he would have resembled some indifferent general, who, having more valour than discretion, instead of directing the efforts of his troops, should seek himself to mingle in the fray.

And now, one by one, those who had been sent to traverse the grounds returned slowly, with the report of their non-success in the discovery of her whom they sought.

"I knew it," said Captain Morton, sadly, to himself, "I was certain of it from the first. She is lost ! Heaven help her, and endow me with strength to bear this calamity. It is that man who has laid some plan for her captivity—that mendicant, who was so nearly my prisoner, but who escaped me."

He turned, and with unsteady and faltering steps was about to seek the parlour, in order that he might there consult with those who could perhaps bring calmer judgments to the task, upon the best means to be adopted for recovering the beautiful girl who had so mysteriously disappeared from her best friends and only protectors. Before, however, he reached that apartment, the thought flashed across him, that amid all the confusion of the household, and among all the servants and dependants upon him whom he had within the last hour spoken to, Rafferty Brolickbones had not made his appearance. There was some comfort in this thought when it first flashed across him, for he considered that Rafferty might, upon the first alarm, have gone to seek Mabel with some better information than any one else as to where it was most probable she would be found.

"It would be just like him," reasoned Captain Morton, "to be off at once without saying anything to anybody, if he knew there was a good chance of finding her in any particular quarter, or, perhaps, indeed, he may be with her; he may, after all, have accompanied her to the village on some errand or other, and she, having him with her as a protection, of course feels not the necessity of hurrying as if she were alone."

Captain Morton drew a long breath of relief as he added, after a pause,—

"Yes, most certainly, most certainly ; there is more of hope in the absence of Rafferty Brolickbones than in any other circumstance. I must convey that information to those who are waiting with trembling anxiety in the parlour."

With a lighter step, because he had a lighter heart, Captain Morton took his way to the room in which he had left his wife and Mr. Vere. He found his wife alone, for Mr. Vere had accompanied Henry in the minute search which the latter wished to make for Mabel.

"My dear," said Captain Morton to his wife, "it is probable we are alarming ourselves and everybody else, and without sufficient reason."

"Indeed," exclaimed Mrs. Morton, with hope beaming from her countenance; "from what do you gather so pleasant an assurance?"

"From Rafferty's absence. I begin to think he must have gone to the village with Mabel. You know how ready she is to listen to any tale of distress, and if she has been informed she can do any good in the village, with the impulsive generosity which forms a portion of her character, she would go there directly, securing, as she has frequently done before, Rafferty Brolickbones as her guard."

"I pray to Heaven it may be so," said Mrs. Morton.

"It is more than probable. You well know the attachment of the honest old sergeant to Mabel—you know the pride and pleasure with which he has attended upon her from childhood, and, therefore, we may fairly conclude that he is with her now, and that she is safe."

"Oh, what a great relief it is," exclaimed Mrs. Morton, as she clasped her hands, "to think even so for a moment."

"Calm your fears ; we may fairly think so."

"But why not send to the village at once to ascertain?"

"Certainly that can be done," said Morton, as he rang the bell ; and when a servant appeared, he added,—

"Tell one of the men to saddle the fleetest horse in the stables, and to go down to the village and inquire for Rafferty Brolickbones ; ascertain what has become of him."

"Master Henry has already saddled the bay mare, and gone off," said the man.

"Oh, that will do—that will do," said Morton ; "we will wait until his return."

Whether it was that Mrs. Morton was not so hopeful as her husband, or that Morton, for the sake of assuaging her fears, put on an appearance of coolness he was far from feeling, we cannot precisely say, but certain it was that, after a few moments, she did not seem to consider there was much consolation to be found in the hope that Rafferty was with Mabel. Of course, she could not say that he was not so; but the supposition that it was, appeared to her to rest upon a very slender foundation indeed. The next hour was one of the most painful anxiety, each moment growing more excruciating, until, at last, Captain Morton, unable to bear the dreadful state of suspense any longer, arose, and announced his intention of going down to the village himself instanter.

"I cannot endure this inaction," he said; "I am a bad hand at waiting for anything; I cannot and will not believe but what all is right and safe; but still, a gallop to the village will do me good."

"You will come back?" said Mrs. Morton.

"Immediately," he replied; "I cannot be delayed. I shall hear directly if there be any news of her; and, indeed, most probably before I get there, I shall receive some welcome tidings. We must really scold her for not telling us she was about to leave the house."

"Heaven send we may have the opportunity," said Mrs. Morton; "I fear the worst."

"No, no—fear nothing—sufficient for the hour is the evil thereof."

"And that is amply sufficient," said Henry, as he suddenly walked into the parlour.

One glance at his face was sufficient there to read the tale he had to tell. Mabel was not to be found. Captain Morton staggered to a seat as he said,—

"Never mind, boy—never mind; you need not speak your errand; you have been unsuccessful; your looks sufficiently proclaim it."

"You have no news, Henry?" said Mrs. Morton.

"None whatever," he said, mournfully.

"And Mabel is lost," exclaimed the captain; "now, Heaven, lend me strength to bear this blow!"

"We will not bear it," exclaimed Henry, in a voice that rang through the apartment; "we will not bear it—wherefore should we bear it? Are we to have the best, the dearest, the most innocent member of our family, thus snatched from us? No. From this moment I dedicate myself to the task of discovering the fate of her who is dearer to me than my own existence. Let me have the means for such an object—I ask not much, but let me have the means—and, be she hidden where she may, I will restore her to your arms."

"Henry, be calm," said Mrs. Morton, as the tears gushed from her eyes; "be calm; we will consider upon what is best to be done."

"I am calm," said Henry; "there are some blows of fate which lift us far above the frenzy of grief, which crush all excitement—Heaven knows I am calm. I would not by one rash word—nay, one hasty glance or movement, risk Mabel's safety. You will see that I shall be wondrously calm, but I know that I have much to learn yet concerning that beautiful girl that destiny has thrown among us. Now is the time to impart to me that information, for now has the period of action arrived. Let me know all, I implore you to let me know all."

Captain Morton and his wife glanced at each other for a moment, and then the former said, in a calm voice,—

"Sit down, Henry—sit down, Henry—shall know all."

## CHAPTER XLII.

THE CONFIDENCE WITH HENRY.—THE DECLARATION OF LOVE.—THE LETTER FOUND ON THE LAWN.

It did not take Captain Morton a long time to put Henry in possession of all those facts and circumstances connected with the manner in which Mabel had come into his hands, with which the reader is already fully acquainted. He was listened to with the most marked and eager attention, and he concluded by saying,—

"You, Henry, who know her well, and how in every way she was calculated to win upon the affections of every one, can easily imagine with what dismay I have always looked forward to the possibility of some one coming forward to claim her, and take her from me. She has imperceptibly become most dear to me, and the very thought that the day might come when I should have, by informing her she was not my child, to break the tie which bound us together, was fearful to me. I live and have lived for some time in constant uneasiness upon that subject, and every chance visitor here, and every circumstance which seemed to be invested with the least air of mystery, had its effect in causing me the greatest amount of anxiety."

"That," said Henry, "I cannot wonder at."

"You will, then, see, that in keeping the secret of her not being my own child from Mabel, I was doing what I thought was most likely to ensure her continued happiness. She was with us as contented as any human being could possibly be, and I know enough of human nature to be quite certain, that despite the affection which I am quite certain she would still have continued to feel for us, had she been really aware that she was not my child, a thousand anxieties would have arisen in her breast concerning her origin, and her peace of mind would have been lost."

" True—most true," said Henry.

" And then," added Captain Morton, whose sense of honour made him more eager than was at all necessary to excuse himself; " and then I was doing her no harm by keeping this secret. It was not as if I could have placed her in the arms of fond and indulgent parents when I pleased, and that I kept her to myself, because, from long association with her, I

had got to love her as if she were a child of my own. I could not have told her who she was—all I could have told her would have been who she was not, and that would have been an amount of information barren of all results, but such as would have given her uneasiness of mind."

" You were thoroughly justified," said Henry, " in the course you have pursued. Who could blame you? The happiness of Mabel was the motive, and what higher, what purer one, could you have?"

" It was my motive, Henry; and, moreover, if any sudden occurrence had deprived her of my care, there; and, more who could have told her what I have now told you; in addition to which, I have reduced all the particulars to riting,

which is addressed to her, and would have been placed in her hands at my death."

" Which may Heaven long avert," said Henry, as he clasped the captain's hands in his.

" Thank you, Henry. I do not speak because I have any apprehension of dying, but because life, we all know, at the best, is but an uncertain possession, and I thought it my duty to leave the document I mention, so that under my own hand Mabel should be made acquainted with those particulars so interesting to her, which, in some respects, if she heard them from any one else, might be susceptible of exaggeration."

Henry was now silent for some moments, and then a slight flush of colour pervaded his cheeks for an instant, leaving them again much paler than before, when it had passed away.

"I will not," he said, "brother, be less ingenuous to you than you have been to me. I feel that if ever there was a time when it behoved me to be candid upon a subject which lies nearest to my heart, this is that time."

"Speak freely, Henry," said Captain Morton. "Perhaps Mrs. Morton and myself can guess what you are about to say."

"You may do so," added Henry; "but whether that be the case or not, what I have to say is, that I love Mabel."

"We have seen it."

"Seen it? I—I never mentioned it."

"Ah," said Mrs. Morton, "the eyes are sad tell-tales on such occasions. You cannot conceal such feelings, Henry. But do not be vexed that your cherished secret became known to us. Your brother and I have talked of it often, and if it be any pleasure to you to hear so much, I can assure you that we have always talked of it with approval."

"Yes," added the captain; "and Heaven send that Mabel was now here to hear us say as much."

Henry looked much affected, and he rose and walked to the window for a few moments to recover himself from the sudden gush of feeling that had come over him. The Captain and Mrs. Morton did not interrupt him, and in a few moments he came back saying:—

"Yes, I do love her; but those simple words fall far, far short of conveying the extent of my feelings towards her. She is dearer to me than all the world besides—she is dearer to me than life itself. There is no peril I would not dare for her sake. Oh, brother, brother, I am poor and dependant much upon you. Place me but in a position to search for Mabel, my heart's best treasure, and I will bless you."

"Henry, you shall want for no means and appliances to prosecute the search; but before you enter upon it, hear further that which I have to tell you,"

Henry listened anxiously, and Captain Morton then told him of the visit of the mendicant, and the attempt he, Morton, had made to capture him, when he made his escape through the open window on to the lawn in front of the house.

"Now," added the captain, "I have I think every reason to believe that this real or pretended mendicant is at the bottom of all these proceedings, and that in discovering him you will discover Mabel. I cannot, Henry, believe for a moment that he has any real claims of close affinity upon her; but he may be the paid hireling o others."

"Great God!" exclaimed Henry; "and can Mabel—my beautiful and gentle Mabel—be in the power of such a man?"

"Hush! Henry, hush! be calm. Nothing is now to be done by bursts of passionate grief or excitement. Be calm, let me implore you. While, of course, I doubt what kind of claim, if any, this man has upon Mabel, it is just possible he might be able to establish a complete one."

"Horrible possibility!"

"It is, I grant you, a horrible possibility; but still a possibility. He evidently possessed a full knowledge of what had accurred on the battle-field, when Mabel, then an infant, was given into my charge. Of course, you will say that could have been acquired from some other source, and so, indeed, it might. But if you can discover this man—this seeming mendicant—I think that in him you will likewise discover the murderer of the traveller at the inn."

"Common feeling," said Henry, "and common opinion point out this beggar as the author of that dreadful deed."

"In such a case, then, could you succeed in discovering him, whatever might be his claims upon Mabel, you can have no difficulty in separating her from him, because you can give him into the hands of justice."

"I will not think he can be her father," said Henry Morton; "I will reject so horrible a supposition as that from my mind. Oh! what would be her sufferings if she were to find that she was the daughter of a murderer."

"Would you love her the less, Henry?" said Mrs. Morton.

He turned his flashing eyes upon her face, as he repeated the question—

"Would I love her the less? Heaven forbid! Could I be so unjust to her, and ever hope for justice myself on earth or in heaven? Love her the less, because she had the affliction of finding one nearly related to her so wicked! Ah! no. If there could be a dearer—a more tender claim than another upon my consideration, it would be that she was battling against such an affliction. I am not one who can condemn the child because the parent may be guilty."

"You take a correct view of this subject," said Captain Morton; "and from the sentiments that actuate you, Henry, I feel convinced that you are in every way worthy of the possession of such a treasure as the heart of Mabel."

"Let me go at once and seek her!"

"Wait yet a little, and hear me. That

She has been, on some pretence or another, eluded away from us, appears to me now to be quite clear ; but whatever pain such a feeling gives me, I do not believe she is in any danger I have not that additional uneasiness upon my mind."

" In no danger !"

" No, Henry. She may suffer, as doubtless she does, much mental distress ; but I believe the main object of whoever has got possession of her will be to extort from me a sum of money for her ransom."

" Indeed !"

" Yes ; the affection I have for Mabel has been too often exhibited to the neighbourhood hereabouts, not to be a subject of common enough observation ; and I am quite convinced that this abduction of her has merely taken place with a view of inducing me to take some steps to recover her at any pecuniary sacrifice."

" It would seem probable, indeed," said Henry, " that that was the case, and the more especially after you have detailed to me what has passed in the interview you had with the mendicant."

" I expect," added Captain Morton, " to hear very shortly something upon the subject, and that the whole matter will resolve itself into a consideration of what I will pay."

" If such should be the case," said Henry, with more of liveliness and hope in his voice and manner than he had as yet exhibited upon the subject ; " if such should be the case, we shall have a clue to where she is hidden, which, if followed up with perseverance, may restore her to us."

" It will be so, and hence is it that I wish you to wait yet awhile before you take any steps."

" Would it not be well," said Mrs. Morton, " to ascertain from the servants which among them last saw Mabel, and where she then was ?"

" Yes, certainly."

This suggestion was at once carried out, and the result of it was, the discovery that a letter by a strange man had been brought to Mabel, and delivered to her by one of the servants. A little more active inquiry among them, too, brought out the fact that one of the women servants had seen her just at dusk walking rapidly from the house in the direction of the lake.

Now it became evident to Captain Morton that she had been most easily and unadvisedly induced to keep some appointment which had been made with her, and then seized and carried off.

This conclusion had scarcely been come to, when one of the grooms who had been looking for Mabel, came to say he had something to communicate to his master, and he was at once admitted into the parlour.

" Well, Robert," said Captain Morton " have you made any discovery ?"

" I don't know, sir, whether to call it a discovery or not. I was searching along the banks of the lake, where the old fi tree used to stand that has been or the lasr two or three years tumbling into the watert and found it had gone at last."

" Indeed !"

" Yes, sir, and about that spot there were evident marks of footsteps. Upon searching more narrowly I found this glove."

" It is Mabel's," cried Mrs. Morton.

" Yes—yes," said Henry, as he eagerly snatched from the man's hand this sad memorial of her he loved. " Yes, it is, Mabel's. Now, God help her, what has been her fate ?"

" Hush ! Henry, hush !" said Captain Morton ; " let us hear what more Robert has to say to us."

" Of course, sir," added Robert, " I was not then content until I had examined all about the spot so thoroughly as to be convinced that nothing there had escaped my observation."

" Certainly, certainly."

" And I did not search in vain. Some few paces further on, I found this papers. It was trampled upon, and seemed as if some one had in the hurry of the scuffle dropped it unknowingly."

Robert handed a folded paper to Captain Morton, who, before he opened it, said to the groom,—

" Have you any more to say ?"

" No, sir."

" Very good. Robert, you can go."

When they were alone again, Captain Morton opened the paper with trembling hands, while Henry and Mrs. Morton waited eagerly to know what were its contents, for it seemed to be written nearly all over ou its inner side.

" What says it ?" inquired Henry eagerly, " what says it ?"

" Hush ! be calm," said his brother " be assured that I will read to you every word of it."

He glanced his eyes down the page, and then he said,—

" This is not a letter. It seems to be a paper of instructions given to some one. It is written evidently by some person of education, and, and——"

" It concerns Mabel ?" said Henry.

" It does—it does. The mystery of this transaction thickens indeed. We cannot reconcile this with anything that has occurred. Listen."—

Captain Morton read from the paper as follows :—

"There can be no manner of doubt that it was an English officer to whom the child was committed on the battle-field; but whether he died of his wounds, and so was compelled reluctantly, no doubt, to abandon the sacred trust that was reposed in him, or recovered to fulfil it, of course I have no means of knowing.——His name was Morton, or Meriton, or Moreton, or some name extremely similar. What his rank in the English army was we do not know. You will, however, upon repairing to England, most probably find sources of information open to you, of which we are here ignorant; and what appears now so troublesome an affair may be easy enough. And now let me implore you, and yet I feel that to such as you I need not do so, to proceed with the greatest delicacy and caution. Our object is the happiness of that child of destiny, and not to overwhelm her with any misery. God forbid that we should dream of harshly tearing her from the arms of those who may have been to her all that the tenderest parents could be.

"But it is in vain for mortals to calculate upon the chances of fortune. There are several considerations which make this pilgrimage upon which you are going a most holy one.

"In the first place, with all the will to do so, this English officer may not have had the power to be to that child all that he might wish. In the second place, he may, from the very nature of his profession, have been compelled to depute to others the duty, which having himself undertaken, he otherwise would gladly and honourably himself have superintended. And in the third place, as a very remote supposition indeed, he may possibly have been tired of his charge.

"I say this is a very remote possibility; for the man who, under such sad and distressful circumstances as he was in upon that sanguinary field of battle, would, in the manner he did, make the generous promise he did, is not a likely man to tire in its performance.

"Therefore, you will understand, my dear E., why it is that I regard this as a very remote supposition indeed, and do not allow it for one moment to vex me, or cause me a pang of uneasiness.

"There is one other state of things which may have ensued, and which of course would be an answer to all inquiries—she may be dead! The lives of young creatures such as she was are precarious : and how long she had to remain on the field of battle in charge of that wounded man, who could not help himself, I know not; or what accidents she may have been exposed to.

"When these thoughts press upon me, I feel all the sadness of my situation. Then it is that I feel that depression of the heart which you have so often noticed in me, and retire to shed those tears in secret, the traces of which you tell me you have frequently seen upon my cheeks.

"And now, dear E., understand me. It is not death that appals me; it is not the fear that she may be dead that strikes such a chill to my heart. Oh, no! it is the uncertainty whether she be so or not. It is the agony of suspense which unmans me. If I knew the worst, I should be calm.

"And now, dear E., I think you know nearly all that I can tell you, to guide you in your search. When she was given into the charge of that generous Englishman, she had a small pelisse trimmed with white fur on her, and around her neck was the little locket you have so often heard me describe to you. I think she will have her dear mother's eyes. I have pleased myself with the hope that she will, dear E.

"And now Heaven prosper you on this pilgrimage you have, for my sake, undertaken. My prayers will always be with you, and if you find her very happy, leave her so, and come and tell me. I will then visit her, and hold her to my heart and bless her; but she shall not find my affection selfish. I will not tear her from those she loves to those whom she knows not, let them love her ever so tenderly. Heaven bless all who have been kind to her.

"Remember, the name I think is Morton. May the blessing of Heaven always attend you, and that you may return to me with the joyous tidings that she whom my heart has so long yearned for is happy, is my daily prayer. Now go, my dear E., my heart is with you."

\*    \*    \*    \*    \*    \*

Not the least sound was uttered by either Mrs. Morton or Henry, while Captain Morton was reading. The simple and affecting language in which this code of instructions which the paper contained was couched, irresistibly claimed their attention to it; and when the captain ceased reading, and with a deep sigh laid down the paper, they felt a pang of disappointment that there was no more in the same strain.

"That is all," said the captain.

There was a dead silence for several moments. Mrs. Morton was visibly affected, and Henry, as well as his brother, were so bewildered in the mental attempt to reconcile the sentiments in this paper with the abduction of Mabel, that they knew not what to say. It was Henry now who first spoke, and he cried,—

"Good Heavens, what are we to think? The writer of this paper, and his agent to whom he has written it, are not the hands into which our poor Mabel has fallen."

"No," said Mrs. Morton, "nor can it be possible that that mendicant can be known to have any connexion with such people."

"I fear not, indeed," said Captain Morton. "The tone of this writing is such that not one of us would have regretted to see its author come to us and claim Mabel as his own child. There is sound judgment in it—correct feeling; and, in every line, there breathe the sentiments of a man of good feeling and profound philanthropy. Oh, if such a one as he who wrote these words had come to bless Mabel with the news that she had a father living, no one would have hailed his presence with more delight than I should."

"Nor I—nor I," said Henry, "Who is this E.?"

"Heaven knows."

"What are we to think? There is some dreadful mystery in all this which defies all conjecture. The person to whom this letter is addressed cannot be that man who has filled the neighbourhood with terror in consequence of the frightful crime he has committed, and who visited you here?"

Mrs. Morton suddenly clasped her hands and uttered an exclamation of grief, which alarmed both her husband and Henry.

They at once flew to her, and begged her to say what sudden thought distressed her. All she did for some moments was to wring her hands and exclaim, in frantic accents,—

"Oh, my poor Mabel—my poor Mabel!"

"Tell us—oh, tell us," said her husband, "what sudden thought or conviction has given rise to this fearful agony of apprehension."

Mrs. Morton's tears fell fast, as she sobbed,—

"The worst thought of all—oh, the worst of all! Does it not strike you—does it not occur to you, with all the force of truth, that this young traveller, who was murdered so cruelly at the inn, is he who in that paper is named E.? Oh, does it not come across your minds with all the force of a horrible conviction that such is the case? The mendicant has murdered him, and, from among the stolen papers he took from the chamber of his victim, he has acquired the information concerning Mabel, which has enabled him probably to impose upon her judgment. Oh, Heaven, have mercy upon our poor Mabel! She is now in the blood-stained hands of a murderer! She is lost—lost to us for ever!"

Such was the agony of grief into which this cruel, but extremely probable, conviction had thrown Mrs. Morton, that, after uttering these words, she fainted away, and every other consideration was forced, for the moment, to be put aside, in the anxiety of Captain Morton to see her conveyed in safety to her own chamber.

Henry remained in the parlour, with his head resting upon his hands, and in such a bewildered agony of thought as regarded the situation of her whom he loved to such an extent of devotion beyond his power of expression, that, once or twice, he almost thought he should go distracted. He had the greatest difficulty to keep himself from rushing out of the house like a lunatic, shouting the name of Mabel, and calling upon all mankind to assist him in finding out her hiding-place. But he did, for a wonder, succeed in restraining himself from so heedless an act, and in waiting till his brother, the captain, after seeing Mrs. Morton partially restored, came into the parlour again, looking so pale, and agitated, and ill, that scarcely any one who had only seen him in the glow of robust health the day before, would have recognised him as the same individual.

---

## CHAPTER XLIII.

### HENRY'S EXPEDITION IN SEARCH OF MABEL.—RAFFERTY BROLICKBONES' DESPAIR, REPENTANCE, AND RESOLUTION.

HENRY sprang to his feet the moment he saw Captain Morton enter the room, and in a voice which proclaimed the state of agony he was in mentally, he cried,—

"Brother, we are now convinced that Mabel is in the hands of a ruffian; the suggestion of my aunt cannot be gainsayed. It has about it too terrible a probability—it must be true. Each moment's reflection adds a world of confirmation to it. Let me now go at once, I pray you, on my pilgrimage in search of her whom I will find, and rescue from the thraldom which now surrounds her, or myself perish in the attempt."

"I will not delay you now," said Captain Morton; "all I ask of you is to be careful to communicate often with me, for some information may turn up in this neighbourhood that may guide you. You shall go by the first dawn of daylight, Henry, and you shall go with ample means."

"Thank you, brother, thank you. I—

I cannot say all I would, because—because my heart is too full."

"I deserve no thanks, Henry. Do you go and snatch some repose now, while you can, and leave all the preparations for your departure to me. You will have need of all the physical energy you can bring to bear upon the matter; and always remember that by acting systematically, you will go through much more fatigue, than by destroying your natural rest, and suffering yourself to be too much led away by your feelings of intense anxiety."

"Do not doubt me for one moment. The stake I have at issue in this matter will teach me prudence. Do not doubt me, brother."

"You shall start at daybreak, be assured; and now let me have the intervening time to myself, and with it, likewise, the assurance that you are making, at least, the attempt to procure some necessary repose before you start upon your expedition."

"The first part of your request, brother, I can easily comply with, and I will leave you; as for the second, I fear anxiety of mind will now place it quite out of my power, unless when the bodily energies shall happen to be completely exhausted by fatigue."

Captain Morton felt fully the truth of what Henry said, but he made no reply to it; and Henry left the room to proceed to his own chamber, without the slightest idea of being able to sleep.

He busied himself in making a few simple preparations for leaving the Hall, and, with a heavy heart, he told himself that it might be a long and a weary time before he again looked upon that home which to him had been one possessing so many charms while Mabel was an inmate of it, but which now, alas! with her absence, seemed to have lost all its charms.

"My beautiful Mabel," he exclaimed, as, after having completed the few preparations he intended to make, he cast himself upon a chair, with a long-drawn sigh—"my beautiful Mabel, I dread to think of what may be your fate, and yet imagination will be busy on that fearful subject. Oh, if but one ruffian hand be raised in unkindness against you, let him who aims it rue the day and hour he so raised it. I will exact a terrible retribution. Surely, with such perseverance, and with such indomitable energy as I shall bring to the task, I shall be able to discover where she is concealed."

This was not obeying his brother's injunction, and trying to sleep; but how could he dream of repose under the circumstances in which he was placed? It would

have been a perfect mockery to have attempted to sink into a state of forgetfulness of the past. And if he had slept, who knows what terrible forms his now too active imagination might not have brought before his mind's eye? His teeming fancy, unchecked by reason, might have tortured him by a thousand painful images. He might have suffered far more sleeping than he would have done waking; and so, perhaps, it was a better and a wiser course to abstain from making even the attempt to court repose under such distressing circumstances.

In the meantime, the captain went to the chamber of his wife, whose indisposition had now become a new source of painful anxiety to him.

Like Macbeth, he could have remarked, that his troubles came not singly, but in battalions. He was much relieved, however, when he did visit his wife's room to find that she was greatly recovered, and to be assured by her that nothing now remained of the sudden faintness which had been induced by the mental shock she had received from the by far too probable supposition that poor Mabel was in the hands of the murderer of the young traveller at the inn.

"I am well in health, Morton," she said, "quite well, except so far as the mind sympathises with the body; but I still cannot help feeling, with all the force of conviction, and clinging tho it, tat poor Mabel is in the power of that dreadful man."

"I cannot," said Captain Morton, "although I fain would, deny that such is my own impression. We now know the worst, and we have but to arm ourselves with resolution to meet it, as well as take what steps we may to avert any of its fatal consequences—for fatal, as regards our happiness, will they be, unless Mabel is restorad to our arms again."

"Fatal, indeed!"

"The love of Henry for Mabel is evidently no boyish passion. I can well perceive that it is more firmly fixed than we ever imagined, and young as he is, and inexperienced in the world's ways, I do not anticipate anything but the best results from the journey in search of Mabel, which I shall provide him amply with the means of at once and effectually undertaking."

"He is very young."

"He is; but the great change that has taken place in him during these few hours, has shown me how much more rapidly agitating and exciting circumstances will occasionally develop the intellect, than the ordinary course of time."

"And has he changed?"

"He has. He now speaks with the firmness of a man. All the boy seems to have left him, and the ardour with which he looks now forward to the pursuit of Mabel, has, I can perceive, exercised the most marked influence upon him."

"Then with you, husband, I will hope the best from Henry's exertions."

"I am sure you may."

"I will; and although I can give him nothing but my prayers, yet I will hope that they may be of some effect in aiding him. When goes he?"

"By daybreak. With some difficulty I have induced him to wait until then, before he prosecutes the search on which he has set his whole heart and soul."

In such like conversation as this Mrs. Morton and her husband passed some time, until the captain, feeling quite assured, now that she was sufficiently recovered from the mental shock she had received, at all events, to dread no recurrence of it, left her to see to the arrangements for Henry's departure.

He repaired to the parlour again, where lights were still burning, and as he entered that apartment somewhat abruptly, he started to perceive some human form between him and the table. Captain Morton could not at the moment see who it was, because the figure stood between him and the lights; but it was only for an instant he recoiled, and then advancing quickly, he cried,—

"Who's there?"

"A fool, your honour," said a voice, which the captain knew well as that of Rafferty Brolickbones.

"Rafferty!" he exclaimed, "is that you?"

"It was me, sir; but I ain't me now."

"What do you mean?"

"Ah, sir, I'm mean enough. I have done it, sir. You can call a court-martial, sir; I wish you would, and have me shot as soon as you like."

"Shot!"

"Yes, sir. Welcome now will be the bullet that finds its way to Rafferty's heart. I wish I had never lived, sir, to see this day."

Captain Morton turned back and closed the door; then advancing to Rafferty, he said,—

"I cannot fail to understand. You know something of the disappearance of our poor dear Mabel?"

Rafferty replied, in half-choked accents—

"That's just what I do know, sir, more sorrow to me. Oh, captain, why don't you kilt me? I won't accuse you of it afterwards, as I'm a Christian."

"Rafferty, I cannot understand what you mean by all these self-accusations. Whatever has occurred, let me implore you at once to give me a distinct account of it."

Rafferty thus urged, told the whole truth, colouring nothing, and concealing nothing, with a view to render himself less blameable, and he concluded by saying,—

"And now, you see, sir, that there's no fool like an old fool, and it's high time I was invalided. I've only come here to tell your honour what I've done, and now I'm going. Good bye to you, and God's blessing, sir, on you and yours, whatever becomes of me."

"Going where?" said Morton.

"Never mind, sir, where I go; it ain't worth an inquiry. To think of staying now, after to-night's business, is out of the question. I can't do it. Don't say an unkind word to me, sir, about it. I can say, and have said, quite enough of such to myself. There is no accuser stronger than my own heart."

"Stay, Rafferty," said Morton sadly, "stay. I cannot but admit that you have made a great and serious error of judgment; but it is only an error of judgment."

"Only, sir! I have sacrificed her, sir. I would let every drop of blood in my veins flow to save her. I have, fool-like, let poor dear Mabel, who relied upon my protection, be carried off by that thief of the world, sir, of a beggar. What can I think of myself? I shan't live long enough to tell myself thoroughly what a blackguard and a fool I've come to be. Good bye, sir."

"Hold! hold! It is now useless to waste time in idle regrets, Rafferty. You certainly took the very worst course you could take. Your plain and straightforward duty was, as soon as Mabel made you acquainted with the contents of that letter, to have reported the circumstance to me."

"I know it, sir; I know it."

"Then upon my shoulders would have been the responsibility of action."

"Of course, sir. But like an old fool as I am, I must needs be too clever by half, and so the dear child is lost."

"You have certainly done wrong; and now that I have said so much on that head, I shall not think of it again."

"No, sir, you won't have the opportunity. Good bye, your honour."

"You must not go. You must remain as usual in my service, Rafferty; and, notwithstanding this most grievous mistake you have committed, I have no doubt but that you will be a great assistance in repairing it, and assisting to discover Mabel."

"Sir," said the old sergeant, in a voice that showed he was deeply affected, "if you must have the truth, I don't mean to leave a square foot of this country unsearched for her."

"Nay, Rafferty, Henry is going on such an expedition."

"Let me go with him, sir. No—no—why do I ask? The boy will hate the sight of me. No—no; I it was that led her, poor thing, into the snare. No—no, I do not ask to go with him."

"You had better remain here. Something may yet occur even in this neighbourhood to give a clue to where she is."

Rafferty shook his head sadly, as he replied,—

"I can't remain here, sir. Every tree, every flower, every blade of grass, sir, about here would remind me of her. It would seem as if I had given her away to somebody, and was trying to enjoy the old place without her. I couldn't do it, sir; I really couldn't do it. My heart's almost broke already, and to stay here would soon be a finisher to it outright."

There was much pathos in what the old soldier said. Captain Morton knew well by the strange, wiry tone in which he spoke, that the effort he was compelled to make to restrain some sudden and violent outbreak of agonised feeling, must be a great one.

He, therefore, having got from Rafferty all the particulars it was in the old sergeant's power to tell, determined upon putting an end to the interview, and saying no more to him upon the painful and harassing subject until the morning should come.

"Rafferty," he said, "I will speak to you to-morrow. What you have related concerning our poor Mabel is but a confirmation of what we suspected before we saw you to-night. Discussion between us can do but little good. Retire to rest, and to-morrow morning I will talk to you again about what is to be done in this sad emergency."

Rafferty moved towards the door, and then he paused, as he said, with evident difficulty,—

"And Master Henry is going, sir?"

"By daybreak."

The old soldier left the room, and Captain Morton paced the apartment for some time in deep thought.

"So," he said, "our worst suspicions are confirmed. Poor Mabel is in the hands of that scoundrel, the murderer of the young traveller at the Morton Arms, while every concurrent circumstance seems to assure me that he is the individual named under the initial E., in that most interesting document which chance has thrown into our possession. Oh, had that young traveller but come here instead of staying at the inn, what a world of misery it would have saved to us all. Upon what slender threads hang our mortal destinies."

The course of reasoning adopted by Captain Morton was the most rational in the world under the circumstances, and no mind of the most ordinary calibre could possibly have missed it. That the young traveller, who had made such eager and anxious inquiries concerning the Morton family, of our friend, Toggs, the landlord, was the " E." mentioned in the mysterious paper, everything went to prove. That he had been dogged to that spot by the mendicant for the express purpose, probably, only of robbery, and getting possession of the documents which should enable him to prefer a claim to Mabel, that he had no other means of bringing forward appeared quite clear now.

That claim was one which, no doubt, the mendicant hoped, and fully intended, to forego for money. His visit to Captain Morton showed that, and his disappointment at the manner in which he was met, resulted in the attack upon Mabel, and her forcible abduction.

Whether or not he from the first intended to take the life of the young traveller, is doubtful. From the manner, however, in which he did the deed, and the general apparent reckless ferocity of his character, we may come fairly enough to the conclusion that, whether it was a part of his plan or not, he, at all events, had no sort of hesitation in doing the deed of blood.

The great care which the young traveller took off the saddle, in the secret pocket of which were those papers, one of which had, no doubt, been dropped accidentally by the beggar at the spot where it was found by the groom, was possibly the cause of the young traveller's destruction.

Perhaps, had the mendicant obtained possession of the papers in any other way, he might not have taken the life of his victim; but, alas! as it was, his determination to have them was evidently for too strong to allow a human life to stand in the way.

And hence he, who had been so affectionately addressed by the writer of the document which mentioned him as " E," had fallen a victim to the murderer's knife, for attempting too well and faithfully to discharge the scheme that had been entrusted to him.

Fearful fate! Unhappy man! Heaven grant thee that grace and joy hereafter, which has been by cruel destiny denied thee here. May thy translation from this world, and all its evanescent joys and feelings, to that which is without end, be to thee a joyful and a holy recompense, for falling in the glorious cause of justice and mercy !

The circumstances connected with the abduction of Mabel were now, however, so far stripped of extraneous matter in the shape of conjecture, that there was a far greater likelihood of some good and practical result now arising from all energetic sarch, than before.

The evidence of Rafferty Brolickbones, painful as it was, confirmed, beyond the possibility of a doubt, that the mendicant was the guilty man, and so far it would be satisfactory to Henry to know of whom he was in search, and that if he could in any way, by dint of energy and perseverance, come upon the track of that man, he would not be far from his much-loved Mabel.

Now, likewise, two crimes were hanging over the head of that most desperate and diabolical ruffian.

The hands of all men were raised against him as a shedder of blood, and he likewise stood before all who knew anything of the circumstances, as the despoiler of the domestic hearth of one of its brightest attributes in the shape of such a being as Mabel.

Oh, it is singular how one fragile, delicate girl, should be the bond which united a whole household. The kind of rallying point, around which are congregated a thousand virtues and happinesses.

But so it was as regarded Mabel. She was gone, and there was now a blank at Morton Hall, which could not be filled up. There was a sadness and a lonesomeness about the house which was melancholy to see. It seemed as if it had been dismantled of one half of its fittings and furnishing.

How strange that one human being should produce so great an effect among so many.

---

## CHAPTER XLIV.

THE DEPARTURE.—RAFFERTY'S NEW POSITION. — ANOTHER MYSTERIOUS DISAPPEARANCE FROM THE HALL.

HENRY MORTON knew not exactly in what way his brother, the captain, intended to start him on his expedition, when he told him he should go with every means and appliance of success that it was in his power to give him. He, however, felt no uneasiness on that head; for well he knew that when his brother said so much, that he was a man more likely to be better than his word than worse.

He waited with extreme anxiety for the coming morn, and as Captain Morton chose to communicate to his wife what Rafferty Brolickbones had done, Henry was without that information for some hour or more after his brother was aware of it.

When, however, Mr. and Mrs. Morton had talked over this new information, or rather what we may call this confirmation of what they already suspected, Captain Morton thought of endeavouring to ascertain if Henry was sleeping or not.

"If he be up and watchful, as I fear he is," he said, "he may as well be at once put in possession of all this new matter on the subject, instead of waiting until the morning."

"Henry is not sleeping," said Mrs. Morton, "you may depend. There is no fear of interrupting his repose. You will find him up, and most probably plunged in melancholy thought."

"Then I will go to his room at once."

The captain did so, but as there was yet just a possibility that fatigue, both of body and mind, might have induced a state of repose in Henry, he moved the lock of the door very cautiously indeed before he ventured upon thoroughly opening it. Gentle and almost noiseless as was that movement, it did not escape the ear of Henry, who had not made even the pretence of seeking repose by divesting himself of any of his clothing. He sprang to the door in a moment, crying,—

"Who is there?"

"'Tis I, Henry," said Captain Morton, "'tis I. You were not seeking that rest which I told you was so essential to you before you started on your expedition."

"How could I so mock myself, brother," said Henry, "as to attempt to seek repose with my mind so harassed as it is?"

"Well, well, I had a suspicion that you would be up, so I have come to tell you something new that has occurred."

Henry's eyes betrayed the eager hope with which he heard these words, for he thought that possibly some good news of Mabel might have turned up; but his brother soon repressed that joyous expectation by the increased gravity of his countenance, and by what he immediately said.

"Do not elate yourself, Henry. What I have to tell you is merely a confirmation of what we expected."

"A confirmation?"

"Yes. There is abundant and undoubted evidence now that, as we have surmised,

our poor Mabel is in the hands of that desperate and unprincipled scoundrel who, with the appearance of a mendicant, has infested this neighbourhood, whether he be really such in circumstances or not."

Henry lent to his brother the most breathless attention, while the latter related to him the story of Rafferty Brolickbones, and when he had finished Henry could not help exclaiming,

"And so the folly of that man, brother, of whose discretion I have heard you speak so highly, has brought upon us all this amount of misery?"

"It is so. But there is no occasion to say anything to the old soldier about it, by way of reproach."

"No occasion?"

"None, whatever. His own feelings are more than sufficient punishment for his indiscretion."

"But his feelings are a poor recompense to me!"

"They are, of course, none at all; but you should consider that the fault of Rafferty was one into which many of the wisest of us often fall. We adopt a course of conduct which we think the cleverest, in preference to that which is the most straightforward and direct."

"True, but——"

"Nay, Henry, if you knew and saw, as I know and have seen, how much compunction Rafferty feels in this affair, you would rather pity than condemn him; or, at all events, you would pity while you did condemn. You know how greatly he was attached to Mabel, and I am quite sure that if now his heart's blood could restore her to us, he would shed every drop of it to accomplish such a result."

"Well, well," said Henry, "I will say nothing to him. God help poor Mabel, and restore her to us."

"Amen to that Henry; and now I shall give you the best horse in my stable. You may pick which you please, and you shall have a sum of money to start with, sufficient to last you some time; and, when you come near to the end of it, you can write to me from any market town where there is a banker, and I will make arrangements through my bankers to have your cheque honoured there."

"Thank you, brother, a thousand thanks; I will not be wasteful of the means you so generously place in my hands."

"Of that I am well aware, Henry; but you will always remember that the errand you go upon is one as dear and as interesting to me, and your aunt, as to you; and, therefore, if any well-timed piece of liberality with money seems at any time likely to advance that object, do not, I pray you, for one moment hesitate lest I should think you are making an extravagant use of the means I place at your disposal."

"I will not hesitate," said Henry, deeply affected.

"That is right. And now we understand each other upon that subject—of money—which is always a disagreeable one, take this pocket-book, and it will be completely settled until I hear from you."

"Thanks, brother, thanks. All I want is, that small wallet there strapped behind the saddle of my horse. It contains all I shall take with me in the way of luggage."

"You are prudent—the less you take the better, of course."

"Brother, it is nearly daybreak; may I go at once?"

"If it so please you."

Henry sprang to his feet.

"Hold!" said Captain Morton. "Ere you go, let me ask you if you have laid out in your own mind any plan of proceeding?"

"I have. I shall proceed from house to house in the village, and I shall ask of every one of the inhabitants if they have seen or heard anything of a party of three who have been in the vicinity. The probability is, that from some one or other I shall get some clue to which direction the men and Mabel have taken, and then I shall follow that clue with the most careful industry."

"You cannot do better. Go, Henry, and may the blessing of Heaven, which surely should belong to such a cause as ours, attend you."

"It will—it will."

Henry left the room with his brother, and then he paused, as he said,—

"Can I wish my aunt good bye?"

"Yes, certainly. Wait a moment."

The captain went into Mrs. Morton's bedroom, and told her that Henry wished to take leave of her, when she desired that he might be immediately admitted. He shook her by both hands, as he said,—

"Good bye, aunt. I think we shall meet again; but you will see me with Mabel on my return, or never."

"Nay, Henry, that is foolish," said Mrs. Morton; "the best cause may fail, and the holiest of purposes may never be fulfilled. Do not say that, because it may please Heaven that Mabel may never again bless us again by her presence, you, likewise, are to be taken from us."

"It was a foolish speech," said Henry. "Forget it—farewell."

He hastily left the room, and proceeded direct to the stables, where he picked out a middle-sized gray horse, which he had been frequently in the habit of riding, and commenced saddling him himself. It soon, however, got hinted about among the servants, many of whom were up, that Master Henry was going away in search of Mabel, and many were the cordial good wishes he received from homely lips.

And now the horse was saddled, and all was ready just as the calm, sweet, gray light of the morning began to steal, with its magic influence, over all objects. He mounted his steed, and as he held his brother's hand in his, he said, as he glanced among the servants,—

"I would gladly see Rafferty before I go—I do not wish to leave otherwise than the best of friends with all here."

The servants with one accord looked round for Rafferty Brolickbones, but he was nowhere to be found; they called him by name loudly, but there was no response; and then Captain Morton said to Henry, in a low tone, so that no one could hear the purport of what he said,—

"Henry, you may depend he will not come, because he knows your affection for Mabel, and he dreads some words of displeasure from you which he could not well forget."

"Heaven knows," said Henry, "I have no such intention."

"I know you have not; but he cannot know so; I will, however, myself call him. He may attend to my voice, when perhaps he would not to that of any one else."

"Do so, brother."

Captain Morton called aloud upon Rafferty Brolickbones, in his clear and manly voice, several times, but there was no reply, so that he felt himself, however unwillingly, compelled to come to the conclusion that Rafferty either would not come, let who might call him, or that he had carried his threat into execution, and had actually left the place, being quite out of sorts with himself for the part he had played in the abduction of Mabel.

"Well, well," said Henry, when he found there was no chance of Rafferty's showing himself; "tell him, brother, that if these were the last words I had to speak, I freely forgive him for the part he has most unintentionally had in inflicting upon me and upon us all so much suffering."

"I will."

"And now, adieu, friends all—adieu, brother!"

The brothers shook hands cordially, and Henry turned his horse's head away from that home in which he had spent the happiest hours of his existence—happy hours that he would never know again.

Alas! that it should be so; but it is a melancholy fact that, as we grow older and mingle more with the great world and its inhabitants, we get an unfortunate kind of wisdom which incapacitates us from enjoying those delicious feelings which make up the sunshine of our youth.

So it is too with most, if not indeed with all the objects of human ambition;—by the time we attain them, we have lost the relish for them, and they come upon us listlessly. We do not find that exquisite glow of feeling and excitement which we pictured to ourselves as the result of certain advancements in life.

We have grown half-wearied with the world before we can ever, by the greatest possible perseverance, obtain some of its brightest-looking prizes; and when we get them, we find them, like the glittering pieces of money given to the adventurer by the fairies, nothing but dried leaves, and all worthless and lost.

Henry Morton might, by some lucky conjunction of circumstances, find her who was his heart's idol. He might find her unharmed, and he might be well and fully able to snatch her from the hands of that man who had so basely torn her from a home she adorned, to misery; but the light of his joy was gone. The rude shock had been given to his mind which despoiled it of most of its romance.

\*    \*    \*    \*    \*    \*

The plan of operations for the purpose, at all events, of making a vigorous endeavour to find Mabel was, although perhaps the only one which, under the circumstances, Henry could adopt, yet probable enough to fail.

If, upon making the inquiry he intended to make of all the villagers concerning the two men who had taken Mabel away, and the road they had taken her, he found that no one could give him that requisite amount of information to guide him on his course, he would incontestibly find himself in a very puzzling situation how to proceed.

Whether to go east, west, north, or south would then be a troublesome question, and this fact occurred to his mind more quickly after he had left the Hall, and, at a gentle canter, was making his way towards the village.

"Well," he said, with a sigh, "I must make the tour of the country first before I start on my direct line of road. If I can but procure a clue to the route they have taken, I can surely by perseverance follow it up, and eventually overtake them; they cannot be always travelling. The expense of conveyance would be great, and if they go on foot, I shall have no difficulty in soon coming up with them."

He now emerged from the grounds belonging to the Hall, and entered a green lane which led by a short cut to the village.

The morning was advancing with great rapidity, and as this lane in which he now was chanced to look to the east, he seemed as if he were riding from darkness to light, so different an aspect had the sky in that quarter of the heavens to which he was going, apparently to that which he was leaving behind him.

There is something to the young always fresh, beautiful, and exhilarating in the early morning, and Henry now, notwithstanding the heavy weight that was pressing at his heart, felt some of the delightful influences of the coming day.

"Oh!" he exclaimed, "how happy might we all have continued at the Hall, but for this most sad accident of evil fortune which has deprived us of our dearest treasure. But I will not despair. I will hope for the very best, and that, like a passing cloud, all this may fade away, and we shall once again have Mabel back to us."

Henry felt that if once he gave way to any dreadful suppositions that he might not be successful in discovering Mabel, he should be lost entirely, and want nerve to continue that search he wished to persuade himself he began promisingly.

Therefore it was that whenever he trusted his voice to speak upon the subject, he took care that it should be in a hopeful strain, for any other would have driven him completely to despair.

As he had reached about half the length of the green lane, and was not looking a-head, he suddenly became conscious that the light of the morning, which had been glancing in his eyes, was obscured by some intervening object. He drew the reins of his horse mechanically, and then, upon looking forward, he saw a horseman in the very centre of the lane, occupying so much room that it would be difficult to pass him; and, indeed, by his attitude he seemed intent, either from downright discourtesy, or other motives, upon disputing the free passage of Henry down the lane.

Our young friend, however, was not one likely to feel much daunted at such an occurrence. He felt the warm blood mount to his cheeks, and giving the reins to his steed, he, with one bound, was close up to the stranger, when he heard a well-known voice say aloud to him,—

"Halt, Mr. Henry, halt. Hear what the old man has to say, and then ride over him if you like."

"Rafferty!" exclaimed Henry.

"Yes, sir; I was Rafferty."

Henry was silent, and after a very short pause, Rafferty added,—

"You don't speak, Mr. Henry; but it's all the same. You might as well say it as think it, sir. I know what's passing in your mind. 'Here's the ould thief of the world,' says you, 'as let the vagabonds go off with Miss Mabel.' That's what you are thinking of."

"No, Rafferty, no," said Henry. "It's more in sorrow than in anger that I look upon you."

"Ah—humph," said Rafferty; "that's a genteel way, I know, of telling me I am an old blackguard."

"You are wrong, Rafferty."

"Well, well, sir; perhaps I am. I am likely enough to be wrong, sir. After a man has made one great mistake, Mr. Henry, he begins to misdoubt himself."

"But what do you do here, Rafferty, at this time in the morning?"

"Mr. Henry, I was going to find you."

"To the Hall?"

"Yes, sir."

"I have just come from there, and since we have met here, Rafferty, you had better tell me at once what you have to say, for it's likely enough the Hall and I may be strangers now for many a weary day."

"Strangers, sir?"

"Yes, Rafferty. After what has happened you could hardly suppose I would remain there in inactivity. I have now a sacred duty to perform. I have a pursuit in life which shall be successful, or it shall last while life itself lasts."

"I understand you, sir," said Rafferty. "It's Miss Mabel, sir, you mean to look for, and till you find her, sir, you won't see the old Hall?"

"You are right."

"Bad luck to me, Mr. Henry, it's once in a way or so I ought to be right, always considering how wrong I have been."

"Well, Rafferty, you cannot, I see, make a remark about anything without remembering what has occurred, and the share you had in it. Once and for all, let me tell you, that, of course, I cannot help considering you were very indiscreet; but as both my brother and myself are well convinced of your affection for Mabel, and the excellence of your motives, we do not wish to utter one word of reproach to you."

"There's no occasion," said the old soldier, as he struck his chest with his clenched fist; "there's no occasion, sir. I've quite reproach enough to last me all my life, let me use it every hour of the day, here."

"Well, well; that I cannot help, Rafferty.

You must do the best you can to relieve yourself from whatever burden o self-accusation you have now to bear. But you have something to tell me, have you not?"

"I have, sir."

"Be quick and brief, then, for my time presses."

"I have been to every house in the village, sir, and have spoken to every man, woman, and child, and I've found out that the villains took the high road, sir, towards Burking."

"You are sure of that?" said Henry, eagerly.

"Quite, sir."

"Then you have saved me the loss of time of making the same kind of inquiry, Rafferty. I thank you; let me now pass on."

"Mr. Henry," exclaimed Rafferty, in so strange a tone that Henry started, for he could hardly believe it came from his lips.

"What would you say, Rafferty?" he asked.

"Sir, I can't know, of course, if you will listen as I wish you to what I'm going to say; but, to begin with it, I can tell you, sir, that until Miss Mabel's foot crosses the threshold, I have taken my leave of the Hall."

"Do not say that, Rafferty, You still stand high in my brother's esteem, A temporary indiscretion, such as you have fallen into, cannot obliterate his sense of what you have done for him."

"I done for him, sir?"

"Yes. You saved his life on the field of Waterloo."

"Oh, bother! I should have done just what I did for anybody besides him, so that's nothing. Don't speak about it, Mr. Henry; but now to come to the point at once. Look at me Iain't so young as once I was, but my heart is every bit. I have yet a tolerably strong arm. I don't know what fear is; the Brolickbones never did. I don't intend to go back to the Hall: let me follow you, sir, and be of what small help I may in finding her, the loss of whom has nearly broken my heart."

Henry was silent for a moment or two, and then he said, gravely—

"Rafferty, this may not be."

"Not be, sir?"

"No—I am dependant upon my brother's goodness to me in a great measure, and, although he is not one who would, even for one moment, make me feel that dependance, yet, unsanctioned by him, I cannot take away one of his servants as an attendant upon myself."

"You won't, sir?"

"I feel that I ought not."

"Well, Mr. Henry, you have given me an answer. I shall take this horse back to the stables, and then good bye to you for ever! I shall go on foot, and wherever good or bad fortune may lead me. I will not beg, for I am an old soldier, and I cannot bring my mind to do that—but I can starve, and till I do I will hunt for Miss Mabel. Farewell, sir, farewell."

It was not so much what Rafferty said, as the tone and manner in which he said it, that convinced Henry Morton of the deep sincerity of the old man, and the amount of suffering his refusal to allow him to follow him gave to his heart. Henry's feelings at the moment smote him, and he told himself that his brother, far from objecting to Rafferty accompanying him, would, most probably, be well pleased that such was the case. And then again, Rafferty, although he had certainly made an error of judgment as regarded the sad affair which had terminated in the abduction of Mabel, was ordinarily acute and right minded. He was brave too, to a fault. On the whole, his company on the expedition presented advantages of an important nature, which now came crowding upon the mind of Henry. He wheeled round his horse and looked after the old soldier—he saw that he was bent down on the saddle of the steed he rode, as if he were overwhelmed with grief. The horse was going at a foot pace, and, probably, was quite unguided by his rider, whose feelings at that moment were painfully absorbing.

"Poor fellow," said Henry, "he will do no good to himself or anybody else if I don't take him. He loves Mabel, I know, with all his heart. How he has followed her about when she was quite a little thing to save her from harm. No—no; I cannot leave him thus—it would be cruel."

He raised his voice and shouted aloud—

"Rafferty—Rafferty!"

If a thunderbolt had suddenly fallen at the old soldier's feet he could not have started more suddenly erect upon his saddle—he wheeled the horse round in a moment, and in a voice which echoed again in the lane, he cried—

"Here!"

Then he saw Henry beckoning him to approach, and at a hard gallop he reached his side in a few seconds.

"Rafferty," said Henry, "I have taken a better thought. You shall go with me, if you please."

A cry of joy came from Rafferty's lips, and Henry saw the sudden gush of tears which came to his eyes in spite of him.

"God—bless you—Mr. Henry," said he; "I'll follow you all the world over, and anywhere else."

"I'm sure you would, Rafferty."

"And never fear, sir, but we will find her—the sweet jewel of all our hearts. We'll find her, sir, between us; and won't that be a happy hour, any way? bless her sweet eyes. Now, sir, I'm a man again, and care for nothing."

"I have great hopes that we shall find her, Rafferty."

"Great hopes, sir—I have great certainties. I wouldn't put up with only great hopes, not I. They wouldn't suit me, Mr. Henry—we must find her, and we will."

"I am glad to find you in such a frame of mind. As soon as we get to a market town, where there is a post-office, I will write to my brother to account for the disappearance of the horse you ride. By-the-bye, Rafferty, you ride uncommonly well."

"I was in the light cavalry, sir, before I entered the line. There's not many a horse I wouldn't ride. As long as the creturs keep their feet, it's little I care what they do, sir."

"Then let us on to the town called Burking, towards which you say you have ascertained that Mabel has been taken. With you, I will hope for the very best."

"Do, sir, and then we are half way, ay, and a good deal more, towards success. A faint heart, sir, never did anything—only never, sir, if you was to live a hundred years, trust to a fir tree."

"I will not, Rafferty."

"I shall never look at one, sir, without a feeling of what an old fool I have made of myself in getting into one. I have been wishing I was drowned all the night, and wondering I wasn't; but now, somehow, the case is different, for I have got something to do that does give me a chance of repairing the mischief I have done, and woe be to the man who now stands between me and Miss Mabel, if I know it."

"When we make a halt, Rafferty," said Henry, "I can inform you of some more evidence that we have, that not only goes to prove that the mendicant who has gone off with Mabel is the murderer of the young stranger at the Morton Arms, but that that very murdered man came into this neighbourhood to look for Mabel, on behalf of those who, probably, are nearest akin to her, and who, from what little we know of them, we should have had no hesitation in receiving kindly."

"Indeed, sir."

"Yes, Rafferty, such appears to be the

case; so that whoever that diabolical scoundrel may be who has taken Mabel from us, he is evidently a man who scruples not at the worst of crimes, and no doubt has succeeded in producing an immense amount of misery."

"The villain of the world, sir. Well, I only hope that I may just come within half-arms-length of him, that's all. It's a mighty convenient distance that to have a fellow at."

"I hope you may."

"But,—but, Mr. Henry, you,—you don't suppose, villain as he is, he could have the heart to injure the hair of our beautiful darling's head—do you, Mr. Henrry?"

"As to his having the heart to do so, Rafferty, it is hard to say what such a scoundrel may not have the heart to do. But my brother thinks, and I am of the same opinion, that a wish to extort money from him is at the bottom of the whole proceeding; and, in that case, the villain's common sense will teach him that to treat Mabel otherwise than well, would be to defeat most completely all his hopes in that way, and to draw down upon his head the very worst personal consequences of his crime."

"True, sir, true—there is something in that."

"It is a great hope, Rafferty. I intend at every town we come to, to obtain an audience with the principal authorities, and give information of the whole occurrence, and a full description of the parties, as well as offer a handsome reward for any discovery that may be made. By such a course you perceive that, in a short time, we may, mounted as we are, spread an alarm through the whole country."

"Certainly, sir, we may, and a mighty good plan it is, too, as ever was thought of."

"Is that Beechey which we are coming to?"

"It is, sir."

"I am not familiar with this line of road, as it does not present those attractions of scenery which the contrary direction does; but let us now push on, Rafferty, and we may get some news as well as some breakfast at that place."

They put the horses to a good canter, and rapidly neared the little market town of Beechey, towards which Rafferty had been informed that parties answering the description of the fugitives had been seen to go.

---

## CHAPTER XLV.

THE INNS AT BEECHEY.—THE PURSUIT.—
THE DISAPPOINTMENT.

THE distance of the market town from where Henry and Rafferty had first ob-

served it, was greater than it looked, for it stood on the rise of a hill, and they were on the slope of another when they saw it, so that they had to descend into the valley below the two, before they made much real progress towards it. About twenty minutes' riding brought them, however, to its outskirts, and then, as the hill was steep, they reduced the speed of their horses, and quietly entered the long, straggling streets of the town.

Henry made up his mind always to stop at the best inn he could see; not that any particular love of creature comforts tempted him particularly to do so, but he was convinced that he would be more likely to obtain information and respect to his inquiries by so doing, than as if he paused at places of inferior accommodation. Besides, he had found, during some short journeys he had made with his brother, at different times across the country, that the only difference in prices at houses of public entertainment, was between the two extremes of the very high and the very low. A second-rate inn charges as much as a first-rate one; and, therefore, he did not accuse himself of any extravagance by going to the latter.

The inn at Beechey, which seemed to have the most pretensions, was named the Lion, and accordingly Henry dismounted at its door, surrendering the rein of his horse to Rafferty, until the ostler should make his gracious appearance. It was a very early hour, and although the officials of the inn were about, they evidently did not expect any visitors so soon in the day. It was, however, as chance would have it, one of those well-ordered establishments which can seldom be put out of the way, and Henry was shown into a private room, and attended upon with more expedition than he might fairly have expected.

He asked for the landlord, who, in the course of a few moments, made his appearance, and to him Henry at once briefly detailed his errand, desiring him to send some one of his household to make inquiry if any one in the town had seen anything of such persons as he, Henry, described.

The landlord expressed his readiness to do so, and left immediately to carry out his instructions.

An ample breakfast was laid before Henry, to which his ride enabled him, despite his anxiety, to do justice; and he gave orders that Rafferty should have whatever he pleased. Henry, so near home, did not think it necessary to trouble any of the authorities of the town he was in, because he knew that it lay within the county in which his brother's estate was, and that, as a matter of course, the captain would lose no time in making all the local magistracy aware of the fact of the abduction of Mabel from his protection; but he waited with some anxiety to know if the landlord's inquiries should result in anything which would further direct him on the road the men had taken with Mabel.

After about half-an-hour the old landlord returned, and brought with him a rough-looking specimen of humanity, in the shape of a waggoner, who made so many awkward bows and simultaneous kicks out with his feet at the same time, when he was introduced to the apartment, that Henry thought he would never leave off.

"This man, sir," said the landlord, "I think, has seen the parties you wish to inquire concerning."

"I am glad to hear it," said Henry. "Tell me, my good man, all you know of the matter, and I will amply repay you for your loss of time, and your trouble."

"Yes," said the man; "I wur a comin, and I seed 'em."

"Yes; go on."

"They wur a scamperin, and they tarned off loike into the wud."

"Into the what?"

"The wud. Doan't ye know what a wud is?"

"Indeed I do not."

"He means the wood, sir," said the landlord; "about half-a-mile on the road you have come there's a wood."

"There is, I saw it. So they went there?"

"Yees."

"And did you see any more of them?"

"Noa!"

"What sort of persons were they?"

"Two ill-fared looking chaps and a gal; she guved a sort of a shreek when they went into the wud, and afore I could say woa, they were all gone out of sight."

"I have no doubt that these are the parties I seek," said Henry; "where does that road lead to?"

"Why, sir," said the landlord, "it leads to nowhere in particular, but to a lot of old cross roads of one sort and another."

"I must pass through it, however, and, by chance, I may meet some one who has seen the fugitives. There is a sovereign for you, my man."

"A—a what?"

"A sovereign."

"Eh! eh! eh! eh!"

"What are you laughing at?"

"Eh! eh! Tain't a gould one, you know."

"Go along with you," said the landlord, as he pushed him from the room. "How dare you insult the gentleman when he behaves so liberally to you? Go along—go along."

Henry now ordered the horses again, for they had had nearly an hour's rest, and had not been in the least distressed by the canter from Morton Hall to Beeehey.

He hastily, when they had mounted, related to Rafferty what he had heard, and then they turned their horses' heads towards the wood which had been mentioned, and which the reader is already aware that Mabel was really taken through by her captors. The distance was so short that they traversed it very quickly, and then perceiving a bridle road in the wood, which appeared to have been well used, as there were numerous marks of horses' feet at its commencement, they at once entered it, and at a slow pace proceeded onwards, hoping and expecting each moment to meet some rustic of the neighbourhood who might possibly have noticed Mabel. The distance, however, which may be traversed across the country, and not upon the line of any of the great roads, in England, without meeting with any one, is quite a matter of surprise to those who have not actually experienced that such is the case.

The wood was of considerable extent, and Henry and Rafferty must have gone nearly through it, before they heard a rustling among some underwood, and saw a young urchin, whose ostensible errand was, to all appearance, nest-hunting. He seemed rather scared at the approach of the horsemen, but Henry called to him, in an encouraging tone,—

"Hilloa, boy! I want to speak to you."

The boy ran slowly forward with that half assured, half shy movement, with which country children approach their superiors.

"How long have you been in the wood, my little man?" said Henry.

"I haven't took none," said the boy, as he pulled very adroitly one pocket inside out to show its emptiness.

"You may take what you please, as far as I am concerned," added Henry. "What I ask you is, how long you have been in the wood?"

The boy hesitated a moment, and then said,—

"Since breakfast."

"And when was that?"

"When we got up."

"And when was that?"

"When we woke."

"Hilloa, Ned!" cried a man's voice; "what's the matter?"

"Nothing, father," cried the boy, as he

turned to meet a tall man who now appeared through an avenue made naturally by the trees; "nothing's the matter."

This man was in that kind of garb which betokened him half labourer and half poacher. He was probably a fellow who did not stand upon trifles as regarded poultry, either.

"Your servant, sir," he said, when he saw Henry. "Lost your way in the wood, sir?"

"Not exactly," said Henry. "Do you live hereabouts?"

"Yes. I think I know you, sir."

"Probably enough."

"Is your name Morton, sir?"

"It is."

"Oh, then, you are Captain Morton's

HENRY MORTON DEPARTING FROM THE HALL IN SEARCH OF MABEL.

brother, and he ain't one of the poor man's persecutors about a piece of dry wood or a wild rabbit. My service to you, sir, and command me in any way."

"The way in which you can be most useful to me is by giving me the information I ask concerning the route of the two men and a female of whom I am in search, if you have the information to give."

"I believe I can do so," replied the man; "but you had better come to my cottage, such as it is, and then I will tell you all I know; it is but little, but that may be of service to you."

"It may, my good man; but why not here, because time is an object?"

"It will save time, sir, because then I can show you the spot, and then you can start again from that point."

"So I can, my good fellow; lead on, and we'll follow you."

The man turned and made his way in another direction from that in which he was before, and then came to a clear spot, whence they could proceed without any of the difficulties, or of a less number of them than before.

"What do you think of this, sir?" said

Brolickbones; "he's a darling of a boy, surely; he'd do any gentleman's estate a great deal of good by getting of the pheasants and hares; that's his line of business, any how."

"I believe that is the truth, Rafferty; but hold your tongue, he may do us a service."

"Dumb as a drum with a hole in it," said Rafferty, and he relapsed into silence, and followed Henry Morton through the wood, but keeping a sharp look out.

"Is it far?" inquired Henry.

"Not very far, sir—about ten minutes will bring us there."

They followed in silence; the only sounds that reached their ears were those made by themselves, the cracking and breaking of wood, the rustling of dry leaves, and the songs of birds that were just rising in the morning air, and filling the woods with the most melodious notes. The blackbird and the high-soaring lark helped to fill the heavens with their grateful sounds.

The air teemed with gladness, and the scene presented a beautiful appearance; not a sound or a sight but what was such as one who had time to look upon it would have deemed the most beautiful.

But Henry Morton had other thoughts passing through his mind; he was thinking of Mabel, the beautiful orphan; and the finest view in the world would scarce have extracted from him even a passing thought.

Brolickbones, too, had much mental occupation; his mind was sorely disturbed by the share he thought he had in the abduction of Mabel, for he believed but for him she would have still been in the society of her friends. Even at that moment he, Brolickbones, would not have been where he was, following Mr. Henry Morton through the woods with a questionable character for their guide.

It was with these melancholy and disagreeable thoughts passing through their minds, that they came to a sort of clearing, or field, in one corner of which stood a small, tumble-down looking place, which might be called a hut.

"Is this your cottage, my good fellow?" inquired Henry, as he looked at it.

"Yes, sir, it's what I live in; poor people can't pick and choose, else, sir, I'd have a better."

"I dare say—I dare say; you are rather retired here, are you not?"

"Yes," said the man.

"I'd go bail you ain't much troubled with company here?"

"No," said the man.

"Don't have many tea-parties," continued Rafferty, "or dinner-parties either?"

"I don't always get a dinner for myself, and, as for anybody else, it's clean out of the question, and no mistake about that."

"You take your steak by yourself, then, and you don't offer anybody a bit."

"Oh, yes, there are *stakes* enough about here; I could accommodate you that way," said the man, with a grim smile.

"Thank ye, but I'm an old soldier, an can take my share in a fray."

"So I should say."

"Should you?"

"Yes; can you swim?"

"Och, murder! can't I though; you should have seen me the other night, worse luck. Och! and I'll—but no matter."

"You're a good hand at anything, I dare say," remarked the man.

"Never mind that, honey."

"That will do, Rafferty. Attention, if you please—you understand—attention!"

"I will—I do, your honour; can I ever forget it? We had lots of attention on that day—the Waterloo day."

"That's it; now, my good fellow, do you mean to say that they came near here?"

"Yes."

"How could they find it out?"

"I'll show you presently, if you'll dismount and tie your horses here; there's some hay, and there's water; it will do them good."

"It will that," said Rafferty, "for we've come some distance."

"This place has its advantages as well as disadvantages," said the man.

"How so?"

"Why, it lies convenient and close to the wood, and I can slip in and out at the most convenient time. A rabbit is soon shot, and dried sticks gathered; and then a fire's soon lighted and the rabbit broiled, you know."

"I see."

"I suppose a hare or a pheasant don't come amiss?" said Brolickbones.

"And why should it? a poor man's hunger is not more difficult to appease than a rich man's."

"Very true; but now my friend, the promised information?"

"You shall have it, sir. It was about midnight that some one knocked at my door last night."

"After midnight?"

"Yes."

"That was, in fact, this morning?"

"Well, it was."

"What did they want?"

"Water."

"Did they say what for?"

"No; but from what I could understand and hear, there were two men on horseback, and, I believe, a female, who was faint and sick."

"Ah !"

"Yes; well, I gave them some water, and then they rode off."

"Didn't you go out to them?"

"No; I was sleepy and tired, and I didn't put my shoes on."

"And that is all you know?"

"It is."

"Show me where they went—the road they took—for I can see none."

"This way, sir."

The man led them to a corner of the field that led round a sort of double hedgerow and plantation, and showed Henry the lane that run along on the other side.

"They must have known you were here else they could not have come in the dark," said Henry, as he looked back at the hut.

"I don't know how it was, I am sure; but they came."

"It is very singular; these people must know the place as well as you, my friend—they know the country?"

"Of that you may be sure."

"Well, well; then all we can do is to return and mount our nags, and pursue the road after them."

"Yes, sir, I am ready," said Brolickbones, and he commenced returning to the hut—"the nags have had a bait."

They now returned to the hut, and the old poacher, for such he really was, went to a small hole in the thatch or boarding of his hut, or perhaps in both; from whence he drew out a small stone bottle.

"It's a raw cold morning, your honour —are you inclined to do anything this way? It keeps out the damp and cold, and prevents rheumatiz."

"Well," said Henry Morton, "I don't usually take anything of that kind; but as I have been riding some hours, and as you say there is some damp and mist arising, I will take a little. What is it?"

"Whisky."

"Och hone, whisky did you say, darlint?—why, it is a damp morning."

"I am sure of it," said the poacher; "and if his honour isn't objectionable, you may wet your lips, though I believe, Irishmen don't like the taste of it."

"The devil they don't!—why, your ignorance is shocking, because anybody who drinks whisky, ought to be able to know that Irishmen are only weaned upon whisky."

"And very good it is, my good fellow; if you don't often get a dinner, you can make it up in drops."

"Oh! sir, it isn't often I do, but this is too good to waste."

"This has never paid duty," said Rafferty, tossing off the contents of another glass.

"At any rate, you don't object to being the receiver of smuggled goods; you ought to have a search warrant sent down your throat in the shape of salts, to discover if there be any there."

"Beautiful!" exclaimed Rafferty, apostrophising the glass.

"I had it given to me, and had it been any other man for miles round, he should never have tasted it."

Henry Morton gave the man some money by way of compensation, and then, accompanied by Rafferty Brolickbones, mounted his horse, and, with the assistance of the poacher, they got through the hedge, and commenced the pilgrimage again.

---

## CHAPTER XLVI.

THE OLD INN AGAIN.—THE MURDER OF DASHING NED.—THE RESUMPTION OF THE FLIGHT.

WHEN the mendicant returned to the kitchen where the guests were, he exchanged significant looks with the landlord, who said, in a low tone,—

"Well, have you taken care to secure your bird now?"

"Yes; the cage is safer now, and moreover, this attempt and its failure has succeeded in giving her a distate for any more, so much so that she is very sick of it."

"That's all right, then."

"Yes. I must be off early in the morning, and when I go I should like to go quietly."

"You shall, my boy, you shall."

"Mind, only give me the signal that all is ready, and then we can give Ned the wink; he talks so much, that I'm afraid he'll let out more than he need."

"I see; Ned is a flashy talkative cove, and when he's a little on——"

"He's no use whatever."

"And, on a pinch——"

"He'll split, and run away like a deer."

"So I've heard; but there ain't many who'll believe that of Ned."

"They don't know him as I do."

"No, I dare say; but we are all safe here," said the landlord, looking round the room at the guests.

"I shouldn't have been here if I hadn't been pretty sure of that; but where I am afraid of Ned is, when we come to any place where we may not be so safe. If a man will but treat him, he would tell him all, that's my opinion. He's to be pumped—that's it—pumped."

"You are right—that everybody knows. It's a pity he has got two faults."

"What are they?"

"Cowardice and talkativeness; lord bless you, he'd talk a mermaid blind."

"By-and-bye I'll get him out by himself, and talk a little to him."

"Very good."

The conversation now became general, and every one took a share in it.

"I say, Dick, did you hear about Joe Jones, eh?—the fat cove."

"No; what of him?"

"Oh, he's to be hanged."

"The devil he is!"

"Yes, yes; I saw him."

"When?"

"A fortnight ago."

"But he's a precious cur, and I never thought he'd have pluck enough to have a pull at the rope."

"He will though, if they carry him to the gallus, like Guy Faux, in a sedan chair."

"Ha! ha! ha!"

"What a rum chap that Billy Knightly is!" said one of the visitors to a companion.

"Yes, he is; I've heer'd him afore."

"What was Joey taken for?"

"Setting fire to a house, and trying to burn his wife," replied the other.

"Ha! ha! ha!" laughed the whole company, as if it were a capital joke. The idea of a man burning another man's house and his own wife at the same time! there was something so very comic, that they all laughed amazingly.

"Well," said one, when the laughter had somewhat subsided, "I do forgive old Joe, for, of all the women ever I heard, his wife beats all; and, besides, she would split upon him whenever she thought herself offended."

"D—n her! I hope he burned her?"

"Yes, he did, and said he was now quite resigned to his fate, and would be hanged quietly, if they would carry him like a gentleman to the gallows: that was what I was told."

"Indeed?"

"Yes."

"How did it come about?"

"Why, in this manner: he and his wife had agreed to rob an oil-shop where there was a large swag, all of the right sort, clear cash, and no flimsies. He got in and got it, but had a quarrel with his wife afore, and she had threatened to peach upon him, and tell all; and he had been thinking what was the best means of getting rid of the jade."

"And quite right, too."

"Very well; when he got the money, the thought suddenly struck him that he might send her up stairs, upon an excuse.

"'Mary,' said he, suddenly.

"'Curse you, can't you hold your mag? what do you want to Mary me for? go on, can't you, you fat fool?'

"'I forgot to look in that curious little drawer inside the desk.'

"'Well, well, what of it?'

"'Only there is money in it; some gold and some diamond rings.'

"'What a cust fool you are,' said she; 'go back, and look into it, then.'

"'I can't, Mary.'

"'You won't.'

"'Well, then, since you will have it so, my dear, I won't go.'

"'I'll go; but, cus my windpipe,' says she, 'if I don't give it you for this.'

"She immediately walked back, and crept up stairs, and then, when she was gone, Joey said to himself,—

"'There's no fear now, but I'm in for it if I don't stop her gab.'

"He at once set fire to a lot of things at the back of the shop; then some wood, matches, candles, gas, and everything he could come near; and then bolted out, and slammed the door with a loud bang. Well, the house was in flames in no time, and the inmates only escaped by getting out at the top of the house. Joe's wife, as soon as she heard the alarm, was down like a shot; but, at the same time, as soon as she saw the fire, dashed through it, thinking she could reach the door and open it. But no; she dropped down suffocated, I suppose, and she was not found afterwards, save, indeed, a blackened back bone, a skull, and arms, and legs—all bones; nothing else, and very black, indeed."

"And so the poor fellow is to be hanged, is he?" asked one, in a sympathetic tone.

"Yes."

"Shame, shame!" burst forth from all parts of the room.

"Well, I tell you what it is," said one; "there's no humanity in the land—they don't care what they do with a fellow, not a bit; they'd as leave hang, draw, and quarter him as they would eat their breakfast."

"So they would—so they would."

"Ned," said the mendicant.

"Well, what now?" inquired Ned.

"I want to speak to you in the yard privately."

"Can't you say it now? It's infernally cold out there, now I've been sitting in the warmth of the fire."

"You must come, Ned. I have some suspicion; don't let anybody notice you going out, Ned—be careful."

"Suspicion of what?"

"That you're a fool; come, and don't ask any questions here."

Ned was not over pleased; but he knew the man he had to deal with, and watched with a sullen expression the eyes of the guests; and when he saw he was not noticed he slipped out of the kitchen.

In a few moments more, he had groped his way out into the yard, where the mendicant had stationed himself.

"Where are you?" he muttered, as he walked about; "I can hardly see."

"Here I am," said the mendicant, as he stepped out from behind a cart; "here I am."

"Well, what is it you want now? The room was comfortable and quite enough."

"I know that, Ned, but this affair is mine, you know."

"I do, but you ——"

"I promised you fairly, and I'll keep my word; but you haven't completed the affair yet, so, until you have, you must do what is necessary."

"Well, but haven't I done so? what more do you want than what I have done? I did all that I could do."

"I don't complain; but it's no use your stopping there with the ale-mug before you. I know how it will be before long."

"I'm right enough."

"Well, but you may not be; now, come this way, and I'll talk to you."

"Why not here, as well as there?"

"Because it's cold, and we may as well walk about; it's better, and we can't be listened to, and that you know is an object."

"Well, well, do as you like—do as you like, but be quick."

"I will—I will."

They now came to a deep well that was uncovered, save that there was a board or two on the side; but for all else it was open.

When Dashing Ned came near this, he started, and moved on one side to avoid going too close; whereupon the other struck him a tremendous blow on the ear. Ned fell very close to the well, but not in it. He was stunned, but not senseless, and made an ineffectual attempt to rise.

The mendicant gave him a kick on the head, and then, seizing him by the legs, thrust him into the well.

For a moment or two he listened to hear the fall of the body, and then, after the lapse of a second or two, the dead fall of the unhappy man was heard; it was a dull, heavy splash, and all was still.

There was no second attempt to rise, or scream, or call for aid. He was stunned, and at once sunk beneath the surface, and all was quiet again.

"And now for the horses," muttered the mendicant, as he turned from the place. "It will not be well to stay long here now."

Before he re-entered the house, he listened long and carefully to assure himself that he was not seen by any one whatever; he then carefully opened the door, and unnoticed took his seat near the landlord, who had not stirred.

"When does day break?" inquired one of the guests, who had just awakened up from a nap he had been indulging in.

"In about another hour."

"That's lucky," said the mendicant to the landlord. "Will you get our nags ready? we are for an instant start."

"So soon?"

"Yes; the sooner the better. I wish to be on the road before day-break. I have a particular reason; the horses are refreshed, and that is the main thing."

"They shall be ready in a few minutes. I'll go myself and get them ready. You'll have a lonely ride this morning, but you will have no objection to that."

"I shall have all the company I care for," replied the mendicant, "and that is saying no great deal, and exerting but little self-denial; however, bustle about the horses, and let me know when you are ready."

"I'll give you the office."

So saying, the landlord left the kitchen, and proceeded to saddle and bridle the horses for the resumption of the journey, leaving the mendicant, who sat somewhat apart from the guests, who were enjoying themselves with their conversation and liquors.

"Did you ever hear of Dick Jackson's adventure?" inquired one of a man opposite to where he sat.

"I don't know; but what was it?" said the man in reply.

"Only this:—Dick, in riding about, suddenly came upon a parson. Well, he got his purse; it was well weighed; but the man of cloth wouldn't give it up without a bit of a struggle."

"Wouldn't he?"

"Oh, no! he stuck to it, and Dick knocked him off his horse with his pistol, and then jumped upon him."

"Ay, Ay?"

"That must have sent the wind out of his body," remarked a third; "because Dick is very heavy."

"So he is. Well, Dick was well satisfied with his luck for one night, and was riding at a decent pace along the road; it was dry and hard, the wind came at his back, and he could hear the sound of horses' feet coming at a thundering gallop along the road

"'Hilloa!' thought Dick, 'my friend likes my company so well he's in a hurry to overtake me and rejoin me; but I will disappoint him.'

"Dick touched his mare, and away he went at a rattling pace for near two hours, but at the end of that time he found they were yet after him, and that he could not shake them off.

"He knew the ground very well, and therefore determined that he would adopt a little stratagem on the occasion. So, having observed his ground, he determined to go into the next field he came to.

"This he did by dismounting and undoing the gate, and gently leading his horse into it, shutting the gate after him. He walked along gently until he came to a high hedge, and then suddenly he and the horse tumbled down headlong into some deep excavation.

"What this was, where he was, or where he was going to, Dick couldn't tell; but he came to the bottom without any hurt. Being there, he determined to remain there, and in about ten minutes, he could hear the whole party gallop by in pursuit.

"'There they go,' cried Dick; 'they may enjoy the ride, but I'll go back and ride the other way.'

"This he did, and got clear off; but he found he had had a very narrow escape from a broken neck."

"Indeed!"

"Yes, he had."

"What was the place he fell into?"

"A large lime quarry, and, when he came out, he was as white as a miller; however, he was safe, and that was all he cared for; but, had he gone a little more on one side, he would have fallen on to some machinery, at about twenty or thirty feet from the top; or had he rolled much further than he did, he would have fallen into a deep well."

"And that would have settled him."

"You're right; but, as he said, 'It didn't matter much; it must be done some-time or another, and one is as good as another;' he's a rare plucked 'un is Dick."

"So he is.'

At this moment the landlord entered the room, and leaning towards the mendicant, he said,—

"All is ready for you."

Giving the landlord the reckoning, he went out into the yard, where the horses were standing ready for them.

"Where is Dashing Ned of Newington?" inquired the mendicant.

"I don't know."

"Confound him, where can he be loitering about, I wonder?"

"Don't know," said the landlord; "ain't he in the kitchen?"

"No, he was not, when I was there," replied the mendicant; "and I want him."

"Well, I'll go and look after him," said the landlord, after a pause.

"Oh, no, no, if he don't choose to be in the way when he's wanted, I can't help it; he must take his own chance; however, if you see him, tell him I shall go on in the road I told him, unless I see any occasion to alter my intention."

"Very good"

"Good morning," said the mendicant, who had brought Mabel down stairs; and seating her on the horse, mounted, and then soon got clear of the old inn.

They now rode along the high road at a tolerably brisk pace, and the morning air felt refreshing; the road was hard, and the sound of their horses' hoofs was sharp and strong, and they proceeded along favourably. One or two incidents did occur on the road, but they led to no result, save to showing the precaution of the mendicant.

It was just after daybreak when he saw two horsemen crossing a hill on the left, but coming towards them. As soon as they were parted by the intervening trees, he dashed into a plantation, and there remained until the sounds of voices and horses were distinctly heard, and then died away again in the distance.

"Now," muttered the mendicant, "we may safely proceed; not that I apprehend any pursuit now—they would scarcely proceed so far as this; but I can't be too sure, or too safe."

Again he emerged into the high road, and pursued his route onwards at a sound pace, that would carry him over a great deal of ground, and yet not hurt the horses.

Thus they proceeded for some distance in perfect safety to the mendicant.

The morning broke and the sun peeped over the eastern horizon, and then the misty vapour that hung over the plain was more distinctly visible than before.

The clouds began to clear off, and the morning sun appeared, the edges of the night clouds were tinted with a brilliant red, and then the sun-light shot upwards and illumined the whole expanse of sky.

"Now," thought the mendicant, "in another hour or two we shall have people about; men will be going to their labour, and farmers will be riding about from place to place to see that their crops and flocks are safe. I must be cautious and avoid them; and yet I have little to fear from them, for Mabel, I think, now will scarce attempt to influence them. She thinks there is a stake at risk, that she dare not interfere with; that she could never know peace of mind if she were. No, no, she will be tolerably quiet now, though I will not trust too much to anybody."

And Mabel, too, was busy with thought; she pondered on what she had heard from the mendicant, and she trembled as she thought on the words that so cruelly depressed her in spirits. He had told her she was his child and the offspring of shame. To Mabel this knowledge was enough to poison and imbitter her future life, and what could she do now, led as she was by that lawless man from place to place, according to his will or his impulses?

Filled with the most melancholy and poignant reflections, Mabel rode forward with this man. She could not avoid shuddering when she looked at him; and could not feel any of those feelings she anticipated on being restored to those who had been the authors of her being. What would be her destination? or where was she to be taken and what done to her? were questions she knew not how to answer.

Her head was filled with contrary emotions, and she knew not how to act. To stay with this man was against her wishes; and to injure him her heart told her was criminal.

To do that was repugnant to her nature, and yet she knew, that he could do nothing for her, and that he only now sought to take her from those who had behaved so kind to her, from some evil motive of his own.

She knew not but some crime might be in contemplation, and she might be aiding in its execution. This, to Mabel, was another source of sorrow, but she was both defenceless and helpless.

"Have you thought over what I have said to you?" said the mendicant, turning suddenly to Mabel, and slacking his pace at the same time, to allow of conversation.

"I have. Could it be otherwise?"

"I think you must have had ample food for reflection. Your destiny is suddenly altered; the source of the stream has some effect upon its course."

"You need not remind me of the hateful connections I belong to."

"Exactly; but you must become familiarized with the ill; however, my safety, you see, does not entirely depend upon you. I have it, in some measure, in my own power to control my own fate, though you may, indeed, be able to influence it for good or evil."

"I would I could influence it for you."

"Remain passive, then."

"Never!"

"Then we are at war? be it so; let the child attempt the life of its newly-found father. Well, be it so; it is neither fond nor filial; but I suppose what is will be. You will attempt an escape, I suppose?"

"Do you imagine that I will voluntarily stay, under such circumstances as these?"

"You ought."

"No. I may be aiding crime."

"And you may assist in the execution of your father. Do you hear me?"

"I do."

"Well, then, I can leave a sting behind that you will find will have a more lasting effect than you can possibly imagine."

"Indeed! It would be unjust."

"But you will find the world is unjust, and that people will act differently towards you; however, you will influence your fate for the worse; experience will teach you a sad lesson."

"Which you are teaching."

"Who?"

"The injustice of the world now begins. You show me what you say is true."

"But I have a title to act with authority over you, and will."

"Which I doubt."

"And which I'll enforce."

There was a pause of a few moments, during which neither party spoke, and then the mendicant, whose policy it was not to drive Mabel to extremes, thought it was good policy to show her how reckless he was, and how little he cared for the worst, which was sure to be a calamity to her as well as to him, and one that would cause some sorrow and regret in her.

"She cannot be what I think she is," he muttered to himself; "if she do bring me into trouble, it will be more than I believe.

"We shall come to an inn soon. Am I to confine you, or will you remain quiet in ordinary apartments?"

"I will give no promises. I am not mistress of my own actions, and have no power to give my promise."

"You have enough freedom to do that. You can say whether you will remain passive or no."

"I will not answer."

"Very well; notwithstanding your obstinacy, I will endeavour to do my utmost to make you comfortable, come what may. I will not be harsher than I can avoid. You are my child, and I cannot do less than this, though you will not do so much towards him to whom you owe so much duty."

"Can I be said to owe any?"

"Yes."

"You admit deserting me to strangers, who have done all the duty of parents to me—who have, in fact, my affection and duty."

"This is mere wildness."

"It may be; but it is the truth."

"Silence; we are approaching strangers."

They now neared a solitary road-side public-house, and the landlord, at the sight of the strangers, came out to speak to them. He looked at the horses and then at the riders. He was a fat old man, not very bright, but uncommonly jolly and polite in his way.

"Nice nags, them, master; you've a good eye for a horse, anyhow."

"Yours is not a bad one, or you wouldn't have found that out."

The landlord was pleased at this, and rubbed his hands.

"Fine morning this, sir?"

"Yes, very. Can I have a word with you, for a moment?"

"Yes, certainly sir, with the greatest pleasure, sir," said the landlord.

"Well, this way then," said the mendicant.

The two stood a few yards apart from Mabel, when the mendicant said,—

"The young female I have here is of unsound mind, landlord."

"Oh, I see! what a pity—she's a pretty gal—touched in the head I suppose? Well, well, we must live and die, as the Bible says,—eh, sir?"

"That's very true, landlord; now I have had a great deal of trouble and difficulty to catch her and bring her this far."

"Indeed, sir—well now, live and be jolly."

"But she is so cunning and so artful—eh?"

"D—n my sign-board! if she ain't off."

The mendicant turned, for the sound of horses' hoofs struck upon his ear. The fact was, Mabel, who had not been dismounted, finding herself alone, thought it an excellent opportunity to attempt an escape; and as quick as thought, she turned her horse's head in the direction of the road and began to gallop.

The mendicant was at no loss what to do,

but jumping into the saddle with a quickness and dexterity that was amazing, he spurred his own beast at a rapid rate after her.

The spur was a more certain means of urging the mendicant's horse on, than the voice only of Mabel, and the former soon overtook the latter, though there was a sharp contest over nearly a mile of ground.

"So, you are at your games, are you?—you must see that I am as quick as you—it is useless to attempt to escape me."

"I have failed," cried Mabel.

"You have, and so you will."

"We shall see."

"In the meantime we will have breakfast; for I should imagine you wanted some refreshment. I do, at all events."

Mabel made no reply, but suffered herself to be led back to the inn, at the door of which stood the landlord, who had been laughing till he was hoarse.

"Ha, ha, ha!" laughed the landlord—"well—ho, ho, ho!—ha, ha, ha!—I never saw anybody do a thing neater in all my life. Well, blow my apron, if she didn't deserve to get off, it was so well done; and he ought to catch her, for I never saw a man leap into a saddle like that—he is a rum 'un;—'tis a pity such a young gal as that should be so bad; she'd make a wise young gal: it's a shame the best are always overcome. I say," he added, to the mendicant, as he returned, "she'd nearly got the better of you this time."

"Very nearly," said the mendicant; "but then I am usually lucky enough to prevent any harm taking place by the attempt."

"Well, well—she's cunning enough any how—ay, as cunning as many people who have their senses; but, however, you have her now."

"Yes, I have her;—just let us have a private apartment, will you, landlord, and a good breakfast."

"Very good," said the landlord. "I'll serve you in a twinkling. Let's live and be jolly—grief is a folly I don't indulge in when I can help it. I haven't grieved this many a long year. Grief and I are strangers, and I don't want any introduction to the stranger. Here's the room, sir. I'll send in the gal to light the fire."

"This, then, is the room," said the mendicant, surveying it; "the fact is, you see, this young lady has been well brought up, and her friends won't like that she should disgrace herself by forming all sorts of low connections; and Heaven knows what mischief she may do herself and other people, especially to children."

"Is she vicious?"

"Why, you can hardly call it vicious; but mischievous and dangetous she certainly is, and very cunning—very cunning indeed."

"Oh, indeed, I can voueh for that, for I never saw a better instance," said the landlord.

The landlord now left the room, and the girl soon entered, and in a very short time a good fire was blazing in the room, and the mendicant threw himself into a chair, and such a train of thoughts seemed to come over him, that for some time he was barely sensible of anything that happened near him.

However, that matters not—his senses were easily recalled at the slightest sound that could be made; he much resembled some cat that was dozing, but that was always prepared at a moment's warning to jump up and spring upon its prey.

He had, too, taken the precauti0n to lock the door, and hence no attempt could be made at an escape, had she been prepared to make one; but as it was, she was much dejected at the failure of the attemtd

she had so successfully begun, and she now thought that there could be no use in maklng another, as nothing but stratagem would have any ehance of success; if she could do anything like tbat, then indeed she might, but the mendicant kept too good a look out to offer her a chancee.

---

## CHAPTER XLVII.

### THE PURSUIT.—THE DISAPPOINTMENT.— ADVENTURRS ON THE ROAD.

HENRY MORTON, followed by Rafferty Brolickbones, rode on for some mlles without any intermission, without even exchanging a single word. The day, as we have said, began to break at the time he lef the old poacher, and now broad daylight, and they could sec over many miles of country.

At the top of a hill, the road ran over the hill itself, Henry Morton drew up and breathed his horse, while he gazcd around him in every direction. Rafferty Brolickbones, too, ascended the hill, and drew up by the side o! Henry.

The sun had some time risen, and all the country around wss now easily distinguishable, and any moving being was detected with certainty within the range of vision. The mists had now in a great measure cleared off, the green fields and shady foliage could be seen, that fell, too, in great luxuriance, beauty, and variety of colour. The hedge rowsdivided the country around into differcnt shapes and sizes, giving a beautiful diversified apearance to the surface.

They both looked long and carefully over the landscape in silence, but they could see nothing that at all excited suspicion in their minds.

"Well, Rafferty," said Henry, "it is a pleasant prospect this, but it wants what we most desire."

"Oh blister! it does indeed, Mr. Henry; it would be much pleasanter if we could see the rascals who were carrying off Miss Mabel. Oh, bedad! I think I could go without breakfast for a week, if I were sure of catching them."

"Ay, Rafferty, what would I not do, if I were sure of catching them; but I will certainly never give over the chase."

"I'll stick to your honour all round the world and back again."

"It seems to me, Rafferty, that there is not much of a chance about here; we had better set off in the direction of yon market-town; we may then inquire if such persons have been seen there."

"Ay, and the turnpikes, too; and yonder is one where you see the smoke rising."

"A turnpike?"

"Ay, sir."

"But is there none before you come to that place? It must be three or four miles."

"Yes, sir, it is: but for a wonder there is none until you come there."

"Indeed!"

"It is, I must say, very odd, especially when you consider the extent of country, and I can only account for it by supposing the trustees are very liberal."

"Liberal indeed; but come along."

"What's that?"

"What's that, Rafferty?"

"That yonder, ahead of us—in yonder cross road, somebody riding fast. I can only see the head now and then rising above the hedge in the openings."

"Where is it?"

"I can't see it now, but it was yonder by the stump of the willow tree."

"I see the spot, but not the rider."

"Look a little to the left as they keep moving, and at some of the openings we may catch a sight of them."

"True, true."

Henry Morton looked long and fixedly towards the spot where the rider had been seen, but could see nothing; however, he and Brolickbones continued to gaze in the direction for some minutes, when they distinctly saw more than one person pass a gap in the hedge at a very rapid rate, and then disappear.

"Can you make them out, Rafferty?"

"There were two of them, I think, sir."

"I thought so, too."

"There were, sir. I saw two."

"And then one was, if I am not mistaken, a female, but I am not sure."

"Nor I, sir."

"Come on, Rafferty," exclaimed Henry; "we must overtake them soon."

"Sure enough we shall," thought Brolickbones, "if we don't break our necks in the meantime. I must say that if I could find Miss Mabel I wouldn't mind breaking my neck."

Rafferty's reflections were cut short; for Henry Morton increased his pace to a gallop, and Rafferty was compelled to pay all his attention to his horse and his ——

They rode several miles, until they had long passed the point where the —— persons after whom they were rid—— now they saw nothing of them, they could not have gone on m—— of them, as they had come so —— a shorter path.

"Well, Rafferty, they must —— on ahead for some distance."

"They must have suspected something, sir, and that's what made them get on; perhaps they've had a gallop, too."

"I dare say—I dare say."

"Yes, yes—follow on, follow on."

They now rode at a round trot, on the back road, for some miles, until they came to a turnpike gate, where they drew up to make some inquiries.

"Well, my friend," said Henry Morton to the gate-keeper—"you are up early."

"Yes, sir."

"Have you many people through of a morning?" he continued.

"Yes, a few."

"Have you seen any person through this morning, accompanying a lady?"

"No, sir, nobody of that description; there hasn't been such by here. What is the matter— a runaway match?"

"Not exactly; but a young lady has been forced away against her will from her friends, and we are endeavouring to overtake them and recover her from them."

"No, sir, I cannot help you. You know they could evade the pike if they thought proper."

"How?"

"By crossing some of the fields at the back. So you would hear nothing of them; they would harly be traced save at any place they might stop at, and the market towns; but they'll be as private as they can."

"Thank you, my friend," said Henry, and he again rode forward.

The morning was fairly up now, and he determined to ride on to the next market-town, and there put up for a few hours, and walk about the town to make inquiries.

In another hour-and-a-half they reached a pretty market-town, through which the high road ran. It was neatly built, quiet, and clean; the houses were irregularly built and straggling; the Town-hall had a clock, and the market was covered over to protect the salesmen and those who bring in the produce of the neighbouring country.

Henry Morton turned into the first quiet and respectable inn he came to, and, dismounting at the door, gave the bridle into the hands of Rafferty, and then entered the public house or inn—for it appeared to partake of the character of both; then Brolickbones led the horses down the yard, where he was met by the ostler.

"You haven't so many visitors, I suppose, that you can't take another horse?"

"Oh, no; we have room enough;—you are the first we have had since midnight."

"Did you have any before then?"

"Yes."

"Oh, then, maybe we've come the same road, and should have come together, had we been earlier," said Rafferty.

"Very likely," said the ostler.

"But was there any female society?"

"No; none."

"Then it would have been no use to me," said Rafferty, who had learned all he wanted to know, now that he had got this answer.

"I should think that female society would be little pleased with your company, Mr. Rawbones."

"No, no—Brolickbones."

"Very well—Broilbones."

"Did you never learn to speak in this country, or did they let your natural talents for mistakes run wild, eh?"

"Have they cultivated yourn?"

"Maybe they have, and maybe they haven't. What's the time of day?"

"Time for giving the bastes their breakfast."

"Rub them down, and set about it in earnest—as soon as you like, for his honour has ridden far, and maybe will do so again."

"My old boy, I'll see to it. What sort of a man is his honour, as you call him? One of the right sort, eh?"

"I believe as nice a man as ever was; if you don't anger him, he's as quiet as a lamb, and isn't a stingy one at all."

"All right. I'll set about it immediately."

"The rapscallions," muttered Rafferty, "would starve the poor beasts because the master was unworthy of them. What a set of thieves!"

With this comfortable reflection he turned from the yard, and entered the house. Here he was summoned to attend his master, who was waiting in the parlour.

"Well, Brolickbones," said Mr. Morton, "have you learned anything?"

"Nothing, sir, save that there's nobody here, or been here at all, that answers their description. I think we had better inquire elsewhere."

"That is what I intend doing, Rafferty. I want you to go and inquire about the roads, and of the different waggoners, as they come in, and ask them if they have seen any one riding with a lady in his company."

"But there were two, your honour."

"There were Rafferty; but, at the same time, they may have separated; in fact, one don't know anything that may have happened. I will myself go, and make inquiries also; and, from one or the other, it will be strange indeed if we do not discover if they have or have not passed through this way; and that is what we want to know;—once get on their track, and we are sure to make something of it."

"Sure," said Rafferty, "your honour knows best, and spakes like a gineral. I'm thinking myself it will be the best thing in the world, and the sooner we are there the better."

"Then we'll soon be there, Rafferty; the morning is yet early, and I doubt if there are many who can have passed, and hence the turnpike-man can have a very distinct recollection of who has and who has not gone through."

Having given their cattle a little time to breathe, Mr. Morton pushed on again at a hard trot towards the turnpike-gate, there to arouse the dormant individual who had taken a watchful occupation.

The morning was early, most certainly, as Mr. Morton said; for though the sun was up, and his rays warm, yet he had not succeeded in dispelling the mists that hung heavily in many places, and they could distinctly see the white mist curl off the meadows and from the low grounds until it melted away in the morning air.

It did not take them above twenty minutes to arrive at the gate they had seen; but the gatekeeper did not at all appear to consider it any part of his duty to rise with the sun, or to hurry himself when wanted.

"Hilloa, Hilloa! Gate, here—gate!" cried Rafferty, after Morton had in vain endeavoured to attract the attention of the somnambulent individual who presided.

Hilloa! Gate—gate!" again cried Henry Morton, in an angry and impatient tone.

" is there any one here?  See if you can open the gate, Rafferty.  Surely they don't intend to keep us here all day."

" I expect if they did they'd be getting mighty little in the way of profit."

" Give him another cry, and knock at his door with the handle of your whip."

" Hilloa!  Gate—gate!" shouted Rafferty Brolickbones, and at the same time he applied himself so hearily to the task of wakening the gate-keeper up, by attacking the upper part of the door with the but of his heavy riding-rod, that it must have sounded most fearfully to those within.

" Hilloa! what's the row?" shouted a stentorian voice.

" Get up and let us through.  Are you after keeping us all day, and that upon empty stomachs, too?  Bad cess to you."

" Do you want me to shoot you?  Because, if you don't, I can tell you, you had better leave off battering my door in.  I won't stand it."

" Get up, then, and let us through; else we'll pitch the blessed pike to purgatory, and lave you there in it, to get out at the day of judgment—may be, a day or two after."

" Come, my good fellow," said Henry Morton, " we want to go through, and you have no right to keep us here so long."

" I'm a coming.  What a hurry you are in."

At that moment they heard the bars undoing, and then the bolts and locks, and, finally, the upper part of the door was opened, and then the lower, when a big, burly man appeared, with an awfully savage countenance, which seemed, in looks alone, to remonstrate against the unnecessary discomfiture he was being put to for their convenience.

" You have kept us a long time," said Henry Morton, " and we are in haste."

" If you had been woke up three or four times, you'd sleep sound too."

" But it is late," exclaimed Rafferty.

" Late!"

" Yes, very late."

" I think it very early."

" The devil!" said Rafferty.  " The gate ought to be open for some time.  Why, the sun has been risen for a long time."

" I know nothing about that.  He don't come through my shutters."

" Then you should come and see."

" I come out when I am called, and not to tell whether the sun or moon is shining. I'm half asleep now; but you never go to bed, I should say."

" Not when there's anything to do that requires being looked after."

" Ay, ay, it's all very fine; but hand over the browns, and don't keep me here. You're in a hurry, ain't you, eh?"

" Yes."

" Then make haste."

" Not so fast," said Henry Morton. " You say you haye been disturbed to-night?"

" Yes, several times.  Cus people as can't ride at proper hours!" said the gate-keeper.

" Well; but can you remember what sort of people they were who went through?"

" I dare say I could, if I chose."

" Then tell me who have been through, and then I shall know if you have seen the people I should be glad to follow."

" And why should I do that?" inquired the gate-keeper, putting his hands in his pockets, and turning away to enter his hut.

" It may be to your advantage to do so," said Henry Morton.

" And it mightn't."

" I'll promise to reward you if you can answer my questions."

" Gammon!"

" Here is a five-shilling piece.  Tell me, if I give you this, will you answer my questions?"

" I will; but tip up the rowdy first, or it's no go.  You grease a cart's wheels before they go, you know, governor."

Henry Morton gave the money, and then said to the man,—

" Tell me, have any two men been through, with a female in company?"

" Yes, there have," said the man.

" There have?"

" Yes, surely."

" How long since?"

" Why, let me see.  It's difficult to count hours while one's been sleeping; but it must have been three hours ago."

" Two men and one female?"

" Exactly.  Were they on horseback?" inquired the turnpike-man.

" Yes, yes.  That's them," said Henry.

" Ah," said the turnpike-man, " then that's them, as you say.  They rode sharp; but their horses were blowed, and they couldn't go far."

" Thank you, my man!  Thank you," said Henry Morton, as he pushed his horse forward, and they again resumed the hard trot.

The turnpike-man leaned against the post of the opened gate as he looked after them, with his tongue out of his mouth, and he said, as he turned the five shilling-piece over in his hand, and then threw it up in the air, and catching it dexterously as it fell,—

" There they go, a couple of greenhorns; however, they have got something for their money. If they will have information and pay for it, why I can't help giving it, that's all; I couldn't do less than earn it. They'll bust themselves and their horses, but what's that to me? I'm a pike-keeper, and knows a thing or two, and can always tell a yarn when anything's to be got by it, that's all I've got to say; and now for some breakfast."

So saying, the turnpike-man turned round, and walked into his wooden house.

In the meanwhile Henry Morton, followed closely by Rafferty Brolickbones, trotted hard on to the next market-town, where they halted; but finding nothing that could gain them the least clue to the fugitives, they determined to hasten on to a small place about five miles further, and then breakfast.

It was yet early, and they gave their horses a bait, while they strolled about the town in search of information. This they could not obtain, and away they went, until they came within sight of a pretty little road-side patch of houses, not more than a village, and hardly that.

There was but one inn; but that was a very singular and antique-looking affair. It seemed one of those structures that grew more bulky the higher it reached from the ground.

The embayed window of the room above the ground floor projected far over the entrance, and was supported by two strong wooden posts, fancifully carved; but the design had become quite illegible, on account of carvings, equally fanciful, but of not so interesting a nature, having been so frequently performed by the rustics who delight in seeing their own initials and names upon every available space. This was no ornament, but an addition; for which, as the landlord said, they ought to have been fed upon bread and water for a month—his notion of extreme punishment.

The house was a large and imposing one, and looked more like one of those old romantic places we read of in the latter ages, where oddity and picturesqueness were often strongly combined, and render the habitation a curiosity and an object of admiration.

Mr. Morton looked at the old inn, saying, as he did so, to Rafferty Brolickbones,—

"Rafferty, this place was never intended for such a purpose; it has belonged to some noble or wealthy family at some period or other, but it has changed hands, as the times; all things suffer mutation."

"Yes, sir, as you say," said Rafferty; "I dare say much mutton has suffered there; but then, by the holy mother, they do everywhere. People will do it as long as there's a sheep to be had, for love or money; and why shouldn't they? Sure, it's lawful; and as for the old house, I'll warrant they used to brew better October beer in those days than they do now."

"Very likely, Rafferty; though I suspect neither to your taste or mine; for in those days the hop was considered a noxious weed."

Rafferty looked cunning, as much as to say, "It might be very well to say so, but he didn't recollect hearing that before."

They resigned their horses to the charge of a groom who came out, and Henry Morton entered the inn, while Rafferty followed the horses, and saw them placed in a good stable and well fed.

"They are tidy beasts," said the ostler, as he surveyed them.

"Yes," said Rafferty; "there may be better, and there may be worse, you know."

"That's very true. In what college was you brought up in, young man?" said the old ostler, who thought Rafferty was quizzing him.

"In Brazen nose," said Rafferty.

"I should say so; then if so be you knows a horse's head from his tail, take the pail up to the other end of the stable before you give him any drink, 'cause I don't think he'll drink at all at that end."

This was said, because Rafferty stood a moment by the horse's flank, to notice the effect of his reply upon the ostler.

"You do know where he feeds, then?" said Rafferty. "Well, I do expect I have seed in one day as many horses as you and your whole family ever saw in all your lives."

"Ah, well," said the ostler, "you are a nice one; but you ain't of this country, and one must pity your infirmities. Great travellers are great liars, at least they say so."

"They may sometimes tell a lie," said Rafferty. "An old soldier that has seen the plains of Waterloo smoking and blazing, and thousands of horses and riders, need hardly tell lies; he has seen enough to talk of without anything else."

"Are you a soldier?"

"I was."

"And at Waterloo?"

"Yes, at the time when it was dangerous to be there—not there afterwards, but in the thick of it, old boy."

"Well," said the ostler, in deep admiration, "I never seed a man afore as had been there; I honour you, mister. What will you take?—you must have a drink."

"Well," said Rafferty, "I don't know;

but the fact is, we have ridden far this morning, and though we have halted for a short time, yet we didn't do the honours of the place."

"Well, what shall it be?"

"I don't care it there be any whisky in the way; if not, anything else will do—don't trouble yourself."

"Don't talk about trouble," said the ostler; "and that to a Waterloo man, too. Oh, pho! I'd do anything."

"Well, he's a rum 'un," thought Rafferty, "but the whisky will be whisky all the same, for that; and if good—why it can't be otherwise, for who would hurt the cratur? Anything but whisky may be meddled with, but not that—not that. Oh, no,—nobody could have the heart to do it: if they did, they would deserve all the pains of purgatory; but here it comes."

As he spoke, the old white-headed ostler came across the yard with a small stone bottle in one hand, and a glass in the other, and, as he entered the stable, he said,

"Here is some of the right sort; you'll say it's like swallowing a cat and pulling her back by the tail; there's no mistake about this; its real, that's the fact."

"I'm glad of it," said Rafferty, as he took the glass that was offered him; "here's to our better acquaintance, ould gentleman."

"Thank ye, the same to you," said the ostler, dropping a glassful to the bottom of his throat, without touching his lips.

"Now, I dare say," said the old man, "you think it rather strange that I should have such a respect for a Waterloo man?"

"I must say it does seem curious to me, since I have met with many who cared nothing about it, at all, at all."

"Well, then, you shall know—I hate the French, for one thing."

"Very good," said Rafferty, coolly.

"And then, we beat 'em."

"Soundly."

"Ay; the best on 'em too."

"So we did, and no mistake; we drove them all, everywhere."

"Ay, that's the best of it; they couldn't turn round because they'd have been pushed on again; they didn't like the mane of the British lion which was on the end of the guns."

"No, no; bayonets were not the most comfortable things to digest."

"Exactly. Well, then, what I have to say is this 'ere, I had a son who was in that battle."

"Had you?"

"Yes," said the old man slowly, and with something like a touch of sorrow in his manners; "I had a son."

"And he fell?"

"How do you know that?" said the ostler, hastily looking up; "who told you that?"

"I only thought so, from your manner," said Rafferty; "you seemed to grieve."

"I thought I had lost all that," said the old man. "I thought time had worn away all appearance of that, and that I never showed any sorrow for the event."

"I judged you did."

"Well, well, I suppose it's no use to contend against one's feelings—but I don't see why I should regret his fall; I don't see that I ought," said the old ostler, with some sadness.

"Did he vex you, then?" inquired Rafferty.

"Oh, dear, no; a better boy a father couldn't wish: no, no, he was a fine lad—a fine lad; he went to the battle, and gave me his bounty money to bury his poor old mother. Poor woman, she's gone, too; they are all gone but me, and I seem to stay till the last."

"Never mind that," said Rafferty: "you shouldn't be sorry for that, you know."

"I don't know that I am," said the ostler; "and yet what good am I here, after all are gone? The young, you know, could enjoy themselves; but, as I was saying, my youngster shouldered his gun, or, I should say, buckled on his sword, for he was a cavalry man, and went to Waterloo; he was a good and a brave boy, but he fell in battle. Yes, he fell, I am told, in the last desperate charge that was made: he and a comrade were, for a moment or two, parted from the main body, and after fighting desperately they fell, covered with wounds."

"Ah," said Rafferty "that was many a brave man's fate; so don't grieve, though I dare say you can't help it."

"And yet he died in his duty, and fighting like a brave man."

"So much the better; take another drop of the cratur, and recollect, however, sad a soldier's funeral may be, it is always left with a quick step and a lively tune. But this is enough—will you tell me something I want to know?"

"If I can I will."

"Well, then, have you had any visitors since last night?"

"No; we ain't had any."

"Not a couple of men and a lady?"

"No."

"Nor have you seen any such?"

"No; if they had even gone through the place I must have seen something of them; there have been none such, you may depend."

"And yet the man at the gate said there had been such through."

"What, a sleepy fat man?"

"Yes."

"With a queer countenance?"

"The same."

"Then you may put it all down as gammon, especially if you gave him any money, and asked questions."

"Yes, yes; that was it."

"Ay, then he did you. He's called cunning Joe, and joking Joe, and he would tell all you wanted to know, rather than not earn his money; he's not nice to a trifle."

"Then I'll tell the governor," said Rafferty, "because he has thrown us out;" and he forthwith left the stables to go to Henry Morton.

Henry Morton having returned to the inn, at once ordered breakfast, and was shown into the very room that had the bay window in it; and here he could sit and watch the road; nothing, in fact, could pass by without his being cognizant of the fact.

The room was a large handsome one. The ceiling was curiously ornamented, and the panelling carved in oak. It was altogether a curious room, and a study, though many would have called it a cheerless and uncomfortable room. But those with warm feelings and good taste, would instantly become well pleased with the room, and it would conjure up a host of reflections.

"This old apartment," thought Henry Morton, "has been the scene of many a merry party, and perhaps sad ones too; but it has been formed for hospitality.

"Time was, when the chief expense a man was at was the entertainment of his friends, and any stranger who might require it, but now they are otherwise engaged; other employments occupy them, and the entertainment of the traveller has fallen to the care of the innkeeper."

At that moment the breakfast entered, accompanied by the host himself, who was a big, jolly-looking man, whose very face bespoke candour and good humour.

"You have been expeditious," said Henry; for he had not been in the house many minutes—certainly not a quarter of an hour.

"Don't like to wait for breakfast myself, sir, and don't think other people do; and, besides, your horses seem to say they have come a distance. I thought you would be unusually in want of it to clear the mists of these heavy mornings, which are so unwholesome."

"I must confess I do stand in need of it, and am glad of its appearance. Can you tell me if any persons have been past here lately?"

"I cannot well say, sir, though I believe not; there have been none here."

"With a lady, I mean?"

"Oh, dear, no, sir: we are sure to know if any such were to stop, because there is no other halting-place within five miles, either way, and so I am likely enough to know."

"I see, perfectly well. You have a fine old house here; it has not always been an inn, I imagine," said Morton.

"No, sir: but it has been one a very long time—a very long time, indeed."

"Has it, indeed?"

"Yes, sir; my father and my grandfather both had it; they lived to be old men, and each of them was landlord here for near forty years."

"God bless me! it is strange."

"But true, sir."

"I do not doubt it. How long have you been landlord, if I may ask the question out of mere curiosity?"

"Twenty years, sir."

"God bless me! then you three have had this house a century?"

"Yes, sir, and I hope more, when I have done with it. One thing, sir, we all live very long and very regular lives."

"That's a good thing: it's few, however, that can be persuaded of that fact; at least, so far as to practise it."

"Yes, that's very true, sir; but we are an odd race, a very odd race; born innkeepers, live innkeepers. Well, that is not all, either."

"Indeed? what else is there singular about you and your race?"

"Only this, sir; we none of us ever had more than one child."

"God bless me!"

"And, what's more, that one is always a he."

"Indeed?"

"Yes, we only have boys—one each; and he never dies till he's not very far short of ninety or a hundred years."

"Well, you are an extraordinary family, I must confess; I am quite honoured by your attention."

"Don't name it, sir; if you want anything, just ring the bell, and I'll wait upon you in a moment."

The landlord retired, and left Henry Morton to his reflections, which were none of the most hopeful. He thought that he had not as yet even discovered the track of the miscreants who had carried off the unfortunate Mabel from those friends who loved her so dearly and so sincerely.

In the midst of these reflections, Rafferty Brolickbones entered the apartment, and seeing his master well employed, said,—

"Bedad, your honour, we have been done this morning, clean."

"What do you mean, Rafferty?"

"The 'pike man.'"

"What of him?"

"Why, sir, he's stuffed you, you know, with chaff, and no mistake," said Rafferty.

"Stuffed me, Rafferty! what do you mean?" inquired Henry Morton, a little surprised.

"Why, sir, he told you a lot of things for the five shillings you gave him this morning, after we had troubled him to let us through."

"Yes, I remember."

"Well, sir, it's all a lie; he's known here as joking Joe, and can lie so fast and thick, that nobody can tell 'em."

"Indeed!"

"Yes, the ostler says no such persons have been through this way, and he must have known it if they had been."

"I am afraid, Rafferty, that we have got no trace of them: but that can't be helped, we will push on, and endeavour to ascertain if they've been seen anywhere from the cross roads, as they might have gone another way."

"Very true, sir: but when does your honour start? the nags want rest; if they are to go on this way, they'll be knocked up."

"Well, then, in the afternoon; we'll start an hour before sunset, so that we can make a rapid fifteen or twenty miles' journey, and then up before or a little after sunrise"

"That will do, your honour: we'll spend the middle of the day in making inquiries."

---

## CHAPTER XLVIII.

A STRANGE GREETING AT A COUNTRY INN.—THE HAPPY LANDLORD.—THE ARRIVAL OF MABEL AND HER COMPANION IN LONDON.

THE position of Mabel was one of the most distressing in which she could have been placed. There were many difficulties and disagreeables, that can scarcely be conceived; but that which most preyed upon her mind was the separation from her friends, and arising from such a cause.

The mendicant left his first resting-place as soon as he well could, for he foresaw that it might not be every one who would be as credulous as the landlord. Besides, it might happen, that some of those who undoubtedly were in search of Mabel would arrive there, and make inquiries; and were he found there, he would be seized, and Mabel would soon be free.

It was, therefore, not without reason that he again put himself in motion, determining to make his way to some sequestered spot, where he could rest more at leisure, and where there could be less danger to be encountered.

Choosing a favourable opportunity, he sallied out, and scoured along the road for about three-quarters of a mile, until he came to a cross-road, into which he immediately turned his horses' heads, determining that at the first favourable spot he would remain all day till the night should again reign; and then by daylight, if the steeds held out, he would be able to hide himself in the labyrinths of the metropolis, where all traces of himself and Mabel would, he well knew, be lost.

"Once in London," he thought, "and I am safe, for there I may live for years unseen and unknown; there I shall find shelter and safety. But the confines of London may prove dangerous to me, if my charge here proves very refractory—otherwise, I fear nothing, be there what cause there may, I will not shrink from it."

They rode down this cross-road for about a mile or two; apparently it had no particular direcion, for its course wound from right to left, and left to right, so repeatedly, that it was difficult to tell whither they were going. However, after an hour's riding, it took a definite course off to the right; and when they had arrived at the summit of a hill, he could see in the hollow below, at a distance of about two miles, a small market-town.

To go there was not his intention, he only wished to get to some little place, where visitors were few and far between, as at such a place he would deem himself safest, and to discover some such place as that he now applied himself.

After gazing some time in every direction earnestly, he found that he had passed such a place as that he most desired, it was so hidden that he had not seen it in passing by it.

It was but a hundred yards or so to go back: that he thought would be but little trouble, and he did that the more willingly as it gave him an assurance that he was the safer for it.

This he did, and a few moments more, he and Mabel rode up a short lane, and paused before the most curious old tumble-down, moss-grown place he ever beheld.

"If one place more than another promises an original, this does: for I never beheld its equal: it is just the thing."

The old inn or road-side public-house, if it could be called either, was a curiously constructed place. The walls ran high and wide, and there was a vast number of small windows that opened outwards: there ran a very high, red-tiled roof, which was covered in a great part by moss and house-leek.

The front was coverd by a large vine, which seemed to be of the most fruitlul character; and on either side was a row of tall poplars and beech trees.

There was a couple of benches for travellers, and a horse-trough filled with water. No one was, however, to been seen, and the mendicant began to consider what course would be best to pursue: at length he determined to call out for some one.

This, for some time, appeared to be a bootless task, until after a great exertion of lung, he produced a sound that succeeded in cailing the attention of the inmates, and a strange, unearthly voice said—

"Weil, and what do you want? Who are you? Where did you come from, and where are you going? Can't you go in, stupid?"

The mendicant was much astonished, and turned from side to side, with anything but a pleased air; and, nad he seen any one, he would have spoken in a rather imperative tone to them.

"Chuck, chuck, chuck!" said the same voice; and then all was still.

The mendicant was really irritated at this treatment, for he thought that they were making a jest of him; and he said—

"If you keep a house of entertainment for travellers, it would scarcely be too much to expect you would attend to them: if you refuse, you have no right to trouble them with your silly string of questions."

"Who are you?" said the same voice.

"What is that to you? I am a traveller, seeking rest and refreshment; and, moreover, I have an authority about me you dare not dispute."

"Chuck, chuck, chuck!" said the same voice.

"Confound you! if I had you, I'd chuck you into the horse-trough," said the irritated mendicant, looking around.

"Who are you? Where do you come from, and where are you going to? Can't you go in? Chuck, chuck, chuck!" said the same voice; and there came a flapping of wings.

The mendicant looked up, and there saw a large jackdaw, poking its head out of the wicker cage, and looking down on the mendicant with great gravity; and, as soon as the bird saw he was observed, he withdrew his head and then hopped about the cage; saying all the while—

"Chuck, chuck, chuck!"

But whether this sound indicatedamusement at the anger it had excited, or annoy-

ance at being discovered, it was impossible to gather from the expression of its countenance. The mystery was now explained, and the mendicant almost laughed at his own irritation.

"Well," said the mendicant, "this is an odd kind of place. I wonder if the bird is the only inhabitant of the place, or if he's the landlord? Is nobody here?"

"Go in," said the bird,—"go in—go in."

"In faith, many a wise man has uttered a more foolish sentence, though it might have been a longer one. We will go in, and see what can be made of the place."

As he spoke, he dismounted, and led his horse towards a shed which lay on one side of the farm, but the entrance to which was concealed behind the trees.

"Upon my soul, this is a very well contrived place, and would do well for many purposes I could speak of. Hilloa, friend! is there any living human being about this place?"

"Yes—I be here," said a sleepy-looking fellow, half boy and half man; "and as for the beans, you can have them, if so be as you want them, and measter's agreeable."

"Can you take charge of the horses?—sort them down and feed them?"

"Yes, I should think so, I's sort a horse down wi' anybody in the country—I don't care who he be."

"Very well, then, sort them down well; and if you do, you and I'll reckon for it. Is there anybody in the house?"

"Yes; there was when I was in there," returned the fellow, scratching his head.

"Indeed! when was that?"

"About three hours since."

"Then I suspect that they are not there now: they must have emigrated since then."

"Ay, measter's great enough, I s'pose; but you'll find 'em if you look for them, at all events."

"Indeed! I called till I was tired, and they never came to me."

"That's like enough—they never do. Go in and find 'em. Did the bird tell 'ee to go in, eh?"

"Yes."

"Then what a fool thee must be to stand outsoid."

"Well, you are a remarkable sort of people about here—civil to a degree."

"Oh, yes—we be."

Seeing nothing was to be made of this specimen of the population of the district, he entered the house, keeping Mabel constantly by his side.

"I would," he said, "have given you more liberty, but it would be dangerous to trust you: you avowed every intention to make your escape from me."

"And ought I not to do so? is there any justice or right that I infringe by so doing? On the contrary, I am now suffering violence and injustice, to a degree undreamed of by almost any human being, and for which you would suffer, if your falsehoods had not prevailed."

"And will prevail," said the mendicant. "You may depend upon it, when I say that I will leave no means unused to retain you in my power. I have set my life upon a chance, and I will stand to it—but no more of this now—come on."

He entered the passage; and seeing several doors, he opened one, which happened to lead into a large kitchen, around which were placed a number of barrels, resting on trestles, with a variety of cellar utensils.

There was a large fire-place; the fire was evidently on the wane, and on either side sat an elderly couple, male and female. They were fast asleep, and tolerably fat.

The man sat in an easy chair, in his shirt sleeves; he was the landlord of the place—that was plain: he wore an apron before him, and no one else would have presumed to sleep at that time of the day.

"Hilloa! what ho! here—what ho! Is there any one alive in this dull house, here? What ho!"

These words were uttered by the mendicant, with such startling energy, that the sleepers started in affright.

"What ho! hilloa!—anybody alive here?"

"I don't know," said the landlord, who had just recovered the use of his speech. "I don't know—I have nearly been killed with fright: but, before that, I was alive."

"Then look alive."

"I can't" said the landlord, "until I have recovered from the noise."

"You sleep sound, here?"

"Yes, I believe we do. We pay attention to it, you see."

"So I should imagine," said the mendicant, "for you were hard to wake."

"Have you come from sea?"

"What do you mean by that?" said the mendicant, with a scowl.

"Why that I should think you must, and that you have been in a perpetual storm; so you've learnt to halloa, and can't forget it."

"Well, I'm blessed! oh, my good gracious me; who ever heard the like of this afore too I should wish to know,—fo think of coming into people's houses, and frightening them out of their sleep? Well, I am sure!"

"I am sorry for disturbing you, my good dame; but if you keep an open house for travellers, you mustn't complain if they walk in at a seasonable hour."

"There's for you," said the landlady; "as if I was to be disturbed by such people."

"Which is your travellers' room, eh?"

"That one afore you. But what are you pulling the woman about for—you are dragging her about after you as if you were afraid of her running away."

Mabel was irresolute, and for some moments spoke not; but at length she determined to speak to them, and said—

"Help to rescue me from this terrible man, he is taking me from my friends against my will, and compelling me to hide with him from those who are in search of me. He is a vile man!"

"Poor thing!" ejaculated the landlady, "I'll see if he shall touch her!" and then she seized a gigantic shovel.

"Oh," said the landlord; "he shall know what it is to come into my house!" and forthwith seized upon the shovel, and flourished it above his head in an attitude of offence.

The mendicant immediately stepped into the middle of the kitchen, and threw a brace of pistols on the table.

"Murder!" said the landlord.

"The wretch!" said the landlady; "he would take our lives; but I don't care for his pistols—they ain't like guns, and make a dreadful noise. I'll give him a taste of my shovel—here Jem! Jem!"

"Jem, Jem, Jem!" shouted the landlord; because that seemed to promise aid.

"Jem, Jem!" shouted the landlady; "let loose the dogs."

"Ay, let loose the dogs. Murder, fire, and thieves!"

During this time the mendicant, who kept a tight hold of the unfortunate Mabel, drew out the constable's staff, which he held within an inch or two of the landlord's nose.—

"Thou stupid! do you know what this is, eh? Do you?"

"Oh, my eye and the bung! why, it's an officer's staff, as sure as hens' eggs are not kidney beans."

"Well! I am an officer."

"In course you is. I see it all now;—the poor young lady's had a runaway match, and you are taking her back."

"I wish it was no worse," said the mendicant, shaking his head.

"Worse!" exclaimed the landlord, dropping the the poker on the stones.

"Worse!" said the landlady, looking the picture of mystified horror and curiosity.

"Yes, and worse."

"And what can it be?"

"She hasn't had a babby, and killed it, has she? Oh, the wretch!"

"No, worse."

"Goodness gracious! say what it is, for I don't know what is worse."

"Well, then, she is mad."

"Poor creature! mad, eh?" said the landlady, going near to her, and looking at her with intense curiosity and pity.

"Don't go near her; she's very artful, and very dangerous."

"Goodness!"

"My good people," said Mabel, "I want nothing unreasonable. He says I am mad. Why not let my friends convey me to my place of destination? Why should I be dragged through bye-ways, instead of having a proper means of conveyance? I only want my friends to see me, instead of being hurried on in this shameful manner; besides, this man tells me he's my father, and ——"

"There," interrupted the mendicant, "you have heard enough to convince you of her madness, and I beg of you not to go near; if you do, I will not be answerable for any mischief she may do; she escaped once, and that is how it happens I haven't got a carriage for her: she bolted once, and I had a desperate job to get her back. Oh, she's dreadfully artful. Have you a strong room?"

"Yes," said the landlord, "I have. There's one next the parlour; and, when once in there, she can't get out again. Oh, the young puss, to be such a tigress!"

"Dear me! what can have made such a young creature mad?"

"Don't name the cause," said the mendicant, "or she'll go off furious. I'll tell you more of that by-and-by; let me place her safe—let her have what she wants, then I will see to my own wants, and talk to you more at leisure."

"Very well," said the landlord; "that seems to be fair enough, wife; show him the room, and then he can see if it be safe enough to his liking, and then I will set about getting the dinner ready."

"Come this way—come this way," said the fat landlady, as she waddled along the kitchen, and her slippers going up and down with a slap every step she took. Bestowing a look of commiseration upon Mabel as she passed her, she said with a sigh, "Oh, poor thing! if it wasn't madness I should have interfered; but that is a thing that cannot be interfered with. Poor thing! so young, and so pretty. Well, well; it's no use grieving for her. She's not sensible, in a manner of speaking, as we should be of the calamity attending such a state."

"You speak very feelingly," said the mendicant; "and I assure you it has cost me some trouble to get her along."

"Indeed! she wouldn't come quietly?"

"Oh, dear, no; she didn't like to come, of course, and she resisted a great deal, as you may see by my clothes—and I defy anybody to say I was rough with her. I have done my duty, and her friends will say so, I am sure; and as soon as I get to London, she shall be well taken care of."

"I am glad to hear that," said the landlady; "it's quite a sin against nature to see her in such a state."

"Is this the room?" inquired the mendicant, as the landlady stopped before a large door, and turned the key.

"Yes, this is it," answered the landlady; "this is the place; it will answer the purpose here very well. She cannot escape, I'll warrant; and there is a bed in it, so she can sleep or do what she pleases."

And as she spoke she opened the door, displaying to their view one of those large wainscoted apartments so often seen in old houses.

"This," she said, "is safe in every point: the windows are barred, and the chimney, too."

"This will do. Let her have what refreshments you have; and, when you wish to send them in, I will come, too—for until we leave, I will retain the key."

"Oh, very well—just as you please. There's nothing more now, I suppose?"

"Nothing."

They were about to quit the apartment, when Mabel determined to make one last appeal to the landlady.

"Stay," she said to her, "oh, stay for one moment, and hear me!"

The landlady paused.

"Are you a woman," she said; "and can you leave me to such a fate?—a fate a thousand times worse than that of the madhouse; to be made the instrument of that mean, wicked, and iniquitous scheme. There's no act of villany that he will not commit, and cause others to partake in it."

"You hear her wild incoherency of speech," said the mendicant. "Can anything be more palpable?"

"It certainly is a very sad thing," said the landlady; "but it can't be helped. I am very sorry for her, poor creature."

"I do not ask you to do anything that will be hazardous to yourselves. But will you not send for me to the next justice of the peace, and let me be examined? I cannot, if I would, allow my friends to know how I am placed, and to take some notice of that man."

The landlady looked puzzled, and knew not what to say, but she shook her head, saying, as she did so—

"I am truly sorry to see you so, and will do what I can for you; but you had better be quiet, and you will not be hurt, I am sure."

"No," said the mendicant; "it is useless to attend to her: but come along. I'll tell you what, just to please her, I have had her before three justices already, and they have been so angry at me, that I should not like to try a fourth. Poor thing, if I thought she was at all to be blamed, I don't know what I should not do."

"Oh, take no notice of her," said the compassionate landlady: "she's very young, and ought to be very tenderly dealt with."

"And so she shall, as far as may be consistent with my duty."

"Oh, we have all our parts to play," said the landlady, as she left the room: "and some more unpleasant than others."

"And mine's one of them, I assure you," said the mendicant, as he locked the door carefully, and put the key into his pocket.

They both descended the stairs and proceeded to the kitchen, where the landlord had got some viands placed before the fire, as well as some cold meat placed upon the table.

"Here," said he, "is the support of life —the grand invention of civilized life—the *panaka* of hungry stomachs and strong appetites. Ay, this here is a blessed sight, better an' the philosopher's stone, which, as I reckon, must have been d——d hard of digestion."

"I think your surmises are correct. I am happy to have found so sensible a man: but what is it you speak in such laudatory terms of?"

"Wittles and drink," said the landlord.

"Oh, I understand you."

"Yes, but I means cooked wittles, not as the savages understand the process; for they cut the steak off the living ox, and eat it warm, which is certainly economic as far as the firing goes, but expensive when you come to think of the ox. I means cookery as applied to farm produce in this country."

"Exactly—a very noble invention: but have you anything in the shape of good October, or any good ale?"

"I believe you," said the landlord: "some of the best in the country. Why, I often send two or three barrels to the houses of the gentry. I'm well known for good ale, bless you—very well, indeed."

"Are you? Well, then, let us have some of the best you have on tap."

"I will, I will," said the landlord; and, with a short wheezing cough, he began to make his way along the kitchen to an antique-looking cask, from which he drew a jug of clear, light, amber-coloured ale.

"Here," said he, "if you don't say you never drank such stuff as that, why, you're a Dutchman, and deserve to be wrecked in salt water; that's all I have to say to you, friend."

As the landlord spoke, he sat down on a wooden chair with a sob that sounded very much like a smack; he then began to eat and drink most voraciously, saying, as he cut slices off a bone which he held in his hand, and dabbed them alternatively in the salt-cellar and the mustard-pot, and finally into his mouth—

"I haven't eat anything since breakfast, and that's three hours and a half ago. Why, my nap, which, by-the-bye, you broke, has given me a delicate appetite, but by no means such a one as I should have had had you let me sleep another hour. Then, indeed, I could have eaten a bit."

"You are by no means a bad hand at it, now. Indeed, you beat all amateur eaters; though, I must say, I never expected to meet with one of your extraordinary capacity. You do credit to your country."

"Well, I think I do; but come, you don't eat. This pork is some of my own feeding; it's uncommon good; as mild as bread and butter. You see you use both salt and mustard. I tells you what, sir, I never pickles my pork till it is so far pickled, that all you can taste is the flavour of the salt or saltpetre."

"Others do."

"Yes; that's because their pork ain't first-rate, or they are afeard of it tainting, eh?"

"Very likely. This is uncommonly good."

"And the ale?"

"Beautiful. May you always preside over such provender as this."

"Well, as long as I live, I think I may; and when they are gone, what's the use of living? I don't care a fig for a life of trials and inconveniences, as some people talk about they have gone through. Oh, dear, no! More 'tother; more fool they, say I. I wouldn't care to live a day beyond comfort."

"You are a philosopher."

"A bit of one, I believe. A short life and a merry one, say I. Let them say a long one of hardships and struggles if they please: I'll warrant I'm the gainer."

"I think you are right," said the mendicant; but I can neither eat nor drink any more just now."

"Can't you?" exclaimed the landlord, in accents of surprise.

"Not if I am to eat any dinner, which I see roasting."

"As you please," said the landlord—"as you please; but I am very sorry for it. The things are good I know."

"They are good. Had they not been so, I had not eaten as much."

"Well, well, I shall finish mine," he said, turning a large knuckle of a boiled leg of pork that yet held a fair pound of meat on it, "and then I shall leave off with an appetite."

"Indeed!"

"Yes, surely. Dinner will be ready in an hour and a half by the clock. Mind, I'm punctual; I never spoil good wittles because people can't keep time."

"I understand you; I will be punctual, never fear. I shall not be away long from the house—I'm only going to look after my horses."

"I understand; but Jem will take care of them; he is a steady lad, and very fond of cattle; cus him, he's always giving two feeds at a time, and that don't pay."

"I think not; but I'll see they are properly cleansed, and taken care of. I must remain till sunset, and then take to the road again."

"Why not stay till to-morrow morning, and go off fresh? Instead of travelling by night, why not have the daylight?"

"I should not even make this stay, but the horses require it; and, beyond sunset, they will not need rest; besides, they'll do their work as pleasantly again in the cool of the evening, and I shall not make a very long stage of it."

"As you please; everything shall be ready."

Having lulled any lurking suspicion which his host or his wife might entertain by these specious falsehoods, the mendicant left the kitchen, and proceeded to the stable to look at the nags, and to see they were properly attended to; for, though he had received a very good character of Jem from his master, and he had promised him a reward, yet he did not entirely lke to depend upon another under such circumstances, but straightway walked into the stable.

For once the publican had made no vain boast; for both horses had been well cleansed down, and good beds were laid under them, and their mangers were filled with good hard corn.

"You have earned your reward, however," said the mendicant, as he looked at the horses feeding.

"I know how to sort 'em dawn, doant I, sir?" said Jem, with a knowing wink and a hideous griffin-like grin on his countenance.

"Yes, you do, and that after something of a fashion, too. Have they had any water?"

"Yes, a little, and they'll have some more by-and-by, not too much at a time."

"That will do: it couldn't be better, Jem. Now, see they are ready an hour before sunset—will you?"

"I will, sir."

The mendicant looked over the garden for a short time, and then entered the house, and threw himself into a chair, in the next room to that in which Mabel was confined, and then fell, after awhile, into a short sleep. It was more than an hour before mine host came to the place where he was sitting, and looking at him, he exclaimed—

"Well, it is a sleep—a beautiful sleep, what a pity to break it! But, then, dinner is more beautiful still; so what's to be done? needs must, when somebody drives. I don't like to disturb human happiness; and yet, what's to be done?"

He walked up to him, and gave him a hearty salutation across the shins, crying—

"What, ho! there! What, ho!"

The mendicant awoke in an instant, and started up upon his feet, and glared wildly around him for a moment or two.

"What, ho!" continued the landlord, "don't you remember where you are? I've come to say as how dinner's getting ready—such a dinner! My eye! I haven't had the like of it for I don't know how long. Three beautiful young ducks; that's one a-piece, you know. A duck is, you see, an odd kind of bird—too much for some people, and too little for others."

"Ah! I see," said the mendicant; "you made such a noise, I couldn't tell where I was. It's all right; I'm ready. I'll just go and see if my charge is right and safe, and then I'll come back immediately."

"Very good. As I was saying, a duck was too much for some, and not enough for others. Now, I am one of these last; but then I've got a share in my missus's; and as for the young woman in the room there, why, she must take snacks with you. A duck ought to serve two travellers."

"And so it will," said the mendicant, "and that very well. It strikes me that you may eat, and eat, until habit enables you to eat an ox, instead of carrying one."

"Well, I don't know but what it does," said the landlord; "and yet I can't recollect the time when a young pullet would have made a good dinner for me: but I suppose there was a beginning; but it's so long ago, that I have forgotten it altogether."

The landlord left the room, and proceeded towards the kitchen, where lay all that attracted him in life—eating and drinking. Indeed, he eat, drank, and slept through his life, with only these alternations, and no other.

The mendicant opened the door of Mabel's room; and, seeing that she had thrown herself on the bed, and from exhaustion alone she had sunk into some troubled slumber, he closed the door softly, and retired. He, too, sought the kitchen, which reeked now with the agreeable odour of the roast ducks and other viands that were in progress of becoming fit articles of human consumption.

"Just in the very nick of time," said the landlord, thrusting his fork into one of the ducks, and removing it again, as a jet of steam followed. "Done to a T."

The three sat down to their repast, and the landlady said, as she held her plate for her share,—

"About the young woman, sir? Hadn't we better take her some up; or would you have her come and sit down here?"

"Neither, if you please; she is fast asleep; and, in her state of mind, you know, sleep is essential to her, and she may possibly be better after it; at all events, it would have a bad effect to wake her now. She can have her refreshments when she awakes."

"That is a good thought," said the landlord; "and the ducks won't get cold, in the meantime; you had better help her off that duck, and put it into the oven, and then take the remainder into your own plate."

Doing as he was directed by the landlord, the mendicant did place some portion by for the unfortunate Mabel; and, following the example of his host, he took the bird on his plate to carve the morsels off as he ate them.

It was curious to see how the landlord ate; the extreme attention he paid to his plate; the haste and noise with which he seized every morsel that was, to his thinking, a little more delicious than another. His whole mind was centred in his repast; his eyes took in no other object, and his head was bent towards the plate, while his thick pendent lips were hanging with a tremulous motion, as if trembling with eagerness for the next morsel that he destined for them.

Such a sight very few indeed had ever witnessed; and even the mendicant, that rough and rude man, paused frequently to gaze upon the voracious animal that sat before him; even he could see and appreciate the intellect of the creature, if any it had.

There was a long silence during the meal,

which was only broken by the clatter of the dinner utensils, and the rather noisy mode of eating adopted by the landlord.

"You are not much disturbed here," said the mendicant.

"Not at this time of the day. Oh dear, no; if I were, what would become of the dinner? I should never know peace."

"What are your busiest hours?"

"An hour or two after sunset, and then as long as I keep open I have the house full of good company; such glorious songs, my boy: you should stay here a night, only for the sake of the treat.

"I wish I could," said the mendicant; "but that's impossible; I must attend to my duty, and sacrifice my pleasure and inclination."

"Ah!" said the landlord; "that is a very hard case, to say the least of it, on your part,—they ought to pay well."

"They ought—but it's discretionary; they may or they may not, just as the humour suits them."

"Ah, it's ill trusting to people's generosity after their turn is served: beforehand they will give you anything, but afterwards, nothing or next to it."

"That's very true," said the mendicant; "and I expect to be out of pocket this journey; it has cost me so much for expenses; they will not believe it, and cut them off because it won't pay, they'll say, and they can't do it."

"May they live upon short allowance," said the landlord, "for their pains."

The remainder of the day passed thus; the refreshments were carried by the mendicant to Mabel, and she ate but sparingly of them, and she was informed that she must be prepared to travel an hour before sunset.

To this she made no answer; but she again lay down, and filled with tears and grief, again sank into a slumber.

The landlord having eaten himself into a state of repletion, though he assured his guest that it was a very abstemious meal, indeed, he fell into a lethargic slumber, from which he only awoke a little before the time appointed for the departure of his guest.

It seemed almost a miracle to see him wake to animation, as if he were some piece of clock-work, and had been wound up for such a time, and when that was out, he suddenly awoke from his sleep.

The landlady had contrived to get some tea ready for the sake of the poor mad young woman, as she called her, and of that Mabel seemed most grateful.

"I don't blame you," said Mabel to her, as she was about leaving the place. "I can-not blame you for your want of any feeling of humanity towards your own sex; but I lament that circumstances should appear in such a light to you, that you should credit what he says in preference to myself. Did you know how I have been dragged away from friends and home, you would pity me! Heaven above knows where I am being carried, and that by one, too, who pretends to be my own father."

"Ah!" said the mendicant, to the landlady—"it is a sad sight."

"Poor thing, poor thing!" said the landlady, with a tear in her eye; "be as gentle with her as you can."

"I will—good evening."

"Good bye," said the landlord. "If you come this way again, give a call."

"I will, you may depend," replied the mendicant; who, immediately he had secured Mabel in the saddle, mounted himself, and was by her side in an instant, and rode gently down the lane, into the cross-road, and cleared the small market-town that he had before seen lay ahead of them.

"You may endanger my life," said the mendicant; "but you cannot alter my purpose, or shake my resolution. I am determined that you shall not escape from me; and let the reflection sink deep into your heart, that, though you have, through the force of circumstances, been separated from me, yet I am still your father—a father that, had circumstances proved better, would have been a kinder one; but they have not, and I know but one course to pursue."

"If you are in need of money, let me return, and, I promise you, you shall be amply rewarded for your trouble."

"It is a delusion, and cannot be done; but it is bootless to talk upon the subject. You know what I have said; you can, perhaps, take my life, and in return for such an act of filial tenderness; be assured I have that which I can and will disclose, that shall make you wish for death, to hide your shame and confusion. It is a secret that would even bring down the abhorrence of your best friends; and though they might endeavour to repress it before you, you would be looked upon as something loathsome and disgusting."

"God of Heaven!" exclaimed Mabel, "can there be any human heart so depraved, so hardened against all kindness and feeling, as to be capable of doing such a deed as that you speak of? Oh! I have, indeed, fallen into very different hands to those I have been used to."

"Can you be so dead to all feeling yourself, Mabel, as to wish to sacrifice the life of your father?"

"But are you so?"

"I swear it!" vehemently replied the mendicant; "I swear it by all you hold most dear and most sacred."

"Heaven looks down upon and can best tell if you be perjured or not; you have not been a father to me, and others have; to whom am I most indebted?"

"To the author of your being," said the mendicant, sternly.

"To my God?"

The mendicant made no reply; the answer seemed to him one that he could not reply to, or he chose not to do so, and they rode side by side at a moderate pace, until they came near the town, and then spurring their horses forward, they went through at a sharp pace, and when they had got a mile or better through, the pace was again slackened to a good round trot.

The evening sun was setting behind them, and threw their shadows on in advance for some distance. The air was mild and serene, and a more beautiful hour and spot could not be well chosen.

The two travellers still rode side by side, the mendicant keeping hold of Mabel's bridle, so that she could not escape.

They rode thus till the sun set, and the twilight hour ensued; then the shades deepened, and then darkness came over the earth, but yet they proceeded onwards,

After a time the moon rose, and shed a flood of soft, silvery light upon the earth, making the chaotic darkness give place to all the splendour of the night.

And yet they rode onwards with the same speed. Their horses were refreshed from their rest and good feeding, and performed their work willingly; the hard road resounded with the beat of their feet. The air was growing cool, but the motion and rapidity of their pace, and, above all, the thoughts which occupied their minds, prevented their feeling any inconvenience on that score, and thus they rode on in silence.

It was midnight before they came to any halting-place, and that was in a wild and desolate spot. A house partaking more of the nature and character of a farm-house than a public-house, was that at which they stopped.

They dismounted, and their reeking steeds were given into the hands of a man, and then a back door was opened for them, and they entered a ruinous sort of place, in which was plenty of lumber, and odds and ends of all sorts.

Then they entered a large kitchen, in which was an oven being heated, and troughs and pans full of dough, and loaves in pro-

cess of being made by some men and women.

They were a strange set that were there—they looked so, at least, to Mabel, They took apparently no notice of any one; but she could see they exchanged glances of peculiar meaning, as they passed and repassed each other. The red light and heat from the oven, whenever it was opened, gave them a demoniacal appearance. They looked like so many demons at work in the infernal regions. They sat some time in silence, until they saw an aged woman come towards them, from some inner apartment.

"Well," said the mendicant, "you are always busy here, I see."

"Yes, we had need be. Had it not been baking night, you wouldn't have got a rest to-night."

"I shall only stay an hour. We have ridden since sunset, and must ride again. Give us something by way of refreshment."

"You shall have what I have got; and it's lucky it's baking night, else I don't know that I could get you anything."

"Well, I'm glad it's baking night, too, since everything seems to hang upon that one circumstance in this place."

The old woman hobbled off, and soon after returned with the refreshments she promised them. These consisted of cold meat, bread, and ale.

The mendicant eat heartily. It seemed as if his appetite was not at all injured by his anxieties and the hard travelling, but that they rather increased it than otherwise. Mabel ate but little, and what she took was not so much from inclination as from a conviction that it was necessary to support her through the fatigues and trials to which she was exposed.

The people in the place took no notice of them, but continued their operations; and after a time they cleaned the oven out of its ashes, and then put in the bread, and then the oven was carefully closed up.

By this time they had been there beyond the time which the mendicant had prescribed for himself, and, rising, he said—

"Well, I'm off, good mother. Good day to you, mother; it's some time since we met, and may be again; but here is something to remind you of me when I am gone."

He gave her some money, and after a few words, they both went out of the place the same way they entered it; the horses were ready for them at the door, and then Mabel was soon placed in the saddle, followed by the mendicant, and, in a few moments more, the road again beat beneath the hoofs of their steeds.

THE MURDER OF DASHING NED OF NEWINGTON

Onwards they pushed with rapid pace, and their horses were refreshed by the short bait and rest they had. The stars shone brightly in the heavens, and the moon now began to wane, and the light they hitherto had began to fail; but, as if to compensate for the loss of the moon's rays, the stars spangled the blue vault of heaven.

After about four hours' riding, they arrived in the outskirts of London, and then the scene changed.

Hitherto, they had seen nothing but the hedgerows, where there were any, by the road-side, or they passed over barren tracts of heath or common land; but now the road-side was lined with houses and villas, and, in some places, as the countryman once said, when he saw London for the first time, "the road was hedged with houses."

The change was great and striking, even at that quiet hour, for it was not yet day-light, though the east began to lighten a little, and the stars in that quarter began to grow paler and less lustrous, as if the very distant approach of the sun took from them every beauty.

In three quarters of an hour they were in the heart of London, and, stopping before a large public-house, the mendicant dismounted, and helped Mabel to dismount also: then he took her by the arm, and hurried her into the house, and along a narrow, winding passage, before she could recover her breath, and thrust into a small room. A light was brought, and then the mendicant said to her—

" Here you will remain for a few hours, and then you will go to your final destination: you can have what you desire here, and can rest at leisure, for, unless you can desire the attendance of any one, you will not be intruded on."

Mabel made no reply.

" Do you want anything ?' he said, after he had paused for some time.

" Since you will not permit me to see my friends," said Mabel, " will you let me write to them? they are anxious—most anxious for my safety. I know they are my real friends and benefactors. Let me write to them, and tell them where I am."

"That will be madness, and I tell you it cannot be done—not in any one particular. I now reiterate what I have said often and often to you, since I first seized you. You are my child—I am your father."

"And yet you have not any of the affection that they have, to whom I do not belong, but whose kindness and tenderness have been of such vast importance and benefit to me, and to whom I cannot be too grateful."

"Be that as it may, I am a fugitive—my life is in danger at every step I take. We have been strangers to each other until this moment; and last, not least, you are unmindful of our relationship, and act in direct opposition to all my wishes."

"But I know you not; you say you are my father; but you are a desperate criminal also, and may not speak the truth."

"Act upon this impression," said the mendicant, "and you are a parricide."

He then arose, and left the apartment, locking it after him; but the key was hung up on the outside.

The mendicant himself, after a whispered consultation with some man in the house, threw himself upon a bed, and fell into a slumber, from which he arose and partook of some breakfast that had been prepared for him. After that, it being late, he went out to visit a house in the vicinity of Hoxton.

He was employed in and about the old house for some hours. He went to different brokers in the neighbourhood, and procured different articles of furniture, of a mean and wretched appearance, enough only to accommodate two persons in the meanest possible manner; and having placed them in the house, he returned to the public-house in which he had left Mabel.

"I now come," he said, "to convey you away from this place, where you are liable to all the inconveniences of a public-house, to one where you will not be so annoyed."

"It matters little to me," said Mabel, "where I am taken to, since, wherever it may be, my presence is compelled."

"Well, well," said the mendicant; "we can converse more about that at our leisure, where we are going. I have a coach at the door, and we shall have but a short distance to walk before we are safe."

He then led Mabel through the same narrow passage, and then into a coach, the steps of which were rapidly put up after them, and in less time than she could seat

herself the door was slammed to and the horses put in motion, and then they rolled along over the stones at a decent rate. They arrived at a lonely spot, the coach stopped, and out they got; the same celerity of motion was observed, and the coach was out of sight in a minute.

"Now," said the mendicant, "walk quickly, and we shall be at home in another minute or so."

They hurried along, and in a few moments came to a desolate, dismal-looking house, and up the steps of which the mendicant hurried her. The key was placed in the lock, and it at once opened; they entered, and the door was immediately closed and secured by her conductor, who led her to an inner room.

## CHAPTER XLIX.

### THE DISMAL HOUSE.—THE DUNGEON ROOM. THE THREAT AND THE PROMISE.

It was almost with a kind of stupefaction of intellect that poor Mabel looked around her, when she found herself fairly within that desolate and cheerless-looking abode to which she had been brought by that man, who certainly, by his consanguinity to her, near or remote, was her evil genius.

The rapidity with which incident had succeeded incident, since her departure from that happy home, which she never fully appreciated until now that she was torn from it, had made her feel as if years had elapsed since last she heard the tones of those well-known voices she feared that she should never hear again, and looked upon those much-loved forms which never again might meet her longing eyes.

Mabel found how strictly true it was, that time must be measured by the events which are considered within a given space, rather than by its actual progress; all her former life was a quiet dream in comparison to the active and frightful reality of her present existence.

Her mind was torn and distracted by a variety of different emotions; almost every impulse of her generous nature was placed in an antagonistic position, as regarded some other feeling equally curious; like some rudderless vessel, she felt herself tossed at the mercy of the winds and waves of doubt and conjecture, and what to think, or how to act, she knew not.

She spoke not, and when she was rudely thrust into this room, she looked around her and shuddered at what she saw.

It was meanly and barely furnished; it contained only what was absolutely necessary for her exigencies; but what was there was of the commonest character. The light only came in at the top of the shutters, a short space being left unopened, or rather a portion of the woodwork had been sawn off, so as to present a shutter to the height of about two-thirds of the window upwards.

Above this space appeared some iron bars, and thus the window was completely secured; she noticed this almost from the first, because her eyes glanced to where the light came from, and this precaution struck her with terror and dismay.

"Have pity on me," she said, "and do not confine me in such a place as this; it will be terrible; it is but a degree better than a dungeon."

"It may be so," was the mendicant's reply; "but it must be your home for some time."

"My home! God of mercy!"

"Yes; you must remain here, if you will call it so, a prisoner, until circumstances change, and you become of a more amiable disposition."

"Wherefore do you do this? Why am I to be thus imprisoned? What can it benefit you that I should suffer?"

"You know not."

"Alas! I do not; but let me write to my friends, and tell them that I am yet alive."

"No, no; that would but excite in them vain hopes of finding you out: it will not do; you must remain alone for some little time."

As he spoke, he shut the door upon her, and quitted the house.

The sound of the door, as it shut with a heavy bang, fell with a sense of loneliness on her heart. That sound fell upon her mind with a sensation she had never yet felt; it seemed as though she was now shut out from the world.

Tears came apace, and, perhaps, it was as well they did, for this abandonment to grief, which came upon her, was so intense, that it destroyed thought, and when she, in some measure, recovered from it, she found the oppression of mind not so complete and appalling as before.

"I will not think," she exclaimed, "or I shall go mad; this misfortune is too great. I will yet do all I can to preserve my reason. I will even find food for other thoughts here. I may yet be released, and if I can but live on, time may, in its round, find me in a happier situation."

She arose, and looked around the room, and espied a door—it might, perchance, lead to some outlet; she opened it, but, alas! it was an old closet, filled with the dust of years, in which were a few books, that had been thrust into it. She took one of them, and opening it, determined to read, and, if possible, evade or prevent reflection upon the past :—

"Two years, Lucy," said a young man; "two years will be the extent of time that will be required: that once past, and then, my love, we shall be inseparable, hand and heart. One voyage, and all will be as we shall desire."

The maiden looked earnestly in the youth's face, as she replied—

"Two years, Charles, is a long, long time to remain in ignorance of the welfare of those we love; a long time to pass without once seeing the face of one so dear to me as you are; but yet I know the necessity of our separation—it is but to meet to be more happy."

"Truly, my dear Lucy, that is the truth. One voyage, and I have then done with toilsome life, and I will then settle down in some quiet line in life, where there will be no more absences—where we can live and love together."

"That—that will be a happy time. Oh! what an age two years will seem, while I am looking forward to such a happy moment! Time does, you know, Charles, seem longer or shorter, according to circumstances; short to the criminal who has a stated time to live, but long to him who has to wait for an event that he hopes and wishes for."

"So it is, Lucy; but as we cannot command events, we must patiently wait for them in their own order. But if you be as true to me as I am and shall be to you, then nothing but death can interfere with our looked-for happinesss."

"I will be, Charles—I will be; I swear it. No one shall be more true than I to you. But shall we not hear from you?"

"I fear not."

"Write."

"If I have any opportunity I will, depend upon that, Lucy : but you must listen to no tales of shipwreck; and even if it seem they are true, yet believe not all have perished, as it may turn out the reverse."

"I will be careful, Charles."

"And then, Lucy, depend upon my return to you in two years."

"I shall—I shall, Charles. You will not forget me—will you?"

"Forget you, Lucy!—impossible—utterly impossible! I cannot, will not do that. Let me find you as I leave you, and then our hopes and happiness are secured."

Thus spoke two lovers, as they conversed in a small arbour, whither they had resorted to take leave of each other, and say those things they would scarce feel at liberty to utter before a third person.

Lucy Williams was the daughter of a small farmer. She was as beautiful as the dawn, and as innocent as the lambs in her father's flocks. She was the acknowledged toast of the neighbourhood, and many a young farmer sought the love of Lucy, but all in vain.

A young seaman, a mate of a large vessel, sought and won her. She was destined to look upon him as her lover. It happened one evening that she met him at a party, whither she had been invited, and thence commenced their acquaintanceship, which lasted one or two voyages.

This was to be his last voyage, as he thought at the end of that time he would be in a condition to settle down in a quiet country life. He had some property coming to him at that time, and that, added to the earnings of the last two years, would make up a goodly sum. Moreover, Lucy Williams was not yet seventeen years of age, which was a consideration with her parents, who thought two years more added to her age would be desirable. All things considered, the voyage was looked upon by all as a thing that would in every way be conducive to their benefit and future happiness.

They parted that morning; but when they left the scene in the garden, a man stepped out from behind, where he had been concealed, and had overheard the whole of the conversation that had passed.

"So," he muttered; "that's it, is it? I always thought there was something that prevented her from being more complacent than she is to me. It's that fellow, is it? But I'll stop their game. The girl shall be mine, or I'll see better reasons for it than I have yet heard or known of. He goes through the wood to-night. Be it so; I'll do for him what he'll not require to be done again. The girl shall be mine; yes, yes— the girl shall be mine—that's settled. I'm lord about here, and that's a very good reason why she should be mine."

Muttering to himself, he cautiously got over the garden fence, and crossed a ditch. He then proceeded under the shadow of a high hedge, and in a short time disappeared altogether.

\*     \*     \*     \*     \*     \*

That evening it was late when Charles Wise left the farm-house, having taken a kindly leave of the inmates. The farmer and his daughter accompanied him about a mile on his journey, and left him to pursue his journey by himself. They watched him out of sight, and then turned back, walking slowly and in silence towards the farm-house.

Charles Wise turned his back towards the house and walked onwards in silence, immersed in thought, with some feeling of sadness and melancholy. The thought that there was to intervene two years before he should again behold one who was so dear to him, was not at all encouraging; but still hope was strong within him, and he muttered, as he went along by himself—

"Come, come—there is no real cause for sadness; the two years will soon run merrily by, and then comes the pleasure of the return, and the events one loves to think upon, and believe to be the happiest that can happen; that will, indeed, make me a happy man for the remainder of my life."

These words were scarcely out of his mouth when he found that he was not walking alone, but that he had overtaken another man who was on in advance. A second glance sufficed to tell the seaman that he was a respectable man in appearance, and, therefore, he had nothing to fear from him. In this, however, he was mistaken, for the event will be seen to have a very different complexion to what probability gave it at the outset. This man was no other than he who had played the eavesdropper in the garden, and who had lurked unseen on the road until he came up.

"Good even, friend," said the stranger.

"Good even to you;" and then a pause ensued, as if the seaman did not desire other company than his thoughts; but the stranger seemed not likely to be shaken off.

"When the moon rises," he said, "it will be pleasant travelling through yon wood."

"Very likely."

"You don't know it, then?"

"Yes, I have seen it before," said the seaman, quietly. "I have been in this country before to-day, I can tell you."

"Ah! I know it well myself, since I was born here, and brought up on my father's estate, which I now own."

"Indeed!"

"Yes, and it's not very far ahead; and if you are going my road, I'll give you as good a glass of October as ever you drank."

"I am obliged to you, but I have no time to lose on the road, for I am expected where I am going to, and shall be causing some inquiries to be made after me."

"Ay, ay!"

"Yes."

"Well, it would not take long to swallow a glass of ale; but you must please yourself about that; nevertheless, you are welcome to it."

"I would take it but for the reason I have told you, and I do not like to run away when I have received a favour."

"Oh, you can please yourself about stopping or going."

They now journeyed onwards, exchanging a few words until they came to a very desolate spot. A wild-looking heath on one side, and a number of stunted trees on the other. It was a dreary spot, and when they arrived there they could hear the wind moaning from afar over the land; the moon, too, at that moment seemed to have risen over some impediment that had hitherto obscured her rays.

"It is a beautiful spot," said the stranger, as he gazed about.

"But very dreary."

"It may be so."

"And very little to make the place at all lively or pleasant."

"But yet it is a lively spot,"

"A lively spot!"

"Yes."

"What do you mean by that?" inquired the seaman. "I don't see anything at all lively about it."

"Indeed!"

"No; unless it's a lively place for a murder or a robbery. I can't see it's any use for anything else."

"Yes, yes; it is good for such deeds—and it's good for rabbit shooting."

"Is it?"

"Yes; I have had many a good day's sport over these grounds."

"Have you?"

"Yes. Yonder you see a fine spot—there, that place, that looks a little sandy spot; there's a stunted tree there."

"I see."

"Then take that."

These latter words by the stranger, who had been pointing out a particular spot, had just caused Charles Wise to look a different way, when he seized the opportunity of dealing a murderous blow on the back of the head, which caused him to spin round and reel for some distance. He then followed him, and struck him again; but now the unfortunate seaman began to struggle and call out—

"Help, help!—murder! What do you want—my money? I will give it you—all—all; but spare me!"

The unhappy man bled from every pore; his head had several large wounds on it, and he bled profusely. As he staggered about, he seemed to hold his hand to one particular place, where the blood came out in a livid stream.

"Help! murder! Oh, have mercy—mercy!—help, help! Oh, my God—my God! Lucy, Lucy!"

These were the incoherent expressions that the unfortunate man uttered, as he reeled bleeding about the road, endeavouring to avoid the murderous blows of his aggressor; but each sound became less and less distinct.

Once or twice he turned round and endeavoured to face and fight with his murderer; but he was half stunned with the blows, and flooded by blood, that the other planted his blows, with his heavy short bludgeon, wherever he pleased.

As the unfortunate man uttered the last sounds, the words reached the ears only of the stranger; and no sooner did he hear the name of Lucy come from his lips than he muttered—

"Ay, ay; it wanted but that name to enable me to finish him. D——n! he will never die!"

He then aimed a deadly blow on the man's skull; and he could hear the crash of the bones, while a shriek of the most terrific nature came from the unfortunate wretch, who fell, without another sound or motion, a corpse, to the earth.

The murderer staggered back, and trembled at the work he had done; he heard the sound of horses' feet and voices. He looked around him, and could see the forms of men in the moonlight at a distance. No time was to be lost; in another instant he dashed across the open heath for a short distance; and then, when he reached the tall furze bushes, he crept along in a bent posture, and thus he got away from the scene of murder.

He could hear the men come along the road; he could hear them most distinctly—painfully distinct; so much so, that he thought them very close to him.

He could hear them at the part of the road where he had left the murdered body—he could hear them stop. No doubt they had done so, to make an examination of the body.

"If he should not be dead—if he should not be dead!" muttered the man; "if he should but rise, only for a short time, and be able to speak; what will become of me—what will become of me? Sure he knows me not, though he might describe me—but he knows me not."

He listened; but no sounds reached his ears. Then again the sound of horses' feet was heard galloping along the road, in the contrary direction.

Then he muttered, "They are going to

raise the alarm; there is not a minute to spare."

He rushed along over fence and ditch, with the most frantic haste; and he kept muttering to himself—

"I have done it now; I have done it now, and shall succeed, if I can reach home unobserved; then I shall succeed—then I am safe."

But how to do this he knew not; there were many servants about, and it was only by extreme caution that he entered the house unobserved, and gained his own bed-room. Here he examined his dress, and saw that he was free from all marks upon his person, except his hands, which were bloody.

He washed himself, and then entered his own parlour, and then rung for his servant, who looked with some amazement at seeing him there.

He asked him why he did not come before—that he had rung for him—and the poor fellow declared that he had not heard him before. However, he gained his object, and sat down to think over the past.

Next day there was a great stir over the country, when the murder became known; every one flocked to the spot to see where the deed was done, and the sort of place it was. To depict the grief and sorrow of Lucy and her father would, indeed, be impossible. They were completely prostrated by the event; for old Farmer Williams looked upon the young man as his own son, added to which, his daughter's grief was a source of great sorrow as well to him.

We will pass over some months, about eight, before any one approached the bereaved Lucy Williams. About eight months had elapsed, and the grief of Lucy had assumed a milder character; but it sat upon her features, and gave her a melancholy appearance. About this time, several of her former admirers returned, and endeavoured to make themselves agreeable to her; and among them was Mr. Blackburn, the squire, as he was called.

This individual was the proprietor of great estates in the neighbourhood; they were, in fact, very numerous. He was young and good-looking in the eyes of many, though there was an air about him that people did not admire, yet none could well have said in what it consisted.

This person sought Lucy, and his presence served to damp the ardour of other swains, who considered that there was little or no chance for them. In the course of a month or two more she had scarce another suitor. This was, however, but of little matter to Lucy Williams, who had a happy home; and she could not yet forget the less of her former lover, Charles Wise, for whom she wore deep mourning.

However, by degrees, the grief she felt began insensibly to give way to the many attentions of Blackburn—indeed, they were delicate and flattering both to father and daughter, and consideration begot attention, and that, in its turn, different degrees of favour, until it insensibly assumed a feeling a little warmer than esteem.

These favourable gradations were not unseen by Blackburn, who seized each one, and now turned them skilfully to account. The previous state of feeling was but the stepping-stone to the other, until, in course of time, he seized a favourable opportunity of making a declaration of love.

He was not accepted, nor yet was he refused; and this state of indecision lasted for some weeks; but in the end he prevailed.

The wedding was a splendid one, and the whole of the neighbouring residents were invited. Farmer Williams was in the highest state of pleasurable excitement. The marriage of his daughter to such a man as Mr. Blackburn, was, in his mind, a great honour to the family.

Lucy herself seemed perfectly happy. She was calm, pleasant, and content with her lot. There was no appearance of extravagant joy, but she was happy and content. What more could be desired? She gave away her heart and hand to Blackburn in the pretty village church that morning.

It was a gala day with many, and with all the tenants of Blackburn's estate it really was; and a houseful of guests were to be seen at the Hall. But Blackburn's happiness was soon to be turned to bitterness and gall—all his prospects blighted—and even that seeming happiness which he really felt for a few days was quickly put an end to, by an event he could not have foreseen, and one, of all others, he would have said was the most impossible.

There was a stranger noticed among the guests—no one knew anything of him, yet no one liked to question him: it was too joyful an occasion to quarrel because there was one more mouth to fill.

There was an abundance of everything, and there could be no cavilling at such a straw. But the stranger seemed to consider himself entitled to something more than the mere privileges of the guests. He looked upon the place as his own, and went always wherever he pleased.

At length, Mr. Blackburn himself noticed him, and inquired who he was.

"Don't know, sir," said the man; "he's

been here some time, and takes it remarkably easy—remarkably easy indeed."

"Inquire who he is."

The servant obeyed, bnt returned in a few minutes, saying—

"He won't tell me."

"Not tell you?"

"No, sir."

"I will speak to him myself."

So saying, Mr. Blackburn walked up to the stranger, who met him with an undisturbed visage.

"Pray, sir, who are you?" inquired Mr. Blackburn, somewhat irritated at the man's careless air; "and by whose invitation came you here?"

"Oh, nobody's, nobody's—that is, nobody's but my own."

"Your own?"

"Yes."

"But no one's but mine will pass current here," said Mr. Blackburn.

"Oh, we'll overlook the informality of all that," said the man.

"But I will not."

"I will."

"I must have you turned out, that is the whole of it. You are either mad or intoxicated," said Blackburn.

"Neither one nor the other, I assure you—besides, I came to see you."

"To see me?"

"Yes; I have a secret to communicate to you when you shall speak to me in private. I can't tell it before all these people here."

"I have no time to idle away with you. Begone at once."

"I have a secret to tell you," persisted the man; "one that will make you stare."

"Indeed!"

"Yes; I can whisper in your ear, or your wife's, the name of the murderer of Charles Wise!"

Mr. Blackburn's face turned of a leaden hue; he could scarcely speak, and he stood gazing upon the stranger with his eyes almost protruding out of his head.

"Well," said the man, "do you understand, eh? I have more to say to you when you have time; but here it is imprudent to say more. Have you got any money? I'm infernally short, and as we are sworn brothers, you may as well be my banker."

"Your banker?"

"Yes; why not?"

"Because I don't know you. I don't understand what you mean; but I will not submit to any extortion. What you you have to say to me must be said before a justice."

"Very good. To a justice I will go; but step this way first, else some of your servants will remember things that happened that night."

Blackburn followed the man out, and when alone, he said—

"Do you know me?"

"No."

"Then I'll tell you who I am."

"Well do so."

"I am Jack Hampstead, the poacher."

"I now recollect you. You were sentenced to a year's imprisonment for poaching, and you cannot have been long out of gaol."

"True enough."

"Then you will speedily go back again on another charge, if you don't take a little care," said Blackburn.

"Then you must perjure yourself. But as I am, or rather have been, a poacher, it will serve to explain to you how I happened to be on the spot when you murdered the man."

"I—I!"

"Yes, you."

"It is false."

"Well, well, no matter. I was on that part of the warren; I heard some persons coming towards me, when I got into the road, and stood beneath or behind a gnarled oak—I dare say you can remember it—to which you were pointing the attention of the murdered man when you struck him."

"Go on."

"I saw all that followed, and heard the voices approach, and saw you escape. I followed you close home, and saw you get in at the window, and I pointed out the fact to your head gamekeeper at the time."

"My head keeper?"

"Yes."

"But he is not with me now."

"No; but I know where he is to be found, and, though he has no suspicion, I could yet recall the fact to his mind; and, moreover, I could bring such a chain of circumstances that would in the end hang you."

Blackburn breathed short and thick as he said, in a husky voice—

"How much do you want? Remember, all this is untrue."

"Oh, yes; of course."

"And I do not wish to be disturbed at such a moment as this. Do you understand, or else—or else—eh?"

"Oh, exactly—hand over the money."

"How much?"

"Something handsome. You are a rich man, and can pay handsomely; and, for keeping such a secret, you ought to pay handsomely."

"And so I will."

"That's good and fair. Give me what you have about you now, and I'll see you when more at leisure, to settle matters upon a regular footing."

"Take that, then; and on this day week I will see you again. Meet me at this hour in yonder wood, and do not be seen at my house, or about here at all."

"I don't care about being seen here; it will be all the better if I am not; and when I see you come prepared to do the handsome, all his right."

As the man spoke he turned away, but he knew not that he had been observed; nor did Blackburn think he was observed when he said—

"He, too, must be sacrificed. I have not steeped my hands in blood to purchase such a bugbear as this to dog me about. Oh, no; he must die, too, as the other did."

He turned and left the spot, when Lucy and her father came from behind a projecting gable of the Hall.

"Father," said she, "let us leave this place; I see it all now. Poor Charles was a victim of this man. Save me, father, save me!"

"I will save thee, child. We will immediately go to the next justice, and relate all we have heard."

"My God! my God!" said Lucy; "and I am wedded to a murderer!"

"It is not too late to save you from this unfortunate marriage. Come, dear Lucy, make haste, and fly this place."

They both immediately left the place, and proceeded to their own home; and then, taking the farmer's gig, they dashed off to the next market town.

In the meantime there was a great stir at the Hall, when the absence of the bride and her father was discovered.

Search was made everywhere; but they could not be found; and Blackburn was a prey to a thousand anxieties and fears. He knew not what to expect, or what was at all likely to happen next.

Farmer Williams laid an information, and stated what they had heard. Warrants were immediately issued both for Blackburn, and Hampstead, the poacher.

Blackburn was almost insensible when the officers told him they had a warrant for his apprehension; but when, in reply to the question as to what for, he was told for murder, he fainted.

It caused much stir among the guests, and the wedding festivities were suddenly brought to a close.

The poacher required but little inducement to turn king's evidence. The pro-duction of the gamekeeper and other circumstances turned up, so that he was found guilty of the crime of wilful murder.

He was executed; but before that he confessed he had committed the crime. Lucy never afterwards married; but she died at an early age.

---

## CHAPTER L.

DISAPPOINTMENTS IN LONDON.—THE RECOGNITION AND THE PURSUIT.—THE ESCAPE.

MR. HENRY MORTON and Rafferty Brolickbones, when once they had arrived in London, and came to their journey's end, began to be painfully conscious that, without a clue of some sort to guide them to the hiding-place of Mabel and her persecutors, they might as well search through the deserts of Africa, or the woods of America, with equal chances of success.

Rafferty looked at the people passing; they both walked about the streets from one end of the town to the other; but what availed it them? they saw and were seen, but this did not say much for success in their search.

They were both dispirited, and yet neither of them would for some time communicate their fears to the other, for, in London, the chance of meeting with any one who was daily about the streets was the merest probability in the world.

After a long ramble through the leading thoroughfares one day, Rafferty Brolickbones had been very much disappointed, and they were both fatigued; and Rafferty, looking up in Henry Morton's face, said—

"I'm sure, sir, there's people enough to fill all the world over and over again, but I'm thinking we ought to double ourselves over and over again, I can't tell how many times."

"Double ourselves a number of times, Rafferty!" said Mr. Morton; "and what would be the result of that?"

"Why, sir, sure couldn't we, then, walk up and down all the streets at once? and even then we may not meet with her."

"Do not talk of that, Rafferty; do not speak of not meeting with her."

"Och, thun'er and turf, but I don't; I only wish I could cut off my limbs, and make a man of each of them, and then they should stand sentry in particular places, and watch for her."

"That would be an original mode of proceeding," said Henry; "but what can we do? It's of no use talking about impossibilities; we cannot perform impossibilities, you know, Rafferty."

"But one might try, you know, yer honour, and that would be doing something, you know, and something is better than nothing."

"That logic is hardly correct, Rafferty," said Mr. Morton.

"Arrah, an' how can you make out that nothing is better than something, faith?"

"That is not so difficult as you imagine, Rafferty, but it is not what I was about to do."

"What was that, sir?"

"Prove that something is not better than nothing; you recollect that being in the water on a certain occasion was something."

"Yes, faith, it was something too bad a great deal; by Jabus, only let me come across the wagabone!"

"Well, but nothing would have been better than that, would it not?"

"Oh, faith! there ain't no comparison; a dip in the lake when you wanted to be on the bank, is purgatory itself, and no less, faith."

"Well, well," said Morton, "this is very sad work, Rafferty. I would we could find some trace, or some clue by which we could exert ourselves, if it led through danger—anything—anywhere, I would not care a jot."

"Nor I, as your honour says; danger, or anything else, would be an agreeable variation; something to enliven this dull sentry-work we have to perform here; we might as well be the stone statties a looking down on the people who are passing, without being able to see 'em at all, at all."

"That is something of the truth, Rafferty Brolickbones, but we may have a chance, and we must not give up the search. We will watch, if it be for years; for, like a skilful angler whose sport has been bad, he stays and angels on, and the last hour fills his basket."

"Ah, well, sir, I wish we may be as

lucky; I hope we may get hold of the blue, as you say, sir."

"The what?"

"The blue, sir; you said you only wanted the blue."

"Oh, you mean a clue; I said I only wanted a clue."

"They are mighty much alike the same; the same clue and blue as I'm a-thinking, anyhow; why there ain't any more than a letter's difference, as far as I can consult my larning."

"And that makes all the difference, Rafferty," said Mr. Morton.

"That may be, yer honour; but mighty little the same, all but, nevertheless. I hope something may come of this weary watching; it seems to me as though we were about nothing, merely sitting down idly and looking about us—it does look a burning shame, anyhow."

"I am much of your opinion, there, Rafferty; yet we have no alternative but to watch for events."

"I'll do it, sir, but I'd rather have to charge into the midst of the rascals that's keeping her away from those who love her."

At this moment there was a cry and noise in the street. Rafferty and Mr. Morton turned to see whence it came, and saw a coach coming along, and at that moment an elderly gentleman was crossing and knocked down.

In a moment Rafferty and Mr. Morton were at his side; the horses were stopped, and they drew him out from beneath the horses.

No particular injury had been done, so they believed, but the gentleman was perfectly senseless, and between them they carried him into a chemist's shop, followed by a crowd of idle people.

These were soon left on the outside, and then the chemist set about administering restoratives to the unfortunate gentleman.

He was an aged and prepossessing man, his hair was perfectly white. In a little time he breathed, and showed other signs of life.

"He has received no great injury," said the chemist, "at least not in the bones; it arises from the shock, no doubt."

In a little while the gentleman opened his eyes, and then he gradually recovered his consciousness.

"I—I—believe something has happened; yes, yes—I needn't ask that question," said the stranger, who spoke in a foreign accent; "is there anything serious?"

"I believe not," said the chemist; "I think you are whole, sir, at least I have been unable to detect any mischief, beyond a bruise; but I dare say you will feel more than you do now, a few days hence."

"I dare say I shall, but I feel more confused and stunned than inability to take care of myself."

"Probably."

"I scarce know how it happened, but I believe I was lost in thought when I crossed the road."

"That is the fact, sir. I was looking across the road myself," said the chemist, "and saw you come over; the coach was not coming very fast, but he shouted two or three times, but you did not hear him, and were knocked down."

"Yes, that fact I am well aware of, if no other."

"And but for that gentleman and his servant, you must have been killed, for it was only by their timely and active energy that the vehicle was stopped at all, and you saved."

"Indeed! ay, I saw some part of it, or fancy I did, where are my preservers? Show them to me, that I may thank them for their service to me."

"This gentleman was one, and this another," said the chemist, as he pointed to Mr. Morton and to Rafferty Brolickbones, the latter of whom stood a little way behind the former.

"To you," said the stranger, turning to Morton, "I am indebted for life and limb; for more—for freedom probably, from a long time of torture: how shall I be able to thank you?"

"Nay," interposed Mr. Henry Morton, "I am to have all you might have had happened to you, and what you have escaped, to be ascribed to our efforts; it was much less to us to do them, than it was to you."

"And that's why I have to thank you the more heartily," said the gentleman; "and you, my good friend," he added, as he turned to Brolickbones, "to you, also, I am deeply indebted for this service."

"Oh, yer honour is very welcome, as far as I am consarned. I am an ould soldier, and have fought at Waterloo."

"Ah!" said the stranger, who was a Frenchman, as a shadow of sadness crossed his features, "that was a bloody day, and a sad day for many."

"Yer honour may say that; there was many a tall fellar shot in shoes, and many a good man on both sides, as ever wore brogues, was cut down."

"Ah!" said the stranger, "you must come, Mr. Morton and you, too, and drink a bottle of wine at my hotel."

"Sir," said Morton, "I appreciate your generosity, but I cannot accept it."

"And why not?"

"Because your condition at the present moment will not, I think, permit you to do so; but we will, if you will permit us, see you safe to your hotel, and then we will take our leave of you."

"You are willing to add to the benefits I am to receive at your hand, but you will not accept hardly of thanks, much less of ought else."

"And good reason, too, sir; but we will not refuse your offer on another occasion, if you will extend your invitation."

"Gladly and willingly," said the gentleman. "My name is Rousilli; I am a native of France; but I am well enough now to leave when I have discharged my debt here."

Then turning to the chemist, he purchased a few articles, and having paid for them, and thanked him for his attention, they all then left the shop, Rafferty Brolickbones and Henry Morton walking on either side of him, and giving him the support of their arms, to enable him to walk more easily.

"Would you prefer a coach?" inquired Morton,—"it can be had."

"No; I would prefer going as I am, if I distress you not?"

"No, no."

"Oh, we are able to help another on each side, if there was any occasion; not that I want anything of the kind to happen just to show you what we could do—on the contrary, I don't desire it; but we could if it were necessary."

"I have no doubt under Heaven but you could do that, and more, too, if it were at all necessary."

"Faith, and yer honour's right, i'faiks!"

Some more conversation passed between them, and in a little time they came to a hotel, where Mr. Rousilli stopped, and said—

"This is my hotel. At least come up stairs with me."

"I cannot refuse you," replied Morton; and all three went up to the room which he occupied.

"Now," said Rousilli, "you will not refuse to take a glass of wine;" and he rang the bell as he spoke.

"You are very kind," said Henry Morton. "And now we are here I will; but in your present disturbed condition I protest against waiting more than a few minutes."

"You shall be at liberty to retire when you please," said Rousilli.

A waiter now entered the room and placed wine and spirits on the table, and then left the apartment at a word from Rousilli, who desired him to be absent.

"And what will you take, my worthy preserver?" said Rousilli, addressing Rafferty Brolickbones.

"Oh, I, yer honour?"

"Yes, certainly."

"Och, if it's all the same to yer honour, I'd rather have whisky."

"Or brandy?"

"Bad cess! I don't know; but I think I'll have the brandy for the honour of the thing."

"Then help yourself, and welcome."

Henry Morton and Rousilli watched, with something like amusement, the manoeuvres of Brolickbones, who contrived, by some means, to approach the glasses in a particular manner, so that he should come to that part of them where there were some long glasses that held about two ordinary wine glasses—champagne glasses—and with the greatest show of moderation he took the one nearest to him, with the observation of—

"First come first served; it's no matter which gets used first."

"No," said Mr. Rousilli; "it matters not where there is a choice."

"Not a ha'porth," said Rafferty, who now took the spirit decanter, and filled the glass to within an infinitesimal fraction of a hair's breadth of the top, and then, seeing that Mr. Morton's eyes were upon him, he said—"It'll require a steady hand, your honour, to carry that to my mouth."

"And your hand, Rafferty, I am afraid, is not only steady, but willing in this affair."

"I'faiks your honour is right again. Here's wishing you out of this mishap, sir," said Rafferty, making a ludicrous bow, that was intended to be something profound, if not sublime.

"I hope I may, I am sure," returned Rousilli, "I have reason to hope it, not for myself, but the object to attain which I have come to this country."

"You have not been long here, sir?"

"I have not."

"Do you intend remaining here?"

A shade of melancholy and sadness came over the face of Mr. Rousilli, as he, after a pause, answered—

"That depends upon so many events, that I cannot tell myself truly; but yet I have every desire to return to my own country to die."

"Oh! I don't wonder at that, sir," said Rafferty; "for I used often to wish I might be buried in ould Ireland; and yet a soldier has no right to wish that; he ought to be satisfied if he is buried where he falls."

"They usually do—they usually do," said the Frenchman, who appeared unusually sad. "But come to-morrow with me, and I will talk to you. I have lost a son in battle; but more of this when next I see you."

They both took their leave of Mr. Rousilli, and, after many kind words on both sides, they left the hotel.

They walked some distance without speaking to each other; and each was intent upon his own thoughts.

"Well," said Rafferty Brolickbones, after they had walked for nearly a quarter of an hour or twenty minutes—"well, of all the people I have seen, there ain't one at all like Miss Mabel, or that rascally thief of the world who threw the tree into the water ——"

"And you, too."

"Bad cess to him!—no."

"But you were in the water. Were you not quite drenched?"

"Arrah, bad manners to the thief! no. An sure wasn't I in the tree, and he shoved the tree, and the tree went into the water, and, in course, I went in too."

"Of course you did. He not only threw you into the water, but the tree too, as I understand it."

"Arrah, and be d—d to him, for an unmannerly bogtrotter! But how could I help it?" said Rafferty, who did not like the idea of his being beaten by another man. "It wasn't so much him as the accident."

"Yes, it was rather an accident, to have got up into a place where you could'nt get out again."

"Whist! Your honour knows we have more important business than that unlucky affair—for most unlucky it was—to look after just now."

"It was an unlucky affair—as unlucky an affair as ever was. I would to Heaven it had never happened."

"And I, your honour. I would have laid down the best limb I have to have prevented her going,"

"I believe that, Rafferty."

"Indeed, your honour, I would," said Rafferty; "but we do things for the best, that don't always turn out for the best, and that's the worst of it."

"So it is, Rafferty. I wish every one's intentions were as good as our own; then Mabel would be with us at this moment, for none would do her the violence of carrying her off against her will."

"That's true again," said Rafferty; "an' if ever I come across the rascal again, by gosh, won't I have a tussle for the love of the thing! Won't I pummel him! Jabus! I'll—I'll be the death of him, and no mistake."

"Rather secure him, and then we may

learn something of the motives that induced him to make such a diabolical attempt. We may even be serving Mabel herself by doing so."

"Does your honour think so?"

"Sure, I do."

"Then I'll take care on him, any how, an' he comes into my keeping."

At this moment a man came by, dressed in shabby garments, which had seen some rough usage, when Rafferty Brolickbones started and stared, and the blood came to his face, and the fire flashed from his eyes; the man returned his gaze, but he could not avoid the recognition.

It was the mendicant.

"Blur and ouns!" exclaimed Rafferty, "here he is; seize the murdering thief!"

As he spoke, he made a rush at the man, who, by a skilful manœuvre round a cart, evaded the seizure,

"Stop the murdering thief; stop him, Master Henry, dear: he's the varmint—I know him; ah, my jewel—bad luck to you, you blackguard!"

This was uttered by Brolickbones, as the mendicant saw that Mr. Henry Morton was close upon him, and dodging round a cart, when chased by two, was a losing game, and he dashed past Rafferty, who seized him by the coat, but, alas! for the article—it was insufficient to hold him by, and away he went, leaving a fair handful of material in his hand.

"After him, Rafferty," said Henry Morton; "after him; keep him in sight. Stop thief! stop thief! stop thief!"

"Arrah, stop the murdering thief, will yer, there; stop the vagabond!"

Away they went, darting through the bye streets, and suddenly turning a corner, close pursued by Rafferty and Morton, who came almost within grasp of him, when the mendicant struck an orange stall as he passed, and scattered the fruit over the pavement from one side to the other.

Rafferty first trod upon one of these emblems of the shape of the world; squash went the orange, and down came Brolickbones, and immediately over him came Mr. Morton at full length.

"D——n!" said Morton, in the anger of the moment.

"Och, murder! you two swindling vagabonds, to go to destroy and murder the property of a poor widdy."

"Keep him in sight; come on, Rafferty—come on!"

"I'm after him," exclaimed Rafferty; "my curses on the oranges—they'd be dear enough at any price, now."

"Stop thief! stop thief!"

This was the cry which Morton uttered

from time to time, and echoed by Rafferty, as he dashed along some few yards behind him.

This cry was uttered from time to time by others who saw the chase, and more than one man stepped out to secure the fugitive, but that was not to be effected, for each, as he opposed him, was levelled by the mendicant as if he had been a child; and on he went with undiminished haste.

This flight and pursuit went on for nearly half-an-hour, and they had arrived in some unknown region. It was a low neighbourhood; the houses were all occupied by the poorest of the population.

The houses were high, black, and dingy; the lower stories occupied as shops, and the upper let to an infinity of tenants who often took in others.

At length they came helter-skelter to places that had no thoroughfare, and then they hoped, indeed, they had a chance of securing their man.

Through these streets little or no effort was made by any one to stay the progress of the fugitive, who seemed to be under no apprehension, but continued his flight among dogs and children, and fowls, that seemed to congregate about for the express purpose of impeding the passengers; and on more than one occasion they had nearly got stopped; and on every occasion there seemed more intention to aid and abet the flight than to stop the runaway.

"Now we have him," said Rafferty. "Now we have him."

But Brolickbones was mistaken. Both parties had diminished to less than half the speed with which they started, and breath was at a premium, and enough could scarcely be had to carry them along with safety. Suddenly the mendicant paused, and balanced himself, and then dashed in at an open doorway.

Mr. Morton had at that moment reached him, thinking he was about to turn and retrace his steps, and was not prepared for his sudden disappearance in that manner, but was compelled to overshoot his mark, and pass the door.

This Rafferty endeavoured to avoid by laying hold of the door, to stop himself, but only did so in a slight degree, and then came with some force against Mr. Morton, who had just recovered himself, and was about to return, and enter the house in pursuit.

"Do not lose sight of him, Rafferty. He went in here. He must not be lost; he must be run down."

"Och, by St. Patrick! I'd nearly run you down, Mr. Henry; but we'll have the villain now, sure enough."

They both entered the house, and could distinctly hear the rapid tread of the mendicant up stairs. This was enough, and away they went after him. They were much distressed, but they were too much interested in the object they had in view to stop in their pursuit, at the moment, too, when they believed they had achieved their object. No, they might sink from exhaustion, but while they had power to walk they would not give in.

Up stairs they went, and heard a great deal of screaming and talking.

"We shall have him here," said Mr. Morton; "we have him, Rafferty. Come on."

"I'm coming," said Rafferty; "I'll go in first, your honour. I'm an ould soldier, and they won't make my phisog worse than it is, in case they should damage it a little; but it is different ——"

"Come on," said Henry Morton, as he flung himself against the door, which flew wide open.

There was no need to say "Come on" to Rafferty Brolickbones, as he entered the room after, or almost with, Henry Morton. They glanced round the room. There were several squalid, dirty-looking children, and a woman with blear eyes, looking all terror and amazement.

In one corner of the room was a shopboard, and beneath it was a bundle of rags, that seemed to have life.

"What's that?" exclaimed Morton, pointing to the object.

"That's him," said Rafferty, as his eyes caught sight of the mendicant's coat.

In another moment Rafferty had rushed forward, and seizing the man, after some tumbling, pulled him out.

"Here he is. Now, my darlint, what do you think of me for a playfellow? Ain't I as good as a friend to stick to you in this manner—eh?"

As he spoke, he turned it over, and to his astonishment, found him so bound up in list and the coat, that the man couldn't move hardly,

"Mercy! mercy! do not kill me. Consider my wife and children."

"Eh?" said Rafferty.

"What's that?" inquired Henry Morton.

"Thunder and turf!" said Brolickbones, who began to unrol the unfortunate tailor; and then the little piece of humanity stood trembling before them.

"Mercy, good gentlemen! I have done you no wrong—mercy!"

"Who are you?"

"I am Joe Smitchy, the tailor."

There was a pause of a minute, during which all parties looked at each other in pure surprise and amazement; Henry

Morton and Rafferty looking at each other by turns; and then the diminutive tailor, who eyed them with fear and terror, cried—

"Have mercy, good gentlemen—it isn't me, I assure you—it isn't me!"

"What isn't you?" inquired Rafferty.

"What you're looking for."

"And what's that?"

"Oh! you know best—you do, indeed. I know you do, good gentlemen. I'm a poor tailor; don't hurt me."

"How came you by that coat?" inquired Henry Morton, pointing to it.

"That coat?" said the trembling tailor; "that coat?"

"Yes—that coat."

"Ah! Why—why—do you mean that coat?" said the tailor, trembling, and looking around him in terror.

"Yes, yes."

"Oh, yes! I see, good gentlemen, you do mean that coat."

"By all the saints in the calendar," said Rafferty, "and Patrick to boot, who was the best of them all, if you don't answer I'll fling you out of the window."

"Oh, mercy! mercy!"

"The coat! the coat!"

"Oh yes, sir, you may have it and welcome. I wish I had never seen it."

"Now," said Henry Morton, pulling out a pistol, and cocking it, "if you don't tell me how you came by that coat, I'll shoot you; so take your choice, life or death."

"Oh, life! life! sweet sir."

"Then tell me, how came you by that coat, will you?"

"Oh, that is death, too!"

"Then take your choice."

"Well, then, he's not here, is—he? Oh, do not let him kill me."

"Who?"

"That man—he—he—is—is—"

"Where?"

"Gone, eh? Oh, do not let him kill me, and have me dissected!"

"This will not do long," said Brolickbones, opening the window; "if this gentleman don't shoot you, I'll fling you out there."

"Well, then, he gave it me."

"Who?"

"The man who came in here a few minutes ago; he seized me and rolled me up in this thing, which he took off, and ran away with one that I had to repair, and said he would come back in the night and murder me, if I said a word about it."

"Eh?"

"Yes, it's horrible to think of it. He rolled me up in some dirt, and threw me into the corner, where you pulled me out."

"Done again!" said Rafferty.

"Oh, I'm a ruined tailor!—undone and ruined. My family 'll go to the workhouse; and that man will return and murder me. Oh, what shall I do?"

"Be easy on that score. He is a fugitive from justice. If you can tell me where he is, I will reward you."

"I cannot tell where he is," said the tailor; "he went, I think, up the trap."

"Up the trap?"

"Yes; the ladder on the landing that leads to the top of the house."

"Come on, Rafferty," said Morton, as he flung some money to the tailor.

"God bless you, gentlemen, you are very different from the rascal who stole my customer's coat, and then offered violence to myself. I can now pay for my loss."

Rafferty and Morton left the room, and the little tailor peeped out of the door, and said, as he pointed to a rickety ladder that lay on one side—

"That's it, gentlemen."

"What—this ladder?" said Rafferty.

"Yes; that's it."

"But no one could get up there," observed Morton; "it's not near the trap. He couldn't get up there."

"I do assure you I believe he did. That ladder is always kept at the trap, and he must have thrown it down when he got up."

"I see it all now," said Rafferty. "Oh, the vagabond! He'll show fight now I'll wager a marrow bone to a piece of tinder."

"Don't let him come here, gentlemen: don't let him loose; hold him tight. He's a desperate murdering thief. I shall shall never sleep in peace till I know he's hanged."

"And that he will be afore long," said Rafferty, as he drew the ladder from its fallen state and placed it against the trap.

In another moment Rafferty's foot was upon the ladder, and he ascended the steps and came to the trap, which he could not lift.

"What! is it fastened, Rafferty?"

"Not on this side, sir; but he's either standing upon it, or he's placed something heavy over it; but I'll have it off in a minute."

"The moment you have it off I'll be by your side, Rafferty; but if I stand on this rotten ladder while you are using your strength it will be gone, and a fall to both would be the consequence."

"All's right, yer honour."

Rafferty now placed his shoulder to the trap-door, or rather his back, for as he stood on the ladder he bent his head forward, and pressing his feet against the ladder, he with some difficulty lifted the trap-door and its burden from its position.

As soon as Henry Morton saw it move he stepped up the ladder to watch if there were any one behind it to do any sudden mischief.

When Rafferty had risen up pretty high, with Henry Morton's assistance, he threw the whole burden off, and then they sprang into the loft, but it was empty.

"The bird has flown, Rafferty."

"Bad manners to him, yer honour."

"Curses light on him," said Morton, in an agitated manner. "And now we have lost the chance, perhaps the only chance of discovering Mabel. Curses——"

"With all my heart, and the pains of purgatory added to them."

They gazed around on every side, but they saw nothing. A large log of wood lay on one side; it was a short thick piece of timber, like the trunk of a tree that had been used as a chopping block. This was the heavy substance the mendicant had thrown upon the trap-door, to impede the progress of his enemies.

"The murderin' thief of the world!" said Rafferty; "he's given us some trouble for nothing, anyhow."

"I'll not leave him while there is any trace of his progress," said Henry Morton; "and while I can say he has gone this way or gone that, I'll never rest."

"Bravo, sir! That's what I calls being thorough-bred. I'll stick to it myself as long as I can breathe."

They immediately disappeared through the opening in the tiles, made for egress and ingress in case of necessity.

"And now," said Morton, "he must have gone either to the right or the left. Which was it? All depends upon our taking the right direction."

"Indeed it does, sir. I wish we had one of those dogs that can smell people's feet through their shoe leather, and the scent that remains on the ground. We should have him then."

"A bloodhound?"

"Oh, ay. But what's that yonder?"

"Where?"

"Ain't that the very identical hat he wore?"

"By Heavens! he has gone this way. Come on, Rafferty."

"I'm wid your honour."

As Henry Morton spoke he scrambled across the roof of the house and on to the next one, in a manner that was truly alarming, and Rafferty followed him as quick as he was able.

"Take care, Mr. Henry—for the love of life, take care. The least slip in the world would smash you to atoms. Holy Virgin! take care. You had like to have had at least a sixty feet fall, and that's much more than any Christian can bear. Be careful for everybody's sake, or you'll be kilt, and what will Miss Mabel do?"

"I see him ahead, Rafferty. I can see the villain."

"Hurrah!" said Rafferty, forgetting, in the excitement of the moment, the caution he had been giving Morton. But the prospect of overtaking the man who had so audaciously served him out, and, above all, run away with Miss Mabel, was so strong an incentive, that it banished all thoughts but that of diminishing, as rapidly as he could, the distance between them.

At length Henry Morton paused, and looked round to see if Rafferty was following him; and, seeing he was close beside him, he said—

"He went in here, Rafferty. We shall have him at last."

"Hurrah, Mr. Henry! I'm arter you. This is as glorious as the field of Waterloo. Hurrah! hurrah!"

His voice was suddenly hushed, for he immediately jumped in at a garret window, and attempted to open the door, but it was locked on the outside.

"Here's a go!" cried Rafferty, trying the door. "He's locked us in."

"Have we made a mistake, and come in at the wrong window? And yet I am sure he came in here."

"Hark! There he is, sure enough."

"Where?"

"Down stairs. There's a row."

They listened, and they heard the sounds of altercation, women's voices, and struggling and screaming, down stairs.

"D——n!" said Henry Morton, wound up to the highest state of desperation. "Burst the door open."

"But it opens this way. If I were on the other side," said Rafferty, "I'd have it open in a minute."

He looked around, and saw a small poker, that had been used till it had become short and sharp.

"Here's the thing. Now 'open sesame,'" said Brolickbones, as he pushed it between the lock and the door. The door yielded, and they were free.

"Now for it," he said, throwing down the poker, "now for the murdering vagabond; we'll have him."

They both rushed down stairs till they came down to the second floor landing, where there was a number of people, men, women, and children, standing talking together.

"Hilloa!" said a man.

"Hilloa!" said Rafferty.

"What do you mean by breaking into people's houses in this style for? I'll have ye all transported, ye vagabond thieves. Ye sha'n't come here."

"Just be aisy, honey," said Rafferty; "if ye are going to fight for the murdering thief, all I have got to tell ye is, you'll have a tough job to get over a Waterloo man."

"Oh, you murdering wretch!" said a female voice; "if you come here I'll kill you outright, I will."

"And then I'm coming."

"My good people," said Henry Morton, advancing, "we are in pursuit of a great criminal, and I charge you all to aid me in securing him."

"And I charge you to go where you came from," said the man.

"You'll be liable for aiding and abetting a felon, and moreover, you'll be punished for your resistance and refusal to aid me."

"Go to the devil," said the man; "you are quite wrong; you'll be put to the treadmill as rogues and thieves, for breaking into a man's house; so you had better go back again."

"Is the man who came in here in the house?"

"Of course not."

"I don't believe you at all."

"Do as you like; but don't give me too much of your cheek, or I'll have you well ducked in the water-tub."

"Any violence you may attempt will be visited on your heads with the utmost severity. I have the means and the will to punish any attempt even to insult."

"We shall see," said the man; "go back, now; if you are wise you'll go back."

"I insist upon searching for this man. I must have him."

"But you can't here; besides, he's not here—he's gone; if you want him, you might have known he wouldn't be fool enough to stop in any place he had been seen or known to enter."

"Then we will go out."

"Not down stairs."

"Yes."

"But I say no; go whence you came. You shall not make a thoroughfare of my house. You must go back."

"You let him through."

"I did not; he bolted past the women, who tried to stop him, but they couldn't; he knocked one down."

"It's no use talking," said Henry Morton to Brolickbones, "we must force our way out; come on, follow me."

Brolickbones, however, suddenly took the initiative, and threw himself with such force against the man as caused him to fall, knocking down others in his fall; like one of the skittles that has been forcibly struck, he upset many more.

Henry Morton followed close upon Brolickbones, and prevented any more violence being offered, and in a few minutes they reached the shop, which was a bird-fancier's, and thence into the street.

"We've missed him, Rafferty," said Morton; "he has escaped us this time."

"Yes, sir; we lost too much time among those rapscallions up stairs. I wish I had time to thrash them all singly."

"Oh, they are all desperately well knocked about as it is; they didn't get thrown down one over the other on the stairs without some mischief."

"I dare say not, sir; but I should like to have had that fellow who escaped; I would have given my right arm to have secured him."

"He would have been glad to have purchased his liberty by informing us where Mabel was, and by giving her up"

"So he would, sir—so he would, or he'd be more fond of hanging than I am, at all events; but we know he's in London, and so is she."

"Yes, I am sure of that much; but how soon, now that he knows that the pursuit is so hot, will he remove her?"

"Bedad, he'd be a great fool if he took her at all away, because, in a smaller place, she would be much easier to find; it is because there is so many that we cannot find her."

"There is much truth in that, Rafferty; but we must now seek some rest: since I have been disappointed I feel the fatigue, which I did not think of before."

"Nor I, sir. Jasus! it was all easy before, but now one's ready to drop into the earth, and I'm wet all over with perspiration, to say nothing of the loss of my hat, which is gone I don't know where. I can't now recollect when it fell off, unless my hair lifted it off when I first saw yer honour go helter-skelter over the house tops."

"I dare say I did, Rafferty; but I didn't think of what I was doing. I wonder how we got over so safely."

"I wonder, indeed, sir. I wonder, too, we haven't both made a line or two in a newspaper, and then the news would have been additional mischief at Morton Hall."

"So it would, Rafferty; but, now we are safe, I never felt exertion so much; you must have a new hat."

They entered a shop, where Brolickbones was accommodated with a new hat, and then they sought some place where they could sit down, rest, and have some refreshment, for their exertion and disappointment had produced a great reaction, mental and physical; they were fatigued, silent, and melancholy.

---

## CHAPTER LI.

MABEL'S MELANCHOLY REFLECTIONS.——
THE SEARCH THROUGH THE VAULTS.——
THE HORRIBLE DISCOVERY.

WE left Mabel in the lonely and pent-up room in the desolate house to which she had been carried by the mendicant, who had made her, in fact, a prisoner, and who declared that there she should remain a prisoner until she became more amenable to his wishes than she appeared at that time.

She had sought a refuge for reflection in reading, but that could only serve so long as it diverted the mind from the saddening topic that would otherwise present itself to her imagination.

But of reading she tired, and, when she had finished the tale in which she was engaged, she threw the book over on one side, and instead of her thoughts turning to what she had been reading, they returned to their original channel, and melancholy once more beset her.

"What can they be thinking of me? they will, perhaps, believe me dead; and yet, if Brolickbones escaped, he would tell them how I was forced away against my will. He, poor fellow, may be drowned, and yet he was hardy and brave; but entangled amongst the boughs of that old tree, he may have been drowned.

"Alas, poor faithful Rafferty! has not my insatiable longing to know what I now regret, if true, been the cause of at least danger, if not of death?"

Then she thought of Captain Morton and Mrs. Morton, and of Henry. What was he doing? Surely they were all looking out for her, but they knew not where she was. Could she tell herself! Alas! she could not. She knew not where she was.

From what had fallen from the mendicant she believed she was in London, and that was all she could form any idea of the locality.

Sad thoughts were these to one so young and so tenderly nurtured as Mabel was. There was she made prisoner by a man who professed himself her father, and who exercised an authority over her not to be

gainsaid; it was absolute and complete; nay, how few parents would think of exercising such a power over their children of any age!

But this man was a criminal! How the thought grated the fine feelings and imagination of Mabel. She shuddered at the bare idea of such a man being her father; and yet how she shrank from wilfully exposing him to great and imminent danger, lest it should be so.

She would scarce have grieved that she should see him taken by those whose duty it was to punish evil doers, and yet she would not have his blood upon her soul; that was even more horrible than all.

She would escape, if she could; she would not remain in such contaminating hands, but she could not do what would lead to the destruction of that man.

Again her thoughts would revert back to her home with the Mortons, and the contrast between the Hall and this miserable abode, if even such it could be called, was not greater than the difference between her late protectors and friends and her present captor, or gaoler—he was no better.

These thoughts were maddening to Mabel; she could not bear to think of them, and her grief was great and bitter; but she found no relief in that now, so she determined, if it were possible, to throw off thought and reflection, or, at least, to throw them in another channel, and thus extract the sweet from the bitter, or avoid the latter if she enjoyed not the former.

She rose up, and examined the room she was confined in, and saw that it was fastened on every side, and presented an entire barrier to egress.

Could she but get out at such a moment, when the mendicant was away, she would not compromise her own feelings by consigning him to prison; at least, if that took place eventually, she would have the consoling reflection that she did not do so, but it was the result and reward of his own misdeeds.

She was actuated by more motives than one to make her escape if she could when this bad man was away.

She, therefore, looked more carefully around, and at the door; after much examination, she thought she observed that the hinges of the door were not strongly fastened in, as usual, as if, indeed, they had been torn out and then replaced, for little blocks of new wood had been wedged in to make all secure.

By good fortune, a small bar of flat iron, strong, but not much longer than a knife, lay in the old firegrate, and with this she essayed to open the door at the hinges.

Having thrust the bar in, she found there was no great difficulty to surmount in opening the door, or, rather, in lifting it out, blocks and all.

She was almost terrified at her own success, and paused for a moment, ere she stepped into the passage, and when she did so, she found it was all dark.

The day was on the decline, and, in that desolate house, she found that all the shutters had been put up, and so deprived it of much light it might have.

She examined the street-door carefully, but it was secured in a manner that defied her utmost endeavours to open, and, after expending much labour and time, she was obliged to give up that as an impracticable attempt.

Then Mabel thought that there might be some more ready means to be found down stairs, and up the area, that part of houses being generally not so well protected; but, at all events, if she could not get out there, she might alarm some persons, and the door could be forced open.

This thought cheered her on, and revived her flagging spirits. In her way back, she stumbled over something in the passage, and, on feeling to ascertain what it was, discovered that, to her great joy, it was the materials for getting a light, which the mendicant had left there for his own use, should the next time he came to this place be in the evening, as it would then be useful.

Mabel instantly took possession of them, and soon obtained a light, and then descended what appeared to her to be the kitchen stairs.

They were very dark and ruinous, and the bare walls appeared in many places, and large portions of plastering lay about in several places, as if the damp had assailed it, and caused the destruction; in some places, the boards were rotten that were placed down on the other side.

At length, she got to the bottom; the candle she held in her hand gave but a few feeble rays in that damp, dark place.

It was a passage, yet it could be said to be no better than a vault, from which ran other vaults; and at the farther end seemed another door.

She entered the first vault that she came near. It was a dark, dismal place; there were several things thrown in—such as a large wooden stool, a broken chair, and a few pieces of boards, and odd matters of that kind.

Mabel held up the light, and endeavoured to pierce the gloom of the place, and listen to any sound that might be heard in that silent place.

There was an occasional dropping of moisture exuding from the brick walls, and falling to the earth; the bricks themselves looked moist, slimy, and slippery; it was a frightful place to look into, and Mabel shuddered, and a cold sensation seized her very heart.

She retreated a pace or two, and then she advanced again to the same place, for she thought the light had fallen upon something she had not seen before.

Once more she looked in the same direction, and saw a sack lying in one corner. It was an ordinary sack, such as might have been used for a variety of every-day purposes.

At length, after much hesitating, Mabel determined to examine the sack, and stepped forward to do so. She trembled, but could not tell why. Placing the candle on the floor, she looked at the sack, and then cautiously opened the mouth of it.

She started with horror at the sight that there met her view—a wild scream escaped her lips, and she stood unable to move.

She was some minutes thus; and now the spectacle that first met her view was presented to her eyes in all its ghastliness and horror.

The contents of the sack which so terrified Mabel were the remains of a human being. The head and face were plainly discernible, but in a dreadful state of decomposition. It was a sight she could never forget, and that thrilled through her very veins.

She stood some moments gazing on the body, as if fascinated, and then she smelt, for the first time, the fœtid odour arising from the decomposition of the body. Perhaps it was the motion she had given it in undoing the mouth of the sack and exposing the features to the air; but certain it was, the stench was almost insupportable.

At length, by dint of a great mental and, apparently, physical exertion, she was able to tear herself away, seize the candle, and quit the vaults, and ascend the ruinous steps that led to the upper part of that house, glad to escape even to her own prison-room again.

The light shook in her hands as she stood in the passage, and her shadow danced upon the wall. The whole place looked more terrible and gloomy than before.

"Oh! how shall I support my confinement in this horrible place? 'Tis most terrible. Every day brings some new cause of terror, and grief and horrors accumulate rapidly. I shall sink—I shall sink. I would I were dead, rather than

live here; and yet the time may come when I shall be released from this place, and then the society of my former friends will indeed be dear to me. Heavens! what a contrast between this and Morton Hall! One could scarce ever believe in such things. Have mercy on me, Heaven, and let me not perish by slow means in such a place and in such hands! The decrees of fate surely cannot be so hard upon those who endeavour to act with conscientiousness and justice. Where are they—where can they be? They cannot have forgotten their Mabel, whom they so tenderly nurtured and loved so well!"

She paused, and sat down upon the stairs, and tears came to her relief. She had been much weakened and affected by her treatment, travelling, and the sight she had just witnessed.

How long she was there, rocking herself to and fro, with great mental agony, she knew not; but the candle burned low in the socket, when she was startled by hearing the sound of footsteps at the door.

She trembled excessively, and could not put in force a momentary resolution she had formed, when the key was put in the lock, of rushing out, when the door was opened, into the street; but she, alas! had not power to do it.

The door opened, and the mendicant stood before her.

This man, her terror and aversion, stood still with astonishment for a moment or two; but speedily recovering himself, he closed the door, and secured it behind him; and then, advancing towards her, said, in a loud and harsh voice—

"What means all this? Why is it I find you thus? Why are you out of the room in which I placed you? There is no other place suitable for you. Tell me why is this, or dread my vengeance."

"I dread not death."

"But that I do not intend shall be your lot; the reverse is the case. You will have a long time of suffering; and, if it so please me, you might terminate them all by such a consummation."

"Why torture me? Why not kill me at once?"

"It does not suit me to do so. Besides, it would be unnatural, you would say, for a father to kill his daughter. But why came you here?"

"Ask the caged bird why it tries to escape to the upper air—to the freedom of fields and action. I would be free, and confinement will be the death of me. I shall droop and sink."

"But we must bear even worse evils than that. We cannot kick against the decrees of destiny. If it be yours to remain here a prisoners you will not escape, though you fret your heart out, and vex your mind with all sorts of schemes."

"And it may happen that our destinies may be reversed."

"And then I'll meet mine as I have met heavier misfortunes than any that can now happen to me."

"Yet death remains."

"To scare the timid and the weak, but not me. I am proof against such weakness—such infatuation of the mind, that cannot calmly contemplate a physical change in matter."

"And you fear it not?"

"I would not encounter such a change, unless it were an alternative, or I paid it as a penalty or wager, having lost my game. I would avoid it; but when inevitable, I will meet it."

"I would avoid imprisonment."

"But must submit for a time. Go in. How came you to get out? But first go into your room."

"Have pity! You will destroy my reason, if you drive me into that horrible room again. Have some mercy on me! I cannot bear it."

"But must."

"Oh, no—no!"

"You shall. Come, go in."

"Oh, no! Do not force me. You cannot imagine the horror I have of this place; it is insurmountable!"

"But it must and shall be surmounted; so go in, I say."

"Monster!"

"Ha! ha!"

"You are a vile monster to use any human being thus."

"Rail on—rail on."

"Can you look at me, and then say you are my father? Oh, monstrous falsity!—utterly impossible! There would be some secret link of sympathy shown on one side or the other of such a relationship; but there is none."

"Your view is partial. Because you feel none, you say there is none. That may indeed be, as far as you are concerned; but this I can say, that there is much on my side."

"Oh, Heaven! who could believe such gross wickedness as this!"

"There," said the mendicant, getting furious, "there, girl, go into that room. I cannot spend more time in arguing with you. You know not what I have suffered on your account."

"And what have I not suffered through you? Let me go—let me go, and you will suffer no more."

"Ha! ha! that would be to forego all the hoped-for reward to my own exertions. No, no; I cannot play the fool thus; you are mine by nature, and you are mine now by possession."

"And what do you intend to do with me now?"

"That is a matter which I have thought of, else you had not been here; but I neither consult you, nor make a confidant of you. You act as my enemy, and I may not trust you."

"You might, if the purpose be good." replied Mabel; "but your answer proves to me that you have none but the vilest motives to make you."

"Whatever they may be, they are sufficient. But, once again, go into that room, or, by Heaven, I'll fling you in!"

"Oh! no, no!"

"Go in."

"I cannot—I cannot!" murmured Mabel.

"Must I use force?"

"Mercy!"

"Yes, such as I show," said the mendicant, as he seized hold of her, and forcibly dragged her into the room, and flung her on the bed.

"Mercy! mercy!"

"Ha! ha! ha! I'm not going to hurt you; but you will not obey my orders, and I must execute them myself. I must take care you do not escape this time; I shall consider the propriety of having a chain made for you, so as to secure you to the wall."

"And can you call yourself a father, and yet commit such horrid barbarities as these?"

"They are rendered necessary by your own conduct."

"I want to go to those friends who have behaved so truly kind to me; who have, in fact, been parents in affection to me; who are, indeed, the only parents I desire to know."

"The romance of the feeling has now worn off, then, of the desire to know who your parents were; and this because they are not what you thought you had a right to expect, as if you had any right at all. Now you have found one, you think, because misfortune has laid a heavy hand upon him, that you have a right to turn your back upon him—to accept the bounty of strangers who know nothing of you."

"They know as much of me as I know of myself—they are contented, and why cannot I be?"

"Ay, you were not; you fancied you wished to know your father."

"I did."

"And now the knowledge displeases you, and you repent."

"I have been taught to love virtue and abhor vice—to do good and to shun evil."

"Your father turns out to be one, you see, whom circumstances have made a criminal."

"Yes; a theft makes a thief."

"But yet your birth is not above my present condition, bad as that may be; and it is worse than you may believe; but yet I am your father."

"Have you not forfeited the character by abandoning me at an age which required the fostering care of a parent until now? I feel I am able to judge, think, and act for myself."

"You believe so, because you fancy you have made a mistake; strange motive—but you can have no other."

"I have many others; and perhaps the thought is, I was then happy; here I am surrounded by horrors, and no hope of their being ended."

"All things have an end, some day or other; do not despair of the end, then," said the mendicant, mockingly.

"But life has an end in this life, at least, and if our misfortunes only end with it."

"Then is life not worth having; that is my opinion; and yet people cling to it to the last."

"That is natural; but why should you drag me into such an abyss of misery, when you might have been a gainer by allowing me to remain where I was? Captain Morton would have given you money if you had made what you say appear true."

"Captain Morton would have hanged me, I dare say."

"Oh, no; not my father. I am sure he would not; that is why I doubt you; I cannot believe you."

"Girl, I am your father, and, though a criminal, I am a father, and have all the rights that a father usually possesses. It matters not what stands between me and society, nothing can stand between me and you."

"But why exert that power which can neither bring profit nor satisfaction?"

"You know not what you say; my motives are my own; they are urgent and satisfactory."

"They never can give you satisfaction: motives that produce such fruit are sure sources of remorse."

"I have heard of such things before, but they are dreams,—the dreams of those who scarce know what life is, or who may have been engaged in one crime, and tremble at their own shadow; not such as I—I have nothing to fear; the troubles of a conscience have long since been spared me."

Mabel clasped her hands, and looked on the mendicant with horror, and she said, half involuntarily and half unconsciously—

"Can such men be! Surely Heaven never let loose upon society such monsters of iniquity and crime, but as a scourge and a plague."

"If Heaven had no better alternative to punish one part of society than by flinging another part upon them, it would have but a clumsy machinery, since all would be punished. It is like creating one set of animals to eat down another, lest the last should get too numerous."

"Horror! what profanation—what impiety is this!"

"Ha! ha! ha! rail on; but do not say the provision is a wise or a humane one. You may shrink from me, your father, yet I am better born than you are."

"Monster!"

"You are the offspring of sin and crime from your very birth."

"Horrible! it is too horrible! I will not—I cannot believe you."

"Ha! ha! ha!" laughed the mendicant, in a strange discordant sound; "'tis strange how slow the mind is to receive any notion of its own lowness of origin, and how it clings to some indefinite hope of what it is not rather than what it is!"

"Be my birth what it may, my life will not be a reproach to me, and shall not. I will perish rather than have aught upon my conscience that shall bring sorrow or shame to me or those who have nurtured me."

"We shall see," said the mendicant; "circumstances govern all things; and I am too well convinced of that to have my opinion shaken, even by the obstinacy of a romantic girl."

The mendicant now turned to examine the door, to detect the means by which she had got out.

"Oh, oh!" he said, as he put the light against the door, "you have had a lever here; you have had a little help; had I known that you had one, I might have anticipated this, and provided against it; but I was not aware of it."

He now lifted the door into its place, and then left the room; but he returned in a few minutes with some nails and a hammer, saying,—

"I will, at all events, make this fast, and it will be difficult, without such an instrument, to make your way out."

"God will aid me."

"He must do it in a very particular manner, then," said the mendicant, with a short laugh; "for I shall take pains that no ordinary means shall avail."

"All this will one day recoil upon your own head; you will be the sufferer from your own iniquity."

"And if I do, I will meet my fate; but you will have the satisfaction of knowing you have helped on the road to destruction your own parent, who, whatever may be his crimes or misfortunes, is still your father, and has kept the secret of your infamous birth to himself, and will do so, unless he finds you have escaped him, and wilfully set his power at naught; then, indeed, he will make the secret known, and those whom you call friends will shrink from you as a thing cursed."

"God of mercy! what horrible secret can this be, that it should cling to the young and the innocent?"

"You shall not know while you are in my power—I would not so far horrify you; but once endanger my life, or escape, and then you shall feel the full power I have to blast your future happiness."

"God of Heaven, and can such horrible atrocity exist!"

"It does, and will be in existence as long as there's any contrariety of purpose in you."

Having secured the door, as he deemed, in a sufficient and careful manner, he replaced it, and tried it with is own strength, and finding it strong, he said—

"And now this is done, I think you'll find it more difficult to move than before, even with the same instrument, which is too dangerous a one even in your hands to be allowed to remain."

He took up the small flat bit of iron, and then, once more surveying his work, said—

"This time, at all events, I leave you safe; if I catch you in an effort to escape, I shall sacrifice your life to my just resentment, and then you may give up all hopes of ever seeing your former friends, as you call them."

He cast a scowling look upon her as he left the room, and then drew the door after him, and she heard, with a saddened heart, the sound of the locks and bolts, as he turned the one and shot the other.

Then the sound of the street-door came upon her soul with a chill, as the heavy bang reverberated through the empty house, and she was once more alone. She felt and knew she was alone—her heart told her so; and the knowledge of the existence of the dead body in the vaults made her loneliness more insupportable.

---

## CHAPTER LII.

THE STORMY NIGHT IN THE RUINED HOUSE.—THE MELANCHOLY OF MABEL, AND HER FEARS.—AN INCIDENT.

THE time hung heavily on the hands of Mabel. She thought and grieved incessantly—indeed, she had no other occupation, save that of recalling to her mind the past, and comparing it with the present, and for one in such a situation it had but a saddening effect.

She was led to contemplate her present prospects, which seemed to be more dreary and unhappy than could well have been anticipated of one of her age and previous habits. The thought often crossed her mind as to when her present imprisonment would terminate, and what could be the result of this confinement. Surely her life could not be this man's object—certainly not, unless he had something to gain by her death; for she could not but believe that he was capable of almost any act—indeed, he had confessed as much on more than one occasion, and he avowed being an outcast from society, and a fugitive from the laws of his country.

She lay on the miserable pallet which the mendicant had provided for her, and in the still hours of the night she would listen, and then the slightest noise, however distant, came with a surprising distinctness on her ear that was startling.

For some hours she had lain, not sleeping, but awake, and her mind was busy in picturing to herself the many scenes of beauty and pleasure she had been a participator in.

But how was the scene changed! It seemed a dream—friends and companions were all gone. The dear scenes of her youthful pleasure—where were they? Gone—vanished, and become mere matters for the imagination to speculate upon.

Then the picture would change, and she fancied she could see the Hall and its inmates after her forced departure—their sorrow and despair—their consternation—all tended to awaken in her breast those feelings of uneasiness and regret she lay there a prey to.

Neither could she forget her present position, the solitary confinement she suffered, and the wretched mode of existence she was now compelled to endure.

She was laying thus occupied, in utter darkness, and hours had elapsed since she had seen the last rays of the setting sun—those few rays which came in at the top of the window—when she thought she heard some one pass along the street, and stand near the door.

She paused for some moments in silent attention, listening to ascertain whether any sound took place that indicated a return of the mendicant.

It was strange how distinct the footfall of any passenger fell upon her ear. They were few and far between, and she was situated but ill for listening to such sounds; indeed, she scarcely heard such sounds before—at least, she had not noticed them, but now they came with a strange distinctness almost startling.

The day had been an inclement one, and the night was worse; the rain and sleet had been pattering down for many hours. Mabel could hear the tread of the pattens as the women passed the house, and then the hollow roaring of the wind in the chimneys claimed her attention.

The wind howled and roared round the house, into which it had obtained a ready access by a hundred different fissures and other places. The house was old, and, it might be said, ruined and dismantled, and the wind whistled through the rooms and along the passage ; and now and then a door would bang to with great force, causing a sound that reverberated through the ruinous place.

" This is very dreadful," thought Mabel. " I am not naturally timid or superstitious, but here I am, away from all friends, without, as I know, a soul near me, save those who may mean me harm. I would I were again with my kind and generous benefactor at Morton Hall."

The wind whistled again through the house, and the rain came in fitful gusts against the windows and shutters; the wind, too, came in fearfully to her apartment, and swept across the floor to the empty fire-grate.

It was cold and chilly. Mabel threw herself, dressed as she was, on the bed, and wrapped herself in the clothes which were there, and they were scanty enough ; but she was there somewhat more out of the draught. and she was thus much warmer than she would have been otherwise ; besides, it was pitchy dark ; there was not even a gleam of light from a neighbouring window ; there was no reflected light to give her, accustomed as were her eyes to the intense darkness with which she was surrounded, the slightest notion of her locality in the room, save what she knew came from remembrance and experience.

The sounds came peculiarly dull and dismal, and well calculated to overpower a strong mind with terror, and poor Mabel, with all the accumulated horrors and dangers of her position, felt herself each moment become more and more a prey to the feeling of dread and despair that was creeping over her despite all the efforts she made to arouse her mind from the torpor of terror—to become alive only the more acutely to the miserable condition she felt herself in.

" I am safe here ; be where I may, Heaven will not desert the innocent. I will no longer doubt its mercy and its power, but resign myself to His direction, come what may, believing that whatever may be my fate, it is inevitable."

Notwithstanding this resignation, she could not shake off the feeling of undefined terror which was, despite all these precautions, creeping over her.

How many were there who had suffered the most horrible and cruel deaths merely because they had given some bandit or robber his due, or not submitted entirely to his will ; and who could say that the man by whom she was captured and detained in this place was not capable of destroying her life, merely from caprice, or some feeling of revenge, arising from disappointment in his schemes connected with herself ; his assertion that he was her father was no bar to that, for it might not be true.

These thoughts were no pleasing companions to such a one as Mabel, situated as she was ; indeed, they were in unison too strongly with the melancholy and dismal sounds that were heard from without and within.

What could all this tend to? what had become of the passenger whose footsteps she had last heard? Had he gone on unheard by her—listening as she had been to sounds of the least import? No; she had listened too attentively—he could not have gone on ; that was unlikely and improbable, unless, indeed, he had stepped into the road, and yet that was scarcely probable on such a night.

Hark ! what sounds are those?—they are human feet ascending the door-steps. She could distinctly hear them, and count them, and then all was still again.

What could this mean? she asked herself. It was not the mendicant—of that she was certain.

It might be some one who was desirous of escaping the sudden pelting of the pitiless storm, which raged without with redoubled fury.

" Ah !" thought Mabel, " there are those who think their case worse than mine, and who cannot imagine a greater evil than one created by exposure to the inclemencies of such a night as this."

Ah ! there they have remained long enough to be impatient, and fear that the storm will not give way that night; indeed, it promised to last many hours.

The footsteps are heard descending, and leave the doorway; but, hark! what sound is that? What is the meaning of that whistle?

There seemed to come on the night air a clear but low whistle, which was three times repeated.

Then again all was still—no sounds met her ears, save such as the storm occasioned. They were palpable enough, and were frequent; but yet they were accountable, but not so the whistle. What could it mean? No good. Some godless scheme of villany was afloat; but what was it?

Alas! poor Mabel could but sit there and fear the worst, and imagine all sorts of things; but at the same time she knew of none—of nothing; and hence her fears were awakened by all the vague conceptions of her mind about something terrible.

Again the low whistle was sounded, and then another was heard in the distance, and then an approach of some other persons towards the spot.

This might be the mendicant, she thought; but why he, who had been so cautious as to conceal his abode from every one, and, even, to prevent his being followed, had adopted several devices—why he should act thus she could not tell; but then, she could not understand his motives, and, therefore, could not judge what might be his acts.

She listened again, and thought, as she lay there, she could distinguish more than two, if not more than three, persons at the door.

There was a shuffling of feet for several seconds, and some bungling attempts at the keyhole.

She sat up in the bed, much terrified at the thought that several men were about to be brought into the house at such an hour, and probably they were in liquor, for the key was more than once tried, and yet they could not open the door.

These were moments of great uneasiness to her, and she sat up listening with almost painful acuteness. The door was again tried unsuccessfully; but then, again, it yielded to repeated attempts, and opened on its hinges, for Mabel was sure of this from the rush of cold air that entered at that moment.

## CHAPTER LIII.

THE MIDNIGHT INTRUDERS INTO THE RUINED HOUSE.—MABEL'S TERRORS AND DANGER.—CONFIDENTIAL CONVERSATION.

THERE was some indistinct kind of noise that Mabel could not make out, and much shuffling and shifting of feet in the passage; the door was then carefully closed after them, and then a whispered conversation was held in the passage.

"I tell you," said one, "the house has been empty for some years; and I am frequently in the neighbourhood, and not a light nor a soul have I ever seen in it."

"It doesn't follow but that there might be, for all that," said another voice; "and it's my opinion we can't be too careful in this matter; you know how Ned Williams was taken in the other day,"

"No, I don't; and don't care, that's more. I know that you are an infernally timid cove, and would start at your own shadow if you saw it."

"That's by no means unlikely. I have known some good men do that before to-day; and, if I hadn't, I couldn't help it, when I don't know what it is."

"Well, then, don't look at it until somebody comes and tells you what it is; that I think, is the best for you; but come on."

"You are a very nice man to say come on. Why don't you help me on with the cove?"

There was a whispered consultation among those who were now in the passage, and they seemed to move with great caution and care.

"Where shall we go, Bill?" inquired one of the men.

"What do you mean? Didn't I tell you I knew of a crib where the job could be done, and where we needn't be seen again if we wasn't fools, and here we are—what do you want more?"

"I mean, what part of the house shall we go—up stairs or down stairs, or in my lady's chamber, as the nursery rhyme has it, eh?"

"D—n you and your nursery tales too. Can't you keep your foolery to yourself, and not give it out?"

"Well, then, let's go in the kitchen, or somewhere down stairs."

"We can't go in the kitchen; it isn't a safe place; besides, it's all open to the area, and that communicates to the street, and that won't do."

"Very good; but they have cellars about where it would be better to go to; there we should be much safer; and if a scream should make its way, it won't rattle in and out the old empty rooms enough to frighten a score of men."

"I tell you we can't go down stairs, and that's flat."

"And why not, Bill?"

"Because I tells you so."

"That's no reason, you know; and none at all for me," said the other, in a somewhat positive tone.

"Well, then, I tell you I have two reasons that will prevent my going down at all, and one which will pervent you, if not two."

"And what are they? Come, Bill, what are they?"

"In the first place, the stairs are all rotten and have given way; if not entirely, quite enough so as to make it almost an impossibility to get back again when once you are down, so you are caught in a trap."

"That's very good. Now for the other eason, Bill. I hope it's a good one."

"It will serve me, and that's enough, for you know when I say I won't, why, I won't, and there's an end on't."

"But why won't you?"

"Because there is something below I'd rather not look upon," said the ruffian, in a short, surly tone; "and now you know as much as it is safe for you to know, or for me to say."

"Ah, Bill! you ain't confidential."

"And ain't agoing to be, so don't trouble your head about other people's affairs, or I shall think you mean something."

"I tell you what it is, Bill; if you had said you had private reasons for not going below, or that there was a secret of your own down below, I shouldn't have been so particular in my inquiries; but there, it's no use of trying to make a silk purse out of a sow's auricular organ, so I won't teach you gentility."

"And you needn't; but come on, we had better go into the back parlour, that's the best for our purpose."

They seemed to be dragging something or somebody along the floor; Mabel could not distinguish which it was; indeed, she was fearfully agitated; she could not tell what to imagine. These men, be they whom they might, were, doubtless, murderers; and if they should find her, they would, no doubt, sacrifice her to their sense of safety, for while she lived, she knew enough to make her very dangerous to them. What, therefore, was there to prevent them from taking her life, when their own lives were at stake, or when they believed so, and that was the same thing to them?

She sat up in her bed, and the feelings

of horror and despair came over her heart with a strength it is difficult to depict. Her eyes were fixed towards the door, for it was too dark even to see its shadow.

"It's d—d heavy," said one.

"Yes," replied the other; "and we mustn't complain of that."

"No, no; his purse was heavy, too; and that's some consolation, though I'm sure I'm very dry and very tired."

"So am I."

"Then let's put him in this room."

"What, the front parlour?"

"Yes."

"'Tis so exposed to the street, that the slightest sound might bring a host of people about us."

"The time of night would render that impossible," replied his companion; "but he has been so well hocussed, that there is no fear of that; indeed, you'll find him no more than a child without a tongue."

"So much the better."

"Besides, I noticed these shutters were all made fast, so we cannot be intruded upon. I wish to sit down a few minutes and taste a drop of brandy before proceeding to work, for I always like to do these things creditably, and not in the hurried and bungling manner that I have known people do them."

They pushed the parlour door open, and dragged somebody in; she could hear the scrapping of the feet of some body that was being partially dragged and partially lifted along the ground, until it was laid on the floor, and then there was a pause, during which she could hear the men breathe, as if they had deposited a heavy burden upon the floor, and they were recovering themselves from the fatigue.

"Well," said one of them, "there ain't much accommodation here—no inducement to stay long."

"No."

"And that's not the proper sort of thing; but as I am wet, cold, tired, and thirsty, I will sit down on the floor for a short time."

"And can you sit down at such a moment?"

"And why not—haven't I got some brandy in my flask? Come and sit down; we may as well enjoy the moments as they fly; I mean to be, you must know, very jolly during to-night."

"You seem strangely full of spirits; you want caution."

"Not a bit of it; come and sit down, and I'll take care to make my company agreeable."

"I can only tell where you are by sound," said the other.

"We will throw a light on the subject, if you please; here's my darkey, it will illuminate us all."

"All?"

"Yes."

"You and I?"

"Yes; and the gemman in the sleepy fit that lies here."

With a convulsive shudder and great mental effort, Mabel restrained herself from uttering a loud shriek, but a suppressed sound, as that of a groan, escaped her.

"What's that?" exclaimed he who was the last to sit down.

"What's what, you fool?" exclaimed his companion; "you are always up to some of these tricks; you're afraid of the least sound; why, d—e, you would fly if you heard the footstep of a man."

"And good reason, too. I thought I heard a groan, or some such thing."

"Very likely you heard a groan; it was the wind wheezing and puffing through the old, deserted house; I am only surprised that we haven't heard more, and doors banging."

"D—n you, I wish you'd hold your tongue; there they go."

At that moment several of the room doors up stairs were driven to by a sudden squall of wind, with a loud noise that reverberated through the empty and desolate house.

"Ha! ha! ha! what a stew you are in; surely one would almost believe you had a conscience, and that you were troubled with it."

"Are you going to play the fool till daylight, until the man gets over the dose we have given him?"

"Come, don't be in a hurry; here is a toss of brandy,—tell me what you think of that. No, no, not so fast, wait a moment—a toast—yes, we must have a toast."

"Oh, never mind that."

"But I do. Come—Prosperity to trade, short jobs, and well paid."

"Ah, d—n!"

"Don't be ungenteel."

Mabel, though shaking in every limb as though an ague had suddenly seized her, by a kind of instinct arose and crept towards a chink in the door that led to the next room.

She discovered the chink in consequence of the light shining through it from their lantern.

There she saw two men dress'd in large white coats, or what had been white at one time, patched over in places. They were seated on the floor; they were big, burly men, with most villanous countenances.

They held the one a drinking cup, and

the other a dram-bottle. On the ground beside them there was a dark lantern with the shade taken off, and it threw a light upon them both, throwing them out into a kind of almost supernatural relief.

It gave them a strange unearthly appearance; the profiles of their countenances were very distinct, and they looked at each other with a combined expression of cunning and villany of a most brutal character.

---

## CHAPTER LIV.

THE MIDNIGHT MURDER.—THE SUDDEN APPARITION, AND ITS EFFECTS.—THE MENDICANT AND THE STRANGE ALARM.

MABEL sickened at the sight of these two men; their countenances bespoke a degree of depravity that can scarcely be credited by any human being. Murderers seemed written upon every lineament; but yet they were apparently unconscious of their own marked character, for they sat with an apparent calmness beside each other.

On the floor beneath them lay the body of a man; he was well dressed and tolerably young, as might be presumed by his hair and dress.

He was living and breathing, but it was heavy and laboured, as though some drug had been given him, or he had been drinking to excess. The unfortunate man was tossed down almost as though he had been a lump of lumber, and there allowed to remain, which proved the strength of the drug that had been given him; and of this these two men must have been well aware.

They were drinking and conversing in low tones to each other by turns, as though something serious now engaged their attention, and they conversed mutually and seriously.

"Well, Jack," sad one; "now, I tell you what it is—my opinion is this."

"Well, what is it?"

"Why, that we might have a chance of being followed."

"But, have we?"

"I don't know, but the chance is everything. Let's do what we have to do now, and at once; we have a distance to travel before we are in a place of safety, and there is a greater chance of being seen the later we go away from here."

"Well, I am ready; though, if you listen to the storm you will soon see that we have little to fear, for the rain is falling fast, and the wind howls tremendously—there'll be nobody about to-night, that s

certain, and more certain that they will not loiter about until this hour."

"I dare say you are right enough; but, you know, Jack, if I am caught, I'm safe for a hempen cravat. I have long escaped, but it is only in consequence of my being so precious cautious."

"Well, business is business; and now I'm ready; this gemman seems to take it quietly enough."

"Yes, he will be more so before long; how shall we do it?"

"That's a question; I don't like cutting his throat, it makes such a bloody mess, and then there are traces, and so forth, which may one day see the light."

"Yes, yes; I think so too. What do you say to a little strangulation—mere choking, you know?"

"It will be better, safer, and quieter; and should he wake up, it will be with no cries,—he will be quieted; and when he does open his eyes, which he will for a moment, they will be quickly closed again."

"Very well, so be it. Where's the rope, and where's the beam?"

"Yonder is a nail that will hold a halter, and a man at the end of it, if ever it would anything."

As he spoke he pointed to a nail over the door, through a chink of which poor Mabel was viewing them, and listening in an agony of fear and apprehension. She could not move nor speak; her whole frame seemed spell-bound; she stood like a statue, immovable, and in one position.

She had remained here ever since they had come, and she had, moreover, heard all they said; she knew they were about to committ murder, and yet she could not raise a single cry of alarm to save the wretched man from his fate.

That the mendicant was not with them she was fully aware, and who these men were, she, of course, could not guess; they were some midnight marauders and murderers, she had no doubt, but they were quite ignorant of her presence. Indeed, they were perfectly assured, in their own minds, that the house was altogether empty of even an occasional inhabitant.

The two men looked at the insensible man, and turned him over and over several times, but nothing more than an occasional deep breath or slight groan escaped from his lips.

"Bill, we should have had a tough job to have had any struggle with this cove, he had some strength."

"Yes, and where could we have left the body? somewhere where we should have had a discovery in ten minutes, and we should have been hunted about in style."

"So we should—so we should," said the other; "and now we must manufacture a halter out of his handkerchiefs."

So saying, he took two from the person of the insensible man, and began to tie them together in a peculiar manner.

"You seem quite clever at it," remarked the other.

"We don't know what may be useful some day or other; but come, just help us, and try to adjust this round his neck in a nice slip knot."

"With all my heart; and now you have it all right, I'll go and try the strength of the nail."

"Do so, and be quick; he seems to be restless; he may wake for a time."

Thus urged, the ruffian arose and walked to the door, and pulled at the nail, and lifted himself up by it.

"Yes," he said; "this is strong enough to hold an ox. Where does this door lead to? The back parlour, I suppose. Ah, it's fast, I see; it hasn't been opened for years, I dare say."

"No; and now I think this noose will do very well; it will run pretty tight, and come just under the ear."

"That is the very thing that will ease him of all his woes; but did you ever hang anybody before?"

"What's that to you? I don't open my mouth so wide as some people; and, if you ask any more questions, I shall be apt to think you are upon the look out for something to split about. Come, come, no more of your prying, because I can't stand it; if I find you up to any tricks, I'll make my knife and your ribs acquainted."

"And I can play at that game as well as you can, if you think it worth your while to quarrel about it; but I had no such intention, and ain't in a condition to peach against any man. I mererly asked you the question, if——"

"I won't answer any such questions, and you had better ask none."

"Ah! very well—perhaps you've a conscience, and have a comfortable time of it, when you are alone; but all is one to me, you can't hang me without yourself, so I don't care for you or your knife; or, if you like, I'll leave you this job to do by yourself. I'll walk out, than I sha'n't see you."

"Come, come; none of this. I've made a bargain, and will abide by it. If you see cause to withdraw and break your word, I can't help it."

"I don't."

"Then why talk about making your knife acquainted with my ribs? Curse me, if I can understand that! I've a notion it ain't over and above civil."

"Well, well; don't ask questions. Let bygones be bygones; and now give us a help up with this cove."

The two men now got the insensible man up in a sitting posture, and began to feel carefully over his person, and turned every one of his pockets out, one after the other, in a very expeditious manner, which showed they were very old adepts at that sort of thing.

When this was done, and the few trinkets that were found disposed of, one of the murderers said,—

"There's not much to be found this time, at all events. The first go was the best. Lift him up, and help me to bring him beneath the nail."

They each took him beneath the arms, and dragged him to the spot indicated, and poor Mabel was horrified to find that they were about to commit the atrocious deed within a few inches of where she stood.

However, she was so entranced, that, had her life depended upon it, she could not move or close her eyes to the awful scene that was about to be enacted; neither could she utter one single shriek to save the unfortunate man's life, so bound up were her faculties.

Mabel could see and hear, but she could not move, she could not speak, and her very breath came and went with a suppressed sound; the current of her blood seemed frozen within her, and she stood glaring on the awful spectacle that was now going on so close to her.

"Come, lift him up higher," said one of the men, as he tried to fix the running knot he had made at the other end of the handkerchief, to catch fast hold of the nail.

"I can't."

"It must be done somehow or other. See, he begins to move. Now should he once fairly open his eyes, he may, very probably, be so much frightened, that he will be thoroughly aroused to a state of his danger, and then ware-hawk."

"What can I do?"

"Either you or I must lift him up on our shoulders, while the other puts the noose over the nail."

"And should it break?"

"We must choke or stab him, as may be best at the moment."

"Then I'll kneel down, and do you put him on my shoulders, and help me to rise again, and then put the loop on the nail safely."

"That will be the best plan," said his companion, who placed their victim astride across his shoulder, and then, with some great exertion, the one who knelt, by the aid of his companion, was enabled to rise with his heavy burden, and then his companion, taking the end of the handkerchief, made a fresh loop, as the old one left the handkerchief too long, and the feet of the unfortunate man would just touch the ground.

"All right," said the man, when he had fixed the handkerchief on the nail securely.

"When shall I let him go?"

"Now; but gently."

Gradually the man withdrew the support he gave to the body, and the sufferer began to kick and plunge, making a suppressed sound in his throat.

"Hold his legs and arms."

They did so; but the nail gave way, and the half-strangled man came to the earth with a dreadful fall.

Then commenced a dreadful struggle. It was now life and death for all. During the struggle the door flew open from the violence of their attempts; but, fortunately, it escaped Mabel, who still stood terrified and incapable of motion, gazing on the horrid and deadly fray.

"Take out your knife, while I hold on by the handkerchief," said one, as he grasped it, and tightened it round the man's throat.

The other made no reply, but took from his pocket a Spanish clasp knife, which he opened with his teeth, and then dashed it, with a heavy blow, into the prostrate man's breast, as he lifted his arms to free himself from the strangulation that he was suffering.

A sudden convulsion passed through the body, and the man was a corpse. He straightened himself on the floor, and the life-blood welled out of the gaping wound which the broad and long-bladed Spanish knife had caused.

"That was a d—d good blow, anyhow. Quite in the right place, and at the right moment."

"Yes," replied the man, coolly wiping his knife on the dead man's leg. "I thought it had been carried on too far, and in another minute or two he would have got his jaw loose, and then the neighbours would be called in. Eh!—"

"What's the matter? Why, d——e, you are as white as a sheet. Have you seen a ghost, or——"

The speaker had followed the direction of the gaze of his companion, whose eyes were nearly starting from their sockets, and his under jaw fell; and on looking round he discovered the object of his companion's terror, which was now also his own. What that was we will now explain.

Mabel, who was unable to move or to speak, had stood staring, with a gaze she could not withdraw, at the deed that had been done, and the bloody spectacle before her.

When she first got off the bed, to peep through the chink in the door, she had wrapped a coarse white quilt around her in the dark, as it was very cold at that time of night—and such a night as it was. Her appearance at the door was, therefore, to say the least of it, in keeping well with the supernatural.

The men, through their falls and struggles with their victim, had forced the door open, yet did not seem to be aware that it really was open, and the first intimation they had of it, was by something unusually white attracting the attention of one, in the way we have described.

Such men are usually superstitious, and when they saw a figure all in white, with a countenance ghastly pale, standing in the attitude of bending forward, with what appeared to them to be supernaturally lustrous eyes, they were paralyzed, and for several minutes could not withdraw their gaze from her's.

Suddenly one jumped up; the spell that bound the other was broken, and they both dashed out of the room, along the passage, and were speedily in the street, and coursing along the town as if a whole legion of devils were after them.

However, Mabel was unable to withdraw that painful gaze which was fixed on an object so terrifying as that which lay before her.

The first thing of which she was sensible, was a strong light before her. She heard some one speak; but who it was, or what was said, she knew not; but then the spell was broken. She looked up and saw the mendicant standing by her in an inquiring attitude, looking alternately at her and the dead body that lay surrounded by a pool of blood.

"What means this?" he said, pointing to the body.

"Murder! murder!" exclaimed Mabel, in almost shrieking accents.

"Hush! hush! not so loud. Who has done this?"

"Murder!—oh, God! oh, God!—murder!"

"I see that; but you needn't trouble yourself about it so much. Who has been here to do it, and how came they here it at all? and how came the door opened, and you safe?"

Mabel made no reply; her eyes were withdrawn from the horrifying spectacle where they had been so long fixed; she was in no hurry to encounter it again, and she hid her face in her hands to shut out the very sight of that which had cause her more misery and anguish of heart than she had ever yet felt.

The mendicant now stooped to examine the body, and was about to speak, when a loud and rapid knocking commenced at the street-door, that reverberated fearfully through the house, and caused him to start to his feet.

---

## CHAPTER LV.

AN EXPLANATION OF SOME OF THE MYS-
TERIES.—THE NARRATION OF THE
OLD GENTLEMAN.

YOUNG MORTON, as may well be sup-posed, from the interest he had already seemed to take in the elderly gentleman, to whom he had by good fortune been enabled to be of so much service, did not forget the engagement he had made with him to pay him a visit, and hear from him some promised particulars of the cause of his apparent dejection, as well as his pre-sence in London.

That there was some sort of mystery connected with him appeared past a doubt; indeed he had himself quite admitted as much; and although far—very far—from being ordinarily disposed to interfere in the affairs of other people, Henry could not disguise from himself that he felt an amount of curiosity, as new as it was irresistible, to know something more of the stranger, whose appearance so greatly in-terested him in his favour.

Notwithstanding the stirring events which had taken place in the pursuit of the men-dicant, the time hung heavily on the hands of Henry until, with propriety, he could seek the elderly stranger, and put him in mind of his promise.

When the hour of appointment drew near, he became extremely impatient, so much so, indeed, as to attract the attention of Rafferty Brolickbones, who inquired in his way what was " after ailing him."

" Nothing particular, Rafferty," said Henry; " but I am very curious to hear what the old gentleman, that we were of service to in the street, has to say to me."

" Oh, is that all?" said Rafferty.

" Yes, that is all."

" Bedad, then, perhaps he wants to borrow a guinea or two."

" No, Rafferty. I am quite convinced that that is not his motive. He is not the sort of person."

" Well, sir, then do you really think he is a Frenchman?"

" It seems so; and I cannot have any great doubts upon that subject. What motive could he have for passing himself off as a Frenchman if he were really a native of any other nation?"

" Why, no, sir, as you say, it's hard to think that anybody in his senses would pre-tend to be a Frenchman, if he were not. But still, sir, you know it might be to excite compassion."

" I suppose, then, Rafferty," said Henry, with a smile, " you think the mere fact of a man being a Frenchman, to a com-passionate mind, is a misfortune of sufficient magnitude to excite sympathy ?"

" Faith, sir, I rather do think that same."

" I thought as much."

" You know, sir, we ain't brute bastes; so we know that when a man is a French-man it's no fault of his. He couldn't help it, of course, sir, or else he wouldn't be a Frenchman."

" And hence you think the gentleman whom we were of service to may be shamming the Frenchman, in order to excite in us an amount of sympathy which we otherwise might not feel ?"

" Well, sir, I don't say so; but it may be, you know, for all that. Howsomdever, you can find out, and I'll tell you how, sir."

" How ?"

" Why, sir, I knew a young woman, sir, as went with a family to France, and they lived at a place called Crootoo."

" Crootoo ?"

" Yes, sir. Now, if you want to find out whether this old fellow is a Frenchman or not, you say to him, ' Do you know Crootoo ?' says you, and if he looks flabbergasted, you may depend he is only shamming being a Frenchy."

" How can you be so absurd, Rafferty Brolickbones? Why, it does not by any means follow that because the man is a Frenchman he is to know every little petty hamlet in France."

" And why not, sir ?"

" There is no reason why not; but there is abundant reason to suppose that he does not."

" Have it your own way; don't say I thwarted you."

This was generally how Rafferty Brolick-bones ended an argument, and a very choice way it was, too, for it saved him any further trouble, besides having about it a very magnanimous look.

Henry now started on his visit; and by walking rapidly he soon reached the temporary abode of the French gentleman, whom he had the pleasure to find had by no means forgotten the appointment, but was duly expecting him, with an impatience that looked almost like a reflex of his own, which had excited so much the surprise and attention of Rafferty.

It would answer no good purpose whatever for us to trouble the reader with the errors of pronunciation incidental to a foreigner with but an imperfect knowledge of our language; therefore, in the conversation which ensued between Henry and the stranger, we shall assume that the one was as well able to express himself as the other; because, where the French gentleman was at fault, Henry was well able to assist him by his knowledge of both languages.

"Sir," said the gentleman, when they were both fairly seated, "I know not how it is, but the fact cannot be disputed, that I feel a strong inclination to unfold to you, above all men, the innermost secrets of my soul."

"Sir," replied Henry, "without asking for your confidence, or officiously attempting to intrude into your private affairs, I can only say I shall listen with the greatest attention to whatever you may choose to communicate to me, and keep your confidence inviolate."

"I am sure of that, sir. And now so strongly do I feel impelled to tell you the whole of a somewhat painful family history, that I should feel the most grievous disappointment if you did not listen to me."

Henry made a suitable reply; and, after a short pause, the old French gentleman said, in a voice of emotion, which showed that some of the recollections that came now thronging across his mind were of a painful nature,—

"My name is Rouselli, and I belong to, or rather am now, the head of an ancient French family, nearly allied to the noblesse. You are well aware of the strife, both external and internal, and the changes and mutations which my unhappy counrty has undergone for many years past, and therefore you will not consider it possible that a family of any importance in the social fabric of the country should escape some of the evils of so disorganised a state of things."

The old man paused a moment or two, as if what he had next to say was of a painful nature, and not to be said hurriedly or lightly.

"I had a son."

Henry was silent. He saw the tear gather in the father's eye, and he knew from the expression which had been used that that son was no more. He felt as if any of the common-place exhortations to fortitude wou d have been an impertinence, and, therefore, he was silent.

"I thank you," sa d the old man, after a pause, "for that silence. An ordinary mind would have condoled with me as if any words that could come from the lips of any human being could reconcile the heart of a father to the loss of his child."

"I can understand and appreciate your feelings, sir," said Henry; "but I pray you to avoid topics which may press too painfully upon your feelings at such a time as this."

"I will, my young friend; I will, as far as possible."

He then continued as follows:—

"I have said I had a son, and, by my use of that expression, you know that now I have him not. He has passed from me, and I am childless in my old age. He died the death of a soldier."

"Did he fall then in any of the memorable battles of the long war?"

"He fell at the battle of Mont St. Jean."

"Which we call Waterloo?"

"Yes—yes."

"A soldier's death is a glorious one, and I am convinced it is far easier than to linger on a bed of sickness, exposed to the ravages of some terrific disease, which slowly but surely saps the foundation of existence."

"You may be right—I think you are. My son was a colonel of cavalry in the army of the emperor. He had followed his imperial master's fortunes on many a well-fought field, and, perhaps happily for him, he laid down his life at last for him before those misfortunes from which Napoleon never again emerged. Some years before Waterloo, as you name it, was fought and won, the imperial army overran the greater part of Germany and Prussia."

"True—true."

"My son's regiment, for a considerable time, found quarters at Berlin, and as a severe winter had set in, the operations of the war were, to a certain extent, in that quarter, at least, suspended.

"It was at one of the entertainments got up by some of the French party in Berlin, that my son first beheld Marie Mendelson, a beautiful and accomplished girl, then but eighteen years of age, and the daughter of respectable parents in Berlin. To see her, as he wrote to me, was to love her, and that love, according as opportunity occurred, soon grew into an unconquerable passion.

"But there were circumstances which placed, to all appearance, an insurmountable difficulty in the way of Marie Mendelson ever becoming his. She was engaged to be married to a man named Sternhold, a Prussian, who was highly approved of by her family, but, as it appeared, not at all loved or chosen by Marie herself.

"This was a painful state of things, and not likely to pass off quietly. Sternhold, the intended husband of Marie Mendelson, was a man of the most violent passions, and he soon discovered that my son looked with the eyes of affection upon Marie, as well as making the more mortifying discovery that she was not indifferent to the attractions of the handsome young officer, who, in manners and appearance, presented so striking a contrast to Sternhold, whom she was about to be sacrificed to, for nothing but a sacrifice could it be called.

"Thus matters went on for some time, until, at a ball which was attended by all the French officers, and by the principal inhabitants of Berlin, who had submitted to the new dominion, these rivals met.

"It became then a struggle between the two which should engross the hand of the beautiful Marie during the dances. She decided in favour of my son, and Sternhold left the ball-room, furious.

"That night an attempt was made to assassinate my son as he was returning to his quarters; Sternhold could not be proved to be the party, but he was more than suspected.

"The family of Marie now took up the business, and insisted upon her at once fulfilling her matrimonial engagement with Sternhold. They were deaf to her entreaties—they were blind to her tears, and she was dragged to the altar an unwilling bride on the same day that orders arrived for a grand movement of the French army of occupation from Prussia to meet the emperor, and concentrate a large force further south.

"Despair took possession of the lovers. They had a stolen interview by the aid and assistance of a faithful old domestic of the Mendelson family, whose heart bled to witness the distress of Marie, and there it was arranged that she should allow the ceremony of marriage to proceed so far as to lull suspicion, and leave her home before the bridal party reached the cathedral where the more solemn rites were to be performed.

"By some unfortunate circumstances, however, it appeared that Marie was compelled to fail in keeping her engagement, and, unable to elude the vigilance of her friends, she was compelled, actually, to allow the marriage to proceed; so that as far as the ritual of the church could make her, she became the wife of Sternhold.

"She had made up her mind, however, that death was preferable to becoming really his; and when the shades of evening wrapped the city in obscurity, and preparations were proceeding at her father's house, for the purpose of celebrating the wedding with magnificence and *eclat*, she watched her opportunity, and being now unsuspected, in consequence of the ceremony of marriage having actually taken place, she left her father's house and fled to my son.

"In another half hour his regiment must have left Berlin, indeed, he might be almost said to have been mounted and ready, although despair and agony were at his heart.

"It is needless to say with what rapturous feelings he received the confiding girl, who had now given to him so convincing a proof of her affection. He made some hasty arrangements for her comfort, and before she was well missed from her father's house, she was *en route* from Berlin, in the acknowledged character of my son's wife, for such he declared her to be.

"Alas—alas! what a world of misery followed close upon that step, which had been prompted by unreflecting affection. Bear with me awhile, sir, my heart bleeds at the remembrance of the past."

---

## CHAPTER LVI.

THE NARRATIVE CONTINUED.—WATER-LOO.—THE CHILD AND THE BATTLE FIELD.

THE old man seemed to pause at this point in his narrative, as if it were the last one upon which he could dwell with pleasure. There was certainly something romantic and ennobling in that love which could induce a girl, so tenderly nurtured, to forsake her home, her friends, and all those associations which render life dear, for the purpose of throwing herself completely and entirely upon the protection of a stranger.

It was a piece of trusting confidence, such as a young heart, in all the freshness of its feelings, could alone have bestowed upon any one.

"I can feel with you, sir," said Henry Morton; "I can feel with you at this point of your narrative, and comprehend the feelings with which you linger over it."

"I do, indeed, linger over it," said the old man, regretfully.

"I can fancy the love and tenderness you would have lavished upon such a daughter."

"Yes—yes," said the old man, with enthusiasm; "in my eyes, had she not been beautiful, as I believed she was, the preference she gave to my son, Adolphe, and the noble confidence she showed in his honour, would have been sufficient to invest her with a thousand charms; but I must not keep you from the sequel of a narration which I have never yet commenced to any human being out of the immediate circle of my own family but yourself."

"I pray you, sir," said Henry, "not to let any fanciful impatience of mine hurry you forward to events, the description of which will give you pain. I own that I am deeply interested in your narrative, perhaps more so than you imagine—the name of your son and yourself, you say, is Rouselli?"

"Yes, that is our family name—a name which my poor Adolphe would have been

glad to bestow, with every dignity, and with every honour that could appertain to it, upon Marie Mendelson."

"I doubt it not, sir. Pray proceed."

"You will perceive, then, my young friend, that, unfortunately, in consequence of that lapse of time which had enabled the marriage ceremony to be performed between Marie and Sternhold, he had a sort of claim upon her, which he was just the man to urge to its very utmost."

"I understand the church had done its part in effecting this union."

"It had; and yet, with all this apparent bar

to her being my son's wife, she so trustingly, you will perceive, flew to his arms.

Notwithstanding that the ceremony of marriage had been performed between her and Sternhold, my son would not be satisfied until he had induced a Catholic priest, who had devoted himself to the army in order that he might pronounce the benediction for the dead over those who might come in his way mortally wounded by the chances of war, to wed them with such rites and ceremonies as the cir-

cumstances in which they were placed rendered possible.

Thus was Marie Mendelson twice married within the short space of almost a few hours; but there can be no doubt she looked upon the first vows as nothing better than a solemn mockery, for she had been dragged to the altar's foot by her friends, there to pledge her faith to a man whom she could neither respect nor love.

It was hard for such a creature, nursed in the lap of luxury, as she had been, to endure the terrors, the privations, and the hardships of a campaign; but with a noble fortitude that surprised all who saw her, and elicited the admiration of the oldest veterans, she bore up against every fatigue and every disaster of a campaign peculiarly fatiguing and disastrous. The emperor was in the decay of his fortunes; disaster followed disaster—treachery, open and undisguised, exhibited itself on all hands; so that a brilliant army was reduced about the year 1814 to a fearful wreck.

It was then that in a miserable cottage

somewhere in Flanders, the beauty, Marie Mendelson, presented her husband with a child.

It was born amid the clash of arms, and the din and horror of war; and his anxiety for fear he should be obliged to leave her, in consequence of his regiment being ordered forward, was so intense as nearly to render him helpless, through sickness brought on by excessive mental anguish. A thousand times he blamed himself for the unthinking affection which had led him to induce that beautiful girl to throw herself upon the precarious protection of a soldier; but when he would thus speak to her, and blame himself for being too selfish in his love, it was she who would chide the expression of such opinions, and who would tell him how much happier she was in his presence, enduring everything, than in the gilded saloons of her ancestors, and surrounded by every luxury the world could offer her.

Long before, under ordinary circumstances, she would have been declared fit to travel, the remnant of the army was ordered forward, in order to effect a junction with the new legions which the emperor had with immense perseverance recently raised.

Marie and her infant occupied a luggage waggon, which was confided to the care of parties whom Colonel Rouselli could depend upon; and thus for some months longer she followed in the fortunes of the army, and was in the immediate outskirts of many a brilliant engagement.

Her fears for the life of her husband, whenever his corps had any affairs with the enemy, were at first of the most agonizing and heartrending description; but as, time after time, he came back to her unhurt, she began to have a sort of confidence in his safety, and to think that Heaven, for the dear love he bore her, would turn aside the deadly bullet in its path, and hold him harmless.

She would tell him jestingly, she knew he had a charmed life—that he was preserved for her and her infant, until, at last, from his impunity in danger, he began to think that such was really the case.

But suddenly, one day, when my son was sitting in his tent along with his wife and child, a hand-grenade was throw into the midst of them, and a loud voice cried,—

" Vengeance for Sternhold !"

With the ready tact of a soldier inured to danger, he threw himself upon his face, and forced his wife to do so likewise, with the child in her arms, close to the death-dealing missile.

It exploded, but left them unharmed.

The camp was searched, but no one answering the description of Sternhold, the Prussian, was discovered. From that hour, however, assassination of sentinels and officers became frequent, and most of the bodies had a placard pinned to their breasts, on which were the words,—

" The vengeance of Sternhold against the nation of Rouselli !"

My son had several narrow escapes of his life—bullets grazed him repeatedly, and once or twice, in the dusk of the evening, he actually caught sight of a figure prowling about on his path.

These were circumstances of alarm which, although but half known to Marie—for he never told her of any danger abroad—had a visible effect upon her health and spirits; she never now parted with Adolphe with her former confidence, but always with a fear that she was looking her last upon him.

It was not engagements with the enemy she dreaded, but the vengeance of the villain Sternhold, who seemed, with a dreadful ferocity, to have devoted himself to the task of destroying Rouselli.

Thus affairs went on for some time, until, after an engagement, it was reported that a dark figure had paraded the field of battle, slaughtering the helpless and the wounded, and that he had been fired at repeatedly, but had hitherto escaped all efforts for his destruction.

A superstitious fear seized upon the soldiers; they called this appearance the Battle Fiend, and the whole of that division of the army became impregnated with a kind of dread concerning him which it was wonderful brave men could give way to.

But events were hurrying on, of a political character, which forced the emperor to make one grand effort for his own existence as a monarch. The battle of Waterloo was near at hand—that terrific conflict, which has exercised, and will continue to exercise, so great an effect upon the politics of Europe.

The division of the French army with which my son's regiment was incorporated was not foremost in the field. It was not till after two o'clock, on that memorable day, that he and his regiment were called into action.

It is well known, to all who made themselves acquainted with the details of that terrible engagement, that, towards the latter part of it, it was fought out by the artillery and cavalry. My son's regiment, therefore, being a mounted one, came in for a full share of the affray.

Marie was in the rear of the French lines; and, from time to time, Rouselli had managed to send her word that he was safe, by those parties who had the care of transporting the wounded to places of security.

At last, these small detachments got so much in the habit of seeking her out, and saying "Colonel Rouselli is safe," that when something of a contrary nature happened, without any direction from any one, the fact was abruptly communicated to her.

The battle was lost; that last grand, decisive charge had taken place, when all the scattered cavalry met in terrific collision. Light cavalry and heavy dragoons, cuirassiers and lancers, all were intermingled, without order or precedence. Thousands fell, and among them——"

The old man paused, and shook like an aspen leaf.

"Enough !" said Henry Morton; "I know what you would say."

"Yes, yes; you can guess."

"I can. Do not pain yourself by uttering words which should never pass your lips."

"He fell," said the old man, with much emotion, "as he always wished to fall, upon the battle-field, gloriously, his face to the foe. But, alas! what glory can compensate the bereaved father for the loss of that child whom he had watched from infancy to manhood with the tenderest solicitude? What is glory but a name, a hollow sound, a poor—a wretched compensation for a tangible affection, boundless as are the limits of God's goodness to his creatures?"

Henry felt that this was not a time to intrude a remark upon the sorrow-stricken man. With a tact beyond his years, he knew that if the mourner found not sufficient philosophy within his own heart to stem the current of his grief, it could be given him by no one.

The old man was silent for many minutes, and then, stretching forth his hand, he took Henry's in his grasp, and said, gently,—

"My young friend, I thank you for this silent sympathy ; it speaks to me more eloquently than any words in which you could have clothed feeling. The pang is past, and I can now proceed more calmly."

"Perhaps at another time," said Henry, "you will be more inclined to furnish me with the sequel of a narrative that has already excited my warmest sympathies."

"No, no; no time like the present. If I told you not all now, I should feel the weight of what I had to tell pressing heavily upon me. I will go on now. The tale is nearly over ; but yet its strangest portion has yet to come."

## CHAPTER LVII.

### THE CHILD AND ITS PROTECTOR.

AFTER a pause, the old man continued, and he spoke more composedly by far than he had done before. It seemed as if, up to the point when he had told how his son had fallen, he had laboured in his narrative, and it had been a pain to him of no ordinary character to bring it to its climax.

Now, however, that was passed, and, as we said, he proceeded with more spirit and determination.

"You must understand, my friend, that these particulars which I communicate to you found their way to my ears through the medium of a brother officer of my son's, in whom Adolphe had ever placed the greatest confidence, and towards whom he felt all the affection of a most attached friend.

"This officer was wounded likewise, but not severely ; and although it was a wound which put a stop to his locomotion, yet it was not sufficient to prevent him, at a distance, from being a spectator of various events that had occurred upon the field of battle."

"Is this officer living?" said Henry.

"He is, but now aged; for at that time he had served for a number of years ; and the wear and tear of campaigns must be expected to make some ravages even upon the stoutest constitutions."

"He's in France, I presume?"

"He is."

"I pray you, sir, to proceed, and to believe that I do not ask these questions carelessly."

"It was towards evening, then, and the scattered host of the French army was flying before the Prussian cavalry, which came comparatively fresh into the field against them.

"That ensanguined plain, upon which the dreadful conflict had taken place, was more deserted than any portion of the surrounding country. It is true that great efforts had been made to carry to places of safety and accommodation the wounded; but when more than sixty thousand men fell upon the field, to complete such a task required days and days of labour from unfatigued men, and not the few hours that the exhausted soldiers could give to it, ere they themselves were compelled to throw themselves down for repose.

"My son's wounds were not mortal, and he lay for some hours seemingly dead, but really only in a trance, upon that field of blood. Marie, from the first moment that she had been roughly told he had fallen at the head of his regiment, had, with the despair of death depicted upon her countenance flown to seek him amidst the dead and the dying.

Grasping her infant to her breast, and with a feeling of despair at her heart that enabled her to tread without sickening, e'en through the pools of blood and the mangled corpses that strewed the plain, she sought the chosen of her heart—that husband who was to her the whole world, and without whom life were desolate indeed.

It was no easy task, amidst such a group of spectral-looking forms, to find any one in particular, but the eye of affection is ready and acute. At last she found him; she thought he was no more, and, with a shriek of agony, she flung herself beside his blood-stained form, and prayed of Heaven to take her, too, to that world which is to come.

It seemed as if God's mercy had granted the mourner's prayer; she moved not, spoke not; insensibility stole over her, and, as Adolphe slowly opened his eyes, upon which the film of death was gathering, and looked upon that bloody field, he became painfully conscious that, beside him, was the cherished idol of his heart.

He saw the child, too; and he saw that it lived, although he believed that its mother was no more.

The wounded officer, who was enabled, from the observations he made, to tell me this much, states, that at that moment a horse, maddened by wounds, and in the agonies of death, rose up and dashed across the field, scattering destruction beneath his sounding hoofs.

He was trodden on by the infuriated animal in its wild career, and the pain he endured sufficiently confused his faculties to enable him to have a faint, dreamy kind of perception of what next occurred.

He thinks he heard the sound of English voices close about where Adolphe lay, and he fancied that some sort of struggle took place, for he distinctly avers that a musket was discharged by some one.

Then he saw Adolphe rise up, or nearly so, but he could not be sure; darkness was coming over the plain, and he was getting himself fearfully faint, as much from exhaustion, in consequence of the want of food for many hours, as from the anguish of his wounds, and that was all he could actually tell me of his own knowledge."

"Indeed!"

"Yes, all; from that moment I have heard nothing definite concerning my son, Marie, or the child."

"But you have heard something, though of an indefinite character?"

"Yes; but, because all inquiries have been fruitless, I'm led to think that what I have heard is founded upon error, and that some accidental coincidence of circumstances must have occurred to give colour to a story which surely cannot be the fact, or diligent inquiry would have been crowned with some sort of success."

"Have you any objection to impart to me those particulars which you thought you acquired?"

"None in the least; listen, I will tell you all; they are simply these :—

My son's friend was taken up by the English, and conveyed to Brussels, where he remained for many weeks in a church, which had been devoted to the purposes of a military hospital.

There, from various parties, who came to speak to him, he learned the following particulars. It was said that an English officer, while lying wounded on the field, and scarcely able to help himself, so badly was he hurt, had had consigned to his care a young child, by a French officer of rank, who, shortly after bestowing such a trust upon him, and getting his promise in the name of Heaven to fulfil it, expired by his side.

This story was currently spoken of among the soldiery; but our friend was disabled, as you will understand, from making personal inquiry. He was told that this very officer lay dangerously wounded in Brussels, and, as his own injuries were not of a very serious character, but, on the contrary, such as promised a speedy convalescence, he made up his mind not to appear anxious on the subject, but to seek out the English officer when he could do so personally, and ascertain if it were indeed the child of Colonel Rouselli of which he had charge.

. Contrary, however, to all expectations, his wound assumed a troublesome, if not a dangerous character, after a time ; a fever supervened, which disordered his faculties ; and, when that subsided by the remedies pursued by the English surgeons, he had the mortification of finding that the British army had left Brussels, on their route to Paris, and that among the wounded officers who had sufficiently recovered to be sent home was this very officer, about whom the story of the child had been told.

This was mortifying in the extreme, but could not be helped, and the only resource of Adolphe's friend now, was to endeavour to discover the name and rank of the party who had accepted such a trust.

In pursuing these inquiries he found how difficult a thing it was to get apparently the simplest evidence upon the simplest affair.

There seemed to be a general understanding and agreement that such a circumstance had taken place, of a child being placed in the care of a British officer upon the field of battle; but no two persons were agreed about his name or his rank.

One person, indeed, a camp-follower, asserted that it was not an officer at all, but a wild-looking Irish infantry man, who had taken charge of the child, and who was about the worst guardian it could possibly have had."

"But what name did the generality agree in giving to the English officer?"

"Martin, or Murton, or some such name; which, however, we could not find as belonging to the British army in any rank whatever, except that of the very lowest, and those individuals, when applied to, disclaimed all knowledge of the transaction."

"Alas, sir!" said Henry, "what unavailing exertions have you made to discover the truth?"

"As many as possible; and my presence here in this country is a proof that, although sixteen or seventeen years have elapsed, I have not forgotten the affair, or given up a hope of one day clearing up the mysteries which surround it."

"And was nothing," said Henry, with great hesitation, "ever heard of Marie Mendelson?"

"Nothing—nothing."

"Alas! her fate seems to have been the most gloomy of all."

"It was—it was. My son, of course, found the death which he knew might be the result of his profession; but to poor Marie, the case was widely different, and whatever fate may have been hers, she is most abundantly to be pitied."

Henry turned pale and red by turns, and could not conceal the agitation into which he was thrown.

"My young friend," said old Rouselli, "you are unwell. I fear I have tried your generous feelings too much by the recital of my misfortunes."

"No, no."

"You breathe faintly. What is it—oh, tell me what is it, that has come over you?"

"It is nothing—a sudden rush of feeling. I shall be better presently. I must confess your narrative has sensibly touched me."

"Ah! you are too young to be afflicted by such terrifying details. I regret I told you all; but I felt, somehow, impelled to do so."

"Nay, sir, do not regret, for a moment, for in telling me all, believe me, you——"

"Wherefore do you pause? what would you say?"

"Nothing—nothing."

"Oh, if you have any consolation to offer to a father's heart, offer it at once. and do not keep me in a horrible suspense."

"I have nothing—I have nothing. Will you, sir, permit me to call upon you at this hour to-morrow?"

"With pleasure. Your society will be grateful to me. 'Tis I that shall feel greatly indebted for such a visit. But let me offer you some refreshment, for I feel convinced that you are really ill. Help! help! He faints—he faints!"

---

## CHAPTER LVIII.

HENRY MORTON'S RETURN, AND CONSULTATION WITH RAFFERTY BROLICKBONES.—THE RESOLUTION.

THE tale that Mr. Henry Morton had heard of the Frenchman, Rouselli, filled him with much astonishment, and he would have endeavoured to have made some explanations then and there, but that he feared to excite hopes that might never be realized. He feared to cause hope in the heart of Rouselli, and he feared to do so for Mabel's sake, lest she, being found, should become interested in this affair, and yet doomed to another disappointment.

He turned towards the house where he left Rafferty Brolickbones, with the intention of questioning him as to the circumstances attending the finding of the child on the field of battle.

"It seems so very likely," he said, "that I have very strong suspicions myself; but I would make them certainty before I spoke of them to any human being. Rafferty will remember the day of which I have so often heard him speak, and he'll remember the circumstances that attended the finding of the child.

"God of heaven! if it should turn out, as I suspect it will, that she is the daughter of the Frenchman who died, this much we know; but, should she have been connected with this family, then, indeed, it will have been an additional pleasure in finding the relative of one so good and amiable as Mabel.

"Alas, alas!" he said, recollecting himself; "we have yet to find Mabel, the beautiful, the good Mabel. I would I knew where at once to find her, and then I would — but no, I must make inquiries first, and ascertain all I believe to be true is true, and then we may indulge in congratulations. I would not name it even to Mabel. I will find out Rafferty Brolickbones; he was badly hurt, and lay by my brother on the field of blood, when the child was consigned to the care of Morton."

He went to his lodgings, and searched about for Rafferty Brolickbones; but he was not to be found. Vexed with the circumstance, Henry Morton strode about, venting impatient exclamations.

"Where can Rafferty have gone? What could induce him to go out? Confound him, he's always away; perhaps the landlady knows where he may be."

Acting on this thought, he descended from the place he occupied, and seeing the woman of the house, he said,—

"Can you tell me where my servant is?"

"No, sir, I can't; but he hasn't been out long."

"He is out?"

"Yes, sir."

"You have no idea, I suppose, when he will return?"

"He said he was only going to take a turn about, sir, and then come back again."

"Thank you."

Henry Morton turned away to conceal his vexation from the woman, and re-entered his own apartment, where he resolved to await the return of Rafferty Brolickbones. In the meantime, he resolved to exert all the patience he was capable of, and again his mind reverted to the loss of Mabel, and the interview he had had with Rouselli.

However, he had not to wait long, for very soon after, he heard the voice of Rafferty exclaim—

"Well, Mrs. Jones, is the governor within?"

"Yes: and he has been inquiring after you, Mr. Rafferty."

"Ha! now who would have thought of that? Mighty bad luck to the length of the streets."

"And why?"

"Because they take so long to get to the end of 'em. Indeed, I think some of them lengthen out as you go."

"Do what?"

"Get longer."

"Nonsense."

"Oh, it's aisy to say nonsense; but I say they are very much like talescope-jointed ones."

"What do you mean by that, Mr. Rafferty? I never saw such a man as you are!"

"Didn't you, agrah?"

"No; but what do you mean? I really don't think you can tell what you mean, nine times out of ten."

"Don't you, my jewel? Well, what would you do if I were Mr. Jones? there'd be a pretty state of misunderstanding. I should like to see it. But the master is up stairs, isn't he, Mrs. Jones?"

"Indeed he is."

"Then he may want me; and it isn't the like of me as 'ud keep a gentleman waiting."

And upon this Rafferty Brolickbones walked up stairs, with a step that was intended to suit a slow march, and when he entered the room where Mr. Henry was, he said,—

"Does your honour want me?"

"Yes, Rafferty, I do."

"Oh, bedad! I've been out."

"Where, Rafferty?"

"Can't say; but I've been looking about, up one street and down another; but when I've nothing to do, you know, your honour, I always go into the street, to look for Miss Mabel, or maybe that rascally beggarman, who got away so cleverly when we thought we had him."

"I understand you, Rafferty; but I want to speak to you about Mabel."

"About Miss Mabel? Oh, yes, your honour; all day, if you please," said Rafferty.

"Not all day, Rafferty, though I could do so. I want to ask you a few questions, will you answer me?"

"Yes, sure."

"Do you remember the day on which was fought the battle of Waterloo, eh?"

"Can I recollect my own self? or, sure now, your honour is poking fun at me, by asking such a question."

"No, no; I mean the evening of the day on which that great battle was fought."

"Murder and glory! I do. Is there anything a man recollects better than a broken leg, a hole in his shoulder, and two or three other things besides?"

"Well, well, that's not what I mean."

"But it's what I mean, especially when I am tired; it comes across me like an old sore."

"I dare say; but do you remember all the circumstances relating to the affair of Mabel?"

"I do."

"Then it is of that that I want to ask you a few questions," said Mr. Morton.

"Oh, as many as you please."

"Do you recollect what kind of man it was that gave my brother the child that he brought away with him from the battle-field?"

"Yes; I mind him, your honour."

"What sort of man was he?"

"A good-looking young man enough,"

said Brolickbones. "I was lying wounded, but he wore a handsome uniform, and said he was Rushhilly, and he belonged to the guarde-shovel, what means horse-guards."

"I hear; well, what else?"

"Oh, begum! Mr. Morton, the child, Miss Mabel; and the captain, then an ensign, swore he'd do for it."

"Do for it, Brolickbones?"

"Yes, sure; he promised to take care of it, and do for it as if he had been its own father. Sure, what would you have more? If that ain't enough, I don't know what is."

"And he had the child taken care of?"

"Yes, sure; and when he came to England, and took Mrs. Morton, that is his lady, you know——"

"Yes, yes!"

"He took the child—a baby, home, too."

"I understand."

"Well, then, all I know about the matter more is, that when she grew up she was beautiful and good, and, if your honour hasn't the same opinion, why, then, yer honour's taste and mine ain't alike."

"Well, Rafferty, you are not far out. She is beautiful; but this Frenchman, to my thinking, is a relative of Miss Mabel's."

"Och, murder! murder! you don't say that, do you?"

"It is the same name."

"Rushhilly?"

"No, Rouselli."

"Well, it's much the same for the matter of that; but then we've been picking up Miss Mabel's grandfather; maybe he'll be after looking after her?"

"It is likely, Rafferty; but I would not have raised any unnecessary expectations in his mind that might never be fulfilled, and, therefore, I never said a word about it."

"Indeed, sir; then we have all the sacret to ourselves as yet; what, is he looking after her at all?"

"Oh, yes; he has come to this country to seek for the child of the officer who was slain, who was the son, I believe, of this gentleman."

"I see, sir; aisy, aisy."

"Well, he has described him, and the situation he was last seen and heard of on the field of battle."

"Ay, ay, sir."

"Well, then, do you know if the clothes in which she was found are still in existence?"

"Yes, sure enough, if they have been taken care of. Oh, yes; bedad, that's likely."

"You do not know, then, for a certainty?"

"I don't know more than I say, your honour."

"Well, then, I hardly know how to proceed, or what to do. I would we could find Mabel."

"And so do I with all my heart, and bad blazes to them as wouldn't, say I; but why not take the road home again, to Morton Hall, sir?"

"And there inquire of my brother for these things?"

"Yes, sure; you'll find it the quickest way, sir. The horses are all right; they have rested well, and will, when I tell them of the nature of their errand, start on the road home with a wind in their tails that'll carry 'em along with a flowing sheet, as I have heard sailors say, though how they are to get a flowing sheet I don't know, except it is when their tails are blown in their faces."

"Well, I think that will, after all, be the best plan," said Henry Morton; "much the best plan, and I will adopt it. My brother can tell me what can be done, or ought to be done, in this case, and to him I'll go."

"When, your honour?"

"To-morrow early."

"Bedad I'll be ready for your honour, and I'll warrant the horses shall be well fed, and their shoes looked to before we start. At daybreak, I suppose, your honour?"

"Yes; as early as we can, the earlier the better, for we shall have advanced upon our road towards Morton Hall, where we shall arrive in good time, and then I dare say we shall have another ride to London immediately."

---

## CHAPTER LIX.

RAFFERTY BROLICKBONES' REMINISCENCES OF WATERLOO.—THE LAST NIGHT IN TOWN.—THE JOURNEY.

WHEN Rafferty Brolickbones had left Henry Morton, to proceed about getting everything in good order for the next day's journey to Morton Hall, where he once more expected to see familiar faces, though not the one which the honest old Irishman would have desired to see, the latter considered what he should do, and how he should act until next he saw Rouselli, and how to apologize for the disappointment he would cause by not calling again upon him.

"He will think it discourteous; I must write to him; but how shall I expect to find him, or what to say without giving him hopes which may never be realized, though I must say something that will induce him to stay ?"

Seeing he could devise no other mode of action, he determined to write to Rouselli, explaining, and requesting his remaining in town for a few days.

" It must be a short and abrupt letter," he said, as he arose to fetch the writing materials, which were at hand, "and he may learn the motive of what to him would naturally appear strange and inexplicable conduct at a future day; but at present it will appear a mystery."

He took a sheet of paper, and wrote as follows :—

"Sir,                          "——Hotel.

" You will doubtless be surprised to hear from me instead of seeing me, for which I must apologize. I am compelled to leave town unexpectedly, but shall not be away many days. Will you permit me to beg of you not to leave your hotel until I return to London ?

" I have urgent motives for making this request, which I cannot state in this letter, and there is not time for an interview.

" Allow me to beg this favour of you, that you will not yet quit your hotel until my return, which shall be in a very few days at the farthest.—I am, sir,

    "Your obliged servant,
                    "HENRY MORTON."

"To M. Rouselli.

Henry Morton rang the bell, and Rafferty Brolickbones soon after appeared at the door.

" Does your honour want Rafferty ?"

" I do."

" Then I'm ready," and Rafferty at once walked into the room, and stood before Henry.

" I want you to take this letter to Mr. Rouselli," he said, as he handed him the letter.

" Oh, mushay Rousehilly !"

" Give this in at the hotel, but do not wait for an answer, and come away directly; do you hear ?"

" Oh, yes, sir."

" To-night you must get all ready, and get to bed earlier, and then you will have less need of rest till you can get at the Hall, as I do not purpose to stop on the road more than we are obliged."

" I'm with your honour ; I can do with as little rest as a horse, I'll warrant," said Brolickbones.

" I have no doubt of it," said Henry ; " and I shall make my arrangements with the same view."

" Very good, your honour."

Rafferty quitted the room without delay,

and was soon on his way to the hotel of Rouselli.

That evening Henry Morton spent in walking about, at least until near nine o'clock, and then he returned with a dejected air to his supper, which was laid before him by Rafferty Brolickbones.

" Rafferty."

" Yer honour."

" You may as well take your supper with me; set it down there, and we can converse about matters we have at heart, and with more freedom."

" Your honour is very good."

" I shall go to bed as soon as I have done, so I can employ the time we spend in supper economically."

" Very good, sir."

Rafferty brought up his supper, which he placed upon the edge of the table, and sat down, with many apologies, which he deemed necessary for the occasion.

" I'm ready, yer honour."

" Eh ?"

" I'm ready."

" What do you mean ? your supper ?—because if you do, why don't you begin ?"

" I have, yer honour."

" What are you ready for —whisky ?"

" Oh, yes, your honour, I'm always so for that; but that was not what I meant ; I meant that I was ready to spake to your honour whenever your honour should spake first, in token of signal to say something."

Henry Morton smiled at the oddity of the Irishman, but said, after a pause,—

" Did you give the letter in ?"

" I did, yer honour."

" That was right ; I wished to ask you if you remember if anything else had happened at the time you and my brother lay wounded on the field of Waterloo ?"

" A good many things, sir."

" Indeed !"

" Yes, yer honour ; there were many things—such a thing as a mad horse galloping over people, without ' with your leave or by your leave ;' men smashed, and the small remains of life left in them only knocked out with their brains."

" Horrible !"

" Yes, that was bad enough."

" Bad enough ! could there be worse ?"

" Yes ; there's nothing so bad but what may be worse, so they say, though I'd rather not carry the inquiry much further, especially if it be at all experimental."

" Exactly; but what could you have worse ?"

" Why, after lying wounded, in several places, your legs broken, and so on, and then——"

" What then, Rafferty ?"

"Why, a woman—ay, a female woman —coming to rob you, if dead, and, if not dead, at least murder you."

"You don't mean to say that such things have happened, and that you have seen them?"

"Bedad, they happen after every battle that takes place, but, for the honour of the sex, you know, I shot her dead."

"Dead!"

"Oh, yes, sir, I couldn't do less; indeed, that one would have been too bad, for she would have murdered Mabel's fa-ther, as he lay dying on the field of battle."

"Good God!"

"And then the captain's and my turn would have come next, and you know neither of us had been here; we should have been all in glory."

"I understand; but Mabel's father died on the field of battle, did he not?" inquired Henry Morton.

"Yes, he did; poor fellow, he was dying when he gave poor Mabel to your brother, Captain Morton."

THE MENDICANT FRUSTRATING THE ESCAPE OF MABEL.

"Did he—and what said he?"

"Oh! poor ignorant fellow: he thought he had been the victor, that the emperor had beaten us; but, bedad! that was not quite the state of affairs; we had beaten him, and a sound drubbing he had at our hands; so we told him it was more t'other, you see, and he spoke after a different fashion."

"Well, Rafferty, those days are past, and let's hope they never will again come."

"Ah! bedad! no, not until the French want another drubbing; but they are always making a stir about what they can do, and what other people can't, until they'll get to such a height that there'll be no bearing them, and then they must be treated as they have been treated before."

"I hope not."

"Hope as you like, sir; it will come to it one of these days, and that's the fact of it."

"Well, well; until those times come, we'll s y no more about it," said Harry Morton.

"As you please, your honour; not that I am at all saying as how Frenchmen can't fight; they can fight, and, what's worse, they can act with great cruelty and treachery; but they can't fight so well as those who beat them."

"That, we suppose, is the truth, Rafferty."

"And so I should think."

Mr. Morton having finished his supper, and given general directions to Rafferty Brolickbones, retired to his chamber to rest himself against the fatigues of the morrow.

\*  \*  \*  \*  \*

The morning came, and by daybreak Rafferty Brolickbones was in the stable, having fed the horses, and was standing by the manger, watching them eat their provender, when Henry Morton entered the stables also.

"You are up, then, Rafferty?"

"Yes, your honour; what should I want to do in bed when there was work to do? Botheration, it wouldn't do at any price."

"When will the horses be ready?"

"In one half hour, yer honour; they have nearly done, but they oughtn't to be run out directly they have had their corn."

"Exactly—well, look to yourself, and get something to eat before you go, as we shall not stop for an hour or two."

"Very good, sir," said Rafferty; "I thought the people at this place were not up."

"They are now."

Accordingly, Rafferty Brolickbones followed Mr. Henry Morton into the house, and was soon, as he expressed it, cheek by jowl to a sirloin and some ale.

"A mighty solid breakfast," said Rafferty, "I have had," as he drank down the last draught of ale. "It won't make me any the lighter in the saddle than I was afore, I'll go bail."

In a few moments more they were both in the saddle, and in the open streets of London.

"The air is keen this morning, Rafferty," said Henry Morton, as they rode leisurely through the streets.

"Yes, sir; and I'm thinking we shall not be sorry we've taken precautions to prevent the entrance of the raw air into our stomachs, by filling 'em up."

"Yes, there's no evil in that; but now we have got clear of the narrow thoroughfares we can push on."

They set their horses into a round trot, and an hour saw them some miles on a good country road, where the sound of their horses' hoofs rang in the air clear and sharp as they rode along at a rapid pace.

## CHAPTER LX.

THE JOURNEY.—THE FIRST STOPPAGE ON THE ROAD.—MORTON'S THOUGHTS.

IT was not the intention of Henry Morton to allow the grass to grow as he went along, but to reach Morton Hall as quickly as he could, and to lose nothing by delays on the road; and but for resting his horse, which was absolutely necessary, he would have ridden on until he had reached his destination.

However, they had ridden a fair five-and-twenty miles before he thought of stopping, and then he pulled up at a roadside inn, saying to Rafferty—

"Do you think we had better stay and give the horses a bait, or proceed onwards?"

"I think you must stop, sir, if you want to get down to Morton Hall without any accident, or knocking up the horse. You ought not to take him out again until the evening; or, at all events, until the latter end of the day, when they may go another twenty-five miles."

"You think they can do so much?"

"Certainly; for two days, certainly," said Rafferty; "and then they will want a day or two's rest."

He dismounted, and giving the horses into the ostler's care, under the surveillance of Rafferty Brolickbones, who would take care that there was nothing wanting in their management, for he was a man you could depend upon for anything that was intrusted to him.

"Well," said Rafferty; "when do you give the horses any corn?"

"After they have been rubbed down."

"After they are rubbed down, eh?"

"Yes; won't that do?"

"Oh, yes; when they do get it, it is convenient at any time; but the greatest convenience is bringing it at all; when I see that I shall say he's got it."

"Well, you know it strikes me you'll get more knocks than you like, if you come interfering with my work."

"It is my work to look after my master's cattle," said Rafferty; "and I don't mind a few knocks in the way of business; but, of course, I can give as many as I can take. An old Waterloo man ain't to be foiled in these matters. So, now, are you going to be civil, and give the animals their corn, or must I go and say you won't ?"

"You may say what you like, but they won't have it just yet, it ain't time : so be satisfied."

"Very well. I shall leave you ; but mind, see the horse is fed, or Mr. Morton is informed of it ; so it's no use your quarrelling or being disagreeable over the matter—I'm going."

The ostler looked after him with a malicious look, and said he'd be even with him ; and if he got no fee, he'd have his revenge, anyhow, come what would.

"Well," thought Brolickbones ; "I'll just see the landlord, and ask him what's the usage of the place."

After a few minutes' search he found the landlord, who was busy preparing for a breakfast that Morton had ordered, and to him he said in a bland manner,—

"Good morrow, Mr. Innkeeper."

"Good morrow, Mr. Irishman," was the reply.

"Eh ?" said Rafferty.

"What did you please to remark ?" observed the innkeeper.

"A good morning."

"A very good morning."

"Well, we are both of one mind," said Rafferty, "and it bothers conversation. I wish to know the custom of the place."

"Oh, certainly. A gallon of ale is the usual price of the initiation," said the landlord.

"You don't mane that ?"

"It is a fact ; only a gallon."

"But, how ? Suppose I'm going to stay long enough to learn—what then, Mr. landlord ?"

"Pay the money ; and I'll warrant you'll know all ; to stand a gallon of ale, is the custom of the place."

"Then put it down in the bill, and ask the govenor to pay for it, will you ?"

"Eh ?"

"Ask him to pay."

"He won't."

"And do you expect me to pay more than he will ? Come, come ; be reasonable, and stand the ale yourself."

"Well, I'm sure ; I never heard the like of this in all my life. You are a nice man."

"Very good. I'm an old soldier, and know a thing or two. Will you allow me to see the horses fed ?"

"Yes."

"Your man says I shall not."

"Indeed !"

"He does so, and threatens that he will be revenged ; now, I fear some damage done to the horses. I have not spoken to my master about this, because it would make things disagreeable ; besides, I thought, as the fault lay with your people, I had better inform you of it."

"Ah, it is all right—I'll see to it ; you'll be called, so say nothing about it."

"Very good ; only don't let him give the horses any sly hurt ; our journey depends upon them, and if anything was to happen, it would make Mr. Morton very angry, and he would spend a hat full of money sooner than not find it out."

"I'll take care."

This matter being settled to Brolickbones' satisfaction, he went to see if his master wanted anything, but he was not required, and Rafferty then sought out the kitchen, and searched for his own breakfast, which was by no means a slight one, for the ride in the open air was a rare sharpener to his appetite.

This despatched, he again sought the groom, who had now finished dressing his horses.

"Arrah, now, honey ; what is to be done next—can I see the bastes fed, myself ?"

"Yes," said the groom, smiling.

"What ! I can, can I ? Has the wind changed, or are you more obliging than before ?"

"You can see, if you open your eyes ; but I don't find you in eyesight."

"Nor I find you in temper or brains," said Rafferty. "I wonder what quarter the moon was in when you where born—the thingamy pointed to stormy, I suppose."

The groom, however, would have nothing to say to Rafferty, but gave the horses their feed, and Brolickbones placed himself beside the manager, to watch the progress of feeding.

Henry Morton, in the meanwhile, sat thinking over the various occurrences that had happened. That Mabel was the child of the dead officer there could be no doubt ; but that the dead Rouselli was the son of the living Rouselli was a matter which had to be proved ; but which he had no doubt could be done, if the clothes and bracelets that were left with the child could be found.

"These and these alone," thought Henry, "could identify the child as belonging to the young Frenchman who had perished on the field of battle, and I trust they have been preserved, as, indeed, I cannot doubt but they have, for my brother would not permit them to be destroyed if he were aware of it ; and, moreover, he knew that it was Mabel's own wish to discover who her parents were, and without these things she could not hope to do so.

"It is strange that such an unexpected, unlooked-for event should ever happen. I can scarcely persuade myself but it is a dream; and yet, if it be so, I am on a bootless errand. No—no, it is all true and real.

"Who could that fellow be who succeeded in drawing Mabel from her home and securing her, and secreting her from the knowledge of her - friends? What could be his motive, and who could he be?"

Filled with melancholy reflections, to which he could not add anything at all of a pleasing character, he arose, having finished his breakfast, and walked out into the yard, where the first person he saw was Rafferty Brolickbones.

"Well, Rafferty, how do our horses get on?"

"Oh, easy and comfortable, sir. You'd like such a bed as they have got under them. I saw after them myself, sir; though they didn't seem to like it a bit. But they've had their food, and are lying down like two kittens asleep."

"Then they will do well."

"Oh, devil a bit of doubt, sir. Do you think we shall be far off the Hall by this time to-morrow night, sir? It's a mighty long way off, I'm thinking."

"Yes; but we shall sleep at the Hall to-morrow night, if we keep to our work. We must leave this place by a little before three."

"Very well, yer honour."

"Rafferty."

"Well, sir."

"What could be that man's motive for carrying away Miss Mabel?" said Henry Morton.

"A mighty bad one, sir."

"Yes, that is plain enough, Rafferty; but what particular evil motive could he have had?"

"Bedad, sir, but I can't tell; the rascal has some object in view. He must mane something, anyhow; he can't have run away with her from any particular pleasure, though there's some folks as would."

"Exactly. But you saw him?"

"I did."

"What did you think of him?"

"Oh, bedad! I thought him one of the greatest thieves in the world. I could have been the death of him, only the varmint pushed the tree into the water."

"Well, you saw him?"

"Oh, bad cess, yes."

"Would you know him again?"

"Faith, and has your honour forgotten the chase we gave him the other day, when we meet this Roushilly?"

"Oh, yes. I had, at the moment, for-gotten it. I was just then thinking of other things."

"Ay, ay, sir. Aisey—aisey. I'll tell you what, sir, I would do, for any sum of money."

"What, Rafferty, what?"

"I'd know him, and swear to him anywhere in the wide world, no matter where; and when I do find him again, he shall find no friend stick to him as I will."

"No doubt of that, Brolickbones."

"And when I last saw him, it was no want of good will that I didn't stick to him then. I did my best; but it was of no use."

"No. We both went through a few odd places before he escaped from us, and he must have been very nearly taken, for if we where so nearly knocked up, how much more so must he have been who had all to do to save himself?"

"Yes, I'll go bail he was bothered. It is certain that he is now in London, and with him Miss Mabel: I feel as sure of the one as the other."

"And I, too, Rafferty," said Henry, as he turned away.

---

## CHAPTER LXI.

THE ARRIVAL AT MORTON HALL.—THE WELCOME EXPLANATIONS.

IT was a little before three on that day, when Henry Morton, followed by Rafferty Brolickbones, left the inn-yard, and proceeded at a brisk trot onwards towards their destination. The two animals they rode stepped out willingly, as if they knew their journey was homewards.

It was near an hour ere they spoke. At length a small market-town came in sight, when, as he approached it, Henry Morton drew his bridle, and slackening his speed, allowed his companion, Rafferty Brolickbones, to come up with him, when he said.—

"Rafferty, I suppose we must halt here for a short time, eh? The horses will be too warm."

"Ay, ay, yer honour—short stages, long halts, and cattle thrive well, sir."

"Ay, Rafferty; but that kind of stage will not do upon affairs in which Mabel is concerned; we must ride for life and death."

"I'm with your honour, then. I've often seen life and death by the score, just the same as though it were pase in a bushel. Och Ochree, I've seen some terrible sights, and heard some queer things in my time, anyhow."

"I dare say."

"But the quarest thing, was a thing I saw lately."

"And what was that, Rafferty?"

"Why, your honour, it was myself, swimming across the water, after having been thrown in by another man. I was nicely caught, like a bee in a honey-pot. Bad manners to the villain, I'll never forgive him that—terrible blue blazes torment him."

"Ah! he'll have his day by-and-bye."

"He has it now, i' faith. But I tell you what, sir; he'd better make the most of it, for, by all that's holy about the four evangelists, and the priest of Ballybothershins, I'll make clane work with him when I do catch him."

"Fair and easy goes a long way, as I often have heard you say, Rafferty. You must not forget your own lessons, you know, or what use are they?"

"Mighty little, sir, I'll consent to admit; only it ain't fair in any case where Miss Mabel is concerned. I can't stand argiment where she's in danger. I'll go the whole animal, and no mistake."

"I cannot blame you, for she deserves all."

"All, faith, and as much again as all is made of, I'll go bail—all, sir?—you can't think of her as I do; you ain't knowed her as I did; when she was a little thing, dipping her tiny fingers in the blood of brave men who were lying about, mangled in a terrible state, and then looking at her fingers as if she wondered how it was they were so red."

"Yes—yes; I can understand all that."

"Then your honour understands a man's feelings that'll do him no discredit."

"Indeed they will not."

"Well, sir; I knowed her as soon as the captain, your brother, knowed her. But we were both wounded on the field of battle, and laid up for some time afterwards. I was very badly hurt; but I am well, and have nothing to complain of; and I have lived to be happy, and see Miss Mabel grow up a credit to all who ever had anything to do with her."

"Yes, Rafferty, she is well calculated to render all happy who know her," said Henry, enthusiastically.

"You may say that, your honour, and no word of a lie in it, any way. I'll swear to the truth of it; but here we are, at the best inn of the place."

They drew up before a large, old fashioned place, with a horse-trough in front of the door; and here they waited about twenty minutes or half-an-hour, and then they again resumed their journey as before.

In little less than another hour, they stopped again for a halt, but without anything particular happening; then came the same thing a third time, until at length the last stage was attained; and here they rested themselves and their jaded steeds until dawn, without any particular incident happening worth recording; but on the second day, they again quitted their quarters early, but pushed on the entire day with only short halts, until, as the sun set, they came upon a hill in the vicinity of Morton Hall.

The sun shone on the windows, and conveyed a pleasing sensation to the heart of Henry Morton; nor was his companion without emotions of pleasure; and yet, each scene had something to remind them of Mabel, and her absence from them.

"Yonder, sir, I'm thinking, is the place for our money. Ay, sir; 'tis a fine old place, after all."

"Yes, Brolickbones, yes."

"There ain't another in the country like it."

"May be not; but there are many others as good, and some better," said Henry Morton.

"Not to my liking, sir, however," said Rafferty, dogmatically; "people as hav'n't seen such places as I have, may think so; but I've seen places that would make a king stare."

"Indeed!"

"Lord love your honour, I've seen places with hardly any walls, and no roofs at all. What do you think of that for an order in architecture?"

"I must admit that in that light the Hall is a most estimable place, and far above any such as you mention, Rafferty—yes, much better."

"Aisy, now; didn't I tell your honour that you'd be of my opinion, if you knew all that I know?"

"And it seems very likely to be so, for all I can see to the contrary; but, however, there is but a couple of miles between us and the Hall, so we must push on; the horses have nothing to do afterwards; they'll have a stable and feeding as they please."

"March on," said the imperturbable Rafferty; "here we go—we are turned into light cavalry."

"And as such we'll do duty, and show how we can ride onward—that's the word, eh?"

In about twenty minutes or a little more, they entered the yard of Morton Hall.

They were immediately surrounded by the domestics and other servants employed in and about the Hall; and many were the inquiries that were made of Rafferty

Brolickbones, who, however, answered in a very indirect manner, and so kept all the curiosity that was crowded into the breast of the inhabitants of that place, alive and active.

"Well, Henry," said Captain Morton; "you have come back safe and well, I perceive."

"And alone!"

"Rafferty is with you."

"Ay; but without her."

"So I feared."

"Have you heard anything of our dear Mabel?" inquired Mrs. Morton, sorrowfully.

"I can hardly give any answer to such a question, without saying something more than the truth."

"Indeed!"

"Yes, it's a fact; but I would wish to speak to you about her. Rafferty, come with me."

"Yes, your honour."

"Now," said Henry Morton, as he stood in the parlour in the presence of his brother, his sister-in-law, and Rafferty, "I will explain to you what has been done, and that seems to be but little, for, as you perceive, we have not Mabel."

"No," said Mrs. Morton, "I know you have not; I have dreamed of her repeatedly."

"Have you? Well, to keep you no longer in suspense, we have seen the villain who carried her away from this place."

"You have?"

"Yes."

"You knew him again? How could you? Because you never saw him."

"I did not; but Rafferty has seen him, and knew him again; and a desperate chase we had after him; but he succeeded in baffling us at last, though we stopped at nothing to catch him. Rafferty had hold, almost, several times, but he contrived to get away."

"He did, bad cess to him. Had I got once a fair hold of him, then he might have squeaked like a cat; but there he got away, and it's no use talking."

"Yes," said Henry, "he got clean off."

"The villain!" said Mrs. Morton.

"He ought to have been shot," said the captain; "I would I had him up at the triangle—he should have his fill of punishment, if he confessed not where she was."

"Well, well, pass by that; the only good we gained there was the knowledge that Mabel must be in the town, else he would not be there."

"And what brought you away when she was there?" inquired Captain Morton, in some surprise.

"This much. You remember the circumstances that preceded the consignment of Mabel to your care?"

"Surely!"

"And what occurred at the time?"

"I do."

"The name of the young officer who gave the child into your hands when he felt himself dying?"

"I do; but what do you mean by asking these questions? You seem eager; ease my anxiety, and tell me."

"I will; listen. As Rafferty and I went along one of the streets, we saw an elderly gentleman knocked down by a coach, and, but for our assistance, he would have been killed."

"Well?"

"The gentleman was insensible, as it was, and we carried him to a chemist's, and after some remedies had been used, he was recovered; and, having seen him home, we were invited to his room next day."

"Very good."

"Then I went, and had some conversation with him, and he related—frankly told me the cause of his coming to this country—he was a Frenchman."

"Indeed!"

"Yes; and he came to seek for the child of a son of his—a young officer in the French army, who died on the field of battle, on that day when the pride and glory of France were crushed beneath the power of England."

"Well, and what was his name?"

"Rouselli."

"Rouselli!"

"Yes, that was the name," said Henry Morton, and then he paused to see what effect this communication would have upon his brother.

---

## CHAPTER LXII.

CAPTAIN MORTON'S DETERMINATION TO GO TO LONDON.—THE BREAKFAST.—THE DEPARTURE FROM THE HALL.

THERE was a pause of some minutes' duration after the communication that Henry Morton had been the bearer of had been communicated to Captain and Mrs. Morton. There was an evident surprise, that almost created a doubt—not of the truth of what Henry had said, but that he heard aright, in Captain Morton's mind. Indeed, he could scarcely believe but that he dreamed.

"What!" he exclaimed, "do you tell me, Henry, that you have seen Mr. Rouselli, the father of the young officer who lay dead by my side on the field of Waterloo?"

"It would seem so, from what he says."

"And you met him by accident?"

"Purely."

"It is a most wonderful thing, certainly."

"It was an accident that gave me an introduction to his society. We, as I said before, saved his life; he was about to be crushed beneath the wheels of a carriage; we were invited to his hotel, and I went next day."

"And what did he say?"

"He told me he was a Frenchman; that his only business in this country was to find a member of it that had never yet been seen by him; that he had a son, who had fought under Napoleon, and who had there died.

"He had married a young lady against the will of her friends, and had one child; this infant was with him on that field, but what became of that infant he could not tell; but he, from some information he had received, was led to believe that the child was in the possession of some officer of the English army, and his business here is an endeavour to trace the infant."

"And his name is, you say, Rouselli?"

"Yes, Rouselli is the name," replied Henry; "and an agreeable, gentlemanly man he certainly is—evidently of rank and standing in society."

"Heaven be praised!" said Mrs. Morton. "How poor Mabel would have been pleased to have heard all this; but then, what can the other man mean who has taken our dear Mabel from us? Who and what can he be?"

There was a pause, during which the whole party seemed puzzled to suggest an answer to this query. It was strange that this man should have endeavoured to have possessed himself of the person of Mabel, and to have pretended to some knowledge of her parents. There was some mystery in it beyond what floated on the surface.

"One would think," said Captain Morton, "that he wanted money. What purpose could he have but that of obtaining money? None on earth; and yet I know not how to reconcile his conduct."

"Might it not be," suggested Henry Morton, "that he does know something of the family, and that there may be large property coming to Mabel, and that he desired to detain her until he can make such exorbitant terms as only great wealth can give to him for the restoration of Mabel?"

"It may be so; but the man's apparent condition bespeaks but little for the possession of such a secret."

"Well, he has her, and we had a desperate chase after him when we were in London; and now I come to think of it, I am surprised we did not fall and kill ourselves."

"Oh, bedad, sir," said Rafferty, "we never thought of it; if we had we were sure to be made cold meat of in a very few minutes, and no mistake at all, at all."

"There is some truth in all that, Rafferty," said Henry Morton; "and yet I wish we could have got the scoundrel."

"And so do I, sir, and no mistake at all, at all; it wouldn't be let ing him go that I'd be after doing. Oh, no, I'd have his bones out of his skin, one by one, until he told me all I wanted to know. There's no doing anything with gentle means with such thaves of the world as that."

"I think not; anything is too good for such scoundrels; but there is one thing I want to know."

"What is it, Henry?"

"This," said Henry Morton: "Have you by you any of the clothes or other things that may have been with the child when the officer consigned her to your care on the battle-field?"

"I have."

"Then they are of the utmost importance. I was to have met Rouselli at his hotel the next day, but I sent him a letter, begging him to remain in town for a few days, as I wished to see him upon urgent matters."

"Will he remain?"

"I believe he will do so. I wrote so urgently to him, that I do not think he would leave his hotel until he has again seen me."

"What does he say to this affair?"

"I have told him nothing about it at all."

"Not informed him of Mabel's existence?"

"No, nothing. I thought it would be unwise to raise up hopes that might never be realised—that it might not be the same person—there might be no relationship, though the names were the same; and, moreover, Mabel is not to be found."

"Not to be found!" echoed Mrs. Morton. "Alas, that it should be so. Poor Mabel not to be found."

"We have not succeeded in finding her," said Henry.

"Nor have we; but that is easily accounted for, since you saw the man who forced her away in London. She surely is there too, Henry—there can be no doubt about that."

"Nor have I any," said Henry Morton; "but I consider, with Mr. Rouselli, we may unite in conducting a search through London much more effective than any that can be done by our isolated efforts."

"That is true enough," said Captain Morton, "and I myself will accompany you to town, and see this Rouselli myself, carrying with me at the same time those proofs, if I may so call them, of Mabel's parentage and birth."

"Exactly: that will be the best thing that can be done. When we reach town, we will all three go and see Rouselli, and then explain to him the cause of my sudden departure, and the, to him, singular request I made, of begging him to stay where he was at that time, which must, indeed, have startled him."

"Then," said Mr. Morton, "you will stay here one night before you go to London again?"

"Yes," said Henry Morton, "we must; and for the sake of the horses, we must take so much time."

"We will have entirely a new relay of them," said Captain Morton; "those you have had must now be pretty well fatigued, and a few days' rest will benefit them."

"It will do them no harm," said Rafferty. "I'll have them ready by early dawn, sir."

"I shall be up at sunrise, Rafferty; but I will give orders respecting the horses, and preparations for the journey; but you see about seeking rest for yourself."

"Rest, your honour!"

"Yes; don't you feel tired?"

"What, of being carried?"

"Of riding?"

"No, bedad, no. I had a good baste to carry me, and do you think I am tired with nothing to do? I may get tired of doing nothing, and be glad of a change, but nothing more."

"Oh, very well; please yourself."

"My dear," said Mrs. Morton to Captain Morton, "do you think we shall ever see poor Mabel again? Poor thing, what she must have suffered we can hardly imagine."

"No; we may, however, think her worse off than she is; but I hope she has not fallen into the hands of any of those harpies who may endeavour to ruin the poor child; but if no unfair or wicked means be used, I am not afraid but she will come out unscathed from the fire."

"Nor I," said Mrs. Morton.

"Nor I either," said Henry Morton. "She is as pure as tried gold, but the wickedness of those into whose hands she may be thrown makes me tremble. God keep her, not so much from temptation, as from the power of others."

"Amen," said Rafferty. "Oh, bedad, let me come across the rapscallions as would touch Miss Mabel—I'd charge clean through 'em, I would, the varmint; but let's get at them, and get her back, and then we shall see what'll be done."

"I should like to see her back again, and I don't despair," said Henry; "but I have as yet been disappointed sadly."

They now separated.

Rafferty took up his usual quarters in the household, where he retailed a variety of anecdotes relative to the adventures that he and Mr. Henry Morton had gone through, that quite amazed his hearers in the kitchen.

"Rafferty Brolickbones," said one, "what, have you come again to see us at the Hall?"

"Yes, faith; is there anything extraordinary in that, my jewel?" said Rafferty, shaking his fellow-servant's hand.

"I thought, as you had set out on your travels, that you wouldn't come back again until a year and a day had passed."

"I'm here."

"So I see; but some said that even then, if you were dead, you'd never come back."

"Wouldn't I, a come back, if it were to haunt you all for your pains."

"Yes, I said you'd haunt us in the shape of an old man sticking out of a hollow tree."

"I'd go bail you'd have stopped there until now, had you been there, you spalpeen; you'd 'a looked like a bear that couldn't get down, and you'd have to be fished out with a long rope, and a piece of lead with three prongs to it."

"Oh! oh! oh! Jack, Rafferty has you there."

"He may be pleased with the notion," said the man, "but I don't care where he has me, so long as he hasn't got me swimming about like a piece of green turf."

"Very well, we shall see; but perhaps you are safe. You wouldn't swim like a piece of turf, but you would like a stone, and so make a good retrate to the bottom."

With much good-natured badinage, the old soldier was installed into the warmest corner by the fire-side, and then he was soon deeply employed in coining fictions for the gratification of the appetites of those who listened to him.

* * * * * *

The next morning the whole party were astir before the sun's earliest rays had passed the line of the horizon, and the cattle had been fed nearly an hour.

Mrs. Morton, too, was busy in preparing those comfortable ingredients that so well agree with the inward man of a traveller.

She thought it was a sin that anybody should ever be out in the cold morning air with an empty stomach. She had heard scientific professor in natural philosophy declare that nature abhorred a vacuum, and, in compliance with this dictum, Mrs. Morton always had plenty of what the same professor might have scientifically denominated "stopping," but which ordinary people would call food, by her in the larder; and when any one betrayed any uneasiness arising from such a cause, instant recourse was had to the remedy, and an effectual stop was put to the gap.

Breakfast was laid, and when Captain Morton and his brother Henry arose and entered the breakfast-room, they found that Mrs. Morton had already been some time employed in preparing it for them.

"Well, my dear," said Captain Morton, "you have been provident in providing for our wants, at all events."

MABEL DISCOVERING THE BODY IN THE OLD ROCL.

"Why, you know, Morton, that when you come to ride, you will in a few hours —ay, in less time than that, find yourselves very hungry and ill."

"I hope not."

"Ay, but jolting on horseback can't be done upon an empty stomach, I am sure."

"We must do without jolting."

"So much the better. Then you will only have to keep out the cold air and damps that float about early in the morning—they are very dangerous."

"We sha'n't hurt now."

"I hope not."

"What do you say, Henry?"

"That we ought to be much obliged for such care and attention, for I am sure I think that such a breakfast is most seasonable; but at the same time I fear we have given unnecessary trouble to Mrs. Morton."

"Oh, no! the trouble was necessary; but now, let me tell you, you must find Mabel somehow or other."

"We will, if it be in our power. No attempt shall be left unmade that could be made."

"I am satisfied that all will be done that can be done."

"You may depend upon that," added Captain Morton.

They finished their breakfast. The sounds of the horses' feet were heard at the door, and then, taking an affectionate leave of Mrs. Morton, Captain Morton, followed by his brother, betook himself to the saddle, and then, accompanied by Rafferty Brolickbones, left Morton Hall for London.

At first they travelled slowly, but after a short time they put their horses to their metal, and the sound of their feet might be heard for some distance in a quick and rapid pace.

And thus they went forward, stopping at different places, waiting only to allow their blown animals to recover their wind, and to cool themselves before they started on their journey again with renewed strength and vigour.

## CHAPTER LXIII.

### THE ATTACK OF THE OFFICERS UPON THE EMPTY HOUSE.—THE CAPTURE OF THE MENDICANT.—HIS APPEAL TO MABEL.

THE knocking at the door of the house in which the mendicant had confined Mabel, and in which so deep and terrible a tragedy had so short a time before been enacted, completely confounded both her and her persecutor.

They stood both in the same attitude in which it had surprised them.

Again came the startling sounds, and they rang and echoed through the old house in a manner that would have led to the supposition that the house was similarly attacked on all sides.

Still the mendicant attempted not an escape. He was so thoroughly bewildered and surprised, that he could not think of safety, but gazed alternately at the body of the murdered man, which lay at his feet, and then at Mabel.

How the body could come there he could not conceive. That it was murdered he knew, and that it was murdered in that room, too, was apparent, from the quantity of blood that lay about the body, and collected in a pool where the flooring lay lower.

Who could have been there to do it was beyond his powers of imagination to conceive, and that Mabel had done it he could not credit. No, no, that was impossible.

She could not have dyed her hands in blood; but at the same time, who could have done it, and who could have brought it there ?

Poor Mabel, too, stood like one in a trance. She could not think she saw the hideous spectacle. She had been an involuntary witness of all that had happened, and could not but feel her heart chilled by the accumulation of horrors that had that night taken place, and surrounded her.

At this moment voices were heard.

"Force the door in," said a deep, stern voice.

"Ay, ay," was the answer.

In another moment there came such a crash, that was proof that those on the outside had succeeded in forcing the door, and were now about to enter the house.

The door, however, still held by some other parts, but ultimately it was thrown down with a tremendous bang, that almost alarmed the neighbourhood.

At that moment footsteps were heard in the passage, and the same voice was heard to say,—

"They came here. I am sure we shall find the murderer in the house, and his victim."

Then, and only at that moment, did the mendicant seem to recover himself sufficiently to think of self-preservation.

"D——n!" he muttered; and then, looking from one way to the other, he seemed to have made up his mind, and darted out to escape by a sudden and desperate effort to rush through the persons, whoever they might be.

In this he had to deal with men who were accustomed to surprises; who, in fact, may be said to be so, and to them a surprise is nothing of the kind.

The mendicant had no sooner got into the passage, than he found himself grappled by a stout powerful man, who seized him by the throat, and from whom he could not free himself.

"Here you are, Bill."

"What's all the row about?"

"I've got one cove, as he was trying to make a dive and get out. Here he is."

"Bring him in."

"I have got him. Just come and put on the darbies. The gentleman won't be quiet, though he knows he can't get away. There, confound you, if you won't take things more quietly, take that, and that, will you, and be cursed to you !"

Immediately following this, was heard a

sound that indicated a bumping of heads against the wall in the passage.

"Hilloa! don't do to much of that, Tom!"

"Oh, no; only a little by way of diversion. Will you stand still, now, eh, you son of the halter?"

The other man spoken to now came, and the mendicant was secured by means of handcuffs, which held him firmly enough, so that he could not get away.

"Now we have you safe," he said, "we will examine the house, and see what you have been up to."

"I have done nothing."

"Then you need not be under any alarm. You are safe enough, so don't put yourself in a fume."

The mendicant certainly did seem to be taken unawares, and had lost his usual presence of mind in this instance; indeed, his whole faculties seemed to have received a shock. It was a tremendous surprise that had taken possession of his faculties, and from this he was but slowly recovering to a full consciousness that he was placed in the last position that he could with safety to his life enjoy; he therefore made use of the only means of escape that suggested itself to him, and this, unfortunately for him, had failed.

"Come, bring him into the room; but one can guard him now, for he has not the use of his hands."

"Here, hold up the lantern."

"The house is empty."

"Yes, empty of all save such as thieves and murderers may have in it, and these must be looked to."

The men now crowded around the mendicant, whom they had secured; and holding the lanterns up to his face, they looked at him, but he returned their gaze steadily and firmly, and said to them,—

"What do you mean by using me thus?"

"Oh, you'll know in good time to-morrow, at Bow-street; it will then be explained."

"It is your duty to tell me, and my pleasure to ask. Tell me, for what I am thus used?"

"You are suspected of belonging to a gang of murderers. A gentleman has been traced here, and several men have been wi h him. If we find him well and sound, you'll only get a month or six weeks as a rogue and vagabond."

"I have committed no murder."

"Oh, dear, no!"

"And I know not of whom you speak."

"How blessed innocent!"

"I'm blowed if he wouldn't do to come out at eight o'clock without an ordinary."

"So he would."

"That a deed of blood has been committed here I cannot deny, but not by me."

"Well, how singular!"

"Only think of that! One or two, perhaps. Come in with him, and then we shall hear what he has to say, and begin to make our search, and find out how true he is."

They now entered the place; the room in which the stranger had been cruelly and brutally murdered.

The first man who entered slipped as his foot stepped into a pool of blood.

"Hilloa, Jem, what's the matter? Keep yourself upright, and we shall know you are safe."

"It's d—d slippy, any how," returned the other; "why, where are you going with the lantern?"

"Hang me if I know, but I tumbled over something soft, and down I came."

"Well, you had better remain there; you are going to put your hand, I see, in a pool of blood."

The officer got on his leg without putting his hand into the pool of blood as his companion had pointed out, and holding his lantern above his head, he examined the room.

"Here does, indeed, seem something of the sort we expected to find," said the officer.

"There's the dead body, too."

"That's what I tumbled over."

"It is hardly cold yet, poor wretch; how savage and brutal must this fellow be."

"No wonder he wanted to get out."

"Yes, and then to feel indignant because we believe him guilty of this; and, upon my soul—but then who will you find that'll tell you the truth?"

"Truth or no truth, I never injured that man."

"Is not killing an injury?"

"Yes, but I never killed him."

"Who did?"

"I don't know."

"What do you do here?"

"I live here."

"In an empty house?"

"Yes, I have no other."

"That may be, but it gives you no right to live here; nevertheless, if you live here, you could not be ignorant of how this unfortunate man came by his death."

"As surely as I am innocent of this crime, I know nothing about it at all how it came there, or how he was murdered; I am utterly and entirely innocent."

"Make those believe you who can, I cannot; you don't mean to say that strangers brought in this man, and after murdering him, went out again, and left you ignorant of the whole transaction?—It's all nonsense."

"I was not here when it was done."

"There he goes again."

"I had come in a few moments before you came."

"Indeed."

"Yes; and I was so amazed that I could not move or stir, else I had escaped."

"Ah, that's all very well. Well, well, you will have an opportunity of trying to make the beak believe all that—I don't believe a word of it."

"There's one that can clear me; she well knows I am innocent. Mabel, say I am innocent."

"Place me as I was among my friends; do me justice, and I will say all I have seen."

"No, I cannot, will not do that."

"You will not place me among my friends as I was formerly—you will not restore me?"

"No."

"Then my lips are sealed."

"There, now, a nice young fellow you are, ain't you? Why your own witness would hang you."

"Come along."

"A pretty job this," said one of the officers, as he looked at the body; "why he's tried to hang him, and then couldn't, and stabbed him; as sure as I am alive he has; what a hard-hearted brute,—but there, look in his face, and you will tell what he is."

"For all you say," said the mendicant, "I am innocent; and as for you, Mabel, this day's work will and must be a bitter one to you when you reflect that by refraining from uttering the truth, you have brought me to death. It will be a bitter reflection—one that will haunt you through the whole of your life. You know that I am innocent; you know that I hurt not this man; but if I had been guilty of the deed, I should not have remained here, and allowed myself to be found in such company, without there was every evidence to prove my innocence of the deed."

"What cunning! I say, my friend, your doubling and twisting about only makes you sink deeper into the mire. Recollect, all you say we shall have to repeat."

"You may say what I say, that I am innocent of this crime, and she who stands there is well aware that I only speak the truth. Justice, Mabel,—justice."

"And justice I say, too," said Mabel; "restore me to the arms of those friends from whom you have torn me; do justice there, and then you may demand justice for yourself."

"There, that's what I call common sense; and, if he can't see it, he ought to be hanged without the benefit of the clergy, though I can't tell what peculiar benefit that is."

"You see he's a double rascal; he's been committing abduction, which is of itself a transportable offence; and were it not that we are sure of his being hung, why we'd have him committed on that score; but I tell you what, we can't have him transported after he is hanged, and, to transport him first, would be to put off the final account, and put the country to greater expense than he is at all worth."

"Well, we had better bring along our prisoner, and leave some one with the body."

"Oh, curse that, do that to-morrow morning."

"Why not to-night?"

"Because none of us want the job, that's the reason; what do you think of that?"

"That you want to create a mutiny."

"Pho—pho."

"What shall we do with the body?"

"Leave it where it is for the blessed jury to see it; they'll be able to see further into a mile-stone than they could have done had we moved it."

"Exactly; and we shall have the credit of being very clever officers for our pains; come on, I'm quite tired, and want to get to bed, and I can't while this fellow hangs about; he must be locked up safely for the night."

"Yes, yes; come along," said another, to the head officer; "we can make this all right."

"Very well; now, then, are you all ready? Now, my amiable looking cut-throat, will you please to move? and to move at our pace, too, for a short walk, and then we'll have a coach; we'll endeavour to indulge you as well as ourselves."

"Mabel," said the mendicant, "remember who I am."

"I know not."

"Good God! can I look upon this as natural depravity or perversion of nature? What can be the meaning of this? I have different motives for my refusal to you of which I could satisfy you at another time, but not now."

"And I have a sufficient motive, too."

"But it is only to speak the truth."

"The truth ain't always easy to be

spoken," said the officer : " and it seems to me your gammon's no us; the young woman hasn't been over well used, and I myself think she would not be acting wisely to commit perjury on account of you— you ought to be ashamed of yourself."

" Well, Mabel, since your mind is made up, remember I have yet a secret that I leave as a legacy to you, but not in your keeping."

" Threats will not do; my lips are sealed; do justice first, and then expect justice in return."

" Depend upon it that is a very excellent maxim ; do as you would be done by, you know, is an old copy-book injunction, and as such it will remain, for nobody ever thinks of doing what they are told."

" I am ready," said the mendicant, turning to the officers.

" And so are we "

" Mabel, be at the police-office to-morrow, and clear me of this foul imputation."

" Where are my friends ?"

These were the last words of Mabel that reached the ear of the mendicant; he was hurried along the passage until they came to the street-door, when there was a stoppage for a moment.

" What's the matter now ?" said one.

" The door."

" What door?"

" Why the one we knocked down when we came in."

" Can't you step over it ?"

" Yes."

" Do so, then."

" What shall we do about it ? It will be open all night, and the place will be exposed to every one."

" If anybody goes in there, I'll warrant they'll soon walk out again. A murdered body is not a very enticing spectacle, and certainly not one anybody would feel inclined to steal."

" It certainly is not."

" Cannot we put up the door again ?"

" No, no."

" But the young woman——"

" Oh, bother the young woman. Well, you may as well just put it up, if you can; it may keep some of the wind out, but nothing else."

" Just bear a hand, Jem."

" Here you are," replied Jem; and the two men began to lift up the door, which they caused to be placed against the open door-way, and they all departed.

## CHAPTER LXIV.

THE MOMENT OF TERROR.—MABEL'S ESCAPE FROM THE RUINED HOUSE.—THE RESCUE.

MABEL heard the retreating footsteps of the officers with a trance-like feeling. She was scarcely aware of her own position and her own freedom. She heard their steps become fainter and fainter, and then she thought she could hear the footsteps of the mendicant; she could, she imagined, distinguish them from the others.

It was a painful feeling that she remembered slowly that she was alone; that, in fact, she was worse than alone; because there was the mangled corpse lying huddled up in a heap not far from her.

Was the mendicant really gone? It seemed a dream; the whole of the occurrence a dream of the most hideous aspect that ever crept over the waking senses of human being; a dream that made the blood run cold, and the flesh creep into knots. No, no; hideous and horrible as it was, yet it was real; there was nothing but what was plain matter of fact.

She listened with breathless attention to ascertain if that fearful man should return to place a bar between her and hope and liberty.

No, she heard no one, no sound—no footsteps reached her ear. She was free; but hark ! the heavy tread of a man is heard approaching.

She listened with dread and anxiety. It came nearer and nearer each moment, but it brought no pleasing emotion to her heart; she thought not the footstep might belong to one who would free her, had there been any bar existing to prevent her quitting the house.

" I am free," she thought, " I am free; and yet what may not this sound portend ?"

It came closer and closer, until within a few paces of the street-door. She paused in breathless agitation, lest her chance should be gone.

Her breathing was suspended, and then she heard the footstep pause at the street-door, for a moment or two, and then come up the steps, and then no further noise directed her attention,

" God of heaven !" she half muttered to herself, " is he come back, or are there any more intrusions ? What may I not be subjected to yet ? But yet they cannot attempt any violence or imprisonment; they have no motive for keeping me against my will."

The individual, whoever he was, had stopped before the door from curiosity, for now he descended the steps, and moved away in the contrary direction whence he came.

"Thank Heaven for that," she exclaimed. "What have I suffered since I have been here? I am free! yes, I am free! Surely there is no hindrance to my leaving this horrible place."

She went into the room again, and sought for the bed upon which lay the only things she had in the way of covering for protecting herself in the open air. It was merely what she had wrapped herself up in when she had left Morton Hall.

So protected she came to the door of that room where she had seen so much crime committed—a deed of the deepest guilt that could be perpetrated.

Here she paused. Her heart beat violently. Could she cross that room, and in all probability come in contact with that dreadful corpse, all besmirched with blood? It made her tremble to think of it. She could not go, for if she escaped the body, there was a pool of blood right across the floor—this she must tread into to go out.

"Horrible! horrible!" she exclaimed. "What shall I do? What shall I do? To walk in the blood of a fellow-creature is horrible; and yet, what can I do?"

This was more easily asked than answered; indeed, it seemed as if, in order to avoid stepping in the ensanguined stream, she must forego the chance of liberty that was now offered to her. She could not refuse to profit by the occasion; but she shuddered to think of what she must encounter ere she reached the door of that dreadful house.

Having made up her mind to encounter terrors that were to be met—for she knew they were but imaginary ones, though they took so firm a hold upon her that she could not shake the feeling of horror off—she stepped slowly and cautiously along the room, but had scarcely got half way across when she felt her foot slip along the floor a short way.

A suppressed scream of terror came to her lips, and died away before she gave utterance to it; for she knew she had stepped into the pool of blood—so cold, so slimy, that a chill of horror crept through her frame.

Great as was her terror, she could scarcely move to escape the clotted gore that lay on the dappled boards; but, by a sudden impulse, she made a violent effort, and rushed into the passage, where the cold air that came in at the door somewhat recovered her.

She paused, and leaned her head on her hand, as she supported herself against the cold wall. The sound of some distant passenger, however, recalled her to herself, and she crept cautiously to the door.

It had been placed so as to lean against the doorway, and so keep itself up by means of its own weight, and it was placed very awkwardly by the men for Mabel's escape.

She could not get out without moving it, and to do that, she must turn it on one side, and open it partially.

To do this would be a thing of some difficulty, and require almost more strength than she could at that time boast of. She was weak, and certainly not in good health, for her nerves were terribly shattered, and her appearance much altered, as may be imagined, and she felt herself much weaker than she had been.

However, opened the door must be, and she determined to set about it immediately; therefore, she made the attempt by lifting it round, and, after much exertion, succeeded in doing so,

"Thank Heaven, I am free," she exclaimed, in a half audible voice; "I am free once more."

"Eh, marm? Did you speak to me, marm? Shall I call a coach, or a wheelbarrow?"

At that moment the door, which she had left standing on little more than a balance, was thrown down by a gust of wind which swept through the passage. It came down with a dreadful bang, that made Mabel start involuntarily, as well as the man who had spoken so suddenly to her.

"Heaven help me!" she exclaimed, "what is that?"

"That, marm? Why that—d—d if I know, marm; it's a cussed sight worse nor shutting a hundred coach-doors all at once. I'm blessed if I don't think the man in the moon has dropped his tooth out."

Mabel recollected now what it was, and said to herself, but audibly enough to the man,

"It is the street-door; yes, it is the street-door. I am glad I am free."

"Ahem, marm! if that's the street-door, all I got to say is, that there ain't nobody dead nor asleep in that house, for it would have brought the dead to life. Why, it would have waked up Sleeping Jemmy. He used to sleep in a manner that beat all I have heered on. Why, marm, you believe me or not, just as you please, but, on the honour of a hackney coachman, we bored a hole through his ear with a red-hot tobacco-pipe, and left the bowl in his ear to make him look ornamental."

Mabel paid no attention to the con-

versation of the man, but turned away be-
[illegible] his anecdote, which,

[illegible]

[illegible]

So saying, he turned away, and walked
onwards, intent upon some small matter
that to him was one of life and death importance and interest.

Poor Mabel, she hurried on from the
vicinity of the house in which she had seen
enough of crime and horror to appal the
stoutest heart. She never heeded where
she was going, she only thought of getting
away from that place of horrors.

The morning air came cool; the streets
were damp and misty; scarce a human
being was to be seen about; chilly, raw,
and wet, a more miserable night could
scarce have been found for any purpose in
the London climate.

What she was to do, or where she was
to go for shelter, she knew not; but,
unable to devise any scheme, she kept
walking on until she felt fit to drop on the
earth.

There were no places open but a few late
houses, and into these she could not venture
to go. At length she came to a complete
stand still—she could not go any further.

There was an archway near at hand, and
in to this she tottered, and upon a step of a
door in it she sat down, to rest herself and
recover from the fatigue she had so unavoid-
ably encountered, completely-exhausted.

Thus she remained. A sense of great
fatigue came over her, and she leaned back
to rest her head. Nature had done her best
to this moment, and then she fainted
away.

\*　　\*　　\*　　\*

How long she remained in this state she
could not tell, but when she awoke from
her trance, she felt herself being pulled
about by some persons.

One was smacking the palms of her
hands, and one was bathing her head with
vinegar, while one poked a burnt feather
up her nose, and a fourth alternately
endeavoured to make her sniff and swallow
hartshorn.

"Ah," said a voice, with a fat sigh,
"poor thing—poor thing, she really is
beautiful."

"Certainly, I don't mean to deny that,
Mrs. Smith, only there's no denying it—
there's something very romantic about
beauty. I'm not fond of simple beauties."

"My husband used to say——"

"Now ladies—ladies."

"Well, Mother Clattershins?"

"No conversation about husbands, if
[illegible]."

[illegible]

[illegible] can bear witness to
that fact; you have a husband, Mrs.
Clattershins."

"Very good; and did anybody ever
hear me pay any attention to him?"

"No, no—never."

"Did anybody ever see me accost him
when he spoke, unless it was to tell him
he was a fool?"

"No, that is all very true."

"Well, ladies, I take pride in myself."

"And so you ought."

"I'll let the men know we ain't slaves,
and that Rule Britannia don't wear
petticoats and a three-pronged toasting-
fork for nothing. I never give an advantage
away—that's my maxim, at any rate."

"A very good one, too."

"It's one my mother told me afore I
was married—that if I wanted to kill my
husband in the surest way, I had only to
worry him, and if he were at close work,
to keep it up for years, and this I have
done, and I have nearly received my reward. My husband's getting weakly and
fretful. Yes—yes, he's going, that's one
great comfort."

"So it is. Mine's gone."

"Has he, now?"

"Oh, yes."

"How lucky you are. Well, I'm sure
you are the most fortunate woman under
heaven."

"They do say I'm favoured."

"Do you intend getting married again?"

"Oh, dear, no, unless——"

"What?"

"There happens to be property in the
case, and then, you know, I might be
tempted to part with my liberty."

This produced a titter, as the individual
speaking was a red-faced, blowsy woman,
of about eight-and-forty, and the very idea
that a man could look at her and think of
marriage was too truly ridiculous.

"About this poor girl—she seems to be
coming to."

"Yes, she'll be carried up stairs after
a moment or two. She can remain here.
She'll do very well; but we must be very
cautious."

"Yes, I think she'll do. She looks well
enough—she's fresh and young, two great
qualities for the town. I don't know how
it is, but I find fresh young girls always
succeed the best."

"Yes, that's generally the case with
people; I don't know how it is, but it is so."

"See, poor thing, she opens her eyes—give her some of this, it will warm her, and do her good."

As she spoke, she forced some spirits and water, of which she had been drinking, into Mabel's mouth, and compelled her to swallow it. Half choked, she was soon brought to, and placed in a chair before the fire.

She looked around her, and found she was in a room with oddly-assorted furniture; there were several females in it, but Mabel could bestow but little thought or scrutiny on them; they were muttering and talking to themselves, and she could barely hear what they said, and that she did not understand.

"She's come to, now," said one. "She has been deserted, no doubt. I dare say she could eat a bit. Are you hungry, my dear—will you have something to eat?"

"No, no," said Mabel. "Tell me where am I. Where am I—how came I here?"

"You ask too many questions in one breath, my dear; you'll only over exert yourself."

"You are quite safe with us; we'll take care of you, for a day or two, till you can shift for yourself. Be quiet, now; will you lie down?"

"Thank you, thank you," said Mabel; "I am grateful to you for your kindness; but tell how came I here? I have no recollection of coming here."

"How should you? You were insensible, and lying on a door-step; the watch would have taken you to the watchhouse for drunkenness; but I knew it was a fit."

"Ah, you are very good and kind to me; I was quite exhausted, and could go no further."

"Ah, it is as I say," remarked another who stood by her; "she's been seduced."

"Have you any friends in London?"

"None, none."

"Were you born here?"

"No, no."

"And you don't live here?"

"No, I have been brought here against my will."

"Ah, just as I thought. But now you are destitute, and wouldn't like to face your friends?"

"Yes; I would desire nothing better than to meet them; if you'll aid me in that, then I shall be under great obligations to you, and my friends will not be niggardly in their reward to you for your kindness."

"Poor thing; she imagines they'd be glad to see her. Well-a-day, well-a-day! My dear, we will talk over this matter more tomorrow. Here's some nice tea and toast.

I'm going to have my breakfast; I've been up all night at a party, and before I go to bed, I shall have some breakfast—you may have some with me, if you will."

Mabel was placed in a large chair, and some tea-things were brought in and laid on the table, some toast was placed before the fire, and some ham on the table. The fat female seemed to have made up her mind to enjoy herself.

"I think, Mary," she said, to one of the girls, "I will have my breakfast alone this morning; this young woman and I will have ours together."

"Very well," was the only reply; "very well, then, I and Margaret can have ours up-stairs."

"Yes."

The young women left the room. They were coarse, showy young women, with a great deal of tawdry dress; but Mabel could not notice much, she was too poorly, too terrified, and too much bewildered to think of anything, save that she was safe from that dreadful man.

Grateful she was for the care that had caused her to be carried to a decent place: and where she could enjoy the comfort of a warm fire and food, things she had not felt since she had been forced away from her home by the mendicant; and then, when she recollected the scenes that had taken place, she shuddered visibly.

Here, however, was a change—a good fire, a kettle, making the hob musical with its vocal sounds, a warm carpet, a fire that threw out a good heat, with food on the tabel—what, under the circumstances, could she desire more?

---

## CHAPTER LXV.

THE CHANGE OF SCENE.—THE COARSE, FAT
WOMAN.—MABEL'S NEW FRIENDS.

MABEL was certainly conscious of the change that had taken place in her position. She knew she was in the hands of strangers. and that she had been rescued from a very dangerous and uncomfortable situation; for she could now well remember sitting down on a door-step, beneath an archway, perfectly exhausted, and there she must have been found, and brought thither.

"Did you," she inquired, "find me?"

"Yes; I and some of the gals were coming home, and we saw a watchman shaking you by the shoulder, telling you to get up and walk quietly."

"I don't recollect it."

"No; I should be surprised if you did; for, as I told him, you were much more likely to be in a fit; but he insisted you were drunk. The beast was hardly able to stand. Well, we took you from him, and carried you here, where you have remained until you became sensible."

"How much am I indebted to you!"

"Oh! we shall make that all right by-and-by. Come, eat; you are half famished, I can tell. I have only to look in your face, and find that out."

"I have had but very little these two or hree days; but I have been too terrified o eat."

"I dare say, but that will all wear off in time—quite wear off, I assure you."

"There is no doubt of that," said Mabel, becoming drowsy before the fire; "I feel it now."

"Eat; here is plenty; the tea is warm and good, and after this you will sleep very well, indeed. I am sure of it. I always do."

Mabel eat and drank as she was enjoined by the woman, who talked of a variety of matters, very little of which Mabel heard or understood.

MABEL ATTENDED BY THE BROTHEL KEEPER'S ASSISTANTS.

The effects of the fire, the warmth of the room, and the reaction from the cold she had felt in the open air, all tended to make her extremely sleepy; and it was only now and then she was able to reply to the questions put to her by the woman who was taking so much care of her.

She had not power to make those discriminating notices of what was said and done by the woman. There might have been some few floating notions in her mind that all was not as right as it should be: but she was young, innocent, and unsuspicious, and, moreover, she was grateful—very grateful for the kindness that she had received at the hands of the female.

Mabel's heart would never allow her to think evil of any one who had done good. It was a species of ingratitude she could not bring herself to commit. She sat by the fire. Each moment rendered her more and more drowsy.

"You are very sleepy?"

"Yes, very."

"And you shall go to bed in a few minutes. One more cup, and another slice of ham."

"No, no."

"I say, yes. I am mistress here, and I will have you make a good breakfast. Why, I have eaten four slices to your one, and I am sure I am no immoderate eater."

This was hardly the fact, for the lady had eaten enormously, and drunk like a fish—of tea, of course—which tea was somewhat qualified and diluted with a little alcohol. Mabel's had a dose of something in it, which, however, she noticed not; her mind was too much absorbed in half-formed reflections upon the scene of horror that was that evening perpetrated.

"I am very sleepy," said Mabel.

"And so am I," said the woman, who had just dropped her last piece of toast out of her hand on the floor, and nodded her head with such a jerk, that she awoke herself by the pain it gave her neck.

"Where can I lie down? for I fear I shall fall in the fire, if I remain here any longer."

"You can go at once. You shall have the little bed-room that runs out of this."

"Thank you."

"No matter; you are welcome—very welcome. 'We will lead a life of pleasure—without mixture, without measure!'" said the coarse female, as she dozed before the fire, and woke up suddenly, in a very good humour.

Then rising, she walked to the door, and opened it, saying as she did so,—

"There it is, as neat and nice a little snuggery as ever you stepped into. I'm sure you will sleep there."

"Yes; I am sure of it," said Mabel, feeling herself compelled to say something, though she was so sleepy and fatigued she was scarce able to stand.

"You'll find it suit you."

"Yes, yes."

"And you'd like to see your friends here, I dare say?"

"Yes; I should like to see my friends; that's the only thing I now want," said Mabel.

"Ay, friends—friends of every degree. No—I mean rogues—rogues of every degree, ain't it?"

It is questionable if Mabel would not have said yes to this; for she was incapable of discovering what was pernicious or not in this woman's conversati; but it so happened that the female was herself drowsy, and did not exactly require an answer to any of her speeches.

"There," she said, pointing to the bed; "that's a peculiar bed that; it's seen some adventures."

"It's very good."

"Yes; it's very good; and you'll say so before a week's over," she said.

"A week?"

"Yes; maybe three days."

"Three days?"

"Yes; that depends upon whether you're a fool or not."

"What did you say?"

"Nothing, nothing; but a good many country gals have made their fortunes on that bed, and when they came here they soon began to see town life."

"I shall be glad to see the country again," said Mabel.

"Gammon!"

"And my friends, too."

"Gammon! But you can lay yourself down; you will soon be asleep, and then as happy as a king, and I, like the queen of trumps, as I am, will follow suit."

With such like conversation did the coarse female lead Mabel to the bed; but it was unnoticed, for she was too far gone in fatigue, both of body and mind, to be mindful of anything that was not forced upon the mental faculties by any display peculiarly suspicious.

Poor Mabel threw herself upon the bed, and her companion threw some clothes over her, for she had fallen asleep as soon as her head had touched the pillow, and she was as much insensible as asleep.

Then, taking a sleepy look at her, she muttered,—

"Yes; she is pretty, and my Lord Dildrum will give me at least fifty pounds for my discovery, and reward the girl herself; and who knows, if she be not a fool, and stand in her own light, she might come in for a good thing, for his lordship may take a liking to the girl, and keep her. More unlikely things than that have happened before now."

So saying, she left the room, and turning the key upon Mabel, with a knowing wink, she said,—

"Safe keep, safe find."

Then she looked out of the window for a few moments, and, as she pulled the curtains on one side, a stream of light came through, and fell upon the floor.

"Broad day, by the holy poker! Well, we do keep it up, at all events—there's nothing like it. Keep the pot a biling. I rayther think this is life. There'll be plenty of time to set things all in trim before the green 'un wakes up. Ha! ha! she won't wake this side of eight o'clock to-night. She's had a little drop of laudanum, that will quiet her and do her good; besides, it's an excellent thing.

"I wonder what she did, now, upon the step of the door. She had fainted, I suppose. She thought she had come to the worst. Perhaps she had been cast off by her lover—perhaps turned adrift by her friends.

"Ah, well! it don't matter; all's one a hundred years hence, and I am precious tired; so here goes!"

As she spoke she closed the curtains, and undressed herself previous to retiring for the night—that is, the day of other people who were more legitimately engaged than she. She then threw herself upon the bed, and fell asleep, after muttering some incoherent speeches.

------

## CHAPTER LXVI.

### THE CUSTOMS OF THE STRANGE HOUSE AND ITS INHABITANTS. — MABEL'S ALARM AND ESCAPE.

ALL was now quiet in the house; no sound was to be heard throughout the various rooms in that place. Other houses were alive with inhabitants; but, then, they were closed to all comers at the usual hour of rest. But not so this. On the contrary, it might be said by the inhabitants, that

"—— Night has grown our day,"

In this case, it was strictly true; and that, too, of nearly all the inhabitants of the house.

Those, indeed, who held the position of servants or drudges in this house were up before the others; but that was all; for they were hours after others of the same class elsewhere, on every side of them.

It was near eleven o'clock before any one was astir in this place; and then the fires began to be lighted. The servants were recalled to life by the fact that it was getting on for midday, at least.

It was near this latter hour that the fat woman, who had locked Mabel in, was awakened by the servant, who came in with a hot meat breakfast.

"Ma'am, ma'am!" said the drudge, as she shook the curtains; "ma'am, 'tis breakfast time."

"Oh, dear!" said the drowsy fat female.

"Very true, as you observe, ma'am; but the steak will be cold, if you do."

"Eh?"

"Breakfast is ready, ma'am."

"No, no; don't be in such a hurry," said the coarse female, in alarm, and opening her eyes.

"No, ma'am."

"But it's so uncomfortable to be woke up out of a comfortable nap. I wish you hadn't got it ready, and I had slept another hour, or, may be, two."

"Well, ma'am, you said twelve."

"Yes, I did."

"Then, what was I to do?"

"Oh, bother! you are always a trouble, night or day. However, I must eat it; so give us hold of it. There is one consolation about it—that I can go to sleep again."

"Yes, ma'am, certainly."

"And I will."

"Very good, ma'am."

So saying, the drudge placed the tray on the bed, steaks and all; while the fat female waddled about, till she righted herself and sat up; and then, drawing the things towards her, she began to eat with an appetite and voracity quite astounding for one so recently asleep.

It did not take long before she had finished; and, pushing the tray from her, she again scrambled into the hole she had been sleeping in, and in a few more minutes she was snoring again.

Thus things continued for a couple of hours more; when the drudge came in again, and shook her by the arm for some moments, without causing the least approach to a wake-up; but at length, she turned, and growled out,—

"What now?"

"It's going on for three, ma'am."

"I can't help it."

"No, ma'am; but you are wanted."

"Who wants me?"

"Lord Dildrum."

"Eh?"

"Lord Dildrum."

"Oh, Lord Dildrum?"

"Yes, ma'am."

"Is he waiting?"

"Yes, ma'am."

"Then, I must get up."

"Yes, ma'am. He wants to see you directly."

"Go and tell him I'll be there directly," said the fat, frouzy woman, who began to huddle about, and dress herself with all the expedition she was able, and finished by wrapping herself up in a large dressing-gown.

Thus accoutred she descended to the parlour, to have an interview with the roué peer, where we will leave her, and return to Mabel.

It was long after dark before Mabel awoke; she had slept a fair twelve hours.

It was near eight o'clock the next evening before she awoke.

And then a sense of drowsiness and oppression came over her senses, and had she been left to her own choice, she would have fallen off to sleep.

"Come, come," said the frouzy dame, who was now dressed in her gayest colours. "It is time to get up."

"It is quite dark," murmured Mabel.

"Dark! yes, you've slept all day."

"Where am I?"

"At home."

"At home!" repeated Mabel; and then, rousing up, she looked around, and repeated the word "Home!"

"Yes, and a very good home too; and one you may have at your own price, if you know how to earn the money. But come, you must have some food, you are nearly starving; and then, when you are quite well and refreshed, we will talk of these matters."

She left the room; and Mabel, becoming somewhat recovered from her drowsiness, got up.

After having washed her face in cold water, she felt herself much better, and began to recall to her mind the events that had happened since that awful event preceding her escape from the dreadful house.

One by one they came upon her mind, in distinct features.

However, there was but little time left her. She was joined by a young woman of coarse manners, whose conversation, if not positively objectionable, had nothing to recommend it to one educated and possessed of the native good sense and purity of heart that Mabel had.

She descended the stairs, and was shown into the parlour, where there were several persons, and all sat down to a hearty meat supper, or dinner, whichever she chose to call it; in fact, it was their dinner.

Here the conversation became disgusting to Mabel, who began to feel some indefinite alarm lest she should get into some even more desperate hands than even those who so lately held a sway over her.

The supper over, the same woman, who seemed from her manners, and the way she spoke to those about her, to be a person of some influence in the house, beckoned her out, and then, as she approached her, said,—

"Come this way, my dear."

Mabel followed her to a small back room, which was very handsomely furnished.

"Sit down, my dear," said the woman, as she drew a couch before the fire, and placed some wine on the table.

Mabel obeyed.

"You are yet, I dare say, scarcely recovered enough to be aware of the advantages that are offered you, or what is best for you. You are not very well."

"I am not, indeed."

"Take some wine ; it will do you good."

"I cannot."

"Don't you like it?"

"Yes, but I never take much."

"That is not much—a glass!"

"What I had last night has left a dreadful head-ache, and I am afraid of it."

"Well, just as you please. I was about to say the other room had too many visitors, and you'd probably like to be by yourself a bit, so I brought you here."

"Thank you." said Mabel.

"You are a very handsome girl," said the old woman; "and if I were only half as young and handsome, I should consider my fortune was made."

"Indeed! you attach more importance to outward show than I do," said Mabel.

"Many a girl has been ruined by her beauty."

"It may be true."

"Then why not made?"

"It may be so ; but what has that to do with me?" inquired Mabel.

"This much; I only am showing you how you may lead a life of pleasure and gaiety, and make your fortune before many years are over your head."

"I do not desire."

"Psha ! psha !"

"You have acted kindly," said Mabel, in a calm tone, "for which I am obliged to you."

"Obliged !"

"Yes; and, as soon as I can find my friends, I promise you you shall be rewarded for your trouble."

"You promise !"

"I can do no more at present."

"Well, well, that's cool, at all events; but we shall soon alter all that ; come, now, young woman, don't attempt to carry the thing with too high a hand here, because we ain't used to it, and we may kick."

"I really do not comprehend you."

"Oh, indeed !"

"No; but if you have any bad purpose in view, you had better defer it altogether, for to none will I submit."

"Indeed! and who has any ill intentions towards you? I only wish you to become a decent, respectable girl, and not one as goes about fainting on people's steps."

"If you will enable me to reach my friends, I can promise you a far higher reward than any that you can gain by acting in a contrary course."

"Ah, that's all very well; but you had better think of it before you refuse his lordship's offer."

"His lordship's offer !"

"Yes."

"Who ?"

"Lord Dildrum."

As she spoke she left the room, leaving poor Mabel in a state of agitating excitement. She now plainly saw that she had fallen into bad hands, and, therefore, determined to exert herself to the utmost to counteract any attempt that might be made by these people.

She was left alone for two or three hours. She had tried the door, and found it was locked. This was a cause of alarm to her, for why should that be, unless they intended some harm to her?

In a short time she heard some footsteps approaching the door, which was suddenly opened, and a middle-aged man walked in.

There was an air of reckless foppery about him, which sat ill upon a bloated and blotchy form. His hair was carefully combed and curled, and his dress of the most exquisite pattern that was known.

He bowed to Mabel, advanced carelessly towards her, and he was about to take her hand, when he paused, for the look she cast upon him was one that caused even him to start, and think he had met with some one who would be no easy conquest.

"What, my charming creature," he began, having recovered the first check—"my dear rustic, be not alarmed; we will here sit, and have a charming conversation."

"You will, I presume, as a gentleman, withdraw, my lord, when I tell you you are an intruder."

"Ah, ah! I see you are shy; I'm used to it; I don't object to it, to a certain extent only."

"I will not hear any more of this, my lord, if that be your title, which your conduct would seem to deny."

As she spoke her features glowed with anger, and she made a sudden spring to the door, opened it, and with a light step reached the street-door; and she heard the slam of this, and yet no signs of alarm.

But this she believed could not last long; she crossed the road and ran up a short street, and crossed into another. She was soon lost to herself, and she could not tell where she was, nor how far she might be from those who had persecuted her.

It was very late, in fact, near morning, when she escaped from the house; and, after an hour or two's walk, she found herself, after sunrise, in the neighbourhood of London, in the outskirts.

How she came there she knew not, but she was very fatigued and cold. Not knowing where to go, she sat down in a doorway to rest, and to shelter herself from the wind that blew so cold.

---

## CHAPTER LXVII.

THE FATHER AND DAUGHTER.—THE DOWNWARD PATH OF CRIME.—THE COMPTER.

THE party of officers who had taken the mendicant prisoner, were in search of a notorious offender, whom they believed to be the principal of a gang of daring and unscrupulous men, who hesitated at neither robbery nor murder.

The unfortunate gentleman who had been murdered was a country gentleman, who had only recently come to town, with the idea of discovering some relative whom he desired to see. It was a female member of his own family; in fact, his daughter. He was a man of some wealth and rank in the county in which he lived.

Mr. Charles Pearson was a gentleman farmer and mill owner, and had amassed some property during his lifetime. He had a decent fortune left him by his own father, and now had nearly doubled the amount by judgment and skill in his avocations, which were to him but amusements.

He married early, and had but one child, a young and beautiful girl, who was the pride of his heart, and the pleasure of his declining days; he loved her as father never loved child, and she, too, was well worthy of a father's affection; she was dutiful and affectionate.

But the day came when the undivided affection of the daughter was shared, and the father was not the only object that she looked up to with love and for protection.

To old Pearson this was a day he could scarce bear to think of, and yet come it must. That day must come, he knew, as well as that of his death, and yet he scarce knew which of the two he would have preferred.

Her mother was dead, had been so for some years, and the widower was thus thrown, for domestic happiness, upon the resources of the daughter, who well acquitted herself of the task.

Thus several years passed in peace, happiness, and felicity.

The day came when the thoughts and affections of Emily Pearson were divided with her father. One day, a young gentleman, the son of a man of rank in the army, came there upon an invitation to shoot over the manor, a sport he was very fond of—a sport for which he would have made almost any sacrifice.

During his stay at Mr. Pearson's he was much stricken with the beauty of Emily Pearson. He watched her, and, from the expression of her features, saw she was as beautiful in endowments of an intellectual character, as she was in personal charms.

Irresistibly attracted together by the secret impulses of their nature, they soon formed a silent and sincere attachment to each other. These feelings were in being before they were well aware of their existence; she loved before their love was apparent to themselves.

Such a passion has no bounds, and no impediment can separate those who are united by such bonds, for they madly loved before they told each other the tale of their affections.

This, however, was told; they mutually embraced and swore to love eternally—to love in good and evil—never to separate, but to live and die for each other, and with each other.

Such were the passionate terms of their engagement. Such was the force of young love—a love so pure and with so little alloy, that neither at that moment dreamed of aught that was wrong.

But another day came, and the young gentleman began to reflect that he was already contracted to a lady of high birth and rank; that to disappoint her would be to involve his father in endles quarrels; also, it would be the ruin of himself as well as the young lady who had been introduced to the world as his intended wife.

What could he do? This was a question much easier to ask than answer. What could he do? He could not debar himself the society of the beautiful Emily Pearson.

This is what he ought to have done; but, no; he knew she loved him, and to leave a woman who loved him, seemed a piece of self-denial unknown to human nature.

What to do, he knew not; he could not neglect either; he loved the one, and he had scarcely less affection for the other; but, at the same time, when the question of interest and expediency was called into question, he decided—the wavering mind of the lover turned the beam against the happiness of Emily Pearson.

He had determined upon seducing the confiding girl, who thus loved him and told him so.

It was a base deed, and yet he resolved to do it—coolly and deliberately resolved to it; and what he did resolve to do, he accomplished, and Emily Pearson was a ruined beaut .

Thus far accomplished, and all was safe, and he then ordered her to leave the paternal roof and follow him to London.

This she did, in the full belief and anticipation of her being there united to the object of her desire, when she could return and brave her father's anger, and beg his forgiveness. But that happy day was never to arrive.

When once in London, the novelty of his situation soon wore off, and he looked upon the unfortunate Emily Pearson as his mistress only, and he never intended it should be otherwise.

However, he was discovered by Mr. Pearson, who upbraided him, and opened the whole matter before his friends, who at once discarded him for being a deliberate seducer, and the destroyer of innocence in the most deliberate manner.

The marriage was put off altogether, and, in fact, he was turned adrift, and forbidden the house of his own father.

Then it was that the evil in his nature shone out most conspicuously. At least, he seemed to be thoroughly vicious. There was not one crime that he did not seem capable of committing. He hitherto had no motive for doing wrong, because he had an abundance of everything, and that removed him from the necessity of doing aught to supply his own wants.

But now that he was no longer the same in position and society—and now that he had no income, save such as he himself could procure, there was nothing that he would not accomplish, or attempt to accomplish, by some means.

He had now lost all cast, and was universally hated by society; but he refused to give up the cause of all the mischief. He would not part with the unfortunate Emily, whom he kept in want and poverty in lodgings.

Often did Mr. Pearson endeavour to find her out, but he could not do so; this criminal prevented it by the secrecy of his motions, for he would not even take money as a bribe to give her up.

He did not love her now; he hated her as the cause of all his misfortunes; but he kept her in misery, and wretchedness, and rags, to gratify his feelings of revenge both against herself and father, whom he swore some day he would destroy.

Often would the money that was offered as a reward for her have been of the greatest use to him; nay he had wanted bread—but no; he would not do it, because he should be able to still feel he had a deep and diabolical mode of revenging himself upon the unfortunate Mr. Pearson.

Often would this man go out into the

highways, and stop passengers, and rob them of their purses. He never took anything but money, and that he would have, somehow or other.

In time he did the same thing in London, in the unfrequented parts, and there he robbed people with impunity and success.

His daring and address soon procured him associates, and these of a similar character to his own.

This could not pass unnoticed, for the officers, having received intelligence of the occurrences, were on the alert to capture him and his gang, wherever they could find him or them.

Mr. Pearson, at length, almost despaired of finding his daughter, when one morning he received the following note :—

"Sir,—If you will bring two hundred pounds to the corner of —— street, and wait for half-an-hour after nine o'clock at night, and then follow the man who shall speak to you, until you come to a house, you may see me and your daughter; but, unless the money be forthcoming, and secrecy observed, you'll see neither.

"Yours, &c.,

"Philip."

This letter was opened by Mr. Pearson, who at once resolved to accept the terms; and, placing the two hundred pounds into his pocket, he determined to go to the spot indicated; but before he did so, he had the precaution to inform a party of officers of the occurrence.

"You had better not trust yourself with him, sir," said one; "you'll find he will rob you."

"Oh, no; I don't think that; besides, I want to find my daughter, and if he get not the money he will ill-use her."

"Well, what had we better do? Watch you at a distance—eh?" suggested one.

"That will be the best."

"And when you enter the house, we'll come in after you?"

"You had better not."

"What shall we do?"

"Wait till I and my daughter come out, and then you can go in and take him; he deserves it—villain as he is."

"He is, indeed, sir. I have half a fear that we shall miss him, somehow or other."

"Oh, no! you cannot, in consequence of this arrangement."

"That may be; but he has the devil's luck and his own," said the officer.

When nine o'clock came, Mr. Pearson went to the spot indicated, and though it rained hard, yet he resolved to brave it out, and stopped the required time—indeed, more than an hour over the time appointed by the villain.

It was just as he was giving the whole affair up as a bad job, that suddenly a man, whom he had noticed on several occasions had passed him, came up to him and said,—

"Is your name Pearson?"

"It is."

"Follow me, then."

And, without any further conversation, he walked away at a quick rate. Mr. Pearson followed at the same pace.

The officers had been concealed in a neighbouring house, and there waited the departure of Mr. Pearson. They feared, if they were seen, the person who was appointed to meet Mr. Pearson would not take any notice; but, seeing them, would walk away.

To avoid this it was they posted themselves in a house, and it was to enable the thieves to watch any person about the neighbourhood, so that there would be no possibility of a surprise.

Seeing no one at hand, the man came up to Mr. Pearson, after he had watched well, and uttered the words above.

Mr. Pearson followed the man for upwards of an hour, when they were joined by several others, when Mr. Pearson seemed alarmed, and endeavoured to get away, when he was suddenly seized, and hurried onwards with a velocity that outstripped the officers, and threw them out.

They then came to the house where the mendicant had confined Mabel, not knowing that any one was there; and then committed the murder.

Terrified at the sudden apparition of Mabel, they fled, and afterwards the mendicant came in.

The rest is known.

The officers who had been thrown out, wandered about for some time, and feeling that they could not be far off, they searched about, and found his hat and gloves. They concluded that he had gone in there, and the house being a deserted one, and seeing a light, they knocked, and finding that no answer was returned, burst it open.

"Come along, my lad; sure you are in for it."

"You have done a nice thing."

"I have done nothing."

"Oh, I dare say not."

"Killing a man is nothing with you: only it is something with other people," replied an officer.

"I have killed no man."

"That man died, I suppose?"

"I suppose so too."

"And not killed?"

"He appeared to be so to me."

"And yet you didn't do it!"

"Well, that's good. There's a man dead—a murdered man, and in his own blood. You are there, and have no right to be there, and yet you did not do the deed?"

"No, I did not."

"And who did?"

"How can I tell?"

"Well, if you can't, who can? It strikes me forcibly that you'll be considered the murderer."

"I did not. I never laid hands upon the man, and was as much surprised at the presence of the body as you, and, probably, much more so."

"Ha! ha! Tell them that to-morrow, and then at the Old Bailey. Depend upon it the story will not save you from the gallows, so you had better think of some other tale to satisfy a Middlesex jury; for that won't do."

The mendicant said nothing more; he saw it was useless to talk to the officers, who would not believe a word that he uttered; but began to think what he should do on the morrow.

This was no easy matter to determine, and he gave up the attempt, and soon after arrived at the lock-up-house.

For security's sake, he was lodged in the Compter, and when he arrived there, he created a sensation.

"What's that the highwayman as robbed old Pearson of his daughter?" cried one of the turnkeys.

"Not him; but another."

"Oh! one of the same sort?"

"Yes; belongs to the same gang," said the officer.

"Anything particular against him?"

"Yes; killed a man."

"Who?"

"Pearson himself."

"The devil!"

"He did."

"The vagabone! We'll have a morning concert for him, then, over the way in the church tower."

"Safe."

"Don't deny it, I suppose?"

"Don't he, though."

"I'm blessed if I know what people can expect other people to be made of when they tell such outrageous lies. I never heard the equal of that fellow, Broad-bottomed Jack, in all my life; he'll beat anybody at a lie."

"Well, what did he do then?"

"Oh! why he boned about eighteen pair of soles, and hid them between his shirt and his skin."

"A cool waiscoat they'd make."

"They were warm; so people said."

"Well, what did he do?"

"Why he was found putting the nineteenth pair under his cravat; and, when taxed with taking more, he stoutly denied it, and offered to take his davy of it. But, when they talked of searching him, why he took to his heels, and away went the soles flying about in all sorts of directions."

"They caught him?"

"Yes."

"And how many soles?"

"Not one; they had all flown away; and then he swears he hadn't a pair of soles in his hands the whole of that morning, and stuck to it, too."

"Well, he is a rum 'un; but what did they do with him?"

"Nothing yet; he'll have six months for it."

"But how could he make them stick in his clothes, eh? That's what I want to know."

"Don't you know?"

"I should think not."

"Oh! he puts them with their tails downwards, and their heads upwards," said the turnkey, gravely.

"Well, heads and tails then. I can't see the utility of that. You are quizzing me."

"No; honour! Don't you see the reason? The scales are so rough that they stick out against the clothing and skin; so that they won't easily slip down, unless with violent exertion."

"Upon my soul, I should never have thought of that."

"No, nor I; live and learn, you see. I say, Sammy, there's more in London than is dreamt of in your and my philosophy."

"You are right, Joey, my trump; but just show this gentleman into a tidy apartment—one that shall be able to contain such a treasure, without any fear of losing him, or his hurting himself."

"Come this way; I've a place that would hold Jack Shepherd, if he were alive now. They hadn't such boxes as these in those days. His escapes were all my eye."

"So they were, Sammy."

This being over, the mendicant was placed in a cell, and then left to himself, to sleep, or think, as pleased him best.

"Well," he muttered, "they have me now; but they have not for what I have done, the fools. They would not have had me so soon, but for some blundering, accidental circumstance. They don't even know me. This may be a dangerous affair, after all; but I have got out of some scrapes before to-day, and why not out of this? I did not commit the murder. Nay, I am quite at a loss to tell how it came there. What can be the meaning of it all?

"It seems a dream," he muttered, "a mere dream, to find a body—that of a freshly-murdered man in that house, when, so few hours before only, I had left it. Who could believe it? Not I. It seems a mere phantom."

He lay some time on a bench in the cell, deeply meditating upon the occurrences that had taken place, and their probable result, and how far they might influence himself, or how far his safety might be compromised by them.

"I am safe," he muttered; "Margaret knows well that I did not do the murder. I am as innocent as she; and yet, if presence with the bleeding body was any evidence of guilt at all, it would be equally conclusive against her, or rather more against her than I, for she was with it before I was."

This seemed in some measure to reassure him, and he fell into a sound slumber—

THE FINDING OF MABEL ON A DOOR-STEP.

one that seemed to be unbroken and undisturbed, notwithstanding the heavy load of guilt that lay upon his soul like an incubus.

And yet he snored, as though he had nothing upon his conscience—as though he were not under circumstances of great peril that might probably endanger his life.

The morrow, he knew, would settle his doubts about the situation in which he was placed, and tell him what he had to expect from those who were to be his prosecutors, and what he should have to fear, and what not.

The morrow came, and with its earliest dawn returned the senses of the mendicant who had slept soundly the whole of the remaining portion of the night that was left him. Daylight did not come very early in the cells in the Compter. It was dull and gloomy in there. No place for cheerful reflection that, and to such an one as the mendicant it was not suggestive of any promising hope or prospect.

However, he rose up and looked around him; he seemed to be somewhat in doubt as to whether what he saw was real or illusory.

The bare white walls of his cell were, however, sufficient proof of the fact that he was in some place of confinement, and a very little reflection enabled him to comprehend the nature of his situation.

An early hour it was, for he could not hear the least sound throughout the whole of the building; at least, no sound reached his cell, and he concluded it must be yet too early for the people to be about, save those whose duty it was to keep watch and ward in the building.

He had full leisure to reflect upon the probable termination of this adventure, which had apparently so little in it to his advantage, and showed so small a chance of his escaping from the entanglements of circumstantial evidence. The case was strong against him, and his denial of any knowledge of his accomplices, or of the deed, would go for nought. It would be what any one would expect of him.

Who would admit the perpetration of a capital crime? No one who was not appalled by the weight of evidence against him; but not so the mendicant, he knew and felt he was innocent, and felt persuaded, moreover, that he would not suffer for this crime; that it was not his; and however Mabel might refuse to bear testimony in his favour, yet she must speak when once the magistrates put her upon her oath, and to refuse, or to speak anything but the truth, was equally unlikely.

## CHAPTER LXVIII.

BREAKFAST AT THE COMPTER.—THE EXAMINATION OF THE MENDICANT.—THE DISAPPEARANCE OF THE WITNESS.

THE time occupied in these reflections brought about the time for visiting the prisoners, and he could hear the various cells unlocked and locked, and the tramp of men as they walked about the various passages.

"It will be my turn presently," he thought, "to be looked after, and then will come my breakfast. Well, considering all things, I am rather tired and hungry; sleep is refreshing, especially when one don't dream. Hate dreaming, it is so uncomfortable, and makes a man nervous."

The cell was soon appproached by the turnkey, and he could hear the key turned in the lock, and then the door was opened, and a red-visaged man peeped in.

"Well?" said he.

The mendicant looked up, but made no answer.

"Well?"

Still no answer.

"Oh, you've got the sulks, have you? wery good; when you've no need of your shoes you will get out of them, but you know it's more your fault than mine that you are here."

"Did they send you to say that?"

"I came on purpose."

"Then you have done."

"In course I have, and so have you, without any breakfast. Good morning; when you're wanted you'll be fetched."

"Stop!"

"Well, be quick; I have something else to do than stand here all day, so give us as much as you can of it as quickly as you please," said the turnkey.

"I want some breakfast."

"Well, what is it to be?"

"What do they allow?"

"Anything you like to pay for," he replied; "the prison allowance will be as good as you can expect."

"That is not very good?"

"That's according to taste and opinion, you know; you'll like it very well if you can't get any better; but if you can, why you had better take the advantage of circumstances and have what you can get; because, you know, in Newgate you may do what you are obliged, and no more."

"Very good; here is some money; if you can put any cordial into the tea to increase its strength, you know it will keep the cold out, and no body know anything about it."

"I understand," said the turnkey, counting over the money; "you may depend upon me."

So saying, he quitted the cell, and left the mendicant to his own meditations, which were of the following character,—

"I do not usually care much about food, but lately I have been sparing, and now I feel as though a hearty meal would give me greater physical strength to go through the scene I have to endure in a few hours' time. I can and will meet them as they should be met, boldly and unshrinkingly. Nay, I can talk of innocence, and all that; surely I am an innocent man for once, and why should it be without its effect? It will not, nay it cannot be; aided by Mabel's testimony, I shall be triumphant.

"What tale can I give by way of answer to the questions that will be put to me? I know not, and 'tis useless to think now on what account I can give of myself; but my life is safe, and as for liberty, that may be recovered at leisure. At the expense of my plans it is true, but what of that? I can recommence them, and perhaps at a more favourable juncture than even now."

While he was thus thinking he again heard approaching footsteps, when the turnkey entered, and said—

"You may as well come out of this into the waiting room, and have your breakfast there, it will be more comfortable than having it here, and, besides, you will be called away presently."

The mendicant rose and followed the turnkey, who conducted him through a long passage until he came to a room on the left, and into this he entered.

Here were several turnkeys who were employed in the agreeable exercise of mastication, and had before them good breakfasts, composed of eggs and other refections.

The mendicant sat down with his back to the light, and then looked stealthily upon the turnkeys, who were there seated, and endeavoured to ascertain if he had seen any of them before.

Having satisfied his mind upon that score, he listened to the conversation with apparent earnestness.

"Here is your breakfast," said the man to whom he had given the money. "It is doctored."

The mendicant nodded, and said—

"All right—thank you."

The man sat down to his own breakfast, close by his prisoner, on whom he kept a watchful eye; not that it was at all necessary, for had he been able to have made an escape through these men, and out of the room, he could not have escaped past the wicket, by any means whatever; besides, the mendicant did not dream of attempting.

"Do you recollect Harry Newman?" inquired one of the turnkeys as he was eating a steak.

"What! Bluff Harry?"

"The same."

"Yes I did."

"Well, then, do you know what became of him?"

"No, I don't; he was had up here for horse-stealing, and got off from something wrong in the indictment, I believe,"

"Yes; the horse was a mare."

"So it was, and he got off."

"He did; it was a narrow chance."

"He would have been hanged."

"No doubt about it. Others were hung for it before, and many afterwards, and so would he but for this misfortune."

"Misfortune!"

"Yes; a lawyer's misfortune you know; but he was afterwards hanged at York, for a murder."

"Indeed."

"Yes, and I believe he was innocent."

"Do you? I suppose he told you so," returned the other, "and you have thought it worth while to believe him."

"I do, to this day, especially as another man, who was executed for another crime, confessed, the night before his execution, that he was the man who committed the deed."

"That alters the case," said the turnkey; "but do you know the particulars of the crime for which he was executed?"

"Yes; I was at York at the time; and he himself related them to me, and he said to me,—

"Buffer," said he, "you know the condition of people like myself, and as I am to be hanged to-morrow, I may as well tell you the truth; I have no secrets to keep, and if I were not innocent, I would at once say I was guilty."

"Very good," I said; "but you knows, Harry, you are not famous for telling the truth, but rather infamous for telling lies."

"Good again," he said; "but I have to quit the world to-morrow, and that, you know, makes a man serious."

"Well, so it does," I said; "and you are serious, then?"

"I am," he said.

"Very good," said I.

"Very good," said he. "Now, listen to me. I have committed many a crime that would hang me if they were known; why should I, then, persist in saying I am innocent of this one?"

"I am sure I can't tell," I replied.

"No, nor nobody else," he said.

"Except," I said, "you wanted to gammon the authorities, and make them get a reprieve."

"No hope," said he, "no hope;" and he shook his head.

"Well," said I, "push a-head, Harry; there's no time to lose; to-morrow morning will soon be here."

"So it will, Buffers, worse luck," said he; "and if they had known how many horses I have had in my life, to-morrow morning would have come long ago. But now it comes for a matter I didn't do, and I think it a very great hardship I should swing for what I never did, and I think I am an ill-used man."

"What can it signify," said I, "what you are scragged for, providing it's all right in the long run? You ought to be lagged, you know, and you will be hanged; that's all about it. What a discontented man you are, Harry!"

"But that ain't all about it, and that's what vexes me. Now, if I had ever killed a man, and was hanged for it, why, well and good; who'd say it was wrong?"

"Nobody."

"In course they couldn't."

"But if you were tried for murdering one man, and found guilty only of murdering somebody else, you couldn't complain."

"I could," he said.

"Well, you are an extraordinary animal."

"Not at all," he said; "when you are well, you wouldn't like to rouse about your inside with physic."

"In course I shouldn't."

"But you might have been ill afore."

"Well, what has that to do with it?" I said.

"This much—that ere is my case, that's exactly what I say—that's my case to a T."

"I don't see it."

"Why, no matter when you are ill; you ought to be physicked, and you are physicked, no matter whether it's the right occasion or not; and I am, as I ought to be, hanged, and am hanged, no matter whether it be the right occasion or not."

"Well," said I, "there's something in that."

"In course there is."

"But, Harry," said I.

"Well," said he.

"You were about to say something about this affair, for which you are to suffer in the wrong."

"Ah!" said he, "I am innocent; but no matter, I am to be hanged, and what does it matter to anybody else but me? I am innocent, but deserve death for other crimes. People will tell you it don't matter, he was a criminal, and not to be believed. However, I was coming home late one evening—that is, I was coming towards York, for I always call York home, because, when about nothing in the way of business, I used to spend my time, and I was born there, you know."

"I see."

"I had been out and settled upon a place where there were some good cattle—where, indeed, I should make a good thing of it, and no mistake."

"I dare say."

"Well, thinks I, this is not quite the thing to-day; I'll have a turn in a day or two after this, and make a good thing of it. I shall live in York like a gentleman."

"And you did?"

"No, I didn't; that's what galls me most. However, after that I secured three geldings and a mare."

"The devil!" said I.

"It's a fact," said he.

"And yet you complain of being hanged?"

"To be sure I do."

"Well, you ought to be ashamed of yourself," I said. "What difference can it make to you?"

"The difference doesn't signify," said he.

"Well, you beat all the discontented people I ever came nigh. You are a nice man, certainly."

"What's that to do with it?" said he; "you won't hear me out."

"I will," said I; "go a-head."

"Very well, then; as I was telling you, I had secured two geldings and a mare, with which I started off for London, and where they are sold for a good price by this time."

"Good, again," said I.

"Well," said he, "I was riding homewards, when I heard cries of 'murder' along the road I was going, and in my way, so I put spurs to my beast, and trotted along at a good pace, until I came to a spot where I saw two men beating another about on the road."

"Ay—ay!"

"Well, they dragged him off his horse, and had struck him about over the head with bludgeons. They did not see or hear me until I was close on to them, and then we had a fight. I got some knocks, and they too; and hearing the sounds of voices in the distance, bolted as well as they could.

"I did the best I could upon the occasion. I endeavoured to help the unfortunate man to rise, but he could but utter some indistinct words, and then he fell backwards and died.

"Hilloa!" said a voice.

"Hilloa!" said I.

"What are you doing there?"

"Helping an unfortunate, who's been knocked about by some men, and sadly ill-used."

"You seem to have got some knocks."

"I have," said I,

"Ah," said he, "'tis a bad job."

"Very."

"Is he dead?"

"I think so," said I.

"Will you wait here if I send for assistance?"

"I have had enough of it just now. I will come on to York myself. Perhaps you'll do duty here as a sentinel?"

"No," said he.

"Well, I shall not; I shall go to York and tell the authorities, and send assistance."

"Very well," he said; but off he scampered as hard as he could go, and left me alone.

"This I thought was shabby; but I drew the man out of the road, and placed him on the foot-path, and then mounting my horse, I set off for York at a gallop.

"I had not gone above half, or two-thirds of the distance, before I met some horsemen coming out from the city towards the place where I had come from.

"Hilloa !" shouted one.

I knew the sound; it was the same man who had left me, and so I shouted "Hilloa !" in return.

"That's him," said the voice.

"That's who ?" said I.

"You were with a man on the road just now, as I came by—he was insensible ?"

"Yes I was; and I asked you to help me with him," said I, "instead of which you bolted."

"And good cause, too."

"What do you mean ?" said I.

"That you are the murderer."

"Murderer !" I exclaimed.

"Yes."

"What do you mean, you cur ?"

"Oh, it's all very well; but I was not going to place myself in your power by dismounting to help you with a dead man. That's the man, officers; he is the murderer."

"This is above a joke, or an excuse for cowardice. I am no murderer; but I heard the cries of murder on the road, and came down."

I then told them what I saw, and what had happened, but it was all of no use.

"He's the murderer," said this man.

"Now, my lad, you must come along with us, and we will give your friends assurances that you are in safe keeping. It's no use making a fuss about it."

"I ain't a going," I said, "because I know I am innocent. I have the marks of bruises I have received in the fray, and the marks of blood I have of my own and the men who were attacking him."

"It's all of no use," said one of the officers. "The bruises may have been received from the poor wretch himself while trying to defend himself from your attack."

"Oh, if that's to be the game," I said, "why, I shall say nothing more. Only keep that cowardly humbug out of the way, or I may knock his crown in with the butt of my riding whip."

You should have seen how the fellow backed his horse into the rear of the officers.

"Take care he does no mischief, officers," said he—"take care, or he will escape; he's a desperate man."

"There's no need," said I, to the officers, "to take any notice of what he says; I am not going to run away. Here I am an innocent man, and, if you please, I am in your custody."

"Yes," they repl'ed, "you are in our custody. It's no use being violent. We have enough men to put you down in an instant, besides the mischief you do yourself in the struggle."

"I am well aware of that. You must do your duty, if he persist in his tale against me."

"He does."

"Then, I am your prisoner."

"You are."

We rode back to the place where the man lay. He was quite dead; but his money had not been taken away. In fact, merely a murder had been committed, and no robbery.

Well, we took him to York, and I was placed in the castle; but I had not any fear as to the results.

I was innocent; and that was, in my mind, enough to bear me up against all the false swearing of this man.

However, I had made a great mistake. I had been up on several charges of horse-stealing; and, though they could not convict for want of evidence, yet the impression was not that I was innocent, but that I was too clever for them.

Well, they thought they had a good opportunity to punish me, and rid themselves of a troublesome man; and they therefore took all possible pains to impress people with a notion that I was a bad character; and I was just the man to commit such a crime.

Of course, it was believed. The marks of the struggle that I had about me were immediately seized upon as evidence of the crime, and gave additional weight to the evidence against me.

You know the rest. I was tried; not a word of my story was believed; I was pronounced guilty; for I could not say where I had been; but, at the same time, if I had done so, I should not have been believed, since I had implicated another person, whose life, as well as mine, would have been forfeited; and, besides, I had no other witnesses save him and me to the fact; for, of course, we don't want to accumulate evidence against ourselves.

"Well, I said no more; but I tell you," he said, slapping his very chest, "I am, as far as this crime is concerned, a murdered man. But I could not get off this occasion, without putting my head into a halter on another account."

"And do you believe him?" inquired one of the turnkeys.

"I do; for, as I told you, a man afterwards confessed to the crime; and this proved him right."

At that moment, there was a bustle in the passage; and one of the turnkeys rose, and left, saying,—

"I dare say this is some man from Bow-street."

"You'll be wanted, I dare say," said the man next to the mendicant. "You had better finish."

"I have done," said the mendicant, "and am ready to go whenever you please. We shall have an early hearing, I suppose."

"That's as may be—if the magistrates get there, and how many night-charges have been brought up."

"How shall we go?"

"I dare say, in a coach."

"I am glad of it."

"You are too valuable to be allowed to have a chair."

The mendicant winked, but made no reply, beyond bidding them to remain silent.

In a few moments more the turnkey came in, and said,—

"Your prisoner's wanted."

"Come along then," said the man. "I thought your time was at hand. Come along; keep up a good heart."

"I never had a faint one," said the mendicant.

"I see you're a trump."

They then left the room, and entered the wicket; and there there were several officers in waiting, one of whom placed on a pair of handcuffs, saying,—

"You now understand you are to go with us to Bow-street. If you make any attempt to escape, we are armed, and can resist you; and it will only result in wounds and perhaps death."

"I am innocent, and have no intention of attempting an escape. I have other objects in view."

"Very well; I am glad of it. We can have a coach; and, therefore, you will not be inconvenienced by walking."

"It matters little—but little; but yet I would rather ride than walk through the streets thus."

"Come along, then."

The officer took him by the arm, and led him down the steps to the coach, into which he stepped. There was an officer in, and one stepped in after him; and away they drove.

Nothing was said during the drive; and when they arrived at the office, and got out,

until the night charges were disposed of the mendicant was locked up in a cell attached to the office.

He remained there more than an hour and a half, when he was taken into the office and placed in the dock.

"Well," inquired the magistrate; "what does this man stand charged with?"

"Murder, your worship."

"State the particulars."

"From information," said the officer, "I and some other officers were placed in waiting to watch where Mr. Pearson should be conducted to, and then to make a capture."

"You had some previous charge?"

"Yes; we were after another man."

"Oh, this is not the man?"

"No, your worship; the affair I was on was of another character, and different persons; this turned up accidentally, and was only committed last night."

"Go on."

"We watched, but were suddenly at fault, owing to the caution we were compelled to use in following, lest we should be observed, and the whole affair discovered, and we lose our man."

"I see exactly."

"We, however, discovered the house, and then we were compelled to force our way in, where we discovered the unfortunate gentleman to be murdered, and this man stood beside him."

"And was he robbed?"

"Yes; everything taken."

"Had he much?"

"We know that he had a heavy sum of money about him."

"And it was gone?"

"It was."

"And the prisoner was with the body?"

"He was."

"How long a time elapsed after you first missed him, to the time you found the prisoner with the dead body?"

"Not half an hour; about twenty minutes."

Some other evidence was gone into, to corroborate the above, by the other officers, and then the magistrate turned to the mendicant, and said,—

"Well, prisoner, what have you to say? I am bound to tell you, what you do say will be made use of against you."

"I am innocent, and the young female, who was in the house at the time, can tell you so. I came in but a few moments before the officers, and was more surprised to see a dead body there than they could be."

"Are you the owner of the house?"

"No; it is a deserted one, and I am in

distress, and slept there for want of means to get a better."

"Well," said the magistrate, to one of the officers, "it would be as well to send for this young woman, and in the meantime we will adjourn the examination."

*    *    *    *    *

In about an hour and a half, the prisoner was again placed at the bar, and the examination continued,—

"Have you discovered the young woman?" inquired the magistrate.

"No, your worship; there are no traces of her."

"Your witness, then, is not forthcoming?" said the magistrate to the mendicant.

"It seems not; I must trust to chance for her arrival; she is a stranger to town, and seeing that I was taken away, she thought that no place for her, especially as there was a dead body in it. She may hear of my peril, and come forward."

"It is to be hoped she may, otherwise she will place you in a very disagreeable position. What are you?"

"I have no business."

"No business, eh?"

"Yes."

"Well, then, there is sufficient ground to commit you at once; but, at the same time, I shall remand you and give you an opportunity of finding out your witness, and in the meanwhile we may ascertain something about you."

The mendicant was then removed from the bar, and reconducted to the cell, where he was left till it was convenient to carry him to the Compter.

"It is a wonder he didn't commit you at once," said the officer; "and I am more surprised at his adjourning for a couple of hours for your witness."

"Yes; I did not expect it."

"Nor anybody else; but it matters not. You will be up on the next examination day, and then you will be committed."

---

## CHAPTER LXIX

### MABEL'S DESTITUTION.—THE LONE ALE-HOUSE.

MABEL was much more puzzled what to do with herself after she had escaped the several dangers and insults she experienced in the streets of the metropolis, than she had been immediately after her escape from the house of horrors in which she had been confined by the mendicant.

Which way to turn she knew not; not a friend at hand to whom she could apply for advice; and she wandered about, not knowing where she was going, and, after a while, found herself again in London.

She felt wearied and tired, and yet she had not the means to purchase rest and refreshment. Now, however, that it was broad daylight, and people were rushing to and fro from all quarters, she could suffer no insult or injury; she felt a sense of security that she had not hitherto felt, but the means of existence again troubled her.

Seeing a goldsmith's open, and an announcement that old jewellery was brought, and a variety of other announcements, she determined to sell a small ring she possessed; and, for that purpose, entered the shop, and, seeing an individual behind the counter, she said to him,—

"Will you purchase this ring of me?"

The man looked very hard at Mabel, and then at the ring, which he weighed in his hand, and carefully examined it over and over, and finally he went to a phial, from which he took a piece of wire, and dropped a small drop of some liquid upon it, and then he took the scales, and, having weighed it, he said to Mabel, in a soft voice,—

"Nine-and-sixpence, miss, is all I can give for it; that is the utmost value of the metal."

"I must trust to you, sir, for its value," said Mabel, "for I do not know it myself. I will take that sum."

"It is your own, I presume?" said the shopkeeper, inquiringly.

"Yes; certainly."

The money was counted out on the counter carefully by the goldsmith, who said when he had done so,—

"We buy those things, you see, for the sake of the metal only, and it is only the price of the gold that we can offer, as the ring will be broken up and melted."

"Thank you," said Mabel; "perhaps you can direct me to the——road?"

She named the road that led towards that part of the country whence she had lately come against her will, being suddenly seized by a vague idea of taking that road back again, and finding her way thither by herself, and unaided. She was conscious that she had not means to insure travelling by any other conveyance than that which nature had provided her with, and she thought she could accomplish it, especially pressed as she was by circumstances.

The shopkeeper directed her on her route, without asking any questions; and she passed through the centre of the great town, amazed at what she saw; for the wealth displayed on all sides of her was so great, that she could not sufficiently admire the wealth of the citizens of

London, who could afford to place so much riches in the windows of their shops.

"There must be surely more riches in London," she murmured, "than in all the world besides."

She walked onwards, however, and never rested until she saw the signs of London were fast fading from before her eyes, and the signs of suburban residences and cottages met her view. She was not ill-pleased to see this. It assured her she was making some progress on her journey, and that, in fact, she was fast leaving London, and going in the country, which was what she desired.

How light her heart felt in comparison to what she had felt when cooped up in that lonely room in that lonely house, where she had seen what she never hoped to see again!

The sun was high up in the heavens, and she felt the fatigue of walking, for her strength had diminished of late, because she had been but poorly cared for by the mendicant, who had supplied her with but poor and indifferent food; her confinement and mental disquietude all preyed upon her, and reduced her strength.

She determined that the next quiet, unpretending looking place she came to she would stop fo refreshment and rest.

It was not very long before she came to one that suited her taste, and appeared all she wanted.

It was a little, lone ale-house, with benches that were unoccupied; and then the house, too, at that hour, was empty. The inmates were employed in their domestic duties, and preparing all for the afternoon.

Mabel entered the little parlour, in which were several highly-polished chairs and tables, and the floor had recently been sanded. There was a good fire in the grate, which burned brightly and pleasantly as she entered the room.

Mabel sat herself down on a seat near the fire, and waited until some one entered the room.

At length the landlady entered. She was a fat, comfortable body, who evidently would thrive, if nobody else could.

"What is your pleasure, miss?" she inquired, as she looked at Mabel with inquisitive eyes.

"I want some refreshment," said Mabel.

"What can I have?"

"Anything you please."

"Have you any cold meat?"

"Yes, miss—cold leg of mutton."

"Let me have some of that, and some weak ale."

"Yes, miss," said the landlady, who was a civil woman, whose natural curiosity was greatly under control, though she felt an itching to make some inquiries of Mabel respecting her situation, and her object in thus travelling alone, which she thought must be curious and well worth knowing; but she restrained herself from doing what she believed would give offence to her guest, and left the room.

"I wonder," she said, "what it is that can have brought such a pretty young creature into a place like this. I don't know, but I am pretty sure nothing but necessity could do it."

However, she set about executing her orders, and carried them into the little parlour, where Mabel was sitting expecting her. And when the meat and other matters were placed upon the table, the landlady said,—

"I have brought you the newspaper to read, if you remain long enough, love. You will find a very horrible murder in it."

"Indeed!" said Mabel.

"Yes, miss; we always have a paper, for people in these parts like to know what's going on in London."

"I dare say."

"Oh, all people do."

"No doubt; but what of this murder you were speaking about just now?" said Mabel, who began to grow interested in the relation, for she remembered what she herself had seen.

"Oh, it's a dreadful thing—very shocking!"

"Indeed!"

"Oh, I never read anything equal to it."

"What was it? Have you read it?"

"Yes, miss."

"Was it a man or a woman?"

"A gentleman; and he was hanged first and stabbed afterwards. Oh, he was killed over and over again."

"That was very dreadful."

"So it was; but they robbed him, too."

"Has the murderer been taken?"

"He has."

"Does he confess it?" she inquired.

"Confess, eh! Bless your heart, miss, you know nothing of them sort of people, if you think they will confess anything. Oh, dear, no; they stand out against everything."

"What does he say?"

"That he didn't do it; he was quite innocent, and knowed nothing about it at all," said the landlady.

"Indeed!"

"Ay, and more than that, he said there was a young lady as knowed he was innocent."

"Did he say where she was?"

"No, miss."

"Have they sought after her?"

"Yes."

"Did they find her?"

"Oh, dear, no; nobody was to be found. It is out of the question to suppose that there could be any truth in what such a man as that could say; of course he would deny it. Nobody liked hanging; and, of course, a man who had committed a murder isn't to be believed on his oath, much less on his mere word."

"Certainly not."

"And, besides, they are sure to hang him."

"But suppose," said Mabel, "this person were to come forward and say he was not the murderer?"

"Why, if such a thing were possible, then indeed he'd be saved, if they believed her," said the landlady.

"And if not?"

"He's sure to be hanged."

"What have they done with him?"

"They have sent him back to prison, and they'll have him up again to-morrow, I believe."

THE OFFICERS FINDING THE BODY OF THE MURDERED MR PEARSON

"What will be done with him then?"

"They will then send him to Newgate for trial, and after that they'll hang him till he is quite dead."

"Are you sure of it?"

"Yes, miss; if you read the paper, you will see it all." So saying, the landlady handed her the newspaper.

"Do you want anything, ma'am?"

"Not at present, thank you."

The landlady left the room and Mabel was left alone. She ate her food, bt the whole time she was deeply embued with the consideration of the condition of the mendicant. The strange conduct of this man was to her unexplainable. He must have known something, even if he were not what he represented himself to be —her father.

Besides, she could not help believing he must be some relation, and yet she shuddered to think what. He was the last man in the world that she would have desired for a father. Indeed, her thoughts revolted from such a contemplation.

The mendicant could not be her father, something seemed to say; and yet she could not bear the idea of leaving even such a man to perish by such a fate.

He had forcibly taken her from her friends; used threats and violence towards her; but he had done no more than was necessary to accomplish that purpose; unjustifiable as that purpose was, she had nothing else to complain of.

Great as this was, it sank before her, when she thought of the death that he would suffer. She could not look coldly on, and see him die a death so horrible as that of a public execution, when it only wanted the breath of her mouth to save him:

True it was, he had acknowledged that he was a criminal, and that he should suffer death, if he were taken; but, at the same time, she knew not but this might have been said from a desire to try her feelings and to prevent her from attempting anything that might place him in jeopardy.

The more she thought of these things, the more she felt that it was highly improper to leave even a bad man to such a fate —to a public death for a crime he was not guilty of. It was unjust in her, nay, criminal in her to permit it.

There was a moral obligation on her to rescue him from the state he was then in, and she had almost made up her mind, before she had finished her meal, that she would turn back, and appear at the principal police-office, and state all she knew.

When she had done her dinner, for such it was, she took up the paper, and then read the account of the remand of the mendicant, and the intimation that on that day, when he was next brought up, he would be committed for trial; and when she had finished, she laid the paper down for a minute or two, seemingly lost in meditation.

"To-morrow," she muttered, "yes, to-morrow, and then he will be again brought up. I will go and save him, though I may be again subject to his power, and yet when I tell my tale, he dare not again seize me. Besides, I may as well take my lodgings up here until I return.

"Well, well," she muttered, "perhaps Captain Morton may hear of my situation, if it got into the papers."

"Can I have a bed here to-night?" she inquired of the landlady, who at that moment entered the room.

"Yes; if you desire it."

"Then I shall remain here to-day."

"You had better by-and-by sit in the kitchen, or come with me into my room, for you will see company here that you will not like to see."

"Thank you, I am much obliged to you."

"You had better come at once, for all the men have left work, and will be here in a few minutes."

Mabel left the parlour, and followed the landlady into a back room, where she had some books given her to amuse her.

This was all that Mabel desired; she felt herself fortunate in going to a place where the people were so thoughtful.

*        *        *        *

The next morning Mabel took leave of the landlady, and bent her steps towards London again, where she arrived at an early hour, and where she proceeded at once towards the police-office.

It was some difficulty for her to find it out; and when she did, she almost shrunk from going in.

One of the officers belonging to the court came forward, and seeing she was strange and excited, said to her—

"What do you want? Can I be of any service to you?"

"Is this the police-office?"

"Yes."

"Will the man who is charged with murder be brought up to-day?"

"Yes; he was remanded to this day."

"And will be brought up again and committed for trial?" said Mabel, with some interest.

"Yes, he will, unless he can produce very good evidence that he is not the man."

"I wish to be present when he is brought up."

"You had better go into this room, and wait. You can sit down; there are only the night charges on now, which have very little in them, save what is disgusting."

"Thank you; I will."

Accordingly she was shown into a waiting-room, and there left to herself for nearly an hour.

Then there was a great stir in the police court, and everybody was in a bustle.

"Make way there—make way for the prisoner," was said frequently by the officers as they followed some one through the crowd.

In another moment the door was opened, and the same officer whom she had seen before now came in.

"You wanted to be present at this man's examination," he said.

"The man charged with murder?"

"Yes, the same."

"I did."

"Then come this way—quick, if you please."

Mabel immediately followed, and was soon in the court, where she was placed by the officer, who had taken it into his head to be very civil, indeed.

She saw the mendicant placed in the dock. He looked much the same, perhaps a little paler, but he was firm and collected, and looked round the court with a careless eye; he did not observe, however, Mabel, and turned from the multitude to the magistrates.

The evidence was read over in the presence of the mendicant, and each witness was asked if he had anything to add to his former depositions, and having signed them the magistrate said—

"Have you any further evidence to offer?"

"None."

"Then let it go to trial as it is."

"We believe the case is complete."

"Yes, it is."

Then, after a pause, the magistrate turned towards the prisoner, and said to him, in a distinct voice—

"Prisoner, have you anything further to say, by way of defence? But I am bound to tell you that whatever you do say may be made use of against you."

"I have nothing to add but that I am innocent of the crime laid to my charge. I had not been in the house five minutes before the officers came in, and I had not recovered from the start and surprise of the first moment, when I was taken."

"Have you any witness?"

"There is one who could prove what I say, but I cannot tell where to find her."

"You will have opportunities and facilities afforded you before the day of your trial, which will take place shortly; for it will be my duty to commit you."

"Very well," replied the mendicant.

"Stay," said a voice in the court.

That voice was Mabel's.

All eyes were turned towards the place where it came from, and all eyes were fixed upon her.

"'Tis she!" exclaimed the mendicant.

"Who?"

"My witness. Now I care not whether she comes as friend or foe; she can but tell the truth."

"Who was that," inquired the magistrate, "that interrupted the proceedings?"

The officer now stepped up to her, saying—

"You must step here, if you please, and tell his worship why you spoke just now."

Mabel did as she was desired, and then the magistrate, when he had fixed his eyes upon her for a minute or two, said—

"What do you know of this matter?"

"That he his innocent."

"Who did commit the murder, then?"

"Several men, who left the house before this man returned to it, after some hours' absence."

"How long had he returned?"

"About three or four minutes; scarcely so much."

"Well, tell us all you know about it."

Mabel then went into a full relation of all that had occurred after the entrance of the murderers into the house, until the entrance of the officers who took the mendicant into custody.

"And why did you not come forward before?"

"Because I felt afraid of that man, and was almost determined to leave him to his fate."

"You felt afraid of him?"

"Yes."

"How came you in that house?" inquired the magistrate.

"I was forcibly taken and confined there by this man," replied Mabel.

"Indeed! Where did he take you from?"

"He took me from my friends."

"What is your name?"

"Mabel Morton."

"Where do you live?"

"At Morton Hall."

"How came you in town?"

"I was forcibly carried away from that place, and was forcibly brought to town by this man, who retained me in custody till he was taken by the officers, and I then escaped."

"You were forcibly confined by him, against your will?"

"I was."

"A clear case of abduction. What motive did he allege for detaining you in this manner?"

"He said he was my father, and thus tore me from the arms of my friends and benefactors, who had been more than parents to me since my childhood. He tore me away from them."

"What do you know of this man?"

"Nothing more than what I have told you. I never saw him before lately, and never desire to do so again."

"Well, your testimony seems to be disinterested enough. It certainly acquits him of murder; but at the expense of a very serious charge of abduction."

"It matters not," said the mendicant. "I am innocent of the blood of this man. I care not for the result. What I have said to this young female in private I now tell her. I have told her nothing but the truth, and that, when I have the will, I have the means of proving."

"You had better set about it," said the magistrate; "for, under all circumstances, I shall not think it consistent with my duty to part with you, even upon bail. You will remain in custody till your trial comes on."

"Do you commit me?"

"No. I shall remand you till this day week, and, in the meantime, we will correspond with this Captain Morton, and obtain from him additional evidence."

The mendicant seemed uneasy.

"Miss Morton," said the magistrate, "you have been brought to town against your will—how have you lodged yourself?"

"I have no lodging, sir. I was about to make an attempt to get back to Morton Hall, as I am quite a stranger, and have neither friend nor means here. When I saw the account of this man's examination, I thought I should be doing a great wrong to let him die such a death."

"Certainly; you were quite right; but you cannot return to the Hall at present."

"Indeed!"

"No. I shall require your attendance at the remand, and at the trial. You have no bail in London, and only you can prove it. I must order one of the officers to look after you. You have no money, I dare say?"

"Scarcely any."

"Well, one of the officers shall provide you with proper accommodation until I can write to your friends; and when they return an answer, or come up for you, you will obtain immediate aid from them. Until that time you will be taken care of."

"Thank you, sir," said Mabel. "You will then write to Captain Morton?"

"I will."

"That will then relieve me of much of my uneasiness as to how I am to get back to them again."

"You will have facilities for writing, also," said the magistrate, "and can do as you please in that respect."

There was a pause for a few moments, after which the magistrate turned to the mendicant, saying,—

"Prisoner, you are remanded until this day week, when you will, in all probability, be committed for trial on the charge of abduction."

"I am prepared. Can I see this witness in private?" inquired the mendicant as he was removed.

"Certainly not," said the magistrate.

"Then, Mabel," said the mendicant,

"remember what I have told you of your parents and your birth."

He was then removed, and Mabel followed the old officer who had before spoken to her.

---

## CHAPTER LXX.

THE JOURNEY TO TOWN OF CAPTAIN MORTON AND HIS FRIENDS.—THE EVIDENCES OF MABEL'S BIRTH

LEAVING now for a brief space the beautiful, but cruelly by fortune persecuted Mabel, we will call the reader's attention to Morton Hall.

Alas! what a wonderful change had there taken place since she who had been, as it were, the very sunshine of the place, had departed from it.

No longer did the old Hall wear its accustomed look of cheerfulness, and every one of its inhabitants felt most painfully the truth of the saying, that we never truly know the worth of anything until we are deprived of its presence.

If, a short six months before, when all was life, and joy, and gaiety, any one had suddenly asked Captain Morton what acted as a principal cause to make it so, he might have hesitated, and not been able exactly to answer the question with satisfaction to himself, or perspicuity as regarded his questioner.

But now, when all was gloomy and sadness—now, when no longer the old house looked pleasant, even in the sunshine, and when no longer the song of the forest birds sounded delightfully to his ears, if he had been asked the converse of the former question, and any one had said to him, in sober seriousness,—

"What makes Morton Hall so dull?" he would at once, and without a shadow of hesitation, have replied,—

"It is on account of the absence of our dear Mabel."

It is indeed truly astonishing what an immense gap in a family circle sometimes the absence of only one member will produce.

One would hardly have supposed it possible that such should be the case; but certain it is, that when Mabel was gone, both Captain Morton and his wife found out, for the very first time, how much they had loved her.

During the first excitement of her absence, and the activity of the search which was made for her, there was a continual hope that she might be soon discovered; but it was as day after day passed, without that hope being realized, that all the terror of deep disappointment, almost amounting to despair, came upon them.

The absence of his brother, too, affected the spirits of Captain Morton, and he likewise missed Rafferty; so that, altogether, he felt himself about as unhappy as he very well could ever, with his disposition, be.

Over and over again he told himself that, by nourishing in his mind so much misery, he was doing a great injustice to his amiable wife, than whom a better could not have been found; and in her presence he frequently endeavoured to assume a cheerfulness he was really far from feeling; but when he found that she, too, felt as acutely as he did himself the loss of Mabel, he told himself there was no occasion to make such an effort, and accordingly they spent many hours of the day in lamentation after her whom they began to despair of ever again beholding and folding to their hearts.

"My dear," Captain Morton would say, "I am sure that we both love Mabel just as much as if she had beeen a child of our own."

"Yes," Mrs. Morton would reply; "and I often and often thought that a kind Heaven had bestowed her upon us as its most precious gift."

In such commiseration as this would they pass hour after hour, until that auspicious day when Henry Morton and Rafferty Brolickbones appeared at the Hall.

What occurred contingent upon their arrival our readers are already aware of; and all we have to do now is, to take up the travelling party on the road to London.

This party consisted of the captain as well as his brother and Rafferty, for the former could not at all control his impatience to assist now in the search for Mabel, and so, perchance, at least have the satisfaction of embracing her some days earlier than he otherwise would be able to do were he to remain at the Hall.

It was strange, and there was really no sufficient ground for such a belief, and yet one common feeling took possession of them all, which was to the effect, that a long time would not now elapse before they heard some news of Mabel.

Rafferty Brolickbones was particularly certain upon this point, and he took occasion to say to his old master, the captain,—

"Faith, sir, don't you think we shall be after seeing Miss Mabel soon?"

"I sincerely hope so, Rafferty."

"Oh, sir, then it's more than a hope I have got—what people call a presentiment, sir; and, as sure as bullets ain't eggs, sir, we'll find her out."

"It will be a joyful moment."

"Faith, sir, you are right there, and the devil a lie, sir. I recollect, sir, having a presentiment once, and sure enough it came uncommonly true, sir."

"What was it, Rafferty?"

"Oh, murder! When I come to think, I've had enough presentiments to fill a mighty big baggage waggon, sir."

"Have you, indeed?"

"Yes, sure, sir. Now I'll tell you one."

"What was it?"

"Why, just this, sir. You know, sir, I was at the battle of Talawera."

"Yes, yes."

"That was before your honour's time, anyhow; but there I was, and towards the close of the skrimmage, sir, a Frenchman mounted made at me; and says he, in French, says he, 'D—n you, Rafferty! there you are, are you?—take that,' says he."

"But, Rafferty, I did not know you were sufficiently acquainted with the French language to understand what a French cavalry man might say."

"I acquainted with the French language, sir!"

"Yes."

"The devil a bit, sir. I wouldn't own such an acquaintance; and if I was to meet the French language, sir, on never such a lonely road, I would not so much as say, 'The top of the morning to you, you incomprehensible blackguard.'"

"Then how did you know what the French horseman said to you?"

"I saw it, sir."

"Saw!"

"Yes, sir; I saw it in his looks as plain as if it was wrote in his face in the most iligant Irish, sir, that ever mother's son spoke."

"Oh, indeed!"

"Yes, sir. And about the presentiment. Presentiment the first was, that I should get the better of him. I had my musket in my hand, but the devil a charge there was in it, so I was forced, you see, sir, to make an application to the but-end."

"Ah! to be sure."

"Well, sir, he hit at me, and I hit at him; and so we cut about, round and round, for ever so long, till at last he says again—'Now I've got you, bad luck to your sowl!' says he; and he gave a stroke at me that might have made a clane end of me, only it didn't. Then afore, sir, he could gather up his sword again, I gave him a knock on the head; and says I, 'Whoop! There's one in honour of the ould family of the Raffertys and the Brolickbones!' So, when he heard that, down he came, and declined any more fighting."

"Declined fighting!"

"Yes, sir; he was kilt entirely; so, you see, he couldn't very well. 'Have you had enough?' says I.—'Yes,' says he."

"Oh! he spoke."

"No; he didn't spake; but silence, you know, sir, gives consent. So, then, I looked about me for my regiment, and the devil a regiment was to be seen. 'Hilloa!' says I, 'they have marched off, leaving me and the Frenchman to settle our own affairs.' Howsomedever, sir, I listened, and some distance off I heard drums and fifes. 'All's right,' says I, 'but it's tired I am.' So I turned to the Frenchman's horse, and I says to him,—'Baste,' says I, 'be still, will you, while I get on your back? You'll be so mighty kind as to convey me back to my regiment?' and the Frenchman's horse says 'Yes.'"

"What! the horse?"

"Silence, you know, sir, gives consent. It was as good as yes."

"Oh! I had forgotten."

"Well, sir, then off I went; but, somehow, I had a sort of presentiment that the French horse, knowing that he had one of the Raffertys on his back, and that me and the Frenchy had been fighting, would try to play me some ugly trick, so I stuck to him, sir, like a barrel of pitch on a hot day.

"Well, your honour, on we went, till I came in sight of the British lines, about a mile off; but I was coming across the country, you see, sir, which was a near cut; and the more I got towards them, the more I felt sure the French horse would play me yet some trick or another, just out of revenge, you see, sir.

"Our pickets challenged me, and one of 'em fired a shot, because he saw that the horse's accoutrements was French. However, sir, I got along till I came to where my own regiment was lying; and some of the boys knew me, and gave a great shout, that put so much heart into me, that to make a near cut I went at a long bar that went across a narrow road-way."

"And the horse went over it, and threw you, I suppose?"

"No, sir; he didn't."

"What did he do, then?"

"Why, sir, French-like, he went at it with a great bounce, as if he meant to go over it and the moon too; but what do you think he really did?"

"Stopped short, and sent you over his head?"

"No, sir—no."

"Then I cannot guess."

"Why, sir, when he got up to the bar, he ducked, and went under it like a shot, shaving me off his back as clane as a whistle. Then he turned round, and came back again, kicking me to death; and off he tore, as much as to say,—'Now, Rafferty, my boy, I rather think I've done for you.'"

"Well, that was a trick, certainly, to play you."

"Ah, wasn't it, sir?"

"A serious one, no doubt."

"Yes, sir; but it was, praise be to God! my head that suffered, and the heads of the Brolickbones have always been as hard as flint stones, sir; so, you see, it didn't do me much harm."

"Well, I should say it would not."

"Right again, sir, good luck to you; so, as I was saying, when I do have a presentiment, there's a mighty good chance of it's coming true, and I have one that, before long, sir, we shall see Miss Mabel, bless her sweet eyes!"

"I say amen to that, Rafferty, with the deepest sincerity."

"Amen, then, sir, for me."

It seemed to Captain Morton quite like old times revived again, to be listening to Rafferty Brolickbones' stories. He knew very well that, like the rest of his nation, Rafferty was not at all particular with regard to the extent to which he embellished what he related, but his little anecdotes were none the less amusing for all that.

During the journey, Captain Morton and his brother held a serious consultation, as to what, if anything, they should say to old Monsieur Rouselli about the murder which had had taken place at the village of the traveller, who from all the circumstances with which they were now acquainted, they could not doubt, for one moment, to be other than he who had been sent by the kind old man in search of Mabel.

Henry was rather inclined to be of opinion that as no good could be accomplished by telling him the tale, it would be a needless aggravation of his distresses to enter into its particulars.

Captain Morton, in reply to this, said—

"Henry, I have a great dislike to concealments. They always breed mischief, to my mind, and so far from thinking that it would aggravate the distresses of old Mr. Rouselli, if I might judge from my own feelings, I should much prefer to be told of the death for a certainty of one whom I loved, than be left to all the horrors of conjecture concerning him or her. You know, Henry, that if our dear Mabel had been taken from us by the hand of death, we should have endeavoured, and been forced, to reconcile ourselves as well as we could to the deprivation; but it is the dreadful state of uncertainty that we have been in concerning her that, as you know well, has been such a prolific source of anguish to us all."

"True, brother; most true."

"Therefore, Henry, I do think that we had better tell Monsieur Rouselli all that we are in possession of concerning anything which is at all likely to be of interest to him."

"Be it so."

"It will be a pang at first only. Then it will by degrees sober down into a mere reminiscence, and ultimately assume the shape of one of those regular sorrows of the mind, which all human beings have their full share of."

"They have, indeed, brother."

"Happy would be the man, and something more than human might he claim to be, if he could lay his hand upon his heart, and say, 'all is peace here—I have no sorrow.'"

"There lives not such a man."

"I do not think, Henry, there does."

"Nor will there ever live such an one."

"I think we may go as far as that, even; experience warrants us in so doing."

"Have you decided upon any course which you will pursue concerning our poor lost Mabel, when you reach London?"

"I have so far, that I am determined to throw aside what I may call the timid policy which we have hitherto pursued, and feeling, as I do, most completely convinced that the bold scoundrel who has torn her from us has no possible right to control her in any degree, I will now, with the consent of Monsieur Rouselli, which I do not doubt obtaining, try what the utmost possible publicity will do towards placing Mabel once more in our hands."

"You will offer rewards?"

"Ample, ample."

"I will hope for the best. Oh, Mabel, Mabel! could I but have the joy of looking upon you once again, I would, for the felicity of so doing, barter one half of my existence."

"We will see her again, and she will be happy," exclaimed Captain Morton. "Surely, surely, Heaven will be good to its own."

---

### CHAPTER LXXI.

MABEL'S NEW ABODE.—THE ESCAPE OF THE MENDICANT FROM GAOL.—THE MYSTERIOUS LODGER.

AFTER Mabel had, in the heroic manner in which we have recorded, saved her cruel persecutor from a fate which he richly de-served—for death, no doubt, would have been his portion had she not interfered—it will be recollected that she was retained in the hands of the police, virtually under their surveillance, although not with any of the degrading accompaniments of loss of liberty.

An officer had been directed to procure for her a respectable lodging, and to supply her with the means of current subsistence, until a full and an ample inquiry had been made into the truth of what she had stated.

This was accordingly done. The officer to whose care she was given was a very civil man, and rather better educated than most of his class; he regretted to her that he could not accommodate her in his own house, where he would have been certain of her safety; but he had not any room to spare; so he felt compelled to do what he could to find her some unexceptionable place of abode.

Of that, as a matter of course, he was a far better judge than she could be, and so she left it entirely to him, telling him that, in her ignorance of London, and all its localities, she had no choice whatever as to where she should reside.

"I only hope," she said, "that those who seem disposed to act kindly to me have no doubts of the truth of what I have related. It would be a most harassing circumstance to me to think that, even for one hour, I laboured under the stigma of being an impostor."

"Why, you know," replied the man, "let people's private opinions be what they may, upon subjects of this nature, it is absolutely necessary that everything should be proved incontestably."

"True, true; but still it would be a most wretched thing for me, after all my sufferings, to think that I was, even for one hour, suspected."

"Oh! you must not make yourself unhappy about that. The magistrates will at once write to the parties you have named in the country as knowing something of you. A reply will, of course, come by return of post, and then you will no doubt feel yourself in a position which will be very much for the better."

"I do, indeed, now hope," she said, "that my miseries are nearly at an end. I think that, if I can once again behold the kind faces of those dear friends who lightened the paths of my early childhood with their love, I should be most supremely blest."

"That is a result which may come about very soon; and now I think, upon recollection, that I shall be able to place you in a house where I know you will receive both protection and comfort."

"A thousand thanks — a thousand thanks," said Mabel. "These are luxuries both which I have been sufficiently long without, most fully to know the value of, and appreciate."

"It is over the water—that is to say, on the Surrey side of the river."

"Where is that?"

"What! do you really know so little of London as not to be aware of the difference between the two sides of the river?"

"I know so little of it that I have but once even looked upon the Thames, with which Londoners, of course, are so familiar."

"Indeed! Well, you shall see it as you go along now, for we shall cross one of its principal bridges. I dare say it is, to one not accustomed to it, a fine and noble sight; but, really, we see these objects of strangers' attention so often, and might see them so much oftener, that I do believe many a person hurries over one of these bridges, without making the least attempt to look at the stream, which to a stranger would be so rich in all sorts of associations."

"Most true," said Mabel; "familarity blinds us to every charm, and is a foe to all interest."

"It is, indeed, miss, and that's what I often say about great people and people holding any high stations; the more they keep themselves secluded from ordinary observation, the more they are thought of."

"That I have no doubt is the case almost universally. But where are we now?"

"This is Blackfriars Bridge."

They were now crossing that ancient bridge, concerning the health of which so many fears were entertained but a few years ago, but which now appears to set age at defiance, and to have become completely recovered, and young again.

There was the accustomed busy scene upon the river, and as Mabel looked through the old balustrades which used to flank the bridge, and saw the numbers of persons who were in boats of all sorts and description upon the stream so famous in historical recollection, her thoughts wandered back in imagination to the primitive time when the banks of that river, now so thronged with buildings for the convenience of commerce, were soft green slopes, adown which the timid deer would quietly steal to slake his thirst in the stream.

Now, what a wondrous and mighty change! Could it be possible that the painted savage had ever hunted his prey among the tangled thickets which luxuriated on spots now occupied by some of the busiest buildings ever reared to the genius of industry, not to say money-grubbing!

The officer kindly indulged her with as leisurely a survey of the river as she pleased, and then they passed on to the densely-populated district lying over the bridge, a district which, to the inhabitants of the Middlesex side of the river, ever presents so odd and different an aspect, and, by some early error of association, is always considered to be a great distance from any attractive part of London.

In one of those streets, which abound on the Surrey side of the water, and are composed of houses that at one time have made vigorous efforts to be mighty genteel, without being able to accomplish that great desideratum, the officer paused, and knocked at the door of a lodging-house.

It was one of those houses kept by decent enough industrious people, who, from some error of judgment, or calculation, fancy that letting on the shabby scale must be extremely profitable.

But people who let lodgings in London are a distinct race. The trade descends, we were going to say, from father to son; but we ought to say from mother to daughter.

Nothing presents itself in more attractive features to the ladies, than doing something which gives them a pecuniary return, independent of their husbands. This is to be done by letting lodgings; and when a young couple marry, they take a house, which they only intend to enjoy superficially; that is to say, they have the doubtful credit of possessing the whole front of it facing the street, while, in reality, all they do occupy is a back attic and the kitchen.

There can be no comparison as regards the independence of the different classes between the lodger and the person letting the lodging. The former is the great person to whom the latter must be extraordinarily civil; for there is such a vast amount of competition in lodging-letting in London now, that they who choose to lodge somewhere instead of housekeeping, may pick and choose like a bashaw with three tails in a harem.

But young women of the low, middling class, if we may be allowed the term, are brought up to look forward to letting lodgings to single men. That, and the grand principle that the sooner they get married the better, no matter to whom, form the most important features of their education.

Well, they do marry some, perchance, decent man, who could support them just tolerably : a house is taken and enjoyed for a little time ; then commences the lodging-letting furor, which, when once it breaks out in a woman, knows no bounds. Gradually the unhappy husband is driven from room to room ; from first floor to second floor ; from thence to the attics. Then, metaphorically speaking, the parlours slide from under him, and he finds himself in the kitchen.

And what is generally—we do not say always, mind—but what is generally his recompense for all this endurance, and this being jostled about in his own house ? Shall we say ? Yes. Well, then, reader, generally his great reward is, that his wife has a number of new dresses and flaming bonnets, with which to astonish her female acquaintance.

It was into a house of people of this description, of whom the officer knew nothing, that he wished to introduce Mabel.

The door was opened by, of course, a dirty drab of a girl, about fifteen, who

answered in the affirmative, upon the officer inquiring if Mrs. Jenkins was within.

These dirty slip-shod girls are kept in London by many persons in lieu of servants ; we presume upon the principle which induces some people to keep a pony instead of a horse, namely, because they would be afraid of the latter, but think that they can safely domineer a little over the former.

Mabel and the officer were shown into a remarkably dingy parlour, each of the windows of which was decorated with a placard, announcing "Furnished apartments ;" and in a few moments Mrs. Jenkins made her appearance.

It was early in the day, and, consequently, Mrs. Jenkins was a melancholy spectacle of faded finery.

She dressed always upon the showy and ornamental principle, so that the gaudy trappings, which had become too dingy to go out in, were used as the home attire, until sufficient leisure arose for the more elaborate and satisfactory manifestations of the toilette.

"Oh! Mr. Long," she said, "how do you do?"

"Very well, thank you, ma'am. This young lady is a friend of mine, ma'am, from the country. I cannot accommodate her at my house, and she wants a home for a few days only. Can you do it, Mrs. Jenkins?"

"Well, let me see. The back room, second floor, is out of town, and the front attic talks of going."

"Anywhere that is clean and comfortable will do. The young lady is not at all fastidious, and you look to me, if you please, for the money."

"Oh, I am quite sure, Mr. Long, that with any friend of yours, that is all right. I think the second floor back will be the thing."

"Very good, Mrs. Jenkins. I will call to-morrow or next day, if you please; and here, Miss Morton, is some money."

He handed a small sum to Mabel, whom he had previously recommended not to take Mrs. Jenkins, or anybody else, into her confidence with regard to who or what she was; but that if she were challenged with the fact, just to admit that she was the person who, no doubt, the next day would figure at some length in the police reports of the morning papers.

But Mabel was in no great danger of being found out in this way; for Mrs. Jenkins very rarely saw a newspaper at all, and when she did, it was one borrowed from a neighbouring public-house, and which was usually about a week old.

When Mr. Long was gone, which was almost immediately after he had made the arrangement for Mabel remaining, Mrs. Jenkins said very graciously,—

"How do you mean to manage, miss?"

"Manage?" said Mabel. "In what respect, madam?"

"Oh, as to meals, and all that sort of thing."

"I really am so completely ignorant of London, and so unaccustomed to do anything of the sort, that I am afraid I shall be very much at a loss."

"Well, then, in course, the best way will be to let me buy in for you whatever you want, and give you a little bill when you go away, you know, so that you will have no trouble at all."

"I should be much obliged by your taking so much trouble," said Mabel, "and, probably, I should have requested you to do so, but that I dreaded imposing upon your goodness."

"Oh, don't mention that. When I pop out, you know, for what I want myself, nothing can be easier than to get you what you want at the same time. One trouble does for both beautiful."

Mabel admitted that it did, and Mrs. Jenkins was in such high spirits at the idea of having got hold of somebody who permitted her to bring in a little bill, that she actually invited Mabel to tea on the identical afternoon, which invitation was duly accepted upon the spot.

A little bill is the lodging-house keeper's delight. They would not give a pin's head for anybody who comes in and merely pays the rent—not they. It is the little bill which presents itself to their imagination in glowing colours; and let you take a lodging where you will—always provided you give the landlady a *carte blanche* regarding a little bill—you will find that the air has had the most beneficial effect upon your appetite; and if you analyse the little bill, you will find that it takes at least half-a-pound of butter to butter a roll, two pennyworths of milk for two cups of coffee, and a half-quartern loaf to make three slices of toast; a pound of tea for yourself and friend twice, and the mutton-chops are three-and-sixpence a pound.

Reader, if you have any doubts regarding such phenomena, go and try it. We have, and know, from dire experience, the truth of what we assert.

But Mabel knew nothing of all this, and she partook of some horrible tea with Mrs. Jenkins, in perfect innocence of heart.

Little did she suspect what a combination of circumstances was then taking place to alter her whole course of life. During the very period when she was at the very extremity of her distresses, Henry Morton and Monsieur Rouselli were holding that most deeply interesting and important conversation, which opened to his perception the whole of her history, and solved some mysteries which, from the long lapse of time they had become so, threatened to remain so to the crack of doom.

The very circumstances which one would have thought tended at once to unite Mabel to those who loved her so well, and who had so deeply regretted her loss, had in them some phases which delayed so pleasant a consummation.

Henry Morton, after his deeply interesting interview with Monsieur Rouselli, was, as the reader may well suppose, in by far too excited a frame of mind to read newspapers, and hence he was in complete ignorance of what had taken place.

The fact is, he left London to go down to Morton Hall on the very day that Mabel with that noble sense of justice which prompted her to do so, came forward to exonerate him who had been her worst enemy from a false charge.

Then followed the coming to town again, and all the deeply interesting surmises connected with the fate of Mabel, so that the concerns of the world, which the pages of a newspaper might contain, were unknown to him. Little did he dream that those pages would contain something of so deeply and personally interesting a nature to himself.

Things, too, will happen most crossly sometimes, and there cannot be a more notable example of their crossness than in a few events which now happened, one succeeding the other with great rapidity.

They were these—

The magistrate who had received Mabel's deposition, with regard to the mendicant, could not, until the labours of the day were concluded, find time to write to Captain Morton, and when he did so it was at some length, and he missed that day's post.

Considering too, as he likewise did, that the subject matter of his communication was of a strictly personal nature—for he had his own suspicions, from Mabel's story, that, after all, she might be, granting the truth of all she said, a child of the captain's—he took especial care to write the word "private" legibly upon the envelope of the letter.

This letter, then, did not reach Morton Hall until after Captain Morton and his brother had left it, and, as no place had been named to which any letter could be forwarded to him, and as Mrs. Morton had been educated in decent society, and so never dreamed for one moment of opening a letter addressed to her husband and marked "private," the epistle of the magistrate remained unfortunately unanswered.

That gentleman, too, had most particularly requested an answer by return of post; and, indeed, it was one of those communications which ought to have been answered at once and without the least delay, inasmuch as it involved some important consequences to several people.

But there the note remained in a drawer in Captain Morton's study, where, by direction of Mrs. Morton, it was at once placed upon its arrival.

Probably, had she guessed that it related to Mabel, she would have felt herself authorised at once in opening it; but such a suspicion never once crossed her mind, and so, devoured by anxiety and tortured by suspense, she remained in the same

house with the very letter which would have given her the greatest amount of contentment, inasmuch as it would have let her know that Mabel was alive and well, and only waiting for her dearest and best friends to come to her and claim her as their own.

As regarded her comforts at the lodging-house, Mabel considered she had nothing to complain of.

She did no, though, it must be premised, contrast Mrs. Jenkins's second floor back room with her own delightful chamber at Morton Hall, where she had passed so many happy hours. Ah, no! but dingy, dark, and, in some respects, dirty, as was her present abode, it came out to her imagination in pleasant relief against the dreadful home she had had with the mendicant.

She, too, waited with all the fever of natural impatience for the reply of Captain Morton, and how often she told herself that that reply would be prompt indeed.

---

## CHAPTER LXXII.

MABEL'S SURPRISE.—THE MAGISTRATE'S DOUBTS.—THE NEW LODGER.

By inquiries of Mrs. Jenkins, who, never forgetting the "little bill," was always particularly civil to Mabel, the latter ascertained when a letter might, in the due course of events, come from the part of the country which Captain Morton resided in.

To ascertain this point was to Mabel quite equivalent to knowing when such a letter as she knew Captain Morton would write would arrive actually; and as the morning came, her anxiety increased to such an extent that the observant Mrs. Jenkins could not but be aware that something of a very strangely interesting nature indeed must be on the mind of her lodger.

In vain, however, she, by all sorts of oblique hints, endeavoured to get out of Mabel what it was that put her into such a perfect fever of expectation. She could get no sort of information or satisfaction.

When, however, tired out at last with fishing for intelligence, she said,—

"Really, Miss Morton, I am quite certain that you have something on your mind which it would ease you very much to tell to some kind friend."

Mabel quietly replied,—

"I am certainly in a state of anxiety about some affair which cannot concern you, and which I have made up my mind not to communicate."

"Oh, indeed! Well, I never—o

course, miss, you are the best judge of that."

"Yes, of course," said Mabel.

"Very good. I am sure it was only for your sake I asked. I am just about the last person in the world to be at all curious about other people's affairs, I do assure you; and if ever I do go the length of condescending to listen to anybody about anything, it's only with a *sanginous* hope, I can tell you, of doing 'em a world of good."

"Mrs. Jenkins, I give you credit for the very best intentions, and beg you will say no more upon the subject."

This was most provoking, just to be given credit for good intentions, and quietly put off with that doubtful compliment without a hope of the least hint of what it was that made Mabel so nervous and expectant.

But there was no help for it. Poor Mrs. Jenkins was doomed to be the victim of disappointed curiosity, and as it certainly would not do to press a lodger too far who had no objection to a "little bill," she felt herself, as she said, taking one thing in consideration with another, and putting this and that together, compelled to give up the affair of finding out Mabel's business in London as a a bad job.

It was something to be relieved from the oblique inquiries of Mrs. Jenkins, which had really, to Mabel, become a serious inconvenience, and she felt pleased accordingly thereat, and waited with more patience than before the arrival of news from Morton Hall.

But, alas! the hour when a letter ought to have been brought to her, or news of one having come to the magistrate, came and went, and nothing ensued.

Poor Mabel retired to her own dingy room, and wept alone for more than an hour. Then she made an effort to shake off such an amount of deep depression, and she paced the room several times, endeavouring to invent some plausible reason which should fully account for the non-arrival of news.

Later considerably in the day the officer Long came and inquired for her. At the sound of his name she flew to meet him, not doubting but that now she would have all her most anxious expectations fulfilled, and that he was the bearer of some message or letter from Morton Hall.

As good fortune would have it, too, Mrs. Jenkins was out, so that Mabel and the officer had the dingy parlour all to themselves, which it would have been a hard case to get had that lady been at home, considering her curiosity.

"You have news for me?" exclaimed Mabel.

"No," said the officer at once.

"No, no—no news—no message—no letter?"

"Nothing of the sort. The magistrate spoke to me about an hour ago about it. He asked me to come to you and say that he had written to Morton Hall, and that he had particularly requested an answer by return of post; but none had come."

"None—none?"

"Nothing of the kind; and now, Miss Morton, mind you, you must not accuse me of doubting you, or of saying anything unkind to you; but the magistrate has serious misgivings, I can see, in his own mind, with regard to the truth of your story."

"Heaven help me!"

"And he has desired me to ask of you if you still adhere to it in the face of this fact of no answer being returned to the application he has made respecting you to Captain Morton, of Morton Hall?"

A crimson flush came over the sweet countenance of Mabel, and she was silent.

"Nay," added the officer, "you consider yourself insulted, I can see, by the doubt merely which has been cast upon you; but place yourself in the magistrate's situation, and then ask yourself what you could do more than he has done."

A moment's reflection went far towards convincing Mabel that, although with her own knowledge of her own truthfulness, and of how much she had suffered, it was hard to be doubted, yet other persons could not have such a knowledge, and she replied,—

"I am wrong to feel myself offended at any doubts that may be expressed concerning my statement so long as those doubts are not expressed offensively, and, after all, are only doubts. I can no more account than you can, or the magistrate, why a letter has not come from Captain Morton; I do hope to Heaven that no calamity has come over them."

"Well, miss, my idea was that your friends would come to town, some of them personally, and that such was the true reason why no letter had been written."

"It is! it is!" exclaimed Mabel, as she clasped her hand with delight. "It is the true reason; oh, why was I so dull as not to think of that? Oh, yes, they will come to see me, to confirm all that I have said, and to take me back again with them to my happy, happy home."

Overcome by an excess of emotion, she sank back upon a couch that was in the room, and burst into tears.

"This is truth," said the officer.

"Yes, yes," sobbed Mabel. "They will come; they will come, and I shall once again look upon those old familiar faces, which are so dear to me."

He said nothing to her for some moments. He preferred allowing the tide of passion to have its way; but when he saw that she was sufficiently composed to speak more calmly, as well as to listen, he said,—

"I am quite sure that such is the case, and I stated as much myself before I came here to the magistrate."

"You did? And yet he doubted me?"

"Why, I must say he did, and for a very insufficient reason, as far as my mind goes in the matter. He said that the only thing which could have induced Captain Morton to come to London, instead of writing, would be to get here sooner than the post, and as such had not occurred, he rather felt inclined to doubt if there were such a person at all as Captain Morton, and such a place as Morton Hall."

"That was cruel."

"Well, well; you will have the triumph of showing him that he is wrong, and as for his supposition that Captain Morton might start to get to London sooner than the post, it is likely enough he might do so, and yet be delayed by a thousand incidents and accidents on the road to which the post would not be at all subjected."

"Yes, yes; you are right."

"I feel pretty sure I am; I have seen a good deal of human nature, Miss Morton, and I think now I can trust my judgment a little; I believe every word that you have said to be the strict truth, and nothing but the truth."

"You do me justice, and you have the thanks of a grateful heart. He, who has been to me all that the kindest of parents could be, will be able to thank you more efficiently than I can; and that he will soon be here to do so I feel assured."

"And I likewise. If he should not come, miss, in the course of to-day, or to-night, I shall be very much astonished."

"Be assured he will."

"I am so assured. I have to go to the magistrate's private house, to report to him my present interview with you, and I will tell him of my own firm impression as regards what you have said being correct in every particular."

"Do so; do so."

"You make yourself as comfortable here now as you can. Don't tell anything to Mrs. Jenkins; she is not, in her way, a bad sort of woman, but then she cannot keep anything to herself, and if she knew who you were, and why you were here, it would be in the course of a very few hours spread over the entire neighbourhood."

"I have resisted her inquiries."

"That is right; I will call upon you to-morrow morning, without fail, and then I hope to have some pleasant intelligence to give to you."

"I hope so, too; many thanks for all you have done for me."

"Do you require more money?"

"No; I have that which you gave me still. I have spent none of it, and, indeed, may as well return it to you; for Mrs. Jenkins, whatever may be her gossiping faults, has had the kindness to save me all trouble by purchasing whatever I require, and she will put down all the items, she says, in a bill."

A smile came over the officer's face as he said,—

"Well, that is kind, to be sure; but it will do just as well. You tell her I will pay her, and she will then go on being as kind in the way of little bills as she is now."

Mabel saw that there was something in the transaction which excited the risible faculties of the officer, but she had not the least idea of what it was; and, as she did not ask him, he saw no necessity for telling her that Mrs. Jenkins would cheat her wholesale.

After a few more remarks, and a reiterated promise of calling on the morrow, he left her; and although all her anxiety could not be said to be removed, yet she felt so thoroughly convinced that the officer's suggestion respecting Captain Morton's coming to town was a true one, that she would not have been at all astonished if he had knocked at the door.

Of course, she considered that, when he came to town, he would lose not a moment in going to the magistrate who had written, and there he would get her address, which, she well knew, he would not have in his possession many minutes before he was on his road to her.

The very possibility, then, that at any moment he might arrive, kept her in a continued flutter of spirits.

But did she think of no one in that family which was so dear to her, but of Captain Morton? Ah, yes! From the very first moment that doubts of her parentage had crossed her mind, she had associated some of her sweetest dreams of future happiness with the image of the captain's brother; and her heart now fluttered with the fond hope that he would come, too, on the wings of affection, to seek her.

But hour after hour passed away, and they came not. She passed a sleepless night of nervous expectation, but no one came to tell her any one wanted her.

True, she did hear a noise in the night, as of some one stumbling up the staircase, passing her room-door to go to the other attic, and that was all that disturbed the stillness of the long and weary hours during which she courted sleep in vain.

When she arose in the morning, her looks proclaimed pretty clearly that she had had no repose, and Mrs. Jenkins exclaimed,—

"I knew it!  I knew it!"

"You knew what, madam?"

"Why, I knew you could not sleep one blessed wink after half-past three, as never was, all on account of that wretch."

"What wretch?"

"Oh! I will get rid of him, I will.  I hate the sight of him, I do.  A good-for-nothing fellow, I'll be bound.  Coming in at such time o'night, too."

"I do not know to whom you allude, Mrs. Jenkins; but, as regards my not sleeping, you are perfectly correct."

"But did you hear no noise?"

"Yes, I certainly heard a noise, as of some one tumbling up stairs."

"Yes, at half-past three, as never was."

"I did not know what was the hour, nor can I say it was that which awakened me, for I was awake when it occurred. Who was it?"

"Why, now, I'll just tell you, and it only shows how people ought to be, in this world, continually upon their blessed guards, you see, Miss Morton.  Yesterday evening there comes a man, wrapped up in a cloak, and he asks for the lady of the house—ahem!—meaning me.  Well, I has him shown into the parlour, and down I goes.

"'Madam,' he says, 'have you any apartments to let?'

"'Yes,' says I; 'the attic went away to-day, so it's well aired,' says I; 'and the first floor back will be vacant in a week.'

"'Ah!' says he, 'the first floor back would have done best for me—I do not like going so far up stairs as the attic.'

"'Well, but,' I up and says, 'cannot you do with the attic for a week, till the first floor back is gone, you see?'

"'Yes, to be sure,' he says; 'give me a key, and I'll take possession at once. There's some rent in advance.'

"And so he makes no more ado, but down he throws a sovereign on the table, which, in course, I takes up; but I says,

"'Well, sir, of course I haven't no doubt in the world but as it's all right; but business is business, and we always does ask for a reference; so, if you will be

so good as to give me one, I shall be much obliged.'

"'Oh, yes,' says he, 'you can go to the Lord Mayor and tell him that his friend Mr. Smith has referred to him, and you will soon be satisfied.'

"'The Lord Mayor, sir?' says I; 'I think I see me going and bothering the Lord Mayor about any such thing.'

"'Well,' he says, 'that's my reference. At all events, I cannot help it if you won't go; am I not to have a lodging because you object to going to the Lord Mayor, especially when I am willing to pay you your own price?'

"Well, Miss Morton, I was staggered; this sounded so very reasonable; and I says to him, 'Sir,' says I, 'I will go to the Lord Mayor; and, in the meantime, there's a key, and you can bring in your things,' says I; for, to tell the truth, Miss Morton, I just as much thought of going to the Lord Mayor, as I thought of going to the great mogul."

"And have you been deceived?"

"I think I really have.  He has brought in nothing, nothing at all in the world. He says he wants nothing, not even a pair of boots cleaned.  He came home in the middle of the night, and he has gone out again now."

"But still, in all this, Mrs. Jenkins, I do not see that there is anything reprehensible, or that can be really found fault with."

"Ah, but it is not at all lodger-like; not the least, I should say.  It's uncommonly mysterious; and if I was to say that I liked it, I should be telling a confounded—a-hem! that I should, Miss Morton.  I can assure you I shall get rid of him; no such lodgers will do for me.  I like a gentleman to come in like a gentleman, and bring all his clothes and his little fid-fads, and say to me, 'Mrs. Jenkins, I want you to bring me a lot of things for my breakfast. I dine out, and sometimes have a friend in the evening.'"

"But does not all that give you much more trouble, Mrs. Jenkins?"

"Yes, it does, in a manner of speaking, but I don't mind trouble, and it's Christian like.  But you do look pale, indeed!  Ah, you are worritting yourself, as I said to——"

"As you said?" interrupted Mabel.  "I do sincerly hope, Mrs. Jenkins, that you will not make me a subject of remark to any one."

"Lor bless me, if you would but hear me out, now; I was going to say, as I said to myself, that was all."

"Oh, I beg your pardon."

"Me talk of anybody to nobody?  I thin

I see me. I do believe I am just about the very last person in the whole world who ever says anything about nobody to everybody. No, Miss Morton, no; if you was to say to me, 'Mrs. Jenkins,' says you, 'I will now tell you all about what has happened to me, and what is going to happen;' it would sink in my bosom, it would, and nobody would know nothing."

"Such discretion," said Mabel, "is a great virtue, and I believe it to be rare, too."

At this moment, and before Mrs. Jenkins could, as the methodist parsons say, improve upon the occasion, so as to present to herself even the ghost of a chance of worming some of her history out of Mabel, there came a sudden and a violent knock at the street-door, and then a ring at the area bell which was sufficient to break the wire.

"Bless my heart and life, what can that be?"

The door was opened by the dirty apology for a servant, and in another moment Long, the officer, came into the room.

"News! news!" exclaimed Mabel, "you have news for me?"

"I have, indeed."

"And—and they have come—they have come?"

"They have not. But the news I bring you is, that the man whom you charged with your abduction from your friends, has managed to escape from prison."

"Escape?"

"Yes; and the magistrate has taken up an opinion now that you would be gone from here; and that, in fact, you and he are in league together, in some way."

"Let him come," said Mabel, with offended pride, "and he will find me here; or, if I am thought so harshly of, let him cast me into some prison where he will know I cannot, a weak girl as I am, escape from."

"Bless us and save us!" shouted Mrs. Jenkins; "what does it all mean? Tell me; I don't know anything about it. Do tell me—do you want me to burst? What is it, eh? What is it, Mr. Long? What is it all about, my good man? Who's escaped? who hasn't come? what's it all about, eh?—eh?—tell me."

"Good God! woman," cried the officer, "will you hold your tongue? Neither I nor Miss Morton here, can get in a word edgeways."

"I hold my tongue!"

"Yes, you. Now do, for Heaven's sake! What is it to you, I should like to know? It can be no affair of yours, so do, my dear

madam, suffer me to talk with Miss Morton quietly."

Mrs. Jenkins looked unutterable things, but she said nothing; and then the officer, turning to Mabel, added—

"Do not be at all alarmed at the turn affairs have taken; I still defend you; and it was in consequence of the state of irritation into which the magistrate had thrown me, that I knocked and rang so violently at the door. I cannot think what has become of your friends."

"No one then has come from the country to me?—no letter—no communications of any sort? Alas! alas! what will become of me?"

"Nay, do not despair. It is odd, certainly, that now two posts should have elapsed, and no sort of notice been taken of the magistrate's communications, and that is what annoys him, and I have no doubt has unsettled him a good deal."

"Well, I am innocent of that neglect."

"Yes; but you know an angry man don't reason. But now, tell me, for I want to go back to him prepared with evidence upon the point; can you suggest any mode of proof of their being such a person as Captain Morton, and such a place as Morton Hall, without the necessity of some one actually going into the country to find out?"

"I really know not."

"The magistrate says that he has looked through the army list, and the only officer of the name of Morton, is now in Canada."

"Captain Morton is out of the army, now. He fought at Waterloo, as I have often heard, and after that memorable battle retired from the army."

"Well, that is something. At the Horse Guards all that can be proved, or disproved, from authentic sources of information; so do you rest contented for the present, while I go to make such inquiries. I will be myself responsible for you, so do not go out of the house, in case you should be wanted. You cannot tell, you know, what may have happened since you came away from Morton Hall. The family may have left it, or a thousand things may have occurred to hinder Captain Morton from receiving your note sent him by the magistrate."

"Yes, yes; most certainly."

"So you should console yourself with the thought that all will be well at last, as I have no doubt it will; and, in the meantime, all the exertions of the police will be directed to a discovery of the hiding-place of the man whom you have declared innocent of one crime, but accused of another."

"When—oh, when will fate cease from persecuting me ?"

"Come, come, you take things too seriously."

"Yes," half screamed Mrs. Jenkins; "she wants a adviser. She wants a sympathising indiwidual. Look at me—look at me, I say!"

"As far as I am concerned," said Long, "it cannot, of course, make the smallest difference, and Miss Morton may tell you or not tell you, Mrs. Jenkins, what it is which now harasses her so much. If she does, I should say that you ought to give the most solemn pledge of secrecy."

"I'll pledge everything," said Mrs. Jenkins.

"Nay, nay, you must excuse me— indeed you must," remarked Mabel. "I am quite unequal to the task of entering into a history of all I have suffered, and of all I now suffer. I cannot, unless some strong and urgent necessity arise, do so, and therefore, Mrs. Jenkins, without any disrespect to you, and fully giving you credit for the best motives, I ask you, as a favour, to ex-cuse me"

The countenance of Mrs. Jenkins fell, and she gave a groan, as she said,—

"Then, I ain't to know, after all."

"Yes," said Mabel; "after all you shall know; but not now. Do not ask me now for a confidence that would distress me much in the progress of giving it."

The case was hopeless. Mrs. Jenkins gave it up in despair as regarded Mabel; but she followed the officer to the door, and said, in a very confidential sort of tone,—

"My dear Mr. Long, what has she done?"

"Done—done? Why, what made you think she had done anything? She is not accused of doing anything."

"Well—but—but——"

"But what?"

"Why, you know, Mr. Long, that there is some dreadful mystery in the whole affair. I knew there was from the very first, and I might just as well know it as not."

"Well, then——"

"Yes—yes, Mr. Long."

"You must know, then, Mrs. Jenkins, as regards her, I mean the young lady in the parlour, she minds her own business, and it would be a good thing if every one else did the same. So good morning, ma'am, good morning."

Away walked the officer, leaving poor Mrs. Jenkins in a perfect fever of indignation and impatience.

"What!" she exclaimed—"what, will nobody tell me anything about anybody? Am I to endure all this in my own house? Am I to be made certain that something is going on that's, perhaps, absolutely terrific, and not know anything about it ? No—no—n—o—I'll put on my shawl and bonnet, and go to my mother's, and ask her what she would do under such dreadful circumstances. I'll warrant she would not put up with it a moment, not she. She's a clever woman, and kept a lodging-house for thirty years."

With this resolve—certainly a valorous one—Mrs. Jenkins retired to her own tiring-room, and, to the great relief of Mabel, she soon after sallied forth, to go to her mother, who was one of those regular old female sharks who had been, for thirty years, "taking in,"—so the phrase goes—"and doing for" the male population of this great city.

Mabel, now, instead of finding the perils and the troubles which surrounded her diminishing, found them daily increasing.

The silence and the non-appearance of Captain Morton, or some, at least, of the Morton family, was to her one of the most inexplicable things in the whole world. Time enough had now elapsed to cover all accidental delays on the road from Morton Hall to the metropolis, and she could only now fall back upon what had been suggested by the officer, namely, that some circumstances must have happened to induce the Morton family to leave the Hall.

This was a supposition which, although it might account for the non-arrival of some of her friends, was, in other respects, anything but consolatory, because it threw off to an indefinite period when she should see those to whom she had but a short time since considered that she was upon the eve of being re-united.

It likewise suggested a catalogue of causes for the Morton family leaving Morton Hall, among which the possibility of some death among them figured most fearfully to her imagination.

Perhaps Captain Morton himself, to whom the letter had been addressed, was no more, or Mrs. Morton, or worse than all, Henry, to whom, she could no longer conceal from herself, she was tenderly attached.

It was no wonder that all these considerations should produce a mental fever, that might with a very little addition become a bodily one, likewise, and to be confined under such circumstances to a bed of sickness presented itself as a calamity of no ordinary character.

More than once she thought of leaving the house in which she was, and making her way to Morton Hall, there to ascertain, personally, why the magistrate's communication remained unanswered.

But when she came to recollect that she had promised the officer that she would not stir from the house, and that he had told her how he had made himself responsible for her, she gave up that plan as altogether unworthy; although, when she should see him again, she made up her mind to broach it.

Thus poor Mabel passed some hours, until, quite exhausted by her previous night's watchfulness, she lay down, dressed as she was, upon her bed, and fell into a sound and peaceful slumber.

In such a state she was likely to remain long, and feeling, as we do, all the sympathy which we cannot but feel for one so circumstanced, we gladly leave her in so composed a condition for awhile, and turn to some of the other characters and events of our tale, which is now so rapidly drawing to its close.

## CHAPTER LXXIII.

### THE ESCAPE FROM THE PRISON, AND THE HUNT THROUGH SOUTHWARK.

THE mendicant was again remanded, as we have already seen, and returned to the Compter; but upon this occasion he was not remanded upon the more serious charge of murder, because the evidence of Mabel acquitted him of that; but he was remanded upon the charge of abduction, and that with all its concomitant evils was serious enough, and dangerous enough, too.

The officers were much surprised at the turn affairs had taken with the mendicant; they knew not what to make of it, whether to believe Mabel or not.

They could not, however, doubt her, for there was so much apparent sincerity and truth in all she said and uttered, that they were compelled to give up their previously positively-made-up conclusion respecting his guilt; but many of them suspended heir opinion upon the point until the inquiries had been made respecting the truth of Mabel's statement, as regarded Captain Morton.

They, however, returned to the Compter the same day, and the officers said to him, as they walked along,—

"You have had a narrow chance for it, at all events, and it's lucky for you, you have somebody to come forward and swear for you, or your neck would have been within the compas of a halter, I can assure you to a certainty."

"I am not guilty," said the mendicant.

"Very well; be that as it may, I'm certain that, but for her, you would this day have been in Newgate."

"But they would not hang an innocent man."

"If you believe what dying people say, there are many innocent men hung at the Old Bailey."

"Then, they would commit murder."

"Well, I don't know; but, with the law, killing's no murder; that's the way with us, and I am by no means sure, whether there may not come up, about you, from Morton Hall, something that will make you look queer."

The mendicant said nothing; he did not appear to be in a very communicative humour, and was lost in deep thought, so as scarcely to hear what was said to him.

"Well, you are a queer being, at all events," said the officer; "you're not even grateful for the change of prospects."

"Change of prospects!" said the mendicant. "What do you mean? I have no change."

"You have," said the officer. "Don't you consider the change of prospects bettered when you have only imprisonment to look forward to, than when you lived in expectation of being hanged?"

"I was innocent."

"But are you of the second charge?"

"It is useless to talk to you about this matter. I am certain that I can gain nothing from you that will aid me in my defence. Seek, therefore, not to ask me questions that I decline answering."

"It is very well to do so, certainly, very well; and, at the same time, safe, though not very indicative of innocence."

The mendicant made no answer to this, but kept silence until they arrived at the Compter. There was little by the way in which he felt interested; indeed, for so supposed desperate an offender as that which the mendicant was presumed to be, he paid but little attention to any chance of escape which might have occurred on the road —he was quiet and docile.

This might have arisen from the fact of the mendicant being so deeply buried in his own thoughts, that he saw not what was passing around him; or else he was so secure of his own innocence that he cared not to make an escape, since it would render him always liable to re-capture.

When they arrived at the Compter, the turnkey opened the wicket gate, and looked somewhat amazed when the mendicant stepped up, in company with a couple of officers.

"Hilloa!" he said, "who would have thought of seeing you here again? One would have thought of seeing the Great Mogul just as soon. Why, how's this?"

"I can hardly tell myself," said one of the officers.

"They couldn't make up the case complete, but have remanded him, I suppose?"

"Indeed, you are out altogether."

"Out! You don't mean he's to remain here until tried, I suppose; because that's gammon—I'll not believe it."

"Oh! dear, no. You are out again. He hasn't come back here on account of the murder at all."

"No! what do you mean by that?"

"Why, he's been acquitted of the crime of murder, and another charge substituted in its place."

"Well, I don't know what to make of this affair," returned the turnkey. "Did they not say the man was dead?"

"Yes, but he didn't commit the murder —he did not, in fact, kill anybody," returned the officer.

"What have you brought him here for?"

"On a remand for abduction," replied the officer, "and not for murder; for the lady he has carried away, and hid in the very house where the murder was committed, came forward and declared he did not do it."

"Oh! the devil; this is a gay deceiver, and not a murderer, after all, though I am inclined to think nature must have intended him for the latter."

"It is a mistake, I suppose," returned the other; "and now you must lodge him for a week somewhere."

"Very well; where will he be safe?"

"In any of the cells. He need not be placed in the same place he was locked up in last night. That is not necessary—you know he's not here for murder."

"No; he is not."

It was arranged that the mendicant should be placed in one of the cells that had been that day vacated by a prisoner who had been committed to Newgate.

Here he was placed, and left to himself to ruminate, until his week should have expired.

When thrust into this place, the mendicant sat down on the only seat there was, but not from any desire to sit. He was lost in deep thought, and remained for some time in silence, without moving a muscle.

"Have I changed my condition for one better?" he murmured. "Am I better than I was? Am I not rather as dangerously placed? and have I not seen all my hopes ruined?

"Yes, yes; everything has failed—utterly and signally failed. I have escaped the charge of murder, certainly; but am I safer now than I was? Certainly not.

"They will make inquires at Morton Hall, and the neighbourhood, and then other matters will come out which will not tell in my favour. At all events, I shall run serious danger, and almost certain detection."

He paused a moment or two, and then considered a few moments, before he muttered again,—

"Oh! it must, it will be so. An escape could be planned and executed, I have no doubt, suddenly and with energy. Yes, I'll make the attempt, at all events. I can lose nothing, though I may gain; it is wise, therefore, to make the attemp to gain my liberty, when its failure can cost me nothing."

He rose up, and walked about for some time. It was now dark, and he could hear a bustling about among the turnkeys, and the turning of locks and keys.

"My turn will come presently," he muttered; "and then now or never—neck or nothing!"

In a few moments more, he heard the turnkey coming towards him, and his cell, which was a secret one, was at length visited by the turnkey.

He could hear the lock turn, and then the bulky form of the turnkey was seen entering the cell.

"Well," he said, "what have you to say for your supper? Here it is, light and wholesome."

As he spoke, he placed some bread and water on the table.

"You'll have some swiggins for breakfast; that will be warm. Ain't you grateful?"

"Oh, yes," said the mendicant; "here's your health!" and at the same time he lifted the water as if he were about to drink it, and suddenly smacked it into the turnkey's face.

The man gasped and staggered from the effects of the water, and then the mendicant felled him by a blow upon the temple, which caused him to drop as if he had been shot.

In an instant the mendicant took the keys and some silver from the fallen man; opened the cell door, and stepped out, at the same time he locked the door, securing the turnkey in the cell, and freeing himself from immediate pursuit.

For a moment he paused; but he recollected which way he came, and he groped his way in the dark, until he came to a place where the passage entered another, which led right and left.

"Which way now?" he muttered. "I forgot which it was we came down; but whichever it was, I cannot now remember—stay!—what sound is that?"

He listened, and he could hear the turnkey in his cell, hammering away to get free.

"He'll cause an alarm if I do not take one way or the other. I'll chance it, as indeed I must. This one to the right seems the most likely of all."

He accordingly walked down lightly and rapidly, until he came to the end of the passage, which terminated in a cross way, that seemed to lead to several rooms.

A door was suddenly opened, and a man came out and went away. He was one of the turnkeys, and when he came out of the door, the mendicant at once saw that this was the wicket-gate which led into the street.

He heard voices in this place, and yet, to get out, he must pass through this place.

There was a door that led into it, but it was only ajar, and he crept softly towards it, and peeped in at it. The door was shut, but the key was in the door, and he determined to make the attempt.

The odds were formidable, because there were three men in the room. He had not expected so many.

He pushed open the door very gently, and walked into the room without being seen, and had seized a large walking stick which lay in one corner.

He hesitated; how to act he knew not. Whether he had better risk a rush at the wicket-gate at once, or whether he should make an attack upon the turnkeys and stun them.

It was a moment of indecision; but there was no time to lose, for there was a desperate noise in the passage, made by the imprisoned turnkey.

"What can all that noise mean?" exclaimed one of the turnkeys. "What can be the matter?"

"I don't know. Some of the visitors are not very quiet. It seems to me as if some of the good fellows, by way of amusement, had begun to kick the doors.

"And, perhaps, think they will keep u

up all night; but the strong room will do best for them."

"That is true—very true, indeed; but it might happen that somebody wants help."

"Ha! what's that?"

This last exclamation was caused by the mendicant having touched the key with his hand, and turned it in the lock, and made a slight noise.

"The devil!" exclaimed one.

"An escape, by G—d!" shouted the others.

"Stop him! stop him!" they all three cried out until they were out of breath, and they made desperate efforts to do so. Before they reached the mendicant, one measured his length upon the stone flooring, while the next shared the same fate, but the third stood up.

"Now, then, my lad, I have you," he exclaimed; "you don't get away from me, at all events."

As he spoke, he seized the mendicant by the collar, but received such a blow in the eye from the handle of the stick that it made him stagger; and, when at a pace or two's distance, the mendicant brought down a swordsman's blow across the head, so that his body immediately collapsed into a heap, as if deprived of life.

In another moment the mendicant had opened the wicket-gate, and made a dash into the street.

However, they had not been idle inside, for the noise had not been heard to no purpose, but just as the last of the three turnkeys was felled to the earth, the first who had fallen arose, and he was joined by some others, who, hearing the disturbance, were hurrying to that one point.

The alarm-bell was rung, and soon there were a number of men who were ready to pursue.

The mendicant had not time to do more than pull the gate after him, and then, finding himself so closely pressed, he made a dash towards Smithfield.

"Stop him! stop thief! stop him!" were the cries of the turnkeys, who made desperate attempts to overtake the mendicant, but he had too great a stake on the issue of the race to allow himself to be overtaken by any one, if human exertion could carry him away.

On they all rushed, the turnkeys keeping well together, and very close after the pursued; they were not, in fact, many yards apart, for the turnkeys could see the flying figure of the mendicant as he rushed through Smithfield with the greatest speed towards St. John-street.

"Hilloa!" cried a man who came from that way; "mad bull! stop the bull! who —a—a——"

As he spoke, he lifted his stick high in the air, and flourished it so that he seemed about to strike the mendicant, who turned to the right, and ran up Long-lane, the turnkeys very nearly catching him, on account of the turn. He made good his pace, and the foremost fell down in an attempt to catch him, and the next ran against another person.

However, the others came up, and soon kept the mendicant at work; he dashed along Long-lane into Barbican, and then among some vehicles of one kind and another, until he neared the streets that led to Fore-street, and others in that quarter.

Onward the mendicant went without stopping to ascertain if he were followed by looking behind, for he felt assured that there would be a steady pursuit made after him; it would be such a circumstance to be spoken of; a description that would bring with it such condemnation by the authorities.

The turnkeys, in fact, did all they could to overtake the fleeing prisoner.

"Stop thief! stop him!"

These were cries that were uttered and shouted repeatedly after him, that made many a person get out of the way, lest he should be in harm's way when the desperate character came up.

Few, indeed, are there who choose to stop malefactors in the street; it's dangerous—decidedly so—because such people never, or at least very seldom, get any recompense who do, and those who do it are seldom punished for the misdeeds.

Seeing the mendicant coming along the street at such a rate, no one liked the encounter; besides, the mendicant rushed from one side of the road to the other in such a rapid manner that nobody knew on which side of the way they were, and only got out of the rush.

They soon got into Cheapside, and thence towards London Bridge, which they went through at a furious rate; there were many attempts to seize the mendicant, yet they were unsuccessful, bringing discomfort only to the attemptors.

One person, indeed, cried out "Stop thief! stop thief!" and made an attempt to stop him. The mendicant had no time to expostulate, but merely placed his knuckles forcibly in the mouth of the same individual, who came on his back in consequence, and there he lay for some time.

More than once he met with the like necessity of destroying the equilibrium of different individuals, who came in his way for the express purpose, seemingly.

They came to London Bridge, and when once on the other side, the mendicant began to think that there was a probability of his being alone.

He paused a moment to look back towards the bridge he had just crossed; but was immediately apprised that he was very closely followed by a hand being placed on his shoulder, and a voice exclaiming,

"I have you, by G—d!"

The mendicant saw how matters were. He dived beneath the arms of the captor, and rushed full speed down a street to the right, running towards Southwark, where he hoped to be able to shake off the pursuers.

By that time the officers had been joined by several other people, who had been seduced from their proper business to follow the chase of an offender, from the mere sake of doing something and seeing something more than usual.

At length they closed upon him very fast, and the mendicant saw that he was likely to be soon enclosed and secured, and there would be no escape.

Suddenly the thought struck him he might make a dart into some of the old houses, and scramble over the roof, leaving his pursuers in uncertainty which way he went.

No sooner thought of than done, and he rushed into a house, and closed the door suddenly.

He was too breathless to do much; but while he panted for breath, he locked and bolted the door. He had no sooner done so than he felt a violent rush at the door, as if some one had endeavoured to push it open.

"Open the door," said a voice,

The mendicant panted a moment or two, as if he were incapable of moving.

"Open the door in the king's name."

"Are you sure he went in here?" said some one else.

"Yes, I think so."

"Be sure, or else he'll be off; while you are getting in here he will be away in the meantime."

"I have no doubt of that; but this is the house I have pitched upon, and I'll search it."

As he spoke, he began to use the knocker and bells somewhat violently, and then shouted, taking them in turns, till the whole neighbourhood was alarmed, and the people of the house at last, who were under an impression there was a fire somewhere, and in another instant every window was opened, and every head thrust out, and every mouth said,—

"Where is it—where is it?"

"Come down—come down and see," screamed the turnkeys.

In this extremity, the people of the house came rushing down stairs to the street door, and the mendicant, in the confusion, had gained the upper story unquestioned.

"For Heaven's sake what's the matter?" inquired a woman, as she rushed out of the attic.

"We rather expect the chimney is going to fall into your room, and you had better make haste down stairs."

"Muster Smith — Muster Smith," shrieked the woman, who began to knock and kick at the adjoining room with all imaginable violence; "Muster Smith, make haste, or you'll be burnt alive!"

When she had done this, she rushed down stairs; and as the mendicant secured the trap-door after him in the loft, he heard rapidly advancing steps.

"He's gone up here," said one.

"Did you see a tall, ill-looking man go up just now. my good woman?"

"A man has just got into the loft," said the woman, "and I suppose he is on the top of the house by this time."

"That's he," said the person who questioned her. "Follow me, lads; we'll soon be after him—we'll soon have him neck and heels—we'll keep him safe this time."

They, after a short loss of time, burst open the trap-door, and got out of the loft on the top of the houses.

The streets were full of people, and all looking anxiously to the roof of the house, and there they could see the mendicant stealing along the house-tops for some six or seven houses, and then they lost sight of him behind some chimneys.

The officers then came along the roofs, directed by the cries of the mob from one spot to the other, until they came to the place where the mendicant disappeared, and then they seemed to pause for a moment.

"There, down there is where he disappeared," said the mob.

The officers, too, presently disappeared from the eyes of the mob, and did not reappear.

The mendicant had got down a kind of platform, that had been constructed for some purpose or other, and then into a house, the door of which opened into a court-way.

Here he was detained in the house by some person who wanted to detain him, and who would have done so, but that the mendicant struck him down, and then made his escape by stepping into the court.

Of course the officers were immediately put upon his trail, and a sharp chase ensued amongst a number of courts and alleys. Hooting and shouting of all kinds were resorted to by the pursuers, but the mendicant kept up a most astonishing speed; he never appeared to flag, while the officers felt all the fatigue men could feel.

They were, in fact, perfectly beaten, but yet they kept to their pursuit. They seemed not to flag, yet they felt a few moments more must settle the pursuit.

A transitory glimpse of the retreating figure of the mendicant suddenly cheered them on with the prospect of a capture after all, but only a sudden exertion of spirit would do it.

Summoning their remaining energy, they did make the required exertion, and found that the more they increased their speed the more the mendicant increased his.

Suddenly he slipped and fell. Here was a triumph—the officer's hands absolutely touched his coat; but, ah! the chance of war—the officer himself fell, and the mendicant dashed into a public-house, and the officers who came up next made a rush into the place, but it was vacant.

Looking round they saw another room. There were three doors, and each led in a different direction.

After a moment's consideration they made a dash through the opposite door, and then out of it; but it led into a court, which led two ways—they scoured down the one that had no thoroughfare at one end, and but one at the other.

No signs of the fugitive could be seen anywhere, and the officers looked at each other in blank dismay. They were done; and panting as they were with exertion, this disappointment was the more bitter; and then inconsolable were they for the great exertion they had made to no purpose.

----

## CHAPTER LXXIV.

MABEL IS ALARMED AT THE NEW LODGER.—THE DREADFUL DISCOVERY.

POOR Mabel's situation was becoming every day one of more and more anxiety and dread. Indeed, every hour might be said to add materially to the difficulties which beset her, and every minute of the hour brought with it its share of evil instead of consolation.

She quite exhausted her mind in vain efforts to discover what could have possibly happened to prevent the Mortons from writing to her or coming personally once again to take her under their protection; but amid all the wild and improbable cogitations that from time to time took possession of her mind, she never for one moment committed the injustice of attributing their silence and non-appearance to a want of affection for her.

Ah, no! she knew too well upon what a rock of sincerity that affection was based. She knew too well that no ordinary circumstances could shake it, and it was in picturing to herself some calamities as having possibly occurred to the Mortons that she produced for herself such a world of mental anxiety.

If another day or two should elapse without receiving any tidings of them, she felt that her situation would become one of a most precarious character, and that she should be open to suspicions of having by no means adhered to the truth in the statements which she had made.

And perhaps it was no small aggravation of her miseries that she should be so situated that she had no one who could counsel her well; that there was no friend near her to whom she could speak in perfect confidence of spirit, and with a knowledge that she was perfectly understood and believed.

Far from Mrs. Jenkins being any such person, Mabel was quite delighted at her absence, if anything could b said to delight her at such a time.

But, by some means, what Mrs. Jenkins had said concerning her new lodger, Mabel could not forget, and without having seen him, or knowing why or wherefore, Mabel began to have a great dread of this mysterious personage.

She ascertained, towards the evening of that same day, from the dirty little apology for a servant, that the stranger was at home, and had been shut up in his room for a considerable time, so that, in consequence of Mrs. Jenkins not having returned from her visit of consultation to her mother, Mabel almost dreaded to go to her own apartment in consequence of its proximity to that occupied by the stranger.

When we say its proximity, we do not mean to say that it was on the same floor, but being precisely above her chamber, she was more likely to be annoyed by the incessant, restless, pacing to and fro which the stranger kept up in his room, than as if he had been on the same floor with her.

If Mrs. Jenkins had been within, Mabel could have gone to her chamber with more confidence; but it was getting rather late in the evening before that, in her opinion, much injured lady made her appearance. That is to say, it was late in Mabel's acceptation of the term; for her simple, country habits had made her think the hours that were kept in Mrs. Jenkins's house of the most extraordinary character.

Like many persons unaccustomed to London life, she could not conceive what induced its inhabitants to turn night into day in the manner they did.

A knock, however, at length announced the return of Mrs. Jenkins; and Mabel having duly ascertained that it was that lady, from the little servant, thought that she might now venture to retire to rest, without much dread of the stranger.

She did not wish to meet Mrs. Jenkins first, as that lady would be from a consultation with her maternal parent, so she at once, and before that lady entered the dingy parlour, took her chamber candlestick, and retired to her own room, satisfied with the fact that she was in the house, and no doubt would protect her from any overt act on the part of the stranger.

And yet, as she ascended the creaking staircase, she asked herself—

"And yet, what on earth can I have to dread from him?  Surely, surely, I must have allowed my fancy to get strangely the mastery of my reason, or I could never have all these feelings of dread for a perfect stranger to me; but, somehow, since that man has been in the house, a nervous tremor has crept over me, which I cannot at all account for, and which is enough to induce me almost to leave it at once."

When she reached her own room she heard her fellow-lodger pacing to and fro overhead with rapid strides; and she felt that, while he chose to continue that exercise, any attempt on her part to sleep would be completely out of the question.

Feeling this, she did not retire to rest; and it was as well that she did not, as things turned out; but she sought a temporary solace from her cares in the pages of a volume which she found in her apartment, and from which she read the following short tale :—

My grandfather died when I was quite a boy.  I remember him, though, very well.  He was a tall, thin man, squinted very badly, and wore a grizzly beard.

No very pretty picture, you'll say; but never mind, there are worse men than my grandfather was, although there were a few queer stories told of him.

Everybody thought him a rich man—the why I can't tell; but I must say they were somewhat justified in believing this of him, because they knew very well that he never did anything for many years, but lived quite comfortable and happy, despite the pressure of the times.

"Go when you would, you would be welcome, and partake of all that was on the table; and if he didn't want you to stay to the next day, he would tell you he was going out, and you must shift your quarters.

However, he always kept a full cupboard, and plenty to eat and drink, and none of the worst; but go when you would, the old gentleman never had any money.

I think he had eschewed money; he never lent any one a penny piece in his life that I heard of—added to which he married young in life, and lost his wife early.

I don't recollect ever hearing him say this was a misfortune, though somebody else might have called it a domestic calamity; but I can't say he did.

It was thought from this that he was rich; he had no drain upon his purse, lived cheerful and contented, though a very odd fish indeed.

I have said he squinted, and wore a grey beard.  Well, he had a hooked noise, a brown, long-tailed coat, buttoned up to the chin, and a broad-brimmed hat—not a quaker's hat; that he would have avoided, had he been compelled to wear a bonnet to do so.

Well, he took ill, and died very suddenly. Nobody knew how he used to live alone, and do for himself, and keep a whole house to himself; and one day he was taken very ill, and sent for my father.

I have heard my father laugh as he described the scene, which he said was truly ridiculous.

My grandfather made most horrible faces, had very expressive features, as I have said, and he rolled them about, so that they produced such terrible contortions and visages that he seemed to be a living panorama of all the odd faces that were ever invented by human nature.

He first put his hand upon one part, and then upon the other, and turning about and swearing, whenever a doctor was mentioned, so fearfully, that nobody could help laughing.

However, poor fellow, he died; what of, I can't say, but he was in much pain.

There was one great discovery made, however, after the death, and that was what had not been thought of before; there was no money.

What could my grandfather have been thinking of, to have died at such a moment; at a moment when there was nothing more to be had? Why, he must have lived to the end of his means, and then voluntarily given up the ghost.

This was another thing that was rather singular in my grandfather, that he could have died off so suddenly, just as if he had calculated to a nicety as to how long he could make both ends meet, and then, when there was an end of the means of life, he had only to die, which he did, as if it were something done to order.

People were much astonished.

"I didn't think he would have done such a thing," said one; "I didn't think it was his character."

"I thought he was a rich man," said a second; "he certainly had money."

"What has become of it?" was the natural inquiry.

"What has become of it?" was the only echo, produced from every man's mouth.

My father was especially vexed; he said, that he might as well have told him the truth, and then he wouldn't have expected anything; but as it was, he was, he felt, very much disappointed.

"I am sure he must have money," he said.

"Where is it?" inquired my mother.

"I can't tell; but I dare say he has it in some of the securities, and has left no memorandum of it, and so it is for ever lost to us, come what may."

This was an aggravating view of the case, but I think a just one.

Time passed on, and my father followed in the steps of his father, and he became defunct.

How the world wags! Some are born, some marry, and some die, and so we go on day after day, week after week, and year after year; and no alteration in the great mass of human beings, save an increase of the population.

I was left alone in the world, left to do the best I could for myself or with myself.

I determined first upon one thing, and then upon another, until I knew not what was to be done.

However, I at length determined to enter the company's service, and go out to India. There was a number of young men of good character wanted, as the bills say; so having nothing to do with myself, and no love match on hand, I embarked my whole fortune—that is, my person—in the Indian wars, which were just beginning.

I embarked on board a vessel which took us out to India, and occupied about five months in the voyage; I was about to say, if I had to travel to heaven from the debateable land of purgatory, by a six months' voyage, I would not go.

Nothing in life can compensate a man for a six months' voyage, where there are so many human beings pent up together; to be sure, a voyage to heaven would not be conducted on the same plan; there would be, for instance, very few passengers.

There would, of course, be more room, and we should not be almost compelled to cut out our square inch of air before we swallowed it, so thick it had become.

I am not surprised at the yellow fever, black and all, and any other disorder on board vessels—transport vessels, when we come to consider the nature of the atmosphere we breathe in such latitudes.

It is evidently rarified to a degree, and we require more of it, instead of which, as was the fact with us, there is less of it.

However, we, I might say, I, landed in India, so terribly disgusted with the sea voyage, that I would not have gone back again for a trip, not for a fortune.

Well, we were in India—lord, what a place! there's no beer or coffee-shops—nothing but jungle and black people, or copper-coloured—it does not matter much which—they were all the same to me.

Here we were marched about under a burning sun, and had a different diet to what we had when in England. Things were in abundance, it was true, and cheap, but I didn't care about them.

We had several sharp engagements, and I had the honour of being noticed by my officer, whose life I saved on one occasion, by spitting the fellow who was about to take his head off below the ear.

For that I got a step.

Well, on we went, fighting and firing some falling and some not; I had more than one wound.

Tight work fighting in that climate; there are but few enjoyments to men in the field campaigning; all is danger, if not from the enemy, at least from the climate, and thus we have two to fight against.

Well, as I said before, we went on fighting, until we came on to meet the great Tippoo Saib.

Tippoo was no fool; he had posted himself behind the walls of Seringapatam; here we were determined to besiege him.

It was good fun for those who were not shot; but, for those who had more lead placed suddenly in their persons than was natural, it was very uncomfortable, for it always put the human machinery out of repair, and sometimes entirely damaging it, so that it was of no use, and thrown aside, or in a hole made in the earth on purpose.

Well, the night before the assault was made, I was off duty. On that night I was in my bed; that is to say, I was lying on a few odd things, under a tent, trying to snatch a few hours' sleep, for the next day we believed would decide all.

Well, there I lay. I believe I had fallen asleep; indeed, there can be no doubt about it—I must have fallen asleep, and much good I am sure it did me.

I dreamed, or rather I woke up after a few hours' sound sleep; while thinking of the past, and the duties of the day, I thought I saw a figure before me.

I started; I must confess it, I was rather more terrified than a soldier in the East India Company ought to be under any circumstances.

However, I instantly recognised the figure before me as soon as it was perfectly discernible, which it was not for some moments.

I seemed surrounded by a mist; but who could mistake the broad-brimmed hat, the brown coat with the old-fashioned skirts, the hooked nose, and terrible squint?

That was my grandfather.

I lay some time looking at him, wondering what he was there for, and why he looked so sorrowful and sad at me.

"Grandfather!" said I, at length; or I thought I said so, which is all the same thing, you know:

"Grandson," said the old gentleman.

"What brings you to India, grandfather—what brings you so far away from home?"

"Ah! boy. boy!" said the old gentleman, looking at me sorrowfully. "Ah, boy!"

"What's amiss?"

"You have come to a sad country; why did you come here? wasn't your own country good enough for you?"

"Yes; but I had no means of obtaining a livelihood there; so I came to India to make a fortune."

"Or be food for saltpetre."

"Very likely," said I; "to-morrow will settle that business, I dare say, for I expect we shall have to mount the breaches in the wall."

"Well, boy, and if you get clear of the hot work cut out for you, you ought not to tempt the chance again; but when you get clear, return to your own country, get my old house, and there stick till I see you."

"Ha! ha! ha!" laughed I; "what could I do with your old house? I, a sergeant in the Honourable East India service commence housekeeping! Ha! ha!"

Upon which the old man frowned dreadfully, and said, in an angry voice,—

"Do as you will, boy, but I know it will be to your advantage to do what I tell you; it will make your fortune, however you may be off."

"W.ll it, by George?"

"Yes, it will. Farewell; already the sun nears the horizon, and I must be in the west when the sun rises. You'll see me no more until you are in my house; then expect me."

"Well," thought I, "you will voyage home much quicker than I came here, and will have more accommodation as regards room; I had none, you plenty."

The figure became gradually indistinct and faded away.     *     *     *     *

The troops were awakened at an early hour, and ready to storm the trenches at the appointed time; when, amid the thunder of great guns, and small arms, the shouts of the victors, and the shrieks of the wounded, we entered the fortress as victors.

There came loud shouts when the place was ours, and then store of plunder—the place was very rich. I got some jewels and some valuables of various kinds, and had enough to buy my discharge.

I was wounded, but not severely as to entitle me to a pension, and I did not care well enough to secure a pension at the expense of the continuance in the service, for seven years, in such a clime.

I took my way to Europe; then I had another long voyage, a voyage that I bore with more equanimity than I had done before, because I had more accommodation; I had the money, in fact, to pay for it.

Thus matters stood, and for many weeks we gazed upon the wearisome sea; everything around seemed like glass, not a tree or a shrub, nothing green to relieve the eye—all was one expanse of water.

One morning there was a cry of land. It was a joyful sound to hear; I ran upon deck almost in a state of nudity, when I was politely requested to return below for my wardrobe, which, in the hurry, I had forgotten to bring with me.

I returned below, and dressed myself entirely, and then I returned to the deck very soon after.

It was a delightful thing to see; how people suddenly came to life who had before been no more than moveable corses, and who languished about the deck with long yellow faces as if they were suffering under the jaundice.

The white cliffs of old England were now to be seen, and much pleasure did we anticipate the moment that we should land upon the shore of our native country.

I was wild with joy.

*     *     *     *     *     *

It would be impossible to relate all the absurdities I committed, from mere joy and delight, to find myself once more in my native country.

After spending a few days in Portsmouth I ran up to town in the Portsmouth mail, and arrived there about daybreak, and entered a hotel, where I had a good breakfast, the first I had had in London for several years.

It was a moment of great congratulation to me to find I was once more so safe and so comfortable.

"What shall I do now I am here?" thought I.

That was a serious question, a question I could not answer even to myself upon so short a notice.

I therefore determined to look about me, and see what there was that could be done, and then determined upon adopting such plans as appeared to me most suitable and most promising.

I had not money enough to live upon, though I had a good round sum; it might bring me an annuity, and that was all; but then to run any risk was a thing I did not feel much inclined to; besides, I was not then calculated for employment when I had any one to attend to, because they would not like my mode of attending to them.

I had acquired odd habits, and who is there who has been in India that has not done so?

"Well," thought I, "now I am here it seems to me I am worse off than before. Work! I don't like a trade because of the risk, and so what to do is really a mystery."

I had walked about for some days, but yet nothing was to be seen. Come what would I was determined I would stick by my money; I would not part with that;

that was my only friend, and to lose that would be dreadful.

I sat one day in a hotel thinking of the past and future, and many old recollections returned, when, suddenly, my grandfather's image presented itself to my mind.

"Ah!" thought I, "my dream, by Jove; I will see if the old house is standing; and if so, I may as well take it. It is very old, but I will chance it; surely my dream, or rather the vision, meant something."

My grandfather wasn't a man to trouble himself about nothing; quite the contrary, he would take no trouble unless it resulted in something.

"My grandfather's ghost," said I, to myself, "never would have come all the way to India, without some great and especial object in view. It may mean something or nothing; but take the old house I certainly will."

Well, it was an odd thought—but one I stuck to, and in an hour I was walking before the old house.

It was very old and dingy, and uninhabited; the doors and shutters were fastened, and there was a notice intimating that those premises were to let; but it was more than half defaced, and I considered some time whether it was intended to remain in force

However, I determined to make inquiries, and I did so.

"Yes, sir, the old house is to let, or to be sold, or something, or anything of the sort, that can be done with it."

"Its not in ornamental repair," said I.

"He! he! no—no, it isn't."

"What do you ask for it?"

"These are the terms," said the man, pointing to the list, "twenty-five pounds a year."

"Twenty-five!"

"Used to let for fifty-five," said the agent, stopping me before I had finished my remark.

"I know—but I don't know that I shall give you that first, unless you'll put it into repair."

"Oh dear no; the owners won't do that; they'd sooner let it tumble to pieces."

"Well," said I, "I'll take it for a twelve month, at twenty pounds, but not a farthing more."

The bargain was struck and upon proper references being given, the key was placed in my hand.

\* \* \*

Once more I entered the house in which my remembrance brought to my mind many early scenes, now many years gone by; but how the place was altered!

I was very tired—very tired indeed, and I threw myself on a temporary bed, that I had placed there.

I was not there long before I fell into a deep sleep, from which I did not awake for many hours. However, it was but for once I fell so deeply asleep, and after a time I become alive to what took place around me.

Then as soon as I opened my eyes, I beheld my grandfather standing before me as large as life, but not with the same expression upon his countenance.

True, he squinted formidably, but then there was a grim smile, as much as to say, he approved of what I had done.

"Well, boy," he said, "you have taken my warning and come back to the old country."

"Yes," I said, "here I am. You told me to come here, and here I am, sure enough."

"Well, you did right boy, quite right."

"You said if I would, that you would make it all the better for me. I have come upon the faith of that promise, and if you do not keep it, I am a lost sergeant, late of the East India service."

"Very well," he said, "follow me, and I'll make a man of you, instead of a sergeant in any company's service."

"Very well," I said, "I have come."

I arose, and he led way towards the door; I followed him through the door; he went down the passage, and then down stairs into the kitchen—the back kitchen; and then he stood still and pointed to the wall.

It was a very old crumbling wall, and seemed as if it had been patched up any how, and by a bungler.

He then pointed above, over the door; there was a cupboard, and in it a kind of crowbar. I took this, and thinking it a hint, I immediately began to pick away at the wall, my grandfather's spirit standing behind me.

In a few minutes I had demolished the wall, and saw behind there was a large closet filled with bags of gold. The spirit gradually vanished away, and smiled with satisfaction as it did so; I, too, for I had found out where my grandfather's fortune lay, and I was a very rich man now.

\* \* \* \*

Some time before Mabel had come to the end of this narrative, the footsteps of the man in the room above had ceased; but just as she closed the book, and was thinking now of attempting to go to rest herself, presuming that he had done so, and would consequently be quiet for the night, she heard a strange kind of cry from the room above, which lengthened into a scream, and then all was still again.

———

## CHAPTER LXXV.

MABEL'S ALARM.—THE IDENTITY OF THE MYSTERIOUS LODGER ESTABLISHED.— MABEL'S ESCAPE FROM THE HOUSE OF MRS. JENKINS.

SUCH sounds as these were quite sufficient in their meaning ever to banish sleep from thr eyes of Mabel. It was quite clear to her that some catastrophe must have happened ; which, as she knew not the extent of, or of what character it might be, whether an accident or a crime, it became clearly her duty to cause some inquiry to be made into.

She remained for some time in her chamber, pondering over the strange noise she had heard, and endeavouring to gather courage to open her door and look out on to the staircase, in order to see if any alarming spectacle were there.

This, however, she much feared to do ; so, as a resource, she rang the bell, and waited most anxiously and expectantly for the appearance of the little dirty servant, whose duty it unquestionably was to respond to the summons.

But Mabel did not as yet know enough of the internal economy of lodging-houses to be aware that an appeal to a bell is rarely, if ever, answered at all, because it is presumed that, if it be for anything very particular, he or she who rings will ring again ; and if it be not for anything particular, why, then, he or she ought not to have rung at all.

This was an arrangement which, we say, Mabel did not understand, although we pledge our reputation to the fact of its being made down below in many a lodging-house, and only understood and found out by the artfulness of people who, from convenience, pass most of their lives in lodging-houses.

This ring, then—and it was a quite, modest one, too, which gave it all the worse chance—produced no effect whatever upon the obdurate nerves of the small domestic, who was an adept at her trade.

She looked up at the slightly agitated bell, which hung in the corner of the kitchen, and at once, with a wonderful amount of ingenuity, she apostrophised by saying,—

"Now, really, Mr. Bell, what can you want ringing at this time of night, I wonder ? Ah, well ; if you want anything particular, you can ring again, I'll be bound. But I dare say it's some rubbish or another, after all."

The small servant was quite triumphnat when the bell, or rather Mr. Bell, did not ring again, and congratulated herself upon the result of a system of tactics which had saved herself all the trouble of giong up stairs, and knocking at every door she came to, with the question of,—

"Did you ring, sir ?"

Thus, then, was Mabel left to take what steps she chose in a matter, which it is not to be wondered at, that her active imagination dressed up in alarming colours. She waited, we were going to say, a reasonable time ; but, the fact is, that she waited an unreasonable time, for some one to answer the bell, and then, as no one came, she did not consider that any good could be accomplised by ringing it again.

And yet she could not reconcile herself to doing nothing ; and so, fancying that the small servant must be out, and that the dignity of Mrs. Jenkins prevented her from answering the summons, she made up her mind, although with some feeling of alarm, as regarded the opening her door at all, to go down stairs and relate to that lady what she had heard.

The strange noise from above was quite of a sufficiently alarming character to justify her in such a course of proceeding, and, accordingly, she hesitatingly approached her room door, and laid her hand carefully and noiselessly upon the lock, intending to turn it as gently as possible, emerge from her room, and get down stairs as quickly as the speed of fear would enable her.

And yet she kept asking herself of what she was afraid ; and, perhaps, it was this very doubt and uncertainty that pressed upon her mind more than anything else, and alarmed her. Had she known what was the matter, she would have been able to come to some definite conclusion upon it ; but uncertainty is always the most alarming circumstance of all, and, to an imaginative intellect, ten times worse than any amount of really known and appreciable evil.

There are, however, such things as presentiments. From frequent examples, who can doubt that strange psychological fact, that in some mysterious manner the mind has a sort of foreknowledge of coming evils, although it cannot be sufficiently prophetic to be able to define their nature or from what quarter the blow of fate is to come.

Mabel did not think of anything in the circumstance being of a nature to affect her personally. All she had upon her mind was the dread that something had happened to some one, or that the mysterious lodger above was afflicted with, perchance, some pangs of conscience which would neither permit him to repose, nor permit him to think with sufficient liberality concerning the repose of other people.

Softly, so as not to make the least noise, she opened her bedroom door. In order to avoid being seen, she had placed her light in such a position that none of its rays came out of the room; but scarcely had she stepped out from her apartment on to the landing, when she heard the sound of a low, a cautious, steady descending footstep from the room above.

The thought that this was the man who had made so much noise coming from his room came instantly across her, and although she certainly had time to rush down stairs and give the alarm to Mrs. Jenkins, if she had felt so inclined, she did not do so, but rather preferred to glide noiselessly back into her own room.

She left the door of her apartment only so far open that, by standing close to the narrow chink, she could look out and see whoever might pass upon the stairs; and in a few moments, while the cautious sound of the footsteps continued, she saw the faint glimmer of a light, carried, no doubt, by the man who was now descending.

Her heart beat quickly, and she stood there almost with suppressed breath to listen and to observe.

It was evident that, from some reason or another, the individual who so soon would be before her eyes, was most fearful of awakening attention to his movements, or he would not have adopted so very careful a mode of getting down stairs.

It seemed as if he were a minute before he would venture to place his foot upon one of the steps, and then it was only by a subdued creaking of it that Mabel could be sure that he was coming.

Now he was close at hand. Now she saw his arm. He carried the candle in his left hand, and was shading it with his right.

Such an arrangement was calculated to throw a strong light upon his face, and it did so. Mabel with difficulty prevented herself from uttering an exclamation of affright; for in that face she at once recognised the too well-known and repulsive features of the mendicant.

He passed on, too intent upon his own footsteps and upon shielding the light from any blasts of wind, to observe that a door was partially open as Mabel's was. And it was well that he did so, for had be paused and chosen to be inquisitive, he must have seen her, as the sudden terror and surprise of seeing him there, for the

moment, froze up her faculties, and she could not move from the spot on which she stood.

That he had escaped from prison she was aware, because the officer on his last visit had said as much; but that he should be there in the very house where she had found an asylum—not a very desirable one, certainly, but still it was one—surpassed all belief.

But she could not be mistaken. She, of all persons, could not for one moment doubt the identity of that man upon whom she had too often looked with undisguised aversion and terror. His every feature was impressed indelibly upon her memory. There could be no possibility of a mistake. It was that fearful man—that man who had wrested her from all she held dear on earth, and who had plunged her in such a sea of terrors and difficulties as had now for some time surrounded her.

He passed on. The light which he carried slowly faded away, and all upon the staircase was darkness again. Then Mabel staggered back till she came to a chair, upon which she sat, with a sigh that told of the agony of apprehension that had come over her.

Then arose the deeply interesting question of what should she do contingent upon this discovery.

"Why is he here," she asked herself, "but to do me some injury? By some means he has found out the fact of my residence here, and yet has power, he fancies, to harm me. Oh, Heaven! protect me against that dreadful man, and all his fearful machinations; for that he is now contriving something against my peace, my liberty, perhaps my life, admits not of a doubt."

She could not think that the coming there of this man was the result of accident. It was too unlikely, and, therefore, if it were by design, there must be some deep-laid plan inimical to her happiness. How could she know but that he might have confederates whom he had even now gone down stairs to admit into the house?

This thought was one full of alarm, and it at once roused her to action.

"I must fly," she said—"I must fly from here at once, and at any risks and chances. Heaven aid me now, or I shall despair indeed."

It was far easier, however, to decide upon the question of flight, than to carry it into execution; and yet she hastily arranged herself for the streets, and walked to the door of her apartment without having, in the agitation of her mind, been able to lay down any fixed course of action.

Flight! Flight! from the place which contained that fiend in human shape, who had been the bane of her young existence, was the only tangible idea which she thought of.

She could not pause to consider its dangers, or if it were a practicable or a safe step, or if by any more judicious course she could save herself from the necessity of adopting it; but she left her room, and with trembling steps, and in a state of mental agitation which transcends description, she commenced descending the staircase, down which, so shortly before, she had watched the disappearance of her enemy.

While she saw no light she considered she was safe from encountering him, and all was darkness, but she knew the staircase well enough to descend by the aid of the balustrades in the dark, so she in a few moments reached the passage unmolested.

The street-door was gained. To open it was the work of a moment, although to the agitated mind of Mabel it seemed as if it never would obey the lock, and then she was in the street.

---

## CHAPTER LXXVI.

THE ARRIVAL IN LONDON OF THE MORTON FAMILY.—THE INTERVIEW WITH MONSIEUR ROUSELLI.

THERE was only one circumstance which cast a gloom over the hopefulness with which the Mortons came to London, and that consisted in the fact, that it became necessary to communicate to Monsieur Rouselli the sad end of the young man whom he had sent to England to make inquiries concerning Mabel.

The necessity for making this communication, after the argument which Captain Morton had used in favour of it, was admitted by his brother, who promised, since he might be said to have a kind of acquaintance with Monsieur Rouselli, to be the medium through which he should, with as much consideration as possible for his feelings, be made acquainted with the painful truth.

It was towards the latter part of the day that the Mortons, with Rafferty Brolickbones, reached London, so that as they felt greatly fatigued, a visit to Monsieur Rouselli was delayed until the morning.

We will, however, do both Captain Morton and his brother the justice to say, that if the news which they had to tell him had not been tinctured by the piece of mournful intelligence they had to add to it respecting the murder of the traveller, of which, it will be recollected, Jim, the ostler, had been so falsely accused, they would not have allowed the old man to sleep that night without the pleasurable reflections which were sure to be induced by news of Mabel.

As early, however, upon the following morning as they thought he would be likely to be stirring, they both, or rather we ought to say all three (for Rafferty went likewise), proceeded to Monsieur Rouselli's lodgings, to make to him those mingled communications of pain and pleasure.

Monsieur Rouselli, when their names were announced to him, at once and eagerly desired that they should be admitted, and he received them with all the warmth and courtesy of a gentleman.

"I am certain, my dear friend," he said to Henry, "that you bring some good news to me, or you would not, as I am free to confess you have done, have awakened expectations such as those I have been nursing in my heart since last I saw you."

"Let me assure you," said Henry, "that you do me no more than justice. I have, sir, some news to communicate to you, which I do hope and expect will be of the most pleasing and satisfactory nature to you; but, sir ——"

"Oh!" exclaimed the old man, "there is a reservation then?"

"There is, sir. Along with that good news I have one piece of intelligence which will grieve you much."

"No, no," he said, "not along with it, and not following it; you shall tell me the bad news first, and when my mind, oppressed with that, seems, as possibly it may, to be upon the point of sinking, you shall restore me to myself with your better tidings."

"Be it so, sir. The young gentleman whom you sent to England to make inquiries concerning Mabel, has, I regret to say, found a grave among us."

Old Monsieur Rouselli wrung his hands, as he exclaimed—

"Alas! alas! he dead? Heaven take him into its holy keeping. Oh, why has the fell hand of disease seized upon the young, such as he was, and left the old withered trunk, such as I, still living? Dead—dead!"

He turned aside to hide the tears that gushed, despite all his exertions to restrain them, from his eyes; and Captain Morton took the opportunity of whispering to his brother—

"He talks of the hand of death coming from disease. Unless he should insist upon knowing the particulars, I would not undeceive him."

"I will not."

"Ward it off if you can."

"Most assuredly I will. He need not have the additional pang of knowing how this person, for whom he felt so much affection, has come to his end."

After a time Monsïeur Rouselli spoke, saying—

"I cannot, sir, say that I am totally unprepared for this blow. The very fact that for so long I had heard nothing, ought to have been, and indeed was, a sufficient warranty of his death. But still, let us anticipate as closely as we may such a circumstance in connection with those we love, the fact itself comes upon us with as great a shock, as if the mind had never dwelt upon it. Tell me of his death, and what he said, and what he did."

"Nay, sir," interposed Captain Morton, "believe me that I speak to you as a sincere friend, when I say to you, why would you seek to know more than that he died, and was placed in the grave by friendly and sympathising hands? Why seek to harrow your imagination by details which have all terminated in the tomb?"

"You are right—you are right," said Monsieur Rouselli. "I will be content with the amount of grief I have, without seeking aggravating circumstances, for the purpose of adding to it. Only tell me this much. Is there the least doubt of the accuracy of the statements?"

"Not the smallest."

"Enough—enough. I—I will not ask more. I am a poor, weak old man now, with no one to whom I can cling, feeling that the bonds of kindred hold them to me. Alas! alas! Even he, as well as my poor son, has gone from me, and I—I am quite desolate, now—quite desolate!"

"Not so," said Captain Morton. "You forget, sir, in this sudden accession of grief that has come over you, that you had a choice——".

"A choice! A choice of what?"

"A choice of which you should hear first—the good news which we brought to you, or the bad. You have heard the bad."

"Oh! what can compensate me for the loss of him whom I loved so well?"

"Another whom you will love as well, if not better."

"Another?"

"Yes, sir; the child of your son lives."

"My son's child! the infant who—who ——Bear with me, gentlemen—I am old. You would not mock me?"

"On my soul I would not. I tell you that the child whom your son, in his last moments, on the blood-stained field of Waterloo, committed to the care of an English officer, lives, and is one who will compensate you for all evils."

The old man rose, and tottered towards Captain Morton. He took him by the hand, and made an effort to speak, but he could not. Tears came in abundance to his relief; and the captain, who was himself much affected, led him to a chair.

"Be composed, sir," he said; "and you shall listen to the most eventful story that probably ever met your understanding. That child, I assure you, on my word of honour, was preserved from the battle-field, by him to whose charge your son committed her, and she grew in beauty and gentleness to be a blessing to him."

"And he—where is he—that noble spirit, who so faithfully fulfilled his trust?"

"Nay, sir you give me too much commendation."

"You—you, sir?"

"Yes; it was I who——"

Captain Morton found himself clasped in the old man's arms, before he could say more.

"You saved that dear infant?" he said. "You have been the generous soldier, who, when lying even on the field of carnage, wounded, sought to relieve the pangs of an emeny by accepting the sacred trust which he committed to you?"

"Nay, sir, be calm. I should have been undeserving the name of man had I acted otherwise than I did."

"Bravo!" cried Rafferty-Brolickbones, springing up and laying hold of Monsieur Rouselli's hand, to which he gave a shake that nearly knocked the old man down. "Bravo! You are the finest old cock for a Frenchman that ever I saw."

"What do you mean, my friend?"

"Why, by the holy poker! I mane that I am ready, any day in the week, barring a Friday, 'cos that's unlucky, to take the devil's own oath that, at some period or another in your history, ould gentleman, some Irish blood has got into your family."

"Irish?"

"Yes; real ould Irish, whoop filliloo! Do you know what that is?"

"I cannot say I do."

"It is the faction cry of the Raffertys."

"Now, Rafferty, do not make yourself troublesome," said Captain Morton; "you are too violent, and I have only, as you know, permitted you to come here, in order that, in consequence of having been present when Mabel was committed to my care on the field of Waterloo, you might be able to answer any question this gentleman might wish to p   to you."

"And were you there, indeed?" said old Monsieur Rouselli.

"I rather think I was, sir; more by token that I got as elegant a rap on the head as ever a Brolickbones would like to have. It's a mighty good thing it hit so hard a place."

"And you saw the last moments of my son—of my dear son?"

"I did, sir."

"You shall, another time—another time you shall tell me all. Not now, my friend, not now."

"Very good, sir; when you like. By Jasus, Mister Henry will never make me believe but there's some Irish blood in his veins. Maybe there was an Irishman of some sort in his mother's family, who knows?"

## CHAPTER LXXVII.

MABEL DISCOVERS THE MENDICANT AGAIN.—THE ATTEMPT TO CAPTURE HIM, AND THE MURDER OF THE OFFICER.

ALMOST maddened by terror, Mabel ran into the street. She knew not whither she fled, or in what direction. Terror alone was the impulse she moved under. She knew not what was going on around her, or whether she was pursued. Fear, indeed, told her she was; but she had no reason for believing she was, beyond that she knew nothing—nay, she attempted not to think.

The mind was in abeyance. Agitated and impelled by fears and hopes, she had no room for reflection or caution. She merely fled, and that with the utmost precipitation.

Her flight would have cost her much observation, and much trouble from passers-by, had it been at any other time in the four-and-twenty hours than it was; for people would have troubled themselves to have stopped or insulted her.

However, she saw but few people about, and the dim light of the lamps seemed confused in her eyes.

At length she was fast sinking, her breath was short, and she felt almost choked from exertion, while her heart panted so rapidly that she could hardly stand.

"Surely," she thought, "no one is following me—no one at all. I hear none."

She paused a moment or two to listen; but no sound came upon her ear that seemed suspicious.

"Thank Heaven!" she exclaimed, as she seized hold of some iron railings to support herself, and leaning her head on her arm; "thank God for having so far escaped the terrors of that man."

She stood some minutes panting and recovering her breath. She was in a violent heat, for the blood coursed through her temples at such a rate that she feared to move. She could now feel the effects of such violent exercise as she had taken, and a sickness at heart afflicted her.

However, she could not long remain here. She was soon reminded of that fact by some one reeling up to her, and tapping her on the shoulder, saying,—

"My dear, you are all alone, here, to-night. You want company; I'll see you safe home."

Mabel started at these words, and saw a well-dressed enough man, who had been sacrificing rather too freely at the shrine of Bacchus, as the newspapers say.

"We won't go home till morning," sang the man, in a doleful tone, which began, by-the-by, very strong, and ended in a whine. "I say, my dear, we won't go home till morning does most decidedly appear."

Mabel turned away.

"Stop; d—n it, stop; don't go away; somehow or other, I don't know how, I can't run; the street goes up and down like a plank in a saw-pit."

Mabel increased her speed, and so did the intoxicated gentleman, but the motion of his feet could not keep pace with the activity of his mind; for after making a dive, head first, for some distance, and following the superior portion of body by means of his posterior and locomotive parts, he found he could not keep pace with himself, but as a last endeavour scraped all the skin off the bridge of his nose against the uncourteous paving stones.

"Hilloa! now, what's the matter? Who's after routing up the potatoes in the cellar below?" exclaimed a private watchman, who had been seated upon a door-step, half asleep.

"Bind up my wounds; my kingdom for a horse!" hiccoughed the gentleman, flourishing his legs in the air, instead of a walking stick substitute for a sword.

"As for your wounds," said the guardian of darkness, "a piece of plaster on your nose will be all you'll require; and as for your kingdom, why it will be all kingdom come in the watch-house before many minutes is over. I must take somebody in charge, or I shall be thought of no use."

"Slave, I've set——"

"Come, come; no names, or I'll not set you down, but let you down with a smack on the stones, my funny customer. Come, stand up and walk like a man, and I'll take care of you; come along."

Mabel was terrified, and soon got out of hearing; but she was compelled to slacken her speed; for the fatigue and terror she had undergone had had its effect upon her, and she was soon aroused to the necessity of stopping.

This, however, was of little consequence when she no longer heard the sound of the man's voice, who had so terrified her, and the fear of pursuit from the mendicant no longer haunted her.

"Where shall I go? what shall I do?"

These questions were easily asked, and they presented themselves in a variety of shapes, but no answer could be readily given.

One thing alone presented itself very forcibly to her, and that was the fact that she ran some danger in the streets, where she was liable to insult and discovery. What could be done, or where she could go for a few hours she knew not; but this she

knew, she must endeavour to hide herself, for she was incapable of much more exertion.

It was near a market that she found herself, and there were many odd corners and places where she could remain in quiet until daybreak.

She entered a place where there were a good many packages and carts, some under a covered way, and others in the open air.

Among some of the former, she contrived to pass, and sat down upon a hamper, and leaning against the wall, she, after thinking

over the events of the last few days, fell asleep.

She did not awake until the day was far advanced, and the hum and noise of people were heard on all sides of her; she got up and walked out from her place of concealment unmolested by any one, there being so many persons, she was not more noticed than the rest.

It was later in the morning than she had imagined, and she determined that she must adopt some course of action, but what that was to be was almost as difficult as the necessity for some course being pursued.

"What will be said," she thought, "when it becomes known that I have left my lodgings, contrary to my express promise? I shall be deemed an impostor; the best thing I can do will be to go immediately to the police-office, and there see the magistrate or officer."

This was certainly the best plan she could adopt, and she at once determined that when it was late enough, she would go to the magistrate and relate all that had happened.

"This man has escaped from prison; he is a criminal of the worst character, and he has committed so many crimes, to make it unsafe that he should escape: and he haunts me; my life is not secure while he is at liberty."

There was some time to spare, and Mabel walked slowly about; but ever fearful of encountering that fearful man, she kept within the vicinity of the office. As soon as the office was open Mabel entered and sat down in the waiting-room. Here she believed she was safe; for the mendicant, now that he had escaped from the hands of the officers, would never willingly run into their power again. In this she was right—she was safe. That morning there was a communication made to the presiding magistrate to the effect that the officer under whose care she had been placed had just been to her lodging to see her, and found that she had suddenly quitted the place in the middle of the night, and had left no trace behind her. There were several minutes' pause after making this communication, and the magistrate seemed to be considering within himself what could be the cause of it.

"What could have been her motive for leaving in so sudden a manner?" remarked his worship.—"I really don't know, sir. She seemed to be very grateful for what I did for her, so that I really did not expect this."

"Nor I."—"She said nothing to any one, and no trace could be found."

"The man has escaped from his prison too," said the magistrate significantly.—"Yes, they are both gone," said the officer; "and putting this and that together, your worship, why it looks like a very black job."

His worship said it did, and took time to consider what he should say next.

"It strikes me," said the magistrate, "that this Miss Mabel Morton is in league with the man, who, after all, may and is very probably the murderer."—"There's no doubt of it now, your worship, and her evidence was all flam—mere moonshine,

your worship, save and except, of course, the perjury."

"Exactly."—"That by accusing him of one crime she gave him the opportunity to escape from the effects of another."

"And he has now adroitly escaped from the punishment awarded to either," said the magistrate.—"Exactly, your worship,"

"And we have been done—defeated, and justice has been completely diverted from its proper course."—"I think your worship is right. In this instance it seems to me as if it was a planned thing between them."

"Well," said his worship, "I must admit I have been deceived—completely deceived, by the manner, appearance, and tale of the girl herself—that I had every reliance upon her."—"Some of our men seemed to have doubted her from the first, and yet they could not tell why they should, save that she had a very unsettled air."—"She had; but that might be ascribed to so many sources, that we could not judge from that."

There was now a long pause, and then the magistrate said,—

"Well, I don't see what can be done, save take measures to follow and apprehend them. Another post will probably confirm the oppinion that she is an impostor."—"No doubt it will, your worship—no doubt of it."

At that moment Mabel being informed that the night charges were disposed of, and that she might, if she desired, make any application to the bench she pleased, entered the court and heard the last sentence or two, and had also some glimmering of a suspicion that it alludded to herself. She, with the aid of an officer, made her way through the crowd to the witness-box.

"A young woman wants to make an application to your worship," said the usher.

The officer who had been speaking to his worship turned round, and at once recognised Mabel, for it was he who had procured the lodging.

"Why, here she is, your worship," he said, with the utmost satisfaction depicted in his countenance.

"Who?" inquired the magistrate, not knowing what was meant, for his eye had been wandering over the paper.—"Mabel Morton—the young woman we were speaking of just now, who had left the lodgings I procured for her by your worship's orders, near the water."

"Ah, let her come up and explain how it is she has left them," said his worship.

In another moment Mabel stood up in the box, and the magistrate at once saw she had been suffering greatly from some cause or other, and he said kindly—

"Your presence here at this moment certainly gives a contradiction to some surmises that were being made as to the motive that induced you to quit the lodging the officer provided for you by my orders."

"I left on the impulse of the moment," said Mabel.

"And you will be able, at once, to explain the cause of your doing so, satisfactorily, I dare say."

"I hope so," said Mabel; who for some moments seemed to be anxious to gain time and strength.

"Where have you passed the night?"

"In wandering about I know not where," replied Mabel, "until the office opened, and since that time I have been here."

"You have been here?"

"Yes, in the waiting-room."

"Is that a fact?" he asked the officer who accompanied her into the office.

"Yes, your worship, she has been here since the office opened."

"God bless me! and here have we been wondering where she could be."

"It is very strange," said the officer, "why she could not have stopped where I left her, because then I could have found her at a moment's notice, when I wanted."

"Exactly," said his worship.

"But as she's here," the officer added, "she can best tell your worship why she did it."

"Certainly. Now, Miss Morton, be so kind as to furnish us with the key to this mysterious conduct on your part,—quitting, without leave, your lodgings."

"I am sorry to have done so, but couldn't help it, your worship; I was compelled," said Mabel.

"Compelled! who compelled?"

"The officer told me," said Mabel, who took no notice of the last question—"the officer told me that the man whom I had so much cause to fear had broken out of prison, and was once more at liberty."

"He told you the truth."

"Exactly, your worship; but in the night I heard some one walking about overhead for a long time. I could not go to sleep; the sound of the feet seemed dreadful, and even familiar to me; I could not sleep."

"Go on," said his worship.

"I determined, at length, to endeavour to ascertain who it was that was thus walking about in that endless and restless manner, by endeavouring to look through the door."

"And you did so?"

"No, I did not, sir. I endeavoured to do so, and for that purpose opened my door with the intention of creeping up stairs; but, instead of that, I was terrified at the sight of that dreadful man from whom I have suffered so much."

"What, do you mean to tell me that you saw the man you accuse of abduction and saved from being committed for trial for murder?"

"I did, you worship."

This seemed to have an astounding effect upon all present, and there was a pause of some moments.

"Did he see you?" inquired the magistrate.

"I feared so at the time, your worship, though I have not seen him since."

"What was he about?"

"He was coming down from the rooms above," replied Mabel, "with a light in his hand."

"And he was the man who walked about, overhead?" asked the magistrate.

"I suppose it was, your worship; at least, I think it was; but I was so terrified that I scarce knew what to do."

"And you quitted the house because you saw that man?" said the magistrate.

"I did," she replied. "I thought he had come there on purpose to secure me again. Indeed—indeed, I was half frightened into the belief that I had been sent there on purpose to be taken back again."

"Upon my word," said the magistrate, "this is certainly one of the strangest affairs I can remember. You knew nothing of this man's being there, of course?" said the magistrate, inquiringly, to the officer.

"I didn't indeed, your worship, else I would have secured him, your worship."

"So I should imagine," said the magistrate.

"I have come here," added Mabel, "thinking I ought to do so, for several reasons, one of which is, I am destitute, and have no assistance until my friends send me aid from Morton Hall."

"Well?" said the magistrate.

"And another is, I ought to come and explain why I left my lodgings, having given my word that I would not do so."

"Very good," said the magistrate; "very right and proper. You have acted very properly."

"And, above all, to let your worship know where this man is to be found at this moment."

"Yes, I see; we'll take care of that. You will have no objection to go back, and to show the officers the man you mean?"

"No, your worship. I never wish to see him again; but beyond that I have no objection."

"Very well, then; let two officer go back with this young lady to the house, and then see if this man is to be found there now; perhaps he may have fled."

"Miss Morton says she don't know whether he saw her or not," said the officer.

"Oh! is that the fact?"

"I really cannot say. I was too terrified to know distinctly what was done on the occasion. I saw him, and that to me was all that was needed to terrify me. I thought—I can hardly tell you what, sir, but I felt as if my whole life depended upon my immediate escape."

"Well," said the magistrate, "I can easily understand your fears; but the officers will protect you—no harm can come to you with them."

"I am perfectly satisfied."

"Are your ready?" inquired the magistrate, of the officer.

"I am, your worship," he replied.

"And you fellow-officer—where is he?"

"I expect him every moment, your worship," replied the officer. "He is just the man for the job."

"Do not lose more time than necessary."

"No, your worship; though if he intend going, he's gone by this time; and if not, he'll be good for a few hours."

"That's true enough," replied the magistrate; "but at the same time, you will do well to be early."

"You may come this way, if you please, Miss Morton," said the officer to Mabel. "His worship has nothing more to say to you. Follow me, if you please."

Mabel followed the officer out into an ante-room, where he said to her—

"We were having some grave conversation about you, before you came in, I assure you."

"Indeed!" said Mabel.

"Yes; about your sudden, and, to us, unaccountable flight, save upon very unpleasant suppositions."

"You thought I had imposed upon you, I dare say."

"Indeed we did."

"May heaven forgive you for the wrong you did me; but you are not to blame. My precipitancy was the cause of it all; but I was so terrified at the sight of that man, and the imprisonment he would force me into, I should have run any risk, any danger, rather than remain when I knew he was there; the idea was really terrible."

"Well, after what you have related as having gone through with him, I am not much surprised at your fears; but his worship, and I too, really thought you had imposed upon us, to screen the mendicant from the punishment of the graver crime."

"Oh, no, no."

"Your presence here now sufficiently disproves that. But what did you do—where did you hide yourself all night?"

"It was very late when I left the house, and the greater part of the night I wandered about, not knowing where I was; but I came to a market, and sat down in a basket, till I fell asleep, and then walked about till I came here."

"And have you had no breakfast?"

"None."

"Goodness me!" said the officer, "yours is a desperate case; why, I should have been dead by this time. Go without eating and drinking all this time! Why, bless my heart, I'm hungry at the thoughts! Sit down, and I'll get you something, before my brother-officer comes in, for we must be off immediately."

So saying, he left the room.

Mabel did feel sinking for want of sustenance and rest. How she had continued to exist through her recent troubles and privations, she could not understand. The fact was, she had been a sufferer beyond the strength of many; but it was the constant and great excitement that carried her through it. She paused in her thoughts as she heard the footsteps of different people passing and repassing, fearful of hearing the one she most of all dreaded.

Presently the officer returned with some coffee and toast he had procured from a neighbouring coffee-shop, which he placed before her, saying, at the same time—

"Eat this, and be as quick as you can, in case Thorburn should come in; because we must start that instant."

The truth was, Mabel felt very ill, and thought at first she could not swallow; but she soon found the coffee refresh her; and, by the time she had hastily finished her meal, the officer re-entered the room.

"Well," he said, "I am glad to see you have finished it. Do you feel any better now?"

"Much, thank you—I am much better. It has given me new life; I was sinking before."

"Well, I'm glad to hear it. You must now come with me, for the officer I was waiting for is come in."

"I am quite ready," said Mabel—"quite."

"Wait a moment, and I'll see if he is."

So saying, he left the room, and was absent about five minutes, when he returned with another officer, a big, muscular man, about his own height and size; he was a powerfully made man, of a most determined character.

"This is Thorburn," he said. "You will please to accompany us to the room you say this man resides in."

"He did do so when I left."

"Exactly. I dare say, if you haven't frightened him, he'll be there now."

"I know no more than what I told the magistrate," said Mabel; "but I am quite ready."

"And so am I," said Thorburn. "We shall have the gentleman tight enough. If we do once secure him, he shall never get loose again; I'll forgive him if he does."

"Yes, yes; he will have no child's play this time. He must be a very devil in frame and nature if he get loose again, after our hands have been once closed upon him."

"No, no; he's safe enough—safe enough."

"Then I am ready," said Mabel, as she stood by the two men, who were each of them a remarkable contrast to her light and fragile form.

They all three left the ante-room, and walked out of the office into the streets. There was the usual every-day bustle; not a sound that could be heard distinctly. There was a Babel of sounds; but the one so confused the other, that it was more than difficult to separate them from each other.

Amid such bustle and noise, they all proceeded towards the bridge, to pass over the water, to reach the lodgings which the officer had selected for her.

"Do you know much of this fellow we have got to take?" inquired Thorburn of his brother officer.

"Not much; but I believe he's a desperate character, and one who would not hesitate at anything that he thought would enable him to get clear off."

"Ah, he's a pretty scoundrel, I see. He must have been something out of the common way to get out of the compter as he did. It's the same, I believe?"

"Yes; it is the same."

"Ah! he'll be in safer quarters, at all events, this time. There'll be no more chances for him, save chances of hanging."

"It's only for abduction."

"Ah, well! it somehow or other strikes me," said Thorburn, "that he'll be under charge of murder, or something of that sort."

"He may, for he has an uncommon disinclination for safe custody. Some other charge may spring up when there are a few inquiries made at any place he may have been at for any length of time."

"It is more than possible."

"And now," said Mabel, "as we are close upon the spot, let me tell you to be careful, for he will not hesitate to make the most desperate resistance. Life is nothing to him; he would destroy any one for the mere chance of an escape."

"Never fear, miss; we will take care of ourselves. We are used to these cases, and have often taken characters as desperate as he. But, nevertheless, we will not run into any useless danger, especially as you will be placed at his mercy immediately; but there is no danger of that, at all events."

They now arrived at the house in which the officer had placed Mabel, and in which she had seen the mendicant.

"Now," said the officer, "you had better keep clear of any struggling that may go on, because ugly blows may be given; and I have seen enough to know that such a man may be a more awkward customer than may, at first sight, be imagined."

"Ay," said Thorburn, "very likely. But I don't think he can get out of our clutches; we are too strong for that."

"Ay, ay," said the other, "we are strong; but you know, Thorburn, there are as strong men as we are, and some stronger; not that I should hesitate about this man; but you are always so confident in your strength."

"And good reason, too," returned the other.

"Well, I know you have done some clever things in your time; but so have other people."

"Yes, I know that."

"Well, then, you needn't make so much noise about it, but say less, and be less of a brute than you are."

"Pho—pho! you haven't courage enough, now. I don't care for man nor devil."

"Nor I."

"Well, but you never say so," said Thorburn.

"No; there is no need when I mean it. I have not any inclination, nor do I see any necessity, for attempting to make people believe what time will show them, without any trouble on my part."

"Well, well—we have both our different ways. Mine's blunt and bulldog-like, I dare say; but then I have done some things by it that I couldn't have done otherwise."

"I doubt it."

"Well, now, wasn't there——"

"Ay, there was that, and this, and the other; but just hold off awhile, for we have work before us. Here is the house. Now, Miss Morton, here we are; have you any objection to go in?"

"I don't see that I need mind," said

Mabel. "I suppose I can go into my own room?"

"Certainly; you will be safe there," replied the officer. "You can shut yourself in."

"And then shall I come after you when you carry him away?" asked Mabel.

"You may as well come and see how he is disposed of, and then your mind will be at ease with regard to that one object of terror, at all events," said the officer.

They now entered the house, and proceeded up stairs without any interruption of any sort, until they arrived at the room in which she lodged.

"Here," said Mabel, "is my apartment," as she opened the door and walked in. "Yes, just as I left it."

"And the room above is the one you mean?" said the officer, pointing upwards.

"It is."

"Then there's our man," said Thorburn.

"Yes," replied his companion. "Now follow up close; but don't make more noise than a cat."

"All right. I'm as dumb as a bundle of feathers. Go on; I'm close to you. Let me go in first."

"You do as you are told," said the other, with much shortness. "I am sent to apprehend him, and you help and aid me."

"Very good. Go on, or else I'll do all the work myself."

"Silence!"

They both crept forward without the least noise, until they came on a level with the stairs, or rather the landing, so that they could see under the door.

There was suddenly a heavy footstep across the floor, backwards and forwards, as if some one were walking across the flooring several times in succession.

"That's him," said the officer.

"Then push on; we are all right—push on. Put your back to the door, and in we go."

"No, no; we may get him to open the door himself, and then we can at once seize him, without giving him any time to arm himself, as I am persuaded that such a character will use any means of inflicting mischief."

"I don't care a curse if——"

"Hush! nor I don't. I must take the most effectual means to secure him, therefore do not be in any hurry. We may as well take him safely as not."

"Go on, old slow and sure."

"Hush!—he hears you. See, he has stopped walking," said the other officer, as he got on his feet and stood by the door. "Come on; we will wait here a moment or two."

They waited a moment or two; but they found that nothing was to be gained by so doing; so he knocked gently at the door and awaited the effect.

Without a moment's hesitation the mendicant stepped to the door and opened it.

It was evident he had not expected such visitors, for he started as he beheld the two officers. His own heart at once told him the nature of their call, had not a glance at the men been sufficient. In an instant, before the officers could make a movement to prevent him, he had shut the door in their faces, and double-locked it in an instant.

"There," said Thorburn; "well now, how do you like that?"—"D—n."

"Ay, that's all very well for quiet determined fellows who can do nothing with spirit."

"Don't be a fool, Thorburn."

"I a fool! well, I'm blessed. I suppose you'll say it's all my fault, and through my hastiness. I'll go bail you'll say it to me in another minute."

"You could have prevented it just as soon as I could, or a little easier; seeing you were nearer than I."

"I thought so. It wouldn't have been you, if it were not somebody else's fault than yours."

"I didn't say it was your fault or mine either; it was no fault, but an act of the man's own."

"Well, then, the next act of the man will be, to throw himself out of window, cut his own throat, or shoot one of us What do you say to that?"

"Why it's very likely."

"Ah! and then, don't you see, it's all because we have been in too great a hurry, eh?"

"No, no,"

"Ah! I have been coming too much of the bulldog, and so spoilt your cautious game."

"Come, come, Thorburn, don't give us any more of your nonsense; what do you think we had better do in such an emergency as this?"

"Sing the old song of 'Dill, dill, dill, come and be killed.'"

"Confound you, what a fellow you are, —instead of serving a fellow heart and head, you only do it with your hand, and never give advice."

"Well, then, knock at the door, and say what you want at once, and if he refuses to open it, go in."

"Your advice corresponds with my own," said the other. "I was about to do the very thing."

"Do it and be quick."

The officer at once knocked roughly at the door, and awaited but a moment for an answer, and receiving none, he at once repeated the summons, saying—

"Open, in the king's name."

No answer was, however, returned to this, and he drew back a yard or so, saying—

"If you do not open the door, I will soon make way into the room."

As he spoke, he made a rush at the door, followed closely by Thorburn, with the intention of bursting it open; but just as they arrived at it, they found it open; they both passed headlong into the apartment several yards, before they could recover themselves.

"Here's a go!" exclaimed Thorburn.

Before anything more could be said or done, a rush was made by the mendicant past the officers, towards the stair-head, as if for the purpose of flight downwards; but before he could reach it, the officers had seized him by the collar of the coat; and then a desperate struggle ensued among them.

"Surrender!" exclaimed the officer. "You cannot escape."

"I will try," exclaimed the mendicant.

As he spoke, he made a desperate effort to throw off one of the men, to get one arm free; but they succeeded in clinging to him, and holding him down.

"Go quietly," said Thorburn, "and you will be carefully treated; but if you go on in this way, you may depend upon it we shall drag you by the heels till the pavement wears a hole in your head."

The mendicant, however, seemed to have no fear of such an operation, far from it; he seemed to imagined it a motive for additional exertion, and the three lay struggling and rolling on the stairs.

Of course this could not be done without causing an uproar in the house. Poor Mabel sat in the room alone, and terrified at the sounds that reached her; for they told her plainly of the desperate nature of the resistance the mendicant was making to the officers.

She clasped her hands in an agony of fear and supplication, praying for a termination to the dreadful struggle, but not a fatal one, which she most feared.

The people in the house, consisting of various lodgers, came out to view the struggle; and, as in all similar cases, they took part with the weakest against the officers. Indeed, some people never can bear the idea of an officer doing his duty. It grates against their feelings, and they fancy they can feel the grasp of the official on their own coats. Thus it was, the offi-cers were assailed with hoots and groans and, as they struggled together, they encouraged the mendicant to resist.

"That's right boy, stick to 'em," said one man; "what your hands can't do, let your teeth."

This advice was taken; for the mendicant suddenly seized Thorburn by the cheek with his teeth, which caused the other suddenly to loose his hold, and exclaim, as he seized him by the throat,—

"You infernal, tiger-like villain, I'll strangle you; and, as for you," he added, addressing those who were advising the prisoner, "if you go on in this manner, I shall be obliged to return for some of you."

"Ah! you're a fine fellow. Why, you are big enough to eat him, and there are two of you, and yet you can't hold him like men."

The mendicant, however, gained his object, and that was to free his arms—one of them at least—for Thorburn's grasp was at his throat, while his companion held him by the neck and one arm.

During this time the mendicant made so much resistance as to keep the two officers well employed, though the grasp on his throat was becoming each moment more dangerous and more distressing. His breath, already short, was nearly stopped; and but for the sudden release he knew he could procure, he must have surrendered. He got his hand into his pocket, and pulled out a small pocket-pistol. With some difficulty he contrived to cock it, and then, placing the muzzle close to Thorburn's body, he discharged the contents full into him.

The unfortunate man suddenly let go his hold, stood upright on the stairs, and placing his hand to the lower part of his body, exclaimed—

"I'm a dead man, by G—d!"

He reeled backwards, and, being on the stairs, lost his footing, and thus fell headlong down on to the next landing, without sense or motion.

The sounds and words were electric—they were heard by all in the house, and a dreadful consternation seized upon all who saw the dreadful occurrence, and they who had offered gratuitous advice instantly disappeared.

The other officer, for a moment, stood up, and gazed at the fallen body of his brother officer. He saw it was of no use offering aid to one already dead.

The mendicant himself felt the release of the hand, and soon gained breath. A few deep and rapid inspirations seemed to restore, in some measure, his strength—

not as it was before, but it enabled him to renew the struggle with the remaining officer.

This was of a most desperate character, for both seemed nearly equal in strength—the officer the stronger of the two, but not much—both were exhausted.

"Murderer! villain! surrender!"

"Never while I breathe. I have killed one man—I know my doom—see you do not share his fate."

"Not if I can hold you, villain as you are," said the other. "I call upon you, in the name of the king, to do so."

No one, however, responded to this appeal, and the officer continued to hold the mendicant.

"If you do not help me, I will have you all punished; you are bound to help me by law."

However, the law was not very potent there; it was, at all events, disobeyed; for no one took any notice of the behest. Seeing that it was a struggle for life and death, the officer did all he could to disable his opponent, who seemed almost insensible to pain and fatigue, though he, in fact, was hardly able to stand from fatigue.

He tore him away from the bannisters, and dashed his head against the wall. The blood flowed copiously from both; and, in a few moments more, the mendicant gave a sudden swing, and they both came with such force against the hand-rails, that they all flew out, and officer and mendicant fell into the passage beneath, where they lay for a minute or two, stunned.

The officer was the first to recover, and taking advantage of the moment, had nearly slipped the handcuffs over the mendicant's hands; but, by a sudden twist, he saved himself from being thus secured.—The struggle was again renewed, and they both fought their way down the stairs.

Scarce a word was spoken by either; they were too much occupied by the desperate nature of the struggle they were engaged in, and which had been painfully prolonged. Had neither of them such strong and exciting motives—the one for capturing and the other for escaping—the conflict must have soon ended one way or the other; but the fact was, mental excitement aided the bodily strength, and made them almost insensible to what they had suffered.

Their struggles were weak and slow to what they had been, and their endeavours grew weaker and weaker, until at length they reached the passage leading to the door.

There was Mabel, waiting like one newly risen from the grave, pale, agitated, and trembling; she could scarcely stand; but when she heard them approaching, she threw the door open, and stepped into the street.

The fresh air that came in from the steet seemed to revive the mendicant, and he began to struggle anew as they came along the passage to the street-door, and when once in the street the struggles of the two men were really tremendous.

This sudden spurt of exertion, after what they had done, could last but a very few minutes, and, indeed, it was quickly over, for, in the struggle, the officer's head struck against a lamp-post, and he staggered a pace or two, and was unable to see. The mendicant found his grasp loosen, and in an instant he was free, and in another moment he was out of sight.

"D——n!" muttered the officer. "Escaped, by Heaven! and, after such a struggle, it's too bad."

There stood the officer, pale and trembling from exertion, the picture of disappointment and vexation; behind him, a little way, stood also Mabel. She, too, was pale and trembling; terror had seized upon her heart, and she could scarcely move or speak, but she could see the flight of the mendicant, and also knew the mischief that had been done.

## CHAPTER LXXVIII.

THE MENDICANT'S ADVENTURES.—THE THIEVES' RESORT.—THE SURGEONS' STUDY.

THE flight of the mendicant, as may easily be imagined, was continued for some distance; indeed, he was by far too fearful to look back. He believed the officers were after him—close at his heels; until he shaped his course through a densely-crowded neighbourhood, where he hoped, by twisting and turning, to gain ground, and throw his pursuers out of the track.

Then, indeed, he did venture to look round, but saw no one whom he could recognise. He could not move—his heart beat violently, and the blood rushed fearfully through his veins, and his temples throbbed. Indeed, he was at the very last stage of exhaustion.

Any less exciting motive would never have carried him through the immense exertion he had made; and for ten lives he could not now have made the exertion that would save one.

"They have missed me!" he said; "they have missed me! I am safe; I have escaped."

Still he moved not—he was bound to the spot—he knew not which way to move—he feared to turn to the right or the left—the fear of meeting some of his pursuers.

It was just probable he might do so; but, to remain where he was, was equally dangerous. What was he to do? He must encounter some danger; and he had better encounter that which seemed to present the best chance of escape.

To choose was a difficulty—between what seemed probable or possible, in either case; and the necessity there was for his moving away, lest he should attract too much attention from those who were near the spot, and thus defeat his own object. He did move away, and toward a part of the town he knew full well—there was an empty house, and in this he thought he could for a time find shelter. To this he made an immediate retreat; not in so rapid a manner as he had before made—**that** might attract more attention than **was at all desirable.**

THE MENDICANT SHOOTS THE POLICE OFFICER IN THE LODGING HOUSE.

Rapid flight through London was only admissible in very urgent cases; but there was danger in being stopped, both by passers-by and also by some accidental encounter in so crowded a place. The mendicant, therefore, assumed a rapid and cautious walk, until he came to a long and narrow lane.

Here he paused for a moment or two, and looked about him. He did not want to be noticed going into this neighbourhood, for it was just possible that he should be waited for by any of the officers, and that would ensure his detection. Seeing, however, no one near, he went down the lane, and stopped before a house he had, on one or two occasions, stopped at before, and where he had concealed himself for some hours, without being detected.

Ah!" he muttered as he looked up at a large, empty house, " this is the place. I suppose it's condemned."

He gazed around him on all sides; but saw no one looking; but he heard a hue and cry of some sort at the end of the street, as if it were approaching, and without a moment's hesitation the mendicant darted into the house.

The door swung back with some violence, and went with a tremendous bang against the wall, and then back again; but there was no lock or asp to catch it, and it swung backwards and forwards several times before it rested in quiet.

In an instant the mendicant, with a light step, was up stairs, and had reached the first floor landing before he paused, and then he stopped to listen to the many echoes that resounded throughout the empty house. But then, when they had nearly subsided, other sounds reached his ears he had not expected.

"Hilloa! who's that?" shouted a deep, hoarse voice from below the ground floor.

The mendicant paused and listened.

"Oh I'm not alone," he muttered. "Who can this be? but no matter, I'll have no companion."

"Hilloa, who's above?" shouted the same voice. No answer. "Is that you, Jack?" No answer still, and the voice below paused a moment or two, and the other appeared to be listening.

"What's the matter?" inquired another voice below, but in lower tones.

"I don't know, only somebody banged the door fit to knock a hole through the wall into the next house."

"The devil!"—"Didn't you hear it, then?" inquired the first.

"I was in the cellars," said the other; "I heard something, but couldn't tell what it was. It was something that shook the place a bit, but where it came from I could not tell."

"I could though."

"Have you been up to see?" inquired the second voice.

"No," said the first; "I haven't heard anybody move. I dare say it was only the wind."

"It may be; but where I you I'd go up and see, and so satisfy myself, at all events."

"And why don't you, yourself?"

"Are you afraid of a sound," inquired the second voice, "that you want somebody else to go and see for you?"

"Oh, I dare say—I dare say it's the wind."

"It may be; but it may be an ill-wind to us, and if you do not go up, I will."

"Just stand back—I'll go; I nave nothing to fear—you have—but you may as well keep close at hand."

The mendicant listened attentively, and could hear they were both creeping up the stairs into the passage, and when there they examined the place, but saw no one that could have caused the disturbance.

"It was only the wind."

"Most likely some one going by gave it a push on purpose, for the lark of the thing."

"Curse their larks."

"So say I; but they will do it, though they know there's nobody here to frighten, but they like to hear themselves or the noise they make."

"So they do; but yet it is possible that they may have gone up stairs."

"It is not very likely, I should think; but yet it is possible, and only possible," said the first voice.

"Listen awhile."

They approached the stairs and stood in an attitude of attention for some moments, perfectly still with suppressed breathing.

"I hear nothing," said one.

"Nor I; but—but what was that—a shadow?—where did that come from?"

"A shadow!"

"Yes, did you not see it? A shadow came between me and the skylight in the roof."

To explain this we may say that the mendicant had stood there in breathless agitation, listening to the conversation that was being carried on in whispers below; but he suddenly peeped over the bannisters, and saw the two men below; with their ears turned upward to catch the slightest sound that might be uttered or made proceeding from above.

The mendicant had not thought upon the sky-light above, and the shadow below; but he saw the two ears turned upwards endeavouring to catch something.

Thinking it would be a pity they should not catch something, he turned about to see what he could oblige them with. There was nothing at all at hand, save one or two large pantiles, and they stood invitingly balancing upon the very extremity of the landing, just over the precise spot where the two men were standing at that moment.

The pantiles had fallen from the roof above, which was not in the best state of repair, as may be imagined, in consequence of their absence from their appropriate position.

The mendicant gently touched two of these, which lay contiguous to each other, and the motion completely turned them over, and down they fell just as he intended them.

They reached their destination exactly, for they fell flat upon the cheeks of the two men, to their intense astonishment and horror; for they were completely beaten down, not only with the force of the blow, but with amazement likewise.

In an instant after, the mendicant, by rapid strides, entered the room on the first floor, and then going into a small closet, he pushed aside the shelves which opened unto a flight of stairs, and then having closed the door, he paused.

He could hear there the voices of the two men who had been listening, and who had been treated so unceremoniously by the fall of the tiles, and who, after the first surprise had subsided, recovered themselves, and one of them exclaimed—

"There's somebody up stairs."

"I think not," replied his companion; "we hav'n't heard a sound, and nobody could move about those empty rooms without being heard, much less kick tiles over."

"You may say what you please, but there's somebody up stairs; but what an infernal blow on the face I have received; why, it was enough to have broken my jaw."

"And mine; see, my face is cut."

"A little."

"Quite enough; at all events, I'll go up; come on, we can't remain in this state of uncertainty; we may have some game carried on that we little think of, if we do not take proper care; I am sure of that."

"Very well; let's make a thorough search over the place, and in the meantime we may as well secure the door."

"Let down the bar."

Having secured the door, the two men then ascended the stairs and examined the staircase closet, for there was one; it was a large, old-fashioned rambling house, where there were capabilities almost sufficient to conceal a troop of cavalry.

"Well, I must say that this is the oddest old pile ever I saw; there ain't a place but what has some hole, or cupboard, or something of the sort; I can't tell how they could have been ingenious enough to have built a house with them."

"Why, it does seem as though the house had been built with a view to the construction of cupboards."

"Ah, it does; I suppose they built it up first, and tried their hand at what they could make of it afterwards, and in all the odd corners they placed a cupboard."

"Here's been nobody here, I think."

"Well, I think not, too; but it was very strange that all that noise should have arisen from nothing, or from no cause at all. I can't understand it at all."

"Very likely some one came by and did it for the sake of amusement, and then turned tail."

"I heard no one run away."

"And you heard no one come in, did you?" inquired the first speaker, in a louder tone of voice.

"I did not."

"And yet you were much more likely to do that than the former, since they would be nearer to you."

"Well, well, we may as well return; but I'll take good care nobody else gets in or out without my knowledge; I'll manage that all right enough."

So saying, the two men left the room, and the mendicant heard them descend the stairs and pass the street door, at which they were occupied for some time in doing something which he could only guess at.

"There, they cannot get that undone at all from the outside," one said, "and as from the inside, I shall be soon called up by the noise, and I am a match for any man, and you for another; eh, is it not so?"

"I should say so; or at all events, I will try."

"Here are the pantiles; would you like to save one of them as a keepsake?"

"Oh, no, I don't need one of them to remind me of them; I'm not so forgetful as all that."

The men descended below, but they were heard no more.

The mendicant came out again into the room he had left, and pondered over what he had heard, and tried to regain his composure, for his recent exertions were not to be easily forgotten, nor would he be likely at all soon to recover from them.

\* \* \* \* \*

He stood in that attitude for more than one hour, with his eyes fixed upon the floor, as if in deep meditation; but yet not the lightest sound passed unnoticed by him.

"What can be the meaning of this?" he muttered. "When I was here last, there was no soul breathing here, nor were there even any signs or traces of its having been used for any purpose whatever; but it is all altered.

"There are no signs of occupation on the outside; the boards are all up before the windows, and it seems, in fact, as if boarded up, because it was dangerous and uninhabitable. Would these men have talked so much, if they came like myself, hiding? No, I think not; and yet they may be merely securing a retreat; and if they are disturbed, they would endeavour to find out the cause somehow or other.

"I'll remain here at all events; they seem to occupy the lower part, and I'll occupy the upper; a fair division is no cause of quarrel, if they shou'd discover me.

Anything but being taken—that would be utter destruction. All things considered, I had better die resisting than undergo the slow torture preparatory to an execution; for if I be taken, that will be the inevitable result.''

Thus, having satisfied himself entirely that the steps he had taken, and was about to take, were the best that could be adopted under the circumstances, he determined to make a more extended but careful search over the upper part of the house, so that he might be forewarned as to what was to be expected from any quarter of the house.

He went up stairs a flight higher, and found nothing that in any way excited his suspicions, and he returned below, and looked very carefully about, and returned to the cupboard on the stairs, which he had not noticed before; for it was by far too artfully concealed to be found out, save upon the closest inspection.

It was with much difficulty he contrived to open it; but he at length, after various attempts, succeeded in doing so, and then, to his joy, he found what he most needed. This was food. He had eaten nothing since the previous day, and now he was half famished, and his tongue clove to the roof of his mouth.

There was a large barrel, in which was placed the tap, and some jugs were at hand. In an instant the mendicant took one of the largest, and filled it with the beer which it contained; and while doing that, placed half a large meat-pie in his pocket, and the jug being full, he closed the door, but had scarcely reached the landing, when heard the men below—

"There—there's somebody at the beer."

"Don't be a fool—there's nobody there —nobody at all. How are they to get at the beer?"

"How can I tell till I see? I tell you, there must have been somebody there."

"Go up with you, or let me pass. I think you are mad, or the house haunted, I don't know which."

"Nor I neither," replied the first; "but I'll find out something or other before I have done. I know I have heard the running of the beer, despite all you can say. I heard the door shut, too, and that's more—so, come on."

The two men came to the cupboard, and the mendicant reached the door of the closet.

"There," said one, "the door is all right, you see."

"Ah! Well, let us see if the beer is all right. Then you may laugh, because I can afford it, when I know the beer has not suffered."

"Ah! you wouldn't care for anything, so long as you got beer with you."

"Indeed I should not."

They now opened the door, and one of the men examined the tap very carefully, and then he said—

"There has been some drawn here. Look, 'tis quite fresh, and besides, I laid the key here."

"Nonsense! you haven't drawn any beer this hour, it is true, but you couldn't tell how long that which hangs on the tap has been there."

"Oh! don't tell me. Give me the stone jug; we'll try it ourselves—I'm thirsty."

"I dare say you are. You usually contrive to be so very dry, that I can't understand your constitution. You must be a sally-mander"

"And what's a sally-mander?"

"Oh! a man as is made of fire. He always wants the hose of a hingin in his mouth to wet his throat. The stone jug did you say?"

"Yes, to be sure; it hung up on the right hand; it's the biggest of the lot."

"I don't see it on the right or left," said his companion.

"Nor I neither now. I'll swear it was here when we came here last. You saw it?"

"I did. I hung it up myself."

"Well, this is a pretty go, at all events. What'll the club say to such goings on?"

"They won't believe a word about it."

"Nothing; but I tell you what it is, there's somebody in the house who are as thirsty as coach-horses, or they wouldn't have taken the largest jug. We must make a careful search all over the house. Come on."

"Yes; let's have some beer, now we are here."

Accordingly, they both drank heartily of the beer, and then, in putting the jug by, their eyes fell upon the dish in which the meat pie had been. No sooner had they become aware of the extent of their deprivation, than they both started, and their countenances changed; a dull, leaden expression came over them, and they looked at each other in dismay.

"What do you think of this?" inquired one. "Didn't we have some of that for dinner—eh?"

"We did.''

"Well, then, where is it gone now? It was there, you know; you'll admit that?"

"Yes, I must admit that—I can't help it. I saw it put there myself. But what shall we do?"

"Do! why, search the house right over —every hole and cupboard, until we find the wretch, and then we'll have his ears or his life."

"He must not escape us; he will know too much If he be permitted to leave this house alive. We shall not be safe, depend upon that."

"I think not, either. There," he added, shutting the cupboard door; "there, now, that is safe; we may as well go up to the first floor, and there commence our search."

Hearing these words, the mendicant closed the door of the closet, and then shut the shelves standing on the stairs behind this closet. This was scarcely effected before the men entered the room, and looked round, and walked across the floor.

"I thought I heard something here," said one.

"Did you? Well, you might. All I can say is, it is a queer affair. The beer and the pie are a mystery to me. But look about—there is the closet."

The closet door was opened, but it seemed the men were not acquainted with the secret of the moveable back, for they did not attempt to open it. Soon after they both quitted the room, to examine other parts of the house. He could hear them go into various rooms, and then return another way.

The mendicant ate the food he had so opportunely come by in quiet, and quenched his burning thirst with the beer. He had suffered dreadfully from the exertion he had made to get away from the officers, and in the continuance of his flight. A less active and powerful man would have dropped dead long ago; as it was he had bled at the ears and nose.

His eyes were bloodshot, and his whole appearance was soiled, and it betrayed every sign of the struggle he had been engaged in, and his dress appeared torn and destroyed, such as it was. He sat there for some time, until he had eaten as much as he required; the remainder he secured, and having emptied the jug, cautiously stole back to the cupboard on the stairs, and deposited it on the shelf whence he had taken it—then he as cautiously retired to the place where he had before concealed himself.

Scarcely had he done so ere the two men descended the stairs, having searched the house to no purpose, and were returning much annoyed, not to say somewhat dismayed at an occurrence that seemed beyond their comprehension.

"There's nobody in the house, that's certain," said one of them; "but that somebody must have been in that's equally certain."

"Yes; but I can't understand it at all.

How they could contrive to get out again is beyond my belief."

"Well, perhaps they may have done with the jug, and put it back again."

"Ah! ah! I dare say, that is a pretty idea truly, but we'll take another jug of beer down, and that will save our having the trouble to come and fetch it when we want it—eh?"

"Well, I suppose a jug won't hurt us, as we have had more than usual exertion."

They both stepped to the cupboard, and then opened the door; one of the men lifted up his arm, with the intention of taking down one of the jugs; but his eye rested upon the one he had before missed. For a moment he was transfixed with amazement; then, starting back, he pointed to the jug, exclaiming,—"There—there!"

"Well, what? Oh, d——e!"

This exclamation was uttered in consequence of the eye of the other man resting upon the jug, to which his companion pointed; and he, likewise, took a step back, and paused a moment.

"Well, I never! What is the matter now? Who's done this? I never was in such a place."

"Such a place! I believe the devil's got loose among us."

"Don't mention names while you are here; you don't know who you might see suddenly."

"Come along. I won't stay up here any longer. My belief is, the place is haunted."

"Won't you have any beer before you go? there is the jug, you know."

"No, no; I'll have none. It may be in the butt, you know. Come down, I have had enough of this—quite enough for once; we don't doubt the fact; do you?"

"Oh, no; but I'll have some beer, if there be any devilry in it or not."

So saying, he drew some beer, and the men descended again below, having first unfastened the door, being apparently convinced that they could do no good by fastening it, and, it was possible, the cause of their trouble might be kept in by it.

When the mendicant became convinced that there was no further search after him, he quitted the place where he had seated himself, and descended the narrow stairs, until he came to the basement-story, and then he emerged into the under-ground rooms, which were old and dilapidated in the extreme; there were many of them.

He could hear the sound of the men's voices in conversation, and to this he for a time listened; but being convinced that it did not concern him, he left the spot and proceeded forward, and found that there was a large range of buildings behind.

These he had seen before, and they now bore the same appearance, save there were traces of persons having been there recently. Broken pipes and tobacco ashes were signs that there had been, at some time or other, a meeting of some persons, who had more than ordinary reasons for secrecy.

In one part of a large room, or cellar, or perhaps shed, for it partook of all characters, a quantity of straw was heaped up in one corner, partially in sheaves, and partially loose. After some consideration and self-communion, he crept into the straw, and buried himself as far into it as he could.

He hoped there to sleep in safety and peace a few hours, and to enable him to recover from the fatigue that he had undergone that eventful day.

How long he could lay there he did not know, but he believed that he was safer there than anywhere else; indeed, there was no other place where he could sleep, save the passage and stairs, and they were not safe, because they must be known to every one who was acquainted with the house, though the door in the closet might not, since it was a communication that was carefully concealed on both sides.

To the very bottom of the straw he crept; there were ample means of breathing, for the straw above was chiefly in trusses, and piled up crossways.

Here, with such a feeling of security as a man, hunted by society from place to place, could feel, he feel into a deep sleep, such as he had not had for some days; exhausted nature required some such means of—not renovation—but cessation from intense exertion of mind and body.

How long he lay here he could not tell; but he was aroused from his slumber by loud shouting and laughter, accompanied by knocking upon the table, and the jingling of glasses, and other noise, and a rough voice said,—

"D—n it all, Giles, you are a rare boy. You make no bones of what you say or do."

"In coorse I doesn't. I never minds—why should I? I'm among friends, ain't I?"

"You are, my boy."

"Then why should I not say what I mean? I means what I say, gentlemen, and I'll stick to it."

"You do, do you?"

"In coorse I does. Now, I'll tell you what, the last feller as I had anything to do with, served me so. He was a pal of mine, but he wanted to split."

"Ay, ay."

"Yes; and what do you think it was all about?"

"Don't know."

"Why, then, it was this ere—I put up the job; it didn't okkipy us a quarter of an hour. We got fifty-three pounds—that wasn't amiss."

"Very good, indeed. Well, I hope I may never have less than fifty-three pounds for a quarter of an hour's work."

"Between two, you know."

"Yes, yes; twenty-six pun' ten, each."

"No; I gave him twenty-six pounds, and took twenty-seven myself. I did the business, and put it up, too. I only had ten shillings more than my share, and that made a pound more than he had, which wasn't much to cry about."

"No, nothing at all; that was right enough—and no more than was right either."

"Well, he took the sulks upon that. He thought I hadn't acted right, and grumbled about it, sorely; so I said to him,—

"'Here, Bill, do you take the sovereign; one on us must know most about this affair, and has done the most—and that must be you; take it. I see it don't set on your stomach—I sha'n't want it, I dare say.'

"No; he wouldn't have it at all; grumbled, but swore he wouldn't have it. Well, I didn't say no more, but I left the matter as it stood, and then I was told next day that I must beware of Bill, because he was getting dangerous.

"'Dangerous!' said I,

"'Yes,' said my friend; 'you and h did a job last night, didn't you?'

"'Yes,' said I; 'who told you?'

"'Bill.'

"'Then he means splitting,' said I; 'if he tells one he'll tell another.'

"'He does. You had better come with me, and I'll show you what he means.'

"Well, I went with him, and looked through a passage window into a room, where he was sitting with an officer. The window was open, and I could hear what was said by either; and I heard the officer say to him,—

"'Well, then, you'll bring him to the bar?'

"'I will.'

"'Well, then, call for what you will treat him with, and say that one good turn deserves another.'

"'I will. You'll know what I mean; he's the man. It's all right between us?'

"'Yes, certainly—I understand—you have helped me to a prisoner before now, and this Giles I want particularly.'

"This was enough for me—I went away

I knew where to see him, about an hour afterwards. I went and saw him—how precious friendly he was—I said to him,—

" ' Come this way, I have a new job for you—one I've just thought of; come along.'

" ' Have you ?' said he.

" ' Yes,' I said ; ' come along.' And we came here, and into this very room—there was nobody here then.

" ' Well,' said he, ' what is it ?'

" ' Why,' I said, ' you haven't any idea of splitting, have you—of selling me, eh ?'

" You should have seen his face ! He tried to keep his countenance; and he said he had no such intention, and wondered how I could think of such a thing, and expressed his willingness to work with me as he had done.

" ' Well,' said I, ' I thought, when you were settling with the trap to-night, you intended so doing; especially as I heard him and you plan how I was to be taken.'

" ' I plan ?'

" ' Yes; and the officer said you had helped him to more than one prisoner.'

" He staggered, and I sprang forward and seized him by the throat, and held him fast; we struggled, and we fell—he was stunned, and I never released my hold of his throat, but held him there till he was dead."

" Dead, eh ?"

" Yes; dead as a herring, and quite entirely. I never saw any one so soon and entirely dead."

" What did you do with the body ?"

" Ah !" said another, " 'tis easy to kill a man, but how to get rid of the body is the trouble.'

" Sack it, but I had none."

" Tell us the secret, Giles; tell us the secret,—it's worth knowing, any how,—isn't it ?"

" Well, I'll tell you. I put him up in a sack."

" A sack !"

" Yes, in a sack; and then I put the sack on my shoulders, and carried it to a surgeon's, who paid me handsomely for the body, and made no inquiries as to how I come by it or anything else; so I made a good thing of it."

" Well, it served him right. I hate a man who'll split upon his pal,—it is worse than anything I ever heard of, no matter what ; there ain't anything equal to it."

" No more there ain't."

At that moment, from some reason, and which the mendicant could not for his life control, he was compelled to sneeze in so loud and decided a tone, that it startled every one present.

" What's that ?" exclaimed one.

" It's very like a sneeze," said Giles ; " and it strikes me it was a man, too; it's a decided case, in my opinion. There's somebody more here than has been invited."

There was a look of consternation among all present, save Giles, who continued :—

" It strikes me, mates, that somebody's on the look out, and somebody may be in the straw ; what do you say to a search ? It's not the right sort of thing to be listening to gentlemen's conversation. I say, pull him out."

" Then that explans all about the jug, the beer, and the meat-pie, eh ? There's somebody about who knows more than we do ; it's dangerous, decidedly dangerous."

" Pull the straw over; see who it is ; don't stand staring like petrified pigs, but go into him at once ! What's the use of looking on ?"

The mendicant now saw he should be discovered, but determined that he would make an effort to escape, by dashing through them, as soon as he found they had removed the straw,—no doubt he thought the onset would take them by surprise, and he should get clear off. He felt the trusses, one by one, pulled off, until he was exposed to their view.

" Here he is !" cried one.

In an instant the mendicant made a desperate rush towards the door, and had almost succeeded in escaping from them ; but one of them placed a stick between his feet, and he was thrown down, headlong, on the bricks.

" That's the plan," said Giles ; " lend us a hand, boys ; one take a leg, another an arm, and then, you know, we can make a subject."

In an instant the advice was acted upon, and four strong men pinned him to the earth by his four limbs. He could not move—it was hopeless; and yet he struggled fiercely for some minutes with such strength as only he possessed, but it was unavailing.

" Eh, you warmint ! so you were listening, were you ? you want to make a market of us, do you ? but we'll make one of you, at all events."

" I had no such intention."

" Oh, no ! of course nobody never does, till they are cotched at it; and then, you see, we believe ourselves, and nobody else, whatsomdever."

" But I have only escaped being taken by running into this house to conceal myself."

" Ay, ay."

" I have escaped pursuit, and crept in here, and knew not that any one was likely to be here."

" Oh, no ; nobody thinks of such a thing. Who could think of telling the truth upon such an occasion! But, pray, what was it you had been doing to merit being looked after?" -

" No one knows my crimes,—they are my own, and I will not divulge them; but I tell you my life is in danger."

"Very considerably so, I should say."

"I had no intention of listening to you —I was asleep half the time."

"You know too much,—a great deal too much; but I tell you what, you had no intention of taking the beer and the meat-pie, eh?"

" He knows too much; he has been here too long; you know he knows the house better than we do, or else you would have been seen; so there's no good denying it."

"It is a very good trap, though," said one, "and very well done; but we are by far too old hands to be taken in in that manner. It won't do."

"You won't take my life?" said the mendicant.

"But we will though," said Giles. "You would have taken ours, or helped to do so, ; but we must do a little in the way of self-defence."

"Good God! you can never mean to murder me?"

"Murdering you, or hanging us, comes to the same thing in the end," said the other.

The mendicant struggled fiercely for a moment or two; he seemed to think there would be no chance of life, save in his own efforts, and, for a moment, he had nearly freed himself from their hold; but the man Giles threw himself, with his knees, on the mendicant's chest. The blow was a dreadful one, and caused him to straighten himself out, and he was instantly secured in that position; when Giles, having pulled out a large cotton pocket handkerchief, instantly covered the mendicant's mouth and nostrils, and then leaned upon him with all his strength and might. The struggle was a short but fierce one, and soon ended. The mendicant was stretched motionless on the earth, without a sign of life.

"He's done for," said Giles. "I expect we shall have a supper out of this."

"Out of what?

"This dead man," said Giles. "A good supper, too, and something besides, as I reckon."

"One such a supper, and I should be quite satisfied with eating that one for the remainder of my life. I should never eat meat again, I am sure of that."

"Well, but I don't propose to eat our dead friend; we can dispose of the body, you know."

"Oh, yes! where shall we take him?"

"I'll show you. Put him in a sack, and we'll manage all else; there will be time enough yet to get to the house. We shall get a few pounds for him; not that that is much, but then we shall have got rid of the body, and it is worth something to do that."

"So it is," was the reply.

They now produced a large sack, into which the body was thrust, with some exertion; such as bending the legs, and so on, until they contrived to secure the mouth of the sack with a piece of cord. This done, a short consultation was held. They all agreed that they would take it at once in turn, as they went along. Shouldering the burden, they left the house, and proceeded to a surgeon, where they knew they could dispose of it; and they were speedily shown into a small room, and awaited the presence of the surgeon.

"Well," he said, as he entered into the room, "what have you got now for me? Some of those short, poor wretches that you have brought us lately?"

"No; you have one here that you won't match every day in the week, even alive."

"Come, that's good."

"Ay, he's long and broad, and a regular good un, and wouldn't have disgraced a grenadier company."

"Well, what is it to be—five pounds?"

"Five pounds! Well, doctor, we must take it elsewhere. I thought we would give you the first chance; but we must do more than clear our expenses."

"How much do you want?"

"Ten; and not too much either; who would run all the risk for less money?"

"No, I'll give you eight. Let me tell you, eight pounds is a long price," said the surgeon.

"But it's a long corpse."

However, it was agreed amongst them that they would take eight pounds, which was paid, and the whole party left the house, after depositing the body on the table, divested of its clothes.

In a short time afterwards, the surgeon returned to the dissecting room, with a couple of pupils. They arranged the body, and then the surgeon, taking the knife in his hand, said, with the air of a great man,—

"You see that body, gentlemen, is a very fresh one, indeed, and I dare say blood will follow."

"I should say, from its appearance, it had never been buried," remarked one of the pupils.

"Why?" inquired the surgeon.

"Because the body has never been

washed, and people are very particular about that."

"It is true; but we don't know where this body has come from,—it's a good subject,—a perfect one,—a strong and well-made man, but by no means fat, you see; the limbs and muscles are well developed; indeed, when a limb is well developed, we mean both bone and muscle." There was a pause, and then he added, "now, we will make the incision."

He held the knife in his right hand, and began to score down the stomach of the mendicant, who, not being quite dead, began to revive with a loud "Oh!" The surgeon and pupils began by degrees to back from the table, and, when the mendicant slowly sat up, the surgeon went down on his knees, saying—

"Holy Ghost!—our Father! for what we are going to receive,—oh, dear! make us truly thankful."

THE RESUSCITATION OF THE MENDICANT IN THE DISSECTING ROOM.

The pupils, ere this, had scampered down stairs, and the surgeon, when he saw the body moving off the table, scrambled on all-fours underneath, until he reached the door, which he secured, and ran down stairs.

For some moments the mendicant stood up and gazed about him unable to comprehend the nature of what had occurred, or where he was. After much confusion of thoughts, he remembered the last scene that had occurred, and then comprehended how he came there. After a little while, he dressed himself, then taking a large stick in his hand, he sat down very quietly beside the door, there to await in patience its being opened.

In about an hour, the surgeon and his pupils returned, having gained courage by means of libations of brandy, and the reflection that there was but one against three.

Opening the door, the surgeon popped his head in to see where the body was, when the mendicant dropped his stick upon his crown, and the surgeon disappeared; in another moment the mendicant rushed out; the pupils making a faint resistance, and receiving a blow or two from the impetuous mendicant, tumbled over each other on the stairs, and amid the confusion the mendicant reached the street-door, which he succeeded in opening before they could move to offer any opposition, and he got clear off.

---

## CHAPTER LXXIX.

THE CONSULTATION AT MONSIEUR ROU-SELLI'S, AND ITS RESULTS.—RAFFERTY BROLICKBONES HAS AN ADVENTURE IN LONDON.

THE information which had been now given by the Mortons to Monsieur Rouselli, partly of a joyous, and partly of a sad character, as it was, at first did not seem likely to produce any bad consequences upon the health of the old man, for he, to all appearance, quickly enough recovered from the first shock that he had sustained; but it was when he was left alone that memory conjured up to him the scenes of the past, and he felt deeply and keenly all his misfortunes,

"What am I," he said to himself, "without the society of those dear ones who should have been about me, gilding my decline of life, and lending all the charm that affection can lend to age? Alas! alas! I am indeed desolate!"

And when we come to consider the melancholy situation of the old man, we can scarcely wonder at his indulgence in such regrets. He had lost that son who had been dearer to him than life itself. That dear son, for whom he would have laid down his existence a hundred times over rather that he should have suffered, and, likewise, that son's child, who might, and from all that he had now heard of her, would have been such a solace and joy to him.

She, too, was gone; perchance dead, or what was, perhaps, worse than a direct knowledge of her death, he was, in her case, left to all the agony of thought, and to all the horrors of a too keen and vivid imagination.

And then, too, as if some fatality hung over all that he loved,—as if to have his affections was a fatal gift that soon hurried the possessor to the tomb,—the young and generous-minded man who, to assuage the father's deep griefs, had devoted his life to the task of endeavouring to discover his son's child, had fallen a sacrifice to his devotion.

Yes; he, too, was dead! and Monsieur Rouselli might well tell himself that he was desolate, or nearly so; for what now had he to cling to but the hope of Mabel being found, after she had been so long missing?

No wonder that he tormented himself with harrowing reflections,—reflections which at his age, were sure to tell most fearfully upon the physical structure; so that when Captain Morton and his brother saw him again, they were surprised at the ravages grief was making in him.

But what could they do? and what could they say to him further than they had said to assuage his griefs? They could only implore him to hope,—that last resource of the wretched,—and when he told them upon what a slender foundation he considered that hope was resting, they could not but very faintly contradict him.

When Captain Morton, an hour or so after having seen old Monsieur Rouselli, was seated by himself in deep thought, and with something of dejection upon his countenance, Rafferty Brolickbones came to him, and with more earnestness of manner than he usually threw into his speeches, he said—

"Sir, if it pleases you, or if it don't, I'm after wanting a matter of a pound or two."

"Money, Rafferty?"

"Bedad, yer honour didn't think I meant *praties*, surely."

"No, no; you shall have money, Rafferty, if you want it. Your wages, you know——"

"Aisy, aisy, sir, if your honour pleases. It's many the long day ago I asked yer honour to call it pay, and not wages."

"Oh, well, certainly, I know you like the military phrase of pay better, and I should have used it, but that I forgot at the moment. Your pay, then, has been accumulating, as you know, in my hands for some time, so that you can have any sum in reason that you like, Rafferty."

"Many thanks to yer honour for that same. It's only a pair of sovereigns that I want to look at just now; I suppose there's some prize money for them as finds out Miss Mabel?"

Captain Morton looked steadfastly at the weather-beaten countenance of his follower, as he said,—

"Rafferty, if you know anything of where Mabel is, it is a piece of needless cruelty, as well as a serious breach of duty, to keep it from me."

"Faith, sir, then I don't know."

"Then what made you ask such a question, Rafferty, as that which just came from your lips?"

"Only for information, sir. Your honour may depend that it ain't long Rafferty Brolickbones shall know anything of where Miss Mabel is, but he'll tell it to you."

"Well, well, Rafferty, I feel sure of that. Always recollect that mystery defeats itself. There is the amount of money you require; and remember, Rafferty, what a dreadful piece of bad management you made of hiding in the tree, instead of letting me know that Mabel was to be in such danger on the banks of the lake into which you fell, and—"

"There now, aisy, sir, again; faith, then, don't I know all about the same? Does your honour think I forget it? By the mass and the holy poker, no; don't be after taking up a poor fellow's misfortunes, sir, and tying them up in a bundle to throw them whack in his eye."

"Well, Rafferty, I was only, quite in a friendly spirit, warning you."

"It's warned enough I am, sir.'

Away went Rafferty, but if the truth must be told, and we see no good or substantial reason for keeping it away from the reader, Rafferty had a sort of plot of his own, which he did hope would lead to some good results.

Since that unfortunate piece of cleverness of his which had resulted in a good ducking to himself, and in poor Mabel being placed in the power of that desperate character, from whom she had so great a difficulty in rescuing herself, poor Rafferty had been upon the tenter-hooks of impatience to do something which should redeem that error, and show that he was not such a bad schemer as such an untoward event would seem to proclaim him to be.

Of course, that something which he wanted to do was to recover Mabel if he could; and from the moment that he set foot in London, he had been unceasing in his inquiries concerning her.

These inquiries he conducted in a very strange manner, for he would walk along the streets, looking up at the people's names over their shop doors till he saw an Irish one, when in he would walk, with all the assurance incidental to his nation, and exclaiming, "The top of the morning to you," or, "it's a mighty fine day," he seldom failed to get into a long conversation.

Then before he left, he took an opportunity of saying,—

"Do you happen to know of a swate young creature of a young lady, anyway that's lost and don't know where to find herself? because if you do, tell me, and I'll find her for herself, the swate creature."

Everybody answered in the negative, until one day he stepped into a milk-shop, which bore above its door the inviting name of Dermott.

"Here's mercy," said Rafferty; "a Dermott! och, murder! I must go in and knock him down, or something. The Dermotts and the Brolickbones have been fast friends since Ould Ireland was made. Och, murder, who'd have thought of finding a Dermott?"

The milkman received Rafferty graciously, and they soon got into a long chat, and then came Rafferty's question about his knowing or not knowing of a young lady who had lost herself.

"A great beauty," said Dermott, "is she?"

"Yes, yes."

"Well, then, it's the oddest thing in life; but there was a servant girl in here for two new-laid eggs this morning, and she said to me, 'Mr. Dermott,' says she, 'you're a man of discretion, entirely,' she says, 'and there's a young lady in our house,' she says, 'as has lost herslf anyway.'"

"Och, murder, filliloo!"

"So I up and says, says I, 'is there,' says I, and that's all I said."

"Bad cess to you, Dermott, why didn't you ask her all about it?"

"Because I didn't, and that's the reason I tell you. But you can ask her yourself anyhow. She's a countryman of ours."

"Is she? then all's right. Where shall I find the darlint?"

"I'll be bound, now, as it's getting on towards the dusk, if you walk past the 'airy' of No. 7, and whistle the 'Groves of Blarney,' she'll come out in less than no time. You are not so young as you was, but you ain't the ugliest man in the word, after all."

"Thank you kindly," said Rafferty; "don't you see me blushing? No. 7. I'll go, and if it should be the same I want to find out, it sha'n't be the worst day's work you ever did, Dermott, to tell me."

"Oh, don't mention it."

Away went Rafferty to No. 7, while Dermott came to the door after him, and flung an old shoe after him for luck, which hit him on the side of the head.

"Thank you for nothing," said Rafferty, as he walked on and soon found himself by the area rails of No. 7.

It was a respectable enough looking house, and he tried the persuasive tune of the Groves of Blarney, as had been suggested to him by Dermott, without, however, producing any apparent effect upon the nymph of the kitchen. He had gone through the whole tune about five times, with all sorts of variations, and then he got tired of it and dealt one of the rails a heavy kick.

This was a more effectual proceeding, for he saw a face at the kitchen window, the contour of which was sufficient at a glance to convince him that it came from the land of praties and buttermilk; so he put on his most insinuating appearance, and nodded and winked with a force that was quite miraculous.

"Bedad," he said, as the face disappeared, "if that don't bring her out she's one of a thousand."

Rafferty now prudently walked away some paces, and he was quite delighted to find that in a few minutes the area gate was opened, and the girl came out with a key dangling on her finger, and a basket on her arm.

"Och, murder!" said Rafferty, as he came up to her, "what a mighty pretty girl you are to be sure. How is the young lady?"

"Oh, good gracious, do you know ?"

"Yes, to be sure, but I'm a friend, you know. Tell me all about her, and then I shall know if you know, and there will be goulden guineas enough for you to roll over and over in."

"You don't mean that ? Will the captain——"

"The what—the captain—did she speak of the captain?"

"She speaks of nothing else but the captain, and she cries all day long. Poor thing, I do pity her, and I wonder how they can have the heart to behave to her as they do. Keeping her locked up in such a way, all to please some wretch that they know, who brought her from the country, —poor thing, for all the world like a felonious felon."

"The villain of the world."

"Oh, you may say that, Mr.——, what do you call 'em?"

"Rafferty Brolickbones, my darlint: at your service."

"Yes, Mr. Brolick—something. You may say that, and never a word of a lie. I'd give one of the eyes out of my head to do her a service. It was but this morning she said to me, 'Judith,' says she,—she calls me that, but my rale name is Judy,— 'Well,' says she, 'if the captain knew I was here he'd storm the house,' says she."

"And so he would."

"Would he, indend ? Is he handsome?"

"As like me as one pea is like another."

"You don't say so? Oh, tell him she thinks of nothing but him. Tell him she does nothing but cry all day long. Has he come up all the way out of the conntry to look for her ?"

"Faith then he has, my dear, and he won't go back again without her, you may depend. You may look upon your fortune as made entirely, you may; for the captain has got lots of money, and is as generous as a water spout."

"Is he indeed ? Oh, what a nice fellow he must be. I do hate missus, and I hate master, and so if you and the captain like to run away with us—— ?"

"With us ?"

"Yes; me and the young lady, poor dear thing. How she does mope, to be sure. She writes lots of letters to him, and then she tears them up and puts them in the fire. They want to kill her."

"I'll tell you what it is, my darlint, I'll come and take her away. She'll know me as soon as she sees me, and then you'll know that it's all right. When shall I come ?"

"Why, suppose you come after they have all gone to bed to-night, you know? Then I'll tell her that the captain has come up from the country for her, and she can step down stairs, for I'll take care to give her something to break the room door open where they shut her up, and off we go and get married."

"Married ?"

"Yes; she won't consent to anything improper."

"By the holy, she wants to have me in spite of my teeth. Och, it's the ould beauty of the Brolickbones; but I musn't undeceive her. My darlint, of course we will. I'll come if you tell me when, if the devil himself was to say 'don't, Rafferty.'"

"At twelve then, to night."

"Amin ! I'll be here, and you tell her that the captain has not known a minute's pace or comfort since she's been gone, and that he would be a dead man in another year and a day if he didn't see her again, for she's the darlint of his heart."

"Yes; I'll tell her. At twelve, mind, and you kick at the area rails."

"I will, I will. Was he a downright ugly chap that brought her ?"

"Ugly ? I never saw in all my life an uglier."

"That's him, then. Did he make out he was her father too, the vagabond?"

"Oh, yes, and I believe he is too, or else our people, I don't suppose, would have took her in as they have, you know."

"Then I can tell you he isn't. He is only a thief of the world; I know him well. He's no more her father than you are. But that's no matter now; I'll come at twelve o'clock, and give such a kick at those rails as shall astonish them, any way; and mind you have the young swate creature ready now."

"Oh, there's no fear of that."

"Adoo! then, as we says on the continent, where we whacked the French. Hurrah for the Brolickbones."

---

## CHAPTER LXXX.

### RAFFERTY COMPLETES HIS ADVENTURE, AND MAKES ANOTHER MISTAKE.

RAFFERTY thought it most remarkably cunning of him to keep this affair a profound secret from Captain Morton. The fact was, that he had never completely got over in his mind, however it might be excused by others, the disgrace of being so completely at fault, as he had been on the evening of the abduction of Mabel from Morton Hall. That he, an old campaigner, and, certainly one who ought to have known better, should have allowed himself to be so, as it were, duped, was one of those things that got altogether the better of that personal vanity which, in common with his countrymen, he possessed to no small extent. But now he flattered himself he had found an opportunity of redeeming the past, and of hearing, that if he had committed an error, that, to use his own words, he "was the boy to put it all right again."

What a triumph it would be to him to be able to bring Mabel back in safety to the arms of those who were anxious to receive her, and who for so long had been in such great distress, solely occasioned by her absence from among them.

"Then," he thought, "they will say something, I rather think, to Rafferty."

In these pleasant anticipations he passed his time until the hour of appointment had very nearly come—that hour at which he was to go and kick at the area rails, and have the pleasure of rescuing Mabel from her state of bondage.

At about half-past eleven Rafferty was on the spot, and most anxiously did he wait until twelve should strike from a church clock which was in the immediate vicinity, so that he should then, without being too much beforehand, and so perhaps risking the success of the scheme, be fully entitled to kick away at the area rails to his heart's content.

"Oh, the darlint!" he said; "when she only once sees my face, won't she be delighted! Och, murder! this will be a pleasant night, any way, for me. Sorrow's the fool they can call Rafferty Brolickbones now."

At length twelve o'clock was solemnly pealed forth from the church turret that could be just seen peeping over the tops of the houses, and in another moment Rafferty was at the area rails, and had given them a kick that made the whole mass of them vibrate again. He had not to wait long. A light flashed from the kitchen window, and then the door leading into the area was cautiously opened, and a voice said—

"Hist! hist! Is it you?"

"Yes, my jewel," said Rafferty, "it's myself, and no one else."

"Where's the captain? She says she won't come unless the captain is here himself, for fear it should be some scheme."

"Well, it is a scheme, and a mighty fine scheme, any way. You tell her it's Rafferty Brolickbones, and see if she won't come."

"Very well, wait."

Rafferty waited for some time, and then the servant came out into the area, and said in a whisper—

"No, she will see the captain before she comes out, she says; as for you, she don't know you from Adam."

"Not know me! Oh, blazes! Not know me? Tell the little darlint not to be after poking her fun at me; I'll take her to the captain before she is ten minutes older, I swear by all the blessed calendar."

"Well, I'll tell her."

Away went the servant again, and this time she was successful; for she came out in a great hurry, and ran up the steps, with a bag in her hand, to open the gate.

"She's coming! she's coming!" she whispered; "and so am I."

"Come along, then, my darlint; you're a mighty fine girl of your size, you are; so I won't be after saying nay to that part of the bargain."

"She is only putting on her bonnet and crying. Here she comes, here she comes. You really ought, Mr. Barleybones, to have brought the captain with you—captains give a sort of confidence to young ladies, you know."

"May be so. But where's the odds? It's a happy man he'll be when he sees her."

From the kitchen now emerged the form of a young female, closely enveloped in a large shawl. With quick step and agitated manner she ascended to the area gate; and, in another moment, both she and the servant were in the street.

"There goes the gate shut," said the servant; "and they shan't say in the morning they don't know where the key is."

As she spoke, she cast the key down the area, and, at the same moment, the young lady laid her hand upon Rafferty's arm, and said—

"Do not deceive me, but take me to Captain Lovemore at once."

Rafferty might at that moment have been knocked down by the smallest young potato that was ever seen. The young lady was not Mabel, and it was all a mistake from first to last.

"Cap-cap-captain who?" he shouted.

"Lovemore."

"The divil! Och, murder! You ain't you, and I'm not myself. We are neither of us anybody."

"Oh, good God! you wretch! what do you mean?" said the servant.

"By Jasus I don't know," said Rafferty; "one—two—three, here goes. The divil take the hindmost."

As he spoke, away he ran, at a speed which, as the puffing shopkeepers say, "defied all competition." The young lady screamed; the servant accompanied her; and, finally, poor Rafferty sank exhausted on the door steps of a house, some two or three streets off, in a state of mind of the most uncomfortable character.

Here was a *denouement* to all his cleverness. He drew a long breath, and wiped the perspiration from his brow.

"Oh, bedad," he said. "I've made a mighty pretty mess of that, any way. It wasn't her after all. And the trouble I had, too—oh, murder! There's nothing but misfortunes coming to the share of the Brolickbones, now. What's to be done? 'I don't know,' as the echo in Munster says."

Rafferty remained in deep thought for some time, and more than once it occurred to him that he ought to go and punish the milkman who had led him astray; but, when he came to think how ludicrous a figure he should cut, if the affair came to the ears of Captain Morton, he, with a long-drawn sigh, saw that he must give it up, and content himself with renewing his search, having now no clue at all, and no more prospect of success than just what he first started with.

And that was little enough; for although, certainly, as far as impudence and perseverance went, Rafferty was a match for anybody in prosecuting an inquiry, yet even he required some clue to go upon.

But where was that clue to be obtained? True enough is it that, in all enterprises, the first step is a difficult one, if not the most difficult; and so Rafferty stood in the streets, quite at a loss for any expedient.

"East, west, north, or south," he said, "which way am I to go now to look for Miss Mabel?"

This was an easy question to ask, but he found it a difficult one to answer. However, as he could not stand where he was all night, he walked on in a listless mood, and not in the best of spirits.

To him, likewise, it was no agreeable reflection that he had brought trouble upon the young lady whom he had mistaken for Mabel, and who had evidently mistaken Captain Morton for some other captain to whom she was attached.

He did think of making an attempt of some kind to repair this error, but, probably, had he, in his Irish manner, really tried to do so, he would have made confusion worse confounded, and it was quite a mercy that he gave up the idea.

"Well," he said, with a sigh, "there's nothing to be done to-night, so I'll just find out a bed somewhere, if I can, and sleep off my disappointment. Oh, Miss Mabel, Miss Mabel! what a trouble you do give me, to be sure; and, if ever I see you again, you darlint, won't it be a happy sight for me! I won't be after letting you go again so easy."

Rafferty did not like at such an hour to go to the lodgings which had been taken for them all by Captain Morton, because he did not wish any one to know of his adventure; and he thought that, if now that he was out he were to remain all night, he could slip quietly in in the morning, and no one be any the wiser.

In London there is no difficulty in procuring a bed, and Rafferty walked on till he came to one of those early breakfast houses which abound in some parts of London, and which, what with being late supper houses as well, are, somehow or another, never shut at all.

An announcement in the window of "good beds" was just what Rafferty looked for, and he at once entered the place. In answer to his inquiries if he could have a bed there, he was told—certainly, if he paid beforehand for it; but he was farther informed that he must sleep in a double-bedded room, one of the beds in which was already occupied.

"Oh!" said Rafferty, "that don't matter to me; I've often slept in a five hundred-bedded room, my good woman."

"Lor, sir!"

"Yes; I'm an old soldier, and have enjoyed many a comfortable nap with my regiment in a field."

"Oh! I understand what you mean, sir. Here, Jem, show the gentleman up stairs to No. 7—you know were the strange man sleeps."

"Oh! a strange man, is he?" said Rafferty; "blood-an-'ouns, he won't disturb me!"

"No, sir; he seems as quiet as a small lamb, and not very well; he isn't strong enough to disturb any one."

"Very well; I'm sleepy, so come on, master Jem, as you are the chambermaid."

A boy, with a broad grin upon his face, lighted Rafferty to the room, which was a low-roofed, long, rambling-looking apartment, with two beds in it, one of which was up at the farther end, a long way from the door; and the other you ran a good chance of tumbling against the moment the door was opened. It was the latter that was unoccupied, and the curtains of the other were all drawn scrupulously close.

------

## CHAPTER LXXXI.

### THE ARRIVAL OF AN OLD ACQUAINTANCE FROM THE VILLAGE.

Now that so much had been discovered concerning the identification of the beautiful and persecuted Mabel, and now that there could be no further doubt at all upon the minds of any of those who were so much interested in her fate, that she was the daughter of Colonel Rouselli, and, consequently, the grandchild of Monsieur Rouselli, there remained nothing now but to stir heaven and earth to discover her.

Captain Morton and his brother held together a long and serious consultation on the subject, the result of which was an organised system of operations to be entered upon immediately, from which they hoped for success.

They hoped that a very short time would suffice to procure some clue to the proceedings of the mysterious man who had been concerned in her abduction, and since nothing now but the utmost publicity could do any good in the way of discovering the retreat of the mendicant, they made up their minds that that publicity should be at once complete and ample.

"I will," said Captain Morton, "cause advertisements to be placed in every metropolitan paper, offering a large reward for any information concerning her; and I will, myself, have a private interview with the principal police authorities, so as to get their co-operation in the matter."

"We shall surely be successful," said Henry. "Oh! if I could but know that any amount of perseverance in any particular direction would afford me the least chance of obtaining a clue to where she is hidden, I would know no rest until I had

adopted it. Each day's suspense is becoming to me more and more terrific."

"Do not torture yourself thus uselessly," said the captain. "Compare your state with that of Monsieur Rouselli. What must he feel?"

"He feel! Can he love her as I love her? Oh, no, no! not the concentrated love of a thousand relatives can equal or approach mine."

Before Captain Morton could make any reply to this enthusiastic speech, it was announced to him that a man was below who wanted to speak to him, and he said instantly.—

"Admit him—I refuse to see no one; for, by so doing, I may deprive myself of some information with regard to the very person whom I seek."

In a few minutes a stout, respectable-looking man made his appearance, and, advancing to Captain Morton, he said,—

"Don't you recollect, sir, the ostler at the Morton Arms, who was accused of the murder of the young traveller?"

"Good God! is it you? I did not really recognise you at the moment, although now I do well."

"I am very glad to see you, sir. I only heard, by mere accident, that you were in town."

"I am very glad to see you, and, if you are not better engaged, I can give you an employment which will, I think, be congenial to you."

"Sir, I have already an employment which I have never yet forsaken—it is that of endeavouring to discover some trace of the real murderer of the traveller at the inn at the village—I have dedicated my life to that object."

"And have you any clue?"

"I had, of course, a clue which you are aware of, and I came up only yesterday, a long way from the country, in consequence."

"A clue that I am aware of! Pray what clue is that?"

"Why, the police proceedings."

"Police proceedings!"

"Yes, Captain Morton; and the principal thing I have called upon you is, to ask Miss Mabel if she can give me a very accurate description of the fellow, so that I may aid the police."

The captain looked at his brother, and his brother looked at him; then they both shook their heads dubiously, as much as to say—

"Poor fellow, he is a little deranged."

"Of course," said the late ostler, "if this request of mine does not meet with your approbation, I must forego it."

"Sit down, sit down," said Captain Morton, kindly, for he really thought his visitor was a little cracked.

"Thank you, sir—thank you. What a joyful surprise the letter must have been to you."

"Letter!"

"Yes; the magistrate's letter. Good God! do you suppose, Captain Morton, that I don't know anything?"

"Humour him," whispered Henry.

"No; I shall not," said Captain Morton.

"Humour who?" said the late ostler to Henry. "Is your brother mad?"

"No; but you are," said the captain. "In God's name, what do you mean by the letter? You are talking of things that have no existence but in your own brain; and as for asking Mabel any questions, I only wish you had the opportunity."

"Well, then, give me the opportunity, or refuse it at once candidly, and let me know why you so refuse it; or if your brother here will tell me that your mind has become deranged, I will go away at once, and no longer irritate you."

"D—n your infernal impudence!" said the captain.

"Well, and d—n yours."

Henry rose and stepped between them.

"Hush—hush!" he said. "I cannot help thinking that there is some playing at cross-purposes here, and an amount of misconstruction, which is likely to proceed, unless you explain what you really mean."

"I have explained," said the ostler. "I came here after finding out, as I tell you, by mere accident, where you were staying, partly to congratulate you upon the recovery of Miss Mabel, and likewise to ask you to allow me to get what particulars she can give me of that scoundrel who carried her off, and who, I have no sort of doubt in my own mind, is the same who did the dreadful murder at the inn of which I was so wrongfully accused."

"And that's what you are come for?" said the captain.

"Precisely."

"If this is a joke, it's a sorry one."

"A joke!"

"Yes, a joke; but if it be really a mistake arising from misinformation of some sort, I can only regret to say, that as we have not yet recovered Mabel——"

"Not recovered her?"

"Certainly not, nor have we the least idea of what has become of her, or of where she is. We have heard nothing of her whatever since she left Morton Hall."

"Am I dreaming?"

"You must be if you take any other view of the subject."

"Then what is the meaning of all this?"

"All what?"

"The report in this newspaper which I have carried about me ever since."

He handed to Captain Morton a newspaper as he spoke, which was folded so that the following article met his eye :—

"Bow-street.—Yesterday, as the sitting magistrate was about quitting his seat, a lady-like young person, of great personal attractions, stepped into the witness-box and made the following extraordinary application with regard to the late murder near Whitechapel, for which, it will be in the recollection of our readers, that a man unknown is in custody, who has vehemently declared his innocence. The applicant stated that she was an enforced resident with the man at the time of the alleged murder, and that he was innocent of it. She stated herself to be named Mabel Morton——"

The paper dropped from the hands of Captain Morton, and he changed colour, so that Henry, who, however, was scarcely less affected, became alarmed.

"Ring for water!" he cried; "ring the bell!"

"No, no," said Captain Morton. "I am better now. Good God! what does all this mean, and how have we not known it?"

"What!" exclaimed the ostler. "Do you mean to tell me that you know nothing of all this?"

"Nothing, so help me Heaven!" cried Henry.

"Nor I—nor I," gasped Captain Morton. "Henry, read it all—read it all."

Henry took up the paper, and with an agitated tone and manner, he continued the police report which had been so abruptly stopped.

"She stated that her name was Mabel Morton, and that she had been abducted from her home by the man who stood accused of the murder, and whom a sense of justice induced her, notwithstanding he had been to her the greatest of enemies, to exonerate from the charge preferred against him.

"The worthy magistrate questioned her closely, and, from the answers which she gave him, a general favourable impression was created in the minds of all present. She stated that the party with whom, from earliest childhood, she had had a home, was a Captain Morton, residing at Morton House, in Oxfordshire; whereupon the magistrate expressed his intention of immediately writing to that gentleman; and as she declared herself to be destitute, he directed that she should be well taken care of."

"And—and," said Captain Morton, "when was all this?"

"Some days ago."

"And I not know it!"

"We have neither of us looked at the papers lately," replied Henry.

"But the magistrate's letter?"

"Is most likely now lying at the Hall."

"Good Heaven! then the very step which we took in coming to town has been the means of defeating our object in a speedy restoration to our dear Mabel. Oh! what may she not have suffered during this period of agonizing suspense!"

"Well," said the ostler, "all this amazes me. I, of course, thought that it was the magistrate's letter that had brought you to town, and as fully expected to find Mabel with you as ever I expected anything in this world."

"Let us seek her instantly," cried Captain Morton, springing to his feet. "Come, Henry, do not let us delay another moment. Oh, what a delightful day will this be to poor old Monsieur Rouselli! Come, Henry, at once."

"Ready," said Henry, "were it to go the world over, if my reward at the conclusion of my pilgrimage was to be a sight of Mabel."

"Well," remarked the ostler, "I am glad I came, and that our cross-purposes have turned out to be of some importance. Why, Heaven knows how long you might have remained without knowing what had happened."

"We might have been days—ay, weeks; and during all that time, poor Mabel might be exposed to the cruellest of suspicions."

They had now reached the door, and the whole three of them—for the ostler asked and readily obtained permission to walk with them—proceeded to the police-office which had been named in the report.

When, however, they reached there, they found that they were too early, for, although the doors were certainly open, business had not commenced.

Appearance, however, does wonders at all public places in England, and with officials of all sorts and grades. There was so much of the unmistakeable gentleman in Captain Morton's aspect, that the officer who kept the door was disposed to be wonderfully civil.

"The magistrate, sir," he said, "has not yet come, but if you will walk in and take a seat no doubt he will attend to any business you may have with him the moment he arrives."

"My name you will find on that card," said Captain Morton, handing him one; "I come to make inquiry concerning a young girl who appeared here some few days since, and gave the name of Mabel Morton."

"Oh, you are Captain Morton, sir?"

"I am."

"She is an impostor, sir, and ——"

"She is not," interrupted Captain Morton; "you know not of whom you speak; she is no impostor. It is impossible that anything she could say or do should be otherwise than full of truth and excellence."

"Then, sir, you have come for her?"

"I have. Half an hour has not elapsed since I first heard of her situation. I was from home and did not get the magistrate's letter, which accounts for its having met no answer as yet."

"And that circumstance, sir, of course, is the very thing which induced us to think that it was a made up story. I beg your pardon for saying so, but one can only take things as we find them."

"Certainly, certainly, and you will excuse me for showing so much warmth on the accusation, when I tell you that she is as dear to me as if she were a child of my own."

"No doubt of that, sir," said the officer, and then added to himself, "and that's, I suppose, just what she is, if the truth were known."

"Now where is she?" added Captain Morton—"you can tell me where she is, although the magistrate is not here."

"That, indeed, sir, I cannot; she was placed in the care of an officer who has not yet come, and if he had he could not give her up to you without the magistrate's sanction; because I know that, since it was found no answer came to the letter sent to you, sir, and your name was not found in the army list, considerable suspicion was excited as to the truth of her story."

"My name is not in the army list, for I have left the army years ago; although people will still politely call me Captain Morton, and from the force of habit I answer to the title, and indeed often call myself so. I presume then I must wait."

He was admitted into the office, where he waited for half an hour with an amount of impatience that was sufficient to make that lapse of time, short as it was, appear to him half a day. Then one of the officers came to him and said that the magistrate had come and desired to see him in his private room. Captain Morton gladly obeyed the summons and was ushered, with Henry, into the presence of the police potentate.

He, the magistrate, happened to be not only a clever man but a gentlemanly one besides, and he received the Mortons with great courtesy.

"I cannot express to you, gentlemen," he said, "how glad I am that you have come forward and verified the story of the young lady who came before me. There was so much of the very essence of truthfulness about her manner that I was myself strongly impressed in her favour, and I must own that it would have been a very great disappointment to me to have found that she was other than what she represented herself to be."

"Sir," said Captain Morton, "for all the kindness and courtesy which you have shown to her, accept my best acknowledgments. And now you may well conceive with what impatience I long again to see her."

"Certainly, certainly."

The magistrate rang a bell, and when it was answered, he said,—

"If Randell has come, tell him to step in here."

"He has come, sir."

In a few moments the officer, to whose charge Mabel had been last committed, made his appearance. He was a respectable looking specimen of his class, and when it was explained to him who the Mortons were, and what they had come about, he really expressed genuine satisfaction, saying,—

"I am very glad to hear it. The young lady has gained very much upon us, and my wife is so convinced of the truth of all she says, that I do believe she'd almost lay down her life for her."

"And where is she?"

"At my house, gentlemen."

"Whither you can at once take these gentlemen," said the magistrate, "and surrender up your charge to them. I suppose you have no news of the fellow who broke out of prison, and against whom this young lady has a serious charge to prefer?"

"None as yet, sir; but we are sure to have him."

"No doubt, no doubt. I trust, Captain Morton, that you and the young lady will remain in town in order that she may give evidence against the fellow?"

"I shall induce her to do so. And I have, moreover, a servant with me who can identify him likewise."

"By all means then remain, and I think it will go hard with us if we do not manage to transport the rascal who has caused you so much uneasiness."

"He fully deserves it."

The magistrate politely bowed them out, and with the officer the two Mortons, still followed closely by the ostler, who had waited for them in the outer office, proceeded towards the house to unite themselves once again with the beautiful Mabel, who had gone through such cruel vicissitudes of fortune at a period of life when she ought to have been surrounded with all its choicest charms.

And most peculiarly hard was it upon her, for there were persons who loved—persons who panted for her society, and who were as fully willing as they were able to adorn her existence with all that could render it a very romance of delight. Surely he who had so cruelly torn her from those beloved and loving friends deserved at their and at her hands no mercy.

And now that Captain Morton had, in consequence of the deeply interesting communications of M. Rouselli, got rid of even the shadow of a dread that the mendicant might really have the claim of a father upon Mabel, it cannot be supposed that any feeling of consideration for that rascally individual was likely to find a place in his heart.

But now, as he reached the door of the officer's house, joy at the prospect of being so soon able to take his beloved Mabel to his arms again, overpowered every other feeling. But what were Captain Morton's sensations of pleasure compared with those of his brother Henry, the joy of whose whole existence was mingled with the thought of Mabel, whom he loved so truely? We should despair of doing justice to his thoughts and feelings.

## CHAPTER LXXXII.

THE MEETING OF THE MORTONS WITH MABEL.—THE UNEXPECTED JOY.

MABEL sat alone in the officer's house absorbed in deep and melancholy reflections, not the least powerful feature of which was the seeming absolute desertion of her by the Mortons. She could not conceive how it was possible that the magistrate's letter should have remained unanswered. That it had been answered, and the answer, somehow, however rare such a thing may be, had been lost in its progress, she for some time strove to convince herself, and that consequently the whole question was only one of a little time.

But when she came again to consider what she would have done under such circumstances, and what she would have expected the Mortons to do, that hope died away from her completely, and she said, with a sigh,—

"No, no; had they intended to take any notice of me, they would, some of them, have most assuredly come to London long ere this. They are either all dead or dispersed somewhere, that the letter has never reached them—or—or they have forgotten me!"

This last supposition was indeed a terrible one; one which brought with it such a wild rush of dreadful thoughts and misgivings that it nearly drove her distracted, and for the sake of preserving the equilibrium of her intellect, she was glad hastily to dismiss it as one utterly unworthy of her consideration—as one which did the greatest injustice to those dear friends who had been so good and so kind to her, and upon whose love she could rely as she could upon the justice of Heaven.

"No," she said,—"no, they have not neglected me; they could not, and they would not. Something has occurred to produce a delay that, when they know of it, will be a source to them of endless regret. Alas! alas! in the meantime what will become of me?"

She leaned her head upon her hands, and wept! The tears trickled through her fingers as deep sighs came from her over-burthened heart; and then suddenly she rose, as a loud knocking at the street-door struck upon her ears, and recalled her to a sense of where she was.

"These are foolish tears," she said. "The time for weeping has gone past. If I am to be henceforward alone in the world, I must gather around my heart such energy as I may be capable of, and meet with what courage I may whatever chances may befall me. Courage! courage! I will not forget that I am innocent of all ill, and that there is a God above, who will not suffer even a sparrow to fall without his will and cognizance. These tears but mar all resolution; I will shed no more."

She dashed some cold water over her face, to clear away the appearance of having been weeping; for she knew that the officer's wife, from a feeling of kindness towards her, never left her for a long time alone, and to be found with the traces of tears upon her countenance seemed like a reproach against those persons who were striving to make her happy, that they had not succeeded even sufficiently to subdue the most violent accessories of despondency.

But let us glance at the Mortons.

With the most trembling eagerness did Henry Morton and his brother reach the door of the house where they were told they again should see the dear object of their utmost solicitude.

It was the officer himself who knocked so loudly; for though on his own account he would not have done so, he felt the impatience of the visitors he brought, and considered that the summons he made resound from the knocker was on their account and not his own.

His wife had no suspicion that it was he who knocked, so she opened the door in a great flutter, thinking that it was at least some of the magistracy, who required the services of her husband in a wonderful hurry.

"Well, I'm sure, John," she said, when she saw him; "you are a nice article to come knocking at that rate, and putting me so out of sorts."

"Hush, wife, hush! here are some gentlemen; it was for them I knocked, not for myself. Will you walk in, gentlemen, if you please? Chairs, wife, chairs."

The officer's wife, when she really saw that there were visitors, guessed at once their errand, and she exclaimed,—

"Oh, it is the friends of the young lady!"

"Hush! for Heaven's sake!" said Captain Morton; "I dread giving her too sudden a shock."

"Oh, where is she? Let me fly to her!" said Henry.

"No, no; pause a moment," added Captain Morton, as he sat down, and looked very pale. "I could not have believed that I should have been so agitated. Pause a moment or two, I beseech you, Henry."

Henry was, however, all impatience, till the officer said—

"I think it would be prudent to prepare her, if possible, by degrees for the joyful and unexpected appearance of those whom she has been so longing for."

"Be it so," said Henry; "but how is that to be done?"

"Leave it to my wife."

"Yes, yes, madam; do you go, and prepare her as well as you can for the news, so that it may not come upon her with too sudden a shock. Tell her—nay, I cannot instruct you; you must tell her what you please, only be as brief as possible in pity to our impatience."

"I will do my best, sir," said the officer's wife; and she ascended to Mabel's apartment, leaving those below in a fever of impatience which it was no easy matter for them to combat, and which Henry at last found required all the strength of mind he was capable of calling to his aid to prevent him from obeying at once the dictates of his wishes.

Had he listened to his own wishes, he would have rushed up the staircase after the officer's wife, and the first intimation he would have given to Mabel of his presence would have been to clasp her in his arms.

As for Captain Morton, he really felt so agitated himself, that he was glad, now that he considered he had Mabel virtually once again at his heart, of some little respite until the full gush of joyful feeling had a little subsided.

"What weakness this is of me, Henry," he said. "I find myself unequal to the task of meeting my dear Mabel just yet."

"Hush! hush!" said Henry, "surely she will come down directly, or we shall be asked to go up. Oh! this state of suspense is really worse than all. Do you not hear the sound of voices, brother? I fancy I can detect hers."

"And I; and like music, Henry."

"Yes; more delightfully melodious than any music that ever reached mortal ears! Oh! why does she not come? Why does she not come at once? This delay is agonizing and insupportable!"

While, then, Henry Morton was counting moments until they seemed like minutes, and minutes until he transformed them into hours, the officer's wife was doing her best, and that as quickly, too, as was at all prudent, to prepare Mabel for the reception of those dear friends for whose presence she had so much sighed, and who she little dreamt were now within hearing of her very voice.

The good-hearted woman tapped gently at the door, and Mabel herself opened it, and made a weak attempt at a smile, for she knew, and felt grateful that she, the officer's wife, had come to cheer her in her solitude.

"Come, my dear," said the woman; "you don't seem so happy to-day, you must hope for the best, you know. I have some news for you."

A cry of joy came from the lips of Mabel, and she said—

"Yes,—oh! yes,—oh! yes,—they have written?"

"They have; and what is more, they have written to say that they are coming to town to see you, and take you home with them.

Mabel burst into tears.

"Come, now, really I have not seen you weep in your misfortunes before this good news came, and you ought not now."

"I cannot help it. They—they are tears of joy. I am rescued; they love me still; they have not deserted me. Oh! what treason it was against all that is just and true, to suspect for one instant that they could."

"I am, I assure you, as glad as if it were my own case. My husband tells me that when they come to town, and he brings them here, he hopes that you will be able to control your feelings."

"Oh! yes,—yes,—yes. All will be joy!"

"Well, then, I'll tell him that, and he shall bring them, as he said he would. 'Wife,' said he, 'I shall brings the friends of Mabel here the moment they come to town, to inquire for her at the police-office, because the magistrate will refer them to me.'"

"Yes; oh! yes."

"'And then I shall come, and you will be able to know who is with me, because I shall knock very loud, and while they remain down stairs, you shall go up to Mabel's room, and just prepare her a little for the sudden surprise,—you understand.'"

Mabel passed her hand across her brow for a moment, and then, while the colour went and came upon her cheeks, like the sweet sunshine of an April day, she looked in the face of the officer's wife, and said, half choked with emotion,—

"Do not, oh! do not deceive me. Tell me, are—are they here? Yes, yes, your eyes bespeak the truth; they are, and this is but a kind subterfuge to prevent sudden joy from killing me. I see it all! They are here,—I know that they are here. Henry! Henry!"

"Mabel!" cried the voice of Henry, from below,—for he had heard his name pronounced by those lips he valued more than all the world beside.

In an instant she had rushed past the officer's wife, and was down the short, narrow staircase, and the next moment,—oh! joy of joys! she was in the arms of Henry Morton, and lay, half fainting, upon his breast.

The feeling that now reigned in the bosoms of these persons we should find it a vain task to attempt to describe. Thought, in a few brief moments, will achieve more in the way of depicting what Captain Morton, Henry, and Mabel felt, than would the most elaborately attempted description. They were very happy!

The officer had left the room, so that, for nearly half-an-hour, they were all three alone, but had all the world been present, they would have forgotten the fact that any eyes were bent upon, or that any other ears than those to which they severally spoke, drank in the words of hope and congratulation that flowed from their lips.

Oh! it was a sight worth a kingdom to see how Henry Morton sat by Mabel, with one of her hands clasped in his, and looked in her face while she talked to the captain, whose whole countenance exhibited the joy that reigned over his heart, too, now that he had once more recovered possession of his lost treasure—his child of the battle-field, who, in the midst of carnage and of danger, had been intrusted to his honour and humanity.

He seemed as if suddenly time had with him taken a retrograde movement, and had gone back many years. The beaming aspect of actual youth was in his eyes, and not in the whole of the vast city in which they were, we are convinced, could there have been found a happier and a more contented group than that.

The multitude of questions that were asked, and the answers that were given in a brief space of time, defy our limits to record. Suffice that they found they had food for conversation for many a day to come.

But Captain Morton was not easy until he had carefully explained to Mabel how it was that the magistrate's letter had remained unanswered; and although she smiled and told him that it was answered fully now, he would tell her the whole particulars of how he came to town to look for her.

But, as he spoke, Henry gave him a glance which induced him as yet to say nothing of old Monsieur Rouselli. The fact was, that Henry wanted to reserve that communication for himself to make, and which, after all, was a pardonable selfishness, so the captain let him have his own way, saying, as an excuse for their coming to town at such a juncture, that extreme anxiety personally to aid in a search for her actuated him.

"I have given you all," she said, with a smile, "far more trouble than I shall now be worth to you."

"Nay, now, I mean to quarrel with you," said Henry, "just as if you were a total stranger, if ever you utter one word that is not in praise of yourself, if you take yourself for a subject."

"Indeed !"

"Yes ; so, now you are recovered, there are only two people in the world who shall be permitted ever to praise you, either, unless they do it very circumspectly, besides myself ; so you see I am going to be monstrously jealous, troublesome, and exacting."

"You are, really, Henry.  And who are the favoured two ?"

"Oh, my brother and Rafferty."

"Poor Rafferty ! is he well ?"

"Yes, the rascal is well enough.  Confound him ! but for his pretended cleverness, we should not have had the misery, dear Mabel, of being so long separated from you."

"But you forgive him ?"

"His intention was blameless ; and I believe the poor fellow has felt ever since most keenly the consequences of his blunder.  Indeed I am sure he would any day since that fatal one which tore you from the arms of those who loved you, have cheerfully laid down his life if by so doing he could have repaired the error which he felt he had committed.  It will be a happy day for him, I am certain, when he looks upon you again."

"Is he in town ? will that day be this day ?"

"Yes, Mabel ; but we are, I fear, very much intruding upon these people.  Have they treated you with kindness, Mabel ?"

"With the utmost kindness."

"Then they shall find that they have laid out this good feeling at good interest. You shall tell us of every one, dear Mabel, who, by word or action, has alleviated any distress you may have suffered, and their reward shall be ample."

"And you shall tell me," added Henry, "of any one who by word, or look, or action, has added in any way to your afflictions, and their reward shall be ample, likewise, or my name is not Henry Morton."

"Nay," said Mabel, "I do not mean to give you any such information. You know that I have but one great enemy."

"Yes, the villain ! who yet, I hope, will become amenable to the laws.  The officers of justice are hunting everywhere for him ; and surely he must be found, for his necessities will not allow him to leave the country."

Mabel shuddered at the very thought of the mendicant, whose dreadful image had, for a time, vanished from her recollection.

"I hope to God," she said, "I may never look upon his face again !"

"Except as his accuser."

"No, no, I do not, even has his accuser, wish to look upon him.  I feel and know that I am now safe, and care not for vengeance."

"He must not be allowed to escape," said Captain Morton, "nor will he.  He cannot leave the country without means, and the police shall want no stimulant in tracing him to wherever he may be."

"I am, of course," said Mabel, "completely in your hands as regards this matter, and will do whatever you choose to dictate to me."

"We shall be able, dear Mabel," said the captain, "to give you abundant and special reasons for whatever we ask you to do ; and now let us come away."

The captain, before he took Mabel away from the officer's house, placed in the hands of his wife a bank-note of considerable value, at the same time, in the most handsome manner, thanking her for the kindness she had shown to Mabel.  These people were quite delighted at the turn affairs had taken, and no doubt the whole circumstances afforded them abundant food for conversation and for congratulation for many a day.

There was now a short conference as to where they should go, and at length it was decided that Mabel, by the name of Morton, and still passing as the captain's daughter, should at once be taken to the handsome apartments in which, in preference to the hotel where the Mortons had at first gone, they had now partially established themselves.

What a change of delight was this to Mabel !  In a few short hours, from actually feeling that she was in a state of destitution, and considering what was the least objectionable mode in which she could gain a livelihood, she now found herself surrounded by affectionate friends, with both the power and the will to place before her every luxury that money could command.

And so, in a bewilderment of new and delightful emotions, and now and then trembling lest all should be but some uncommonly vivid dream of felicity, we will leave Mabel while we proceed to detail what befel Rafferty Brolickbones at the place where, after his unlucky adventure, or rather misadventure, he had taken a bed for the night.

---

## CHAPTER LXXXIII.

### THE FELLOW-LODGER.—RAFFERTY'S EX-ULTATION.—A SCENE.

RAFFERTY, although he had said to the persons of the coffee-shop that he had no sort of objection to the double-bedded room, yet was a little curious to know who his companion was. The curtains, how-ever, of the bed which was occupied were all drawn so very close, that not the least vestige of the party who there slept could be perceived, and Rafferty did not like the idea of actually going up to him, and saying,—

"Come, now, I want to see what sort of a fellow you are, before I consent to lie down and go to sleep in the same room with you."

He thought of doing so; but, as he him-self said, when he afterwards told the anecdote, the natural bashfulness of an Irishman (?) kept him back, and he didn't. He then thought that it would not be a bad plan to make so much noise as to waken him up, and so induce him to look out, and be a little abusive, which would enable him, Rafferty, to come to some sort of judgment regarding him.

Acting upon this idea, he sang a popular air; but it had no sort of effect, and there-fore he took off one of his boots, and tossed it up to the ceiling, to which it gave an odd-looking contusion, and then came down on the floor again with a heavy blow one would have thought quite sufficient to awaken anybody.

But the man who was in the other bed never moved.

"The deuce take him," thought Rafferty. "I cannot stand this at all, anyhow; I must go and give him a shake."

As if then the sleeper had been by some means able actually to know what Rafferty thought, he uttered a low groan.

"Oh! he says something at last," re-marked Rafferty. "Well, he's alive, and that's something. But who knows?—he may be ill, poor devil. Hilloa! Mr. What's-your-name, is there anything the matter?"

"Go to sleep," said a voice.

"Oh! thank you—the same to you, and many of them. Eh?—eh?—what did you say—eh? Oh, nothing! Very good; if you are pleased I am."

Rafferty now commenced undressing himself, which was a process his military habits enabled him to do with great celerity, and in a few minutes he plumped into bed, and prepared himself for a good few hours' repose. Before he shut his eyes, however, he called out again,—

"Good night, you devil!"

A deep groan was the only answer.

"Bedad, and that's hardly civil, any way," said Rafferty. "However, every man to his liking, as the ould woman said when she kissed the cow. If you ain't enough of a Christian to say 'Good night,' keep it to yourself, and the devil go lucky with you. A bad night to you, if you like that better."

Having delivered himself of this speech, Rafferty closed his eyes, and with a facility which was the effect of long habit, during the campaigns on the continent in which he had been engaged, where it became very desirable to catch a little sleep, without any coquetting with it, when it could be got, he was off in a moment or two.

How long he slept Rafferty had no means of calculating. All he knew was, that something awakened him, and that when he opened his eyes, which he did without moving, he found that the grey light of early morning was in the room.

He lay with his back towards the other bed; but immediately facing him was a dressing-glass, in which he saw it clearly reflected. As he looked—and surely a watchful Providence must have broken his slumber at that moment—he saw the curtains of the other bed, as they were reflected in the glass, slowly opened.

A hand appeared grasping a long, murderous-looking knife, then a foot came out, and finally the whole figure of a man, partially attired, crept from the bed on to the floor, and began to come cautiously towards the bed on which Rafferty slept. He evidently had not the least idea that the looking-glass was betraying him, for he kept his eyes fixed upon Rafferty, whom no doubt he now considered to be a per-fectly easy prey.

A second glance told Rafferty not only his danger, but from whom it arose. That man in the same room, with whom he had slept some hours, was no other than the mendicant—the very man whom he most wished to find, and who, doubtless, know-ing him, Rafferty, had now determined upon taking his life, as the surest way of escaping from him, as well as for vengeance.

Had Rafferty slept but for another five minutes, his doom in this world would have been sealed.

"Fair and easy," thought Rafferty, who

was too old a campaigner to be flurried; "fair and easy. That's it, is it? Come on, my darling."

Step by step the fellow came, and Rafferty gradually freed his feet from any entanglements among the clothing as he did so. With a calmness that few men, under such trying circumstances, would have been equal to, he waited until two steps more would have brought the fellow sufficiently close to him to inflict the blow that, no doubt, from the hand of that practised assassin, would have been almost immediately fatal. Then, as suddenly as if he had been impelled by some mechanical contrivances of great propulsive power, he sprang from the bed on the opposite side to that on which was the assassin.

This movement of Rafferty was so utterly unexpected on the part of the medicant, who no doubt thought him profoundly sleeping, that on the impulse of the moment, he uttered a cry of despair, and then a pillow, thrown by Rafferty, came with such a dab in his face that it nearly blinded him.

"Whack, filliloo!" said Rafferty, as he ran round the bed, seizing the tongs from the fire-place in his progress; "you murdering thief of the world, I've got you, have I?"

The fellow did recover sufficiently to make a desperate attempt with his knife, but happily he missed Rafferty, who gave him such a ringing blow on the top of the head with the tongs, that his faculties evidently became confused, and he reeled like a drunken man, uttering, as he did so, the most diabolical curses, and stabbing at the air with his knife.

"Aisy," said Rafferty, "and don't tell anybody I hit you. There you go now."

Rafferty put out his feet, and tripped him up on to the floor with a heavy fall, where he lay, apparently, unable to move.

All this scarcely occupied a minute in transacting, so that, although the disturbance was heard in the house, which, being an early one, was open, no one had really time to come to see what it was about.

Rafferty, however, now that he had conquered his enemy, quite forgot that he was not in a presentable state; but, with the tongs in his hand, opened the door of the bed-room, and walked down into the coffee-shop, which was full of people, saying, as he made his appearance to the woman of the house, whom he met,—

"If you please, ma'am, there's been a little bit of an action up stairs, and a gentleman wants to be taken up."

The landlady gave a scream, which was echoed by the girl who served in the coffee-shop, while Rafferty looked at them both in amazement.

"What the devil now!" he said, "I wasn't used to be so ugly."

"How dare you come down here, in your shirt?" said the landlady.

"Oh, murder!" said Rafferty; as he, for the first time, became aware of the impropriety, and then, turning at once, he bolted up stairs again amid a roar of laughter from some people who were in the coffee-shop, enjoying some abominable mixture which they flattered themselves was coffee.

The mendicant still lay upon the floor, as if in a state of exhaustion, but as Rafferty was putting on his own clothes, he saw the villain slowly put his hand towards the knife which he had dropped from his grasp when he fell.

"Hilloa!" said Rafferty; "jist tell me now, as we have had a fair fight, whether you surrender or not?"

"I surrender," said the fellow; and, at the same instant, his eyes gleamed with satisfaction, for he thought he succeeded, unobserved, in dragging the knife towards him, with which, no doubt, reckless and desperate as he was, he would have made another attack upon Rafferty had the latter not observed the treacherous movement.

"Very good," said Rafferty; "as you have surrendered, then you'll jist allow me to say, I don't allow my prisoners to be armed. Come out of that."

He walked up to him, and gave a touch with his foot to the hand which partially concealed the knife. With a shriek of baffled malice the fellow made a stab at him, but Rafferty stepped aside, and the sharp blade went deep into the floor.

"Why, you vagabond," said Rafferty; "anybody but me would jist stamp the life out of you. But where's the odds? I mean to see you hanged, and I will before I have done with you, you may take your oath. Will you? just do try to get up, that's all; and be after laving that knife alone."

The villain now gave up all attempts against Rafferty. He felt that he was thoroughly foiled; and closing his eyes, while he made his teeth nearly meet in his lower lip with passion, he said nothing, but awaited quietly whatever might occur. Rafferty's statement below had induced the people of the house to send for a constable, and now that official personage made his appearance at the door of Rafferty's room.

"Hilloa!" he said; "what's the row?"

"Nothing," said Rafferty; "only that gentleman wants a little accommodation to-day in some gaol or another."

"Oh, does he? Come, get up. Who is he?"

"Why, he's the fellow that used this mighty nice little pocket-knife here."

"Oh! why—why—let me see, I think I know him."

"I wish you joy of the acquaintance then."

"No, no! I don't mean that way. But I think I know he's a desperate malefactor."

"Oh, murder, what a discovery!"

The officer took a printed handbill from his pocket and read it, every now and then looking at the mendicant.

"'Fifty pounds reward.—To whoever shall take and lodge in any of his Majesty's gaols a man, name unknown, who was committed to prison on a charge of abduction, preferred by Mabel Morton. He is five feet eight inches in height, of a

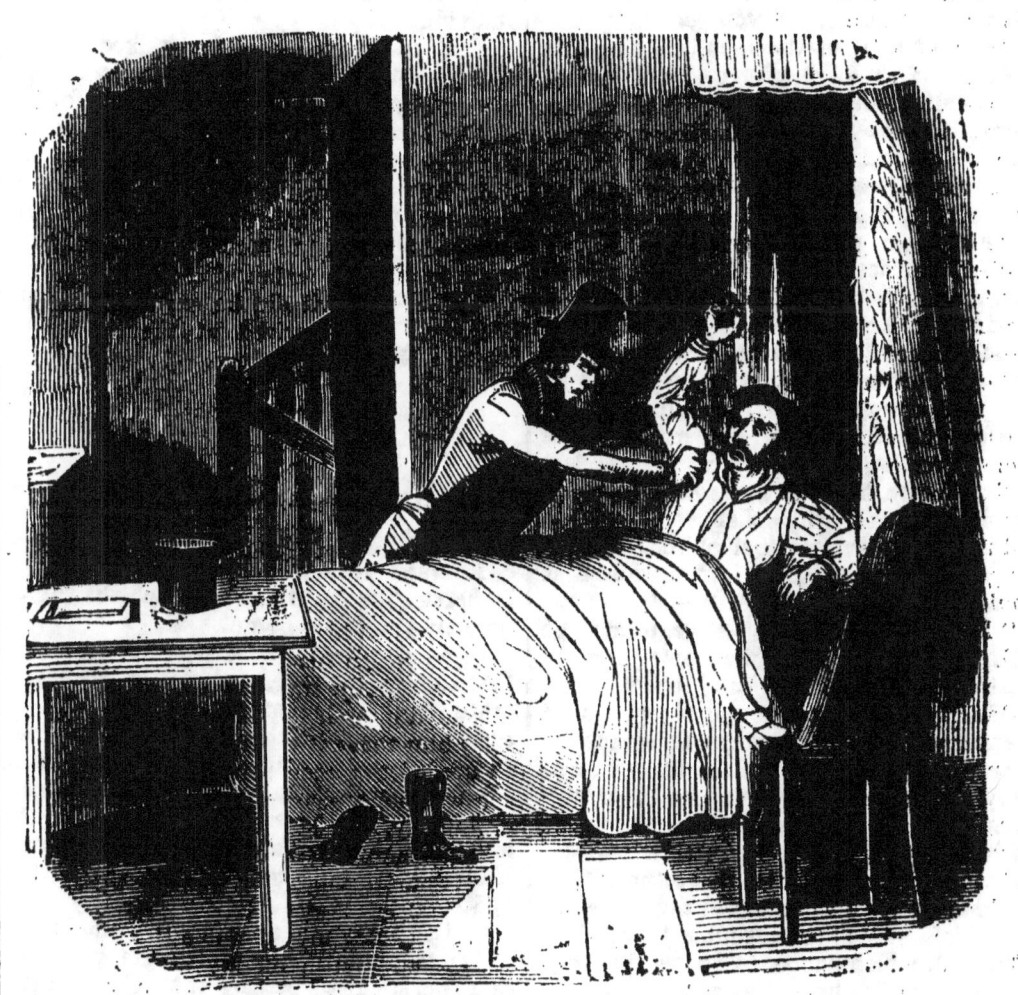

dark, yellowish complexion—squints—has a scar over the left eyebrow.' That's him! Here's a go! I've caught him."

"Have you?" said Rafferty.

"Yes; I have him. Don't you see I've caught him?"

"Well," said Rafferty, "that's modest. You've caught him, have you? Pray how did you catch him?"

"Oh, come, come, you won't chisel me out of my prisoner."

"Chisel you! By the holy, he'd soon have chiselled you if you had had to catch

him; but we won't quarrel about trifles. Take him away at once, and we'll be after settling who caught him some other time."

The officer looked mortified, for he knew well that it was Rafferty and not himself who was entitled to the reward; so he said, as he placed handcuffs upon the prisoner,

"I tell you what, Mr. what's your name, we'll go halves. There, now, will that content you?"

"Remarkably handsome it is," said Rafferty. "We'll spake about it another time."

"D—n you, then, take him to prison yourself."

"Very good, I can do that same; but mind me—there's Captain Morton that's in my service is as intimate with the Secretary of State as you are with any blackguard of an acquaintance you may have; and if you don't do your duty, and take this fellow away now, quiet and aisy, you'll be hung some fine morning as sure as you are a fool."

"Oh, d—n all the world," said the officer. "Get up, will you, get up."

He laid hold of the mendicant by the collar, and dragged him to his feet, and then, half dressed as he was, he took him away, in by no means an amiable mood, or one which induced him to show any indulgence *en route* to the fellow, who, if he had caught him himself, would certainly have been a good fifty pounds in his pocket, besides a hundred pounds which not two hours before Captain Morton had made up his mind to pay to whoever should succeed in capturing the fellow who had caused him and all that was dear to him such a world of anxiety and pain.

Upon the whole, now, Rafferty, when he came to review his adventures for the last twelve hours, had every reason to be well enough satisfied with them, although he had failed in his principal object, namely, the getting possession of information that would restore Mabel to her friends.

"I have caught that blackguard," he said, "at any rate; and he won't get away again easy, I'm thinking."

Rafferty was right enough there; for a prisoner who has once made an escape is, when caught again, looked to rather carefully, so that now we may consider the mendicant is at length fairly in the hands of justice.

It appeared afterwards that the officer to whom Rafferty committed the charge of the villain had no little trouble to get him to a gaol, which happened to be the very one from which he had escaped.

Had he not, indeed, had the precaution, while the desperate man was in a state of mental depression that made him resist nothing, to handcuff him, it is doubtful if he would have got him with safety to the gaol at all, for on their road a dreadful accession of fury came over him, and handcuffed as he was, he threw himself upon the officer, trying even with his teeth to inflict upon him some injury.

The assistance of several other police officers was finally required to convey him to prison; for, when he found he could, in consequence of his manacled condition, do no injury to any one, he threw himself down upon the ground, and threats nor entreaties could induce him to move an inch.

Not at all, therefore, in the tenderest manner he was carried, and it may be supposed that his appearance was hailed with satisfaction by the officials of the prison, who considered that the escape of a prisoner from their custody was a stain upon them of a very serious character, and one which could only be wiped off by the recapture of the daring and fortunate individual.

And now Rafferty, as he walked homeward, began to turn over in his mind what the officer had said about Mabel; for it will be remembered that as yet he was in the same ignorance which Captain Morton had, by so singular a coincidence of circumstances, remained in concerning all that had happened to Mabel, so as to bring her into any connexion with the police.

"What the devil did he say?" thought Rafferty, as he arrived at the door of Captain Morton's lodgings.

## CHAPTER LXXXIV.

### RAFFERTY'S INTRODUCTION TO MABEL.— THE FORGIVENESS.

IT was a very early hour indeed when Rafferty thus reached what might be temporarily called his home.

In answer to his inquiries, he was told that the captain was not up, so he congratulated himself that he should be sure to see him the first thing, to tell him of the capture of the mendicant. But as that even was not a piece of information which he, Rafferty, considered to be of sufficient importance to warrant him in disturbing his master's slumbers, he went to his own bed-room.

"I'll just lay myself down," said Rafferty; "and finish off my night's sleep, that was so disturbed by that blackguard with his long knife, and by that time the captain and Mr. Henry will be up and stirring, and I can tell them all about it, barring how I was took in about the young lady that ought to have been Mabel, but wasn't, poor thing, more the misfortune to her."

With this resolve, Rafferty lay down in his clothes just as he was, and soon fell off into a sleep so profound, that it was an exceedingly doubtful case indeed if he should awake in anything like time to tell the captain before he went out what had occurred.

Now Rafferty would probably have been

awakened, but that in the house there was an Irish servant, who had so much feeling for him, that hearing he had come in late, she was willing that he should have as long a sleep as he wanted, and without interruption, too, if she could possibly ward off any for him.

With that delightful facility which her countrymen and women have in little subversions of the truth, she had told Captain Morton, when he inquired for Rafferty, that he had got up early and gone out.

Then came the events on that morning, which we have had the pleasure of recording, and it has been a pleasure because it has resulted in the union of Mabel again to those dear friends from whom she had been, for so long, so cruelly separated by adverse circumstances.

And Rafferty slept on as sound as a church, as he himself afterwards remarked, while those events were ensuing that constituted a most admirable addendum to his capture of the mendicant, who was the original author of all the evil that had befallen Mabel. Indeed, so prolonged was Rafferty's repose that Mabel had been brought home, and was fairly installed in the comfortable drawing-room before Rafferty awoke; but then he had not slept many hours, for although so much of a highly important nature had been transacted, the day was yet young.

The captain was surprised at what, from the information he had had, he believed to be the continued absence of Rafferty, and he asked Henry what he thought of it.

"I can hardly hazard an opinion," said Henry, "he is so extraordinary and erratic a personage that I don't really know what to say. He seemed to me yesterday to have something on his mind, which gave him peculiar satisfaction. I do hope sincerely he has not blundered into any scrape."

"I hope so too."

The footman came in at this moment to attend to the fire, and Captain Morton said to him—

"Has my servant come in yet?"

"Oh, dear yes, sir; long ago."

"Long ago!—why a servant here told me he had gone out long ago."

"Oh, that was Biddy, sir; you see, sir, she's Irish, and so is your servant, sir, so she would not tell of him."

"Tell of him! Why, what has he been about?"

"I don't know, sir; but he came in at about daylight, early this morning, and has been in bed and asleep ever since."

"Oh, indeed, very well. It's no matter; don't disturb him."

"No, sir."

In about another hour Rafferty awoke of his own accord, and he was a little alarmed when he found it was so late, and much wondered that he had not been aroused. However, he whisked himself up as well as he could, and with serious misgivings as to what his master would say to him, he crept down stairs; and walking into the back drawing-room, which was only separated from the front by some folding doors, which were closed, he gave an intimation of his presence by whistling an old Irish air, and pretending to be wonderfully busy in putting the various articles of furniture to rights.

"They shall speak first," thought Rafferty; "I'll know what sort of humour they are in before I condescend to say a word to them, and maybe I won't tell them if they ain't mighty civil what news I've got."

"Hark," said Henry; "that's Rafferty."

"Let me see him," said Mabel, who was seated by the window with Henry, while Captain Morton was writing a note to old Monsieur Rouselli, in which he desired him to come to him as quick as possible.

"No, no," said Henry; "don't say a word, I am certain that he has been at some mischief, or at something which he considers exceedingly clever; whenever he whistles in that sort of way, it is to show his great independence, and how little he cares for anybody."

"It is so," said the captain, as he folded his note. "You go up stairs, while we find out what he has on his mind, for that he has something I'll be bound, and that it concerns you, I think I should be safe in saying, for I believe the poor fellow thinks of not much else."

"Yes, do, Mabel, do," said Henry.

Thus urged, Mabel, although she would rather have given Rafferty the pleasure of seeing her at once, glided gently from the room, and passing the half open door of the back drawing-room without being perceived by Rafferty, she gained her bedroom at last; the bed-room which she was told was to be hers for that night, although she had not yet slept in it. When she was fairly gone, the captain called out aloud—

"Rafferty—Rafferty!"

There was no answer.

"What can he mean by that?" added the captain, and then he called again, upon which Rafferty condescended to come into the room, saying—

"I'm thinking you called, did you?"

"You know I did. You are very inattentive, Rafferty. This is the first that we have seen of you this morning."

"The first, sir?"

"Yes; where you have been, nobody knows. You are of very little assistance, Rafferty, in our attempts to find out poor Mabel."

"Little assistance, sir? Bedad, if I don't find her out myself it is not any of you that will do that same. Oh, I'll find her; wasn't I all the blessed night looking for her, and didn't I get a—what do you call it,—an idea?"

"Did you really get an idea, Rafferty?" said Henry.

"Aisy now, aisy, Master Henry, wid your jokes; you know you never had but one idea in your own life, and that I made a present to you one day in a fit of confidence."

"Come, come, Rafferty," said the captain, who could scarcely forbear a smile. "If you were really looking for Mabel, you can tell us where you looked and what success you had."

"Oh, of course, sir."

"Well, proceed, then. Our own opinion is, that we shall find her before you have the least idea of where she is."

"Oh, the vanity of some folks. You really think so, sir, do you? Now, I'll tell you, sir, I partly know where she is."

"Do you? Then, perhaps, you will be so kind as to communicate to me the information."

"Not yet; it's a secret I can't tell you yet; but some of these days I'll bring her home to you, never fear. By-the-bye, I ——"

"Stop, Rafferty. I'll make any wager with you you like, that you won't find her."

"And so will I," said Henry. "You will just go blundering about as usual, Rafferty; and far from finding her and restoring her to us, no doubt you will make yourself as ridiculous as you did when you hid yourself in the willow tree."

"Och, murder!"

"And fell into the water," added the captain, "while Mabel was carried off before your very eyes."

"Aisy—aisy! What's up now, that a poor fellow is to have his misfortunes thrown in his teeth in a handful in that way? Now, I'll confound you both. You want to find Mabel. Well, you want to find that thief of the world as took her from us all—good. Now, sometimes I can do a pair of things at once, and sometimes it ain't convenient at all—at all."

"If you do one we shall be satisfied."

"Then it's done," said Rafferty, as-suming a cool and indifferent air. "I haven't found Miss Mabel exactly yet, but I have found the other fellow."

"What other fellow?"

"Why, the fellow that took her away. Match that if you can. Bedad, and you'll find it mighty difficult to get the better of Rafferty Brolickbones. You'd need to get up early, you would."

"Well" said the captain to Henry, "since Rafferty, then, puts us upon our mettle to match what he has done, I don't see what recourse we have but to do our best."

"Certainly—none other," said Henry.

"Then perhaps you will step up stairs and ask our dear Mabel to come down and speak to this fellow Rafferty, who pretended to take such care of her, and then got into a tree, while he let her be carried off by Heaven only knows who."

---

## CHAPTER LXXXV

MABEL'S INTRODUCTION TO MONSIEUR ROU-SELLI.—THE HAPPY FAMILY PARTY.—THE PRIVATE EXAMINATION OF THE MENDICANT AT THE GAOL.

To describe the effect which these words of the captain had upon Rafferty is far beyond the ordinary power of language. He stood as if he never intended, on any account, to shut his eyes again, and he bent forward in an attitude of listening, as if he might well, and actually did, doubt the evidence of his own senses.

Both Henry and the captain were much amused to see such an aspect of intense astonishment sitting upon the countenance of Rafferty; for he generally made a sort of boast that nothing surprised him. Oh, no, he was too old a soldier for that, and had seen too much of the world, &c. But now the tables were turned completely, and instead of him, Rafferty, causing all the astonishment, he was completely outdone by this cool acknowledgment that Mabel was actually in the house.

"You must be after saying that again, sir," he said.

"All I said," repeated the captain, "was to request Henry would desire Mabel to step down stairs, in order that she might hear the no doubt gratifying intelligence of the capture of the man who has wrought her so much uneasiness."

Rafferty turned to Henry, and touching his forehead with the point of his finger, he said in a tone of genuine commiseration—

"So the poor captain has gone at last, Master Henry?"

"What do you mean, Rafferty?"

"It's what do I mane, is it, sir? Why the maning is clear enough. The captain's given his senses leave of absence, that's all. I only hope they'll come back again soon, and report themselves at head-quarters."

Had his life depended upon his keeping his gravity, Henry could not have done so. He was quite upset, and laughed aloud as he cried—

"Well, Rafferty, I do think you are right; but so far as regards going up stairs for Mabel, I can do that."

"Yes, Master Henry, you can go up stairs, devil a doubt, for Miss Mabel, but as to coming down stairs again with her, that's quite another affair altogether."

"We shall see."

"Yes, sir, we shall see, God willing, sir. I don't think it's decent for either of you to be poking your fun at the likes of me."

"Well, well—you go, Henry, at once."

"Yes," said Henry, and he left the room.

Rafferty looked at the captain with an odd bewildered look for some few moments, and then walking closer up to him he said, in a voice that evidently struggled with emotion—

"Captain Morton, I may be an old fool. I'm old, I know, and perhaps not far from being a fool; but I loved that girl, sir, better than I loved my own heart's blood. She is dearer to me than all the world, and to save her a pain or an ache, I'd lay down my life, sir. The very sound of her voice is music to my ears. Don't trifle with me, sir—don't trifle with me, but tell me the honest truth. Have you found her?"

"She shall answer for herself," said the captain, as the door was opened, and Henry appeared, leading in Mabel by the hand.

Rafferty staggered back as if he had been shot.

"It's she!" he cried—"it is—it is. Oh! Mabel, Mabel! how could you?—Never mind. Here's a day!"

He rushed up to her, and before she, or Henry, or the captain, could in the least degree stop him, he had clasped her in his arms, and kissed her so many times, that whenever Henry thought of it during the remainder of that day, he felt positively envious and furious.

"Hold, Rafferty!" he cried. "There if you please—that will do. Confound your impudence!"

"Oh, don't mention it," said Rafferty; "and so you're come back again, dear Mabel, have you, after all the trouble I've had about you, you darlint? But where's the rosy colour that used to sit upon the cheeks of you?"

"That will soon come again, Rafferty, when I am in my happy home once more."

"Hurrah! hurrah!"

"But you forget, Rafferty," said the captain, "that this is the first time you have seen Mabel since you so unhandsomely got into a tree when she was in danger, instead of protecting her."

"Do I forget, captain?" cried Rafferty. "Miss Mabel, you may have a shot at me if you like, and I'll forgive you. The captain has got a pair of duelling-pistols snug at home."

"Rafferty, I have no quarrel to make with you," said Mabel. "You did all for the best, and that is all that Heaven asks of its creatures, Rafferty, so I have no fault to find with you, had the consequences been ten times worse than they have been."

"Now there you are wrong, Miss Mabel," said Rafferty; "I'll own to you, of course, that I did it all for the best. There's no manner of doubt about that; but it was mighty bad generalship for all that; and I haven't from that time to this known a happy hour."

"Well, Rafferty," said Henry, "you see that with all your cleverness we have beaten you, and succeeded in finding out Mabel first."

"Oh! be aisy," said Rafferty; "I shouldn't wonder, after all, that you just heard of her by some accident, which can't be called finding her out. How was it now, Master Henry? You may as well tell the truth, you know, just for once in a way."

"For once in a way! Why, Rafferty, do you think I am like you?"

"Like me, sir! Oh, oedad, not like me. It's a proud man you'd be if you was. Why, the paving-stones in the streets wouldn't be good enough to hould you up, if you thought you was like me. Conceit would get the better of you entirely, and you'd be put in some lunacy asylum, you would."

"Henry," said Captain Morton, "I think you will find yourself no match for Rafferty, so you had better let him have the last word at once."

"True for you, sir," said Rafferty; "an' if you never say a bigger lie than that, sir, you'll do well."

"Agreed, agreed!" cried Henry. "And now all is forgotten and all forgiven, and I am sure no one can entertain a more lively sense of all that we owe to you, Rafferty, than I do; but for you, both Mabel and my brother would have perished on the field of Waterloo."

"Oh, botheration!" said Rafferty. "That's all such a mighty long while ago, that it ain't now worth remembering at all, at all. But where's the ould gentleman?"

"What does he mean?" said Mabel.

"He alludes to a circumstance, dear Mabel," said the captain, "of which we have as yet said nothing to you, because you have really not been with us long enough to enable us to do so; but now, at once, I will tell you that we have another most agreeable surprise for you"

"What! don't she know all about that?" said Rafferty.

"Indeed she does not."

Mabel turned pale, as she said, in anxious tones,—

"Do not tell it to me, if it be any news that in its results may have the effect of taking me from you. If it be any news concerning my real birth, keep it a secret still, and let me rather be the unknown child of the battle-field, and the object of your kind bounty. I do not wish now to make new friends or new associations. My heart is already as full of affection as it can be."

These were delightful words for Henry to hear, but he took up the subject, as the captain was silent, and said—

"Mabel, do you suppose that I could look so joyous as I look now, if I were in possession of any intelligence which would have the effect of taking you from us? Oh, no! The news that we have to tell you is of no such character, although it is information that clears up every mystery connected with your birth."

"Be composed," said the captain. "Henry, you tell our dear Mabel all."

Mabel sat down, with Henry by her side, and he, as rapidly and concisely as he could, related to her all the story connected with old Monsieur Rouselli. She listened to him with the most absorbed attention; and when he had concluded, her eyes filled with tears, as she said—

"My poor, poor father! and my mother, too! Oh! what cruel, cruel misfortunes! I cannot, even on this joyous day, refrain from tears."

"They are natural tears, dear Mabel," said Henry, "and such as honour those who shed them. You must make no excuses to us, who know your kindly heart so well, for any such emotions."

"Don't be after crying, Miss Mabel," said Rafferty; "you don't see me crying, do you? Your father died as a soldier should,—on the battle field, and that's, to my thinking, a mighty deal easier and pleasanter than being laid up in a bed for the Lord knows how long, with some of the machinery in your inside wrong, and, at last, dying by quarters of an inch at a time."

In a short time, Mabel recovered from this flush of emotion that had come over her, and she was confirmed in her wish to see old Monsieur Rouselli. A carriage was procured, and they all, including Rafferty, who would sit on the coach-box, and the ostler, too, who had remained domesticated in the captain's lodgings, went together.

While they are proceeding towards where the old, bereaved man resided, let us take a glance at him, and see what he is about. There can be no doubt but that the agitating news he had heard from the Mortons had much shaken him. He was not, partly in consequence of his advanced age, and partly in consequence of the bereavements he had had, strong enough to fight up against all the intelligence; first, of the manner in which Mabel had been preserved on that dreadful field of slaughter, and secondly, how, after growing into youth and beauty, so as to be beloved by all, she had been suddenly snatched from those who had so long fostered her with the tenderest care.

There was great alteration in his appearance, and a physician whom he had consulted had candidly told him, that if he allowed the mind thus to prey upon the fading energies of his physical system, he would soon be completely worn out.

"You must make all the possible effort in your power," he said, "to turn your thoughts into other channels, and I can recommend nothing to you as a means so likely to bring about such a result as change of scene, and a cultivation of literature."

Monsieur Rouselli felt fully the necessity of this advice; and, although he could not prevail upon himself to change his place of abode from London, while there was a chance of the Mortons discovering where Mabel was hidden, the other suggestion of the physician was fully open to him.

He accordingly surrounded himself with the works of English authors, and, while Henry and Captain Morton were relating to Mabel the fact of his existence, and by what a strange accident they had come across him, he was seeking a temporary solace from the miseries of memory in a work of fiction, from which he read the following tale:—

"The cottage on the moor," said an old man, "was once the abode of a hardy, and bold huntsman; he was well known for strength and courage, and his wife was as well known for her beauty and good sense.

The cottage had not long been inhabited by them at that time, for Hugh Grayling was but recently married, and he held service at the castle, a few hundred yards further back.

It was called a castle, and the owners were called the Lords of Goffet, from olden times, and they were so termed then, and could, formerly, have brought into the field some score or two of hardy retainers, besides many others who held land under them upon military tenure; and those who held the lands now paid rent in money or in kind; the old military tenure had been exchanged, but there were yet some remains of former absolutism in the manor.

Here, then, Hugh Grayling served the Lords of Goffet, as the head huntsman, and as principal attendant in all field musters and exercises, and attended the lord when he rode over his estate, to examine the condition of the soil and tenements.

In fact, Hugh Grayling was a great man on the estate, and his cottage on the moor was comfortable and snug, beyond what many in those times would have considered necessary, or, indeed, what by many would have been unhoped for.

Hugh Grayling's wife was a pretty woman; and many did say she was much more than pretty,—that she was, by far, the handsomest girl within many miles of that place,—whether in hall, or cottage, she was, in beauty, peerless.

The Lord of Goffet heard of Hugh's bride, and he determined, in his own mind, he would go to the huntsman's cottage, and there ascertain the truth of what he heard so many talk about, and, with his own eyes, satisfy himself.

It was not often the lord of the manor visited the cottages of his tenantry, or of his retainers, but his huntsman, Hugh Grayling, was a favourite with his lord, for he was well acquainted with the chase and its duties, and, moreover, he was a strong man, and could take part in his lord's quarrels with some effect.

These were qualities that were not likely to be passed over slightly, but which gained him consideration at the Castle of Goffet, as the old, fortified building was called.

"Hugh," said the Lord of Goffet, one day to his man, "Hugh, to-morrow we will go down to the marshes, and fly a hawk, and see if we cannot find a heron or two."

"There ought to be some there," said Hugh; "for the river has not been disturbed for many a-day."

"I think we may count on sport," said the lord; "I shall begin right early; the sun's rising will be time enough."

"Yes," said Hugh; "before that, and you may lose your birds in the fogs and mists that hang over the river, both hawk and heron, and those are not easily replaced."

"No, they are not, good Hugh."

\* \* \* \* \*

The morning came, and Hugh Grayling, according to the orders he had received from his lord, repaired to the marshes soon after sun-rise, where he expected to meet with his lord. The Lord of Goffet, however, instead of going to the marshes direct, made a call at the cottage of Hugh, determined to ascertain if the truth had been spoken in the report. He, therefore, knocked at Hugh's abode, and it was opened by Hugh Grayling's wife.

"Is Hugh Grayling up yet?" he inquired, as he stepped into the cottage.

Hugh's wife, Margaret, stepped back with all humility, for she was well acquainted with the Lord of Goffet by his dress and his authority, though he knew not her.

"Yes, he is up and out, my lord," she answered.

"Up and out? I thought I told him I would meet him here, to go out soon after sunrise."

"He said his orders were to be in the marshes soon after sun-rise, my lord, and there he is gone."

"Well, I must go there too; but are you Hugh Grayling's wife?" he inquired.

"Yes, an it please your lordship," said Margaret; "I am Margaret Grayling, at your lordship's service."

"And a very pretty wife Hugh Grayling has got, too. Why, Mistress Grayling, you would grace a hall."

Margaret hung down her head, but was not displeased at this compliment paid her by so great a man.

"Why, mistress, your good man must keep a sharp look out upon his house, for I don't know any one that would not try and run away with such a treasure as you are."

"Hugh is a very good man," said Margaret; "I have nothing to complain of in him."

"Nor ought you, mistress; but who would not love and be kind to such a beauty as you? Why, Margaret, you have been shut up among boors all your life; people who don't know how to prize such a jewel as thou art."

"Oh! my lord," said Margaret, "your

condescension is very great, but I am not deserving of it."

" But you are, Mistress Margaret."

" I am only your huntsman, Hugh Grayling's, wife; your lordship must recollect that."

" In truth I do, mistress, and more's the pity, for were you not, I would at once offer you my heart."

" My lord!"

" I would, by Heaven; you are just such a one as would do one's taste credit; it would indeed."

" Fie! my lord."

" Well, good Mistress Margaret, I must away to the marshes, and watch the sport with the hawks; I would I had such a mistress to return to, as Hugh has got."

" My lord!"

" I mean it; a kiss, good Margaret, and then I am gone; one morning salute; come, Mistress Margaret, no coyness, such a salute as this can never spoil your beauty." He caught her round the waist and kissed her lips; there was but a faint resistance, just sufficient to qualify and render it the more pleasing.

" Oh, fie, my lord; you would anger my goodman, if he were here; I don't know what he would say."

" What the eye never sees, the heart never grieves at," said the Lord of Goffet, as he turned away. " Farewell, Mistress Margaret; you ought to be in a better place than this, and were it not for the goodman, as you call him, you should be in a better place or have the refusal in your own power; but farewell till another day."

Mistress Margaret dropped a curtsey when the Lord of Goffet left the house, and then watched him till out of sight.

" He's a fine gentleman," said Mistress Margaret; " a little gay, and soon taken with a pretty face; but there's worse men and worse faults than he or his."

Mistress Margaret, when she could no longer see the Lord of Goffet, returned to her occupation in the cottage.

The Lord of Goffet then took his way to the marshes, and there he found Hugh Grayling waiting for him with the dogs and hawks.

" Well, Hugh," he said, " you are here in good time?"

" Yes, my lord, and there are many herons about; I have counted over five or six myself."

" Indeed! we may reckon upon some sport then; see, here is a fine bird, Hugh, and toss him up yourself; let us see how you can do it."

Hugh did as he was desired, and the bird was shown the object he was to chase in the air, and tossed off. Away he went until he soared high in the air, each bird trying to soar above the other.

It was a long flight, and well maintained; but the power of the hawk was greater on the wing than the heron, and his enemy gained the ascendancy.

Then high soared the hawk; when at a sufficient height he commenced the swoop towards his victim, who was endeavouring to escape, but, seeing this impossible, the heron, as an act of desperation, turned and faced its enemy. Floating in the mid-air, he poised himself a moment with his long sharp beak pointed upwards towards the hawk, who was within a short distance.

" By Heaven! he's no craven, Hugh," said the Lord of Goffet; " he'll face his enemy."

" 'Ware hawk," said Hugh Grayling; " he'll be spitted."

" Wait a moment; the hawk is an old, though a staunch bird, and may be fortunate."

At this moment the hawk made his stoop and came down upon his enemy, who adroitly caught the whole weight upon the point of his beak—long and sharp as it was—so that the hawk spit himself on the beak as clean as if he had been run through by an iron skewer.

" Ah! he has been done this time," said Hugh; " shall I throw up another hawk, my lord?"

" No, Hugh, let the heron have his life; he has fought bravely for it, and deserves to get off."

" See how they come tumbling down together."

This was the fact; for the heron was not able for some moments to disengage itself from the dead hawk, as its beak was secured in its body. However, just as they reached within a few yards of the earth, it contrived to separate itself from its enemy and soared gallantly away.

" Well done, heron," said the Lord of Goffet.

" And well done, poor hawk," said Hugh Grayling.

" Sure, he was staunch; but he is gone; he was a good hawk, his death proves that."

" It does, my lord."

" Get his body if you can; his feathers shall grace the halls in memorial of the past."

Hugh Grayling was well pleased with the order, for he was fond of the hawk; it was one upon which he had bestowed much care and more caresses than any other in the eyrie.

After some walking across the swamps

and wet grass, Hugh discovered the body of the bird. It had been transfixed through the lower part of the body. He presented it to his lord, who looking at it, said—

"Ah! poor bird, he would have struck his adversary with his talons, and have held him, I'll be sworn, like a vice until he had been released."

"Will you have another tria', my lord?"

"Yes; we must take home one heron, else we shall be considered cravens. The herons must not have it all their own way. So far we'll give the enemy the advantage; but we'll have one heron, or I'll lose every hawk in the eyrie."

"Then here is another bird, and a majestic one, too; hark at his sharp cry—and his long neck—his legs—see, all are plain—this will be a short chase," said Hugh.

As he spoke he threw his hawk into the

THE REUNION OF HENRY MORTON AND MABEL.

air, and he caught sight of his victim on the instant, and flew upwards with a sharp cry, which the heron instantly caught and attempted to fly; but after a short flight the hawk made a stoop, and struck him to the earth in an instant.

"So far so well; and now, Hugh, we will return home, and another day we will try all the birds one after another, so as to give each of them a chance."

"It will keep them in order, and healthy, too, my lord."

"It will, Hugh; perhaps to-morrow I may try them again. Go forward, and I will follow you to the castle. I will speak to you at the castle."

"Very well, my lord."

Hugh Grayling walked towards the castle; and the Lord of Goffet bethought himself how he could best make himself acceptable to Mistress Margaret, Hugh's wife. This seemed to be a matter upon which he had made up his mind to attempt.

It could not be denied but Hugh's wife was a very beautiful young woman; she was simple and good-natured, addicted to flattery: but then what woman is not? The only difference is the mode in which it is administered.

Mistress Margaret, therefore, must not be deemed worse than her sex in general on that account. She was pretty, very pretty, and her simplicity led her to believe everybody meant what they said; and she had been particularly struck by what the Lord of Goffet had said to her. Already she began to imagine she was intended for a lady, but she had been stopped in her career of fortune by her husband, who was now a stumbling block in her way.

"I won't tell him a word about his lordship's being here this morning, or what he said. He'll be jealous."

Having made up her mind and come to this conclusion, she set about her work, thinking it might have so happened that she might have had all that done for her by the servants to the Lord of Goffet.

\*     \*     \*     \*

When the Lord of Goffet had reached his castle, he had made up his mind as to what he would do. Hugh Grayling was waiting for him, and his hawks were all put up, and he was ready to receive his orders.

"Hugh Grayling," he said, "you don't mind going upon a few weeks' journey for me, do you?"

"My services are your lordship's, when and where you may require them," replied Hugh.

"Then I wish you to go to a certain nobleman, who is about to sell all his hawks and hounds off."

"Ah!" said Hugh; "are times changing that they should do that? Give up his hawks and hounds?"

"Yes, Hugh, he is become half crazed by an accident he received when out hawking—broke his leg and fractured his skull somehow or other, and now gives up keeping them."

"But he has guests sometimes, I suppose," said Hugh; "but every one to their fancy."

"That is true," said the Lord of Goffet; "and that being the case, you must be my messenger, and purchase some of the best hawks. I must replace the one I lost this morning; and then others are getting old, besides losses on other occasions."

"Very true, my lord. When am I to start on my journey?" inquired Hugh Grayling.

"You may start this very day, Hugh. Indeed I think it will be necessary to do so; you had better be there a day too soon than too late."

"Your lordship is quite right as to that,"

said Hugh; "I shall be prepared to start almost immediately, if your lordship will permit me to return home for a short time; I have a few matters to set to rights before I go."

"Very well, Hugh; and as soon as you can get back here I will have your instructions ready for you, and you will have nothing to do but to mount and ride off."

Hugh Grayling quitted Goffet Castle and went to his own cottage, which was at no very great distance from the former, and informed his wife of his intended journey with something like satisfaction.

"I should have liked it better than all things," said Hugh; "but I shall be obliged to leave you here."

"And here you'll find me when you return," said Mistress Margaret; "along with the cottage."

"Why, yes, I shall expect that," said Hugh; "to be sure. But I sha'n't be long; a few days, I dare say, will bring me back again, or a week or two at the most."

"I shall be glad when you do come back again, for it will be very lonely until you do so."

"I won't be longer than I am obliged to stay, you may depend upon me."

"I shall expect you soon. Farewell, Hugh; God speed you safe back again!"

"Good-bye, Margaret! and be sure you take care of yourself until I return to you," said Hugh.

As Hugh spoke, he imprinted a kiss upon her cheek, and then with a hearty good-bye quitted the cottage, and hastened on his road to the Castle of Goffet.

It was past mid-day when he reached the castle hall, and announced to his lord that he was ready to undertake the journey he wanted him.

"And I am ready, too, Hugh; you will find, that in this paper, I have explained to you all I want you to do; your journey will be three days."

"Am I to go alone, my lord?"

"No; you had better take a couple of assistants with you to take charge of the hawks."

"Yes, your lordship is right; so much is needed when you come to consider the care that must be taken and the chances of the road."

"Yes, that is right; take any two you like, and set forward at once."

Hugh Grayling having chosen his two companions, they all three left the castle together.

\*     \*     \*     \*

Now the morning's sun again shone on

the broad lands of Goffet, and the lord of them rose and looked around him, and then bethought him of his huntsman's wife.

"She must be mine," he muttered, "there can be no doubt but she will; she may be coy; so much the better, but not very unwilling, I'll swear."

He quitted the castle, and walked towards Hugh Grayling's cottage, which he found open, and Mistress Margaret standing on the outside, as fresh and as blooming as the dawn.

"Margaret," said he, "you are as bright and genial as the morning sun."

"My lord, you are very complaisant."

"I ought to be when I see so fresh a flower blooming in such a spot; it warms my heart to look upon you, fair Margaret, you are the pride of Goffet!"

"You are our lord, and it is a condescension in you to say all this," she said.

"Say rather I had not done so had I recollected that; but that I forgot it—and hence, I spoke what I thought, Margaret; you ought to have lived elsewhere; silk would become you better than woollen."

"I am content."

"Another good quality; Hugh Grayling has got a prize, and ought to treat you as a goddess."

"I'm afraid he believes me a mere mortal," said Margaret, laughing, "but I suppose he's right."

"Be that as it may," said Goffet, "here's a purse, fair Margaret; I award it you for the kiss I had yesterday, and must have another to-day. I will give it you to spend as you please, and when the evening comes I will come and endeavour to find out how you have disposed of it."

Margaret laughed, but caught the purse that the Lord of Goffet threw her, and then he caught her in his arms and kissed her lips while she was struggling faintly to free herself from his grasp, yet half permitting him.

Before he let her free he whispered something in her ear; she blushed, but there was a laugh upon her countenance, and she retained the purse he threw her.

\* \* \* \*

That evening, after the sun had gone to the western hemisphere, and there lit up the morn of some other country, and the moon was high in the heavens, the Lord of Goffet left the castle of his ancestors and proceeded towards Grayling's cottage, at which he stopped. Tapping at the door, he said,

"Margaret! Mistress Margaret! 'tis Goffet who knocks; open the door and let me in."

The door was slowly opened, and the Lord of Goffet entered, and then the door was closed quickly.

\* \* \* \*

It was nearly dawn before the Lord of Goffet was seen to leave the cottage of Hugh Grayling for his own castle of Goffet. That night Hugh Grayling was a miserable being; his happiness was for ever blasted, and Margaret was a guilty creature, instead of the pure, light-hearted girl she had been, for such she really was.

Riches and rank had prevailed over poverty and humility, but the day of retribution was at hand, and she who had caused so much mischief, met with her reward, as did her paramour.

Day after day did the Lord of Goffet visit the house of his huntsman, or falconer, and it became known to more than one of the same condition of life as the inhabitants of that cottage, and it caused comment.

Hugh Grayling returned to Goffet Castle a few days earlier than was expected, and finding his lord was not to be found, hastened to his own cottage, as it was late; determining that he would pass the night at home, and then to go to the castle betimes.

He entered his cottage; to his amazement he found the door was still unsecured; the light stood on the table, and there was a good fire.

"Hilloa!" thought Hugh, "what can all this mean?—no good, I'll warrant—eh!"

This last exclamation was caused by the sudden appearance of a sword and bonnet, such as were worn by the gentry and people of distinction.

"As I live,—the sword and bonnet of my Lord of Goffet!"

Hugh Grayling seized the sword, which he drew from the scabbard, and rushed towards the other room—the inner room—his sleeping room, where he could at that moment hear voices, which he recognised as being his wife's and the Lord of Goffet's.

He pushed the door open, and there beheld a sight that for a moment or more completely paralysed him—he stood still while he gazed.

For some moments the guilty pair were not aware of the presence of the injured husband. A shriek from Margaret announced to her paramour that something was wrong, and he started up from his recumbent position, when his eye encountered the angry and flushed features of Hugh Grayling.

"Hugh," exclaimed the Lord of Goffet. "I'll make your fortune,—you shall have houses and lands,—forget the past, and the future shall be happiness and gaiety."

"I'll forget the past when I can forget myself," said Hugh; "but you'll never remember more, for this moment terminates your lives;—you have dishonoured me, and I will avenge myself."

So saying, he rushed upon the guilty pair, and thrust his sword through the bodies of both Goffet and Margaret, and then returned to the castle, where he spent the remainder of the night.

*       *       *       *

The next day the dead bodies were found, and as the position of both was not to be mistaken, there was never any inquiry set afloat as to who was the perpetrator of the deed. Hugh Grayling lived many years there; but he was a morose man, and few spoke to him without need, or he to them.

Old Monsieur Rouselli looked up with a sigh.

"All persons find some solace in their misfortunes," he said, "but I. Alas, I have no hope. My dear son is lost to me, and Heaven only knows what has become of that child which he has left behind him, and who, had fortune dealt kinder by me, might have been the joy and solace of my old age."

A sudden feeling of agitation came over him.

"What is this?" he said—"what shakes me thus?—my heart beats tumultuously! —What is going to happen now?—Is it death that is thus shadowing forth its insidious approach?—Let it come! Let it come!—The great destroyer has little to destroy."

Then came the sound of carriage wheels in the street, and they paused at the door of the house; and surely there must have been some hidden sympathy in the old man's breast, which made him aware of the approach of some event of deep importance to him, for his agitation increased to such an extent that he was compelled to sit down again, after rising from his seat, and do his utmost to reason himself out of such a nervous state of mind.

---

## CHAPTER LXXXVI.

### THE MEETING.—THE OLD MAN'S PENETRATION.—THE GIFT AND ITS RECEPTION.

In a few moments from the time that old Monsieur Rouselli sat down, to try to overcome the nervous feelings that so suddenly had crept over him, the room door was opened, and Captain Morton was announced. He was always glad to see the Mortons, and welcomed the captain with all that bland kindness which is so indicative of the gentleman.

The fact was, that the captain thought it quite as necessary that old Monsieur Rouselli should not be subjected to the shock of seeing Mabel, and being told who she was, as that she should have been gradually prepared, as she was, by the officer's wife, for an introduction to those dear friends from whom she had been so long separated, and whom she so earnestly desired again to see.

With this intent he left Mabel and Henry in the coach below together, while he went up to the old man, and gently told him of the joy he now could bring him.

This was an arrangement which Henry by no means objected to, inasmuch as it left him with Mabel, and gave him an opportunity of saying things to her which he only intended for herself.

To be sure, he made a slight error of judgment in this instance, and did not calculate well his chances, for after making a speech of the most affectionate character to Mabel, and in which there was some highly poetical language, Rafferty, who was upon the coach, rapped his knuckles against the front glass of the carriage, and said—

"Mighty fine! Master Henry, mighty fine! only some of it wants putting into Engli sh, for, by the holy, I can't make out above half of it. Is that what you call making love?—For shame! Master Henry, why don't you spake your mother-tongue, and not put any of your French and Latin nonsense along with it. I wouldn't have thought so of the like of you."

"You villain!" cried Henry.—Mabel blushed and laughed as she said—

"You see, Henry, I warned you to pause, and now you have made a confident, unwittingly, of Rafferty."

While this little incident was proceeding below, the captain had drawn a chair close to the other side of the table at which Monsieur Rouselli sat, and affectionately inquired after his health since last they had met.

"Oh," said the old man, "I have tried, but all in vain, to withdraw my mind from viewing my domestic affairs in the most gloomy light, and I feel that I shall know no joy, and not even an hour's serenity, until that dear child of my son's is restored to my heart."

"Which we all expect will be soon."

"It will need to be soon if I am now to see her with mortal eyes."

"Now, monsieur, cannot you guess that, since I have been in town I have striven in every possible way to discover her? Cannot you suppose that I have set every means at work in such a cause?"

" Yes, and all in vain."

" Not so."

" Not in vain—not—not—you have heard something ?"

" I have ; and expect that the clue which I have obtained will be one followed very shortly by the pleasure of again having her in our possession."

" Oh, tell me again. The very thought of such joyful intelligence takes a load of years off me. I am better now."

" You may, from what I know, Monsieur Rouselli, hope for the best, and that more speedily, too, than you at all imagine."

The old man rose and advanced towards the captain. He laid both his hands upon his breast and looked him earnestly and scrutinizingly in his face. Then, with a cry of joy, he tottered back to his seat again, as he exclaimed—

" I see it all—I see it all. You have found her—you have found the dear child ! It was kind of you to spare the old man too sudden an accession of joy. But you cannot deceive me ; you have found her."

" Be composed, my dear sir—be composed. You are right ; be calm."

" Where, oh, where is she ? My child—my own child, where is she ? Oh, take me to her !"

" She shall come to you."

" Now, now—at once. A moment lost is much to me, for I am old. Oh, fetch her to me. My own beautiful child, sole relic of my dear son, where is she—where is she ? Sir, do not trifle with my feelings ; fetch her to me ; oh, let me clasp her in my arms. I am as one only lingering for a brief space on the grave's brink, and before I sink into its recesses, let me, I implore you, once look upon her !"

" You shall, sir—you shall, indeed."

" Now, now."

" Control your feelings for a short time. I will bring her to you. She is close at hand, sir. You, doubtless, heard a carriage stop in the street below. I will now make no disguises with you. We have found her, and she is as anxious to come to your arms as you can be to receive her."

As he spoke these words, Captain Morton rose and left the room. He made good speed down to the door, and looking into the carriage, he said—

" Mabel, your grandfather is prepared to see you."

" I come—I come," said Mabel, as, by the assistance of the captain, she sprang lightly from the vehicle, being closely followed by Henry.

" Oh, sir," said Rafferty, " it's a murdering shame."

" What Rafferty—what ?"

" Why, sir, there was as nice a bit of colloguing, sir, going on as you'd wish to hear of, sir, in the carriage, sir ; a kind of courting, your honour. I will tell you all about it another time. It's Master Henry, sir, it is."

Captain Morton shook his head at Rafferty, but made no reply to what he insinuated. He knew quite sufficient of the state of Henry's affections to make him receive Rafferty's information as anything but doubtful ; and one of the hopes nearest to his heart was, that Mabel would be induced to become, by a marriage with Henry, really one of the family of which she was, in all love and tenderness that could be bestowed upon her, already one of the most cherished members.

" And how did he receive the news ?" said Mabel, as they ascended the staircase.

" Better than I could have expected. He found it out himself by my countenance, which I had no idea told tales so easily."

They reached the room, and Mabel springing forward prevented the old man from rising ; but, sinking to his feet, she looked up in his face as she said—

" Dear grandfather, will you love me ?"

Sobs of joy choked his utterance. He folded his arms about her, and pressed her to his breast. He kissed tenderly that beautiful brow, and when he could sufficiently command his feelings to allow him to speak, he said—

" Will I love you, my dear child ! Can you ask, when the old man's heart is all yours ? You—you have your father's eyes, dear Mabel. God's blessings on you. I—I never thought to see such a happy moment as this. My beautiful Mabel, I should ask you rather will you love this old withered form so near the grave ?"

" Yes," she said. " Oh, yes ; are you not the only being to whom I can claim affinity, dear grandfather ? I feel now that I am not a nameless thing thrown upon the kindness of those, who, God knows, have been dear friends to me, but yet who know me not."

" Yes, my Mabel, you are now known ; you are the daughter of a brave and honourable man ; one who has left you a name of which you need never be ashamed ; a name recognised in the annals of his country, and which he has left to you free and spotless."

" Yes, yes."

" Young man," he then said to Henry ; " you have many times said kind and gentle words to me, and I have delighted in your society, but I never could think of how to return you some favour for those you have bestowed."

"Oh, sir," said Henry, "I want no thanks."

"No, grandfather, Henry was only too happy," said Mabel, " to give you any pleasure."

"Mabel, you have only, I may say," continued the old man, "been mine a few short minutes, and yet I am about to cast you away again."

"Cast me away, grandfather?"

"Yes; what can you desire to cling to an old man for, who is already familiar with the aspect of approaching death? I shall make you a present, as the most valuable of my possessions, to Henry Morton, if he does not despise the gift."

"Despise!" cried Henry; "Oh, joy."

"And if my dear girl does not object to being so disposed of, and think it unkind of the old man to get rid of her so soon."

Mabel said nothing, but she stretched out one hand to Henry, and he held it in his grasp, as he said,

"Sir, the world contains not so precious a gift."

"But she does not agree to it," he added.

"Yes, yes," said Mabel. "That is—I mean—no—no."

"Oh, that will do; go, my children, and be happy; and may the blessing of God be upon you, Mabel."

"A—min!" said Rafferty, putting his head in at the door. "By the powers of Pat Mulligan, and he was the late Irish giant, I thought what it would come to."

"And you have been listening?" said the captain.

"To be sure I have; it's not much news of what was going on I'd have had, if I had not listened; nobody had the civility to say, 'Rafferty, walk up, sir, if you please;' so I just invited myself as far as the key-hole. Master Henry, a word with you, sir."

"Well, what is it?"

"I claim the first kiss of the bride, sir, and for fear some other blackguard should try to get it, I think I'll have it now, sir, if it's all the same to you."

"No, you won't," said Henry, "and it is not all the same to me; so go about your business, Master Rafferty, and leave the bride alone."

"Och, murder; the jealousy of some people, now, only to think."

---

## CHAPTER LXXXVII.

### THE EXAMINATION OF THE MENDICANT.— THE MOMENTOUS QUESTION.

AND now that Mabel was duly restored to those dear friends who had grieved so much for her absence, and who would have given all the world's wealth to hold her again to their hearts, we will turn our attention to that villain who had caused so much mischief, but who now, in consequence of Rafferty's singular adventure, was consigned to that durance he so richly merited.

Foiled and disappointed in all his hopes, one can well imagine the desperate state of feeling into which that man was thrown, now that, for the second time, the law had him in its grasp, and he could entertain no hope of being so fortunate as again to escape its clutches.

No doubt to him death would have been far preferable to the state of things that had now ensued. No doubt he would gladly, if he could have done so, have now hurried himself to another world, despite the consequences of adding that additional crime to those with which already his soul was stained.

But he was too well watched by the authorities to permit of such a thing occurring, and in the absence of all means of self-destruction, he was compelled to endure, as best he might, the load of vexation and despair that had come upon him.

Although Mabel, with the feeling of forgiving kindness that formed a portion of her disposition, would have forgotten all the past, now that she was in the arms of her nearest and dearest friends, they could not permit the course of justice to be impeded, and therefore was that Mabel was induced to consent, at last, that she would appear as the accuser of the man who had caused her so much woe.

It was some days before the mendicant was in a state to be brought before a magistrate, for he refused at first to take any nourishment, and it was only when, at length, so pressed by hunger that his resolution gave way and he eat something, that it was considered expedient to make him undergo an examination at a police-office.

In order as much as possible to spare the feelings of Mabel, and repress the rush of public curiosity, the proceedings were commenced at an early hour, and the desperate and wretched man was placed at the bar to be accused of divers crimes and misdemeanours.

Mabel was there, for she had been brought by the captain and Henry, both of whom had taken great pains to prepare her, as well as possible, for the disagreeable hour or two that was to come.

"You ought to remember, Mabel," was the correct argument that Captain Morton used; "you ought to remember that it is not in revenge for any personal wrongs of your own that you are supposed to appear against this man, but simply as a member of society, cognizant of an offence committed against the laws which bind that society together."

"Yes," she said; "yes, that is the view that I would wish to take of it."

"And it is the correct one, Mabel, you may rest assured; so do not vex yourself, as I know you did at first, with the idea that a prosecution of this man looks on your part as if you wished to take what pains you could to punish him for all that he had done."

"I understand that now," she replied, "and will state all that I know concerning him, although I shall dread the task."

"And I," said Henry, "wish it was in my power to state anything about him that would put a rope round his neck, the scoundrel! He has made me suffer more in anxiety than he can now be made to suffer."

"All I wish, Mister Henry," remarked Rafferty, "is, that if they don't hang him, they'd let him go altogether; because in that case we would have a mighty good opportunity of catching him somewhere, and doing that piece of work for him."

Old Monsieur Rouselli was persuaded as much as possible, by Mabel and the captain, not to trouble himself to come to the examination of the man who had heaped for a time such misery upon Mabel, but he begged that they would cease to combat his desire to be present, saying—

"I own that by going I may only inflame the passionate feelings that already, as regards that man, have found a home in my heart; but I wish to see him, and want to know if he is like what I have to my mind's eye pictured him."

Of course, after this, the Mortons made no further opposition to the old man going; and as Rafferty went, whether he was wanted or not, the whole party was assembled at the police-office.

The captain had had a long conversation with the ostler of the village inn, who was so strongly of opinion that this same man would unquestionably turn out to be the murderer of the young traveller, of which murder he had himself been so wrongfully accused, and the last words which had passed between them on that subject, had been to the effect, that he, Captain Morton, should say nothing upon that subject, until he saw him, the late ostler, again.

"I will post down to the village, captain," he said, "and get up all the evidence I can as to the identity of the supposed murderer; and I hope I shall be back in time to be present at the examination before the police magistrate, which is about to take place. But if I cannot, he is not at all likely to be discharged from custody."

"Not at all, I will take care of that."

"Then I shall go with perfect confidence, sir."

"Are you certain, now, that you have sufficient means of your own to prosecute the necessary inquiries?"

"Quite, sir," said the ostler, with a smile; "various circumstances which, some day when we have all gone back again to the village, for there I shall fix my habitation, I will relate to you, placed me in the position of life in which you first knew me, but all that is changed now."

"I am extremely glad to hear it."

"Of that I am certain; and now I will be off at once, with the hope of getting back quickly."

The only circumstance which at all annoyed Captain Morton as regarded this business of the murder at the village inn, was that the whole affair would have now, with all its painful and aggravating circumstances, to be told to old Monsieur Rouselli, and so he would have the pang of knowing that one whom he had esteemed, had, in consequence of placing himself in a position of danger for him, come to a cruel and terrible death.

This was a sad thing to think of as regarded Monsieur Rouselli, but it was not to be weighed for an instant against the vindication of the ostler, who had never forgotten the words that were uttered to him by the committing magistrate, viz. that it ought now, for his own vindication, to be the special business almost of his whole existence, to find out the real murderer, and satisfactorily bring the crime home to him.

When, therefore, so unexpectedly, the ostler had made his appearance, and all the circumstances concurrent upon that appearance had taken place, Captain Morton felt that it would be no longer possible to keep from Monsieur Rouselli a knowledge of the fate of his young friend and relative.

He, besides, in a great measure reconciled himself now to that result, because the punishment to which the mendicant was obnoxious, on account of the abduction of Mabel, would, indeed, have been exceed-

ngly inadequate to his deserts; and it
would have been a thousand pities to have
allowed such a fellow to escape, perhaps,
after all, with a year's imprisonment.

But still there was no necessity, as
regarded such communication, to take time
by the forelock, so Captain Morton made
up his mind not to disturb the serenity of
Monsieur Rouselli with the new narration
of the murder until the ostler should
return, and it became impossible any
longer to keep the affair a secret.

To Mabel he spoke of it as well as to
Henry, so that, with the exception of the
old man, all were prepared for some
denouement of a description that would
relieve Mabel from the pain and the
annoyance of prosecuting the mendicant,
by involving him in a charge of so much more
serious a character, that it would take precedence of the one which she could bring
against him.

And now, by half-past nine in the
morning, according to appointment with
the magistrate, who had fixed that early
hour in order that there should not be
sufficient time for a crowd of persons to
collect, Mabel and her friends had arrived
at the police-office.

When they got there the first news they
heard was, that it was doubtful if the prisoner
could be brought up, for he was alarmingly
ill, and had again refused to partake of any
food. An officer was even then gone to
the prison to know if the surgeon of that
establishment would sanction his being
brought to the police court.

Mabel much hoped that he would not
come; but the messenger returned with
the news that he would be there shortly,
having considerably rallied after being told
that it was proposed for him to undergo a
preliminary examination that morning, and
that he had expressed a great desire to do
so.

In another ten minutes or so it was
announced to the magistrate that the
prisoner was then within the precincts of
the court.

Very few persons were admitted besides
those actually interested, so that there was
none of that inconvenient pressure which
is so commonly the case when cases involving any serious points in their details
or their results are likely to come on.

So far as regarded the feelings of the
Morton family and of Mabel all was well,
and now the magistrate gave orders that
the prisoner should be brought before him.

There was a slight bustle at the door of
the court, and then, held by two officers,
that most desperate character was ushered
into the place usually set apart for

criminals. Of course the eyes of all present were immediately fixed upon him.
He was frightfully pale, and from the
neglected state of his beard and apparel, it
was evident that he had been in a despond-
ing condition of mind. He looked like a
man thoroughly beaten by fate—a man who
had nothing to hope for—nothing now to
do with the world, and who cared not how
soon he left it.

At first he did not seem to have any
notion that the Morton family was present,
but after a few moments of haggard glancing at the magistrate, he glanced round the
court, and then he saw them all. There
was a faint flush upon his countenance as
he looked upon Mabel, and saw that she
was now again, despite all his exertions,
surrounded by her best and dearest friends.
Then his eyes lit up with a savage sort of
ferocity, and he exclaimed in a voice louder
than one would have supposed, to look at
him, he would have been capable of
assuming,—

"On what charge am I thus
ignominiously brought here? Is a man
criminal because he escapes from a gaol in
which he is confined for an alleged crime
only, and of which he knows his own
innocence?"

"The charge against you," said the
magistrate, "is for the abduction of a
young lady from the hands of her friends."

"What young lady?"

"She is here present herself to make the
charge, and to substantiate it, I presume."

"If you allude to my daughter, it does
seem somewhat strange to me that she
should make such a charge against me."

"Your daughter?"

"Yes, that young girl, towards whom
you look now, is my daughter. She is now
under age. I claim not only my own discharge from custody, but I claim the legal
guardianship of her."

"Indeed."

"Yes, sir," said a spare man, advancing,
"I have the honour to appear here for the
much injured prisoner at the bar."

"Oh, you are Mr. Meadows, the
solicitor," said the magistrate, "and have
advised him to make the statement?"

"I have advised him to state the truth,
and either he or I will now relate to your
worship the grounds upon which he
substantiates his claim to this young
person."

"You, you," said the mendicant.

"Very good," added the attorney.
"Your worship must know, then, that my
client's name is Leroux, and that he was in
the French army at the period of the battle
of Waterloo. He is a German, but was

naturalised in France, and obtained a colonelcy in a regiment which fought in that great engagement. My client was severely wounded and lay upon the field of slaughter, when his deeply attached wife sought him, carrying in her arms their only infant. So deeply affected was she at observing the husband of her affections apparently in the agony of death that she fainted at his side, and he, believing that she was no more, crawled to a British officer with the child in his arms, and implored him to protect it. That officer has been ascertained to be Captain Morton. The child is now the young lady who, with all the natural feeling of a father, my client strove to obtain the society of."

"Pray be silent," said the magistrate, as he saw that Captain Morton was about to speak; "pray be silent, and allow things to proceed regularly, if you please."

"Certainly, certainly."

THE LORD OF GOFFET HAWKING.

"Prisoner, I have heard this statement which has been volunteered by you on this occasion, and now I shall proceed with the case. Will you come forward, madam, and give your evidence?"

Mabel stepped to the magistrate's table, and was sworn.

"What is your name," he said.

"Mabel Rouselli," she replied in a calm voice.

The effect upon the prisoner was instantaneous and terrific. He stretched out his arms, and his whole countenance became convulsed with passion as he cried,—

"No, no, not Rouselli. Who gave you that name? what fiend whispered to you such a name as that? No, no, it is a wild and desperate guess to drive me mad. I have not heard that name for many a day. Rouselli—Rouselli; who said Rouselli?"

"If you are not silent, prisoner," said the magistrate, "I shall be compelled to have you removed, and to carry on this investigation without you. Miss Rouselli, can you state to me who your father was, and with whom you are now residing?"

"My father was a colonel in the French army of the empire, and I am now under the protection of my grandfather, Monsieur Rouselli."

"'Tis false, false !" cried the mendicant —"all false ; a plot to deprive me of my only defence. She is mine—mine, I tell you. There is no Colonel Rouselli. There never was such a one. She belongs to me."

"I can swear," said Captain Morton, "the prisoner's not the man who gave into my charge the child on the field of Waterloo."

"And so can I, your honour," shouted Rafferty.

"Really," said the magistrate, "this is most irregular. You will please to go on with your evidence, Miss Rouselli. No one, of course, for a moment can be deceived by the impudent fabrications that he, the prisoner, has given utterance to."

"I beg your pardon," said the attorney. "I think your worship is a little premature in coming to such a decision. We have proofs."

"Of what nature?"

"I have a witness here—a French soldier, who was on the field of Waterloo, and saw the whole of this transaction. He has now been settled in this country for some years ; but he lay wounded on the field of battle, and he happened to see all that passed, and can swear that the prisoner at the bar was the person who gave the child to Captain Morton, and that he is what he represents himself to be, namely, an officer in the French army, or at least was such at the date of these transactions."

"Where is your witness?"

"Here."

An old weather-beaten man, tanned by age, stepped forward, and bowed to the magistrate, who, after a moment's consideration, said—

"I will swear you and take your evidence, but not now. When the prisoner in regular course is called upon for his defence, you can be produced."

"And in the meantime I do hope," said the attorney, "that the Morton family will not attempt to interfere with this witness."

Captain Morton, who felt his honour touched at this speech, would have made an angry reply, but the magistrate checked him, saying—

"Never mind, never mind, Captain Morton. You must let these sort of speeches go in at one ear and out at the other in a police-court."

Mabel then related clearly and distinctly the manner of her abduction from home by the mendicant, and how he had forcibly kept her a prisoner for a long time, until she made her escape with great difficulty from him.

Rafferty was then called, to his great chagrin ; for he had to give an account of how remarkably clever he tried to be, and succeeded only in falling into the lake.

"By the holy fire-irons," he muttered, when his examination was over, "if I'd have thought I was going to be persecuted in this way, it's not myself that would have come."

His testimony, however, was an important corroboration of Mabel's, because it fixed the identity of the prisoner.

Captain Morton then deposed to the prisoner being the same man who had previously called upon him, and offered to take money to forego a claim upon Mabel of relationship.

"This is a clear enough offence," said the magistrate. "Now, prisoner, what have you to say in reply to all this ?"

"This is my daughter. This is my witness."

"'Tis false, sir ; it is false," said Monsieur Rouselli, stepping forward and confronting the French witness. "She is my dear grandchild ; blessings on her. It was my son who gave her into the care of Captain Morton. My only brave and gallant son, who died upon that blood-stained field."

The old French soldier, who had come forward again at the call of the mendicant, shrank back from before the gaze of Monsieur Rouselli, and uttered the words "Mon Dieu !"

The magistrate observed his emotion, and had him immediately sworn ; after which he said to him in a solemn voice—

"Now, tell your version of the story ; and remember, that you have sworn in the name of Heaven to tell the truth."

"And he will tell the truth," said the attorney. "I am willing to stake my professional reputation upon the honour of this brave old soldier."

In a low voice the witness began :—

"I was wounded, but not badly, at Waterloo. I lay upon the field close to an English officer and some soldiers, although a gun carriage that had been upset hid me from their observation, while it did not prevent me from observing all that passed. They, if present, will admit that I was there, when I state that I saw one who would have robbed the dead, and murdered the living, shot by a sergeant."

"That's me, any how !" cried Rafferty.

"Yes," said the old French soldier, fixing his eyes upon Rafferty, "you are the man. I know you by the tone of your voice."

"Go on, go on," said the magistrate.

"I was tolerably well acquainted with the French officers in my division of the army, and among them was a Colonel Leroux."

"Ah," said the attorney, "ah, to be sure."

"I knew him well by sight. There was likewise unquestionably a Colonel Rouselli. I knew him, likewise, well by sight."

"Ah, to be sure! ah, to be sure."

"I will thank you, sir, not to interrupt the witness. This is quite insufferable, really," said the magistrate.

"Very well, sir, very well."

"I say," continued the old Frenchman, "that I knew both these officers well, and was present when the circumstance alluded to to-day took place. This gentleman, who told me he was a lawyer, found me out yesterday, and brought me to give my evidence.

"As I lay upon the field, I saw a French officer in the uniform of a colonel crawl, as well as the state of his wounds would permit, towards an English officer, who was likewise wounded. With many recommendations to his kindness, he placed an infant in the Englishman's arms. The Englishman promised to take charge of the child, and the French officer called down upon him the blessing of Heaven."

"Very proper," said the attorney, in a low voice.

"Could you identify the parties?" said the magistrate. "That is the grand question. There is no dispute about the circumstance you mention having actually taken place on any side."

"I could not identify the child."

"No, no, we don't expect you could; but the other parties, can you swear to them?"

"I can, so help me Heaven! I know them all."

"Then distinctly state, if you can see in this court the English officer to whom the child was given in charge."

"Yes," said the Frenchman, pointing to Captain Morton, "it is years ago, but that is the man."

"You are right," said the captain.

"And now what," added the magistrate, "was the name of the French officer in the colonel's uniform who gave the child to Captain Morton?"

The Frenchman paused, and took an old, miserable-looking snuff-box from his pocket, and raising the lid, he handed to the magistrate a small folded piece of paper.

"Why," said the latter, when he had unfolded it, "what has this to do with it? This is one half of a twenty pound note."

"It is. That gentleman," pointing to the lawyer, "gave it to me yesterday, with a promise of the other half to-day if my evidence was satisfactory, and I am only anxious to request you, sir, as I am a poor man and the money is of consequence to me, to see that I get it from him."

"Fool!" whispered the lawyer, "you should not have said anything about that," and then he added, aloud, "at all events, your worship, I presume we may pay our witnesses what we like for their time and attention?"

"I have nothing to do with all this," said the magistrate, "whatever may be my private opinion. Witness, will you answer the question I have asked of you?"

"I will, sir; the French officer who handed the infant to Captain Morton, was, to my certain knowledge, Colonel Rouselli!"

"Thank God!" cried Captain Morton, "the truth has triumphed."

"No, no!" shouted the solicitor; "you mean Colonel Leroux. Think again."

"Colonel Leroux was not there at all. He belonged to Grouchy's division—that was not on the field of battle."

"And that man now at the bar—who is he?"

"He is not Colonel Leroux."

The attorney gave a groan, and the prisoner turned perfectly livid, as he clutched the front of the bar for support.

"Who is he?" added the magistrate.

"He is a Prussian by birth, and his name is Sternholde."

---

## CHAPTER LXXXVIII.

THE PROCEEDINGS OF THE OSTLER AT THE VILLAGE.—THE SLEEPY WITNESS.

JEM, the ostler—who, by the way, we ought not now, in his altered fortunes, to speak of so irreverently—posted to the village, for the purpose of troubling Tom —to whom everything was a trouble— upon the affair in which he felt himself so much interested; and this was, to produce evidence of the mendicant's identity as the murderer of the stranger at the Morton Arms.

This object—that of bringing the murderer to light—had, as our readers are well aware, been a strong and stern feeling with him, and he had long desired to produce the man who did do the deed, and so, beyond all suspicion, clear himself from any doubt; for though the evidence of Troubled

Tom went far enough to secure his liberty, yet there were many who, if they were silenced, were not convinced. They couldn't say he was the man, nor did they suspect him; only they couldn't tell who it was that did do it.

This uncertainty caused a doubt to remain on his own mind, as to whether or no he ought to consider himself honourably acquitted of the charge. He seemed to have an idea he was pointed at, and could imagine people to say—

"There, you see that man; well, he has been in custody for murder, but there wasn't evidence enough to convict him, and he was discharged."

Thus making it appear that, after all, he might have been guilty, only proof was wanting.

Actuated by mingled motives, he determined to set out; and now he thought of the mode in which he could reach the village.

At first he determined to go into the Morton Arms quietly and unobtrusively; but then he thought he might be recognised too soon, so that he might not be able to secure the object he had in view so readily. He therefore came to the resolution of posting down.

Ordering a post-chaise, he quickly threw himself into it, and, while posting down, he indulged in many thoughts upon the strange mutations of circumstances that had taken place. Day after day, some new change had sprung up, or some new position, from which men and things were viewed in a very different light.

What would they think at the Morton Arms when they saw the former ostler posting down as a man of fortune, and as one who had been used to the possession of wealth?

"My old master," he thought, "will be somewhat astonished. He thought there was scarce a dignity that could compete with an innkeeper, and nothing was more difficult to conduct than a well established inn. A man who had never been an innkeeper, and had been in a subordinate station, could never, in his mind, become one, though he would admit he might easily become a gentleman—it was much the easiest transition."

Time flies by, and even a journey by post came to an end; and the sun was sinking near the horizon when the post-chaise at length drew up before the door of the Morton Arms.

There was an instant bustle, and a couple of waiters came out and opened the door, and caught a glimpse of the face of the new comer, and then looked again, and then at each other, and again at the stranger.

They couldn't believe their eyes, and merely stood by bowing, in amazement, from habit.

"Is the landlord in?" inquired the stranger.

"Yes, yes, sir," stammered the waiters; for the voice sounded familiar enough in their ears.

"A private room?"

"Yes, sir; certainly." And they followed the ostler—now a gentleman—into the inn, and saw him into a private room.

"Send the landlord in—I want to speak to him," said Jem; "and tell him an old friend waits for him."

"Yes, yes, sir," said the waiters; and out they rushed to the landlord, whom they met below.

"Well, where are you going to in such a hurry?' inquired the landlord, over whom they had nearly run; "where are you going to, and where have you shown the gentleman?"

"Into the blue room, sir."

"Beg pardon, sir," said the other; "but he says he wants to speak to you, sir; and he says, sir, that he is an old friend, sir; and, beg pardon, sir, but if he ain't our Jem, the ostler, why, sir, he's the devil in his likeness."

"You are a pack of fools," said the landlord; "I'll go to see what he wants, however."

So saying, the landlord went to the blue room, and, opening the door, walked in. Jem was sitting with a decanter before him, with his back to the door, so the landlord didn't see his face at first, and he said—

"Beg pardon, sir, but understood from my waiter you wanted to see me."

"So I did; walk round and take a seat."

The landlord did walk round,—his curiosity was more than excited, and he thought that if that wasn't Jem's voice, it was nobodys; but he said nothing, only opening his eyes wider and wider at each step he took, as the form of Jem came more and more in full view.

"Well, no—eh?—it must be—no—yes—it must be!"

"What did you say?" inquired Jem.

"Ah! it must be; yes, I see now; why, I am—Mr. What's-o'-name, how are you? God bless my heart, who would have expected to see you! Why, you've come into a fortune! Well, that's right; I'm glad to see you, anyhow."

"Thank you," said Jem, as he held his hand out towards the landlord, which the latter shook with much good-will.

"Well, Jem—but I mustn't call you Jem, now."

"Never mind that! I am what I was in all but circumstances; you know nature don't alter and change, though our positions may."

"That's uncommonly true, and I'm glad to hear you say so; fortune will do you good,—you can't think how glad I am to see you."

"Won't you sit down and have some wine with me? I have a few words to say to you. I have come down to these parts for a particular purpose."

"Of course you have," said the landlord, as he sat down on a chair, which he drew to the table, and took a glass of wine; "of course you have,—you've come down here to settle buying a large estate, or something of the sort."

"No, no; that is not my object, at present," said Jem.

"Then what can it be besides, save to see your old friends, and show them how fortunate you are?"

"Nor that, either."

"What then?" said the landlord, tapping his head with his fore-finger. "I don't know of anything more—nothing so good, certainly."

"Well, then, it's to claim the assistance of my friends, especially of Troubled Tom."

"That will be a trouble to him, poor fellow," said the landlord, laughing; "I never knew such an original as that—quite a new idea is Tom."

"Yes; but I shall trouble him to go all the way to London, and that is an affair that will be beyond anything he ever dreamed of."

"It will; there's nothing under heaven that isn't a trouble to him, though, somehow or other, he contrives to rub on, and get through the world."

"Exactly; but do you remember the events of the murder that took place here?"

"I do very well."

"It is about that, then, that I want to see Tom; because he saw the man who escaped, and stepped on him in doing so, as he lay in the pigsty."

"Yes, yes; he did; but I doubt very much how far Tom can recollect him."

"That is just what I want to ask him about," said Jem; "and what I have come about."

"I will send for him."

"Do you see, I have a peculiar interest in bringing this man to justice; you know I suffered from suspicion, and, but for Troubled Tom, I should have suffered much; and there is no knowing the length that might have been run; my

race might, and would, in all probability, have ended with the gallows-tree."

"Ah! that would have been a fatal termination to your career, at last. So it would have been to any one else under the same circumstances,—but I'll go and call Tom."

The landlord took a glass or two more wine, and then talked over old times, and then declared he would go and call Tom, and then he talked again, until, at length, a waiter entered the room to say he was wanted.

"Can't come," said the landlord, peremptorily; and then added,—"go back, and tell Tom I want him."

"Troubled Tom, sir?"

"Yes; certainly."

Away went the waiter, and soon after—as soon as could be expected for Troubled Tom—they heard the worthy very languidly ascending the stairs, and approaching the door, which he opened, and, thrusting his shock head in, said—

"Want me, sir?"

"Yes; come in, Tom," said Jem; "come in. How have you lived—in trouble ever since?"

"Oh, lor, who would have thought; but no—beg pardon. Yes, it must be Jem. Oh,—Jem—what a trouble things are, to be sure; I wonder where we can find a quiet place; but I'm glad to see you, though you've come back quite the gentleman."

"Ah, Tom, I came here especially to trouble you."

"On purpose?"

"Yes; I have come here all the way. You have done me a service before; I want you to do me another, and I will do one for you."

"There, now, I never see any one, but some trouble springs out of it. Why, troubles spring up like nettles in a ditch."

"So they do, Tom; but tell me, do you remember the occurrence of a man stepping out upon you, when the murder was committed here?"

"Yes; I do."

"Well, do you remember the occurrence well enough to describe the form and dress of that person?"

"I believe I do."

"Well, then, do you think you could remember the man if you were to see him?"

"Well, what a trouble; but I dare say I can do so, if I were to see him; but, at all events, I couldn't tell till I saw the man, and that won't be yet awhile, I reckon."

"If you can do so much, I expect you'll be required to come to London, for there is a man there who has been taken into custody upon other matters."

Then Jem related some of the occurrences that had happened, that amazed both the landlord and Troubled Tom, who stood gazing upon Jem, and, at length said—

" Well, now, you have contrived to escape the greatest share of your toils and troubles. Well, we ain't all born with a silver spoon in our mouths ; but I'm glad of it, and I'll do it for you, though it's a nation trouble."

There were many recognitions made, and all were glad enough to see Jem, though he benefitted alone by the accident of fortune, still he did not fail to give them cause to praise his generosity.

While down here he remained at the Morton Arms, and visited many of the old spots which had been so familiar to him, while he was there under very different auspices to those under which he now entered the village, and some there were who knew him not at all; Troubled Tom, however, did not complain so much as might have been expected.

## CHAPTER LXXXIX.

THE REMAND OF THE MENDICANT AND THE RECOGNITION BY THE SLEEPY WITNESS.—THE TRIAL.

WHEN the French witness uttered the name of Sternholde, the whole party of the Mortons started in amazement, for that name brought back the most terrible ideas to them, connected as it was with so much of the terrific, as had been recorded of him by the grandfather of Mabel.

At once they seemed to see before them, not only the persecutor of the beautiful girl, but the unrelenting foe of her parents —the man who had earned so dreadful and so unenviable a notoriety by the most atrocious actions that could disgrace human nature.

They had suspected him of the murder of the traveller at the Morton Arms, but the truth is, they had not suspected him of the dreadful reputation which he really enjoyed. They all continued gazing upon him for some moments in silence, for there was no exclamation which the human language was capable of which would have been sufficiently strong to convey their detestation of one, concerning whom they had heard so much, and who, for the honour of human nature, they did hope was no longer in the land of the living.

The magistrate saw with wonder the effect which the mere pronunciation of the name of Sternholde had upon the persons present, for it was an entirely new name to him, and as unconnected as possible with any previous ideas.

But if upon the prisoner's accusers the pronunciation of his name had so marked an effect, it had, if possible, a much stronger one upon himself, for from that moment that he heard it declared who he was, he appeared to consider that all further attempt to disguise his real character was perfectly useless, and that the most desirable thing would be to glory in the dreadful reputation he had achieved.

He drew himself proudly up, and no longer seemed at all anxious to avoid the glances of those around him. The attempted subornation of a witness had failed completely, and since he could not escape the worst consequences of being known for what he really was, he appeared to derive a gloomy satisfaction in showing that he was really, and to the full, as fearful a character as he was represented to be by all who had heard of his ruinous and desperate career.

" Yes," he said, and his voice sounded hoarsely and discordantly, far above its ordinary tones. " Yes, I am Sternholde, and I care not who knows it. I am Sternholde, and I have one other name, which is, the Battle Fiend! I glory in both appellations, but most do I glory in the latter, because it is that name which has grown out of my revenge."

" What is the meaning of all this ?" said the magistrate. " I must confess that I really cannot comprehend it."

Then, before any one could reply to this observation, there stepped up to the prisoner old Monsieur Rouselli, and while his head shook with emotion, and his white locks were scattered in the air, that waved them as though they had been shreds of flossy silk, he looked him steadily in the face.

The old man did not speak, but he did not withdraw his eyes for a moment from the countenance of the man who had worked him so much woe. And he, Sternholde—the villain Sternholde, the murderer, made a faint and an inefficient effort to look steadily in the countenance of Monsieur Rouselli.

For a time—but a short time only—he did succeed, and then he began to waver; gradually he drooped and trembled— cowering beneath the gaze of the old man, as if it had brought with it some withering blight which it was not in human nature to withstand.

It was quite clear that no word need be spoken. The villain was subdued by that steady, uncompromising gaze alone.

And then, indeed, did he exhibit all the power over the physical frame of an evil conscience, for while he shook like one in an ague he turned his head aside, saying,—

"Enough! enough! I have nothing to say to you."

"Murderer!" said the old man. "Can you breathe in my presence, and yet know the amount of misery you have brought upon me?"

"Away! away!" said Sternholde, for so we may now as well call him. "Away! away, old man, I have no words for thee."

"Will some one," said the magistrate, "explain to me the cause of this most remarkable change in the manner of the prisoner?"

"I can do so, sir," said Captain Morton; "but as the details will occupy some time, and as they cannot be said to apply to affairs recognisable in the jurisdiction of the English laws, I will, in private, communicate to you who and what this desperate man really is; I have only now to pray that you will remand him, for I expect I can produce evidence, so as to prove him guilty of a crime which the English law can take full cognisance of; I shall be able to prove him a murderer."

"'Tis false!" cried Sternholde. "I have done nothing here, and being not an English subject, all acts that may be laid to my charge in other countries have nothing to do with the magistracy of this."

"I shall grant the remand," said the magistrate, "upon your oath, Captain Morton, that you believe you will be able to produce evidence of this man's guilt of a higher crime than the abduction of this young lady."

"I did not abduct her," said Sternholde. "I had as much right to the custody of her as they who arrogate such a duty to themselves."

"You are remarkably incorrect there," said the magistrate. "Captain Morton,, by the laws of this country—and, I expect for the proposition is really too reasonable a one to entertain a doubt upon, by the laws of every other European state—became the natural guardian of Mabel Rouselli. The dying request of her father, that he would accept such a trust, and his ready acceptance of it, were amply sufficient."

"I know well," said Sternholde, "that every point will be strained against me. This is the country, of all others, in which the poor and friendless have no chance against the rich and powerful. But do your worst. I defy you all, and may thwart you yet."

"For how long would you like the prisoner remanded?" asked the magistrate of Captain Morton.

"In one week," said the captain, "I am confident that I shall have all the evidence which it is in my power to procure. The murder of which I accuse him was perpetrated at an inn in the country, called the Morton Arms."

Sternholde looked at Captain Morton with such a savage expression of countenance, that it was quite evident he would have gloried in inflicting upon him some injury; and no doubt his powerless condition, which so effectually prevented him from doing so, was no small aggravation of what he suffered.

He was about to say something else; but as the first few words were those of invective, the magistrate would not hear him, but ordered that he should be immediately removed; at the same time, he directed the officers to look most specially to his safe custody, for there was all the appearance about him of one brewing mischief.

This the officers were pretty sure to do, for their own sakes; and they were quite sufficiently acquainted with such characters to deal with them properly.

Captain Morton made an appointment with the magistrate, in order that he might relate to him the whole particulars of the career of Sternholde, and how he had rendered his name so extremely obnoxious to the Rouselli family.

They then left the police-office, and they soon perceived that the proceedings there had had a most prejudicial effect upon old Monsieur Rouselli. He had supported himself firmly while there, and in the presence of the man who may be said to have brought upon him almost all the distress he had suffered, and he got home tolerably; but when there his firmness forsook him, and he fainted in the arms of Henry Morton.

It was fortunate that Henry was so close at hand as to be able to save the old man, or he would have fallen heavily to the floor. All was confusion for some moments among the Mortons; for the state into which the old man fell so strongly resembled death, that for some time they feared that either it had arrived, or was about to do so.

They, with all the tenderest solicitude, had him conveyed to bed, and a physician of eminence was immediately sent for, who looked upon the case rather seriously.

"The mental shock," he said, "which in a younger subject would pass away, leaving behind it no bad effects permanently, may prove fatal here. I do not say that it will, because the vital energies may rally; but all I have is a hope that way."

This was quite tantamount to an adverse opinion. Indeed, it was saying quite as much as any medical man could be expected to say of a very bad case, the chance of which ending favourably was very remote indeed.

The Mortons consulted together whether they should let Mabel know the worst, or keep her in ignorance of it, until something of a more decided character occurred to prevent them from being able to do so with effect.

"Tell her all," was what Henry said. "Mabel is not a child. She has a heart full of the best and dearest affections; but yet she has a mind which it would be an insult to not to inform of anything which nearly concerns her."

"I of course yield to you," said the captain. "You have, Henry, a right to dictate our conduct to Mabel."

Henry was pleased to hear this recognition of his engagement to Mabel from his brother's lips, and he took upon himself the task of breaking to her the adverse opinion of the medical man regarding her grandfather.

Tears gushed to Mabel's eyes, and, for a time, she seemed completely to gainsay the expressed opinions of Henry, that she had mind enough to govern any affliction. The affections alone seemed to dictate to her.

"Alas! alas!" she said. "This will be a cruel blow of fate to me. I shall then lose the only being to whom I can claim kindred, and I shall be alone in the world!"

"Alone, Mabel!" said Henry, reproachfully; "is this kind to me? or I may go so far as to ask, is this just to me, who have loved you well and constantly? Oh! Mabel, Mabel, I did not think to have heard such words from your lips!"

"Forgive me, Henry," she said, imploringly, as she placed both her hands in his; "forgive me, that for one brief moment I forgot your love. I have never doubted it, and never shall doubt it; but what I said was wrung from me at the instant, by the feeling that, as regarded my lineage and race, I should be alone."

"It is I, dear Mabel," said Henry, "who ought to ask you to forgive me for uttering the shadow of a reproach to you at such a time as this. But love such as mine is foolishly sensitive, and feels even a fancied slight worse than a wound."

"I will strive, Henry, to deserve the affection you bestow upon the orphan, friendless, girl who, but for you, and those connected with you by the nearest and dearest ties, must have long since perished."

"No, Mabel, no; Heaven does not make its choicest creatures to perish. If you had not fallen into our hands, to bless us as you have, some others would have been fortunate enough to become your protectors, and the only happiness I could have hoped then for would have consisted in the ignorance of the greater happiness I had lost."

"I will go at once to the chamber of my grandfather," she said. "Who but I should watch now by his couch?"

"No, Mabel—no, Mabel. Let me implore you not to do so. I know the kindly and noble feelings of affection that prompt you, but strangers, such strangers, I mean, as can form a full and intimate knowledge of them, and can be relied upon, are ever the best to attend upon the sick; I know that in saying this much, I am saying what is adverse to general opinion, but yet I think that I am right."

Mabel answered that he might be right, but still it did not influence her, and, in a few minutes more, she had taken up her station by the bedside of her grandfather, and commenced her task of tending him with all the solicitude of a daughter.

He remained for many hours in a strange apathetic sort of state, but then suddenly all his faculties seemed to return to him, and, turning his eyes upon Mabel, he pronounced her name.

She heard him utter that word, Mabel, with a revived hope that he might yet baffle the enemy, death, which showed so strong a disposition to assail him, and to conquer him. She leaned over him, and looked long and wistfully in his face.

"Speak again, dear grandfather," she said. "You are better than you were, and you can now speak again to your own Mabel. Oh! let me hear your voice once more."

He turned his eyes upon her, and was for some moments silent. Then he made an effort to utter some articulate sound, but it was evidently a painful one, and his voice was sadly and strangely altered from its usual tones.

"Mabel, my Mabel," he said, "do you not regret that I am going from you? The old, withered tree, once the strongest of the forest, must, in time, make a place for the young sapling that shoots up so green and verdant, and full of youthful vigour by its side."

"Oh! grandfather, do not speak thus. You will stay with us long yet—I know you will. You will stay with us to bless us. It would be hard, indeed, to part with you so soon!"

"But, my Mabel, you are young and

beautiful, and I know that you are surrounded by those who love you well,—those who will never let a cold world frown on you again, but encircling you in their arms, will save you from all the frowns of fortune. You will be happy, my beautiful Mabel! you will be very happy!"

Sobs came from Mabel's heart, for she felt a conviction creeping over her that could not be resisted, to the effect that these words she was listening to from those revered lips were the last the old man would utter in this world.

She knew, at least she had been told, that, at his age, the shock he had received from so suddenly confronting the man who had been such a foe to his happiness—the villain Sternholde—was one not likely for him to wholly recover from; but still she had entertained, until now, a hope, at least, that the prediction might not be verified. But when she marked the altered

RAFFERTY'S SURPRISE ON THE RECOVERY OF MABEL.

voice, when she looked upon the face so strangely changed, she could no longer cherish the idea that this last one of her race would be long spared to her, and she already, in imagination, mourned him as gone from her.

And yet Mabel could not call herself desolate, while such dear friends as the Mortons lived; she could not pretend to think for a moment that she was friendless, while shs knew that she was the heart's idol of one who would die rather than she should suffer a pang. But yet, to her mind, there was a something sadly, fearfully melancholy in thus taking leave of the only one to whom she could claim the affinity of kindred. She knew that it was one of those feelings of the human mind which will not stand argumentation, and yet, like many others which exercise the strongest influence over us through life, powerful in its mere instinctive character, and sets itself up strongly in our hearts in defiance all philosophy.

After he had uttered these few words which we have recorded, the old man's

some extra expense and some loss of time; but he met each by increased exertions and labour; the consequence was he lost nothing by the determined manner in which he met all new calls upon him.

I was his first child, and on this occasion there was a little display of finery and expense; but that was to be expected; he was expected to do so by all, and such was the thought of my mother, and she would have been much mortified if he had not done so.

The result of all his care and punctuality in business was he throve well, and acquired a comfortable independence; and when I was about four years old, he determined upon retiring from business, and living a small distance from London, and there enjoy himself.

About this time my mother died and left me, at that early age, in the care of my father, who was as unused to children as a man could be; and though he had every disposition to do what was right—to take care of me, and to indulge me, yet he could not play the man-nurse, or feel at all at home with such a charge as myself, and he resolved to send me to school.

I think he was right in this; for he was not fit to have the charge of a boy of my age. It was altogether a thing he had not been used to, and he was out of his element.

Let me do him the justice to say that a better father never existed, and I am sure he loved me tenderly; he was to me most just and indulgent. I am sure he was fond of me, but he could not nurse and fondle me.

This caused him to send me to school much earlier than I otherwise should have gone; but at the same time I think it was the making of me; for, instead of making a fool of me, I soon became a clever lad.

At least such was my character at school; so I think his judgment was unbiassed when he resolved upon sending me there. He had none of the silly feelings towards a child which many people have if they are pleased with fondling them.

I was his first, and he never forgot it. But he soon grew weary of a single life; he had no sort of home—no place where he could retire to and enjoy himsel; he had been used to the domestic comforts of home during my mother's life, to a degree, I have heard him say, that he never could bear living single again; and he resolved upon marrying a second time.

There were plenty who would have no objection to become the wife of a retired tradesman, a man of means, and a steady, good hearted man as he was; he had many attempts made upon him, but it was useless; there was but one who could succeed, and many must, therefore, be disappointed since they did make the attempt.

On one occasion a young lady—a beautiful creature she was too, as I am told, and she certainly married well afterwards—fainted away in his arms.

This, however, had not the desired effect, for he was terrified, and it caused him to believe she was troubled with fits, and he became very shy of her for ever afterwards. She, however, made several attempts upon him, but he was not to be caught in that manner; he was determined to have nobody that promised any illness.

"I have lost one wife," he used to say, "and I won't lose another if I can, in any way, avoid it. I will endeavour to avoid it if it be at all possible; fainting is a sign of weakness, and constitutional weakness will cause a wife to die. I'll have no more mourning—I hate the colour of black."

Thus he was resolved, and the young lady soon after married a young man, and is at this day in excellent health.

However, my father now set about seriously looking for a wife; and, as many persons were well acquainted with the fact that he had it in his mind—that he contemplated marrying again—he wanted not for invitations, and friends to welcome him wherever he went to.

It was strange what a number of acquaintances he made; and they were all families—it was the easiest thing in the world to find a new friend whenever he wanted one; but yet he never chose one of the daughters or sisters.

One day, accident alone introduced him to the woman he afterwards married.

He was riding in a gig, when his horse shied and kicked when whipped, and then upset him into a ditch; where he was dragged out by the servant of a family residing close at hand. His distress was seen, and he was on the point of perishing from suffocation in the mud in the ditch —the vehicle being thrown over on the top of him.

With some trouble and difficulty, he was got out, and carried in doors, and taken care of by the inmates, who had seen the occurrence, and came out to his assistance.

My father was, I believe, insensible, and was, after some trouble, brought round to himself, having been stunned, or nearly so, for a short time; and now he became conscious of what had happened; and yet he could not tell where he was. He looked around, but saw none upon whom he could rest his gaze with any signs of recognition.

"Where am I?" he inquired; "where am I?"

"In safety," replied a voice close beside him; and the curtains of the bed were, at the same time, drawn by a light hand, and the form of a young female was immediately present to his sight.

"And whom have I to thank for so much care?" he inquired, as he surveyed her; "who was it that saved me, and placed me here? Tell me, to whom am I indebted for this?"

"I was seated at the window," she replied, "and heard something like a noise with the horse, and was just in time to see you thrown, and the servant did all the rest."

"I am your debtor," he replied, "nevertheless. What was done was done at your bidding. You are my saviour."

"You say more than I ought to hear upon that point; but, if you think I have done you any service, you will remain here quiet a few hours till you have rested, and slept a natural sleep for a few hours, and then, if you are able, you shall rise and leave, if you desire to do so."

"You are kind—very kind. I will be guided by you," he replied; "I am your prisoner."

The result was, my father was induced to remain there all that afternoon, and the next day too. He was well-pleased with the people; and the young lady, who was about four or six-and-twenty, he took an especial liking to.

They became acquaintances, and he was frequently there to see her; but he was now also not without having fixed his affections a second time upon a female, and this person was to be his future wife.

He explained to her friends who and what he was; that he had one child—that is, myself; but that was no possible objection to the lady, who was fond of children, and who declared she should love me as if I had been her own.

This was very satisfactory—very satisfactory, indeed, and promised a very good prospect. My father was happy, the lady seemed amiable and handsome, and they loved each other. They married. He was not to blame. He could not know anything but what came under the cognizance of his senses, and he took his wife home to him.

Things went on very well for some time. When my vacation occurred, I was brought home and presented to my mother-in-law, who received me very graciously; but I thought there was more show than real feeling in her manner. I was resolved, young as I then was, that I would never treat her as if she had my entire confidence, but that I would be reserved, and never trust her.

Of course this was a childish resolve, but still I remember just so much; but, at the same time, I never intended that she should know anything about it, or my father.

My vacation over, I returned to school, without either sorrow or regret at having to leave home, though I had certainly no reason why I should desire to go back to school.

Time flew by, and I returned home, and there found my father had increased his family; he had another son by his second wife, and I soon found out that there was a change in the house as well as an increase of its inmates.

My mother-in-law seemed to have taken a fancy that I was an impediment to her plans, and to remove me from my father's sight was her object. If she could get me out of the way that would enable her to have a complete command over him; do that and she would be satisfied.

Well, sir, she did all she could to succeed; all things were in her favour; my father was fond of her, and of the child. I do not quarrel with him for that—it was natural—perfectly natural he should; but it blinded him to some of my mother-in-law's faults; she had acquired a sort of command over him, and he got at length in the habit of surrendering his will to hers, and his inclinations were rather curbed, or they were entirely suppressed, as she appeared to oppose them more or less energetically than before.

She used to show her ill-will to me by informing him, upon every possible occasion, of the little peccadillos of which I had been guilty, and especially commenting upon them.

At length my father grew so weary of my enormities, and the trouble and the long lectures they brought with them, that, I believe, he began to imagine that I was born especially for the purpose of tormenting him.

This, I have no doubt, was the cause of his permitting me to do as I pleased, and allowing my mother-in-law the full power of disposing of me to save himself the trouble of having anything to do with an unruly boy; he was somewhat of an indolent disposition, and averse to any contention whatever.

I say he was of an indolent disposition. I shall explain that this was an acquired habit, rather than otherwise, because, while in business, he was exact and punctual, and never idle.

It was a plan of my mother-in-law's that I should be sent away; she wished me to go to sea, and I had an objection to that; I was, moreover, too young for that, which my father said himself, and he thought I might do elsewhere.

"Do elsewhere!" I remember her very words, "do elsewhere! he never will do anywhere; you had better send him to sea than let him stay here to be hanged."

"But he did not do so badly at school," said my father; "he's not old enough to be taken away from school yet, and he was never complained of by them, but has had a very good character; he is bad here; well, let it be so; all children are worse at home than they are when they are out."

"Then send him out, if that be true," said my mother-in-law; "send him out."

"Very well, he shall go," said my father, who was by no means pleased, yet he knew not how to oppose it after he had been thus nailed, as it were, to an assertion of his own.

"What will you do with him?" inquired my mother-in-law; "what do you think he will learn?"

"I will consider about that; I can't at this moment tell what he is best fit for; but I think school is the best place, after all; however, I will think of it."

"He may remain all his life at school—all his life; and what would he be fit for when he left it?"

However, it never came to a choice of my father's; for he died, and I was still at home. This event happened somewhat suddenly. My father died, I believe, of apoplexy—very suddenly, at all events; and I was then left at the mercy of my mother-in-law, who was now a widow, and possessor of everything.

My father had not died without a will; but I knew nothing of that at the time—was a mere child, and did as I was desired. My mother-in-law immediately put me into some situation—a mere menial capacity of some sort or other—where I was compelled to knock about in a manner never contemplated by my poor father; and I verily believe she hoped I should die, and then there would be no one who could dispute the possession of the property with her.

I knew nothing of that at the time—I was a mere child; but knew this much, I was compelled to earn a hard living; for wherever I was, I boarded in the house, and was compelled to be at every one's beck and call. I had no time I could call my own; all was work or sleep with me at that time.

The widow would never permit me to come home, if she could avoid it; and it was only at stated times that she could do so; and then I had to come as one soliciting a favour.

My half-brother, in the mean while, grew up healthy and strong; he was not a bad kind of youth to look at; but he had a bad and vicious temper, which she appeared to foster.

It was seldom I went home; I did not like my father's widow well enough for that—she was too harsh; and I found that, hard as I was used elsewhere, I was unlikely to be used any better there. Indeed, I am sure I was much worse used; and, at length, I hardly ever went there.

Time wore on, and I grew up; my half-brother grew up, too, and he was a strong hearty youth, and always at home, living in idleness, whilst I worked hard for a scanty living.

I could not help contrasting my state and his, and then inquiring within myself the cause of such a difference. I began to canvass the matter, and to ask how it was my mother-in-law contrived to live so gaily, and to keep her son at home, in handsome apartments.

This was a puzzle. Whatever she had, must come from my father; and if so, was I not entitled, at least, to a share of it? Why should I not be as well off as my half-brother? Surely they could show me no good reason why I should not.

I determined to see about this; and, having consulted a few of my acquaintances, I found they were of my opinion. I had some rights; and they said it was no more than proper that she should restore them to me.

Upon this I determined to question her at once, and ascertain if she had any property. I never thought of the effect this would have on her. I thought only upon the result of the inquiry, which, I believed, must be answered in the affirmative.

I went home—home I call it—though it was no home to me. I went to her, and saw her. I inquired how it was she contrived to live as she did. She opened her eyes, and stared at me.

"You insolent puppy!" she exclaimed; "do you come thus far to annoy me and my son? What do you mean by such a question? Do you want to know what money I have got, that you may break into the place and rob me?"

"No," said I, "I don't."

"What do you desire, then?" she asked, angrily.

"I want to know what my father left; because I have as good a right to it as he or you," said I, boldly. "He stops at home with you, and is kept in idleness. What more is there in him than in me that he should be so much favoured?"

"Because his father wished, and I chose he should. But you were the death of your father; your conduct has been so very bad—most infamous. I have nothing but what is my own, and you are entitled to nothing, because you are not the eldest son."

"I am," I replied.

"You are not, for you were not born in wedlock; you are a nobody."

. I was so enraged that I so far forgot myself that I struck her hard in the face, and struck her down; the imputation upon my mother was too great and gross for me to bear; for though I could recollect little or nothing of my mother, yet I had heard her spoken of, and knew well this was a falsehood.

"Where is my father's will?"

"Leave the house," she exclaimed—"leave the house, and never enter it again; if so, you shall be transported for an attempt at murder and robbery, you scoundrel, you shall."

So violent and so strong was her paroxysm of passion, that I was completely amazed, and could hardly believe my senses. But I left the house, quite convinced that my father had property, but that it was safe in her hands, and that I must first find out what it was, and where placed, before could do any good.

Again, I must ascertain if any will had been proved; but to do all this required money, and I had none to spare. I had scarce enough to enable me to secure a decent living.

"Well," thought I, "time and attention will do something; if not, I will be unknown and unseen by her; she shall not have the evil gratification of seeing that I want anything. She will glory in my misery and misfortunes, and my half-brother will do no less than endeavour to make my situation worse than it was."

It was strange to say he had taken a dislike to me, and appeared to hate me in proportion as his mother did. She hated me, I knew, and he derided all my wishes for independence. He dressed like a gentleman, and rode his horse, while I had to attend one; there was all the difference between us as there was between master and groom.

We were not in actual contact; no, no, he kept clear of that. But I heard he had run through a good deal of money, and he treated her, his mother, very badly.

I got away from all the places I had formerly frequented, and endeavoured to settle somewhere where I was not known, until time or some circumstances should happen that would make my return to society probable.

I often heard of my mother-in-law. She palmed off her own son as the eldest son of my father, and got some friends to avow it; they believed what they said. I had been kept out of the way, and was unknown to most of our family friends.

The mother wanted to marry the son well, and then secure a good fortune; but he was perverse. He ran about the town committing great extravagancies, and flagrant acts of dissipation and debauchery.

I am assured that his mother did all she could to prevent this; she was an unscrupulous and ambitious woman, and desired to see the son settled in life without any loss of time, because she knew, though she might succeed in keeping me from my own, yet she could not reckon upon any transfer of property; or, at all events, when people stand over a mine, they are always in dread lest it blow up.

This was her state, I am sure, but she had unruly materials to act with; she could not bring the son to do what she desired. She had so indulged him, and permitted him to have his own way when he was younger, he had not now learned to curb his own will, or conform to that of others.

His own passions were strong, and he only sought their gratification, and that was his sole study—his sole pursuit; and in this pursuit he did not flag, but spent all his time and all his money.

Frequent were the calls upon her purse, and she used to lecture him every time she was compelled to replenish his exhausted finances; his extravagance knew no bounds, and, while money lasted, there was no means of staying his course.

In all my life I never heard of any one who could get through so much money in so short a time, taking into consideration the amount of fortune he was entitled to.

Often did his wily mother instil, or endeavour to instil into his mind the necessity there existed for a wealthy alliance; she could not tell him all; she could not explain to him her fears or her wishes. She was compelled to keep all to herself, and she had no confidant.

All this, of course, did not occur in a day. I had withdrawn myself from them for some time. I had resolved I would see neither, nor would 1; and I was, moreover, certain, in my own mind, that something would happen some day that would put me in possession of my own, for such

I was sure I was entitled to, for she must have secreted about her my father's property, or have a schedule of what it consisted in, though it could not be found.

Moreover, my father had papers which were of importance, and without which his heir could not take possession of his property.

Well, my mother-in-law was still at her work. Incessantly did she endeavour to induce him to marry, but he would not; and his demands for money became more and more pressing, until there was, I fancy, some terrible disturbance between the mother and son, from which time I have not seen him."

"Not seen, but have heard, doubtless, of your mother-in-law?" said Mr. Morton.

"No."

"That is very strange, is it not?" inquired Captain Morton; "is she dead, think you?"

"No, I fancy not; I have at length obtained some papers, and I gave them into the hands of a solicitor who had some dealings with my father, and who knew something about him.

As may be expected, I had much difficulty in convincing them as to who I was; but I succeeded, at length, in doing so; the papers which I possessed somewhat reassured them. They had all heard that my father had a child by his first wife; and his second wife, now his widow, had all along insisted that the other was the child—that there was now no other.

Thus he had been palmed off upon the friends of the family, and had taken my place; and my absence had aided the deseption; however, there was no help for it now, and my personal efforts were of no avail. It was a long affair; but my claim was good, and apparently I was entitled to some heavy sums of money; I was, in fact, heir to a good property, but the litigation was still to be lengthened, and after some conversation, I have allowed me two hundred a year, until this matter is settled."

"Then," said Captain Morton, "you are, after all, pretty sure of your cause, since you have so great an allowance."

"Yes, I suppose so; and yet I am in continual danger of being unable to prove that I am the eldest son of my father, as well as the will that I feel convinced he left; and if not, I am at least entitled to a full eldest son's share."

"You are, certainly."

"But there lies the difficulty; my father's property consisted of various matters of which I have no information; and then this young fellow being considered the eldest son, he will obtain so much evidence to what I can."

"That is unfortunate; in this respect it would have been better had you remained among your friends."

"But, could any human being have calculated upon the duplicity and fraud of such a description?"

"It was unlooked for, certainly."

"And, moreover, I should have met with a similar fate, do what I would, for who could tell what other scheme would have been put in practice; I am sure they would have tried, and then 'where there's a will, there's a way.'"

"That is very true."

"However, I must now wait until the events turn up, and place me in a yet better position than I now occupy; one great thing to me is, it will place me beyond any fear of a reverse—that is what I should most dread."

"It would be most to be feared, certainly," said Henry Morton; "and contentment, with a small certainty is far preferable to uncertain wealth of any description."

"So it is, sir."

"What has become of the young man, your half-brother?" inquired Captain Morton; "have you ever heard of him?"

"I have never seen him—I have never applied to him, for I was too proud to apply to him. No alms would I take; what I wanted I would earn, or I would not have it at all."

"I commend your determination and independence," said Captain Morton; "and you adhered to this determination?"

"I have."

"It is the resolve of a strong mind," said Captain Morton; "but suppose we take a walk through the streets, and so change the scene for a time; what do you say, Henry?"

"I am well pleased," said Henry; "but I did not hear your answer; where is this young fellow now?"

"Somewhere about town. I believe he has ill-used his mother very badly, as, indeed, he would anybody, who gave him the chance of doing so,—he's a complete ingrate."

They all now sailed out, and walked through the streets, conversing upon a variety of matters which happened to become of interest at the moment, the while they were filled with pleasing emotions as they walked and talked.

Suddenly they were startled by the sound of some one groaning, and on looking about them, they could discover nothing but what appeared a bundle beneath the doorway of a deserted house.

"What can be the meaning of all this?" exclaimed the captain. "I thought I heard some one groaning, as if in distress or pain ; surely it cannot come from yonder heap of rags."

"I think so," replied Jem.

"Indeed ; we had better go over and look at it ; surely it must be a woman," said Henry Morton.

"Yes, probably, if anything at all," said the captain, "and upon the point of death if suffering at all."

They all three crossed over the road, and walked towards the doorway, where the object they perceived was now rocking itself to and fro, as though in great pain.

"What is the matter, my good woman ?" inquired Capta'n Morton, in a kind tone, of her ; "what is the matter with you ?"

"Oh! God!—Oh, God! I am dying!"

exclaimed the woman, in despairing accents; "I—I, who have done so much wrong!"

"You! you! who and what are you?" inquired Henry Morton; "what is it that ails you?"

"I am dying!—dying!"

"Well, what can be done?" inquired Henry, turning round; "she ought to be taken somewhere,"

"To the hospital."

"Yes, that is the most proper place for aid; she is evidently dying from disease. We cannot aid her here at all; she must be carried away to the hospital; we had better get some men to carry her."

"No, no;—I'm dying!—I'm dying!" said the woman; "it's no use—it's no use moving me, I am dying!—I cannot recover! Ah! I would I could see one whom I have so much injured."

"Where do you come from ?"

The unfortunate woman gasped for a moment, or tried as if to get breath and speak, and then she mentioned the name of the village from which they had all come from.

"Good Heaven!" said Jem, the ostler,

as he stepped forward, "'tis the strange and mysterious woman that lived in the cottage in the village. How, in the name of Heaven, came you up here?"

"Here!" echoed the woman, "here!—Oh, God! I came to find one who is no longer to be found;—but how came you here, Jem?—is it, indeed, you?"

"Yes; and that is Captain Morton, and this, Mr. Henry Morton, if you have anything to confess."

"I have much—I cannot die until I do so! My life is now ebbing, but yet I linger to tell the truths I have come to tell. I have sought him, and have not found him."

"Found who?" inquired Jem.

"My step-son."

There was a pause of some moments, as if each were considering what was best to be done, when Jem said—

"Where shall we take you—and what shall we do? You had better go to the hospital."

"Yes," said Captain Morton, "but after having taken her there, we must leave her, and then we shall not be able to ascertain what it is she is desirous of confessing to us."

"I will get something to give her," said Jem; "a little stimulant, or something of that sort; and then we can carry her into this house; it is close by."

"You had better seek the aid of a chemist—there is one over the way," said Henry Morton.

"I think we had better carry her over there," said Captain Morton, "for we can have the use of the surgery, I dare say, to sit and listen to her confession."

"Yes, yes," muttered the almost unconscious object of their attention; "put me anywhere, but be quick, and hear what I have to say. Let me say all, and then I can die. But now my head is like the hell you speak of—the whirl of phantoms that crowd my brain will drive me mad."

No more was said, but the whole party immediately lifted her up as gently as they could, and walked with her to the doctor's shop, on the other side of the way, into which they introduced themselves and the patient. The moment, however, the medical man put eyes upon her, he said, without hesitation.—

"I can do her no good, gentlemen—she had better go to the hospital; she is dying."

"She is," said Captain Morton; "but cannot you administer some little stimulant? She has something upon her mind which she wishes to confess; it may be of importance to some one."

'I do not like doing so, but it may revive her for a time," said the chemist; "and if there is any real utility in doing so, I will; though it may turn out the means of her going faster than she even is at this moment."

Then going to some bottles, he poured out some liquids, which he gave her, and, after which, her eye seemed to look brighter, and her pulsation quickened.

"I feel already better," she said; "I feel stronger. Oh! that my step-son were here, that I might do him justice!"

"Who?"

"My step-son; he whom I have so much injured—he who is now suffering undeserved poverty through my machinations—through my frauds—and all to serve one who is utterly worthless of my regard, and who has turned out ungrateful for all the sacrifices that I have made. He scorned my advice, and even raised his hand against me. He is worthless and abandoned; but could I expect other treatment? I ought not to have done so."

"Who was your step-son?"

"He was ——" replied the old woman. in an audible tone, that was heard by all present; and the eyes of all were turned upon Jem, whose eyes were fixed upon the form of the old woman in speechless amazement, and at length he said—

"It cannot be!—impossible!—you are not, you cannot be her whom I have looked upon as my bitterest enemy—the woman that my father took as a second wife!"

"What do I hear?" exclaimed the woman, starting up with an almost frightful energy; "you the son of ——?"

"I am."

"My step-son?"

"The same," said Jem; "but have you anything to say that concerns me? If so, say it at once; and let me know if Heaven has decreed that justice shall be done."

The old woman paused, and muttered unintelligibly to herself for some moments, and then, fixing her eyes upon Jem, she said—

"And is it he? I never saw the least trace—I never looked for it, and now I can see the likeness strong enough and plain enough. I must have been blind—idiotically blind; but no matter—it shall be done—he shall know all."

She again paused, as if to recollect something, and then she began again the thread of her narrative,—

"When I married your father you were to me a stumbling-block. I will confess the whole truth to you. It is my wish now to do justice. I cared not how soon you could be got rid of but took no steps or some time; but endeavoured to destroy your father's affection for you.

This was a difficult task, and I never entirely succeeded; but he became, for long periods, indifferent, and would willingly consent to my demands, so long as he enjoyed peace and quietness in return.

I got you away from home, and my own child took your place, and, in time, became acknowledged by all to be the heir of your father; in fact, you were utterly forgotten by all, and I question, then, if your father was hardly aware of the fact.

He never mentioned you for months at a time; save when you came home; and then, as there were words about it, he used to be glad when you were gone away again. He died while you were young, and he left, I found, a will, in your favour."

"In mine! it was as I suspected, then."

"It was; and a schedule of his property, as well as some other papers that would place you in instant possession of the property.

My first impulse was to destroy them; but I altered my mind; I carefully secreted them where I knew they were safe, and I determined that, come what would, I would retain them.

I wished my son to be the heir to all your father's property. I thought that if I could secure all that to him, I should for ever retain his gratitude, and should have an ample share, too; and should have, in fact, a splendid house, and the complete control of his house.

This was my ambition; but I little thought of the untoward disposition I should have to deal with in my son, who was as obstinate and self-willed, and who turned out as heartless as any child could possibly be to a mother.

He grew up reckless and untoward. I was constantly in fear, lest something or other should turn up to deprive me of my property, or rather that which I had possession of; and I urged him to settle himself—to get married into a wealthy family, as I was sure he could do so, for there were several young ladies of good fortune who would have had him.

This was an especially easy matter to him; for every one believed him to be the heir of large property, and he would have had no difficulty in thus securing himself for ever an independence, if not a handsome fortune, which he could have done.

Well, I thought all this was enough; but it only required one element, and that was willingness to do what I pointed out; but he was obdurate and obstinate.

I had not calculated upon his opposition; and, moreover, I had never anticipated his extreme extravagance; profligacy was a matter I had never anticipated; he seemed to have picked up all the profligate and low habits a man could pick up, with extravagance and a brutal disposition.

He hunted me for money; I administered to his wants, which I found were without end; and, in consequence, began to limit the supplies of money; then it was I found out his ingratitude—I then reaped what I had sown.

Money, money, was his constant cry; nothing but money was of any use to him; and that he spent in the worst debaucheries; he cared for nothing, and while the means lasted, for weeks together I should not see him at all.

At length I determined to make one effort more to save him from the infamy into which he was about to sink, and for that purpose I determined to appeal to his sense, and when he next sought me for money, I told him the whole truth—that he was entitled to a bare subsistence, and that one day or other he would be deprived of even that.

"Why not," said I, "endeavour to secure yourself from the destruction which is more imminent in your case than you seem to imagine possible? I tell you what it is—if you do not reform and obtain the hand of some one in marriage, you are lost."

I shall never forget his look as he spoke to me.

"Fool," he said, "give me all the deeds, and I'll raise more money than you can get in twenty years. I'll have some signature that shall make them all right. I will live a roaring life; and, as to marriage, I dare say I shall——No, no; I'll not tether myself to a log, because other people do so, I assure you."

I refused to give him the papers.

"You will not give them to me?" he said, bending a look of fury at me.

"I cannot," I replied.

I had scarcely uttered the words, when he struck me down with a blow that laid me insensible.

When I recovered from my insensibility, I found myself covered with blood. I wrung my hands with sorrow and in tears.

"This, then," I said, "is the reward of my crimes; I have deserved it, but he shall not go unpunished; he shall be stripped of all that I have heaped upon him; I will do an act of justice."

My repentance was bitter and sincere, and I resolved that I would spend my time in finding out my step-son, and restore to him what I had so unjustly detained from him. I would return to him his father's inheritance.

I did attempt to find you, but I could not succeed; and then, my passion cooling against my son, I determined to hide myself from him altogether, and give him a chance of repentance and amendment; in the course of years he might do so. I should, at any time, have it in my power to restore the deeds by a dying declaration, which I was resolved I would make, if my son showed any signs of amendment.

I was compelled to hide myself from him; for, could he have found me out, he would have gone the length of murder to compel me to give him money, so that I feared him.

After some time, I found my way to this place, where you found me; and I came here to make some attempt to discover you; but my end was approaching, and I could do no more; but should have sunk in the open streets, but for this providential meeting."

"Where are the documents?" inquiried the captain.

"Here," answered the old woman, as she presented a small packet, sealed up, to her step-son; "here they are; he for whom I have done so much is unworthy."

"But," said Jem, "you showed me a child under the floor of the cottage. You have never explained."

"Oh, my God! my God! name not that now. I have been guilty enough; but the addition of a crime of a still heavier character——"

"It can be no lighter by concealment, now," returned the captain. "You had better confess the whole truth, and thus make a clean breast of it at once."

"That child was my own!"

"Your own!"

"Yes, my own," repeated the old woman, in almost a scream; "and I murdered it. Yes, yes—I—I—I!"

"Good God!" exclaimed Henry Morton, starting back; "she is going mad. What an unfortunate creature she is."

"Unfortunate! who calls me unfortunate? I am a hateful criminal," she uttered in a wild tone, and then paused.

"That child," she said, after she had somewhat abated in her terror and excitment; "that child I had before I was married to your father, but not very long—a twelvemonth."

"You had a child before my father married you?"

"I had."

"Heavens! but he knew it not?" said the late ostler.

"No, no, he knew it not; but I murdered it—ay, I murdered it, because he should never know it; for I had had my eye upon him, and had made up my mind that I would be his wife; therefore I murdered the child, and fearing to put it anywhere or bury it I had it always about me—that is to say, concealed somewhere in the house."

"That child was somewhere in the house with my father?"

"The whole time he lived. I had it under the attic stairs, and I wished to have it buried; but yet feared to do so, lest it should cause a discovery in consequence."

The old woman had been speaking very quickly—she appeared to speak in a hurry, as though she had but a little time to say much in. Suddenly, however, she stopped, gave a convulsive struggle or two, and made one or two ineffectual attempts to speak, but could utter no articulate sound, but fell back in the chair—the rattles were loud in her throat, and in a minute she was no more.

"She is dead," said the chemist. "I did not think she would have gone off so suddenly."

"Nor I; but what can be done with her now she is dead?"

"Send her to the workhouse."

"Will you send a messenger? I will pay all expenses," said Captain Morton, "you may be put to. There is my card."

"Very well, sir," said the chemist, who immediately sent his assistant to the nearest workhouse for people to come and fetch her away.

Captain Morton and his brother Henry, in company with the late ostler, Jem, left the chemist's shop, with food for contemplation sufficient for the present, as well as for congratulation for the recovery of the papers which were of so much importance to the latter, and which he had before so distant a chance of ever recovering, and that alone made the tenure of his fortune so insecure.

"It is a fortunate occurrence," said Captain Morton, "for you and for the old woman; for had she not died as she did, I don't see what kind of death or end she could have hoped for; it is far better as it is."

## CHAPTER XCI.

THE TRIAL OF THE MENDICANT, AND HIS CONDEMNATION FOR THE MURDER AT THE VILLAGE.

AND now the day on which the trial of Sternholde—as we may continue to call him, since he has been so particularly well identified as that atrocious character—came, and the most intense interest was excited amongst all classes of society, to hear what should transpire concerning one, whose name, at one time or another, had been heard by every English officer who had been engaged in the great continental campaigns, which terminated at the battle of Waterloo.

Of course, the newspapers had been from the first day of the apprehension of Sternholde busy in catering for the amusement of their readers, by finding out particulars, and additional particulars, of the life and adventures of a man, who, from a feeling of private revenge, had, no doubt, committed a greater amount of absolute cold-blooded murders, than any other human being actually in existence.

His conduct, since his committal to prison, had been gloomy and taciturn, except when he fancied he was observed, and then he was seen occasionally to smile to himself, while a bitter and spiteful expression would cross his countenance, as if he yet should be able to do something to inflict more pain and anguish upon those whom he had already doomed to so much.

The chaplain of the prison being a busy-body, and not able to keep anything to himself as he ought to have done, took upon him to communicate to Sternholde the death of old Monsieur Rouselli, which produced from the prisoner a bitter and exulting laugh, as he said,—

" Yes, I know it; I had made up my mind that the Rousellis should not outlive me, and I hope that not one of the race will do so."

" You forget that the young lady whom they call Mabel," urged the chaplain, " is a Rouselli, and you may depend that Heaven has in store for her many blessings yet."

" Amen!" said Sternholde, mockingly, " she shall have my benediction, holy sir, yet, before I leave this world, I assure you."

The chaplain could make nothing of him. When he fancied that he had been quietly listening to some religious dogmas which he wished to impress upon his mind, he was off in a tangent, talking of some other object, or adopted suddenly the gloomy taciturn aspect which was most habitual to him, and would not utter one word upon the subject whatever.

On the morning of the trial, he appeared anxious and excited, muttering to himself something continually, which they could not make out, although they made great efforts so to do. He scarcely ate anything; and to the efforts of the chaplain to get him into a serene state of mind, he replied now by downright rudeness.

" Away! away!" he said, " I have something more to think about, and cannot be troubled by muddle-headed priests. Go—go at once! I want no more of your exhortations. I believe in nothing, and, therefore, all that you say falls on an idle ear."

It was a most uncomfortable thought for poor Mabel, that she would have to come into a court of justice, and confront Sternholde. But she was told that it could not be avoided; for although what he was placed upon his trial for was the murder of the young traveller at the inn, of which she knew nothing, yet it was considered desirable she should identify the prisoner as the man who had been evidently lurking about the neighbourhood, and who had stopped her in the plantation close to the lake near Morton Hall.

This evidence, combined with that of Brolickbones, and that of the late ostler, and last, although far from least, that of sleepy and Troubled Tom, it was considered, formed a circumstantial presumption of the guilt of Sternholde, which would be extremely difficult for him to get over.

The avenues to the court were crowded to the greatest excess some hours before the trial took place, so much so, indeed, that it was only by the assistance of the police, and they had to make the greatest possible exertions to accomplish so much, that Captain Morton and his little party could find a way into the body of the court.

However, they did at last accomplish that much, and were admitted at once, before the dense body of persons who were without obtained liberty to attempt an entrance.

All persons who know anything of our criminal courts in London, are well aware that they are small and inconvenient, and many are the complaints arising from such causes; but few people are aware that they are constructed so on purpose.

Yet such is unquestionably the fact. The object is to discourage the courts of law being infested by persons, who come there merely to pass the time, and in a criminal court, where order is absolutely necessary, it would in a large expanse be difficult to obtain it.

The consequence, however, of this arrangement, on the occasion of the trial of Sternholde, was that not one-tenth portion of those who had gone with a hope of being present at the proceedings could obtain an entrance to the court.

It was filled completely, notwithstanding all the efforts of the door-keepers, in the course of a few moments, and then the people who were within shut and barred the doors themselves against the pressure from without, exerted by their less fortunate brethren.

The judge had not yet taken his seat, so that there was not such an amount of silence and order insisted upon as would be when he had done so, and it partook something of the ludicrous, to look down from some place of security, and witness the frantic struggles of the people to pack themselves up, as it were, into a smaller compass than their anatomy rendered at all possible.

Let people do what they will, a certain number of them will occupy a certain amount of space, and the struggle was an unavailing one, although productive of no small share of inconvenience to those who engaged in it.

The ushers became mere nonentities on the occasion. They were, themselves, so wedged in the crowd, that they felt their occupation was gone; and even the pompous individual, who now, at the Central Criminal Court, has his hair so elaborately curled to enable him to cry Hush! silence! with more dignity, would have been pushed about, no doubt, to his great horror, just the same as any ordinary mortal, which he evidently considers he is not.

But when the judge, and one of the Court of Aldermen, and a sheriff took their seats on the bench, some effort was made to preserve composure among the multitude, and the judge censured the officers of the court for allowing so many persons to come in, although he said "he did not like to order any one out again who was quiet, for fear of making invidious distinctions."

"Please, my lord, we could not help it," said one.

"That's nothing to me," remarked the judge. "It's your duty to help it, and whether you could or not is quite another matter."

The officer was forced to be contented with this piece of logic, since it came from the bench, and he would have bowed, but there was not room enough to execute so courteous a feat. It was completely out of the question, and he could only stare and look very hot and indignant.

A number of prisoners were placed at the bar, and pleaded to different indictments; after which, the name of Sternholde was mentioned.

At this there was an unusual movement of curiosity among the people; that is to say, as well as they could, considering that they were so wedged together, they all turned their heads towards the dock to get a sight of the malefactor

In about a minute he made his appearance, and the sinister aspect of his countenance struck every one present. He had all the stern, dogged looks of a man whom one would just suppose to be capable of almost any crime.

He advanced, with a firm step, towards the front of the bar, and then, sweeping off, with an impetuous gesture, some of the herbs which were there placed before him, he glanced fearlessly about him. His dress was plain, but somehow, during his imprisonment, he had contrived to attire himself well enough; and he had got rid of much of the abundance of hair which used to disfigure his visage, so that, with the exception of a large pair of moustachios, he presented no striking peculiarity of appearance beyond that of a man with a very forbidding expression of face.

The formalities of the court, as regards the reading of the indictment, &c. against the prisoner, we must not at all trouble our readers with.

Suffice it that he was arraigned for the murder of the young traveller at the Morton Arms, and that when asked to plead, he said, in a loud, clear voice,—

"Not guilty."

Then, and not till then, he looked to where the Mortons were all seated, and his countenance changed a little when his eye met Mabel's. Probably he did not expect that her presence would have been at all necessary, but certain it is, that the sight of her was the first circumstance that seemed at all capable of moving him. He avoided, after that one glance, which let him know where she was sitting in the court, looking in that direction, but, with a moody appearance, he leaned upon the bar in front of him.

The prosecuting counsel rose.

"My lord," he said, "and you, gentlemen of the jury,—

"The statement which it is my painful duty to make to you this day, will, I am inclined to believe, be as decisive as it will be short. The prisoner at the bar can be identified as a man of the name of Sternholde, a Prussian by birth, and one who, from a train of peculiar circumstances, it will be shown to you was just the very individual to commit the crime which is laid to his charge.

"It is necessary that I should briefly, in order that you should be able to come to a just decision upon this most singular and mysterious case, relate to you some circumstances which occurred a considerable time since.

"From feelings of jealousy, the prisoner Sternholde vowed vengeance, somewhere about the year 1812, against a colonel in the French army, named Rouselli, and it appears, all of which, if necessary, I can prove to you in evidence, that he made several attempts upon Colonel Rouselli's life.

"But not only did he conceive this mortal hatred against Colonel Rouselli, gentlemen of the jury, but, by some most diabolical obliquity of intellect, he carried it out towards all Frenchmen, because one had injured him; and the dastardly and cowardly manner in which he conducted his revenge, was to follow the French army during the continental campaigns, and, after an engagement, slaughter the wounded.

"Yes, gentlemen of the jury, that was the dreadful, and detestable as dreadful, occupation of the prisoner at the bar. He has been so repeatedly seen by wounded men on the field of slaughter, who have only escaped him by feigning to be actually dead, that he got the name of the 'Battle Fiend,' and many of the soldiers considered him as something more than mortal.

"It so happened that the battle of Waterloo, as you all know, put an end to the long war, which for so many years, with so little intermission, had raged on the continent; and, after that contest, the occupation of the assassin was gone.

"At that battle Colonel Rouselli received a mortal wound. His wife sought him on the battle-field, with an infant in her arms; she fainted, and he, believing her dead, crawled some short distance to where he had heard an English officer speaking, and solemnly entrusted the child to his keeping. There can be no doubt then, whatever, but that Colonel Rouselli died of his wounds.

"The English officer was a Captain Morton, and he at once accepted the trust reposed in him, and, like an honourable man, fulfilled it to the very letter, as well as to the spirit. He brought the child to England with him, and in all respects educated it, and had it tended as if it had been one of his own."

"Faith, then," cried Rafferty, when the counsel had got this far, "faith, then, you are right there, any way, and the devil a word of a lie. You can go on now, sir, and it's a mighty illigant speech you are making."

"Who is that?" said the judge.

"Is it me you mane, sir? I'm Rafferty Brolickbones, and saw it with my own eyes, sir."

"If you cannot be quiet, Mr. Brolickbones, I shall be under the necessity of having you turned out of court."

"Si—lence!" said the crier.

"Hold your tongue, then," said Rafferty. "Who's spaking, I'd like to know, but yourself? I only said ——"

"Be quiet," whispered Captain Morton. "How dare you interrupt the court, Rafferty?"

"Oh, bedad; I don't want to interrupt the court. You may go on, all of you."

"Gentlemen of the jury," continued the counsel, taking no notice whatever of Rafferty's interruption, "the family of Colonel Rouselli had no difficulty in hearing of his death on the field of battle, but, to them, the fate of his wife and child was an impenetrable mystery. Captain Morton had no means of knowing that the child had any friends more attached to it than he became himself, and so years passed on, until this infant, which had been committed to his care at that dreadful field of slaughter, became a beautiful girl, admired and beloved by all who knew her."

"Right again," muttered Rafferty.

"She resided at Morton Hall, with the family of Captain Morton, a residence which is in the immediate vicinity of the village of Morton, which was the scene of the murder which we have this day met to investigate.

"On the evening immediately preceding the night on which the murder at the Morton Arms was committed, a man, travel worn, and meanly looking, and attired in rags, presenting all the appearance of being wretchedly poor, made his appearance at the Morton Arms.

"Neither his looks nor his manners were relished by the landlord; and he was told to take himself away, which, however, he did not do, until he had made an attempt to steal the saddle of the stranger's horse, who was murdered that night at the inn.

"This man, I have witnesses who can swear to you, was the prisoner at the bar.

"The gentleman who put up at the inn that night asked some questions of the landlord concerning the Morton family, and although, then, he and his object were alike unknown, it has been since ascertained that he was sent by the Rouselli family, on a mission to endeavour to discover the lost child of Colonel Rouselli, who they at length heard was taken care of by an English officer, of the name of Morton, or something resembling that name.

"Gentlemen of the jury, this young emissary of the Rouselli family was brutally murdered that night at the inn, and, by a combination of circumstances, which have since been all explained, consistently with innocence, the ostler at the Morton Arms was, at first, suspected of the murder; and it was clear that the actual criminal took some pains to shift the onus of his guilt on to the shoulders of an innocent man, a proceeding always received with the greatest abhorrence and detestation by every Englishman who deserves the title.

"An investigation took place, ending in the exculpation of the falsely accused man, and the expression of a determination, upon his part, to leave no spot unsearched for the real author of the murder, who, it was strongly suspected, was still lurking in the neighbourhood.

"Several times did this ostler of the inn catch a sight of the man, so that he was in a condition to swear to his identity with the prisoner at the bar, whose object, in the commission of that cold-blooded and diabolical murder, seems to have been to possess himself of the documents which the young stranger had with him—documents which proved the name and paternity of Mabel Morton, as she was then called, but whose real name was Mabel Rouselli.

"Then, gentlemen of the jury, the young lady herself, Mabel Rouselli, was accosted by this very man in a kind of wood which skirts the estate of Captain Morton, and is, consequently, likewise able to swear that about that time he was there. She was only saved from some rudeness on his part by the courage of a dog.

"Then, again, as showing to you, gentlemen, clearly that the game this fellow was playing was to get either possession of Mabel Rouselli, or a large sum of money from Captain Morton, to be allowed to retain her, he actually had the unparalleled assurance to go to Morton Hall, procure an interview with the captain, and offer by the production of the documents he had committed a murder to possess himself of, that he was the father of Mabel.

"On that occasion he made his escape, although the captain, of course, made an effort to detain him, and then, finding that he could not extort money so easily as he imagined, he adopted the plan of awakening in the mind of the young lady herself all that natural desire which she was sure to feel, to know really who and what she was, and he prevailed upon her to meet him, on the pretext that he could, and would, reveal to her such information.

"That unhappy meeting, through a train of circumstances which I need not detail to you, ended in this young and beautiful girl being carried off by the villain Stern-holde and a comrade of his, whom there is every reason to believe he afterwards murdered, in consequence of finding him troublesome.

"From that time, nothing was heard of him for a considerable period, and the affair of the murder remained without any further elucidation, because no tidings could be got, either of who the murdered man was, or of his supposed murderer.

"It has, however, been since ascertained that his name was Adolphe Ford, and the man at the bar of this court stands accused of his murder, a charge which it is now my duty to bring witnesses forward to substantiate."

The counsel sat down, and. after a slight pause, he directed that our old friend, the landlord of the Morton Arms, should be called, and he accordingly, after some struggling to get out of the crowd, into which he was fast wedged, made his appearance in the witness-box, looking much as he did when last presented to the reader.

"You are the landlord of the Morton Arms?" said the counsel.

"Yes, sir, I were, and, in a manner of speaking, my lord, and gentlemen of the jury, at this here blessed moment, I may take upon myself all for to say that, leastways ——"

"Good God, when are you going to stop?" cried the counsel. "Will you be so good as to answer plain yes, or no, to the questions which I shall put to you?"

"Well, then, as I was saying ——"

"Witness," said the judge, "pray understand me. I shall be under the disagreeable necessity of at once committing you to prison, if you do not answer, in a plain and straightforward manner, the questions which counsel may consider it to be their duty to put to you. Do you comprehend that?"

"Why, yes, my lord, I ——"

"There, that will do."

"Do you remember what guests you had," continued the counsel, "at the Morton Arms, on the day named in the indictment?"

"Oh, dear, yes."

"Now, really, could you not say yes, without prefacing it with ' oh, dear?'"

"Oh, bless you, certainly."

"The witness is incorrigible," said the judge. "I see no plan but that of letting him have his own way."

'State, then, who you had as a visitor at the Morton Arms, on the night in question."

"Towards evening, there came as ill a looking fellow as ever I saw, and wanted something to drink. He was about as saucy as he could be, because I did not half like to serve him."

"Very well. Now look at the prisoner at the bar, and, upon your oath, tell the jury if that is the person, or not, to whom you allude."

The landlord had no doubt in the world that Sternholde was the man, but he considered that, under the circumstances, it would be very wrong of him to say so all at once, so he turned and looked at him fixedly, as if only then he had seen him for the first time; and then he shaded his eyes with his hands, and shook his head cunningly, from side to side, as he said—

"In course; in course."

"What do you mean, witness?"

"That's the man."

"You swear that to be the man who came to the Morton Arms on the same night that the young traveller was murdered?"

"Oh, yes, of course I do. I should know him among a thousand. He left, as I thought, and then I saw him again. When the young gentleman came on horseback, he wanted to carry the saddle somehow for him, but he was prevented, and then he had a sort of a row with Ostler Jem."

"Did you have any conversation with the young traveller?"

"Lord, yes. He told me he had come a long way, and asked me who lived in the neighbourhood; and when I told him about the Mortons, he seemed quite pleased, as if he had heard of them before."

"And that night this gentleman was murdered in the house?"

"Yes, he was; all the world knew that. There was lots of beer drank afterwards. I was nearly murdered first of all, because I had too much beer; and then I was nearly murdered because I had too little. But mind you, Jem, though he was took up, no more did the murder than I did; I can tell you that."

"I have done with you; your recognition of the prisoner at the bar as the man who made himself officious about the stranger's saddle, is quite sufficient."

"Thank you, sir; if ever you come our way, I ——"

"Will you attend to me, sir?" roared the counsel for the defence, who was a bully of the first water, and bent upon confusing the witness by violence of manner. "Will you attend to me, sir?"

"Yes; I cannot help it, and should say, by your bellowing out so loud, that all the parish is forced to attend to you."

There was a laugh, in which the judge himself could hardly refrain from joining. Indeed, his lordship had to make up a very curious face, and pretend to cough a number of times before he could recover his composure.

"Come, come," said the counsel; "we don't want any of your remarks. Now, answer us, sir. Do any beggars come begging to the Morton Arms?"

"I should think so; of course they do."

"Will you swear, that in twelve months as many as one hundred beggars come to the Morton Arms?"

"Well, perhaps there may; that's only two a-week."

"Will you swear that two a-day do not come?"

"No, I won't."

"No, you won't! And you wo'nt swear that upon an average four a-day do not come, or five a-day, or six a-day. Eh—eh—eh?"

"Well, I won't. They come in a gang sometimes."

"And yet you deliberately come here, and pretend that out of 2190 beggars, you can point out one, and swear to him after a considerable lapse of time."

"What! I never saw so many beggars in all my life."

"Why, you will not swear that six a-day do not come?—and six a-day amount in twelve months to the number I have stated."

"Oh, bother! I never knew such a fool as you are, in all my life. Why, one would think you want 2000 beggars all at once. I tell you that's the man, and it's no use your putting yourself in a pet about it."

"The jury will see what the testimony of this witness is worth. He has completely failed in identifying the prisoner, as the intelligent jury will perceive in a moment."

"I haven't done no such thing."

"You have, sir," roared the counsel, "Go down directly."

"Oh, go down yourself—d——d fool!"

There was another laugh, and the crier called the ostler, who deposed to having had a fracas with the prisoner at the bar, whom he recognised at once. He likewise fully identified him as the man he had tried in vain to capture in the church-yard.

This witness's evidence was given in so straightforward a manner, that the counsel for the defence did not endeavour to shake it further than by saying—

"You were, yourself, accused of the murder of the young traveller at the inn, I believe?"

"I was so."

"And you feel still that, in the minds of some persons, your character may suffer, unless the deed be brought home to another?"

"It is possible."

"You will see, gentlemen of the jury, that this witness is largely interested in procuring a conviction of the prisoner at the bar. You may go down."

"Before I go down," said the quondam ostler, "no power on earth shall prevent me from hurling back in your teeth with indignation, the base assumption you have given utterance to. The man who, like you, for a few paltry guineas will come forward with all the wicked effrontery of which his nature is capable, to oppress the innocent and screen the guilty, is alone capable of giving utterance to such a diabolical falsehood."

"Go down, witness," said the judge; "the court cannot listen to such remarks."

But the court had listened, and a buzz of applause greeted the ostler as he stepped from the witness-box.

The next witness called was our old friend, Troubled Tom, and in vain was his name shouted by the crier within the court, and the officers without it. He could not be found, and the counsel for the prosecution looked about him despairingly, until he received a note from the ostler, and after perusing it, he said—

"If there be any one asleep in any corner of the court, it is probably the witness, who has a great aptitude to pass away his time in that way."

"Please, here's a boy in this corner has been leaning on my back, and snoring for this half hour," said a voice.

"That's our man," said the counsel.

With some difficulty, Troubled Tom was aroused to the necessity of putting in an appearance in the witness-box; and, when he got there, he rubbed his eyes and winked a great many times before he was awake enough to know what he was about.

"Now," said the counsel for the prosecution, "do you know where you are, my man? I ask you, because I wish the jury to be convinced that you are wide awake."

"Oh, ah! it's a good deal of trouble."

"Very likely; but do you know where you are, and what you came about?"

"I should think so. In the piggery at the Morton Arms, and I comes to have a jolly good snooze; but, somehow, nobody will let me sleep at all, that's a fact. I haven't had a good sleep never."

"Come, come; you have been brought to London to give evidence, and have just taken an oath that what you shall say shall be the truth, and nothing but the truth. Do you remember, on the night named in the indictment, being in the farmyard at the back of the Morton Arms?"

"I believe you. How should you like your stomach trod upon?"

"Stop a bit; we shall come to that in due time. What time did you go there?"

"Oh! I felt a little sleepy, cos I hadn't had anything like a rest for ever so long; people is always, somehow or another, disturbing o' me, so just about dark, I thought I'd go there, and have a little sleep."

"What happened to you?"

"Why, somebody put his foot on the outside o' my inside, and that rather waked me up, you see. Then I seed a jolly row."

"Should you know the person again?"

"Oh! yes; I never forgets nobody—not I. I should know him—a ugly fellow with a knife in his hand."

"Look at the prisoner at the bar, and tell the jury if that is the man."

Troubled Tom looked, and then nodded his head as he said,—

"Oh! they've caught you, have they? It sarves you right; I'm glad they've caught you. You won't tread on people's outsides again when they is trying all for to get a wink o' sleep. You know you killed the young man while he was trying to get a wink o' sleep, and you killed the dog 'cos he was a-trying to rest himself a little. I wouldn't trust a man with a bad farden as was a enemy to sleeping,—that I wouldn't. Oh, Lor! what a trouble all this here is, to be sure!"

"You can swear, then, distinctly that the prisoner at the bar is the man who aroused you from your sleep on the night in question?"

"I believe you; only ask him. He knows it well enough. Ask him: he can't deny it. Only look at him. Ain't he jolly ugly?"

"You gave evidence, I believe, before the local magistracy upon this subject?"

"Yes; oh! yes. Isn't that all? I am so precious sleepy, I am. Hav'n't you

done? You know he did it; what's the use o' bothering any more about it? Oh! dear, what a trouble."

"I'm afraid my learned friend for the defence will trouble you more than I have. I have no more questions to ask you."

"Well, sir," said the counsel for the defence; "don't you think sleep one of the finest things in the world?"

"Of course I do. Any fool knows that."

"But I suppose, now, you dream something, eh? I do,—all sorts of comical dreams.

"Ah! ah! so don't I."

"You don't? You mean to tell me you don't dream?"

"No, I couldn't think of taking so much trouble, all for nothing. You may dream, though, if you like. My not liking it ain't no rule, you know."

"Come—come; now you are only joking. You do dream sometimes. You know we all dream occasionally. Why, no human being sleeps always without dreaming."

"I ain't going to argufy with you. It's too much trouble. Besides, you seem rather a stupid-head, you do."

"On your oath, sir," cried the counsel, in a loud tone. "On your oath, were you asleep or awake on the night in question, when you say you saw the prisoner at the bar?"

"I didn't see the prisoner at the bar."

"You did not?"

"No; I seed him in the piggery at the Morton Arms."

"Come—come; don't prevaricate, sir. On your oath, I say, were you awake or asleep?"

"Neither."

"Oh! neither. Come—come, I thought we should have it. You hear, gentlemen of the jury, that the witness upon whom the prosecution most relies admits that he was neither asleep nor awake."

"What a crammer you are telling!" said Tom. "You wouldn't let me go on. You asked me if I was asleep or awake upon my oath, and I said neither, 'cos I wasn't on my oath at all, but on a blessed bundle of straw! I tell you I seed him, so don't bother any more. You don't know what to say, so you'd better go to sleep, and let me go to sleep, too."

"You have been well tutored, I presume. I am inclined to think that you are more knave than fool."

"Well, I don't think you is; for I never come a-nigh such a jolly old hass in all my life. What do you want? Haven't I told you I seed him? haven't I told you he trod scrunch on my blessed stomach?

haven't I told you he had the knife? Bother you! can't you make yourself comfortable, and go to sleep like a Christian, and let other Christians do so as well?"

The counsel saw that nothing whatever was to be made of Troubled Tom, and thought that the best part of valour was discretion, so he sat down, amid the stifled laughter of every one in court.

The further progress of the trial consisted in the production of papers found upon the person of Sternholde, which were of such a nature as proved they must have belonged to the young traveller at the inn. They related to the history of Colonel Rouselli, and contained the written instructions of the old Monsieur Rouselli, in order to enable his young relative to trace out the abode of Mabel.

These, no doubt, were the papers that incited Sternholde to do the deed of blood with which he stood that day charged. His intentions had been to harass the Morton family by his claim of relationship, in the new capacity of father, to Mabel, but, finding that he was not listened to, he had altered his tactics, and obtained possession of her, as we know, by the aid of the confederate, whom he afterwards murdered.

Thus a train of circumstantial evidence against him was produced, which was as perfect as any case depending upon circumstantial evidence could be, and every one felt, when the counsel for the defence rose, that he would, indeed, have a difficult task to perform if he thought he could do away with the strong impression of Sternholde's guilt, which was in the minds of the jury.

The whole conduct of the prisoner was incompatible with an idea of innocence, and it would be a matter of impossibility to strain the circumstances that had been sworn to into a presumption otherwise than unfavourable to him.

But still, difficult as was the task, counsel was bound to essay it, and, accordingly, with an assumption of confidence and cheerfulness which only deceives the most ignorant of spectators of legal proceedings, the already much discomfited counsel for the defence rose to speak in favour of Sternholde, the murderer,

Perhaps curiosity to know what he would say as much influenced all present to preserve the death-like stillness that they did, as any other feeling; for upon the real question, as regarded the guilt or innocence of the prisoner, no unprejudiced mind entertained a doubt.

The learned person seemed fully aware of the bad impression he had created by the utter failure of the cross-examination to which he had subjected the witness for the prosecution, and his first efforts were evidently devoted to the task of doing away as much as he could with that unfavourable impression.

"My lord, and gentlemen of the jury," he commenced, "I cannot but be aware that there are great difficulties in the way of an advocate, who rises to defend an individual so painfully situated as is the prisoner now at the bar.

"I am fully aware, gentlemen, of how strong a circumstantial case has been made out against the man who awaits, at your hand, that decision which shall restore himself to the world, or withdraw him for ever from it by means of a dreadful and violent death. But, gentlemen of the jury, it has been held as a principle by our most correct legal authorities, that the more conclusive a case of circumstantial evidence against a man may be, the more careful should we be in arriving at a decision, in order to discover if some of the circumstances, which appear to make out so excellent a case, be not accidental.

"It must be borne in mind that the history of criminal jurisprudence in this country furnishes us with some most dreadful and most melancholy examples of innocent persons being condemned, because some one accidental circumstance has appeared to connect together a host of others, which, without that one, would be but disjointed and inconclusive.

"This, gentlemen of the jury, is the case of my client, who does not attempt to deny that a murder was committed on the night in question, at the Morton Arms. We do not attempt, for one half moment, to deny that that murder was a cold-blooded and an atrocious deed, but what we do deny is, that the prisoner at the bar was the perpetrator of it.

"Gentlemen, far be it from me to hint, for one moment, that any of the witnesses for the prosecution are foresworn. No, gentlemen, I do believe, and I have great pleasure from the fact that I am able to believe so, that those witnesses have stated what they think was the truth.

"But we know well how fallible is human judgment; we know how amongst the most devoted persons, how amongst persons of the most pious and the most logical intellects, differences will arise with regard to the most simple facts.

"Gentlemen, my client, the prisoner at the bar, is mistaken for another. He is mistaken for another who was, at the time of the murder, very similarly attired to himself; and another, who, from the state of poverty to which he was reduced, and the state of rags which he exhibited, might very easily be mistaken for the prisoner at the bar, who was then in a similar condition.

"Now, my lord, and gentlemen of the jury, it is rather a remarkable circumstance, that the learned counsel for the defence has not thought proper to call a witness who could have proved that, in connection with all these circumstances that are related by the various witnesses, in order to fix guilt upon the prisoner at the bar, there was another individual who appeared, but who has not yet been mentioned.

"Now, gentlemen of the jury, I am quite sure I need not call your attention to the fact, that the character of the prisoner at the bar—that what he is, or what he is not, or what he has been, have nothing whatever to do with the charge, to answer which he this day appears before you.

"The simple question for your consideration is, and the only question is, did he, or did he not, commit this murder at the Morton Arms?

"The case, as no doubt the learned judge who sits on the bench will tell you, narrows itself, so that in the end we have no right, whatever, to take into our consideration, whether such and such a man was likely to commit such and such a crime. Did he do it? is the sole question for you. Have you such proof that he did it, that, without any doubt, you can conscientiously condemn him to death?

"Now, my lord, and gentlemen of the jury, I shall relate to you, without disguise or reservation, the real facts of this most unhappy case.

"The prisoner at the bar did, certainly, in early life, receive some of the most cruel and unprovoked injuries from the Rouselli family, that any man could receive. All the angry passions of a jealous man were aroused at the object of his fondest attachment being taken from him by a fop of a French officer, who then sneaked away without having the courage to give Sternholde that satisfaction to which he was entitled.

"Disappointed in all his expectations of happiness in this world, Sternholde did follow the French army, and possibly he may have fought against all Frenchmen, for it is no uncommon thing for a man to take a dislike to a whole nation, because some one individual belonging to it may have inflicted upon him some serious injury.

"Gentlemen of the jury, my client admits that he did arrive at the Morton Arms on the day named in the indictment. He admits that he came to that neighbourhood, to try and possess himself of Mabel Rouselli in order to better his fortunes by making terms with her friends for her restoration. Years had elapsed, and the revengeful feeling that he had at all times cherished was all gone. He was poor, and was not scrupulous as to the means of gaining a livehood.

"Well, gentlemen, he did recognise the young traveller at the inn as a messenger of the Rouselli family. He did, from the care which he saw that young traveller bestowed upon the saddle of his horse, suspect that it contained documents of importance, and he did, he has to me admitted, seek to possess himself of it.

"He failed, gentlemen of the jury, in doing so; and then after that failure he left the inn, and at that point his connexion with the whole of the circumstances that followed really ceased.

"He made the only attempt he chose to make, or considered it safe to make, to obtain possession of the documents, which he fully believed were in the possession of the young traveller at the Morton Arms. And so, gentlemen of the jury, the unhappy individual who now stands before you, accused of so very serious a crime, was actually making his way from the scene of that crime's commission, and would have escaped all the consequences of his present situation, but for an unfortunate accident over which he had no possible control.

"That accident, gentlemen of the jury, was the meeting with an old and valuable acquaintance, valued more on account of many scenes which they had passed together, than for any real merits which he, as an individual, might possess. To this man he stated frankly the circumstances in which he was placed, how he was most anxious to obtain possession of the papers which he knew to be in the possession of the young traveller, how he had failed to obtain possession of them by fair means, and how, disliking the adoption of foul ones, he was wandering away from the spot the same beggar he came to it.

"This, gentlemen of the jury, is the real state of the case, and such as I can pledge my professional reputation to you is the truth. This old acquaintance, however, whom the prisoner at the bar met, at once exclaimed against the folly of leaving such an enterprise unaccomplished. He told the prisoner at the bar that he could procure the papers for him—that he would do so without the commission of any violence, and that if he retraced his steps, and waited for him in the village churchyard, he would most assuredly bring to him the documents he wanted.

"Gentlemen of the jury, it is awful to contemplate such an amount of criminality for so poor an object; but there can be no doubt that this individual, not having the fear of retribution in this world, or in the next, before his eyes, did actually, and *de facto*, commit the murder with which the prisoner at the bar now stands charged.

"And now, gentlemen, I shall proceed to call to you the only witness who can prove to you that, engaged in these infamous transactions, there were two persons of similar appearance as regards costume, and outward appearance of absolute want. Two persons, either of whom might be mistaken for the other, by those who might not pay marked and particular attention to their appearance; and here, gentlemen, it unfortunately happens that the crime is of so serious a character, it is not likely, even if this acquaintance of the prisoner at the bar was in existence, he would come forward to take upon himself the punishment of death to screen another. We cannot expect, gentlemen of the jury, such heroism of virtue, and if we did, we should not get it, for the individual unfortunately is dead.

"Now, gentlemen of the jury, I consider that I have thrown sufficient doubt upon the guilt of the prisoner, to make you pause before you think of convicting him. You will reflect how truly dreadful a circumstance it would become to yourselves, if, in the course of years, such an amount of doubt was to arise in your minds concerning his guilt, as to make you regret your judgment against him, I call upon you to acquit the prisoner upon the ground that I have presented to you.

"I shall now proceed to call Mabel Rouselli, and you will bear in mind, that although that lady has it in her power to accuse the prisoner at the bar of another offence, namely, her abduction from those who had legal custody of her, that has nothing to do with the charge of murder now brought against him."

The counsel considered that this was a point, and so having had his say, like a man of discretion he sat down, leaving certainly behind him a sort of bewildering impression on the minds of the jury, that what he had said might be true, and, probably, a great dread of convicting an innocent man.

We before stated that Mabel had been subpœnaed on this trial by both sides, but that the counsel for the prosecution, considering that she could prove nothing but what he had it fully in his power to prove from other sources, declined harassing her by legal examination.

He had not the least idea, of course, of the nature of the defence to be set up; but still, if Mabel now were called, it gave him an opportunity, if he thought proper, of putting any questions to her, as well as of commenting upon her evidence.

"Courage, Mabel," whispered Captain Morton to her, as he felt her small hand tremble in his, when she heard the announcement that she was to be dragged forward to take part in the criminal proceedings. "Courage, dear Mabel; you can have no difficulty in stating that which you know, whether it work for or against the unhappy man at the bar."

"I will not shrink," she said, "I will not shrink—no one should under such circumstances; I will do my duty."

"That is no more than I expected from you," he returned, encouragingly. "Now, Mabel, now—you're expected."

The name of Mabel Rouselli resounded through the court, and when she stepped into the witness-box, and the oath was administered to her, her exquisite beauty attracted the attention of all who saw her.

She was pale—very pale for a few moments; but then, as her colour gradually returned, there was not a heart in court that did not feel a reluctance at the idea of one who was so young and so beautiful, having to go through so uncomfortable an ordeal.

"I will detain you," said the counsel, "Miss Rouselli, as short a time as possible; but it has become absolutely necessary, for the furtherance of the ends of public justice, that you should occupy the position you now do."

The counsel paused, as if expecting a reply; but Mabel merely inclined her head, and he then proceeded.

"Were you, at the period of the commission of the murder, which is now the subject of judicial investigation, at Morton Hall?"

"I was."

"And it was soon after that circumstance that the occurrence took place, which forced you from the care of Captain Morton and his family, to place you under the doubtful guardianship of others in whom you had no confidence—the prisoner at the bar, in fact, I believe, by a stratagem, took you from your home?"

"He did."

"Was he alone in that adventure? and, if not, will you explain, as nearly as you can, to the court and to the jury, the kind of associate or associates he had in it?"

"He had one associate—a desperate man, like himself, of strange appearance, and ruffianly manners."

"And this man, I presume, in costume, presented no flourishing appearance; in fact, I suppose he assimilated somewhat to the ragged aspect of the prisoner at the bar, when first you saw him?"

"He certainly did so."

"I have no further questions to ask of you; perhaps my learned friend for the prosecution may be anxious to say something."

"Not in the least," said the other counsel. "I'm quite content to let you assume all the advantage you can from this circumstance, and have no comment to make. The case is over, unless you have more witnesses to call."

"None—none—there must be an acquittal."

The judge proceeded now to sum up, and spoke nearly as follows:—

"The prisoner at the bar stands charged with wilful murder—the evidence against him is purely of a circumstantial nature. But where it happens that a positive crime has been committed, and it follows that it must have been committed by one of a certain number of persons, such a train of evidence as will fix it upon one of this number, although what may be called circumstantial, is quite admissible.

"It is proved by the prosecutor, and admitted by the defence, that the prisoner at the bar was at the Morton Arms on the evening of the murder. Witnesses likewise, whose testimony I do not see any circumstances to induce us to cast a reasonable doubt upon, swear unhesitatingly to the identity of the prisoner at the bar with the man who must have committed the deed, unless we can jump to the extravagant conclusion that some individual, not the prisoner at the bar, must have taken great pains to surround himself with all the insignia of guilt, yet, in reality being guiltless.

"The story of the counsel for the defence is uncorroborated, even in any of the minutest details, and I cannot see how the calling forward a witness to prove that the prisoner, Sternholde, was connected with another in the perpetration of a serious, but a minor offence, in any way invalidates the testimony which makes him guilty of a more serious and a major one.

"Gentlemen of the jury, I shall leave the case in your hands, merely saying, that if you have any rational doubt upon this question, regarding the guilt of the prisoner at the bar, that I am sure it will be your pleasure as much as it will be your duty, to give him the full benefit of such doubt; but, at the same time, gentlemen of the jury, if you feel that the defence set up says more for the ingenuity of counsel than for the majesty of truth—if you feel that such a story as is told by the learned gentleman who has so ably conducted the defence is entirely and totally without the corroboration of evidence, and that it would have been quite possible for that learned gentleman to have concocted that story with the assistance of the prisoner at the bar—it will be necessary for you, unflinchingly, to return a verdict of guilty.

"Gentlemen of the jury, with these few observations, I leave the case entirely to your decision."

This was so strong a summing-up against the prisoner, that no one in court could entertain any doubt as to the result; nothing but a pig-headed jury could save him.

There was that look upon the judge's face, too, when he had finished, which showed that he considered an awful duty would soon devolve upon him, and that he would be quickly obliged to condemn a fellow creature to a painful and an ignominious death.

The jury looked as solemn and stupid as juries usually do, and the fattest man, who was, of course, elected foreman, shook his head as if there were really anything in it.

They turned round in the box to consult, and during that brief period, the agitation of Sternholde was most excessive. He clutched the front of the bar till his finger-nails cracked again, and a death-like pallor overspread his countenance.

Then the jury turned round and looked more solemn than before, and the foreman having a great bald head, wiped it with a flaming yellow silk handkerchief, and looked very hard at the clerk of the arraigns, as he said—

"Gentlemen of the jury, have you decided upon your verdict? Do you find the prisoner at the bar guilty or not guilty?"

"Guilty."

Sternholde drew in his breath with a strange, rigorous sort of sound, and the judge put the black cap upon his head, briefly pronouncing sentence of death upon the unhappy man, whose career of crime seemed at last about to be brought to a close by his death upon a scaffold.

---

## CHAPTER XCII.

THE CONDEMNED CELL.—THE JESUIT.—THE FRUSTRATED ATTEMPT TO ESCAPE.

IN another half hour, Sternholde occupied one of the condemned cells of Newgate. The rapid alteration of adventure that had taken place, was now likely to be brought to an end by one of those awful catastrophes which terminate the career of all great criminals, however long may have been their career of crime; and few could boast of a much greater or longer career than the condemned man, nor none more deserving of his doom.

Sternholde sat dumb and motionless; he seemed stunned, and yet he was not the man to be bowed down by difficulties of any kind; danger of the most imminent character he had faced, and even then he was not the man to sink in weak repinings and tearful repentances; he could not do that.

He sat for some time thinking of the past, and revolving in his mind what prospect there was of escaping the doom that awaited him so very nearly. He sat, and his dark thoughts were revolving in his mind. He looked around the cell, and saw the bare walls and the small barred windows.

There was nothing in the whole place that gave any hope, and then he looked at his fetters, as if in utter despair at what seemed insurmountable difficulties.

Little hope, indeed, is to be derived from the appearance of the interior of the condemned cell; its name alone would bring a fearful thought or two to the mind.

The condemned cell! how many have there been who know all the horrors of death, by their acquaintance with the condemned cell! There he sat and pondered over the death that was soon to take place, as a fearful retribution of the past, and by far the greatest punishment that can be inflicted upon man.

Death is the end of such a state, and by no means the worst part of such a punishment; 'tis the contemplation of the means to the end that makes the thing so awful, so terrible; 'tis also the great uncertainty of the future that strikes terror into the soul of many a brave man—that unmans many.

Sternholde heard the steps of the gaoler as he neared the cell for some purpose or other. He doubted not but that he was coming there to him for the purpose of inquiring what he wanted.

He guessed rightly—it was the turnkey. He came to the door, and he could hear the key placed in the lock—the heavy bolts turned, and then the door opened softly upon its hinges, and the turnkey entered.

"Well," said the turnkey, " do you want anything?"

"Nothing," said Sternholde.

"I come to tell you our chaplain will be here in a few minutes to do what he can for you."

Sternholde took no notice of the communication whatever, but sat on the bench, with his eyes fixed upon the stone walls of his prison; and the turnkey, after a few moments, which he spent gazing at the prisoner, retraced his steps, muttering as he shut the door—

"He seems rather stunned—but that is nothing new, they are often so, and he is no exception. A St. Anthony's tippet don't agree with his courage or his constitution."

Sternholde, again left to himself, appeared to be no better or different than he was before. He still fixed his eyes upon the wall, and looked long and steadfastly there, but it was evident he saw nothing; his eyes was fixed, but his mind was far away and engaged on other matters; he was absent.

Again the lock turned, and the door opened. There were two persons this time, and one said—

"You'll find him there, sir."

An elderly man entered, and it was evident, from his gait, that he was a clergyman—the prison chaplain.

"My friend," said the clergyman, advancing towards Sternholde, "is there anything that I can do for you? your awful state requires some preparation. Permit me to give you such consolation as a man can receive, who stands upon the brink of eternity."

"I don't want any," said Sternholde.

"But consider the state of your immortal soul; the time is short in which you have to live, and short is the time in which you have to make your peace with Heaven."

"I am a Catholic."

"Cannot at this moment the distinction of creed be forgotten, and cannot you receive the consolation of the dying from the hand of a fellow Christian? The blessings of God flow upon all alike, Protestant as well as Catholic. Cannot ——"

"You can do nothing, sir. My creed forbids me to hold any religious communication with you, else I would; but if you would do me a favour—if you would afford religious consolation to a dying man, do it through one of my persuasion."

"What do you wish?" inquired the chaplain,

"A priest."

The chaplain paused a moment, and it seemed as if he considered in his own mind the possibility of effecting a change in the prisoner's mind; but apparently he considered the matter hopeless, for he said—

"I will send the governor to you, and to him you must make your request; you will have every facility given you for such a visitor, I am convinced."

"Thank you, sir; I am beholden to you."

"Nay, it is your right. I would I could have granted more, but your position binds my hands. Farewell! and may Heaven show you its mercy."

The chaplain left the cell, Sternholde was again alone, and then he resumed his former immovable position for some time. But in about half an hour's time, the cell door was once more opened, and on this occasion, the governor himself appeared.

"I come to see you," he said. "I understand you have a request to make respecting a confessor or priest."

"Yes," said Sternholde, ; "I am a Catho'ic, and, as such, if any religious consolation be afforded me, I can only receive it through the hands of a priest."

"I will obtain you a sheriff's order for his admission, since you desire it," said the governor; "that is the usual course."

"Whatever that may be," said Sternholde, "I shall be perfectly satisfied. I

THE OLD SEXTONESS DELIVERING THE TESTAMENTARY PAPERS TO THE OSTLER.

desire earnestly that I may have the consolation of confessing and receiving pardon, before I quit this life."

"Have you any priest in particular whom you desire to see?"

"I have."

"Then, when I bring the order to you, you must endorse it with his name, and then he shall be sent for."

"Thank you."

The governor then left the cell to execute his promise of obtaining the order, while

Sternholde himself now leaned back against the wall, and seemed to be meditating.

The time passed by slowly, and the monotony of the place was not broken by one sound. Not even the movement of an insect seemed to show that aught living was there. Even he who sat living and breathing showed no signs of life, save that he breathed, and not any other motion did he make.

There was as little time lost as possible by the governor in obtaining the order and when that was obtained, he went straight to the cell a second time to see the prisoner, to whom he showed the order, saying, as he did so,—

"There is the order; now write the name of your priest upon the back of it, and I will have it conveyed to him by a special messenger, so that no time may be lost."

"It is as I wished," said Sternholde, "and I am beholden to you. I wish to see Father Andrea Minto."

"Is he a Catholic priest?"

"He is. You will find him at the chapel in Queen-street, or at his lodgings in the neighbourhood—they will tell you where at the chapel. Will there be any difficulty now?"

"None."

"Then if you will allow the priest to have instant access to me, I shall be glad, for I have much to say and communicate to him."

"It shall be done," said the governor; "and anything you require compatible with the prison regulations, shall at once be awarded to you."

"I thank you again; your kindness will be remembered by me. I can but thank you."

The governor left the cell, and proceeded to send to Father Andrea Minto, and to inquire first if he were a priest or not; and when assured upon this point, the order was lodged in his hands, and he was informed that his aid was in immediate request.

The priest came and entered the cell. The day was fast declining, and the hour for clearing the prison was at hand; but the priest could not be affected by the general orders. He had the sheriff's order, which admitted him at all hours that the prisoner desired it, save at such hours as people are left asleep.

"My son," said the priest, "I have come at your sending, and do so willingly, to give you such consolation as the state of your soul may require, and be permitted by Heaven."

"You are a Jesuit, are you not?"

"I am an humble follower of the holy order of Jesus," said the priest; "but what of that, my son? Down upon your knees and confess your sins, that I may ——"

"Brother," said Sternholde, "I am a Jesuit, too."

"You?"

"I am—I am a Prussian; but have lived in all countries, and have travelled so much, and seen so much adventure in search of a certain object, that it may be difficult to fix my country; but that is the fact."

"And where were you educated?"

"In the Jesuit College at Gottingen. I was there received into the holy order, and made one of yourselves."

"Convince me of this."

"I will. At that time when I speak of, Father Gregory ruled the college, and he and some more proposed that so many of the order should have dispensations to throw off all their vows, save those which bound them to their order, so that they should mix in society the same as other men, to enable them to propogate the doctrines, and to increase the power and prosperity of the order."

"Good."

"Well, I am one of those monks. I have followed it forward; I have carried my way onwards; I have done what I could for the support of the order, even in military circles, where you know they had less power than anywhere else."

"I do know it, brother."

"And, moreover, I have been engaged in military affairs as well; and it is well known among the few at Gottingen that I have advanced the order in a manner that could not be done by other means; and, moreover, I have sown seeds that will in the future produce the more lasting results, because they are slower of growth, in the same manner that the hardest wood is longest of growth."

"True, brother—true: but I must hear some of the secret signs of our order before I can give my entire credence to what you say."

"You are hard of belief."

"It is the rule of our order not lightly to betray our confidence to any one; give me the word——"

"I will do more; incline your ear, for even stone walls of a condemned cell may not hear what I have to say."

The monk inclined his ear towards Sternholde, and the latter bowed towards him, and uttered some words, in a low tone, in his ear; he paused a moment, and then said something more. The monk started, and looked pale.

"Are you convinced?" inquired Sternholde.

"I am—I am—quite."

"I am your brother in the college, and you are bound by your vow to aid me in my great object; you see it is not yet completed. I call upon you to assist me."

"In what can I advantage you?"

"In providing me the means of escaping from this place. If I once get outside the walls, and unencumbered by these fetters, I will ensure you that I will get clear of them. I know this city too well."

"What do you require?"

"Saws and files,—the best, and most portable you can find."

"I will go and seek for them; you must make the best use you can of them. I will return, and see you again as soon as I can obtain them, and I know where I can obtain them."

"Then hasten, brother, hasten."

The Jesuit arose, and knocking for the turnkey, left the cell, after the other had seen it was all right, and then secured the prisoner.

"I shall be back again to visit him in an hour," said Father Andrea to the turnkey; "I have a dying penitent to whom I must pay some attention, for our people require our aid at such a time more than any other, for they are pleased to see the face of the priest at such moments; it is a sign that Heaven smiles upon them."

The turnkey said nothing, for he had nothing to say, merely to have expressed his notion of a catholic, which was that it was all sheer gammon—mere humbug.

The priest returned in less time than he had said, and was again conducted to the cell, and, when about to leave them, the turnkey said to him,—

"I will call you, sir, when the time is up."

"You may call me, and I will tell you if I can leave my penitent; if not, you must not disturb the confession of this man. I will tell you if we are ready—I will come; but woe to you if you disturb me in the performance of my ministry."

"Oh! bless my soul," said the turnkey; "nobody is a-going to disturb you; only I sha'n't be within call, and then you will not like to be left all night with the prisoner, I suppose?"

The priest entered the cell, and the door was opened and closed upon him, and when the footsteps of the turnkey were heard to die away, the whole scene was changed.

The priest was busily engaged in filing off the fetters of the prisoner, who held out his hand, while the other worked, with good will, to get them off. In less than ten minutes they were off.

"Now," said Sternholde, "my hands and feet are free."

"But how will you get out of this place?"

"Through that window. I will saw the bar, and, when that is done, I can get through anything that may interpose itself as a barrier."

"And, as to myself, I shall be detained?"

"You can seize him by the throat, and knock his brains out, before he can make any noise, or give any alarm, whatever;

and you have only to present yourself at the gates, and you will be permitted to go out at your pleasure."

"Yes, that will, indeed, be the case," said the priest; "therefore, hasten, and I will retard the discovery as much as I can."

There was no time for words; the mendicant, or, Sternholde, as we will call him, aided by the priest, soon removed the bars, and then he got through into a kind of narrow yard, near which was fixed a ladder. In an instant he ascended, and, after much danger, he got to the roof.

Workmen had been making repairs, and thus the ladder had been left, but it was believed in a secure position.

In the meantime, Sternholde had scarcely got out of the cell, before the turnkey came and knocked at the door, saying,—

"Time is up; are you ready, Mr. Andrea What's-your-name? are you ready to leave?"

"Not yet," replied the monk, who sat muttering some prayers, which the turnkey thought was giving absolution, and listening to catch the words, but, finding that he could not, he went away without having his curiosity gratified, and left Sternholde to escape, if he could.

He met with greater difficulties than he had anticipated, and more than once he gave it up as a bad job, and thought of returning, or of throwing himself from the summit, and thus put an end to the life struggle he was undergoing.

The turnkey came again and again, for the third time, when he became impatient, and entered the cell, and before he could express his surprise at the disappearance of the prisoner, he was seized by the throat, and then grappling with him, endeavoured to throw him back upon his head and stun him; but the first surprise over, the turnkey, in his turn, grappled with his antagonist, and being the stronger man, the priest was thrown down, and then an alarm was given.

Several turnkeys came running in, and the priest was quickly secured in irons; the whole prison was alarmed, and a search was commenced in a very short time.

It was surprising how quickly they detected the route of the mendicant, and in a few moments more they were beside him before he was aware of it, for all his faculties were concentrated upon the means of getting safely out of a position of the most imminent peril, which he had got into in his endeavours to escape.

He was quickly seized and thrown down and secured afresh with irons, despite his most vehement and desperate struggles.

"We have you safely enough, now,"

said one of the turnkeys: "and it's quite useless to attempt to struggle; you had better take it quietly, like a man."

Then came the fierce reply; the denunciation of the whole human race, the frantic attempts at self-destruction; the shout and laughter and the exultation in his admission that he had killed hundreds of men; that he had baffled them all for years, and that they could not count more days in their lives than he could count lives he had taken.

The men were all astonished at the occurrence, and the governor ordered him to be taken and placed in a strong room, with extra irons, and two men with him.

His ravings were terrific, and the men did not believe in the horrible tale he told of his own criminality, but looked upon it as a species of phrenzy or madness, during the continuance of which, visions of all that was dreadful visited him, and he believed himself a monster of crimes even greater than they took him to be.

## CHAPTER XCIII.

THE RETURN OF THE MORTONS TO THE HALL.—RAFFERTY BROLICKBONES GETS UP A SENSATION.—THE FESTIVITIES, AND THE SCENE IN THE ARBOUR.

CAPTAIN MORTON thought it prudent, as, indeed, it was, to take Mabel away as quickly as he could from London, and spare her all the unpleasantness that was likely to arise from the knowledge that any man, however well deserving he might have been of his fate, should suffer the extreme penalty, in whose apprehension and punishment she had even been forced into becoming the cause. This, Captain Morton rightly judged, would give her great pain, and a shock to her system that might take time to recover from.

He, however resolved to travel slowly, and taking his own time in doing so, so that the fatigue should not be felt, either by himself or Mabel, whose troubles and adventures had already given her a severe shock, as well as to render her mind susceptible of any sudden emotion or alarm, and, moreover, it would give time to send Rafferty Brolickbones onwards and prepare the Hall for their reception, and to acquaint Mrs. Morton with their coming.

What a change had taken place since last they were all assembled in the Hall; how much had been done, endured, and discovered since that time! What an epoch had it been! There were events enough to fill volumes, crowded into so short a space

that the mind had scarcely time to take cognizance of them. But now they were likely to end, and the even tenour of their former life was likely to return, and that happiness was like to be continued, which had been so suddenly and rudely broken in upon. The future was a smiling prospect, the past a darkened picture, in which were many dangers which were almost hidden, and from which escape was difficult.

Now, however, beside the captain, and in her altered position she felt all the confidence and happiness she was capable of enjoying.

Rafferty Brolickbones was well pleased to travel forward at his own pace, which, had it at all met his own desires, he should have flown home, he said, on the wings of a carrier pigeon; but Rafferty was not angelic enough to be treated with a pair of ærial flappers, and he couldn't fly; and, moreover, it was so incongruous, that it was difficult to imagine how he could, in a future state, even think of becoming a cherubim or seraphim.

However, Rafferty pushed forward with all the haste he could, as if heaven and earth depended for their existence upon the speed with which he could reach Morton Hall. At length he did make the best of his way to the village. This was the last stage, and then, after that, he could bear no more delays, but he hastened on foot to the Hall, where he arrived, and in an instant he rushed into the parlour, where Mrs. Morton was seated.

"Hurrah, ma'am—hurrah! The lost found. Oh, bedad, mistress, dear, have ye heard the news?"

Mrs. Morton looked up in amazement at the sound of the well-known voice of Rafferty Brolickbones; but her surprise was by no means lessened when she beheld the heated face and the excited actions of the faithful serving man; for he was, as some of the servants afterwards declared, like a barrel of yeast which had forced the bung out, and was working its way out of its place of confinement.

"Why, Rafferty, have you come?"

"Oh, bedad! haven't I; the captain, Mr. Henry, and Miss Mabel, and all. Yes, we are, or soon shall be, which is all the same, or next to it. Oh, bedad—but——"

"Stop, Rafferty. Where is your master, and Mabel, and Henry—where are they all? Tell me that, Rafferty."

"Indeed, ma'am, they're all on the road; and I was sent forward to prepare you all against their coming. To get the old Hall in proper order; to get the people together; and won't we have eating, and drinking, and dancing, and shouting, and guns firing?"

"Goodness, me, Brolickbones, you have gone mad! Your master will be here directly, then?"

"Oh, bedad, no. The captain won't be here to-day—he'll be on the road—it may not be to-morrow; but, at all events, we'll have such a glorification over the whole affair; it shall be as grand a day as ever the anniversary of the battle of Waterloo, or St. Patrick's day—bedad, if I know which."

"They are not likely to be here to night?"

"Oh, no, ma'am—oh, no. They come down very slowly. They had been so fatigued and worn out in London, and Miss Mabel has been so ill-used, so locked up and put about, that I wonder she is a living sowl at this moment."

"Poor thing—poor, dear child! The captain wrote to me, and informed me of a great deal; but he said there was much more to be told than he could possibly find time to write."

"Ah, indeed, he may say that, ma'am. He wouldn't get it all into a bible, if he were to try. I'm sure it'll take him a blessed time to tell it. It'll go back from Easter to Easter and a Whitsuntide over, I'll warrant."

"Well, well—you had better go and get some rest, and some refreshment, since you have nothing more to tell me, and, as I know they are well and coming, I must rest satisfied."

Rafferty, upon this, went into the servants' hall, where he became an object of great admiration. The servants collected around him in great numbers, to hear all he had to relate, which he did, never suppressing anything that came uppermost in his mind, which greatly increased their wonderment and admiration.

"Lor, Rafferty!" said one.

"Did you, indeed, Rafferty?" said another. "Why, you are a regular fire-eater, you are, to be sure."

"Ay, bedad, so I had need be, for there was no chance of getting away; it was hard work at such a time. Queer work it was over the top of the tiles, I tell you."

"Oh, ah! to be sure. Were you on the tiles, Rafferty? But that was very wrong, you know."

"Oh, you don't know that London, else you'd know it is a sea of tiles. Besides, an old soldier would follow an enemy anywhere, and there is no mistake about it. But come, we are going to have a feast. Get the people together—get them together. I've got the captain's orders. We'll have a cup to begin with; there's a barrel of ale on tap, we'll finish that now, and we'll have another to-morrow—one tapped on purpose."

There was a great shout given by the servants at this, and some others came in at the moment, and a scene of joyous riot and disorder ensued instanter.

The exuberance of Rafferty Brolickbones' spirits were so great, that when the beer was drunk out, he got upon the cask, and executed an Irish jig upon the end of it, with such right good will that he knocked the head of the barrel in, and he disappeared suddenly, to the great joy of the spectators, some of whom thought he had done it on purpose. However, he soon rose again, and convinced them it was quite an accident, for the edge of the barrel had taken the skin very cleanly off the end of both his nose and chin, as they disappeared in the barrel and close to its edge.

\*     \*     \*     \*     \*

The next day was a scene of better conducted mirth. All who knew anything of the family of the Mortons—all who were employed on the estate, and many more, who only claimed kindred to the servants, were present, and the place was crowded.

Good, substantial viands were handed about, and there was no stint of anything. There were plenty of viands and drink. Joy, like sorrow, is dry, and the best course is, in either case, to wet it, and, therefore, the guests at the Hall did wet it.

The strong compounds were all superintended by Rafferty himself, who failed not to taste if they were all good, and if each can of ale was as strong as the last, and as that was usually the case, he expressed great satisfaction, and proceeded to pass encomium after encomium, until he began to speak with such wonderful fluency that even astonished all who heard him.

"Well, Rafferty," said one, "how came you to let them run away with Miss Mabel, eh?"

"Oh, bedad, did you think I could help it at all—at all? Not I, or else the rapscallion should have died before he should have so much as seen her beautiful face."

"But you were neither killed nor dead?"

"No I wasn't, bedad!"

"Nor were you far from it?"

"No, bedad, I wasn't. But I couldn't get near her all the time; if I could have done so, I would have had my hands hacked off, before she should have been taken away by the spalpeen."

"I can't understand it at all, how you, an old soldier, should be done in that way. I cannot understand—indeed, I think you must have been to blame, else you would have made the matter more plain and comprehensible to our comprehension."

"Well, then, bedad, darlints, if you'll come with me, I will tell you all about it. I will show you the tree; I will show you all about it, and then, if you can blame Rafferty Brolickbones, why it's more than he himself can do—good luck go with him!"

This was agreed to on all hands; for it was getting late in the afternoon, and every one seemed inclined for some practical joke, and everybody was rife for any mischief, and hoped there was some in the wind, though none could tell what.

They all left the Hall, and proceeded in a body to the lake at the end of the grounds, to that well known spot where Mabel first met the mendicant, and where she was carried off by him and his accomplice, and where Rafferty himself fell into the water.

They soon arrived at the spot and looked around.

"There," said Brolickbones—"there is the identical tree. Up that very tree I got to watch for any one coming to Miss Mabel. Ay, there I sat, sure enough."

"Why, it is not large enough to hold you, Rafferty. You are coming some of your blarney over us."

"Push it up," said Rafferty, "and hold it; you will then see it could and did hold me, until the dirty blackguard, that's going to be hung—bad manners to his ugly face —pushed me and the tree together into the water."

"Ha, ha, ha!" laughed the crowd.

"You may all laugh; you haven't had a ducking maybe. By all that's unlucky, it's uncomfortable at night time, and that, too, when you are in a hurry. But push it up, and then you will see what I say is true as the words of St. Patrick."

They pushed the tree up into its place, and, when up, it took but little trouble to hold it there.

"There, you spalpeens, don't you see where I sat there, up in that hole; and so, when I chose, I could pop my head out of the hole, and see who was a coming, and what was the matter."

"And hear all that was said," suggested another.

"Yes, certainly. I should like to know who could help it. But, independent of that, I wasn't a going to allow Miss Mabel to be imposed upon. Besides, she could take the person who was conversing a little way from the tree, where I could not hear a word, but yet be within call."

"Well, well, get up and show us how you did it, Rafferty, and that will put it out of the question."

"Bedad, so I will," exclaimed Rafferty, in high glee. "So I will, bad manners to me. Oh! ye spalpeens, I'll show you what it is to doubt the word of a Waterloo man."

So saying, Rafferty got upon the tree without any aid, and then he let himself down in the hollow, as he had done on a former occasion, and then the mob of guests shouted and halloed, to see him, and those who held the tree quietly retired, leaving it standing for some minutes.

"There," shouted Rafferty; "now you unbelieving bogtrotters. Bedad, do you see now, and do you believe?"

"Believe what?"

"Why, how I fell into the water."

Rafferty could not hear the reply, but he heard a great shout, and he found the tree moving towards the lake, and before he could speculate what was the matter, over the tree went, and Rafferty Brolickbones was once more immersed in the ornamental piece of water, from which he arose snorting, and spluttering, and shaking himself like a great water dog, much to the amusement of the spectators.

*     *     *     *     *

There was a beautiful arbour in the garden, and one that had been a great favourite with Mabel. It was impervious to the eye, and was a cool, sequestered, and sweet retreat in summer.

But who are the occupants now? They are lovers—the volumes of unspoken love that beam from their eyes stamp them as the happiest of the happy. They seem to have given up the restraints of ceremony —they are accepted lovers. And who are they?

They are too well known to the reader. Harry Morton and Mabel. In a quiet moment he had followed her to her favourite bower, and there declared, fully and impassionedly, the love he felt. He knew she loved him—she admitted it; and, moreover, he had induced her to name the day, and, as he snatched a kiss from her lips, and as they rose to leave the bower, he said—

"Then, this day month, dearest Mabel, will see me one of the happiest men that the earth contains. Between this and then, how shall I not pray for the time to fly; and, after that, may it linger long—ay, longer than any impatient lover ever knew it to do so, when it stood between him and the object of his wishes."

## CHAPTER XCIV.

### EXECUTION OF STERNHOLDE.

THE fate of the wretched, but pre-eminently guilty Sternholde, is fast drawing to a close; his hours are numbered, and then he, whose hand was never stretched forth to alleviate human misery, or to spare human life, would shortly cease to beat with the pulsation that, while it lasted, gave life to a spirit as stern and unyielding as it was unpitying in itself.

But the hour was at hand when should close the career of one of the most ungrateful, most ruthless, and most merciless of men. But how did he meet his approaching end? As men do.

After the recent attempt to escape by means of the priest, double care and caution was observed. He was placed in another cell, and as his frantic efforts were directed against himself as well as others, he was secured against any such attempts being made successful, and a strait waistcoat was the result.

His fierce and bitter denunciations were followed by the voluntary confession of crimes that were too horrible to excite belief even in the minds of those who were well versed in the annals of crime—the men whose duty led them daily to have intercourse with the worst and the most hardened offenders.

He would not submit to anything, save upon compulsion. The priest had been denied access to him; the chaplain of the prison endeavoured to reason him into a better frame of mind than that in which he was then in, but it was useless; he refused all intercourse upon religious topics, save to scoff and laugh at them.

"Bring me none of your coffer-loving priests, or table-fed parsons, or your pensioned dignitaries, who league together to enchain the world, and to gather together the loaves and the fishes."

This language, of course, did little to appease the incensed prison authorities, and the chaplain was especially scandalised, and his calling entirely disgraced by such conduct.

However, he did all he could to reason with him; but it was unavailing, each new attempt being met by a corresponding increase of scorn and derision.

"I know how to die," he would say, "and care nothing for your regimental readings and orders—all are framed alike to obtain one end—a luxurious profession for the traders and professors in your faith. You are all alike, waiters upon Mammon."

Thus would he turn away the endeavours of the good man with the utmost contempt; and yet there was a something of noise and boast in all this; he required to hear the sound of his own voice to assure him, and to cover his own weakness, and to aid in giving him that appearance of courage of which he boasted.

At length the day before the execution arrived, and the governor and chaplain visited him.

"Sternholde," said the former, "there is no hope for you—you must die to-morrow."

"To-morrow!" echoed Sternholde.

"Yes; your time is now short. Consider well how you had best employ it, for opportunities now lost are irrecoverable. Time soon, with you, will cease to be."

"Away, away; you cannot take away my life—'tis charmed."

"If you can think so, you are in a lamentable state of error," said the clergyman; "you cannot bear a life charmed against the penalty of the law; never was such a thing heard of, or dreamed of, depend upon it. You have your faith founded upon a rotten basis; be warned in time; the hours are few. Oh, repent; seek for that mercy which you seem never to have shown to man, and may you find Him more merciful than his creatures."

"When must I die?"

"To-morrow, at eight.

"So short a time?"

"It has been long; that is, quite as long as usual; and you must have known that there was no chance of mercy being shown to you—you could have none to expect."

Sternholde said nothing, but leaned back against the cell, and seemed lost in thought. The clergyman thought he might be yet induced to change his mind; that the certainty of death, so near at hand, would work a change in that man's mind, and stood hopefully in expectation that some such occurrence would take place, and be indicated by some expression on his part.

But nothing but sullen silence and a wandering eye was observable in him. Then, after having awaited patiently for some time, the governor said to him, in a kindly tone,—

"Can I do anything for you, Sternholde? Is there anything at this moment that can be done for you, or that you would desire?"

Sternholde shook himself, but answered not.

"Think," added the worthy chaplain, "think of the awful moment so near at hand; think upon the little time you have to make applications to the throne of grace —let me beseech you."

"Too late—too late," said Sternholde.

"Not too late for repentance. Be true; say but the word, and I will sit up with you all night. I will not leave you till that awful moment arrives when you quit the world for ever."

"Away, away; none of your hated jugglery here. I am what I have been, and a change now would be impossible; but it will advantage me nothing, and I will not consent."

"But it would advantage you something hereafter."

"I'll have none of it."

"Wretched man! hour after hour will your courage fail; hour after hour will death seem more terrible and more fearful; and, without the consolation of repentance, and the promises of Heaven to aid you, your last moment will be one of bitterness and gall. Think again—think again, if there can be no hope of your repentance. Time is short—fearfully short; yet, to those who ask it with a contrite heart, the mercies of Heaven are surely promised."

"Ha, ha, ha! Leave me, I have heard enough of this. You may frighten timid hinds, but I have had enough of your cloth; away, away, I have done—leave me to myself."

The chaplain and governor looked at each other with sorrow on their countenances; the former whispered—

"He is, I fear, a hardened sinner; but what an end!"

"His courage," said the governor, "is only assumed, and not real. I cannot believe he will be the man to hold out in this manner to the end—he is much too furious."

"He is, indeed, a wretched man, but I fear further offers would be unavailing; and yet it is dreadful to see him die thus; but there is no help for it."

"None," said the governor, as he quitted the cell, leaving the wretched Sternholde to all the horrors of his fate.

When alone, Sternholde looked around upon the cell in which he sat; not a single ray of hope beamed from any quarter; no possibility of escape presented itself, and, had there been plenty, he would have been unable to have taken advantage of it, since he was so secured that he could do nothing. His limbs were not at liberty, lest he should commit some act of self-destruction.

"I am indeed cooped up here, and there is no chance of getting out of this. I must stay and die. Die, eh? Well, I have had a long career; I have been successful in many things, but this has been fatal to me. I would I had never attempted it, and yet it was a bold game, and, had it been successful, what a result!"

The wretched man endeavoured to find consolation in the reflection that it would last him but a short time, for the knowledge that he must in a few hours die—it was a dreadful knowledge—kept forcing itself more strongly upon his mind, and the more dreadful did it seem.

However, the hours passed by, and the evening came. His meals were brought him, but though he drank, he ate but little. He seemed feverish, but not hungry. His eyes became red, and his whole appearance became disordered.

At night the turnkey came in to sit up with him. It was the custom then to do so, and he felt this was an annoyance to him, for it forced the hateful knowledge upon his mind that he was compelled to die in a very few hours.

"What is the time now?" inquired Sternholde, suddenly speaking, for the first time, to the turnkey who had to sit up with him all night long.

"A little after six."

"And to-morrow at eight I am to die?"

"You are," replied the man. "There is scarce fourteen hours before you cease to live," said the man.

Sternholde felt himself weak; he knew not how it was, but a sudden weakness seized him; he felt a sinking at his heart, as if his strength were not enough to enable him to retain his seat. Indeed, it seemed as if he were about to sink through the earth, such a dreadful sense of trepidation now came over him.

He staggered, rather than walked, to his pallet, and there lay down; and as he did so he thought he heard some confused noise in the court-yard. He thought there was the sound of workmen—of hammers, and hammering, and the dreadful truth flashed across him.

"What—what noise is that?" he inquired of the man who sat up with him during that night.

"They are erecting the scaffold," was the man's reply.

Sternholde felt a shudder creep over him, which he tried to suppress, and which he could no more stop than he could have carried himself suddenly away from that dreadful place.

Slowly passed the hours away, and as they passed decreased the short span of life that remained, and with it fled much of that courage or scorn of death that served to support him during his previous career.

But now the certainty of death was so great that there never had been such a scene presented to his eyes before,—death in every hour that fled, in every object that he saw, and in every sound that he heard.

The sounds of the workmen became painfully distinct, and he could hear—nay, almost feel, every nail that was driven, and every beam that was raised. He could not bear to listen to these sounds, and yet his mind was chained down to them, and he could listen to nothing else—he could think of nothing else.

How painful was the sweat that bedewed his brow alone could testify. The man that sat up with him alone attempted once or twice to speak to him, but finding he was not inclined to talk, said no more, though now Sternholde wished he would speak, but he could not induce him to do so. He could not speak himself—he could not

utter a sound—his tongue cleaved unto his mouth, and he could not say one word to him.

He lay motionless—no sound was heard, save those made by the workmen, and the solemn sound of St. Paul's cathedral clock, and some of the neighbouring church clocks, which came at that dead hour of the night with awful distinctness upon his ear. Little did he do, save count the hours and the quarters as they chimed, and think how fast was life fleeting from him.

The hours came and went with frightful rapidity, and he found morning dawned long before he would have believed half the night could have been passed; but he had counted the chimes and the strokes, and he knew it was now past five.

He yet lay on his pallet; he seemed to have no strength left, not even to rise. Could death be so near at hand—could he be going to die? Yes, it was too certain; there was all the busy preparations being made for his execution.

The noise of the workmen proceeded as

their labours neared their termination. The morning, too, was cold and wet, the rain fell heavily, and London was enveloped in misty gloom.

The authorities in the prison now came and went; doors were opened and shut, and at length the chaplain and governor again entered the cell, to see the wretched man.

"What can be done for you, Sternholde?" inquired the governor.

"Save me," said Sternholde.

"Nay, I cannot do that; no earthly power that can do so will be exerted for you. Let me beg of you to employ your last moments in endeavouring to make your peace with Heaven."

"The moments are few and short," said the chaplain; "make the most of them, and beseech the throne of mercy for pardon; do not die in this horrible state—seek mercy where mercy can be shown."

"You shall not frighten me," exclaimed Sternholde, "by all your preparations, by all your jugglery. I will have nothing to do with you; I will not acquiesce in one single act that goes towards aiding in my own death."

The governor and chaplain exchanged looks, and then quitted the cell. The time passed by, and soon came the sheriffs and all the officers connected with the occasion.

A breakfast was provided in the press-room; but all that Sternholde could take was a cup of tea, and so great was his agony that he bit a piece out of the cup.

The ceremony of pinioning was about to be performed, and the irons knocked off; but the moment they made the attempt to place the rope found his arms and hands, he threw himself on them, exclaiming, as he struggled with them:—

"I will not die this death; you shall not drag me to the scaffold; I will not tamely submit."

However the men secured him, for his strength was too far gone to be able to maintain any struggle with them; but he refused to stand; he could hardly do so, and he trembled excessively at the near approach of death, and talked incoherently and rapidly; but he was scarcely audible.

The moment arrived when the procession was about to be formed, when the various officers of the prison approached him; but he did not wish one of them farewell.

"I will not go," he muttered; "no, no, I will not go. You may drag me, but you shall not take me to die if I can help it. I will resist; you may murder me, but you shall not do it cheaply."

The wretched man was too far gone; he trembled while he struggled, and at the same time the officials found but little difficulty in carrying him along the passages.

The chaplain began to read the burial service, and the procession moved forward; the sound of St. Sepulchre's church bell came heavily on the ear, and not a sound was lost; Sternholde was carried forward, faintly struggling in the arms of those who bore him along.

Abject cowardice seemed to have come over him, and he could not think of death with calmness. They now came upon the platform; Sternholde was supported to the drop.

It rained fast, but there was a dense mass of people, who saluted him with a groan. He had pulled off the cap which had been drawn over his face, and he yet struggled with his supporters now more violently, as the moments grew shorter, and the mob hooted and howled dreadfully; the rain came down heavily; the dismal tolling of the bell came more dreadfully and more distinctly than ever.

The preparations for the execution were complete, so far as the prisoner was concerned, and then the signal was given, and the wretched man, by some misplacement of the rope occasioned by his struggles, swung to and fro, horribly convulsed, for the space of one or two minutes, notwithstanding the executioners hung to his legs, and thus added their weight to his.

After a short and sharp struggle he was no more, and the spirit of the wretched culprit was launched into eternity, clothed in all its crimes and hardihood.

## CHAPTER XCV.

### THE PAPERS LEFT BY THE BATTLE FIEND.

THERE was one subject of anxiety connected with Mabel's history, which her friends had kept from her, because they feared no satisfactory solution to the mystery would be found.

This was as regarded the fate of her mother, and from all the authentic particulars which the Morton family could gather, although there was every presumption that Marie Rouselli was no more, yet no authentic record of her death could be ascertained.

They well knew that to doubt upon such a subject would be to produce in Mabel's mind a great amount of anguish, and therefore was it that, with a pardonable duplicity, the Mortons had never hinted to her a doubt but that her mother had expired upon the field of Waterloo.

Captain Morton, however, had made it his special business to see the chaplain as well as the governor of Newgate, and the sheriffs, in order to beg of them, if any opportunity should present itself, to get from Sternholde some particulars with regard to the fate of her whom he had once pretended to love, and the fact of whose becoming the wife of another seemed to have awakened all those angry passions which he possessed, and which otherwise might not have made so violent an exhibition of themselves.

Captain Morton thought it possible that, if he were watched closely, some moment would arise when a thought of the dreadful doom that awaited him might banish some of the sullenness of his disposition, and make him communicate it.

The question was put to him on several occasions, and no doubt he at once concluded that it was dictated by the Morton family, against whom he entertained the most unextinguishable hatred.

His reply was to the following effect:—

"I do know the information which is sought. Spare my life, and I will tell it."

He was, of course, informed that that was impossible, and then he declined uttering another word upon the subject. And so he went to death, and a communication was immediately made to Captain Morton that no information could be obtained with regard to the subject of his inquiry.

But a singular circumstance converted that no information into the most ample. The Morton family had not been many days at the Hall when, late one evening, it was announced to the captain that a stranger wished to speak to him; and feeling some curiosity to know who it was, as the servant told him the man appeared as if he had travelled far, and really wanted to see him, the captain ordered him to be shown into a private room.

By a strange coincidence, that room was the same in which Sternholde so long before had had the insolence to make his daring attempts upon the credulity of the captain, by passing himself off as the nearest relative of Mabel.

It required but a glance to see that the travel-worn man who appeared before Captain Morton was a Jew, and if anything might be fairly gathered from the expression of his sharp, cunning features, it would seem as if, notwithstanding his fatigue, he were well pleased with his errand.

Upon the entrance of Captain Morton, he saluted him with some show of respect, and then said—

"Sir, I have come all the way from London to see you."

"For what purpose?" said the captain. "I've no recollection of you."

"No, sir; but you knew Mr. Sternholde, who was hanged. Now, my name is Solomon Isaacs, and I always buy the clothes of people who are executed; they are the hangman's perquisite, and I take them of him at a fair valuation."

"Well, Mr. Solomon Isaacs, you have come a long way to give me a piece of information that I care nothing about now I know it."

"Don't you, sir? Just look at me; this is the identical suit that Sternholde wore when he was hung."

"What! do you mean to tell me that you have on the dead man's clothes?"

"Yes; and remarkably well they look, and comfortable they are. You see I wanted to bring them down here to show you, in order to convince you that all was right."

"Really, Mr. Isaacs, you have taken a world of trouble for nothing. I was quite satisfied before you came, and I want to hear nothing more of Sternholde, or of his family."

"Don't you, though; we'll soon see that, Captain Morton. What now if I was to tell you that, in a concealed pocket in the breast of his coat, I found some papers rather interesting to you and to the young lady you call Mabel?"

"Secret papers of Sternholde's!" exclaimed Captain Morton. "Give them to me at once. They will, indeed, be most interesting to me. You have exercised a sound discretion, Mr. Isaacs, in coming here with them, instead of placing them in the hands of any one else."

"No doubt—no doubt; I thought you'd say that, Captain Morton; I was sure you'd say that; but don't be in a hurry; we must make a bargain. I have come a long way, Captain Morton, a long way, and you must understand that I have gone to some expense in this matter."

"Well—well; I dare say you have; I will repay you all that, and give you something for your trouble as well; give me the papers; we shall not disagree about remuneration in any moderate way."

"Ah! Captain Morton; ah, that is very good; very good, indeed. I am sorry to have to say anything that may seem to be at variance to that, especially as you are a liberal gentleman, I am sure; but we had better come to some understanding at once; one had better disagree before the agreement to purchase has been made; you and I have different notions as to what may or may not be moderate; besides, I have the papers, and you have the price, if you think proper to part with it, Captain Morton."

"What you say is very true," said Captain Morton, who saw the Jew's drift; "I can understand what you mean. Pray tell me what you require for these papers?"

"What do I want, Captain Morton?"

"Ay, ay."

"Well, you see, independent of the trouble and expense that I have gone to in this matter, the value of the papers is—something—because they contain, first, something you want to know, and something you don't want others to know."

"Well, I am a man of a few words; say at once, your price, and I will, if I think it not exorbitant, pay you."

"Exorbitant, Captain Morton? I make an exorbitant charge! So help me goodness gracious——"

"Come, come, have you any price at all, or are you going to keep them yourself? I have no more time to waste upon you; I will have the papers, if you will sell them; but it appears you only desire to talk about them."

"Well—well, captain, you are a funny man; I declare I never saw such a man before, and that is the truth; I cannot sell the papers under twenty pounds, Captain Morton."

"Twenty pounds! that is a heavy price for pieces of paper, that are of no earthly use to you or anybody else."

"That has nothing to do with the matter," said the Jew.

"Well—well, you shall have the twenty pounds, since that is your price, for them; I would not give it, were it not you must have expended some of it in coming here."

"Yes—yes; but I have given you the papers; I want my expenses as well."

"What!" exclaimed Captain Morton, looking at the Jew, in intense astonishment.

"Yes, my expenses; ten pounds more; it is but just; I cannot come all this way and not clear my expenses."

"You would get nothing if I were not to buy them."

"No—no, certainly not; I should not, Captain Morton; nor should I, perhaps, even if I were to sell them to the publications; but I should try, or even give them away, rather than make a bad bargain with them who could pay and won't; but that is not your case, Captain Morton, I dare say——"

"How much do you say you want in all? my patience is very nigh exhausted; say it at a word."

"Thirty pounds," said the Jew.

"Then, there are thirty pounds," said the captain, as he laid down the three bank notes he had taken out of his purse; "give me the papers, and let us have done with this business."

The Jew handed over the bundle of papers, and took the notes, which he counted over and held them severally up between himself and the light, and said, as he did so,—

"Well, Captain Morton, these are all right and good; hope I shall have the honour of drinking your health."

"You may," said Morton; "there is a pump in the yard, and any of my men will assist you to as much as you please."

"So help my good gracious," said the Jew; "may I never again eat pork—if I like anything so cold; it settles cold on the stomach; well—well, I must wait till I get to the Morton Arms, where I can have what I pay for."

So saying, the Jew walked away, apparently vexed at Captain Morton not having given him some drink, after exacting the heavy price for some, to him, useless papers.

*      *      *      *      *

"Well," said Captain Morton, "we will see what these papers consist of, and whether they throw any light upon the fate of the unfortunate Rouselli."

So saying, he undid the bundle, and began to examine them one after another, but they were of an entirely fragmental character, and apparently written at moments when the writer had committed some deed of a more than usually diabolical character, which seemed to have excited a degree of pleasure that could have only been felt by one lost to all sense of humanity, and urged on by some deep-seated passion, which knew no satiety.

*      *      *      *      *

Captain Morton took the first of these papers, and so on, reading them one after another, unless he should miss any one that was important to the object he had in view. The first ran as follows:—

*      *      *      *      *

It is done! My first act of retribution —nay, of vengeance, if you will—has been performed on my French enemies. To no one of that hated race will I ever show mercy; but pour out their blood in all places, and under all circumstances, till as much blood shall be shed as would deluge the earth, and redden it till the day of judgment.

It was after my first battle, while fighting in the Russian service against the French, who have my immortal hatred, that I have done this, my initiative deed.

When darkness came over the field of battle, then I stole out, and wandered over the sanguinary spot, to see what French blood I might pour out upon the yet reeking plain. The first I met was a wounded officer.

" Save me !" he said. " I am an officer, and am rich, and can pay you well for your service. I am dying for help."

" What will you give me ?"

" A thousand francs," he replied.

" Not enough—not enough."

" Two thousand."

" Not enough—not enough," I again replied, and was about to raise my sword to plunge it into his breast, when he screamed out—

" Five thousand—any sum I am possessed of ! I give you my sacred honour that it shall be paid you. Oh, save me— save me! I see you will. Thank you— thank God !'

" Frenchman," I replied, " know that you have met the enemy of your race; one who hates you for your nation. I have received wrong at their hands, and all whom I meet I shall slay, destroy, and pour out their blood without remorse. Take your death from my hand."

As I spoke, I plunged my sword into his breast. He gave a sudden, convulsive start, and then he sank back with an expression of agony on his countenance.

\* \* \* \* \*

The same evening I destroyed no less than fifteen Frenchmen, who fell beneath the point of my sword—they fell to rise no more. They might have lived, had assistance been offered them ; but I killed them. The French deserve this retribution; they are ruthless, and they have no mercy themselves—let none be shown them.

The last man who fell was an officer of rank. I know their hated tongue well. 1 know how they place their watches and guards—they are familiar to me.

The night was dark, pitchy dark, and I left our own encampment and went over to the enemy, at the same time being well acquainted with all that appertains to their mode of encampment; at the same time they would have let me pass, had I presented myself in the character of a deserter.

I stole into their camp, and stood by a tent that was but dimly lighted, and I heard two officers conversing together. I listened to them, and heard the following words pass :—

" Well, Lavolt, I am glad it is no worse. You will be well in a week or two at the farthest. I was afraid, when I saw you carried by, that you might have been mortally wounded."

" I thought I was done for," said Lavolt; " but I think I shall get over it, though my wound looks bad."

" The surgeon told me the reverse of all this. He said, for all he could tell to the contrary, you would be well enough to resume your duties in a fortnight."

" I hope I may, for the Lady Julie's sake."

" It was for her sake I made such particular inquiries concerning your wound. Had it been worse, I would have written to inform her brother."

" Thank you; but I now hope that I shall not be compelled to resort to such a proceeding. She will be quite affected when she hears I have been wounded and got over it."

" She will. I am sorry too, Lavolt, that you ever entered the army. It is not the place for a man of your prospects— your hopes, and your wishes."

" You know the cause. You know the cause. But why should I not do as well in the army as any other, though I have ten thousand francs a-year ?"

" Because you are too fond of domestic happiness. You have not the ambition of a soldier."

" Do you doubt my courage ?"

" No; if I did your conduct to-day would teach me to respect it. But I know you have not only courage, but capacity also. You have a home—a beautiful girl, and have every prospect of all the happiness you could wish."

" I have."

" And you entered the army in a fit of spleen."

" I did."

" And you think because you have done your duty that that will in time make you a general. Well, you will find that it will not; and though a lover's quarrel can make a soldier, it cannot make a general of a division."

" You are joking with me."

" Not I; but I must seek rest for myself. I have gone through much to-day. Good bye. May you rest well. I will see you in the morning, and hope to find you better."

" Adieu !" said the wounded man.

The other came near the opening of the tent—I was standing close by it. The moment I saw him advance, I drew my sword and passed it through his body, and he fell to the earth without a groan.

I stepped over the body, and entered the tent. The wounded man had turned in his bed, and lay with his back towards me. I stepped up to the bed.

" I thought you had gone," he said to me, without turning.

"I am just come in it," I said.

My voice caused him to turn round. There was so much of bitterness that he seemed terror-stricken.

"Who are you," he inquired; "and what do you want?"

"Do you see this weapon?" said I, as I held up the sword before his astonished eyes.

"I do—help!"

I permitted no other sound to pass his lips, for with one blow I clove his head in two. Voices were heard outside the tent—I put out the light, and ripping an opening in the tent with my good sword, I quitted it as others came in.

\* \* \* \* \*

Again did the sun set upon another bloody field, over which lay the strewn corses of mangled men and beasts, who lay in confused masses—the wounded entangled with the dead.

It was here I had been seen fighting with all the spirit I could. It seemed to astonish our officers. The men looked at me in awe—they all declared I had a charmed life, that many a Frenchman had levelled, and fired, but they never hit me.

They rushed on to the attack with me, and many a Frenchman fell by my efforts. I hate the cursed nation to a man!

The evening is come, and my brother officers are all reposing after the cares of the day; but what are they to me? It is fine recreation—enjoyment—pleasure—to kill Frenchmen; it is my delight! Nothing on earth can give a calmer feeling to my mind!

There lies a French officer—he has a broken limb, and yonder are the relief parties. He must never see them, save to feel in the moment of death how horrible is the pang of disappointment at such a moment as this.

"Yonder," said I to him, "come the relief parties."

"I see—I see—thank God! Oh, my leg—it is broken! What agony! But are they far off?"

"No."

"Will you call, stranger? my throat is parched. I can hardly draw my breath! My mouth is encased with a crust."

"I am the destroyer of your race! Take your death from my hands!" and I plunged my sword's point through his body, just below the left breast.

\* \* \* \* \*

On the same evening, as usual, I stole in the enemy's encampment, and made my way from tent to tent, destroying four or five, until I came to another, when I heard the sound of voices in conversation.

"You think our plan of operations to-day, then, not the best that could be adopted?"

"Certainly not."

"And what do you deem grounds sufficient to enable you to say so?" demanded the first.

"Because it has been a mere series of assaults, one mass of men thrown upon another, until they are projected forward, and another being compelled to retire. Nothing but fresh men, fresh regiments—no matter what amount of human life may be sacrificed, the emperor thinks not of that."

"No; but we have gained a victory."

"We have, we have; but our laurels are dyed deeply in the gore of our own people."

"Granted; and so must all such victories."

"That is incontestible. But France must in time cease to pour out such countless numbers to fight her battles; the enemy has lost a battle, but they will be ready to fight again in a week. Each new victory appears to beget us new enemies, and we must go on increasing our strength, while, in point of fact, we are decreasing it each battle by the loss of our oldest and best soldiers."

"Well, well, will say no more now; the time will come when you will be convinced of the fallacy of all these dismal forebodings and opinions. Adieu."

"Adieu; may you be preserved against the fate of many a friend of ours who has fallen this day."

"But covered with glory."

"Adieu; it is so."

The speaker, who was a staff officer, came out of the tent, and as he did so, he faced me. He started, for I was in the Prussian uniform: he laid his hand on his sword.

"Sacre! whence come you?"

I pointed upwards, and said, while his teeth seemed to chatter, and his whole body shook with fear,—

"I am the avenger; I hate your race."

As I spoke I thrust my sword through his body, just as his friend, hearing the words he had spoken, came up, and caught him in his arms.

He stood still for a moment, and seeing his friend dead, threw the body down, and drawing his own sword, and shouting to some one to aid him, he rushed on me.

This was needless, for my sword was drawn, and as he came on I transfixed him with my weapon just below the breast, and its point came out at the blade bone behind. He fell dead and never spoke, but hearing a disturbance, I walked into the tent, and there saw a French woman; she lay on a bed with an infant on her arms.

"Curse of mankind," I muttered, "and belonging to an accursed race, never will I spare French blood; you die as others have died before you. Curse! curse! curse you!"

The female looked up; but a feeling of horror came over her, and she could not speak. I raised my sword, a shriek came from her lips as I plunged it into her breast, and the warm blood gushed up into my face.

I should have destroyed the child, but there was no time for that. I cut my way through the tent, and had scarcely got on the outside when others entered it on the other.

There was an alarm given, and parties were sent out everywhere. The death of the staff-officers in the midst of the camp, with the wife of one of them, was a matter that could not be very well accounted for by them.

I escaped to my quarters, after destroying a few sentinels, upon whom I came unawares.

\* \* \* \*

The day is over; many men lie slaughtered; the French are often beaten, but their officers preserve the appearance of victory. The indecision of ours often happens through the ill effects of councils of war, that limit the operations of men who should be free in their choice of alternatives, but which is not allowed them.

We were presumed to have had the worst, and yet our commanders are ready to fight to-morrow. We are encamped within a mile or two of the French, and I have walked over the field of battle. The French usually conceal their loss from people when they can; it never reaches the papers, they are suppressed, and none know of it, save the officers, and they dare not speak out respecting it, even if they would.

This day had been a terrific one, and men fell by hundreds. I was among the thickest of the fight. I do not say so to gain applause, for who shall applaud me? and, moreover, who shall know aught of it, even should these papers fall into any one's hands after my death? I leave them as memorials of my vengeance, and not as witnesses of my courage; that I care not for; but my revenge is sweet, and for that I live, and for that will I die.

This evening I walked over the field, and saw many wounded near, and they seemed to be able to read in my eyes that I showed no mercy; that I was, in fact, the bane of their race. They seldom asked help of me after they saw my visage, and when they did, the point of my sword gave the answer.

After having destroyed many Frenchmen, I came to a lonely part of the field. Here a charge of Prussian cavalry had done much execution among the French. I found a wounded officer, supported by a youth of about fifteen or sixteen; they were anxiously awaiting the arrival of the relief parties.

"Are they coming, Theodore?" inquired the wounded man.

"I do not see them, father."

The wounded man groaned, and the boy looked anxiously around, and I stood in the shadow of a tree.

"Shall I go, or shout for assistance?"

"No, no, boy, it is useless to do so; you would only miss your way, and you would not find me again. Wait with me—wait with me until you see them."

"I will—I will, father."

I left the spot where I stood concealed, and walked forward until I came close to them. I could see they were father and son, both serving in the same regiment.

"What do you desire?"

"Aid for a wounded officer," said the boy.

The man turned round, and gazed at me for a moment, and then at my uniform, saying,—

"A Prussian—here, too; and yet we have the victory."

"You have; and yet you see I am on the field; the French are every day weakening themselves with their victories."

"And their enemies also," said the officer.

"We shall see that; but your time is come. I never permit a Frenchman to live. I am the avenger. I have received great wrongs, and I spill French blood meet it when I may."

"Will you draw your sword against a defenceless enemy?"

"Look at my sword. Is it not bloody? Are not the gouts of blood fresh and moist?"

"Yes—yes."

"Well, then, you see it is so, because it has let out the life of many a defenceless Frenchman."

"Cowardly wretch!" said the officer. "Theodore, draw your sword, boy; I cannot aid you. God be with you; defend yourself to the last. I see by his eye you have no mercy to obtain."

"Nor do I want any," said the youth, who drew his sword, and advanced upon me with the fury of a young tiger; and had I not been prepared, or had I been a less active swordsman, I might have been overcome; but the fight, though furious, was short; I plunged my sword, after a few thrusts, right through his heart.

I saw the officer turn pale as he saw the youth fall, and he turned his head, saying,—

"May you die the death of a felon, dastard as you are! You cannot hurt me now; I wish to die."

"You shall have your wish," said I, as I thrust the point of my sword through the body of the wounded man, who died cursing me; but I laughed, and left the spot.

Many more Frenchmen fell beneath my sword; none could stand against me in single fight, and few ever escaped from me when in front of battle. I was ever victorious.

\* \* \* \*

Marie Rouselli! What is there in a name that causes so many emotions to arise in my brain? Why should I feel all the glow of anger and revenge? Why should I feel all the horrors of a bursting but steeled heart? Away—away! with such beginnings of a train of reflections, that even I cannot bear with calmness, nay, without madness.

She has come to a sad end. It might have been otherwise, but she could not be turned from her purpose; she could not avoid the consequences.

I have seen many ends, many lives lost, and have taken hundreds; yet I cannot pass by this one as I would some others. I cannot but remember that time was, when even I was not what I am. I am, however, what I shall ever be to the end of life.

Marie Rouselli went mad; yes, raving mad. She knew nobody, and nobody would befriend her. The loss of the child preyed so deeply on her mind, that, resolved to find it, she began to wander about in all the most unheard-of places that could be imagined, and her life was continually in danger.

She was taken to a madhouse. She died in Berlin; carefully tended, certainly, but under restraint; and yet she could not have been conscious of the fact, for she seemed to have no desire to leave the place. She was not violently mad.

"My child—my child!" was the cry all day long—in her dreams by night—until she became exhausted, and nature, unable to bear up, sank beneath affliction so deep and so continuous.

She remained there some years. She was always known by the name of the mad mother, and many used to wonder who she was; but I knew who she was, and her family, and others would have given something to know it. But no matter, so long as I can inflict vengeance upon Frenchmen; it is all I care to do.

Her race is run; her pilgrimage is o'er, and she has become a mass of corruption. She is most truly no more.

My days of vengeance are not complete —the time is not yet run out; but should these wars continue, many a hundred Frenchmen will fall beneath my hand. Their fate will be bad; but Marie Rouselli's fate has been worse than any. To die in a madhouse is a fearful end—even I—I should shrink from that.

\* \* \* \*

My days of vengeance still come round; there is no battle in which I do not take a part, or in which I do not attempt to become a volunteer, if I cannot obtain a post with any command; but be it how it may, there are few of the fields that I do not walk over, and destroy many French lives.

"But here I must end for the present," said Captain Morton; "they seem all alike of the same sanguinary nature; but we have discovered the end of the unfortunate Marie Rouselli. She died in a madhouse, eh?"

---

## CHAPTER XCVI.

### MABEL'S MARRIAGE.—A STRANGE INCIDENT.—THE SECOND WEDDING.

THE month of probation which Mabel had appointed for Henry Morton, was soon expired, though it might seem long to the impatience of the lover, who counted the minutes which divided the present from the moment in which his future happiness was to be completed; when, in fact, there should be no longer time to intervene between the object of his love, where no doubt of the future could cross his mind.

This time was come; the morning of the marriage was come, and the old Hall looked gay; and there were not happier faces to be seen round the whole country, than were to be seen at Morton Hall.

Rafferty Brolickbones was at the head of all the fun and blunders of the day—that is, up to the hour of the marriage ceremony. There was a peculiar life and oddity about Rafferty on this morning, that no one could understand. He appeared to be bursting with all sorts of fun, and every now and then he broke into loud expressions of mirth.

What was the cause of all this nobody could tell; but whenever Rafferty passed any one, he would look at them very hard, and burst into a fit of laughter; and when about to speak, would appear as if he were bolting his own words, and choking in the process.

"Well, Rafferty," one would say, "what ails you this morning? Are you unwell? You seem as if you had an earthquake in your stomach, and can't digest it."

"No," said Rafferty, "it isn't that, but it has been so long in coming; that's what I'm thinking about."

"What has been coming?"

"Ah! that's my affair; do you mind your own, as the bull said to the dog when he ate up the calf."

"Never heard of such a case in all my life—never knew that the creature would do so; but never mind; you haven't got over that ducking you have had in the pond."

"Do you mind your business."

"Oh! we haven't any business at all

THE MENDICANT CONDUCTED TO THE PLACE OF EXECUTION.

now, Rafferty; it's all pleasure—it is high treason in you, Rafferty, to talk about business on such a day as this."

"Well, well, who's got nothing to do? I'll soon give him something to do, if it's only to hold his tongue."

"That seems to me to be much like doing nothing."

"Oh! you don't know how hard it is to do so, sometimes, honey, or you would not say so," said Rafferty, with a knowing look.

"Well, I never thought so until I saw

you this morning, walking about, a-boiling over with something or other."

Thus Rafferty was attacked by one or the other the whole morning; but when the hour for the marriage—which hour was an early one—came round, then all was bustle, and the party to the church was a numerous one.

Captain and Mrs. Morton went with them to the church, and then the happiness of both was completed, and they were now united to each other for life.

The whole party left the church—th

village church where so many incidents had taken place—where the man Sternholde had more than once been seen to seek concealment, and from which he had been chased by the ostler of the Morton Arms.

The house—the hall—had been open the day or two previous to the calls of such as chose to go, who were in any way connected with the estate, and Rafferty, being the head man, had a controlling influence upon the character and extent of the proceedings that were exerted for the benefit of his patron, and the comfort of all who came there.

However, when the marriage was over—when the newly married couple came home to the Hall, Rafferty was no where to be seen. But Captain Morton remarked that Rafferty Brolickbones was somewhat eccentric in his motions, and, therefore, he thought nothing of that, though, on that occasion, it did somewhat surprise him.

No more was said at that time, and the bride's health was drunk round in some of the finest champagne, and that with the utmost good will. Many were the good and kind wishes that were, on that day, uttered towards the bride and bridegroom. They were both beloved by all who lived within the sphere of their influence.

The mirth and happiness was at the highest; many a smile, and many a joke was seen and heard, when suddenly the whole party were terrified by the bride's screaming out, and rising, and attempting to move away, but, from the excess of her terror, appeared to be unable to do so.

"What is the matter?" exclaimed Henry Morton, starting up to Mabel, and unable to divine what was the cause of her sudden outcry and starting up.

"Good God!" exclaimed Captain Morton, "are you ill, Mabel?"

"Oh! my dear Mabel, exclaimed Mrs. Morton; "my dear girl, what—what is the cause of this?"

"My leg!" exclaimed Mabel, suddenly releasing herself, and flinging herself into Henry's arms.

"Her leg!" exclaimed Captain Morton; "her leg! Good Heavens, what can be the matter? Oh!"

"Ho! ho! ho!" echoed the visitors all round, as they looked at the sofa upon which Mabel had been sitting.

We will endeavour to explain the cause of the mystery, and of the cause of the surprise and amazement of all present.

On the previous night, Troubled Tom, whose choice of a bed was certainly singular and recherché, for some object had been to the Hall, and there he had business with Rafferty Brolickbones; some message or other from the Morton Arms, of no consequence to the reader at all.

After spending an hour or two there, and partaking of the cheer that was to be had there, Troubled Tom and Rafferty Brolickbones found themselves, notwithstanding the hour and the trouble, discussing old ale, to a very pretty tune.

"It's time to go," said Rafferty. "We shall not be able to get up in the morning; there's plenty to do."

"Oh! what a trouble," said Tom.

"It can't be helped," said Rafferty; "we must have our troubles now and then, you know."

"Ah! but mine have lasted since I first recollect, and even that's a trouble to think of; but as for going home, Rafferty, I shall not. I shall drop down somewhere by the way, and have a sleep, out of which I am sure to be awoke by somebody, or something."

"It is a sad thing you are so much disturbed in your sleep. I am never served so."

"Very likely," said Tom.

"But I suppose it is because you choose such out-of-the-way places to sleep in; but good Tom, it's all one, as the showman says, and it's past twelve o'clock."

"Well, good night, Brolickbones," said Tom; "but it's a nation trouble to do so."

So saying, Brolickbones left Troubled Tom to find his way out by himself; but Troubled Tom did not feel himself so inclined, but feeling drowsy, and in anything but a pedestrian humour, and seeing the breakfast-room door open with an inviting air, he walked in.

Now, after looking for a few moments in one direction and then in another, he came to the conclusion that the only safe place to sleep in would be under the sofa.

"There I shall not be seen," he murmured. "I shall sleep till morning, and shall be handy when the feast comes on. It will save a world of trouble."

There was no resisting such arguments, and he accordingly crept under the sofa, and there remained sleeping, for once in his life, an untroubled slumber; but it so happened that he on this occasion found it too much trouble to wake, and slept on, regardless of passing events.

It was not until the bride's health had been drunk, after their return from church, that Troubled Tom suddenly awoke, and was quite oblivious as to his whereabouts—how he came there, and all about it.

Then, in a fit of desperation, or something more like a conglomeration of all his faculties, he began to crawl out just beneath the spot where Mabel was sitting, and finding an impediment, had seized it, and that turned out to be Mabel's ankle which he had seized with his hand.

This, then, was the cause of the outcry that had been raised, and the subsequent amazement and astonishment which the mysterious appearance of Troubled Tom was so sure to raise.

"Troubled Tom!" exclaimed one and all.

"Ay, it is Troubled Tom, sure enough," he muttered, rubbing his eyes, and staring wildly about him; "and yet I can hardly tell whether it be myself or anybody else."

"What do you do here, Tom?" inquired the captain.

"I really don't know, Captain Morton. I just this moment awoke, and can't tell how I came, or where I am."

"You are in Morton Hall. Perhaps I shall be able to assist your memory, or give you time to recollect, if I consign you to the keeper of the Bridewell."

"No, captain; that would be the worst trouble ever I had to go through yet. I meant no harm, nor any wrong, but how I came here I can't tell, but I suppose it was the ale."

"Ah! the ale; I declare, upon my honour, it always is the ale. If anybody is found out poaching of a night, it is the ale; if an odd child comes into a family belonging to the eldest daughter, oh! it's the ale; to be sure, the ale does more wrong than anything else, and now here's a man says the ale has put him under a sofa. That may be true enough, but how came he here to get the ale? He must have come voluntarily. Whom did you come to?"

"Rafferty Brolickbones."

"I see how it is," said Mabel; "he has come to see Rafferty, and they have had too much ale."

"Is that the case?" inquired the captain.

"Yes, captain, it is."

"Well, then, I am afraid it is an aggravation of the case."

"For my sake, sir, and for Rafferty's sake, you must pardon him; remember it's all owing to me that they have done a little wrong."

"A little wrong? Well, never mind. I will overlook it, for Mrs. Henry Morton's sake; but you must go below, and take some more ale, by way of punishment."

"That he will easily submit to," said one of the visitors.

"But where is Rafferty Brolickbones?" inquired the captain.

Nobody knew; he was called for every-where, and search was made, but no Rafferty was forthcoming, and, by dint of much inquiry, it was decided that he had disappeared suddenly and mysteriously, immediately after the ceremony had been performed that morning, and had not been in since.

"And what can have become of him?" said Captain Morton. "I am anxious about him, because I am sure, had not something happened to him, he would have been present upon such an occasion."

"Arrah! and sure yer honour is right. I'fakes! where would Rafferty be if not at a wedding when a wedding was going on? but, carracovaky! here I am. I have been doing a little business on my own account!"

As Rafferty spoke, he pushed the door open and stood on the mat—oh, ye gods! with as fine a specimen of George the Fourth's choice as could be found in any county in the three kingdoms—namely, fair, fat, and forty.

The lady was indeed all these combined in one; but had, perhaps, a little more of each of these ingredients than that monarch would have desired. She was very fair—very fair indeed, her face being something more than the colour of the "red, red rose," being a very red rose indeed that could match the vermillion of her cheek.

And as for "fat," goodness gracious! think of her and a five-mile walk in the dog-days, and think of Shakspere's fat knight "larding the lean earth," and you have some notion of her condition.

And then for the "forty" part of the business—gentle reader, excuse us, this is forbidden ground. A lady's age is a thing quite sacred, and men have no business with it. For my part, I never heard rightly the age of any of the feminine gender after fifteen; after that period it was always wrapped in mystery, and it is difficult to come to the truth when that is the case. So, for our parts, we never even believe in a tombstone when we see the age mentioned on it, being convinced what was difficult to learn while the object was living was more difficult and apocryphal when dead.

"Well, Rafferty, what have you to say for bringing this unfortunate friend of yours into trouble?"

"Arrah! sir—captain dear, I have been in trouble myself—that is, I may be before I die; but I have been doing a little in the matrimonial line myself."

"Eh, Rafferty?"

"I have been to the parish church, captain, dear, and ladies and gentlemen, and this," continued Rafferty, taking the fat hand of the blushing Phœbe—"and this is the bride."

"The bride, Rafferty—did you say the bride?"

"Bad cess to me, yer honour, if she's any less."

"Then you've got married, Rafferty?" exclaimed Captain Morton, in extreme and almost ludicrous astonishment.

"Arrah! an yer honour's just hit it; and why shouldn't an old soldier get married as well as another man?"

"Oh, certainly, Rafferty, certainly; no reason on earth why you should not get married, and I hope you will be happy with your choice. You shall not be without my good wishes, Rafferty."

"I am sure of that, yer honour."

"And of something more substantial too."

"Yer honour is always kind and generous," said Rafferty; and turning to Mr. Henry Morton and to Mabel, he continued, —"May yer honour live long and happily; and as for Miss Mabel—arrah! I mane Mrs. Henry Morton—I can never forget. I nursed her when she was a child, and, though a poor body, I shall always think of her as if she were my own child. May she live to be as happy as I am sure Mister Henry will try to make her."

"You are right, my good Rafferty," said Henry Morton, who could not hear unmoved, nor any one else, the words of the honest Irishman—"you are right; she shall and will be happy if it be in my power to make her so; and allow me to wish you, my honest old friend, all the happiness you deserve, for your fidelity and courage have never been questioned."

"No," said Captain Morton, "they have not; and this last act of his in carrying away the presiding priestess of the bar at the Morton Arms, to my mind, required no little of that excellent quality. We will not keep you and your bride, Rafferty, to whom we wish all joy, any longer. Go and make yourselves as merry as you please, and how you please; you have ample means below."

With this generous hint, Rafferty quitted the wedding party, and each retired, and the day passed off happily.

---

## CHAPTER XCVII.

### CONCLUSION.

AND now let us imagine three months to have elapsed, and look again at the young and beautiful bride, to see if she is happy.

It is a pleasant evening, and the shadows of the tall trees, that are in front of Morton Lodge, are thrown far across the beautiful green sward, where, upon some rustic chairs, sit a happy party. We will look into the face of the young bride, and we shall see at a glance, that it is beaming with contentment. There is a quiet, placid look of domestic happiness about the whole group, that is rarely seen; and most worthy would it have been of the pencil of some gifted lover of his art and of humanity, to paint that happy group, as there, in gentle converse, which in the evening air sounded scarce above a whisper, they passed a pleasant hour, ere the night closed in, and told them to seek the indoor enjoyments of the mansion.

Captain Morton and his wife were walking to and fro conversing together; while Henry, as he leaned over the back of the chair on which Mabel sat, was bringing to her mind recollections of the past.

"Does it not seem, dear Mabel, long, long ago since we were separated, and the envious fates appeared for ever to have conspired against us?"

"It does, indeed, Henry; and this season of joy and tranquillity which we have passed, appears to have cast something of the halo of its own beauty over those events which preceded it."

"It is so with myself, Mabel, and a happy thing is it that we forget suffering quicker than we forget joy. The reminiscences of happiness will cling to us when the remembrance of grief holds in the chambers of our brain but a dim and shadowy existence."

"It is so, Henry, it is so; and yet there are times even now, when I look back with something of a shudder, and wonder how I had the resolution and the courage to bear up against the trials that beset me."

"In many minds, dear Mabel—and I can well perceive yours to be one of them —there is a natural capacity to find sufficient energy to meet the occasion, and that strength, energy, and courage, comes but with the occasion. We cannot imagine its existence, although we imagine the incident that would call it forth."

"I understand you, Henry; and thus it is we shudder at things which, when they happen, we meet gallantly and courageously."

"Yes, Mabel; imagination, as well as conscience, doth make cowards of us all."

Mabel was silent for a few moments, and then she said, gently,—

"I would not dwell upon a painful reminiscence, or even awaken one, but what would I not give if old Mr. Rouselli could look upon a scene like this."

Mrs. Morton was near at hand, and heard the wish. She approached Mabel, and took her by the hand.

"My dear child," she said, "you utter that wish as if you were hopeless of its accomplishment."

"Its accomplishment!" said Mabel, with surprise.

"Yes, dear Mabel, its accomplishment. Do you not believe that one so good and excellent in all respects as your dear grandfather, enjoys all the happiness that can be promised in that world which is to come for all of us—that world in which there is no grief, no sorrow, no tears, Mabel, and from which it has ever been a favourite idea of mine to think that it will be one of the choicest pleasures of the good and great, who have gone before us, to look down from their star-spangled home upon them they loved on earth."

"Oh! it is a charming theory," said Mabel, "and I will cling to it."

"Do so, dearest; it is one that may be believed by the purest and the best. If it be a delusion, it is heaven-born, and pardonable for its beauty."

"You have awakened me to a better sense. I will no longer, dear mother" (Mabel still loved to call Mrs. Morton mother), "I will never again, dear mother, wish, with a sigh, that old Mr. Rouselli were here to look down upon us in our happiness. But when the feeling comes across me, that we are more than usually happy, and I feel that heart-gushing tenderness towards all things that can scarcely express itself in words, I will not say I wish he saw us, but I will say he does see us."

Henry saw a tear trembling in the eyelid of his young wife, and he drew her arm gently in his, as he said,—

"Come, Mabel; let us walk on yonder mount, and see the last of the setting sun."

"Who can this be?" said Captain Morton; "there's some man coming from the house with a stable-jacket on whom I don't know."

"Why, good heavens! it's Rafferty," said Henry.

"Rafferty—impossible! he went and settled in the next town, twelve miles off, with his wife."

But it was Rafferty, who, when he came up to the party, said,—

"Would you be afther having candles lighted in the dining-room, or are you going to set a light to the new chandeleree? A mighty dash it cuts, like a lot of broken glass bottles hanging from the ceiling."

"Why, good God, Rafferty!" said the captain, "you left my service three months ago, and got married, and went to live twelve miles off, and here you are in your old costume, asking us if we'd have candles in the dining-room, or the chandelier lighted."

"It's the dress, is it?" said Rafferty. "Faith, then, and I found that in my old room, on the same peg that I left it. You see, sir, I've been in your sarvice a good while, so I thought I'd take you on again. Where's the wonder of that?"

"But where's your wife, Rafferty?" said Mrs. Morton. "I'm afraid we cannot have your wife."

"Afraid, marm—afraid you can't have her? Faith, and I'd be damnably afraid if you could, marm. God forgive me for swearing before the likes of you, marm. Amen!"

"Well, but, Rafferty, where is she?" said the captain.

"Atween you and me and the post, captain, it's not worth asking about. Here I am again—let bygones be bygones. Sorrow take the Christian as would throw a fellow's misfortunes in his face!"

"But you must tell us," said Henry; "we can't encourage men leaving their wives."

"You can't encourage, Mr. Henry? Nobody asked you, sir. It be a few, indeed, would be encouraged by you, sir. I wish I'd had Miss Mabel myself instead of you. She couldn't have took to British brandy like Mrs. Rafferty, and fell down a trapdoor and broke her neck!"

"Oh, that is it, is it?" said the captain; "then you are a widower, Rafferty?"

"Yes, sir; and what's happened is a what's-a-name to me—a great something;" but he added something about beer or ale.—"oh! I have it, sir, a great morale lesson, I've been through a campaign or two, captain, but this has been just the worst; so say no more about it."

They did respect Rafferty's feelings now they really found what had happened, and Rafferty himself quietly slid into his ordinary employments again; and nothing could give him greater offence than any allusion to his brief sojourn in the realms matrimonial.

It was a great pleasure to Mabel, as well as to Henry, and, in fact, all the Morton family, to provide for Troubled Tom; but the great difficulty was, how to provide for him; for, although they got him a great number of employments, he went to sleep so perpetually that he was really of no use to any one, and at last it became quite a puzzle among the family to know what to do with him; and then Troubled Tom, in an extraordinary fit of wakefulness, came out with a suggestion him-self.

"Oh, dear," he said, "it's a great bore to have to say anything. I—I should like a little bit of sleep somewhere, only nobody'll let me have it. Now, I tells yer what——"

At this juncture, Troubled Tom gave evident symptoms of leaving off and taking a nap; but, after being well shaken, he resumed, and actually proposed that a chair should be appropriated to him in any field, the produce of which was likely to be much attacked by birds, and there be allowed to fall asleep all day, doing the duty of an animated scarecrow.

This, of course, the Mortons would not agree to; so he lived at the Hall, and dozed away his time by the kitchen fire, alike insensible to the boiling over of pots and pans and the scolding of the cook.

\*     \*     \*     \*

Reader, we have brought our eventful history to a close, and those who have followed our heroine through her many perilous adventures know well how deserving she is of the happiness that has certainly fallen upon her.

It will be seen, in the course of her eventful career, how, in the time of utmost need, friends will rise up for the unfortunate, so that none need despair; for what could have been a more destitute and pitiable object than a young infant upon the field of carnage, from whence Mabel had been plucked, and whom death had bereft of one parent—despair of another.

Nor was the happiness we have depicted of short duration; but, as years passed on, and she became a happy mother, seeing the living images of herself and husband in the little prattlers that clustered round her knee, she would shed those tears of joy which come from the overflowing heart—tears so different from those which grief produces; and many a time she would tremble as she crept closer to her husband's heart, and whispered,—

"Is it a sin to be so happy?"

And he would smile, and, pointing to the blue heavens above, would tell her that that omniscient Being, who preserved the Child of the Battle Field, preserved her to be what she now was—the happiest of the happy.

THE END.